ON OPPOSITE SIDES

CAT SCHIELD

ONE COLORADO NIGHT

JOANNE ROCK

MILLS & BOON

First Published in Great Britain 2022
by Mills & Boon, an imprint of HarperCollins*Publishers* Ltd
1 London Bridge Street, London, SE1 9GF

www.harpercollins.co.uk

HarperCollins*Publishers*
1st Floor, Watermarque Building,
Ringsend Road, Dublin 4, Ireland

On Opposite Sides © 2022 Harlequin Enterprises ULC
One Colorado Night © 2022 Joanne Rock

Special thanks and acknowledgement are given to Cat Schield for her contribution to the Texas Cattleman's Club: Ranchers and Rivals series.

ISBN: 978-0-263-30381-0

0622

MIX
Paper from
responsible sources
FSC® C007454

Cat Schield is an award-winning author of contemporary romances for Mills & Boon. She likes her heroines spunky and her heroes swoonworthy. While her jet-setting characters live all over the globe, Cat makes her home in Minnesota with her daughter, two opinionated Burmese cats and a goofy Doberman. When she's not writing or walking dogs, she's searching for the perfect cocktail or travelling to visit friends and family. Contact her at catschield.com

Joanne Rock credits her decision to write romance after a book she picked up during a flight delay engrossed her so thoroughly that she didn't mind at all when her flight was delayed two more times. Giving her readers the chance to escape into another world has motivated her to write over eighty books for a variety of Mills & Boon series.

ON OPPOSITE SIDES

CAT SCHIELD

For my dad.

One

Chelsea Grandin was proud of the fact that she could outrope, outride and outlast half the men on her family's ranch. Unfortunately, none of her abilities had ever impressed any of the male members of her family. Eldest of her siblings, she had all the first-child traits. An ambitious, responsible know-it-all, she was always the first one out the door in the morning and the last one in the door at night.

Take today, for instance. She'd left the house at 4:00 a.m. so she could get all her work done in order to take off the afternoon for Royal's Fourth of July celebration. With the sun at its zenith, she'd already put in a full day with no sign of her brother, Vic.

"Oh, to be the only boy and presumptive heir," she muttered, wincing as she lost control of her seething resentment. No matter how hard she worked, her father made it clear he intended to turn control of the ranch over to his son. And because of this, Vic behaved like it was his due. "Entitled jerk."

The siblings had different management styles. Chelsea loved working side by side with the ranch hands, believing if she contributed significantly to the daily activity, she was more in tune with the pulse of the ranch. Plus, she took satisfaction in all the physical activity. Vic, in contrast, preferred to delegate. While she wasn't deluded into thinking she was the only person who knew what was going on, Chelsea was convinced she was far more informed than her brother. Not that this had ever given her a leg up when it came to impressing her father or her late grandfather.

Grief gave her heart an agonizing wrench. They'd buried Victor John Grandin Sr. two short months earlier, but Chelsea continued to miss the family's strong patriarch. He'd been such an enormous presence in her life, inspiring her to work ever harder to prove herself, even though the patriarchy was alive and well on the Grandin ranch.

Chelsea slipped out of her truck and approached the front porch, where her sibling sat with his feet up on the railing.

"So I guess you're taking today off," she said, slogging up the steps to the porch, feeling her early morning catching up to her.

"It's the Fourth of July," Vic said, arching one eyebrow at her.

"Your point?" Chelsea hated being constantly irritated with her brother.

Daily she grappled with the certainty that their father would bypass her and hand the reins to Vic. It was just so unfair that being born a girl meant she had no shot at being in charge of the ranch, no matter her qualifications or dedication.

Equally frustrating was the lack of recognition she craved. If she'd been born into another family, she'd be basking in her parents' approval. Instead, both her father and mother saw her contributions as something to keep her occupied until she got married and moved out. They didn't recognize how tied she was to the land her family had owned for generations.

"The point is," Vic began in the unruffled tone that always set her teeth on edge, "today's a holiday, and I'm not working."

As if that explained it all. And maybe it did. With her working so hard, did he really have to?

"No," Chelsea grumbled, "it's not like you're working."

Entering the massive house she shared with her entire family, Chelsea contemplated the moment when Vic took over. How she could possibly stay, knowing that every time they butted heads he would win? Yet the ranch was her everything. What would she do instead?

As Chelsea crossed the spacious living room, her gaze fell on a recent family portrait taken at Layla's engagement party. Her sister Layla was buying her own spread with her fiancé, Joshua Banks. Like them, Chelsea could strike out on her own.

Or she could start a business like her youngest sister. Morgan owned a successful fashion boutique in town called the Rancher's Daughter. Chelsea suspected that her sister had realized early on that with three older siblings managing the ranch, there wouldn't be room for her. The feisty redhead seemed perfectly happy doing her own thing. Could Chelsea find joy being anywhere but here?

She angled toward her bedroom, hoping a shower would clear her head and revive her flagging energy. She had a full day of celebrations ahead of her. The whole family was attending the town's annual Fourth of July parade and picnic. Later, they would head to the Texas Cattleman's Club. Every year the club hosted a barbecue and fireworks to celebrate the holiday.

As she reached the hallway that led to her bedroom, she spied her mother coming down the hall toward her.

"I was just looking for you." Bethany Grandin made no attempt to hide her disappointment as she surveyed her daughter's disheveled appearance. "Oh, you're not ready to go."

"I just got back from…" She trailed off, seeing her mother wasn't really listening. Bethany shared her husband's resistance to their daughters working the ranch. Chelsea had long ago learned to just do things and stop explaining herself.

Bethany glanced at the gold watch on her wrist. Diamonds sparkled on the twenty-fifth wedding anniversary present from her husband. "The parade starts in an hour."

"I know. It won't take me long to shower and change." Chelsea eased past her mother. A garment bag lay on her bed. "What's that?"

"Just a little something from your sister's boutique that I thought would work for today." Bethany adored shopping and often bought things for her children to wear.

Clearly her mother believed that Chelsea was neglecting her appearance. And maybe Bethany was right. As much as Chelsea enjoyed dressing up, lately, when left to her own devices, she wore jeans, boots and whatever shirt came to hand.

"That's really nice of you."

Bethany seemed to relax at her daughter's response. No doubt she'd been expecting a battle. Chelsea sighed. Was she really that prickly and difficult to deal with? She didn't want to be. She just wanted to be appreciated for who she was, not ignored or changed into somebody else's vision of her.

"I saw it at Morgan's boutique, and I immediately thought of you." Her mother unzipped the garment bag and pulled out a red halter dress with a full skirt.

"Wow." The obligatory smile she'd pasted onto her lips turned into an oh of appreciation as Chelsea pictured how great the bold color would look against her dark hair and brown eyes.

"And there's lipstick to match." Bethany scooped up a gold tube from Chelsea's nightstand. "I looked all over until I found the perfect shade to go with the dress."

Chelsea took the lipstick and opened it. The bright red color triggered her anxiety. She was not the family beauty. Layla and Morgan were the ones who'd inherited their mother's delicate features and fair coloring, while Chelsea and Vic favored their father, with dark brown hair and eyes. But where Victor John's strong bone structure and eyebrows made her brother handsome, their boldness left Chelsea feeling far from dainty and feminine.

"I know it's not something you would've chosen," her mother said, fondling the soft material. "But you have the perfect figure for this dress, and I thought you might like it."

Translation: *it would be nice if you went back to dressing like a girl again.* Chelsea knew her mother was right. She just hated falling short when compared to her beautiful, stylish sisters.

"It's very nice." And she would definitely get noticed wearing the dress. Unfortunately, it wasn't the type of recognition she craved. Chelsea briefly wallowed in regret. She wanted to stand out for her achievements, not her appearance. "But is it a bit too much for a parade and TCC barbecue?"

"Too much?" Bethany's face fell, and Chelsea silently cursed.

"You have such wonderful taste." Seeing her mother was only partially mollified by the compliment, Chelsea cast about for a way to distract her further. "In fact, I was thinking that maybe you could help me with something else."

"Of course I'll help. What did you have in mind?"

Spying the outdated Paris-themed wallpaper and matching decor in her room, Chelsea latched on to an idea. Little had changed since she'd gone off to college seventeen years earlier. At the time she'd been obsessed with Paris and even considered spending a year studying overseas, but in the end, she'd decided to be more practical and selected an agriculture major that made sense for a future rancher.

Now the room was a vivid reminder of paths not taken. Perhaps it was time to erase this reminder of the possibilities she'd once embraced. Time to forget that her dreams had involved something besides running Grandin Ranch. She just needed to redouble her focus and convince her father to listen to all her ideas to improve the ranch.

If he heard her out, he'd see the value in instituting new pasture rotation techniques to maximize the quality of the grass their herd fed on and agree to incorporate new bloodlines to strengthen the quality of their stock. Already she'd implemented a number of technology-based applications that allowed her to monitor the health of the cattle.

"I was just thinking that maybe I should do something with my room. It could use a makeover." Seeing her mother's eyes begin to glow with excitement, Chelsea impulsively rushed on. "I honestly don't know what I would do in here. And you are so good at decorating."

"Oh, that's a wonderful idea. I've been dying to renovate this room for a while now." Bethany didn't add that Chelsea's room was the last one in the ranch house lacking her mother's creative flair. In fact, many rooms had been through two or even three renovations.

Chelsea winced at her mother's obvious enthusiasm. "I guess it's a little bit like a time capsule in here."

"A bit." Her mother gave a relieved laugh before enfolding her daughter in a spirited hug. "I'll leave you to get ready. Do you want us to wait for you?"

"I'll drive myself." If she took her time making herself presentable, Chelsea didn't want to hold any of them up.

Bethany looked worried. "You are planning to come?"

"Yes, I promise I'll be there." She pumped extra cheer into her tone to be convincing. "Wearing that." She indicated the dress and then held up the lipstick. "And this."

"You're going to look fantastic."

Her mother's prophecy turned out to be closer to fact than Chelsea expected, which was confirmed by her best friend as the two women rendezvoused on Main Street to watch the parade.

"Girl, you look amazing." This was quite a compliment coming from Natalie Hastings, who had a stylish wardrobe that would be the envy of the pickiest fashionistas. "Where has this Chelsea been hiding these last two years?"

Tall and curvy with long, dark hair and flawless tawny-brown skin, Natalie shared Chelsea's ambition when it came to her career, but she hadn't abandoned her personal life entirely. It was just that the younger woman had an unrequited crush on the elusive Jonathan Lattimore, Chelsea's neighbor. But if Natalie lacked confidence when it came to love, she was always on the prowl for her friend.

"Hey."

The parade had been underway for half an hour, and Chelsea had let her thoughts drift back to the ranch and what it would take to convince her father that she—and not Vic—should take over running things when he retired.

"Ouch." Chelsea hadn't responded to her best friend fast enough and received an elbow nudged into her ribs. Scowling, she shot Natalie a frown and found her friend's attention wasn't on the parade. "What?"

"Don't look now, but Nolan Thurston has been staring at you for the last ten minutes."

"Nolan Thurston?" Icy dismay raised goose bumps on her arm. "Are you sure?" Chelsea was glad her gaze was hidden behind designer sunglasses as she scanned the crowd across the street. "I don't see him."

"He's standing in front of Royal Gents."

A float interrupted her view, and Chelsea shook her head. "I'm sure it's nothing. Or maybe it's because of what's going on between our families."

Nolan had returned to Royal right around the time Chelsea's grandfather had died and had joined his brother, Heath, in making the Grandin family's lives hell. Nolan and Heath had produced documents claiming their mother, Cynthia Thurston, owned the oil rights beneath the ranches belonging to the Grandin family and their neighbors the Lattimores.

"I don't know. It was more like a sexy stare." Natalie's lips pursed. "Like he saw something he liked and wants to get it naked."

Natalie's assessment was a bottle rocket zipping

straight at Chelsea's head. Adrenaline shot through her, prompting a shocked laugh.

"That's nuts."

Although she'd seen Nolan around town and at the Texas Cattleman's Club, they'd never once spoken. She'd gone out of her way to avoid both the Thurston brothers, not wanting to vent her wrath at whatever they were up to and get into a public argument.

"Is it?" Natalie sounded wistful.

"Layla is more his type." Once again Chelsea was searching through a gap in the parade for Nolan. "He hit on her when he first came to town."

"Because he wanted information about your family. Not because he was interested in her."

The mysterious granting of the oil rights by Chelsea's grandfather had shaken all parties. At first the Grandin family had suspected the whole thing had been a huge scam perpetrated by the Thurston twins, but soon it became apparent that Chelsea's uncle David had actually had an affair with Cynthia around the time she'd gotten pregnant with her daughter, Ashley. Mysteriously, the document hadn't come to light until after mother and daughter had died in an accident. Now Heath Thurston, in concert with his twin, was determined to grow their wealth at the expense of the Grandin and Lattimore ranches.

"Maybe since he struck out with Layla, he's coming for me next?" Chelsea proposed.

"You know, there's another possibility…"

"Such as?"

As she asked the question, her gaze found the darkhaired twins standing on the opposite side of the parade route. Even with the width of the downtown Royal street between them, she could tell that Nolan was indeed staring at her. Something dangerous and exciting lit up her nerve endings. Strangely short of breath, Chelsea barely registered Natalie's answer.

"It's possible he didn't recognize you all gussied up like this. We've been best friends forever, and I almost walked past you earlier."

Chelsea didn't think she'd deliberately downplayed her femininity because of her father's unfair prejudice against her gender, but for the last few years, she'd ignored her closet full of dresses in favor of strutting around town in jeans and cowboy boots. It was foolish to think by dressing like a guy that her father would see her as a capable rancher first and his eldest daughter second.

"Maybe he's just a gorgeous guy interested in a sexy gal." Natalie's gaze bounced from Nolan Thurston to Chelsea. "With his yummy dark eyes and those bold eyebrows, combined with your fantastic bone structure, you two would make beautiful babies."

Chelsea was a second too slow to stop the bark of shocked laughter that burst from her. "Oh, jeez." She rolled her eyes dismissively while her stomach did a disconcerting somersault. "Whatever. I don't have time for anything having to do with Nolan Thurston and his luscious bedroom eyes."

"Not even if it meant getting a leg up on your brother?"

"I'm listening." Chelsea brought her full attention to bear on her best friend.

"What's the biggest crisis on the ranch right now?"

"The oil rights claim."

Natalie nodded sagely. "So Nolan offered to take Layla to lunch to 'talk things out.' But obviously Layla knew he just wanted to get information. What if you turn the tables on him and do the same thing to him? If you save the ranch by stopping the oil rights claim, your dad would have no choice but to put you in charge."

Most of the time she used straightforward tactics to try to beat out her brother for control of the ranch. She wanted to win through hard work and good judgment. But sexism cloaked in tradition was alive and well in her family. And thinking about it now, Chelsea reckoned if she didn't give it everything she had, maybe she didn't deserve to be in charge.

Resolve blazed inside Chelsea. "I like the way you think."

Whatever it took to beat Vic. That was what she'd promised herself.

Her gaze flicked toward the Thurston twins and skimmed over Nolan. A little weakness invaded her knees as she thought about what dating him might entail. One thing was for certain—spending time with such a handsome man would be equal parts pleasure and satisfaction.

And in the end, she'd save her ranch.

Maybe it was about time that being female became an asset.

Chelsea linked arms with her friend. "How do I go about casually bumping into Nolan Thurston?"

The heat that consumed Nolan Thurston had nothing to do with the ninety-four-degree temperature radiating from the pavement or the confining press of the parade crowd around him. No, the cause of the inferno was that the sizzling brunette in the sexy red dress had finally noticed him. Damn, the woman was striking. He liked his women tall, lithe, but with curves in all the right places, and she looked to be the perfect blend of all that. Her dark brown hair fell in sexy waves over her delicate shoulders, and he imagined himself twining the silky locks around his wrists as he pulled her in for a hot, deep kiss.

When was the last time he'd gazed at a woman and felt something hit him like a brick wall? A long, long time. A float interrupted his view of the woman who'd sparked his interest, and it was as if a cloud had passed in front of the sun. Suddenly Nolan was desperate—he had to get across the street before she vanished. He simply had to get up close and personal to see if she was as bewitching in person.

As Nolan began to edge his way forward, a hand caught his arm. "Hey! Where are you going?"

Nolan glanced over his shoulder at his brother. Being apart from Heath for fifteen years had made him forget what it was like to look at his twin and feel that crazy disorientation of seeing himself reflected in another's features. It was a little like looking in the mirror but not recognizing yourself.

Heath had always been the more serious and responsible brother. These days the somber stranger with the weight of the world on his shoulders bore no resemblance to the mischievous twin of old. The brothers might share the same features, but they each wore the years differently.

"There's a woman I'm dying to get to know." Nolan indicated the opposite side of the street, where the lady in red stood.

A grin transformed Heath's features, making him much more approachable. "Who?"

"That's what I'd like to find out."

Between the two of them, Nolan was the flirt, the one women flocked to because of his easy charm and daring ways. Heath's more serious demeanor didn't scare away the ladies—his handsome features and rugged physique always attracted attention—but he wasn't usually focused on romance.

"Which one is she?" Heath eyed the crowd opposite them as if he might be able to guess his brother's taste in women.

"The one in the red dress across the way." Even as he spoke, the trailing edge of the float moved by and revealed her once more. A bottled-up sigh slipped free. Absolutely stunning.

"Let's see. A red dress, you say... Whoa!" Heath gave his head a vigorous shake. "You definitely cannot go there."

"Why?" Nolan felt his insides clench at his brother's emphatic declaration. "Did you date her?"

"Did I date...?" Heath gaped at him. "Don't you know who that is?"

Nolan was utterly confused. "Should I?"

"That's Chelsea *Grandin*."

Hearing the emphasis his brother put on the last name, Nolan narrowed his eyes and inspected her once more. "Are you sure? That looks nothing like Chelsea." Where was the no-nonsense rancher's daughter in sensible denim and boots? This vision in red had wayward, touchable hair, big brown eyes and glorious, full red lips. "She's a knockout."

"I'm sure." Heath's statement sounded like the fall of a judge's gavel. The decision was final. Nolan could have nothing to do with anyone in the Grandin family.

Two months ago, he'd been stunned when Heath explained about the document he'd found among their mother's things granting her rights to the oil beneath the Grandin and Lattimore ranches. And when Heath had asked him to come to Royal, Texas, to help him make the claim, of course he'd said yes. The brothers had not been on the best terms even before Nolan left town at eighteen. Nolan was hoping to repair that.

While Heath had always felt connected to their family's ranch and worked hard not just to keep it going, but to make it thrive, Nolan had a completely different passion. Unconcerned by money or the need to hold tight to things, he'd packed up his limited possessions, slung a backpack over his shoulder and headed west. A few weeks later, he'd landed in Los Angeles.

For many young hopefuls, Tinseltown was the end of the journey, but for Nolan, it was only the beginning. Within a week, he'd connected with a guy looking for crew to help him deliver a yacht to Singapore. With the experience he gained during that voyage, Nolan then spent the next three years working a series of private yachts doing charters. It was during one of these voyages in the Mediterranean that he'd met wealthy studio executive Skip McGrath and embarked on a career in reality TV production. Scouting filming locations gave him the opportunity to work in any number of exotic areas. Seeing the world had been his dream since he was a kid, and making a living while doing so was absolutely perfect.

The only dark spot in an otherwise idyllic life was his estrangement with his twin. The only time in fifteen years that Nolan had returned to Royal was to attend the double funeral of his mother and sister two years earlier. He'd been worried how Heath would react to seeing him again, but grief had provided a bridge for the brothers to reconcile. Since then, their relationship had improved somewhat. The shocking loss had sparked their communication, and they'd spoken more often, but they had a long way to go. Which was part of what had spurred Nolan to return to Royal. He hoped that a shared goal would reignite the close bond they'd enjoyed as kids, but

Heath's obsession with getting the full value of what was theirs left him prickly, and Nolan couldn't seem to gain his brother's trust.

That his mission was going to stir up the town and compel their friends and neighbors to pick sides didn't seem to worry Heath at all. Small-town living wasn't for everyone, and all the reasons Nolan had put Royal behind him came rushing back. Even though Royal was an affluent town with sprawling ranches, high-end shopping and luxury hotels, Nolan had felt confined by the community. Maybe it was how everyone knew what was going on with their neighbors, or the way his family was tied to the land they owned.

Nolan had been obsessed with getting beyond the city limits and seeing what the world had to offer. He'd been lucky that a series of opportunities had landed him in Skip's orbit and led to Nolan traveling to some amazing parts of the world—as well as some seriously sketchy locales and rough terrain. He'd loved every dangerous, uncomfortable, eye-opening moment of his years spent adventuring. But the cost of living his dream was losing the brother he loved.

"You really think she's attractive?" Heath's thoughtful murmur caught Nolan off guard.

"Yeah. Of course." He glanced toward the attractive brunette only to realize that she'd disappeared. His mood dipped. "Don't you?"

Heath shrugged. "I've never really thought about it."

"If I recall, you were always more attracted to blondes." Nolan thought about his own failed attempt to cozy up to Layla Grandin in an effort to gain some insight into why their mother, Cynthia, had had a document granting her rights to the oil beneath the Grandin ranch. "Maybe you're the one who should've taken a crack at

Layla. She's pretty enough, but my heart wasn't really in it. I think that's why I asked Layla to bring Chelsea along, but I had no idea Chelsea could look like that."

As sexy as he found beautiful, confident women, when he'd seen Chelsea around town, she'd hidden her expression beneath the brim of a Stetson, and he realized that he'd seen more of her backside heading in the opposite direction.

Confronted by this new insight, Nolan frowned. Could she have been avoiding him? Given the conflict between their families, it would make sense that she might not wish to have anything to do with him. His senses tingled in anticipation of a chase.

"What if I get to know Chelsea a bit?" Nolan proposed, glancing toward his twin. "I might have better luck connecting with her than I did with her sister."

"This isn't a good idea." But Heath wasn't as emphatic as he'd been earlier.

"Look, I can do this. Half my job is negotiating."

"Just remember, don't give up more information than you get."

Since he had very little knowledge about his brother's strategy or motivation, that wasn't going to be a problem. And maybe if he found out something that would help their cause, Heath would start treating him like his twin again instead of keeping Nolan at arm's length.

"I've had dinner with billionaires in Istanbul, spent weeks living in the jungle while hunting for the perfect location in Indonesia and been confronted by crocodiles in Australia. I'm lucky, resourceful and persistent."

"Chelsea is smart and will see you coming from a mile away."

Nolan shrugged. Why waste time touting his skills

when he could let his success speak for itself? "No harm in taking a swing."

"You'll strike out."

"It's a chance worth taking. And you never know—" Nolan shot his brother a cocky grin. "She might have a taste for adventure."

Heath snorted. "I doubt that."

"Challenge accepted," Nolan crowed, mentally rubbing his hands together.

Two

Nolan hadn't imagined a knockout in a red dress would all be that hard to spot, but he hadn't taken into account that most of the town would be wearing an assortment of red, white and blue clothing. Still, after coming up empty after half an hour of searching, Nolan was starting to worry that she'd already left. Disappointment hit. He hadn't realized how much he'd been looking forward to encountering Chelsea Grandin until his hopes had been dashed.

Hoping he'd have better luck at the barbecue, Nolan headed for the Texas Cattleman's Club. On the drive, he realized a lot of women had passed through his life, some more memorable than others. He wasn't accustomed to pursuing any of them with anywhere near the enthusiasm that drove him to search through the barbecue attendees. Nolan acknowledged that he had a mission. They needed information—or, better yet, an ally. He also recognized that he'd keyed into her before discovering that she was a Grandin.

Someone bumped into his back. The impact jarred him out of his thoughts. Given the crush of people milling about the gardens, he wasn't surprised by the contact.

"Oh, sorry," came a husky female voice.

Nolan caught a whiff of passion fruit and was transported to Brazil. He'd spent nearly a month in the southern end of the country, scouting a location near Iguazu Falls. The scent of wild passion fruit had hung heavy in the air as macaws had flown through the dense canopy above his head. He pivoted to face the woman who'd run into him.

Chelsea Grandin.

His heart did a crazy jig at his first glimpse of her large brown eyes, soft with apology. Although he'd been searching high and low for her, Nolan hadn't been prepared for the lightning that went through him at suddenly finding her within arm's reach. A smudge of sauce near her mouth drew his attention to her ruby-red lips. Shocked by the urge to bend down and lick the barbecue sauce from her skin, Nolan backed up half a step.

"It was all my fault," Nolan responded, a little short of breath. An irrepressible smile twitched at his lips as he noticed a dimple appearing in her cheek at his suave counter.

"Not true. You were standing still. It was entirely me. I think I stepped in a hole."

Nolan's gaze followed hers as she glanced down at the ground near her feet. Given the fancy dress she wore, he expected her to be in high-heeled sandals. Instead, she wore a sensible pair of cowboy boots in cognac leather, inset with white stars.

"I just lost my balance for a second." Her enormous

eyes went impossibly wide. "Oh, I didn't get any barbecue sauce on you, I hope."

Before he could assure her he didn't care if she had, she slipped around him, her fingers trailing over his shirt as she checked for damage. Nolan stood frozen while a thousand nerve endings blazed beneath her light touch.

"Oh, good," she declared on a relieved sigh. "Looks like we dodged a bullet."

Had he?

His clothes might have been all right, but the hit to his equilibrium rocked him. Thunder rumbled through his muscles as she completed her inspection and returned to stand before him.

"I'm Nolan."

For some reason he'd left off his last name. Maybe given his immediate, intense physical reaction to her, he was reluctant to see her open expression slam closed when she realized he was a Thurston. Yet he and Heath were twins. He scoured her expression for some sign of recognition. When he glimpsed neither caution nor hostility, he grew suspicious. His brother had overset her entire family by pursuing a claim for the oil rights beneath her land. Why wasn't she treating him like the enemy?

"Chelsea." Her wide lips curved in a genuine smile, further confusing him.

After making sure her right hand was free of barbecue, she held it out to him. The rough calluses on the palm that connected with his affirmed that this wasn't a woman who sat back and let others do the work. His interest in her flared still brighter, making him regret the animosity between their families.

"I've seen you around town," he said, dipping his toe into the murky situation. "But never dressed like this." He let his appreciation shine as he flicked his gaze along her slim form. "You look like a firecracker ready to explode."

Her husky chuckle raised goose bumps on his arms. The bold interest lighting her eyes twisted up his insides. Lust at first sight wasn't an unfamiliar phenomenon to him, but few women presented the sort of intriguing danger Chelsea Grandin embodied.

Heath's warning filled his thoughts. Nolan wished he understood his brother's obsession, but Heath hadn't been all that forthcoming with explanations, and Nolan hadn't wanted to rock the boat by demanding answers. When Heath trusted him, Nolan would get clarity. Until then, he'd support his brother and hope that when he'd proved his loyalty, Heath would confide in him.

"It's hot enough that I just might." She sent him a smoky look from beneath her lashes before indicating a nearby booth. "Feel like buying a girl a glass of lemonade?"

"Sure."

Without a backward glance to see if he was following, she headed off. Obviously, she was confident he wouldn't let her get away. Nolan hesitated a brief moment, just long enough to admire the way her hips flared out from the indent of her tiny waist. Loath to lose her in the crowded garden, he shot after her, neatly navigating between two converging groups to reach her side.

At the lemonade stand, he exchanged a bill for two paper cups adorned with lemons.

As they moved away, Chelsea scanned the nearby picnic tables. "Let's find a place to sit down?"

"How about there?" He indicated a narrow space that they could both just squeeze into.

She eyed his selection and then gave an approving nod. He waited for her to settle before joining her. Although he was firmly sandwiched between her and a beefy cow-boy, Nolan only noticed the soft, feminine body pressed against his left side.

"Here," she said, nudging the plate his way. "Have some of these. It's way too much for me to eat all by myself."

He considered refusing, but as the scent of the fragrant barbecue reached his nose, his stomach picked that moment to growl. "I am a little hungry." A pause. "I could go get my own…"

Even as he offered, he hoped she'd repeat her invitation to share. He was afraid she'd disappear again if he left her even briefly. What if someone approached her while he was gone and filled her ear with warnings?

To his relief, Chelsea shook her head.

"Help me finish these first."

"Sure."

The meal that followed went into his memory as one of the most delicious, carnal events he'd experienced. Not only were the ribs tender and perfectly smoked, but watching Chelsea's even white teeth tear the meat off the bone made the July day even hotter.

"What do you think of Royal's Fourth of July celebration?" Chelsea asked when there was nothing left of the feast but a pile of bones. "Did you enjoy the parade?"

"To be honest, I wasn't paying attention."

"Too small-town?" she teased.

Nolan shook his head. "Too distracted."

"Oh?"

At one point during the parade, he'd been certain that she'd noticed his interest, but since she'd been so far away and wearing sunglasses, he couldn't say for sure. Equally mystifying was the way she was acting as if she had no idea who he was.

While the oil rights claim that had put their families into conflict loomed large in his thoughts, he hesitated to bring the matter up. If she didn't mention the elephant in the room, he wasn't going to. Maybe she, too, wanted to explore the attraction between them—or could it be that she was planning on pumping him for information?

"There was a certain woman across the way who caught my eye, and I couldn't seem to look away."

"Can you describe her? Maybe I know who she is."

Was this one big flirtation, or was she as ingenuous as she appeared? As a tactic, it was working. The uncertainty had thrown off his rhythm.

"Long brown hair. Scorching-hot red dress. Kissable red lips. She blew my mind."

"From thirty feet away?" Chelsea blinked in surprise. Color had bloomed in her cheeks at his description. "Wow! She must have made quite an impression."

He set his elbow on the table and dropped his chin into his palm. With his gaze resting on her, Nolan said, "She was a total knockout."

"So, if you found this woman, what would you want to do with her?"

She was testing him, trying to decide what sort of man he was. Nolan realized that, for all her banter, Chelsea Grandin was cautious, guarded and maybe even controlling. In many ways she reminded him of Heath. Although his twin wasn't firstborn—their sister, Ashley, had been five years older—but Heath had been the firstborn boy, and where Nolan had been outgoing and self-centered, Heath had shouldered responsibility without complaint."

"I'd like to get to know her better." A shiver stole down his spine as her red lips curved into a crooked smile.

"And if she's already spoken for?"

Her counter caught him off guard. Was Chelsea dating someone? Heath hadn't mentioned a boyfriend, but then, his brother's singular focus kept him from visualizing the big picture.

"Obviously if she's married, it's my loss. But any other relationship status I consider fair game."

"You're pretty sure of your appeal. What do you bring to the table that might interest her?"

Damn. This woman was making him work. Not that he was afraid of a challenge. He'd tackled the Bhutan Snowman Trek, a twenty-five-day journey over eleven passes of forty-five hundred meters in elevation that defined the border between Tibet and Bhutan. He'd trained for six months before attempting it.

"Adventure. Excitement. Romance."

With each word he spoke, eager curiosity grew in her soft brown eyes.

"Hmm," she murmured. "Sounds nice."

Convinced he was taking the right tack, Nolan stroked a strand of hair off her cheek and slid it behind her ear. "What do you say, Chelsea? Are you game?"

Chelsea found herself shockingly short of breath beneath Nolan's intense regard. Was she game? Hell, yes. Maybe too game? She'd need to watch herself with this one. Even without the troubles between their families, he was not the sort she'd usually choose to go out with.

The men she preferred to date were structured and predictable. From the moment she'd met him, she'd decided Nolan Thurston was going to be anything but.

"What did you have in mind?"

"Dinner?" His eyebrows rose. "Unless you'd like to try something more adventurous."

Excitement ignited at his dare, sparking her uneasiness. Chelsea had never met anyone as intriguing as

Nolan. Which probably explained why, since seeing him at the parade, she'd avoided thinking about the ranch and the problems filling up her bucket of woes. Now she reveled in his engaging grin and come-hither dark brown eyes. With his solid, muscular body pressed against hers in the narrow space, she had a hard time keeping her wits about her.

She took a second to remind herself that spending time with him was a means to an end. She'd approached him because of the oil rights claim against her family's land. Still, there was no reason she couldn't enjoy herself while convincing him that pursuing their claim wouldn't be worth their while. A successful outcome for her family would demonstrate once and for all that the Grandin Ranch should be hers to run.

Chelsea shook herself free of his spell. "Let's start with dinner and see how it goes."

"Wonderful. Are you free this week?"

"I'm available Tuesday or Thursday." She didn't want him to think that her social schedule was wide-open, and a weeknight was more casual for a first date than a weekend. Plus, to keep him wanting more, she could always cut the date short, claiming that she started her mornings early. Which she did.

"Tuesday, then. I don't want to wait any longer than I have to." His wolfish smile curled her toes.

Did he really not know she was a Grandin? Granted, they hadn't exchanged last names, but he'd been standing next to his brother at the parade, and Heath knew exactly who she was. The fact that neither one of them had acknowledged their connection or brought up the oil rights claim reminded her to be wary of trickery.

They exchanged phone numbers, but neither made any move to part. Instead, they stood smiling at each other like a couple of smitten teenagers while the sounds emanating from the crowded garden faded to white noise.

"This has been fun." Chelsea heard equal notes of pleasure and reluctance in her voice as she attempted to extricate herself from Nolan.

Sharing the plate of barbecue with him had proved as distracting as it had been delightful. What it hadn't been was productive. Neither one of them had acknowledged the connection between their families.

"A lot of fun," Nolan agreed, pinning her with a smoky gaze. "I can't recall a meal I enjoyed more."

Chelsea told her feet to move, but none of her mental goading convinced her muscles to function. She'd gotten him to bite, now she just needed to set the hook. That meant walking away. *Leave him wanting more.*

"We could get dessert," she suggested instead, cursing her craving for more time with him.

"It is a hot day." His gaze glanced off her lips, making her shiver. "Ice cream back in town?"

"Perfect." The drive should give her time to start thinking straight.

He dropped the remains of their shared barbecue into nearest trash receptacle. She gave him directions to her favorite ice-cream shop on Main Street and told him she'd meet him there.

In the shop's cool interior, Chelsea breathed in the vanilla scent of freshly made waffle cones mingling with the rich aroma of hot fudge. They each chose their favorite flavor—Nolan surprised her by choosing cookie dough.

With the sweet taste of chocolate melting on her tongue, Chelsea and Nolan meandered along the shady side of Main Street where the parade had passed several hours earlier and settled on a bench outside the bank.

While Nolan half lounged with his long legs stretched out before him, one arm draped over the back of the bench behind her, Chelsea perched on the edge, knees primly locked together, and surreptitiously peeked at his magnificent physique.

Having no idea what to say, she couldn't believe it when she blurted out the first thing that came to mind. "What is your favorite color?" She quickly used her tongue to chase a drip running down the side of her cone to hide her embarrassment.

When Nolan didn't immediately reply to her question, she glanced over and caught him watching her with intense fascination. Something sexy and primal vibrated behind her belly button as she imagined gliding her tongue along his skin in a similar fashion.

"Red. I spotted you across the road and couldn't take my eyes off you." His voice dipped into husky undertones as if he truly meant what he said.

"Oh." Chelsea was at a loss. Despite knowing that he was trouble, he seemed so damned genuine, and she wanted to be swayed by his openness. In fact, several times over the last hour, she'd lost track of the real reason she'd approached him in the first place. "Are you always this direct?"

"Usually. When I see something and immediately know in my gut that it's right, I tend to be single-minded and straightforward."

Should she infer that she was that something right for him? It was flattering to think a glimpse of her from so far away could have caused such conviction in him, but maybe that's exactly what he intended for her to think. Hadn't their connection formed a little too smoothly? He had to know who she was. After all, he'd been in town for a couple months. Heath would've pointed out the entire Grandin clan to Nolan. This sudden burst of insight triggered Chelsea's guards. And just in time. She had been on the brink of believing all his romantic chitchat.

Recalled to the dangerous nature of her mission, Chelsea reviewed their conversation. What tidbit of information had she let slip that might've given Nolan something he could take back to his brother? Nothing came to mind. But she'd been pretty swept away by his charm.

He'd proven to be far more charming and interesting than she'd expected. Chelsea was no longer confident in her ability to manipulate Nolan.

The Texas heat prevented Chelsea from lingering over her ice-cream cone. The frozen treat was melting fast, and she had to gulp it down before the sticky mess dripped all over her. As she popped the last bit of sugary cone into her mouth, she decided it was a blessing in disguise. If she delayed her exit much longer, he might get the idea that she was smitten.

"This has been fun, but my family is probably wondering where I got off to," Chelsea said, getting to her feet. "I guess I'll see you on Tuesday."

"No guesswork needed." Nolan's slow smile made her vibrate with anticipation. "You definitely will."

Chelsea made no effort to hide her delight as she flashed him an answering grin. Playing games wasn't her forte. That being said, it was exactly what she'd committed to doing with Nolan. Still, if she hadn't found him attractive, she'd never have been able to flirt with him in a genuine way.

She'd walked a block before realizing that she'd headed in the opposite direction from where she'd parked her car. Cursing her addled brain, she traveled another half block to her sister's boutique and ducked into the Rancher's Daughter. The tinkling bell over the door notified the salesclerk that someone had entered the shop. Kerri looked up from the accessories she was unpacking and smiled when she caught sight of Chelsea.

"Is Morgan around today?" Chelsea indicated the dress she was wearing. "I just wanted to show her the dress Mom bought for me here."

"She's in the back." Kerri's attention returned to the necklaces she'd been pulling from their plastic wrapping.

Chelsea found the youngest Grandin sibling in her small office at the back of the store. Morgan was perusing an online catalog of dresses and jotting notes on a legal pad beside her keyboard.

"Working on a holiday?" Chelsea asked from the doorway.

With seven years and two siblings between them, Chelsea and Morgan had never formed the tight bond that Chelsea shared with Layla. It didn't help their relationship that Morgan sided with Vic all the time. Not only was he her older brother, but they were close in age, and as such the pair was thick as thieves. So it wasn't a surprise that when it came to the debate on who should be in charge of Grandin Ranch, Morgan thought her brother was the right choice.

"I've got a few things I wanted to check on before heading to the Texas Cattleman's Club for the fireworks." Morgan sized up her sister's ensemble and nodded in approval. "The boots are a surprising choice, but they work. You should really dress up more often."

Chelsea thought about her upcoming date with Nolan and decided she would buy something sexy and sophisticated to boost her confidence. "You're right. I'm going to take a look around and see if anything catches my eye."

When Morgan nodded absently and returned to work, Chelsea headed back into the shop. Buzzing with anticipation, she selected several dresses and went to try them on. Once again, she marveled at her sister's fashion sense as she narrowed her choices down to three. After much deliberating, she couldn't settle on which one to buy. It wasn't like her to dither when making decisions. Of course, lately all her decisions had been to benefit the ranch. There, she could weigh the pros and cons of various strategies and formulate the best solution.

This was different. She was trying to create an emotional reaction in someone she didn't know at all. What would appeal to Nolan? Did she hit him with something flirty and romantic or drop-dead sexy? Did she want to win his heart or scramble his brains with lust? The latter seemed far easier and less emotionally treacherous.

As the full impact of what she was doing struck her, Chelsea sat down in the dressing room. What had seemed like a perfectly sensible scheme when Natalie proposed it was quickly becoming complicated. Was she really considering hooking up with Nolan under false pretenses? She was both excited and horrified at her daring, but the potential to save the ranch and win her father's approval was hard to ignore.

She balled her fists in her lap and told her racing heart to chill. There was a lot at stake, both for her and the ranch. She'd never balked at high stakes before. Why start now? As long as she kept her own emotions under control and her eye on the prize, nothing would go wrong.

Three

After parting from Chelsea, Nolan headed to his rental. The thousand-square-foot converted loft in a former furniture store off First Avenue was similar to his place in downtown LA and more familiar than the ranch house he'd grown up in. He'd been worried that living with Heath would bring up too many uncomfortable memories. Sharing tight quarters with people for extended periods of time could be stressful—a little something he'd learned while crewing on a luxury yacht for nearly a year.

Unfortunately, he'd forgotten this lesson three years ago when he'd agreed to produce a documentary about a research vessel studying whale migration near the South Pole. Four months of flaring tempers and personality conflicts had reminded Nolan why he preferred to travel solo.

No doubt most people would find his lifestyle lonely and undesirable, but Nolan liked the freedom to do as he chose. He wasn't used to having his comings and goings tracked, and even though he wasn't living on Thurston Ranch, Heath was keeping close tabs on him. Maybe his brother was worried that Nolan would vanish into the night again. Whatever Heath's concerns, Nolan was finding that being back in Royal was proving to be more of an adjustment than he'd expected.

It brought up the same urge to hit the trail as when he was eighteen. Back then Royal had felt small and confining despite its proximity to Dallas. Looking back, however, Nolan thought his discomfort had been less about the town and more about everyone's expectations. Not that he'd felt pressure to take over the ranch. Heath had stepped into their father's shoes after he died, but having to decide about college and a career had made Nolan feel constrained. The last thing he'd wanted was to be tied down.

His phone chimed to indicate an incoming text as he shut and locked the front door behind him. As he dropped his keys onto the counter, Nolan wondered if he was heading back to LA. He was waiting to hear about several reality show projects that would soon need him to scout locations. If the studios were ready to head into development, Nolan would have to decide if he should turn down the lucrative work and stay in Royal to help Heath, or leave his brother to fend for himself.

Passing on the scouting jobs could mean the executive producers would be less likely to reach out to him later. He needed to figure out how long he expected to stay in Royal. He was on a month-to-month lease with this loft, so he could pick up and go at any time. Of course, it was also a risk to abandon his brother to battle the oil rights claim alone against the Lattimores and Grandins. This might set their relationship back to square one.

To Nolan's relief, Heath was the one reaching out. He wouldn't have to make a lose-lose decision today.

How'd it go with Chelsea Grandin?

Although the question was straightforward, Heath's tension came through loud and clear. Nolan's twin had been consumed by the oil rights for reasons he hadn't made clear. It wasn't that Heath needed the money. The ranch was doing well, even better than it had been when Nolan left. He wished his brother would confide what was really going on. Not that he blamed Heath for his reticence. It wasn't like the twins had communicated in the years since Nolan's precipitous exit from Royal at eighteen.

I have a date with her Tuesday night. Any idea where I should take her?

Below his text message, a trio of blinking dots indicated his brother was typing a message. Nolan watched it for several seconds, anticipating a reply. When none came and the seconds ticked by, he set the phone down and went to grab a beer from the refrigerator. By the time he picked up his phone once more, there were no dots and no message.

Nolan was about ready to give up and do his own research when his phone lit up with a call.

"Tell me everything she said," Heath demanded without preliminaries.

"I don't know that I remember everything," Nolan hedged, suspecting Heath wouldn't appreciate how much energy Nolan had expended flirting with Chelsea and that they'd not discussed the oil rights or even mentioned that their families were connected.

"Well, what do you remember?"

Nolan sighed. Sometimes Heath was too direct. Could he convince his brother that an investigation into her family history was going to take time and finesse? And maybe even a little seduction.

"We didn't talk about the document you found, and I didn't bring up our shared family history." Nolan paused for a second, hearing his brother's heavy exhalation. "Look, I need to gain her trust, and that's not going to happen over a plate of ribs."

"I get it." Heath sounded resigned—unsurprised. "Thanks for trying."

That his brother was already throwing in the towel made Nolan grind his teeth. It was just like Heath to dismiss Nolan's abilities. He was one of the most sought-after location scouts in the industry and a stellar negotiator, but Heath only saw his twin as his younger brother.

As a kid, Heath had never hesitated to voice his strong opinions and bully his twin if Nolan's ideas differed. Several times in the last couple months, Heath had offhandedly disparaged what Nolan did, not understanding how his twin could make a good living while getting to do something he loved.

"Oh, I'm not done," Nolan said, growing all the more determined. "I fully intend to figure out everything Chelsea knows. That way we can establish a strategy for winning the legal battles that are sure to be waged against your claim."

"*My* claim?" Heath sounded taken aback. "You're part of this family. This involves you just as much as it does me."

"Sure." A lump formed in Nolan's throat. His relationship with Heath was neither straightforward nor easy, but that didn't stop Nolan from wanting to improve it. "But I've been gone so long I didn't really think you considered me part of the family anymore."

A silence greeted his statement while both men processed the doubts that Nolan had dared to voice.

"I'm sorry you feel that way," Heath said at last. "I'll admit that it's been hard without you around all these years, but Mom often reminded me that you had your own path to follow. You always did have a restless nature, and there's not a lot of new ground to discover here in Royal."

An overwhelming surge of relief and sorrow washed over Nolan. For the first time since he'd returned home, Nolan felt as if Heath at least understood his need to leave Royal, even if he didn't like that his twin had gone.

"I'm sorry I took off and left you holding the bag."

Heath huffed. "I don't believe that for a second. You always had your eyes on the horizon. I can't imagine that you gave any thought to how I would take being left here without you."

Nolan winced at the shotgun blast of guilt his brother had unloaded on him. "Actually, I did think about it," he said, forcing down his resentment. "I almost didn't leave, but then I thought about how miserable I would be and how you had everything under control with the ranch. Also, I never expected to be gone so long. I thought I'd see some of the world and eventually come home. Turns out there was more world for me to see than I anticipated."

"Considering we're twins, you and I are completely different people," Heath said, sounding unusually thoughtful. "The ranch is where I belong. I have no interest in leaving Royal. Even with all the troubles we've had in the last few years, with the storms and droughts, and then losing Mom and Ashley, I never even thought about selling and doing something else."

"Of course not," Nolan agreed, unable to imagine Heath as anything but a rancher. "You were made to be a cattleman."

"So, Chelsea Grandin agreed to go on a date with you," Heath mused, bringing them back to the original topic. "Interesting."

"We hit it off."

"I wouldn't have guessed you'd have any luck with her."

"I'll be honest, I'm a little surprised myself." Despite their significant chemistry, Nolan presumed the trouble between their families would've been too great a barrier. "But she was definitely into me."

"She's a little too practical to be swept off her feet," Heath said, his voice dry. "Even by a charmer like you."

"So what are you saying?" Even as he asked, Nolan anticipated Heath's answer.

"That she might be using you the same way you're using her."

"That occurred to me." Nolan decided to play it cool. Heath had made it clear that he didn't trust any of the Grandin family. No need for Nolan to divulge his eagerness to get acquainted with Chelsea. "But she also might be looking to have a little fun."

"That doesn't sound like Chelsea," Heath said. "She's the most sensible of all her siblings. And she's devoted to the Grandin Ranch. She'll go to great lengths to keep it safe."

"Including dating me?" Nolan cursed the trace of disappointment audible in his voice. Although he recognized that his brother was right to be cautious, Nolan was convinced that the attraction between them was real.

Heath waited a beat before replying, "Just watch yourself."

"I'll be careful."

"Where are you off to?" Chelsea's mother looked up from the crossword puzzle she been working on. Her eyes widened as she took in her oldest daughter. "Dressed like that?"

For her first date with Nolan, Chelsea had decided on a body-hugging long-sleeved dress in midnight blue with a reverse V neckline. Viewed from the front, she looked sexy but covered up from collarbone to knee. The drama came when she turned away—a gold zipper ran from the low point of the back V to the hemline, just begging to be undone. She'd gotten a little thrill putting it on and imagining Nolan's reaction. Would he see it as an invitation or a challenge?

"I'm having dinner with somebody." Chelsea was proud of her nonchalant tone, even though her insides were churning with excitement and anxiety.

"She's having dinner with Nolan Thurston," Layla piped up. She'd come for dinner since her fiancé was working late.

"You're dating a Thurston? Why would you do that with everything that's going on?" Her mother looked scandalized.

Chelsea shot her sister a withering glance. She'd explained to Layla her plan to go out with Nolan in order to gather some inside information on his brother's strategy regarding the oil rights. Since Layla had been Nolan's first target a couple months earlier, Chelsea had been hoping to get some insight from her sister.

"You could have your pick of any bachelor in town,"

her mother continued. "Why did you choose someone who is trying to ruin us?"

"It's for that exact reason that I'm going out with him." Chelsea hated feeling like a misguided teenager. Why couldn't her family ever see her as an intelligent, competent individual who knew exactly what she was doing? "Honestly, you can't seriously believe I'd be interested in dating him otherwise."

"Well." Bethany sniffed. "You don't have the best track record when it comes to picking men."

Chelsea didn't need to be reminded of her woeful dating blunders. She'd had more than her fair share of being ghosted by men she'd dated. It had happened often enough to make her reluctant to go out with anyone. But Nolan was different. She wasn't actually dating him.

"I'm hoping to get some insight into what he and Heath are planning."

Layla smirked. "If he's anything like his brother, he's not gonna tell you a thing."

"You don't know that," Chelsea fumed. "We had—" Damn. It sounded idiotic to say it, but what the hell. "—a connection."

"It's more likely that he's going to try and use you to get information the same way he tried when he asked Layla for a lunch date," her mother said, sending a speaking glance her daughter's way.

"Hey!" Layla exclaimed. "I knew exactly what he was up to, and I'm sure Chelsea does as well."

"I do," Chelsea agreed. "I don't need any of you worrying about me. Sometimes I think you all forget that I'm a capable thirty-five-year-old woman who knows how to take care of herself and this ranch."

"You should just let your father and Vic take care of

this oil rights business," her mother said, returning to her puzzle.

Chelsea ground her teeth together, frustrated by her mother's persistent exclusion of Chelsea's participation in major decisions surrounding the ranch. It was bad enough that her father and grandfather had clung to the notion that a male heir should be in charge, but Bethany Grandin was just as old-fashioned.

Just because their mother's sole ambition in life was to marry a rich rancher and manage his personal life didn't mean that her daughters were cut from the same cloth. Not that she'd stood in the way of Morgan opening the Rancher's Daughter. It was just when it came to Chelsea's dream of running the ranch that her mother couldn't get on board.

It stung that none of her family valued her input or gave her any credit. Especially after the changes she'd made to the land and animal management had improved the quality of the stock they raised. How maddening that her father refused to acknowledge a more efficiently and productively run ranch if it meant that any of the daughters—and not the son—were responsible for the improvements. To Chelsea's mind, this was incredibly shortsighted. But what could she do when her parents' mindsets were firmly entrenched in traditional patriarchy?

"Besides," Chelsea continued, tabling her resentment for another time. "Haven't you heard the old saying 'keep your friends close and your enemies closer'?"

"Which category does Nolan fall into?" Layla asked, arching a skeptical brow.

"Do I really need to answer that?" Chelsea snapped, rising to her sister's bait.

"Just watch yourself," her mother said. "Those Thurston boys are out for blood."

Chelsea thought over her initial meeting with Nolan. While her mother had every reason to judge the brothers harshly, Chelsea couldn't help but wonder if they had the Thurston twins pegged accurately. Sure, their potential ownership of the oil rights threatened the ranch, and that of their neighbors and dear friends the Lattimores. But wasn't it possible that Nolan and Heath were couching the matter as a business venture rather than some sort of vendetta.

On the heels of that question came the realization that she was already giving Nolan the benefit of the doubt—and that was certain to play straight into his hands.

No, her family was right. Chelsea needed to keep her wits about her. She had too much to prove and their ranch to save.

"I didn't fall for Nolan Thurston's charm," Layla said, coming to her sister's aid at last. "And neither will Chelsea."

Although Chelsea could see their mother wasn't convinced by anything she had heard in her daughter's defense, she left the ranch filled with a greater sense of determination. All her life she'd been living with her family's lack of faith in her. She hadn't let it get her down before. It certainly wasn't going to affect her now.

Chelsea had agreed to meet Nolan at the bench in front of the bank where they'd eaten their ice cream. She arrived five minutes early and discovered Nolan was waiting for her. She'd parked a block down and made her way slowly along Main Street. It had been months since she'd put on a pair of heels, and she was unaccustomed to walking in the five-inch stilettos.

"Wow!" He studied her with open admiration as she

drew near. "I didn't think you could get any more beautiful, but I was wrong. You look gorgeous."

She'd styled her hair in artful, beachy waves and swept the entire curtain over her left shoulder. With her large eyes, strong bone structure and overly wide mouth, Chelsea knew she was more striking than beautiful.

For a long time she'd resented her ugly duckling status and the praise her prettier sisters received. While she'd eventually made peace with her shortcomings and learned to enhance her best features, being told she was beautiful by a handsome guy who also happened to be sexy and charismatic was going straight to her head.

"You look pretty great yourself." She took in his charcoal-gray suit and black button-down shirt. The dark shades combined with his swarthy complexion gave him an edgy look. With the top button of his shirt undone, it was a struggle to tear her gaze away from the exposed hollow of his throat. If his dimples hadn't been flashing, she would've reconsidered going anywhere alone with him. "I was a little worried that I might've overdressed."

Taking her hand in a familiar grip, he leaned forward and placed a warm kiss on her cheek. A searing zing snatched her breath away. Feeling as giddy and idiotic as a naive teenager on her first date, Chelsea wondered what had come over her. Was she really this susceptible to the man's over-the-top sex appeal?

"You're perfect." Another sizzling smile melted her bones as he gestured toward a rugged black Jeep that looked like it could tackle any terrain Texas decided to throw at it. "Shall we go?"

"Sure." Chelsea had nearly reached the passenger door before realizing that Nolan hadn't followed her. Wondering if she'd mistaken which car he'd meant, she turned and found him rooted to the sidewalk, his

espresso eyes wide, his full lips pursed in a silent whistle. "Are you okay?"

"Am I okay?" He set his palm against his chest and
staggered dramatically. "That dress is the sexiest thing
I've seen all year. When you walked away, you nearly
killed me."

"Did I?"

As Nolan strode her way, Chelsea caught herself grinning with feminine satisfaction. Okay, she'd achieved the
exact effect she'd been after, but was it merely delight
that her plan was working or was she testing her sexual
power on a man she desired?

She might be in trouble if she was doing something
other than scoping out how much Nolan knew about his
brother's intentions or discovering the truth of his mother's connection to her uncle Daniel. Better still if she
could convince him to leave her family's ranch alone—
or persuade him to encourage Heath to drop the claim.
Her main purpose in dating him was to achieve any or
all of these goals and to prove to her family once and for
all that Grandin Ranch should be hers.

But as Nolan reached her side and skimmed his fingertips along her spine, to the top of the zipper, and gave the
tab a little tug, she wasn't sure where ambition stopped
and hunger began. Trembling with yearning, she bit her
lip. The temptation to beg him to unfasten the zipper was
both dangerous and all-consuming.

Nolan lowered his head and murmured, "Sexy as hell,
Ms. Dreamy."

The endearment tickled her. "Isn't it a little early for
nicknames?" she queried in a shaky rush as his breath
puffed against her neck.

"I call 'em as I see 'em. And you are definitely as
dreamy as they come."

Four

Damn the woman, Nolan thought with grudging admiration as he fingered the tab at the top of the zipper. He hadn't been exaggerating when he declared that she'd nearly killed him with this dress. As soon as he saw that gold zipper stretching from neckline to hem, all he could think about was snatching the tab and sliding it all the way down. She'd caught him off guard, and that rarely happened these days.

Maybe she needed a lesson in what happened when he was provoked.

He slid his finger along the vein in her neck, feeling as well as hearing her breath catch. Her eyes lifted to meet his, and her look was direct and unwavering. Not quite a challenge, but not exactly consent. But then she leaned just ever so slightly in his direction, and he saw an invitation in the subtle curve of her lips.

Now it was his breath's turn to hitch. Rationally, he

knew they were playing a game, but she'd reeled him in. Before he could give in and taste her, Heath's warning blasted through his mind.

She might be using you the way you're using her.

Nolan pulled back before temptation led him into trouble. "You know, we never properly introduced ourselves."

She nodded, as if seeing where he was going. "Chelsea Grandin."

"Nolan Thurston." He watched her reaction to his name and saw no surprise. So, she had known who he was from the start. "Is this going to be a problem?"

"Probably." Her wry smile made his pulse race. "I'll just have to see if you're worth it."

Her reply stunned him into laughter. "I guess I'll have to be on my best behavior."

With that out of the way, he helped her into the passenger seat and circled to the driver's side. Nolan appreciated the brief respite to restore his equilibrium. Chelsea Grandin had taken a blowtorch to his cool control, and he had to figure out the best way to find his way back.

"Where are we off to?" she asked as he backed out of the parking space and headed for the highway leading out of town.

"I thought we'd have dinner at Cocott in downtown Dallas. I've heard the food is pretty good."

"Cocott?" Chelsea's frown was equal parts confused and concerned. "You do realize that it's so popular it's impossible to get a reservation."

Nolan nodded. "I've heard that."

"So…do you have a reservation?"

"I do." Nolan shot her a smug grin. "I'll bet you're dying to know my secret."

"I am curious."

"The owner is a friend of mine. I don't know if you're

familiar with the travel show *Fork and Backpack*? I worked on it with Camila Darvas. She and I crisscrossed France for several months while she filmed it." The series had featured the cuisine and culture of small towns, and he'd had a blast learning about the various regions in France. "She opened Cocott shortly after the show aired, and it sounds like the restaurant is doing very well."

"What is it you do, exactly?"

"I scout international locations for television shows. Reality TV mostly, but I've worked on a few film projects as well."

"That's a very unusual career. And one that must require a lot of travel."

"The amount changes every year and depends on how busy I want to be. On average I'm on the road thirty to forty weeks."

Chelsea's eyes went round. "I can't imagine being away from home that long." Her gaze turned thoughtful. "Although I did go through a phase in high school when I wanted to spend a year studying in Paris."

From her wistful expression, he could see she regretted not doing so.

"What happened?"

"I decided it didn't make sense if I intended on majoring in agriculture. Ranching is in my blood, and it's all I've ever wanted to do." She gave a half-hearted shrug. "How did you get started scouting locations for TV?"

"I was eighteen when I left Royal. I was a man without a plan. Maybe that helped me. I don't know. I was open to whatever opportunities came my way. All I knew is that I wanted to see more of the world."

Chelsea shuddered. "I don't know whether that's brave or insane, but I could never have taken a leap of faith like that."

"Don't forget I was just out of high school. And prone to rash behavior." Nolan thought back to those first few months living on his own and couldn't imagine too many people who'd embrace that sort of freedom. "I went to LA and took a job working on a private yacht as a deckhand. The captain took a liking to me, and when he got a boat in the Caribbean, he took me along. From there I got enough experience to bounce over to Europe, where I worked the summer in the Mediterranean. It was during a private charter off the Amalfi Coast that I met a studio head." Nolan smiled, remembering that fortuitous meeting. "Skip McGrath took a chance on me, and I never looked back."

"It must've taken a lot of courage for you to strike out on your own at such a young age. It was hard enough for me going off to college." She fiddled with her gold bracelet. "I have no idea how I would've survived the way you did."

"Everyone has their own path. Even though I got into several schools, college wasn't for me. My mom encouraged me to take a gap year to decide what I wanted to do with the rest of my life."

"I'll bet she never expected that you would go and never come back."

"Things might have ended up different if I hadn't stumbled into an industry that pays me very well to do what I love. Can't get much better than that."

"With that amount of traveling, how often do you get back to Royal?"

"I don't get back to Royal at all. My mother and sister's funeral two years ago was the first time I'd been back."

She gawked at him. "But why? Were you that busy or was it something else?"

Her question hit too close to home. He knew Chelsea

was tight with her family. Hell, there were three generations of Grandins living together on that ranch. She probably could never imagine anything that would put them at odds.

"I felt like I let them down, given the way I left. And I wasn't sure I'd be welcome." Nolan wasn't sure what possessed him to confide such a painful truth, especially when he didn't know if he should trust her.

"What happened?"

"None of them knew about my plans to leave Royal until after I was gone." He nodded at her aghast expression. "It wasn't the best way to handle things, but I knew that it would be hard enough to go without them putting pressure on me to stay. And then the longer I stayed away, the harder it was for me to face coming home."

From Chelsea's stricken look, it was pretty clear that she perceived his absence as upsetting. No doubt someone who'd surrounded herself with family and never considered leaving Royal would find it hard to distance herself from home.

"Weren't you lonely?" She frowned. "I mean, what did you do for holidays?"

"I had friends who I spent time with. Also, a lot of times I was out of the country. I kinda got accustomed to it after a while. And I was always comfortable being alone."

"So you and Heath aren't close?"

Inwardly, Nolan flinched at her dismay. Her need for family and his need for individualism were at odds. It was just one of the many things they didn't have in common.

"I think people expect twins to be the same. Given the shared DNA and all. But Heath and I are quite different. I was held back a year before entering first grade."

"How come?"

"Heath and I were born on August 20, and my parents thought while Heath was ready for first grade, I wasn't." Although studies claimed that keeping a child back a year wouldn't affect him in the long run, the decision had caused a rift between the twins.

"That must've been an adjustment for you both."

"More so for me than Heath. We had different friend groups and were never studying the same subjects. I always felt as if I was behind him, even though we made similar grades all through school. It definitely meant we weren't as close as we had been."

"I guess that's why I didn't recall you growing up. I kinda remember Heath..."

No wonder. His brother had always been the more outgoing twin.

"I would've been a lowly freshman when you were a senior. Even if we'd gone to the same high school, I wouldn't have expected you to give me the time of day."

"I'm sorry." She sounded more confused than apologetic. "I feel like I should've noticed you. I mean, Royal isn't that big."

He was unsure if she was merely flirting with him or if he should trust the confusion underlying her remark. She genuinely seemed perplexed by her limited memory of him.

Nolan's own recollection was quite different. Chelsea had been a cheerleader and president of her school's student council, and pretty in a way that had started his teenage hormones buzzing. "A two-year age gap isn't anything now," he said, "but back then it was a lifetime. I'm not surprised at all that you don't remember me."

"I guess you're right. Huh."

Her pensive expression faded away, replaced by a dawning realization. She fixed her keen brown gaze on him and quirked an eyebrow. But whatever was turning over in her mind remained unspoken.

"What are you thinking?" he prompted, intrigued by the vibes rolling off her.

Her brow puckered. "I've never dated a younger man before."

The level of sexual tension between them ratcheted up a notch as she bit her lip and shot him a smoky glance. Nolan was having a hard time keeping track of his purpose in asking her out tonight. Heath had described Chelsea Grandin in a way that didn't jibe with the flesh-and-blood woman seated beside him.

"Seems like you might be interested in giving it a try." At least, he sure as hell hoped that was the case.

Her low hum filled the car as she gave the matter serious thought. "I think I just might."

Cocott definitely lived up to its stellar reputation. The decor was simple—dark gray walls adorned with enormous sepia images of Paris. Indirect lighting in the tray ceiling. Basic white tablecloths. A votive candle glowing on each table. The star of Cocott was the exquisite food.

The hostess led the way to a table in the back and left them with a warm smile. Nolan gallantly helped Chelsea settle into her seat before taking the chair opposite her.

"No menus?" She looked at Nolan in confusion.

He shrugged. "When I called Camila, she said she'd prepare something special for us."

"Mysterious," Chelsea murmured, a little thrill chasing across her skin.

She'd suspected that tonight's dinner would be one to remember, but she hadn't anticipated this level of intrigue. Then again, she'd never imagined Nolan would be well-connected enough to get a reservation at a place like Cocott, much less secure them a private tasting by a world-renowned chef. If the man was trying to impress her, he'd scored huge.

As she was mulling over her dinner companion, a waiter arrived with a bottle of wine.

"Good evening. I understand you are special guests of Cocott tonight." The man had salt-and-pepper hair and a lean smile. "My name is Richard, and I will be your waiter. Chef Darvas has prepared a special menu for you tonight. Starting off, I have a pinot gris from Alsace for you."

What followed was course after course of the most delicious food Chelsea had ever eaten. Seared Hudson Valley foie gras, a salad with kale and white truffle honey, and then salmon with leeks, dandelion and green apple.

While they ate, Nolan described his months of travel with Camila and all the fascinating places she'd taken him. The stories stirred young Chelsea's longing for a year spent studying abroad, and she wondered how her life would be different if she'd let her heart guide her instead of her head.

As the waiter was taking away their empty entrée plates, a beautiful woman in chef's whites approached their table. Given the success of her television show and this Dallas restaurant, Chelsea had expected a much older woman. Instead, Camila Darvas looked to be close to Chelsea's age, thirty-five. Since Nolan had his back to the kitchen, he didn't see the chef approach until Camila set her hand on his shoulder. Nolan sprang to his feet and exchanged a set of cheek kisses with her before throwing his arm wide to introduce Chelsea.

"Nice to meet you," Camila said in her accented English, her warm smile encompassing both Nolan and Chelsea.

"Your food was fantastic," Chelsea gushed, liking the Frenchwoman immediately. "I'll be honest, my sisters and I have been dying to come here, but getting a reservation is nearly impossible."

"I'm so glad you enjoyed it," Camila said. "I was a little surprised when Nolan called me to say he had someone he wanted to bring to my restaurant."

"Why is that?"

"When we traveled together, he didn't exactly appreciate my cooking."

"How is that possible?" Chelsea gaped at Nolan. "Her food is fantastic."

"I'm not a fan of all the sauces."

An affectionate look passed between Camila and Nolan that made Chelsea's heart clench. Had they been lovers? If the talented chef was Nolan's type, Chelsea questioned why he'd be interested in her. Wouldn't he be drawn to someone who shared his passion for travel and adventure? Did this confirm that he really wasn't attracted to her at all, but that he was only using her because of the oil rights?

Chelsea's chaotic thoughts were interrupted by the arrival of dessert. Her mouth watered as Camila described the final course, a bittersweet chocolate marquise with anise-scented cherries and crème fraîche ice cream.

"Nolan said you enjoyed chocolate," Camila said, her hand on the back of his chair. "I think you'll really enjoy this dessert."

"I'm sure I will," Chelsea assured the chef even as she told herself to not get too excited that Nolan had noticed her love of all things chocolate.

With a fond smile for Nolan, Camila took herself back to her kitchen. As much as Chelsea had liked the chef, she was glad the woman was gone. While meeting her had been enjoyable, it had also raised too many questions when it came to Nolan.

If he noticed that she was quieter on the way back to Royal, Nolan made no mention of it. Perhaps he assumed she was in a food coma, which wasn't far from the case. The delicious meal, combined with the different wine pairings with each course, had put Chelsea in a blissful physical state that lasted until they arrived in Royal.

"I'm parked over there." She indicated her truck, dreading the evening's end.

Despite the disquiet fluttering over Nolan's motivation for asking her out, she'd had a wonderful time. Far better than she'd expected. The type of man she usually dated had a stable profession, was pragmatic and tended to be a little dull. Nolan had fascinated her with stories of the exotic locations he'd visited, and his disarming charm had put her at ease. His adventurous spirit had sparked something restless inside her, and that, combined with her earlier worries about his reasons for asking her out, made her more than a little uncomfortable.

So, what was her next move?

Tonight, as if by mutual assent, they'd steered clear of all talk of the oil rights he and his brother were pursuing. If her whole purpose in dating him was to find out what they planned to do next, she'd abjectly failed. Instead, she'd flirted away as if she'd been on a regular date. She couldn't trust him. Planned on using him. And must avoid getting burned in the process. But damn if she didn't want a good-night kiss.

While she'd been locked in a fierce battle between her head and her hormones, Nolan had brought the Jeep to a stop behind her pickup and thrown the vehicle into Park. He turned his torso to face her. As they stared at each other in silence, Chelsea wondered if he, too, was struggling with how to end the date.

Nolan broke the silence. "Thank you for tonight."

His deep voice rumbled through her like an earthquake. She quivered in the aftermath.

"That's supposed to be my line," she responded, devouring his strong masculine features with her gaze, appreciating how his well-shaped lips softened into a small smile. Chelsea was pretty sure she could drown in his dreamy brown eyes. Had she ever dedicated so much energy to just appreciating the way a man looked? "Thank you for dinner. It was just perfect."

"I'm glad you enjoyed it."

"I really did."

Impulsively, she cupped his cheek in her palm. He drew in a sharp breath but didn't move a muscle. Her stomach clenched at the intense light in his gaze.

"I'd really like it if you would kiss me," she said, unsure when she'd decided to go off script.

"I can do that."

She stroked her thumb over his lower lip, tugging at it. "A slow kiss. One that tells me I am worth breaking the rules for."

She didn't explain what rules, but he had to recognize what they were doing was going to make their respective families unhappy. She was convinced this was why he'd decide to take her to Dallas for dinner rather than dine at one of Royal's excellent restaurants. The fewer people that saw them together, the easier it would be to deny they were dating.

If that's indeed what they were doing. Dating. Her breath hitched. Worry intruded. Maybe his mind was on something different. One way to find out…

She tilted her face and leaned ever so slightly toward

him. To her relief, he dipped his head and stroked his lips against hers in the softest, most tender of kisses. The gentleness made her senses ignite. She wanted more. For his lips to own her. His hands to learn every inch of her skin. For his tongue to glide over all her sensitive areas.

Moaning as hunger flared between her thighs, Chelsea sank her fingers into the soft texture of his hair and pressed hard into his mouth. He groaned low and deep, and suddenly he was with her in the kiss, sliding his tongue across her lower lip, taking the tender flesh between his teeth and then claiming her with a deeper contact that she could feel sizzling through every cell in her body. Feverish and wild, she longed for more, for him to slam her against a wall and run his hands all over her.

By the time he broke off the kiss, Chelsea had lost track of time and place. Groggily, she opened her eyes and caught sight of her surroundings. Whoa. She and Nolan had been making out like horny teenagers in full view of anyone wandering Main Street at nine o'clock at night.

She cursed.

"You okay?" he asked, holding her face with the tips of his fingers.

It took a huge amount of willpower to pull away. "Perfectly fine. It's just this is pretty public…"

"And Royal is a small town." He nodded in understanding. "It's still early. Do you want to go back to my place?"

Chelsea immediately perked up at his offer. She'd enjoyed spending time with Nolan and really didn't want to head home so early. "I'd like that."

Whoops. Did agreeing to go back to his place after that passionate kiss give him the idea that she intended to sleep with him on the first date? She'd better correct that assumption fast. Still, she hesitated. All too often she was criticized for speaking her mind. Would being blunt turn him off? Or maybe she didn't need to worry with Nolan. He seemed the sort of guy who could handle a little straightforward communication.

"Uh-oh," Nolan said, peering at her with a slight pucker between his eyebrows. "What's wrong?"

Chelsea blinked. "Wrong?"

"You got really serious all of a sudden."

"Oh."

She focused on his handsome face, and the concern reflected in his gaze made her want to start kissing him all over again. Damn the man for seeming too good to be true.

"I don't want you to get the wrong idea." Despite her best intentions, heat rose up her throat and burned in her face. Still, she managed to keep her tone casual. "I'm not agreeing to sleep with you."

To her relief, his teeth flashed in a broad smile. "Ever?" he teased.

The warmth in her cheeks lanced straight to her belly and coiled there like a purring cat. The vibration hit all the right spots, turning her on like crazy.

"Not tonight."

When his dimples flashed, she realized what she'd given away. Her mouth popped open, but it was too late to take it back. A second later she decided she didn't want to. Her body longed for Nolan Thurston. Good or bad, she was not strong enough to withstand the attraction between them. She just hoped when she gave in, she'd be able to survive the coming storm.

Five

"I'm surprised you're not staying at your family's ranch," Chelsea said, glancing around the loft's open floor plan. Her gaze ricocheted off the king-size bed at the far end before returning her attention to him.

They sat sideways on his couch, facing each other, their knees a whisper apart. The energy between them crackled and popped. Nolan drank in the bold drama of her features and traced the length of her slender neck to the delicate hollow of her throat. He recalled the graceful flare of her shoulder blades and the gentle wave of her spinal column as it disappeared behind that tantalizing gold zipper.

"I thought it might be a lot to expect that I would stay there after being gone for fifteen years."

Nolan hoped he'd imagined the fleeting speculation in her eyes at his remark. He wanted to believe that she was here without an agenda.

"So, how come you're still single?" he asked, deciding to distract her with personal questions. "Is every man in Royal blind?"

A startled laugh burst from her. "Thanks for the compliment, but once you get to know me better, I'm sure you'll realize that I'm no one's idea of a catch."

"Not from where I'm sitting." Nolan cocked his head and tried to suss her out. "If you're single, it's because that's the way you want it."

"Let's just say I'm so focused on the ranch that my personal life suffers." She smoothed her palm along her skirt.

He leaned his upper body forward and spoke softly. "Maybe you just haven't found the right guy."

The way her lashes fluttered and gaze zipped away, Nolan sensed he'd struck at a sore spot. Given her strong will and confident nature, he couldn't imagine any guy getting away with breaking her heart or bruising her spirit. Could he be wrong?

"Sure…" After grappling with something, she released a huge sigh. "Or I'm the problem."

Her admission startled him. Obviously, she had a story to tell. Still to be determined was whether she wanted to share it with him.

"Why would you say that?"

"The men I date have a tendency to disappear."

"Maybe you have a secret admirer who's taking them out." He made an exaggerated martial arts move with his hands and drew a faint smile from her.

"It's more like they dump me for someone less complicated and demanding to date."

"Or they're not man enough to handle an intelligent, accomplished woman."

"And it's really not that things don't work out," Chelsea said, her lips tightening with remembered annoyance. "It's more that instead of having a conversation and breaking up like civilized people, they ghost me. A couple of enjoyable dates where it feels like something might be developing, and then nothing."

"That's a crappy thing to do," Nolan said even as he wondered if he'd been guilty of that in his past. He'd assumed the women he'd gone out with had understood the nature of his business, but it was possible he'd vanished from their lives in a similarly abrupt way. "How many times has it happened?"

"Four. But the worst was Brandon. We'd dated several months before he disappeared. And I think I'm making it worse because I expect it now. I have a really hard time trusting anyone, and that gives men the impression that I'm an iceberg."

"But you're not." Half statement, half assurance. Nolan felt her relax and knew he'd struck the right note. "Trust me. That kiss earlier was dynamite, and the chemistry I feel with you tells me that you're a smoldering volcano."

"You are great for my ego," she told him with a wry smile that didn't quite mask her relief. "And a breath of fresh air."

"Maybe what you need is to date someone different from your usual type. What sort of guys do you usually go for?"

"I gravitate toward serious types who are focused on business. Men like my dad, I guess." She looked slightly dazed by her sudden insight. "As much as it drives me crazy that he's so traditional, I keep dating men that don't appreciate women who are serious about their careers."

"And that's not you."

"Far from it. I'm always trying to do things better. Most of the time I forget that every second of my day and every thought in my head doesn't have to revolve around cattle."

Nolan reached out and took her hand in his. Turning it palm up, he drew circles on her skin. "Sounds like you haven't met anybody who could take your mind off your problems."

"It's not an easy thing to do." Her lashes fluttered at his caress, and rosy color stole into her cheeks. "I'm always working twice as hard as my brother to get noticed." She made a face and looked uncomfortable with the admission.

"Why are you competing with your brother?" Nolan smiled as his light touch lured her into revealing more about her family dynamic. "It seems to make sense that as the oldest you'd be in charge."

"It's my dad. I described him as traditional." She bit her lower lip as he slid his fingers between hers. The contact was disrupting her wariness and loosening her tongue. "He believes the only person who deserves to be in charge of the ranch is a man. That means my brother."

"That seems very shortsighted of him. There are four of you, right?"

Chelsea studied their entwined hands. "Three girls and one boy. My youngest sister, Morgan, has no interest in running the ranch. She owns a boutique on Main Street. The Rancher's Daughter." With her free hand, Chelsea indicated what she was wearing. "This dress is from there."

"I think you already know my opinion of it," Nolan murmured.

"I don't dress up very often anymore." Chelsea made a face. "After Brandon ghosted me two years ago, my parents started pushing eligible men at me. I think they hoped I'd find a husband." The disgust in her voice came through loud and clear. Clearly this was not her goal.

"You don't want to get married?"

"I don't have anything against it." Chelsea shrugged. "But I don't like my parents' assumption that it's what I was born to do."

Obviously, she was a modern woman whose contemporary ideas were in conflict with her family's perception of what their daughter ought to do.

Chelsea grimaced. "Maybe that's why I've put my personal life on hold. The last thing I want to do is prove my parents right. At least not until I've achieved my goal of taking charge of the ranch. Even though it's an uphill battle, I'm convinced that I'd be completely out of the running if I started dating someone my family found acceptable."

Although Nolan doubted she meant to point out that her family would never approve of him, she had to be thinking about it. As the brother of the man who was trying to interfere with the smooth running of her ranch, she was courting trouble by not keeping her distance.

Of course, this left him wondering if, for all her casual air, she had an ulterior motive for being here with him. His chest constricted as disappointment trickled through him. He had no reason to feel this way. Hadn't he approached her with the idea of getting into her good graces and finding her family's weaknesses?

"I'm not sure why I told you that," she murmured, tunneling her fingers into her hair and giving the dark locks a sharp tug.

"You're not what I expected," he said spontaneously.

"No?" She tensed. A frown appeared to mar her smooth forehead.

He immediately saw that his offhand remark had made her wary and recalled what she'd revealed of her insecurity. "You have a reputation around town for being all business. I thought I'd have a hard time getting to know you."

She let loose a rusty laugh. "I guess that's a fair assessment. My focus has always been my family's ranch. I went to college to study ranch and animal management with the intention that I would be in charge someday." A dark cloud passed across her features.

He thought of his own ambitions and how Heath had stepped up when their dad died. "It was never a question between Heath and me. He was always going to run our ranch."

"So he's older?"

"By about fifteen minutes."

"You two never considered sharing responsibility?" Nolan shook his head. "Never. I wasn't keen on ranching, and Heath likes to do things his own way." He paused and shot her a wry smile. She was a lot like his brother. Another thing that might cause trouble between them in the future. "It worked out for both of us," Nolan continued. "Heath got the ranch, and I was free to let my wanderlust run wild."

Chelsea sighed. "I wish my brother, Vic, felt the way you do."

"You mean you wish he would give you the ranch and go do something else?"

"Frankly, yes. I'm the one with the passion for ranching." She practically growled the last word.

Obviously, Nolan could tell this was a sore subject, but one that provided much-needed insight into the Grandin family dynamic. "Does he want to be in charge?"

"I'm not sure he wants it the way I do. He's just always assumed the ranch would come to him. It's frustrating. Between all my siblings, I have the best vision for where the ranch should go. Yet my father can't imagine handing over the reins to me. I don't know if he assumes I'll one day get married and move out." Resentment poured off her in waves, an abrupt shift from the mellow mood she'd been in all evening. "It's what Layla has done. She and Joshua are getting a ranch of their own. What my dad doesn't understand is that he left her no other choice."

As if concluding that she'd shared enough about her family, Chelsea turned the conversation to things Nolan enjoyed doing when not traveling. She seemed unsurprised that his favorite activities involved adventure and often took him off the beaten path. Several times he glimpsed a wistful flicker in her eyes as he shared his pastimes. It was almost as if she regretted the lack of excitement in her life. This didn't seem to jibe with the no-nonsense businesswoman Heath had described. Nolan was quickly discovering that Chelsea Grandin was beautiful, intelligent and complicated.

"I should probably get going," Chelsea said, indicating the large, decorative wall clock. She slipped her feet from beneath her and settled them into her high heels. "I can't believe it's two in the morning."

Although he was loath to end the evening, he stood and held his hand out to assist her. "It's pretty late. Why don't I walk you down to your car?"

Up until the offer spilled from his lips, he'd planned to escort her as far as his front door and say goodbye with a lingering kiss that would leave her craving another date with him. But as he opened the condo door and gestured her through, Nolan could already feel himself missing her. The ache unsettled him.

Chelsea glanced up at him as she passed. "I'm sure I'll be okay."

"I insist."

"That's very gentlemanly of you."

There was laughter in her voice and speculation in her gaze. Nolan hadn't figured out yet if Chelsea was wary because of her dating failures in the past or of him in particular. Maybe both.

"You'd be the first woman who'd think so."

"I don't believe that. I saw the way Camila looked at you tonight. She was very happy to see you."

"We never hooked up," Nolan confessed, sensing it was important to reassure Chelsea of this. As they strolled side by side along Main Street in the direction of her car, Nolan peered at her expression. "She's great fun to travel with, but I don't cross professional lines."

"What about after the show was done? Did you have any interest in seeing her?"

Nolan shook his head. "We are great friends, but that's it for me."

"Are you sure?" Chelsea stared at him as if she didn't believe he could be so clueless. "She's beautiful and talented. Or is it because she's here in Texas and you're based out of LA?"

"She's too serious for something casual, and I wasn't interested enough to want more."

"Huh." Chelsea looked as if his answer had thrown her.

"What?"

"Just huh."

His travels had given him plenty of opportunity to meet and romance women of all kinds. Not that he was a player. Far from it. He truly enjoyed the company of women and didn't put scoring as his top priority for spending time with any of them. It just seemed as if he drew women who enjoyed sex without strings. Uncomplicated fun. Which had been great in his twenties, but since turning thirty, he'd begun to feel a different sort of restlessness.

Sitting still for the last few months had given Nolan time to mull his future. He'd caught up with some of his high school friends—many married and starting families—and gained a different perspective on his love life. He'd never imagined himself going down that road. Settling down had never been his plan, but he couldn't deny that his old classmates really seemed to enjoy having someone to come home to.

Yet Nolan recognized that domestic bliss wasn't for him. He had a globe-trotting career that kept him on the go. Sustaining a relationship under those circumstances would take a special woman. One Nolan had yet to meet.

All of a sudden, Chelsea stopped walking, jolting Nolan out of his thoughts. Looking around, he realized they'd arrived at her car. She was seconds away from escaping. He couldn't let her go without something to dream about. Catching her arm, he drew her toward him. He set his forefinger beneath her chin to tilt her head up and dropped a light kiss on her full lips. A sigh puffed out of her as he dusted a second kiss across her cheek.

"Do you want to go out again?" she murmured, sounding drowsy and content. She'd rested her palms on his waist right above his belt, and her touch seared straight through his fine cotton shirt.

He kissed her earlobe and felt her shiver. "I was going to ask you the same thing."

"Great minds…"

"Tomorrow?"

She gusted out a chuckle. "It's already tomorrow. How about Friday?"

"You're going to make me wait three whole days?"

"I'm sure you'll manage." And then she was pulling free and turning toward her car.

Nolan received another gut-kicking glimpse of that damned gold zipper running down the length of her dress before she unlocked her truck and climbed in. There was something so damned sexy about a well-dressed woman in a pickup, he thought with a grin. He might have been out of Texas nearly half his life, but some things remained the same.

"Text me when you get home," he called to her before the driver's door shut.

Chelsea leaned out to frown at him. "I'll be fine."

"You're already better than fine," he insisted, a trace of steel entering his tone. "Text me."

"It'll take me half an hour. You might be asleep by then."

"I won't be able to sleep unless I know you're home safe." Seeing that his request had spurred some sort of conflict inside her, Nolan stepped up to her car door. "I know you are capable of taking care of yourself, but I always insist my staff check in at night when we're on location. Humor me."

Her eyes softened. "I'll text."

With a satisfied nod, Nolan stepped back and watched until she'd driven off. Then he headed back to his loft to ponder what he was going to do with the dreamy Chelsea Grandin.

Despite the late hour, Chelsea was wide-awake as she drove back to Grandin Ranch. Her senses buzzed in the

aftermath of Nolan's kiss, a dangerous intoxicant for a
levelheaded woman like her. What if she grew addicted
to the high and lost her way? Maybe she was more tired
than she realized. A couple kisses weren't going to turn
her head. She was dating Nolan as a way of finding out
more about the Thurston brothers and their strategy for
going after the oil beneath her family's land. Yet it bothered her that she found him so attractive.

She'd learned a lot from Nolan, more than she'd expected. The most important item had been that the relationship between the brothers wasn't as tight as her
family believed. Chelsea felt a rush of optimism. Maybe
there was an opportunity to win Nolan to her side.

But how?

The obvious answer lay in the chemistry percolating
between them. Unfortunately, tonight had demonstrated
that she was woefully out of practice at flirting. Look
how she'd confessed that she refused to fall in love until
her father accepted her as an independent woman capable of running the ranch. She'd also shared how much
she hated the way her parents had tried for years to set
her up with every eligible man in the county.

Overcome with remembered humiliation, Chelsea
clenched the steering wheel. Why couldn't her father
open his eyes and see her as his equal instead of a
commodity he could use to cement relationships in the
community?

To her dismay, lights still burned in the living room
when she got home. Wondering if her mother had left
the light on as a courtesy or if someone was actually
waiting up for her, she parked her truck and braced herself as she entered the house.

Vic sat in their father's favorite chair, acting like he
was already head of the family. Irritation bloomed at

the sight, but it was his scowl and the fact that he was obviously waiting up for her that caused heat to steal into her cheeks. Honestly, she'd done nothing wrong, yet here she was blushing like a wayward teenager.

"What are you doing dating Nolan Thurston?"

"Not that it's any of your business," she declared coolly over her shoulder, keeping her voice low, "but I'm not dating him. I'm looking out for our family's best interest."

"How? By getting into bed with the enemy?"

Chelsea counted to ten even as she kept walking toward her bedroom. She didn't owe Vic an explanation. Still, she should've expected that with her family on edge about the Thurston brothers, they would've discussed what she was up to.

Despite all she'd learned from Nolan, Chelsea wished she'd come straight home after dinner. Or anytime in the five hours that followed. No doubt rolling in after two in the morning looked suspiciously like she'd slept with Nolan. Hell, she couldn't even deny that's what she'd wanted to do. Chelsea couldn't remember the last time a man intrigued her the way Nolan did. He wasn't like any of the men around town. All the things he'd seen on his travels had inspired her imagination and made her question the way she'd let her ambition monopolize her life.

"I didn't get into bed with anyone," Chelsea said, cursing as she paused to defend herself rather than head straight to her bedroom.

"What do you call spending all night with Nolan Thurston?"

It hadn't been all night. Vic was just trying to push her buttons. And as usual, it was working.

"Reconnaissance." She forced her lips into a smirk

while her stomach roiled at the picture she was paint-ing of herself. Coming off strong and ruthless was a defense mechanism. Their father ran Grandin Ranch like his father before him, with an iron hand. If she ex-pected to be taken seriously, she must appear tough and determined. "I think he's the key to getting through to Heath about dropping the claim."

Vic was looking less sure of himself. "Or it's just an excuse because you're into him."

Chelsea rolled her eyes. "Give me some credit." The phrasing of the comment made her wince. She shouldn't be asking Vic to give her the benefit of the doubt. She didn't need to convince him of anything.

"Everybody thinks you should stay away from him."

"Then everybody is wrong." Chelsea was used to fighting for recognition in her family, but this path she was walking with Nolan left her feeling more alone than ever. "Anyway, what does it matter? It's not like I'm going to ever stop fighting their claim. The destruc-tion that would happen to our ranch if they lease those oil rights to a drilling company would ruin our land forever. *I'm* not gonna let that happen."

"Maybe, but what if you fall for him? Maybe he's planning to seduce you in the hopes that he can change your mind."

For a split second, Chelsea considered arguing fur-ther. But why bother wasting her breath when the power belonged to her father? "You know that everything is going to be in the hands of the lawyers."

"Still, it looks bad, you hanging out with the enemy and all."

"Then I guess I'll just have to be more careful about being seen in public with him." She meant the remark to be sarcastic, but Vic took her seriously.

"It'd be better if you didn't see him at all, but if you can get some intel, then I guess it might be worth doing whatever."

Doing whatever? Chelsea felt a little bit ill. Had she gone too hard at the do-whatever-it-takes-to-win attitude?

"I don't think you and I should discuss the topic of my spending time with Nolan Thurston anymore."

"Why not?" Vic smirked. "Afraid to admit I'm right?"

Her brother was a little too cocky when it came to throwing his weight around. Maybe if he worked harder than she did on the ranch she might feel differently, but he was assuming their father would put him in charge, and that left him resting on his laurels.

Mired in his sense of entitlement, Vic didn't push himself, and his unwillingness or inability to take the initiative, think things through and make decisions drove her crazy. She'd respect him more if he behaved as her equal instead of just insisting he was.

"Because I don't answer to you," she replied. "Which means it's none of your business."

Her phone chimed. Reflexively, she glanced at the incoming text and caught her breath. It was from Nolan. Her heart fluttered as she read his message.

Home yet, Ms. Dreamy?

Cursing the nickname and her breathless state, Chelsea fired off a response.

Just arrived.

I had a great time tonight.

Me too.

Sweet dreams!

You too.

The text exchange made her forget all about the argument with Vic.

"Is that Thurston?"

She tore her attention away from the phone, her irritation returning in a rush. "It's late, and I have to be up in three hours. Unless you want to oversee the feeding this morning? Believe me, I'd be happy to sleep in for a change."

"I've got my own work," Vic grumbled.

"Of course you do. So, I'll see you around ten?" And then before her brother could reply, she stepped into her room and closed the door in his face.

With adrenaline surging in the aftermath of her fight with Vic, she wondered how long it would take for her to get to the sweet dreams Nolan had wished for her. She smiled again as she recalled the brief exchange.

Was it worth using someone to achieve her goals? Of course, there was always the possibility that Nolan was using her in turn. If they were both playing an elaborate game of cat and mouse, she might be the one in danger of getting hurt. Was she brave enough to continue?

Once upon a time, she'd let her heart lead her down a treacherous romantic path. Given the strong chemistry between her and Nolan, it would be easy for her emotions to lead her astray once again. Dating him would be a lot less complicated if she kept in the front of her mind the myriad reasons they could never work out. That way she wouldn't give her heart a chance to betray her.

And yet, did any of that matter if she succeeded in preventing the Thurstons from acting on the oil rights? Her father couldn't help but notice if she saved the ranch. Then he would have no choice but to put her in charge.

Wasn't a little heartache worth achieving everything she'd been working for all along?

Six

Nolan glanced at the woman occupying his passenger seat. Today, Chelsea wore a buttery-yellow sundress with thin straps that showed off her toned arms. She had a body built by hard work. All lean muscle beneath smooth, tan skin. He loved her athleticism and suspected she was one of the few women he knew who could match him for endurance.

"Where are we off to today?" she asked as Royal disappeared behind them.

While it wasn't unusual for him to plan fun adventures—ferreting out once-in-a-lifetime experiences was what he did for a living—he wanted every date with Chelsea to be memorable. Still, as he'd helped her into the car, a glimpse of her long, sleek thighs had set his pulse to dancing. Every instinct shouted for Nolan to bail on his plans for the evening and head straight to his place.

"I have a special surprise for us."

He'd found a company that specialized in gondola rides in Irving, Texas. It wasn't Venice, but he hoped the Italian meal, served while cruising the city's Mandalay Canal and Lake Carolyn, would appeal to her. Normally the cruise lasted two hours, but he'd paid extra to double their time. He had no intention of rushing anything with Chelsea.

"Sounds quite mysterious," she replied, delight shimmering in her wide brown eyes. "Do I get a hint?"

"Nope. I want you to be surprised."

Nolan reached across the space between them and captured her hand. Her fingers meshed easily with his, as if they'd done this a hundred times, and he brushed a kiss across her knuckles. A slight tremor went through her at his romantic gesture, and he felt a spasm of guilt. She'd been hurt several times by men she'd thought she could trust, and he was doing his damnedest to tear down her walls.

Dating Chelsea was like walking a tightrope without a net. With their families soon to be engaged in some pretty hostile conflict over the oil rights Heath intended to claim, she had to wonder if Nolan had ulterior motives for taking her out. Her intelligence was one of her strongest features. Yet the chemistry between them was real, and she seemed to be going with it. Something like that was incredibly hard to fake, but he had to consider that she might be playing him in turn. Nolan hoped the latter wasn't true.

Even as the thought popped into his mind, he knew he was in trouble. When Heath no longer needed him, Nolan planned to go back to his regular life. And with Chelsea completely bound to her ranch—and her family—it was unlikely that she would give up either one to follow him around the world. Which meant he'd better not get any more attached to Chelsea Grandin.

This realization should've made it easier for Nolan to temper his interest in her. Yet the sexual energy between them was hungry and strong. And he wasn't all that good at resisting adventures. When something called to him, he had no choice but to answer. And what he sensed about Chelsea's hidden depths called to him. He wanted to explore everything about her and, once seized by determination, no challenge was too much.

Nolan just had to keep his fascination with her on the down low. No need for Heath to know that his brother had strayed from their original mission. As long as Heath thought Nolan was simply using Chelsea to get intel on the Grandin family, the fledgling relationship between the two brothers would remain untested. At least where Chelsea was concerned.

Heath's obsession with the oil rights was a different matter.

It wasn't that Nolan didn't want to pursue the claim. He just didn't understand why their mother had owned the rights for years and never once mentioned them or tried to do anything about them. Surely, the millions a contract like that would be worth could've helped in the days when the Thurston ranch had gone through hard times.

In Nolan's opinion, too many questions remained about the situation. He wished he understood what drove his brother's obsession. He sensed more to it than the potential of adding to his wealth. Yet every time Nolan tried to raise this point with his brother, Heath refused to discuss the matter. Not wanting to upset their tenuous rapport, Nolan squashed his curiosity. Heath wasn't responsible for their falling-out. Nolan's absence from

Royal had put distance between them. That made repairing the rift Nolan's responsibility, and he wasn't going to fix anything by arguing with his brother.

"Ever been here?" Nolan asked an hour later as they strolled hand in hand toward the dock where the gondolas waited.

Her voice was husky with awe as she murmured, "I had no idea this existed."

A man dressed as a traditional gondolier smiled as they approached. "Good evening," the man intoned in a passable Italian accent and extended a single red rose to Chelsea. She accepted the token with a bemused expression and turned to glance over her shoulder at Nolan.

"We're going in that?" She nodded toward the long, narrow boat. Since it was evening, he'd opted to go with the traditional open gondola rather than one of the covered varieties.

"Since a trip to Venice was a little much for a second date, I thought this would do."

He shot her a sideways glance, eager for her approval. His heart clenched when she gave his fingers a brief, fierce squeeze.

"I absolutely love it."

"I'm glad."

The gondolier handed Chelsea into the boat, and as she settled in a comfortable seat at the middle, Nolan stepped in. While the waitstaff placed plates loaded with their three-course meal on the intimate table before them, Nolan scrutinized her expression and decided he'd chosen well. For someone who didn't stray far from home, he sensed that Chelsea was actually enjoying getting outside her comfort zone.

"To your first gondola ride," Nolan murmured as the

boat glided away from the dock. He touched his champagne flute to hers, enjoying her delight.

"I could get used to this," Chelsea said, humming in appreciation as she eyed the delicious plates of food. "Although I'm not sure how we're supposed to get through so much."

"I ordered a variety of dishes, unsure which you'd prefer."

"I'm not sure, either. I think I'd like to taste everything."

With the sun dipping toward the horizon, the July heat eased as they skimmed across the lake surface. A light breeze ruffled the hair framing Chelsea's face, and he used the excuse to slide a sable strand behind her ear. With a long sigh, her soft body relaxed into his side.

"Earlier, when I said I could get used to this," Chelsea said, gazing at him from beneath her lashes, "I wasn't just talking about the food or the boat ride. I meant you."

Should he take her declaration at face value? This was only the second time they'd gone out, and while he was feeling the strong vibe between them, she might be deliberately trying to give him a false sense of security by pushing the impression that she was more into him than she was.

Before he could decide how to respond, she added, "I'm just not sure that's a good idea."

Nolan registered a silent curse. Just when he had her figured out, she switched things up. Was she truly conflicted, or was this just a bit of gamesmanship?

"It's sensible of you to feel that way."

"That's the trouble. I struggle to feel sensible when I'm with you." She spun the stem of her champagne flute with her fingers. "We haven't talked about what's going on between our families."

"We don't have to get involved," Nolan stated, ignoring the fact that he had already agreed to help Heath by gleaning her family's strategy for opposing the claim. "You've already said you don't have control when it comes to the ranch and the decisions being made."

"That's true." She tensed as he probed this sore spot. "But the same can't be said for you."

"Heath is the one who wants to claim the oil rights."

"Are you trying to tell me you'd walk away from millions of dollars?"

He heard her skepticism and for a second wondered if their pleasant evening was over before it began.

"Yes." That wasn't a lie. If the decision was left up to Nolan, he would drop the matter. "I've made enough money with my scouting company to live comfortably for many lifetimes. But my brother is determined to fight to the bitter end."

Chelsea let out a long, exaggerated sigh and shook her head. "I wish I understood why my grandfather and Augustus Lattimore turned over the oil rights to your mother. It makes no sense."

"Maybe it was for child support. She was pregnant with your uncle's child."

"Was she?" Chelsea stared out across the water. "Other than the right timing, there's no real proof that your half sister was Daniel's daughter. And he claims he didn't know Cynthia was pregnant."

"Or maybe he knew and fled to France all those years ago to avoid the responsibility." It wouldn't surprise him. Nolan was no stranger to running away from obligation, implied or not. "How come he didn't stick around to help your father run the ranch?"

"I could ask the same of you," Chelsea countered.

"Even if I'd wanted to stick around, I don't know how much Heath would've let me help."

The instant the words escaped his mouth, Nolan regretted it.

"You know, I've been wondering why you never came back to Royal all these years." Her eyes gleamed with curiosity. "Something happened between you and Heath, didn't it?"

"Not really between us. I don't honestly think he had a clue…"

Nolan didn't talk about his family with anyone. When asked, he usually gave a pat answer about how his family owned a ranch in Texas and that ranching wasn't his thing. He should've known that Chelsea could inspire him to spill more than he usually shared.

"Heath was Dad's right hand and spent every spare second following him around the ranch, learning how to run it. When Dad died, even though we were only in elementary school, Heath stepped up and helped Mom a lot, eventually taking over running of most things by high school." Nolan thought about the ranch journal his father had kept and how he'd specified that it should go to Heath.

"I know firsthand what it's like to compete with a sibling. Even though my father loved Heath and me equally, there was no question that they were more in sync."

Chelsea leaned into his understanding, and her head settled against his shoulder, as if to take comfort from being close.

"At the time, our mom couldn't afford to hire a manager, and besides, Heath was convinced that everything would fall apart without him overseeing the operations." Nolan recalled how he'd sometimes felt like an outsider when he and Heath did things with their father. Dad and elder son had so much in common and so much to say to each other that a lot of the time Nolan just retreated into his own imagination. "I was jealous."

"Jealous? Why?"

"He was always closer to my dad. They had so much in common, and I always felt like a third wheel. It caused me to pull away from them. Even my mom and sister." This fact hadn't occurred to him at the time, but looking back on it, especially after losing his mom and Ashley, he acknowledged that his resentment had caused him to build walls.

"I get that," Chelsea said. "I've never been close with my dad, either. While he showers my brother with his time and attention, I had to learn about ranching from the foreman and at college." She toyed with the silverware as she continued, "But what really kills me is when Vic gets the credit for things that I've done. I still remember the shock I felt when I realized that being the oldest gave me no extra edge. I committed to doing whatever it took to prove myself. The problem is, no matter how hard I work, my father is blind to my achievements."

"I'm sorry your dad is like that. Even though I wasn't interested in ranching, when it came to fishing or running around on ATVs, the three of us had a blast. There just wasn't always time for fun. In the end, it all worked out. I got to see the world, and Heath gets to run the ranch he loves."

"I guess we are just destined to find our way based on what we want out of life. You are interested in seeing the world, and I'm interested in running it." Her lips curved into a wry grin. "Or at least my corner of it."

It bummed Nolan out a little that they were both so different in this way. Eventually, he would have to leave Texas. He couldn't ignore his business forever. Many of the projects in the works would begin to ramp up, and he would start to scout locations. He thought about traveling with her, sharing many of the places that he'd loved. But she was so tied to her ranch. And with her locked in competition with her brother, he couldn't imagine convincing her to leave it, even for a few weeks. Was it crazy that this was only their second date and he was already uncomfortable at the thought of leaving her behind?

"Have you ever considered doing anything else?" Nolan posed the question as much to himself as to her and was unprepared for the stark anxiety that streaked across her face.

"Lately, I've been spending a lot of time wondering what I'm going to do if my father hands the reins over to my brother."

Her admission took him by surprise. Nolan reached out and took her hand. "That won't happen. He's going to come around."

But even as he reassured her, part of Nolan was hoping that one day Chelsea might lose the ranch and be forced to look for something new. He'd recognized that his stories had ignited her sense of adventure, and he wondered if a future existed where he could convince her to leave Texas and venture into the big, wide world. With him.

Chelsea stood on the back porch of the ranch house and stared across the side yard in the direction of the twenty acres her grandfather had gifted her on her twenty-first birthday. She'd planned to build a house there and demonstrate to her family that she was dug in. Although she enjoyed her close connection with her family, having three generations living in fifteen thousand square feet made for little personal space or privacy. Liking the idea of owning a home where she could be separate, yet remain close to her family, she'd hired an architect to draw up plans, interviewed contractors and had even gone so far as to pick out finishes. Yet she'd never pulled the trigger. In part because these last few years she'd focused so exclusively on the ranch that there was neither time nor energy for anything else. Plus, with her grandparents aging, she knew her time with them was limited.

Now, however, since starting to date Nolan, she wished she'd gone forward with the house. Every time she left for or came in from one of their dates, she ran into someone with an opinion about her activities.

"Chelsea!"

At the sound of her name, she wrenched herself out of her thoughts. Turning her head, she spied Layla standing beside her. "Sorry?"

The entire Grandin family had gathered for Sunday dinner to talk about the Thurston brothers and the oil rights claim. Anticipating the dread moment when the conversation would turn to her decision to date Nolan, she'd almost given in to his dinner invitation and bailed on her family. Instead, for the last hour, over predinner cocktails, she'd been defending her actions and reiterating her motivation while each one of her family members—with the exception of her grandmother Miriam, who at eighty-eight was having health issues—had dumped a truckload of censure upon her.

Simmering with frustration, she'd escaped to the back deck to cool off before dinner.

Her sister frowned. "I've been talking to you for ten minutes."

"Sorry."

"What is up with you? You've been so distracted lately." Layla gave her an odd look. "Ever since you met Nolan Thurston. It's like you're into the guy."

With her stomach in knots, Chelsea shrugged dismissively. "If I'm fooling you, then he's not going to catch on to what I'm doing."

"Are you sure it's him you're fooling?"

Chelsea sucked in a sharp breath. "What is that supposed to mean?"

"It's just that he's really different from all the guys you've dated before. It wouldn't surprise me if you fell for all his smoldering sexiness and masculine arrogance."

"I mean, he's sexy, sure." Her sister's description of Nolan made Chelsea frown. "But I don't see him as arrogant."

In fact, being with him left her awash in comfort. He seemed to understand her better than her family did. Having someone on her side was amazing. So much so that it only felt the littlest bit scary to let her guard down and allow herself be taken care of for a change.

Layla rolled her eyes. "Are you kidding? When he approached me a couple months ago, he was all, 'You and I should go out to lunch and discuss the oil rights claim. And bring your sister.'"

The commanding baritone Layla adopted sounded nothing like the Nolan Chelsea had been dating. Goose bumps rose on her arm. Was it possible that she wasn't seeing his true self? It wasn't unimaginable that he was playing her. In fact, the thought had crossed her mind often. After all, she was playing him.

As much as she wanted to reject her sister's insight, Chelsea would be unwise to ignore this reminder to be careful. If only it wasn't so easy to forget everything except her growing desire when she was with him. Simple things like the way he slipped his hand around her waist to guide her or his fondness for tucking strands of her hair behind her ear. The fleeting touches combined with the intensity of his gaze sometimes caught her off guard. He made her feel attractive and desirable, and she thrilled to the sizzle of their chemistry. He treated her as a woman he wanted to possess while reassuring her that he appreciated her intelligence and opinions.

"I thought the whole point of you dating him was so you could get in with the enemy."

"He never wants to discuss the oil rights," Chelsea told her sister. "I think we both recognize that we are on opposite sides of a fraught issue."

Her sister had driven a stake straight into the heart of Chelsea's dilemma. She had originally decided to go out with Nolan with the idea that she would dig for information. Instead, she'd avoided asking any questions that might disturb the positive energy flowing between them. Which meant she was doing exactly what her sister accused her of—she was dating the enemy and loving every second of it.

"Oh, for heaven's sake," Chelsea said, tossing her hands up in exasperation while her heart pounded erratically against her ribs. "It's been like a week and a half, and we've only gone out a few times." The actual number of official dates was six, but Chelsea kept that to herself. "It's going to take time to gain his trust."

"Time is of the essence," Layla reminded her.

"I know." Chelsea pinched the bridge of her nose to combat a growing headache. "I don't want them to ruin our ranch, but nothing is going to happen in the next few days."

Layla gave her a searching look. "This isn't like you."

"What isn't like me? I've never been one to rush into anything. I think everything through and then put a plan into place."

"Sure." Her sister sounded worried. "But you usually have a plan. I have not seen any sign of one. You are simply going out with that man and…" Layla cocked her head and studied Chelsea. "Enjoying him."

Chelsea made a strangled noise. "Don't be ridiculous."

"Deny it all you want, but I think you like him."

The only sound Chelsea could manage was some unimpressive sputtering. It was one thing to lie to her parents and Vic, but convincing Layla that she had everything under control was way harder.

"I do like him," Chelsea admitted and sighed. "He's been everywhere and has these amazing stories about all the things he's seen. Plus, he's easy on the eyes, and we've got great chemistry…"

"I knew it." With each syllable Chelsea had uttered, Layla's expression had grown more worried. "I just knew it. You are falling for him."

"*Falling* is a little extreme."

"You are falling for the guy. Why would you do that when you know the Thurstons can't be trusted?"

"I know they can't be trusted." Chelsea groaned softly. "Listen, I have everything under control. Honestly, when have you known me to do something rash?"

"You have always been the most sensible of any of us, and I know you're far more guarded since what happened with Brandon." Layla grew pensive. "But when it comes to love, none of us can see it coming."

Two months earlier, Layla had found love with Joshua, but a misguided ruse involving a twin switch nearly ruined their romance before it truly began.

"Whoa, no. Who said anything about love?" Chelsea waved her hands, desperate to ward off her sister's misguided assumptions. "There's no way I'm going there. I think he's hot as sin, and sure, I'm not going to deny that I wouldn't mind sleeping with him. But he's only in

Royal temporarily. Eventually, he will have to get back to his globe-trotting ways. And my life is here. I'm not getting emotionally involved."

"I guess." Layla didn't seem all that convinced. "But I've seen you date other guys, and this is different. You're relaxed and seem really…secure."

Her sister's description made Chelsea flinch. Despite knowing their fling had an expiration date, she did feel secure with Nolan. Maybe because she had no possibility of a future with him, she could date him without expectations.

"I'm worried about you," Layla finished.

"You don't have to be. I just have a lot on my mind. Now that Grandpa is gone, Dad's timetable for choosing which of us will get control of the ranch has moved up. He's going to want to make sure his successor is thoroughly trained before he retires. Which means I have even less time to convince Dad that Vic doesn't deserve to be in charge. That's the only thing on my mind. Well, that and what might happen to the ranch if Heath succeeds in laying claim to the oil rights."

"Heath…? What about Nolan?" Layla never got her question answered, because Chelsea's phone began to ring.

When she glanced down and saw the caller was Nolan, her pulse jumped in anticipation of his whiskey-smooth voice in her car.

"I have to take this." Chelsea stabbed her finger against the green button. Not until she spied her sister's astonished expression did she consider what her actions had revealed about her feelings for him.

"This is exactly what I'm talking about," Layla protested, adding an exaggerated eye roll to further punctuate her disgust.

"Hey." Chelsea shot daggers at her sister before turning her back and striding the width of the house away from Layla. "What's up?"

"I just wanted to finalize our meeting time tomorrow."

She liked that he never left her hanging regarding plans. She'd dated guys in the past who left things until the last minute or never bothered to call when they were running late. To her mind, that was the height of rudeness. She knew that some men didn't communicate well, but what was the big deal about letting a girl know that you couldn't make a date? And then there was Brandon. She'd thought they were serious until one day he'd neglected to show up and then didn't respond to her texts or calls asking him what was going on.

"I'll be by your place around two o'clock."

"Can you give me a hint what we're doing?" he asked.

"Nope. It's your turn to be surprised."

"I guess I'll just have to be patient. And speaking of that, are you sure you can't come by tonight?"

A surge of heat coiled in her midsection. His voice had taken on a smoky tone that drove her mad with longing.

Chelsea glanced toward her sister and sighed with regret. "No. The whole family has gathered for Sunday night dinner, and there's no way I can sneak away."

Layla was gesturing toward the French doors that led from the deck to the great room. Chelsea waved at her to go ahead. Instead, her sister stood beside the doors with her arms crossed, looking like she planned to scowl at Chelsea until she ended the call and came inside.

"Then I'll just have to wait and see you tomorrow."

"It'll be worth the wait, I promise."

"I'm counting on it. G'night, Ms. Dreamy. Sweet dreams." His warm goodbye sent pleasure spiraling through her.

"You, too."

It seemed hard to believe they'd only gone out a handful of times, and each time was more amazing than the last. Not that they'd all been as noteworthy as the gondola ride or dinner at Cocott, but Nolan was fun to be around and made even the most mundane activities a lot of fun.

If only she'd been able to find this sense of camaraderie in someone who wasn't trying to mess with her family's ranch. The unfairness of it all felt like being clocked in the jaw. For a brief second, her chest grew uncomfortably tight.

All too aware that her sister continued to radiate disapproval, Chelsea composed her face into bland disinterest and headed for the house. After one final look over and an *uh-huh* of disgust, Layla—and her opinions about Chelsea's feelings for Nolan—preceded her sister into the house.

To Chelsea's relief, Layla made no attempt to bring her concerns up to the family over dinner. This didn't mean that the conversation wasn't at the forefront of Chelsea's mind. Was she too wrapped up in Nolan? Well, obviously, she found him handsome, charming and intriguing, but while every inch of him appealed to her, he was in league with his brother to ruin her family's ranch. That should bother her so much that she found Nolan detestable. Only she didn't.

The man had a body to die for and the engaging personality to match it. He made her laugh at a time when she was too stressed to even smile. She in turn made excuses for what he and Heath intended to do to her and to her family.

Why was she doing this to herself? Even without the feud between their families, it was never going to work between them. And yet she couldn't bring herself to stop seeing him. Despite knowing he would eventually run off in search of adventure. In spite of the worry that he could be using her to further his family's claim to what lay beneath her family's land.

Layla was right. Chelsea was becoming emotionally invested in Nolan. The game she was playing was a perilous one, because the person most in danger of getting fooled was her.

Seven

When Chelsea showed up at his door in tight jeans and a red crop top that bared her chiseled abdomen, Nolan had no idea how he was going to get them both out of the loft before he lost his battle with lust. The top was held together by a line of tiny strawberry buttons, and Nolan imagined he could hear them pinging off his walls as he tore it open. Did she have any idea how much he adored her in red? Before meeting her, his favorite color had been blue. Now he was obsessed with shades from crimson to scarlet, as long as they encased Chelsea's lean curves.

"I hope you're ready for anything," she said, her eyes glowing with excitement.

They'd been out to dinner several times when she could get away from the demands of the ranch for a few hours. Today, they had a longer date planned, an outing Chelsea insisted on keeping a surprise. Her saucy grin broadcast how much she liked being in control. In fact, Nolan enjoyed it as well.

Nolan raised an eyebrow as he gestured her inside. "I'm game if you are."

"I'm so game."

Not only was she a treat for the eyes, she smelled good enough to eat. Her shoulder brushed his chest as she passed by, and he caught a whiff of her berry-scented lotion. Suddenly besieged by the need to nibble his way up and down her fragrant skin, Nolan took in her playful updo and red lip as she sashayed into his living room. Her cowboy boots gave her hips a gentle rolling motion that seized his attention and wouldn't let go.

"You look great," he rasped, losing control of his voice.

"So do you." Her gaze held smoky approval as she took in his worn jeans and snug V-neck T-shirt. She reached out and picked up the medallion he wore around his neck, the light brush of her fingers singeing him through the thin fabric. "This is cool. Something you picked up on your travels?"

"Tibet. It's a Kalachakra, a powerful mantra for peace. It reduces suffering by calming negativity and conflict." He covered her hand with his so that they held the necklace together. "These represent the moon, the sun and the flame. It's a symbol of good fortune and protection for the wearer."

"All that sounds like something I could use." A wistful sigh puffed from her lips. "Next time you're there, pick me up one, will you?"

"How about you just take the one I'm wearing?" He lifted the chain off his neck and dropped it over her head. The pendant settled amid the column of strawberry buttons between her breasts, and Nolan gave himself several seconds to admire the way the silver chain looked against her tan skin.

"Are you sure? It came all the way from Tibet. Are you sure you can part with it?" She turned her big brown eyes on him, and Nolan knew he'd give her this and more to make her happy.

"It looks like it was made for you."

"Thank you." Sending her fingers tunneling through his hair, she drew him down for a grateful kiss. She nipped at his lower lip before opening her mouth to the thrust of his tongue. Eager to take things further, he groaned as she eased away, whispering, "I'm going to treasure it."

With his hormones dancing in appreciation of her soft breasts grazing his chest, Nolan smiled down at her. Her lips remained softly parted, and Nolan knew if he kept staring at them, he'd claim her mouth all over again. He was close to surrendering to the urge to scoop her into his arms, carry her to bed and rip off every one of those strawberry buttons with his teeth. His fingers twitched as he imagined himself giving the top one a fierce twist. One by one, they would fall to the floor, exposing her beautiful breasts. He was mentally sliding his lips over one lush curve when the fingers gliding down his cheek fell away. The sudden loss knocked him out of his trance.

"Should we get going?" From her bright tone, Nolan suspected she had no sense of the fierce hunger raging inside him.

With the imprint of her final caress lingering on his skin, Nolan scrubbed his hand across his jaw and somehow summoned the strength to croak, "Sure."

If he didn't get them out of the condo, he would never know what surprises she'd organized for him. And from the gleeful anticipation sparkling in her gaze, she was looking forward to whatever she had planned.

Nolan watched her charming butt as she descended the stairs ahead of him. Damn. It was going to be a long afternoon.

Since Chelsea knew where they were going, she drove. Whatever she'd planned must've been a doozy, because she was bubbling with excitement. Nolan liked this take-charge side of her, mostly because reveling in her power made her that much more attractive. Her brown eyes glowed with satisfaction while a mysterious smile teased her lips. Her high spirits were infectious, and Nolan found his nerves humming as they traveled a series of two-lane roads.

"Almost there," she assured him, casting a teasing look his way. "You are going to be so surprised."

She turned off the highway onto a road that ran parallel to a well-maintained landing strip.

Mystified, he searched the small airfield. "Are we flying somewhere?"

"You might say that."

They flashed past a sign. "Skydiving?" The one-word question burst from him on a laugh. "This is what you want to do?"

"You're certified, and I called and confirmed that with your credentials we can jump tandem."

Nolan's entire body flushed with anticipation. She'd been intrigued when he talked about his experiences, but he'd never imagined she'd be interested in jumping herself.

"Are you sure about this?"

"Aren't you?"

"Of course. I've made nearly a hundred jumps…"

He trailed off as she parked. "You trust me to keep you safe?"

It wasn't just the jump he was asking about.

Flashing her even, white teeth, Chelsea shut off the engine and turned to face him. "There's no one I'd rather jump out of a plane strapped to."

Nolan slid his fingers into her thick hair and tugged to draw her closer. "You, Ms. Dreamy, continue to bewitch and amaze me."

"I'm glad." Her lashes fanned her cheeks as his head dipped and their lips grew steadily closer. "With everything you've seen and done, I wasn't sure I could find something adventurous enough for you."

He dusted soft kisses across her lips, mingling their breath. "If you're doing this for me, it's not necessary. Being with you is adventure enough for me."

"That's sweet." While her fingertips traced a line of fire down his neck, she nipped his jawline and then lightly raked his earlobe with her teeth. "But being with you has inspired me to be a little reckless, and I want to test the mettle of my bravery."

Nolan shuddered as his nerves went incandescent in response to her tantalizing touch. "I've been trying like hell not to ravish you these last few days, but I can't promise to be good after jumping out of an airplane with you strapped to my body."

"The anticipation has been killing me, too," she whispered, her eyes blazing with hunger. She took his hand and placed his palm over her breast, then moaned as his fingers kneaded gently.

For the last week, he'd been reminding himself that anticipation could heighten pleasure. When he at last slept with Chelsea, he intended the moment be absolutely memorable. For both of them. But he was near the end of his rope, and skydiving with her was sure to push him beyond the limits of his control.

"We could just go park somewhere deserted and take the edge off." His fingers roamed over her abs and teased the waistband of her jeans. She rotated her hips in his direction and slid her foot over his leg. The console between them was a problem.

"I think about you at night," she whispered, her voice fierce and urgent as her tongue flicked against his neck. "I imagine you doing all kinds of things to me."

The sexy words made him desperate for her. "Do you come when you think of what I'm doing?"

He dipped his hand between her legs. She gasped as he stroked her sensitive flesh, the heat of her no less tantalizing for it being muffled by the fabric of her jeans. They both panted as she rocked against his palm. Nolan sent his lips roaming down the delicate column of her neck. When he reached the spot where her shoulder started, he eased the edges of his teeth into her skin, gently but with enough pressure to leave the tiniest of marks.

"Yes," she moaned on the thinnest whisper of air, and even more softly she added, "Again."

As he gave her what she wanted, Nolan found himself spiraling into another reality, a sensual, intoxicating realm that existed for just the two of them.

Nolan dimly noticed the sound of a car door slamming, and a second later he was jerked back into awareness of their surroundings by the staccato blast of a horn as someone locked their vehicle. He set his forehead against hers, all too conscious of his ragged breathing and unsteady pulse. They sat that way for a long time while their bodies calmed. But even as his heart rate steadied, his need for her continued to smolder.

"Being with you is all the rush I need," he told her, wondering how she'd feel about him after jumping out of a plane at ten thousand feet.

"That's music to my ears." She dropped a brief kiss on his lips. "Now, let's go skydiving."

Chelsea barely felt the impact as she and Nolan landed in the empty field that had been designated as the landing site. Her entire body was lit up with adrenaline and desire. The jump had been spectacular, a breath-stealing plunge through the heavens, followed by a leisurely drift along the thermals after the chute had bloomed above them. For someone who normally kept her feet firmly planted on the ground, the experience had electrified her. And left her pondering all she'd given up by choosing to focus her energy on the ranch.

"That was crazy," she yelled as Nolan released her harness from his. "Amazing."

Robbed of his strong, reassuring presence behind her, Chelsea stumbled and would've fallen, except he caught her and spun her into his arms. Her heart fluttered wildly at the intensity of his expression as his arm wrapped around her, squeezing her against him once more. Before she had a chance to say a word, his lips crashed down on hers. Wild, intoxicating emotion exploded through her, and she pushed into the kiss, wrapping her arms around his neck and feasting on his mouth.

He lifted her off the ground, and she wrapped her thighs around his waist. Her arms encircled his shoulders as the press of his erection against the most sensitive parts sent her body into spasms of joy. She wiggled her hips, driving her heated core against him. Nolan dropped to his knees and, with his arm binding Chelsea to his chest, lowered her to the cushion of grass in the big, empty field.

His lips coasted down her throat. She cupped his head and arched her back, offering him more of her skin to nibble on. The heat of the July afternoon was unbearable, but it was nothing compared to the inferno raging inside her. Chelsea squirmed in an effort to free herself from the binding harness, and sensing her distress, Nolan rolled them until he lay beneath her.

With a triumphant gasp, Chelsea sat up, popped the catch in the middle of her chest and ripped the straps off her shoulders. Panting, she attacked Nolan's clasp. His fingers curved over her bare waist between the crop top and her jeans, thumbs riding the ripple of her ribs, making her hands shake as she struggled to get her hands on his skin in turn. Seconds later, she let out a satisfied sigh as she successfully tunneled her fingers beneath the hem of his shirt and rode his six-pack to his impressive pecs. As he groaned in pleasure, she curved her fingers and lightly raked her nails across his nipples. She grinned as a sharp expletive escaped his parted lips.

"I want you, right here, right now," she told him, leaning down to seize his lower lip between her teeth.

"You're killing me, you know that, right?"

"I'm glad." She didn't mean to come off all cocky and was glad to see he didn't take her words at face value. His crooked smile gave her a second to gather her wits. "What I mean is every time you touch me, I go wild, and I'm really glad I can do the same for you."

"Trust me, you do."

Nolan lifted his hips and drove his erection against her tender flesh. She met his thrust with a little twist of her own that made them both moan with frustration and pleasure.

"As hot as it would be to do this here and now," he said, "we really are not gonna have time to do it right before we're picked up." Yet even as he said this, he sank his long fingers into her hair and pulled her close for a sizzling kiss. After a long time, he released her lips and murmured, "And I want all the time in the world to make love to you."

Chelsea shuddered at his declaration and recognized that he was right. As hungry as she was for him, a frantic coupling in a field was not how she wanted their first time together to happen.

"So, back to your place right now, or dinner first?" She'd planned for the latter, but with desire raging through her veins, she wasn't sure she could eat anything. Not while she was starved for the six feet of sizzling male who'd slid his fingers beneath her crop top and cupped her lace-covered breasts.

"Definitely dinner," he teased, whisking his thumbs over her nipples. "I want the anticipation to build."

"You don't think it's been building?" she asked, finishing with a little gasp as he nibbled on her ear.

"It has for me from the moment I set eyes on you across Main Street."

His admission sent a familiar thrill up her spine. She wasn't used to having a man seduce her with words. She'd always been so practical with those she chose to date in the past.

"Please, can we just go back to your place?" She made the request in a small, breathless voice, unaccustomed to begging for what she wanted. "I can't wait any longer to be with you."

"I'd like that more than anything."

As more kisses followed, each one hotter and deeper,

Chelsea wondered if he had any idea that she'd shared more with him than with any man she'd ever known.

She'd confided how her father's lack of faith in her abilities saddened her. Voiced the question if Vic became the sibling in charge, what that meant for her future. Most days she got up and applied a tough persona along with her mascara and lipstick. None of her family knew about Chelsea's deep anxiety, but she'd drawn back the curtain and put her fragile confidence on display for Nolan.

It should terrify her that she'd revealed her insecurity. Yet maintaining her defenses with Nolan hadn't seemed necessary. He'd given her a safe space to explore her fears because he'd been willing to share his concerns about his relationship with his brother, the pain of losing his mother and sister and his regret that staying away these last fifteen years had robbed him of precious time with them.

They were oblivious to the vehicle that rolled up on them until the light tap of a horn roused them from their sex-fogged delirium. Chelsea and Nolan jerked apart, laughing as they resettled their clothes and got to their feet. Another time, a different man, and Chelsea would've been mortified to be caught making out in public, but being with Nolan was so easy and fun that she didn't mind the knowing looks cast her way by the driver and his passengers.

Hand in hand, she and Nolan headed to the van. They settled into the back and grinned at each other in delight, but the intense gleam in his eyes made Chelsea uncomfortably aware of the throbbing heat between her thighs. How was she supposed to survive the hour-long drive back to Royal? Anticipation, hell. She was in serious distress.

"Let's get out of here," Nolan whispered in her ear once they were back at the skydiving base. He slid his hand into the back pocket of her jeans and gave a little squeeze. "I need to be inside you before I lose my mind."

His sexy words made her breath hitch. "I want that, too." She handed him her keys. "Feel like driving? I don't feel all that steady at the moment."

Taking the keys, he planted a quick, hard kiss on her lips before nudging her toward the passenger side of the truck. If the drive back to Royal seemed to take forever, at least she was lost in a blissful daze. She distantly heard herself asking Nolan about his other skydiving adventures and tried to pay attention to his answers, but with her blood pounding hot and fierce through her veins, she struggled to concentrate on anything but what would happen when they returned to his loft.

They barely made it through the door before Chelsea launched herself at him. She dived her fingers into his lush, wavy hair and reached up on tiptoe to press her mouth to his. The kiss started hot and hungry but quickly slowed down as Nolan gently caressed her burning cheek and ran his tongue along her bottom lip. A breath eased out of her tight chest as he played with her lips, pressing and nibbling kisses that were both tender and hungry.

Instead of moving them to his waiting bed, Nolan picked her up and set her on the nearby kitchen counter.

"Here?" she squeaked, losing control of her voice as he stepped between her parted thighs and ground his erection into her.

"For a start."

Eyes glowing with wicked intent, he gripped her boot
and slid it off her foot. She barely heard the bang as it hit
the wood floor above the pounding of her heart. While
he loosened the second boot, she shimmied out of the
crop top, letting it fall. His eyes lit with approval as he
scanned her pale breasts encased in red lace.

"Damn," he murmured. "I do love you in red."

She reached behind her for the clasp. "How do you
feel about me out of it?" In seconds the bra had come
undone, and his gaze found hers as he peeled the straps
down her arm, exposing her.

"You are perfection," he murmured, his lips easing
onto the delicate skin behind her ear, making her quiver.

His palm pressed hard between her thighs, inviting her to rub her tender parts against him. In a rising frenzy of desire, she realized how close she was
to coming.

"Nolan," she panted. "This is… You are… I'm…"
She fumbled with the zipper on her jeans, needing his
fingers inside her. Before she'd done more than popped
the button, an orgasm broke over her like a wave, shattering her into pieces. "Damn." Part relief, part protest,
the curse made him chuckle.

"Most women enjoy coming," he muttered before his
mouth clamped down over hers. He drove his tongue
forward to tangle with hers, and she half sobbed as af-
tershocks pummeled her.

Her release was only partially satisfying. What she
truly craved was his possession. To be filled by him
and made whole. And Nolan seemed to understand,
because he finished stripping off her jeans and underwear, hooked his fingers in the waistband and tugged
the denim off her hips and down her legs.

A startled laugh escaped as her naked butt connected with the cool stone countertop, but then his hand found the heat between her legs and she went up in flames.

"You're so wet," he said, sliding his fingers across her.

A greedy moan poured from her lips. "That feels so good. I've been waiting so long…" She captured his face in hers and kissed him hard. "You know what would feel better, though? If you got naked, too, and we went over to that big bed of yours. I need your skin against mine." Their hearts beating together.

That last bit was too romantic to say out loud. As much as she might enjoy talking dirty in bed, she was terrified to send him running by divulging that her need for him was more than physical.

Nolan bracketed her hips in his strong fingers and lowered his forehead to hers. "I want that, too."

She reached between them to unfasten his jeans and worked feverishly until she had them off his hips. Hissing in appreciation at the impressive tent his erection made in his boxer briefs, she carefully released it from the confining fabric. He set his head against her shoulder and shuddered as her hand closed around him.

A curse slipped from his lips as she explored his hard length, learning its velvety surface and the shape beneath. All too soon he covered her hand with his and pulled it away from him.

"No more." He lifted her palm to his lips, nibbling on the sensitive mound near her thumb. "There's only so much willpower available when I'm with you."

"I don't want you to hold back."

He snorted. "Ms. Dreamy, I'm just trying to hold on."

And then he was stepping out of his jeans, ripping his T-shirt over his head. She barely got a chance to appreciate the impressive cut of his biceps, the rolling muscles of his shoulders or the toned beauty of his abs before he slid his hands beneath her butt cheeks and lifted her. With a surprised murmur, she wrapped her arms and legs around him as he carried her—at long last—to his bed.

Eight

Nolan set Chelsea down on her feet beside his bed and took a step back, astonished at his rapid heart rate and the irregular cadence of his breathing. "Let me look at you," he said, his eyes roving over her naked perfection, seeing the effort it cost her to hold still beneath his scrutiny. "You are gorgeous."

"You're not so bad yourself."

"I can't wait to get to know every inch of you."

"I want that." She blew out a ragged breath. "Can we get started?"

"You're in a hurry?"

"I'm suddenly really nervous."

This was his moment to reassure her, so Nolan stepped closer and cupped her cheek in one palm. "You don't need to be nervous. I'll take care of you." He threaded her long hair through his fingers and gave a gentle tug.

"I know you will," she responded, edging closer until

the heat of their skin leaped across the narrow distance between them and burned away her hesitation. She smoothed her hand over his chest, fingers dancing over his pecs. "In fact, I'm counting on it."

Nolan drew in a deep breath and sighed as she raked her nails down his abs, letting her nerves settle as she explored his hard planes, the structure of bones beneath his overheated skin. At last he could take no more and took her by the shoulders, pivoting her toward the bed. As the backs of her knees encountered the mattress, she flopped backward, spreading her arms wide as she landed. Nolan stared hungrily at her firm breasts, watching her nipples harden beneath his regard. Shooting him an enticing grin, she wiggled her way toward the middle of the bed.

Reaching into the nightstand, he pulled out a condom and slid it on. Her eyes flashed, feral and wild, as she watched his every movement.

"Nolan." Greedy and impatient, his name was a growl torn from her lips. She arched her back and drew her fingertips from her navel to the cleft between her breasts. "Touch me, please."

He smiled wolfishly. Setting his knee on the bed beside her, he caressed along her thigh and into the indent of her waist, riding her ribs to the soft curve of her breast. She sucked in a breath as he cupped her gently and then squeezed before feathering fingertips across her tight nipples.

"This is where I've wanted you from the first moment I saw you," he murmured, his voice hot and hungry. Nolan captured one rosy bud between his lips and flicked his tongue over it. "Naked, in my bed."

"I want you," she whispered, her thighs falling open as she rocked her hips. "Make me yours."

Her plea lanced through him like lightning. It felt so

good to have her hands roaming over his body, but he'd waited so long to have her, and holding back much longer might have catastrophic consequences. He shifted between her thighs, settling his hand on the back of her leg, opening her wide, making room for himself. She obliged with a soft purr of delight, raking her fingers through his hair.

He took his erection in one hand and teased her with the head, coating himself in her wet heat. She gasped as he sank into her, and he stilled.

"Does it hurt?"

She shook her head. "You feel amazing. More. I want all of you."

"I can give you more." He circled her thigh with his fingers and hitched it over his hip, opening her up so he could go deeper.

"Yes." She gave a breathless nod and sank her fingers into his forearm as he pulled back and stroked forward once again. "Like that."

This time, as he lay fully embedded in her, he brought his hand to her face and dragged his thumb over her soft lips. He'd never felt this closeness with anyone before and knew she'd gifted him with a glimpse into the tender emotions she kept hidden.

"You're incredible."

Her lashes fluttered. "You make me feel that way."

And then desire took over and Nolan had to move. He kept his strokes smooth and rhythmic, watching her reaction to each thrust. A delectable smile curved her soft lips, and she lost herself in their lovemaking. Watching her, Nolan found his own grin forming. What was it about her?

"Harder," she commanded.

With a reverent groan, he obliged, pumping faster,

harder, aware that she was dissolving beneath him, her cries growing more reckless and abandoned. Panting as he surged toward the threshold of ecstasy, Nolan had just enough presence of mind to make sure Chelsea came with him.

"Come for me," he coaxed, each second carrying him nearer his climax. He loved how the world had fallen away and there was only Chelsea.

She wrapped her legs around him tighter, signaling she was close to the edge as well. Nolan watched her, waiting for the telltale signs, feeling her body quickening as his own screamed at him to let go. And then she was there, her body bucking with the power of it, her inner muscles contracting on him, drawing him deep and hard into her as an orgasm tore through her like a tornado. Nolan took it all in for several heartbeats, watched her shatter and then let himself be pulled apart in her arms.

In the aftermath, Nolan's lips drifted along her damp skin, smiling at the salty taste of her, breathing in the sexy musk of her arousal. He wanted to know all her scents and sounds and flavors. To hear her snore softly in her sleep and press her round backside against his morning erection. So much to learn. Yet he couldn't help but hear a ticking clock in the background. A warning that stolen moments like these wouldn't last forever.

"You know, I could get used to this," she murmured, nuzzling into his throat, her teeth nipping suggestively. She'd draped her arms over his shoulders, and despite her boneless lassitude, he could tell her thoughts were spinning. "Let's stay in bed like this forever."

As Nolan processed her statement, a wave of goose bumps rushed over his skin. Little by little she was shedding all the protective layers she wore to keep herself safe. Originally, he'd thought he could romance her, get the information Heath needed and move on. Assuming what was between them was strictly physical, he'd stupidly believed that afterward, he could walk away. But each hour in her company had brought him to a new level of understanding, of appreciation.

"I wouldn't mind that." His palms glided over her silken curves, noting the hard muscle beneath.

Her body was the exact opposite of her personality. She presented the world with this fierce toughness, while inside she was tender and vulnerable. No doubt most people believed she was hard as nails. It's probably why she got hurt over and over. This was how she'd allowed herself to be misunderstood in the past. She'd fallen for men who never saw or couldn't appreciate the fragility hidden beneath her thick skin.

"But of course, that's truly unrealistic," she went on as if he hadn't spoken. Her breath puffed against his skin as she sighed. "I mean, I can't let myself get used to this, because I don't know how long you're going to be around."

Nolan's gut clenched as he heard the resignation in her voice at their inevitable separation. "I haven't really decided what I'm gonna do," he said, which was the first time he'd voiced his inner turmoil out loud.

"You don't expect me to believe that you'd consider staying in Royal. Not after being gone for fifteen years. Your business involves location scouting around the world."

He'd known she was too shrewd to believe such a glib response. "Being back here has been nice." Claiming he'd had a change of heart and intended to stick around might've worked on another woman, but not Chelsea. Still, that didn't stop him from trying. "I've enjoyed reconnecting with my brother, and meeting you has given me food for thought."

She set her chin on his chest and hit him with a solemn gaze. "I don't believe you."

Her declaration really did give him food for thought. She'd been burned so often that winning her trust might be nearly impossible. And he wanted her to believe him. Not to help with his brother's plan regarding the oil rights, but because each glimpse past her shields had touched his heart. It made him want to enclose her in Bubble Wrap and take care of her, even as she claimed she needed no one's help. He'd never put another person's welfare before his own, and the change in his perspective rattled him.

"You don't believe people can change their minds about things?" he asked.

"I'd be every kind of fool to be that pessimistic when I am doing everything in my power to change my dad's mind about letting me be in charge of the ranch." She rolled her head to the side so that her ear rested over his steadily beating heart. "Yet there's a big part of me that doubts I'll be successful."

Her expression grew so pensive that Nolan decided she was unaccustomed to coming clean about her own inner demons. His gut tightened. That she'd trusted him with something so private warned him to tread carefully.

"I've learned that getting what you want often involves making compromises. Sometimes when I find a perfect place to shoot, convincing the owners to let us disrupt their property for several months means we have to find some way to make it worth their while. Maybe it's as simple as writing a big check. Sometimes they want to be a part of the action."

"Are you saying I'm wrong for wanting it all?"

"Never. I'm just saying that sometimes what you think you want isn't what you need. Like, our budget was super tight on one shoot and we found the perfect spot, but the property owner asked five grand for two weeks. He was an aspiring songwriter, so instead of paying him the money he wanted, we arranged for him to write one of the songs on the soundtrack."

"What I want is to run the ranch." She paused, and her eyebrow quirked in challenge. "What do you think I need?"

"Me."

"Hello, stranger," Natalie teased, but her tone wasn't at all lighthearted as she slid into the booth opposite Chelsea.

The women had decided to meet for lunch at the Royal Diner, a popular eatery in downtown that was decorated like an old-fashioned 1950s diner with red faux-leather booths and black-and-white-checkered floors, where owner Amanda Battle served classic diner meals.

"What do you mean, stranger?" Chelsea protested, her enthusiasm for this lunch with her best friend dimming. "I saw you just the other day. We went shopping, remember?"

"For an outfit you could wear on your next date with Nolan."

"I thought we had fun trying stuff on. I didn't realize… I mean, does it bother you that I'm dating him? You were the one who suggested he was interested in me in the first place."

"I know." Natalie made a face. "I thought you'd have some fun with him and loosen up a bit. All you've done for months is obsess about your dad picking Vic to run the ranch. But it just seems like you've traded one obsession for another."

Chelsea's mood dipped still further. She was tired of everybody harassing her about Nolan. Why couldn't her family and friends just accept that she knew what she was doing?

"Don't you realize that the two things are connected? If I can convince Nolan that he and Heath shouldn't pursue the oil rights, then I will have saved the ranch and my dad will have to put me in charge."

"I know." Natalie frowned. "It's just that ever since you and Nolan started getting serious—"

"Serious?" Chelsea interrupted, panic stirring as she contemplated Natalie's take on what was happening between her and Nolan. "We aren't serious. I mean, we've only been going out for a couple of weeks."

"A couple of weeks where I've never seen you so preoccupied. Not even after Brandon ghosted you right before you were supposed to meet his parents." Natalie paused and frowned at her. "You've changed a bunch since you've started seeing him."

Chelsea considered the way Nolan brought out her adventurous side. "Maybe I needed to change a little. I mean, for years people have been telling me to lighten up and have some fun. Why is it the minute I start taking that advice, you all get on my case for it?"

"I don't think anybody begrudges you some fun." Natalie looked uncomfortable. "I just wonder if you should be having fun with Nolan Thurston. You are moving really fast."

"Fast?"

She thought about her friends from college who jumped into bed with a guy on the first date. At least she'd waited until the seventh date to sleep with Nolan. Okay, so it was fast for her. She'd dated her last boyfriend for three months before taking things into the bedroom. And look how that one had turned out. Brandon had been the perfect guy on paper. Well educated. A great job. Sophisticated. They'd gone to the best restaurants. Attended concerts and the theater. Things had been going great until they slept together. And then, after arranging for them to have dinner with his parents, he'd just vanished.

"Yes, fast."

"Well, maybe it is." Chelsea reflected on the last two weeks. "The fact is, I like him, and he makes me feel things I've never known before."

She'd never connected with anyone this fast or with this level of confidence. Natalie might think Chelsea had fallen hard for Brandon, but in fact, she'd turned a blind eye to many warning signs. Nolan aroused no such misgivings. Well, except for his part in claiming the oil rights beneath the Grandin ranch.

"And that's my point," Natalie continued, oblivious to her friend's turmoil. "You usually start dating a guy armed with a checklist and a clear idea of the sort of future you could have with him. Have you considered just how complicated any sort of relationship with Nolan would be? He and his brother are coming after the oil beneath your land."

"And I'm hoping that I can change his mind about that."

"Have you considered that maybe he's hoping to get you on his side?" Natalie's look of utter pity shoved Chelsea hard against the back of the booth.

"He's not." But her claim lacked conviction.

"You don't know that. You don't know anything about him." Natalie sighed in exasperation. "It's crazy that you are throwing yourself into a relationship with him when you have no idea what tricks he has up his sleeve."

Was she misreading Nolan's signals?

"First of all, we're not in a relationship. You don't think I realize that he's not going to settle down in Royal?"

Chelsea's throat tightened. She had grown accustomed to Nolan and hated contemplating the day when he'd have to go. But she wasn't unrealistic about it. For the moment, she just wanted to enjoy their time together. And having everyone throwing their suspicions in her face was making that damned hard. "Maybe he is using me. Maybe I'm using him. It's not like I'm clueless. Maybe I'm not being my normal sensible self, but I'm sick of playing it safe. It hasn't gotten me anywhere, and I like the way Nolan makes me feel."

Natalie shook her head. "I just think you're asking for trouble."

"A little trouble is what I need at the moment." Before Nolan came along, she'd been making herself miserable fighting an upward battle against her family's patriarchal leanings. What if after all her hard work, Vic ended up in charge and she'd never taken the time to ride on a gondola or jump out of an airplane? "What's so great about playing it safe?"

"You don't get hurt." Natalie's voice had taken on a hollow tone.

"But you don't have any fun, either." Chelsea leaned her arms on the table and pinned Natalie with her gaze. "Maybe you need to take a risk. Why not jump-start your own social life with somebody interesting?"

"Interesting like who?"

"Jonathan Lattimore comes to mind," Chelsea said, paying close attention to her friend's reaction. "You've had a crush on him for a long time. Why don't you make the first move?"

The Lattimore family owned the ranch next door to the Grandins. Victor Sr. and Augustus Lattimore had been best friends. Like Chelsea, Jonathan was the oldest child of their generation. The families had a warm relationship—so much so that both sides had hoped Jonathan would marry either Chelsea or Layla, but the trio had never been anything but good friends.

Although Natalie hid it well, Chelsea knew her friend well enough to recognize that she had a crush on the eldest Lattimore son. It had often surprised Chelsea that her confident, beautiful friend had never let Jonathan know she was interested in him. Maybe she hadn't had the courage to do so before Jonathan got married, but now that he was divorced, Natalie still hadn't made her feelings known.

"I don't want to talk about Jonathan," Natalie grumbled. She picked up her menu and deliberately stopped talking.

"Oh, so you can badger me about Nolan, but I make one comment about you asking Jonathan out and that's the end of the conversation?"

"Jonathan isn't interested in me." Natalie was sounding as annoyed as Chelsea had felt moments earlier. "Nothing could ever happen between us."

In Chelsea's opinion, Jonathan had been so devastated by his failed marriage that he'd closed himself off. "Maybe he'd be interested in you if he had some inkling you had a crush on him."

Natalie looked aghast. "I can't let him know I'm attracted to him. What if he's not interested and it gets awkward between us?"

"You don't think it's awkward between you now? Well, maybe not on his part, because he has no clue how you feel." Chelsea wished her stunning, talented best friend had half the confidence when it came to romance that she demonstrated in her career. "But I've seen you when he comes into the room—you get completely tongue-tied."

"I know what you're doing. You're trying to distract me from warning you about Nolan."

Chelsea sighed. "Not at all. I am simply trying to point out that taking a risk with your heart might be better for you than you think."

"You are falling for Nolan Thurston, aren't you?"

"I don't know if I'd say I am falling for him," Chelsea demurred. "I know that we don't have a future. He will eventually return to his international travels, and I will remain in Royal and hopefully be running Grandin Ranch. No matter what happens, I will always cherish this time with him."

Chelsea was proud of herself. She sounded so practical and matter-of-fact, just the way she approached everything in her life. But thinking about the day when Nolan would leave tore her up inside. The old Chelsea would've stopped herself from becoming invested long before her heart had gotten engaged. But getting to know Nolan had changed her, opened her to joy and optimism. Her spirit soared in his company. His passion for adventure had awakened something exhilarating and irrepressible inside her.

There were moments she could actually imagine herself traveling with him to all the exotic places he visited in search of film locations. Of course, she would never want to experience the rough conditions he had told her about, but she could imagine herself on safari in South Africa or riding an elephant in Indonesia or camels in the Moroccan desert.

"Maybe that's the secret," Natalie murmured.

"The secret to what?"

"You're happy dating Nolan because there's no pressure from expectations. You recognize that eventually you'll both go your own ways, not because of some dramatic breakup, but because your lifestyles are incompatible."

Chelsea was glad she hadn't confessed to Natalie about the tiny seedling that had taken root in her subconscious. If her dad put Vic in charge, Chelsea might not end things with Nolan. She'd be in for even more lecturing if anyone got wind of that.

"I think the secret," Chelsea continued, "is to recognize what makes you happy and go after it."

Nine

Nolan was alone in the living room of the house he'd grown up in, talking on the phone to Chelsea. He'd agreed to have dinner with Heath but planned on joining Chelsea at his place later for dessert. They'd been together every night this week, but tonight was different—she was staying over for the first time. Since it was Friday night, she had the weekend free and was planning to spend her time off with him. The sleepover marked another stage in their relationship, and Nolan was surprised how smoothly things were progressing between them.

"Looking forward to seeing you later," he murmured into his phone, unable to resist a smile as he added in sultry tones, "And, of course, I mean *all* of you."

"The feeling is mutual," Chelsea replied in the throaty purr that drove him wild. "Eight o'clock. Don't be late."

She often said things like that, a holdover from other

men she'd dated, who'd disappointed her by either being late all the time or not showing up at all. Nolan recognized it as a defense mechanism turned habit and promised he'd never give her a reason to doubt him.

"I won't."

The more time he spent in Chelsea's company, the harder it was to imagine any man standing her up. When they were apart, his thoughts were filled with her. No woman had ever appealed to him more. Her combination of intelligence, practicality and directness kept him on his toes, and their sexual chemistry was off the charts, leaving no doubt in his mind that she was as into him as he was into her.

In fact, the only negative thing about dating her had to do with her family and his being on opposite sides of the oil rights claim.

"You're seeing Chelsea again?" Heath asked, carrying two beers into the room and extending one to Nolan. He'd been in the middle of his own phone call when Nolan had arrived a few minutes earlier, a quick update from the lawyer, from what he'd overheard.

"Later tonight."

"Are you making any headway?" Heath's closed body language and the way he asked the question suggested he already knew Nolan was no longer on task.

He wasn't wrong.

As much as Nolan wanted to be on Heath's side, he could also sympathize with how afraid Chelsea was of what might happen to her family's ranch if Heath granted the rights to an oil company. That company would then be able to use the surface above the oil deposit as "reasonably necessary," and it was legally murky what that meant. After yesterday, when Chelsea had shown him a photo of her horse on her phone and told him all the things she loved about the ranch, he'd done some research and discovered that an oil company that leased the mineral rights could enter the property, build roads, use caliche found on the leased property, install pipelines to transport products from the lease, store equipment and inject salt water in disposal wells. Further, unless provisions were spelled out in the contract, an oil company could select the locations of wells and pipelines to be placed on the property without input from the surface owner.

The amount of destruction that could happen if Heath leased the rights to an oil company could devastate the Grandin and neighboring Lattimore ranches.

"I don't know if I'm making the sort of progress you'd be interested in." Picturing Chelsea as she'd looked the night before in his bed, Nolan sighed.

"You're sleeping with her." A declaration rather than a question, and one wrapped up in concern. "I suppose she's trying to win you over to her side."

"She's told me a few things about the ranch, and we've talked about the repercussions of having an oil company drilling on the land."

"I should've talked you out of getting to know her when you first spotted her on July Fourth." Heath looked grim as he studied his brother's face. "I was wrong to think you and I were on the same page."

The last thing Nolan wanted to do was disappoint his brother, but after Chelsea had explained the potential devastation to her ranch, he was no longer as committed to his brother's plan. Nor could he imagine a choice that would make them both happy.

This was the sort of conflict he usually avoided in his private life. Was it any wonder that he rarely stayed still long enough for trouble of a personal nature to manifest?

With his profession running him all over the world, he rarely formed attachments with women. He could keep up with his friends via text and video calls, but romantic relationships required him to be present in a way his business didn't permit.

Chelsea was different. With each day that passed, he was more consumed with wanting to be with her. To make love to her every day and sleep with her in his arms every night. Being away from her brought him physical pain and emotional distress. She was on his mind nonstop. He constantly caught himself wanting to send her links to interesting stories or ridiculous memes that he hoped would make her laugh.

"From the research I've done, it's bound to disrupt their operations and do permanent damage to their land," Nolan argued. "It just seems like there's enough destruction in the world." In the fifteen years he'd roamed the globe, Nolan had witnessed the slow-moving devastation that mankind was doing to the planet in the name of progress and capitalism.

"I really thought you were on my side."

"I am on your side," Nolan insisted, starting to realize that as long as he was involved with Chelsea, Heath would never believe him. "It's just that I have concerns."

Tension invaded Heath's body with each word Nolan uttered. The last thing Nolan wanted to do was worsen his relationship with his brother, but he couldn't turn his back on what was best for Chelsea and her family, either. Trapped as he was between a rock and a hard place, Nolan suspected if his feelings for Chelsea continued to grow, he would be forced to make a devastating choice.

"Have you wondered why Mom didn't assert her claim all these years?" Nolan asked. Was she too proud to take anything from Victor Grandin? Had Ladd Thurston known about the oil claim? Or had the couple decided that exercising the rights would've been more hassle than it was worth? "I mean, there were some lean years when the money would've been helpful."

"We'll never know why Mom stuffed the document in a drawer and never did anything about it." Heath's brown eyes hardened into smoky quartz. "Maybe she was bullied and afraid to take action."

Given the way the families were fighting against Heath, Nolan could see where the scenario played into his brother's narrative about why they should treat the Grandins and Lattimores as their enemies. Which didn't help Nolan's quandary. The thought of having to battle with Chelsea's family made Nolan's stomach twist. He didn't want to be stuck in the middle of a bitter fight.

"Or she didn't want to take anything from the Grandins," Nolan pointed out, hoping his brother might see the logic of this.

"I know there's no hard proof that Daniel Grandin was Ashley's father," Heath said, restating the premise that motivated his action. "But Mom's papers, and the fact that Victor Grandin gave her the oil rights, point to it."

On that they both agreed. Yet the circumstances that had led to the creation of the legal document were less clear.

"While all that's true, both Mom and Ashley are gone…"

Nolan couldn't imagine how awful the loss of their mother and sister had been for Heath. Even though Nolan hadn't been home for years, their loss had hit him hard. But Heath's grief had taken him to a very dark place. In the grip of strong emotions, when it came to the oil rights, there was no reasoning with him. Yet Nolan was determined to try.

"And I, for one, don't need the money." Nolan braced himself for the next part. "I'm loath to do harm just so we can become wealthier."

"I'm not doing this for us." Heath looked disappointed by Nolan's assumption.

"You're not?"

"No. All this is for Ashley. She started a foundation but died before getting it off the ground. The money will fund her legacy."

"Oh, wow!" The knot in Nolan's chest began to ease as Heath went on to explain Ashley's vision for the foundation.

Heath's explanation shone a whole new light on his obsession. Two years ago, after burying their mother and sister, the brothers had talked long into the night about their mutual loss. Sadly, their shared grief hadn't been enough to bridge the chasm between them created by misunderstanding, resentment and distance. Now Nolan wondered if he'd done even more damage by misreading Heath's motivation.

Yet he couldn't be sure if that's all there was to his brother's crusade. If all Heath wanted was to ensure Ashley's foundation lived on, then why hadn't he come out and said this earlier? Nolan wondered if Heath knew perfectly well the destruction an oil company could do and wanted to hurt the Grandins. It worried Nolan that Heath might have lost his way.

"I want to do right by our sister," Nolan said. "And I know it's important to you that she live on through the foundation, but is it worth destroying someone else's dream in the process?"

"You mean Chelsea's dream?"

The accusation hit home, but Nolan pictured her beautiful face and worried brown eyes, his resolve hardening. "She's just trying to save her family's ranch."

"You realize that both sides can't win." Heath looked unconcerned by his brother's dilemma.

"Yeah, I guess I do."

Chelsea lay on her stomach, legs bent, feet in the air while she flipped through the Sunday paper. Beside her on the king-size bed, Nolan drank coffee and read the sports section. He wore only a pair of boxers, and Chelsea had a hard time focusing on the headlines.

"You know," she said, giving up trying to read and ogling Nolan from beneath her lashes. She adored all his rippling muscles and bronze skin. Nibbling on her lower lip, she pondered how wonderful it had been to wake up snuggled against him that morning and savor his fingertips roving over her curves. "Of all the things we've done these last few weeks, I think this is my favorite."

"Personally, I liked the cowgirl museum." Nolan looked absolutely serious. "It gave me a much greater appreciation of all the contributions the women of Texas have made."

If another man had said this, Chelsea might take it as sarcasm, but Nolan had shown such a genuine interest in all the exhibits. In fact, the entire time she'd known him, every reaction he displayed rang true. It was refreshing to date someone and not have to speculate where his head was. If she wanted to know his opinion, all she had to do was ask. He would give her insight into what was on his mind.

"That was nice, but I'm happiest when we're hanging out. Like this." She gestured with her hand to indicate the bed. "I hope we get a lot more weekends like this." She noted his fleeting frown, and doubt crept in. "I suppose that's not likely to happen. You are probably going to be contacted about a project anytime now." He'd mentioned that several of the production studios he'd worked with in the past were in the development stage for new and returning shows.

"I'm not sure I'm ready to leave Royal," he said, inflating her hopes once more. "But I've been thinking how much I'd like to take you to all the places I've loved the most, and then I remember you don't want to be away from the ranch."

His comment zipped through her like an electric shock. It was exciting to hear that she wasn't the only one pondering their future. The connection between them seemed to grow stronger every day.

"I've been thinking about that, too," she admitted. "Ever since meeting you, I've realized I need to expand my horizons beyond Texas. Maybe after things are settled with…" She trailed off in horror.

By mutual consent, neither of them had mentioned the oil rights issue during their time together. Chelsea recognized that eventually being on opposite sides of the issue was going to blow up in their faces, but she'd been enjoying Nolan's company far too much to make waves.

Nolan put aside the paper and rolled onto his side, facing her. He took her hand in his and brought her palm to his lips. "I think we both know that the situation between our families is going to get worse. Heath told me he's doing this for Ashley. She started a foundation before she died, and Heath wants to use the money from the oil rights to fund the charity. He wants her name to be remembered."

"That's a wonderful gesture." Chelsea snuggled against Nolan, buried her face in his neck and breathed in his warm, masculine scent. Just being near him brought her comfort. "Enough talk about families. Let's live in this moment and forget everything else."

"I'm down for that," Nolan said, capturing her lips for a long, lingering kiss. "What do you wanna do today?"

Breathless and giddy, Chelsea grinned. "You."

"I'm down for that, too."

Chelsea quivered as his fingertips drifted along her bare thigh. Immediately desire awakened, and a hot hum of longing throbbed between her thighs. She sighed as he stroked the hair off her neck and nuzzled the sensitive skin below her ear. No matter where the man touched, her body came alive. He took her hand, and she thrilled to the physical connection that sent her emotions spiraling. She loved the way he toyed with her hair. This lightest of touches caused goose bumps to break out on her body.

His hands roamed down her chest, long fingers circling her breasts. Pleasure shot through her as he gently captured her nipples through the thin T-shirt she wore and tweaked with enough pressure to make her gasp. The pain awakened her desire, and Chelsea dug her nails into his sides as he skimmed the shirt off her body and closed his mouth over one tight bud.

She parted her legs and rocked her silk-clad core against the steely length of him. He moaned as wildfire streaked through her veins, setting her on fire. Her breath hitched as he sent his fingers diving beneath the waistband of her panties. He caressed the seam between her thigh and body, tantalizingly far from where she needed him most. Anticipation of his touch made her vibrate. Every fiber of her screamed for him to stroke into her wetness and fill her up. As he continued to deny her, Chelsea squirmed in an effort to show him how badly she needed him.

"Look at me."

Her lashes felt as if they were dipped in concrete as she struggled to obey his command. The heat in his eyes made her feel unique and desirable, as if she was the only woman he'd ever wanted like this. It changed her, turned her on, took her to a place of reckless bliss she never wanted to leave.

"Now say my name," he demanded in a rough voice.

"Nolan."

His smile broke her into pieces and then made her whole again. It was an expression of satisfaction and wicked eagerness. He slipped her panties down her thighs, the silky fabric grazing across her feverish skin, making her burn even hotter.

"You are gorgeous," he murmured. "The most amazing woman I've ever met. And I'm dying to taste you." He shifted downward, sliding along her body. "Spread your legs for me."

Chelsea did as he asked, biting her lip as he set his hands on her thighs and moved his shoulders between them. She was spiraling up to heaven, and he hadn't even gone anywhere near her. Her breath caught as he bent down and sent his tongue lapping through her wetness. Momentarily blinded by a lightning strike of pure pleasure, Chelsea forgot how to breathe as her entire world narrowed to Nolan and the sensation of his hands, lips and tongue driving her mad.

She sank her fingers into his thick, dark hair, anchoring herself to him as he drove her burning need hotter and hotter still. Nothing had ever felt as true or as real as Nolan making love to her. He transported her to places she'd never dreamed existed. Her hips bucked as he flicked his tongue against her clit and then sucked. Incoherent babble broke from her throat as he slid two fingers into her. She bucked against him, her head falling back as she lost herself in the scrape of his stubble, the softness of his lips and the driving hardness of his fingers.

His name poured from her lips and careened around the walls of the loft. She'd never been so glad that the building was built so well as her climax built and her frantic ramblings grew louder. Then she was coming on his mouth, driven by his tongue into a wild, moaning frenzy as she begged for more, rocking against him, tugging on his hair, writhing harder, faster, panting erratically as she fell off the edge and soared.

She was shaking in the aftermath as he kissed his way up her body and nuzzled into her neck. Belatedly, Chelsea realized she'd never released her death grip on his hair and was shocked at the effort it took to unclench her fingers and send her palms gliding over his bare shoulder.

Despite the rigid length of him pressed against her hip that proclaimed he was ready for round two, Nolan seemed content to let his hands and lips drift over her skin.

"That was amazing," she murmured as his tongue drew lazy circles along her collarbone. "You are incredibly gifted."

His breath puffed against her skin as he chuckled. "Glad you think so."

Being with Nolan made her more deliriously happy than she'd ever imagined possible. This was the relationship she'd longed for all her life. The one that had always seemed so elusive. They connected so perfectly that she was convinced they were soul mates.

Chelsea snatched the thought to her chest, imagining how such a declaration would be ridiculed by everyone she loved. Until meeting Nolan, she hadn't realized how narrow her focus had become. By contrast, Nolan's outside-the-norm experiences fascinated her. He meditated unusual deals, acquired amulets to protect the wearer from harm, spoke three languages and had done things most people only read about.

With the amount of time they were spending together, they both realized their need for companionship had been growing. They'd discussed how their contrasting perspectives about family had led to regrets. He'd admitted that although he'd spent half his life avoiding Royal, he felt guilty about the time he'd lost with his mother and sister, adding that he wanted to mend his relationship with Heath. In response, she'd shared that her competitive nature had put her at odds with her siblings. And she'd begun to realize that by focusing all her energy on the ranch, her work-life balance was skewed.

Chelsea found him a great listener. She shared her passion for her family's long history on the land. She knew he wouldn't truly be able to appreciate what it meant to have deep roots and multiple generations growing up on the same acreage. Although he had grown up on a ranch, unlike his brother, Nolan had no attachment to the land. His values weren't in acquiring and maintaining property but in discovering new places and enjoying experiences. Still, she had hoped that her enthusiasm for growing her family's ranching legacy would persuade him to her side.

Although Chelsea hadn't gone so far as to ask him if

he'd be willing to convince his brother to drop the claim, she was certain that he'd been sympathetic when she discussed her fears about how her family's land would be damaged by oil companies drilling on the property. He'd seen the devastation wrought by the deforestation of the rain forests in Brazil.

Yet even as she thought she'd won him to her side, Chelsea wasn't sure his help would matter in the end. According to Nolan, Heath was bulldozing ahead with the claim, and although Nolan contended that his brother wasn't solely motivated by wealth, he hadn't explained what was driving Heath.

Oh, why had her grandfather given the oil rights to Cynthia?

"You're tensing up," Nolan commented, his lips gliding into the hollow between her breasts. "What are you thinking about?"

Although she'd spoken freely about so many of her secret desires and the insecurities she kept hidden, the one thing Chelsea couldn't share with Nolan was her anger with Heath over the situation he'd inflicted on her family. The last thing she wanted to do was create conflict between herself and Nolan over something that wasn't his fault. The fact that both of them would eventually have to pick sides was a dark cloud hanging over them.

So she projected an image that she was fine. Pretended to be strong and confident while, inside, her emotions were a Gordian knot of dread.

And instead of confessing what was at the top of her mind, she tackled something that had been brewing for several days. "Do you think we should come out of the closet, so to speak?"

Nolan lifted his head and arched one dark eyebrow at her. "What do you have in mind?"

"Maybe drinks at the Texas Cattleman's Club." Chelsea let out her breath on the suggestion, relieved that he hadn't balked.

"Followed by dinner?"

"We could…" She trembled as his fingers trailed over her abdomen. Reaching up, she stroked her palm over his shoulder, appreciating the solid muscle beneath his warm skin. "It might kick up a whole lot of dust, but I'm so happy that we're dating, and I want everyone to know it."

Plus, if her family saw how good things were between them, how great they were together, surely they'd come around. Her parents were always telling her they only wanted her to be happy. This would be a quick way to see if that was true.

When several seconds had passed and Nolan hadn't responded, uneasiness stirred. Had she misread their relationship? Maybe Heath didn't know Nolan was dating her and he wanted to keep it that way to avoid conflict.

"Unless you don't want to go public," she said, offering him a way out.

"You have to live here. It's more of an issue for you."

Chelsea wasn't sure how to take his response. He wasn't wrong that she had stronger ties to the community than he did, but should she infer that he didn't care about other people's opinions because they weren't important to him—or because he wasn't planning on being in Royal much longer?

Instead of mulling over the issue, Chelsea decided not to spend any more of her Sunday worrying about what might happen in the future. She was in bed with a sexy, half-naked man who deserved her full attention. Making love with Nolan was a much better use of her energy. Chelsea reached between them and took his erection in her hand, loving the way he sucked in a sharp breath as she circled her fingers over the velvety head. She could deal with the rest of the world later.

With a smile, she bent down and flicked her tongue over the bead of moisture on the tip.

Much later.

Ten

Nolan's phone rang as he slid his Jeep into an empty space in the Texas Cattleman's Club parking lot. He glanced at the display as he shut off the engine and grimaced as he recognized the caller. Lyle Short, a producer for GoForth Studios, had warned him a week ago that the studio was close to green-lighting the latest season of their unscripted series *Love in Paradise*. When Nolan had left LA a couple months earlier, he'd left behind several projects in the development stage that would eventually need his attention. Before heading to Royal, he'd submitted preliminary reports on the reconnaissance he'd accomplished, but none of the studio heads had settled on any locations.

"Hey, Lyle," Nolan said. "What news do you have for me?"

"We reviewed your reports and have decided to locate next season in Bora Bora. Can you meet with us at one o'clock tomorrow? We just forwarded all the specs to your assistant, so you will know what we are looking for."

"About that…" The pressure to immediately jump on a plane and head to the South Pacific constricted his chest like a hungry python. "I'm still in Royal. Things here are a little out of sorts at the moment. How much time do I have before you need the location finalized?"

"By the end of the month." Lyle chuckled. "I guess that's the end of next week. You'll see our notes in what we sent to you. We've made some changes to this season's scenario, so there will be a few more arrangements for you to make."

Nolan cursed silently. "That quick?"

He hadn't been prepared to exit Royal so abruptly. It wouldn't sit well with Heath, who was counting on his support in dealing with the Lattimore and Grandin families. Of course, Nolan wasn't handling his dealings with Chelsea to his brother's satisfaction. Which brought up the other reason he was reluctant to leave Royal at this moment—his connection to Chelsea was growing each day. It was too soon to decide if it made sense to take their relationship to the next level, but if he left now, based on how her relationships had ended in the past, Nolan suspected she'd be resistant to a long-distance relationship.

"What's going on, Nolan? It isn't like you to hesitate."

"I know I've always been the first one on a plane, but my brother asked me to come home to help him out with some things, and I really need more time."

"How much time?" Lyle's frown came through loud and clear.

"A couple months."

"I'm not sure that's going to work for us. What's the soonest you could be available?"

"I'd like to give my brother a heads-up. Can I let you know tomorrow?"

Although Nolan used his brother as an excuse for stalling, he recognized that his reluctance centered on Chelsea. The feelings she aroused in him were too new and too scary for him to speak them out loud.

"Sure. But, Nolan, you've already put in a lot of work on this project," Lyle reminded him. "If you can't meet the deadline, we may be forced to turn the job over to someone else."

"I get it." Nolan didn't feel threatened at all by Lyle's ultimatum. It was the nature of the business that production studios were hog-tied by impossible timelines, tight budgets and the constant pressure to produce the next hot thing. "I promise I'll let you know tomorrow if I'm going to do the job or pass."

"Because I know you and how you work, we can wait until tomorrow morning for your answer." Lyle sounded regretful, as if he sensed that Nolan was going to turn down the project.

"Thanks. I owe you one."

He'd come to a crossroad. He either needed to leave Royal and return to his old life or attempt some sort of hybrid situation so he could stay in town part-time while scaling back his traveling and relying on his staff more. Nolan's gut was telling him he was going to pass on this one. He just wasn't ready to leave Royal. Staying away for so long had done too much damage to his relationship with Heath.

Although he'd made inroads with Heath, the brothers had a long way to go before they could be considered close again. If he left now, he risked alienating his brother again. One thing Nolan had decided in the last few weeks was that he didn't want to keep isolating himself from those he cared about the most.

And then there was Chelsea. He'd never been so preoccupied with a woman before. He wanted to be with her all the time, and when they were apart, he struggled to keep his attention focused on matters at hand. If he left now, he might never find out if they could work. Yet was he being a fool to risk his business for a woman he'd only known a couple weeks?

With uncertainty jangling his nerves, Nolan headed toward the entrance to the Texas Cattleman's Club clubhouse, where he was meeting Chelsea for drinks. Choosing to meet at this particular location meant they were publicly stating that they were seeing each other. Up until now, they'd kept a pretty low profile by going outside the city limits of Royal for their dates. While Nolan was ready to let everyone know he was into Chelsea, he recognized that the decision didn't carry a lot of risk for him. He was a relative stranger in town, and with the exception of his brother, Heath, no one really cared whom he was dating.

Chelsea, on the other hand, had family and friends to answer to. No doubt letting everyone know they were a couple was a greater risk for her. Which was why it had surprised Nolan when she'd suggested they be seen together at the Texas Cattleman's Club. Yet despite his surprise, he was also deeply moved that she didn't want to keep the relationship hidden anymore. That had to mean she was serious about him. Which was why he was so conflicted about the project in Bora Bora.

Riddled with clashing emotions, Nolan crossed the threshold and entered the cool dimness of the lobby. After the brightness outside, he was momentarily blind and paused to let his eyes adjust. A shape blocked his path before he'd fully transitioned, and Nolan stepped aside to let the other pass. To his surprise, instead of walking past, the man stopped and greeted him.

"Here to meet my sister, Thurston?"

Nolan might not have recognized the unfriendly voice, but the question made his identity clear. Vic Grandin, Chelsea's brother. Was this the first of many confrontations with a member of Chelsea's family?

"I am," Nolan replied, maintaining a neutral tone as his instincts warned him to be cautious.

"You know that Chelsea is only dating you to find out what you and your brother are up to about the oil rights."

Vic's words went through Nolan like lightning. He flushed hot and then cold as the disquiet he'd suppressed these last few weeks awakened with a roar. At a loss for what tack to take as a response, Nolan arched an eyebrow and struggled to keep the hit from showing on his face. If Vic was telling the truth, Nolan had been an idiot to open his heart to Chelsea. Yet their time together had been so perfect. Too perfect?

"Don't tell me you're worried about my welfare." Nolan could see his sarcastic rebuke hadn't shut down the other man. Vic was too determined to make a point.

"I just hate to see a guy get played."

"What makes you think that's what's happening?" Nolan was proud that his voice didn't reflect how Vic's insinuation had twisted him up inside. The gut punch of this exchange with Chelsea's brother had shattered the romantic bubble Nolan had been existing in. "It could be your sister and I are merely enjoying each other's company."

"Maybe you're into her, but Chelsea is all about the ranch. She has no personal life. Doesn't give any men in town the time of day. And then you come along, and suddenly she's taking time off and neglecting her responsibilities." Vic sounded put out by this last part. "Don't get me wrong, it's been great to see her screw up. She's always so organized and efficient. But she always puts the ranch first."

Nolan slid his hands into his pockets and regarded the other man in silence.

"Chelsea always thinks she knows best." As Vic continued his rant, his bitterness came through loud and clear. "She thinks she should be the one in charge of Grandin Ranch."

"She's right," Nolan replied calmly, seeing his matter-of-fact reply struck home.

"She believes if she's the one who saves the ranch from you and you brother, our dad will be convinced that she should run things."

Taking Vic's words at face value was tricky, but the explanation was too plausible for Nolan to ignore. Given what Chelsea had shared with him about her struggles with her brother over control of the ranch, it made sense that she would do whatever it took to win. Even use Nolan.

"Do you know this for a fact or are you guessing?" Nolan had entertained the same conclusion in the beginning.

"It's a fact. She told my whole family that's what she's doing."

"Maybe she told you that to keep you all off her back about being with me."

"Well, well, well." Vic's hearty chuckle was riddled with mockery. "Looks like she has you good and fooled."

Incensed that by defending his relationship with Chelsea, he'd played into Vic's hands, Nolan ground his teeth. "If that's true, and I'm not saying it is, seems to me that by giving me a heads-up about this, you're making trouble for your sister. You must be nervous that she's going to win."

"The ranch is mine."

This glimpse into the other man's motivation didn't ease Nolan's disquiet. Nor did it make his own regret any less potent.

"Maybe if you spent less time sabotaging your sister and more time working as hard as she does, then you wouldn't have anything to worry about." Nolan saw his retaliatory strike hit home. Not surprisingly, this didn't ease the ache in his own chest. "Now, if you'll excuse me."

Nolan brushed past the younger man and headed toward the bar, but as he walked along the wide hallway, he couldn't help but replay his conversation with Vic. Perhaps both he and Chelsea had started out misleading each other, but somewhere along the line, his emotions had engaged.

He was no longer merely interested in her as a way to help his brother. He'd actually begun to consider what sort of relationship she would want when determining his future plans. Given what was going on between their families, he'd known their relationship would be buffeted by negative outside opinions. Nolan had believed that they could weather the storm together. That their ever-strengthening connection would be the bedrock they could build a foundation on. Now it appeared as if the whole thing had been nothing more than a fantasy.

His steps slowed.

So, if he was being played, like Vic claimed, the question of whether he should stay in Royal or take the job in Bora Bora might have just been answered. It might be smart to get away for a while and clear his head. Suddenly, Nolan found himself veering away from the bar.

Heath would not be happy, but Nolan could make him understand. He would just assure his brother that after the location scout, he would return to Royal. He'd only be gone a few weeks. Surely that would be enough time to sort out his feelings for Chelsea and lead with his head and not his heart.

Convinced he was making the right decision, Nolan retraced his steps through the clubhouse and shoved open the door to the outside. He hit the redial button on his phone. The call rolled into voice mail.

"Lyle, hey, it's Nolan. Things have changed here, so I'm available to head to Bora Bora as soon as I can assemble my team. I'm headed back to LA tonight, and I'll see you at the 1:00 p.m. meeting tomorrow."

Chelsea had dressed with care for her rendezvous with Nolan at the Texas Cattleman's Club. She'd borrowed from Natalie a ruched, off-the-shoulder dress in black that hugged her curves, and paired it with black-and-white sandals. Although Nolan loved when she wore her hair down, he also loved plucking the pins free and sending it cascading around her shoulders. Tonight, she'd fastened the mass of chocolate waves into a free-spirited bun with face-framing tendrils. Big gold hoops swung from her ears, and a gold tennis bracelet sparkled on her wrist.

When Chelsea had suggested she and Nolan meet for drinks and dinner at the social hub for her family, friends and neighbors, she'd been on an emotional high after spending the weekend with him. They'd had an amazing time together, and Chelsea's confidence in their strengthening relationship had led her to feel invincible. As long as they faced all opposition together, she was convinced they could overcome everyone's negative opinions.

Unfortunately, two days later, Chelsea was seeing the situation from a more pragmatic point of view, and the excuse she'd been using with her family—that she was seeing Nolan as a way of spying on him and his brother—was going to fall apart when they saw the fondness Chelsea couldn't hide. So she'd convinced Natalie to join her and Nolan for drinks, hoping that having a third person along would prevent anyone from making a public scene.

She'd thought she was prepared for anything, but Nolan neglecting to show blindsided her.

Natalie's gaze flicked to her watch. "You're sure he knew you were meeting at six?"

"He confirmed this afternoon." Her voice sounded as if it was fraying around the edges. "He always texts me to verify we're on. Even before I told him about how Brandon ghosted me, he was great at touching base. He knows it's a sensitive issue for me."

"It's a little after seven," Natalie said cautiously.

Chelsea was well aware what time it was. She felt the tick of each second like the poke of a needle against her skin. For the last forty-five minutes, her emotions had run the gamut between panic, annoyance and deep hurt. Logically, she knew it was ridiculous to let herself be bothered by his lateness, but Nolan was either on time or early, and if he was running late, he would've let her know. Since he'd confirmed that they were meeting at the Texas Cattleman's Club today, all she could think was that he'd gotten cold feet at the last second. This was a big move for them. Today they were broadcasting to all of Royal that they were seeing each other.

"I'm sure he's just running late," Chelsea said, refus-

ing to entertain that it was anything other than an un-
avoidable delay.

She was convinced that if he'd been able to, Nolan
would've let her know what time he'd arrive. Maybe he
was having car trouble and was stranded in a zone with
no cell service. There were numerous places around
Royal like that. Or he could've been in an accident or
damaged his phone. She told herself to be patient. Just
because he hadn't yet arrived, and hadn't called to let
her know he was on his way or that he couldn't make it,
didn't mean anything dire had happened.

"It's weird that he hasn't called or texted," Natalie said,
her musing scraping Chelsea's raw nerves. "You said he's
really good about staying in touch."

"He really is." Chelsea picked up her phone, hoping
she'd just missed the notification of his text. Nothing.
"It's possible he lost track of time."

"Sure." Pity flickered in Natalie's brown gaze. "That
must be it."

Or should she surmise from his delay that he really
didn't care about her? Had his innate charm led her to
read too much into all his romantic gestures and the
amazing sex? What if she wasn't special to him? No
doubt she was the most recent in a string of women he'd
hooked up with and moved on from. Since he probably
didn't linger in a single place for more than a few days,
she wouldn't be surprised if she was his longest relationship ever. Rather than flattered, Chelsea felt ashamed of
herself for ignoring all the signs.

"You're really bugging out right now, aren't you?"
Natalie was peering at her in concern.

"No. Of course not." Chelsea huffed out a pathetic
chuckle. "I mean, he's just running late. No big deal."

"For many people, it's probably not a big deal, but

you hate tardiness, and I'm sure you're feeling panicky right about now."

"A little panicky. He's never done anything like this before." But then, she'd only been dating him a few weeks. Shouldn't she have suspected that dating a man who was constantly on the move made for an unreliable relationship? "I'm worried something has happened to him."

"Do you want to message him again?"

"I already sent him a text, but he hasn't responded." Chelsea ground her teeth, fighting her worst instincts. "I'm sure he will when he gets the chance."

"And while we wait for him to reply, why don't we have another drink?"

They'd been sipping red wine, but when Chelsea got the bartender's attention, she ordered a shot of whiskey. Ignoring Natalie's worried frown, she tossed back the entire drink. Her eyes teared up as the strong liquor scorched her throat. She gave an inadvertent cough and blinked rapidly.

"Smooth," she muttered, hitting the bartender with a determined stare and gesturing for another shot.

After the second whiskey, a comforting warmth spread through her body, transforming her agitation into reckless disregard. Damn the man. She'd actually let herself trust him. So much so that she'd opened up her heart. She'd ignored everyone's warnings to be cautious. Instead, she'd plowed straight into danger, confident in her judgment. Which, in hindsight, had been completely idiotic. When had she ever done the right thing when it came to her love life? As shrewd as she could be when making decisions for the ranch, the instant she turned over control to her heart, she stopped perceiving reality and created a fantasy based on what she craved.

"Okay," Natalie said, waving the bartender away when Chelsea tried to order her fourth shot. "I think you've had enough."

With her head buzzing, Chelsea was consumed by a sudden urge to emote. "I really love you. You know that, right?" Although she was feeling fairly foggy around the edges, she maintained enough of her faculties to rationalize that keeping her emotions bottled up had led to the explosive pressure that resulted in her making bad decisions regarding Nolan. Maybe if she'd opened herself up more all along, she wouldn't have been so needy when he entered her life.

"I love you, too," Natalie said, laughter edging her voice. She put her hand atop Chelsea's and squeezed gently. "I'm really sorry Nolan did this to you."

It just couldn't be happening. He'd seemed unruffled by her suggestion that they take their relationship public. Had she misread him? Worse, had she pressured him? Was that what had caused Nolan's abrupt change in behavior? The logical part of her tried to shut down her overly emotional response to Nolan's absence and his lack of communication. But she'd been here before, geared up for a relationship-changing event, only to be left hanging. Was it any wonder she couldn't slow the torrent of insecurity and doubt that washed away every joyful moment she'd spent in Nolan's company?

"You know, it's fine," Chelsea ground out, resentment racing through her.

The dark emotion exploded outward from her aching heart and speared straight into her insecurities. Ghosted again. And by Nolan. What made it worse was that he knew how sensitive she was to being dropped. She'd trusted him and spilled all her fears and self-doubt.

"I mean, it's not like he and I make any sense whatsoever," she went on, grief making her swing wildly. "He's never going to settle down in Royal, and I'm never going to leave here. Everybody got on my case about why I was seeing him and telling me I was so foolish to get involved. Except I'm not foolish." She jabbed her finger into her chest, bruising her breastbone in the process. "I'm Chelsea freaking Grandin. I was using him to find out what he and his brother were planning about the oil rights. That makes me the smartest woman around."

"Ah, Chelsea." Natalie's gaze had gone past her friend, coffee-brown eyes opening wide in concern.

"I'm never going to get played by any man," Chelsea continued, her rant barreling forward unchecked. Damn the man for messing with her heart. He'd actually made her believe he cared. Bastard. "If anyone's doing the playing, it's me."

"That's good to know," came a hard voice.

As the deep timbre of Nolan's tone cut through the fog of Chelsea's misery, regret blazed through her, dispelling much of her self-pity. Enough remained, however, that she wore a scowl as she turned on her bar stool to face Nolan.

The hard planes of his face had never looked more chiseled as he stood like a statue before her. Only his eyes glittered with reproach, making her heart cower. But instead of apologizing for anything she said, Chelsea tilted her chin and went on the offensive.

"So, you decided to finally show up."

He nodded tersely. "I didn't want to leave town without seeing you in person one last time."

"You're leaving?" She heard herself sounding like a small, disappointed child and cursed. "When?"

"Tonight. I'm flying back to LA. There's a project

waiting for me, and I have to meet with the producers to get all the specs before I head out to Bora Bora."

The moment she'd been dreading. He was leaving Royal. Leaving her.

"I guess I shouldn't be surprised. You were bound to go at some point."

"Yeah." A muscle jumped in his cheek as he stared down at her. "Too bad you didn't get what you needed before I left."

For a second, she had no idea what he was talking about, and then she realized that he'd heard her whole speech about how she'd only dated him to find out what he and Heath were up to. She froze in horror. She'd stopped pursuing that angle almost immediately. His company had been too enjoyable for her to jeopardize by scheming.

In the weeks since they'd started dating, she'd recognized that her desire to run the ranch had become so important because it was a substitute for the love she wasn't finding in her personal life. She couldn't control her romantic victories, but she could work damned hard to convince her father to give her Grandin Ranch.

"So, you're done with Royal? You're not coming back at all?"

"I don't know." His gaze raked over her. "I still have some unfinished business here."

Chelsea trembled as a familiar heat burned her up. She loved this man. She'd gone and done the one thing she shouldn't—she'd fallen hard. And now she was going to lose him unless she was brave enough to explain that his not showing up had triggered all her insecurities.

"What sort of unfinished business?" She held her breath and waited for the answer she craved.

"I came back to Royal to help out my brother—"

"Of course. It's all about the claim. All along, I figured that's why you hit on me in the first place. Was it your idea or your brother's?" Chelsea couldn't stop her stupid fear from continuing to push him away. "Did Heath tell you about my terrible track record with men? You probably assumed I'd be easy to charm. And I guess you were right."

Nolan scowled at her. "That's not it at all."

"No?" Chelsea couldn't bring herself to confront him directly. Staring into his gorgeous brown eyes always made her melt inside. She couldn't afford to be weak now. "Seems to me after you struck out with my sister, you decided I'd be easier pickings. And I guess I was."

"I never once saw you as easy pickings. And I never hit on your sister. I approached her with the idea that we should talk about the claim, not because I wanted to date her."

"So you're saying you wanted to date me?" She gave a rough laugh. The ache in her chest grew with every syllable he uttered. "Or maybe getting me into bed was just a side benefit to your scheme."

Beside her, Natalie gasped. Tears sprang to Chelsea's eyes, but she blinked them back. She was saying all the wrong things. They both were. In the deepest levels of her heart, she didn't for one second believe that Nolan had been manipulating her. They were both attacking because they were afraid and hurt. And neither of them was brave enough to stop.

"You're accusing me of scheming after admitting that the only reason you started seeing me was to use me to get my brother to drop the claim?" His lips twisted into a sneer. "That's really rich."

"So you're telling me that you never once considered I could be useful where your family's claim was concerned?"

"Maybe in the beginning—"

"Ha!" she interrupted, crowing in satisfaction even as his confirmation made her cringe inside.

"I said *in the beginning*," he reiterated. "Once I got to know you, and you explained the potential damage to your ranch, I really didn't want to pursue the claim. I tried to talk to my brother—"

"Stop. Please just stop. None of that matters. You're leaving, and that's all there is to it."

"Chelsea," he began, a deep throb in his voice that touched off a wildfire of sorrow inside her.

"Please don't. Whatever it is you want to say, just don't." Even now, after he'd admitted his true motivation for asking her out, he was still trying to charm her. But it was all lies. "No matter what motivated us to get together, we had fun. Let's just leave it at that. We took a swing and missed. No harm, no foul."

As she spouted platitudes, Nolan's expression grew ever more grim. "I guess we're both a couple of players. We used each other, and neither one of us came out the winner." He held out his hand like some sort of sports competitor.

Chelsea didn't want to touch him. To do so, to feel the warm, strong clasp of his hand around hers, would remind her of every time he'd ever touched her. Of the passion that burned so hot between them. Of how she'd loved waking up in his arms. Of the way she'd started dreaming of a future for them.

"It's a draw." She gripped his hand, squeezing hard as she focused on pretending he was nothing more than a business associate in a busted deal. "Good luck in Bora Bora."

She didn't realize until she was halfway to the exit that she'd left her friend behind. Chelsea was so close to losing it that there was no way she could hesitate or stop. Her heart was slowly shattering with each step she took. As the distance between her and Nolan increased, she was terrified that if she looked back, she wouldn't be able to prevent herself from breaking down. As it was, she barely made it to the ladies' room. Her stomach began to turn as she pushed through the door and scrambled for a stall.

The three whiskey shots came up, acid burning her throat in the aftermath of her encounter with Nolan. Tears stung her eyes while ice raced through her veins, making her shake uncontrollably. Her entire world had just ripped apart. Losing the ranch to Vic wouldn't have hurt a fraction of what she was going through as her relationship with Nolan ended. Chelsea stuffed her fist into her mouth and bit down on her knuckles to stop herself from surrendering to the sobs that threatened.

"Chelsea, are you okay?" Natalie had entered the bathroom without Chelsea hearing the door open.

"Of course I'm fine. Why wouldn't I be?" Her overly perky tone failed to mask the bitterness beneath. She'd spent too much of her adult life being strong and never showing weakness. When it came to the ranch or her personal life, she couldn't bear to let anyone think she was anything other than one hundred percent in control.

This outward show of strength, however, didn't work on Natalie. The two women had shared all the ups and downs of both career and personal lives. Natalie was probably the only person on earth who knew all Chelsea's demons.

"Because for the first time ever, you didn't play it safe?" Natalie suggested, her tone gentle and sympathetic. "You let Nolan all the way in."

And in the process, she'd let herself be blindsided.

"I am such an idiot," Chelsea moaned, resting her head against the cool metal of the stall wall. "Why didn't I listen when everybody told me not to get involved with Nolan?"

"Because you two are the real deal."

"Did you not listen to what he just said?" Chelsea unlocked the stall door and stepped out. She avoided Natalie's gaze and stared at her own reflection. Pale face. Enormous, haunted brown eyes. She looked dazed, as if she'd been kicked in the head by a horse. "It was all just a big game to him. And I made such a fool of myself, thinking we had a future. I'll bet he and Heath had a great time laughing at how needy I was."

Natalie let out a weary sigh. "He didn't much look like a man who'd come to gloat. In fact, while you were talking, before you knew he was there, he looked like he's been hit upside the head with a two-by-four."

"No doubt he was surprised that he'd been played in turn."

"I don't think so. He didn't look angry or chagrined. He really looked devastated."

"Well, he's a good actor. He had me completely bamboozled."

"What if the same thing happened to him that happened to you?" Natalie asked. "What if he started out dating you to see what he could find out about the oil rights and ended up falling for you?"

"I'd be more inclined to believe that if he hadn't declared that's why he'd been dating me."

But her words were sheer bravado. Chelsea wanted to believe that at some point he'd begun to care for her. Surely, after all her dating failures, she wouldn't have slept with him if she hadn't sensed genuine emotion.

"Maybe he was just reacting to what you said to save face," Natalie argued. "The way you did. I mean, it's not like after you went on and on about how you were playing him that he would come clean and admit that he had real feelings for you."

Deep inside she hoped Natalie was right. But as she recalled what he'd said, her confidence shrank.

"No. It's not like that." Chelsea shook her head, locked in the grip of her past romantic disasters. "And it doesn't matter, anyway. He's leaving. I'm staying. It was never going to work."

"That's a load of crap and you know it," Natalie declared. "That man makes you happy."

"So what if he does?"

"If you let him leave without telling him how you really feel, then you are not as strong and brave as I thought." Natalie fixed her with a challenging glare. "So, what's it going to be?"

Eleven

Nolan cursed the impulse that had prompted him to return to the Texas Cattleman's Club in time to hear Chelsea confirm her brother's accusations. After his confrontation with Vic, Nolan had been consumed by the need to get as far away from her as possible, so he'd headed back to his loft and made arrangements for a late-night flight to LA. But as he began to pack, it became pretty obvious that much of what he owned was tangled with a number of items Chelsea had left behind.

His instinct had been to toss everything. In fact, he'd been in the process of stuffing a pair of her jeans into a trash bag when he'd come across the T-shirt he'd bought for Chelsea at the cowgirl museum. Emblazoned on the red fabric was the slogan Well-Behaved Cowgirls Rarely Make History, and Nolan recalled how she'd sauntered around the loft in the shirt, silk panties and her boots. That memory of her was only one of a hundred that had been burned into his brain like a brand. Her brand. He belonged to her in a way that was permanent and irreversible.

The initial shock following his conversation with Vic had worn off by then. He'd rationalized that Chelsea's brother had been making mischief. What better way to mess with his sister than to interfere with her love life? Especially when she was already extraordinarily vulnerable from being treated badly by the previous men she'd dated.

It was then that he'd decided he couldn't leave Royal without seeing her. In retrospect, he should've texted or called her as he was on his way to the airport. He might've saved himself the pain of hearing her brother's accusation confirmed. She had been using him from the start in an effort to save her family's ranch. As much as Nolan had wished it otherwise, Vic Grandin had not been wrong. His sister had played him and nearly won.

Nolan decided to call Heath to let him know he was heading back to LA. While he waited for his brother to answer, Nolan let himself back into the loft to finish packing. Being on the road as much as he was, he was accustomed to packing light. When he'd arrived in town two months earlier, he'd brought little more than his clothes, his electronic devices and a few personal items. He'd signed a month-to-month lease on the fully furnished loft, which meant there was only a week to go. Even though the project in Bora Bora was a quick turnaround, Nolan wasn't sure when he'd be back in Royal. Or if he intended to return at all.

"Hey," Nolan said when Heath answered. "Just wanted to let you know that I'm on my way to LA to take a meeting with some producers. They want me to head to Bora Bora to scout a location for their upcoming show."

The abruptness of Nolan's decision must've caught his brother off guard, because it took him several seconds to respond.

"How long are you gonna be gone?"

A brusque intensity had entered Heath's tone. Was Nolan's brother recalling the first time the brothers had parted? A time when Nolan had disappeared, not to return until their mom and sister's funeral. He couldn't help but feel a familiar urgent need to escape Royal and clear his head.

Nolan wasn't sure what to say to his brother. Given what had happened with Chelsea, Nolan couldn't promise Heath he was coming back. Avoiding entanglements had kept Nolan from slowing down. He liked adventure and experiencing different cultures, but there was also a part of him of him that knew if he kept moving, it was nearly impossible to make the deep connections that lead to expectations, disappointments and heartache. Look at what he was feeling now. If he hadn't let down his guard and gone all in with Chelsea, he wouldn't feel like his insides were being shredded.

"I'm not sure." Feeling the way he was at the moment, Nolan didn't want to come back to Royal at all, but he also didn't want to disrupt the healing relationship between him and Heath. "It depends on the scope of the project."

"I see." From Heath's stiff response, Nolan could tell that his brother wasn't happy.

"I'll know more after the meeting tomorrow." Nolan hated that he felt guilty about disappointing his brother. Strong emotions like this were the exact thing he usually avoided. Yet he couldn't deny that reconnecting with his brother these last few months had made him happier than he'd been in quite some time. Maybe he could learn to take the bad with the good. Surely it would all balance itself out, and in the end, he would have a stronger relationship with his brother. "Look, I know it probably seems like I'm running out on you, but I really do need to get back to work."

"I thought maybe you'd stay in Royal and join me on the ranch."

For a second, Nolan couldn't breathe. He'd never imagined that Heath would offer up such an invitation. Heath had been managing the Thurston ranch since their father died. He'd never needed or wanted Nolan's help before. Why would he include him now?

"I don't think I'd be any help," Nolan said, unsure what to make of the offer. "I've forgotten more than I ever knew about ranching."

"That may be true, but it's been good having you around." Heath's admission was another blow Nolan hadn't seen coming.

"It's been good being back here with you," Nolan echoed, his chest tight as emotion swept through him. "Makes me wish I hadn't stayed away as long as I did." Swallowing past the lump in his throat, Nolan fought down anxiety. Ever since his mom and sister had died, he'd been buffeted by an emotional storm. Coming home had stirred it further. Reconnecting with Heath was both a blessing and a curse. He liked feeling as if he belonged somewhere, yet at the same time the old tension between the brothers couldn't be resolved without talking through why Nolan had left in the first place.

"I get that work is taking you away. Don't worry about anything here. I just hope you know that you can come back anytime."

"Thanks. I appreciate your understanding. I'll be in touch."

Nolan ended the call and tossed his cell phone on the bed. The conversation with Heath had briefly taken Nolan's mind off his encounter with Chelsea, but as he emptied the closet and dresser drawer, his mind replayed the statements she'd made.

If asked, he never would've pegged her as someone who played games. She'd always struck him as straightforward, someone who believed in hard work and dealt with people honestly. To hear Vic's insinuations confirmed by her had absolutely blown him away. Maybe if he hadn't trusted her and given her the benefit of the doubt, he wouldn't feel like she'd carved out his heart.

A knock sounded on his door. Since the only person who ever visited him was the one person he didn't want to talk to at the moment, Nolan considered pretending he wasn't home, but no doubt she'd already seen that his car was parked in his reserved spot. So, he opened his door and found Chelsea standing in the hall.

"What are you doing here?" he asked, not bothering to moderate his unhappiness.

"I didn't like the way we left things and wanted to clear the air before you left."

He narrowed his gaze and took her in, recognizing her unsteadiness and trouble focusing. "You've been drinking."

"I was drinking before you showed up," she explained. "It's why I said what I did." Her gaze avoided his. "I didn't mean what you heard."

"So you didn't start dating me because of the oil rights claim?"

"Okay, that part was true. But once I got to know you, I stopped thinking of you as a means to an end."

Nolan heaved a sigh. "Why did you come here?"

"I didn't want you to leave Royal with us on bad terms."

She looked absolutely wretched, and Nolan remembered all the times when she'd let herself be vulnerable with him. When she'd shared the most humiliating, heartbreaking moments she'd been through. Had that all been an act to garner his sympathy? To make him want to cherish and protect her? Nolan no longer trusted her or his own reactions to her.

"What does it matter? I'm leaving and we're over."

She made no effort to hide her wince. "Is that what you want? For us to be over?"

What was she playing at? Nolan scrutinized her expression, seeing frustration and hopelessness. For someone who was usually so forthright, Chelsea was certainly dancing around whatever was on her mind.

"I don't know. After talking to your brother—"

"You talked to Vic?" Her eyebrows crashed together. "What did he say to you?"

Nolan was a little taken aback by her vehemence, until he realized this was a symptom of her fierce struggle for control of the ranch. "Exactly what you told Natalie in the bar. He said you've been playing me all along."

"When did you talk to my brother?"

"I was on my way into the Texas Cattleman's Club to meet you when I ran into Vic. He was pretty convincing." Nolan crossed his arms over his chest and stared down at her. "So much so that I decided to head to LA without saying goodbye."

Chelsea glowered while her hands clenched into fists. "He had no right to say anything to you."

"It took me a little while to realize that he might've been actively trying to cause trouble between us. But imagine how I felt after deciding to give you the benefit of the doubt, to show up and hear you echoing exactly what your brother had told me."

"I was upset. You didn't show up when you said you would, and you weren't answering my texts. It brought up all the times that Brandon did the same thing before ghosting me entirely. I thought the same thing was happening all over, and I went a bit crazy. I had too much to drink and started spouting stupid stuff."

Nolan braced himself against the misery in her eyes even as his heart lurched. Her acute distress was causing his resolve to waver. He'd been ready to give her a chance to explain, even though logic told him her brother had been completely right.

"All great excuses, but the fact remains that you did date me in order to get information on what Heath planned to do about the oil rights."

"Are you trying to tell me that never crossed your mind when we were together?" Chelsea gave him a skeptical look. "Or that your brother put no pressure on you to spy on me in return?"

"So we're both a couple of opportunists." Nolan refused to feel guilty for his part in the scheme. He'd come back to Royal to support his brother, and he'd done a terrible job so far. Both he and Chelsea had known that one day they would have to pick a side, and today he was choosing Heath's.

Chelsea's warm brown eyes dominated her face, unshed tears making them appear larger than ever. "Does that mean everything you said to me was a lie?"

"No." She was amazing. Beautiful. Brilliant. As the tightness in his throat bottled up the words, Nolan's heart ached for what he was pushing away. "It's just that we landed on opposite sides of a bad situation, and even if we wanted to be together, too many things stand in the way."

"That was true in the beginning, and it's no different

now," she agreed. "But we could make it work. I really want to give us a shot. Would you be willing to try?"

Would he? His life was a lot less complicated without her in it. The entreaty in her eyes almost sold him, but the turmoil in his chest was a discomfort he couldn't ignore. Was it possible that a mere hour ago he'd been heading to the Texas Cattleman's Club to declare to the public that he and Chelsea were a couple? He'd been happy at this big step in their relationship. Now, all he wanted to do was get away from her and ease the chaotic emotions roiling in him.

"I have this job in Bora Bora to do." It wasn't any kind of an answer, and from the way her shoulders sagged, it wasn't what she hoped to hear. "I don't know how long I'll be gone. If some of the other jobs come through while I'm there, it could be a long time."

"You sound like you're not coming back." She looked stricken. "Is this the end for us?"

Although Nolan had already accepted that they were finished, he reeled at the finality in her question. Before, he'd been so angry with her that he hadn't considered what being parted from her would truly mean. Now, with his outrage fading, he was at the mercy of all his memories of their time together. No woman had ever burrowed so deep into his heart, and the thought of leaving her behind was a knife twisting in his gut. He'd been ready to change his lifestyle for this woman, to make compromises and plan a future with her. But if he'd learned anything in the last hour, it was that the forces at work to keep them apart were stronger than their desire to be together.

"I guess we're lucky we didn't let ourselves get carried away," Nolan said, doing his best to keep his voice light. "At least this way we can part as friends."

"That's not what I want," she said, frowning as she realized how her statement came across. "I mean, I don't want to be parted from you."

Nolan hardened his heart against her entreaty. "So, you're willing to leave everything behind and come with me?"

Her expression said it all.

"I didn't think so." All of a sudden, he had to get away. From her. From Royal. From the longing that made him feel so empty inside. "I have to get to the airport. My flight leaves in a couple hours." He couldn't control the impulse that compelled him to bend down and place his lips against her forehead. "Take care of yourself, Chelsea."

And then he was walking out the door and out of her life for good.

Twelve

Nolan had never thoroughly scouted a location so fast in his life. Nor could he have managed to do even half of what he accomplished without his stellar staff. They worked tirelessly and seemed unfazed that their boss was being an unusually demanding asshole. Perhaps that was because after filling in his assistant about his legal and personal problems in Royal, he'd made sure his employees understood that his distraction and bad mood had nothing to do with the project or them.

It also helped that he'd bought several rounds in the resort bar where they were staying by way of apology.

Every one of the seven days after arriving in Bora Bora, he'd been beating himself up for how he'd left things with Chelsea. She'd pleaded with him to find a way to compromise so they could be together, and he'd been too afraid of his strong emotions to meet her half-way. Telling himself it would never work and that he was better off ending things before he was in too deep was idiotic. He'd never been so miserable. Usually getting on a plane to an exotic location was a cure for whatever ailed him. For the first time in his life, he couldn't wait to get home. And that *home* meant Royal, Texas, instead of Los Angeles was yet another hit to his belief system.

Yet what he longed for wasn't a place, but a person. Chelsea. She was the home his heart craved. The safe haven for his restless soul. Except he'd gone and blown it with her. The one thing he'd promised himself he'd never do, he'd done. He'd made her doubt him. Worse, he'd made her feel less than thoroughly desirable. Even if he returned and somehow convinced her to take him back, that breach of her trust would always be between them.

All that and more should've convinced him to get over her and move on, but with each hour they were apart, he was consumed by the need to run back to her. He hadn't achieved closure by leaving her behind in Royal. Her refusal to give up her life there and follow him around the world hadn't settled his mind about their lack of a future. He kept wondering what would've happened if he'd given in.

Which was why, after most of the details had been handled to his satisfaction, he'd turned the project over to his capable assistant and hopped on a plane back to Texas.

After landing in Dallas, he picked up a rental car and headed for Royal. Conscious that he couldn't speak his heart to Chelsea without first clearing the air with Heath, Nolan headed to the Thurston ranch. He found his brother in the barn, chatting with his foreman.

Heath looked surprised to see him. "You're back? From the way you talked, I thought you'd be gone for quite a while."

"I was running away again," Nolan admitted. "It seems that after fifteen years, it's something I still do."

"At least it didn't take you fifteen years to come back this time."

"Nope. This time I realized that what's most important to me is right here. I love you." Nolan wished he'd declared himself sooner. "I'm sorry I went away for so long. I want us to be close again." He paused to read Heath's expression, and although his brother was nodding in agreement, he seemed to be waiting for the rest of Nolan's intentions. "But this fight you're in with the Grandins is not for me."

"This is about Chelsea, isn't it?"

"I love her." He'd been tossing those three words over and over in his mind for the last few days, but it was the first time he'd said them out loud to anyone. To his surprise, he felt empowered by the announcement. "Being away from her even for a day has been eating me up. I can't go back to living my life the way it was. I want to be with her."

"How does she feel about that?"

"I don't know. I came to you first. I want to clear the air with us."

"This fight with the Grandins is only going to get uglier," Heath warned. "What if she chooses her family over you?"

Nolan was ready with his answer. He'd thought long and hard about his divided loyalties and planned to go with his heart. "Then I'll have to prove that I'm on her side. I'm always going to choose her."

The silence that followed ate into Nolan's soul like acid. Two months earlier, he'd come back to Royal to fix his relationship with his brother, and here he was shattering their alliance into pieces. This wasn't how he'd wanted things to go. But who could've predicted that he would fall in love with Chelsea Grandin?

"I see."

"I know you need to do this thing for our mom and Ashley, but is it worth doing if it tears apart everything that you have built? The Grandin and Lattimore families combined have so many resources to fight with. Is there some way we could just let it go?"

"I can't. Ashley was ignored and denied her birthright." The pain in Heath's voice rang through loud and clear. "She was a Grandin, and they ignored that."

Seeing the bright light of determination burning in his brother's eyes, Nolan decided it was the years he'd spent away that kept him from picking up the same torch that Heath raised. Both their mother and Ashley were dead. They would not benefit from the money. But Nolan understood that his brother's grief needed an outlet, and funding her foundation with the idea that their sister would be remembered was what Heath needed to heal.

"You're right," Nolan said, "but Mom never did anything about the claim."

"She didn't have the strength to take them on," Heath countered. "But I do."

Heath's fervor was getting through to him. Nolan understood more and more what drove his brother, and yet he couldn't believe that Heath would be happy to destroy the Grandin and Lattimore ranches in order to achieve his goal.

Nolan reminded his brother, "I don't think she'd be happy if we end up hurting someone."

"Someone like Chelsea Grandin?" Heath asked. He didn't seem particularly angry at Nolan's attempts to talk him out of pursuing the oil claim rights. More like disappointed.

"Chelsea. Me. You."

"Nothing's gonna happen to me or you." A muscle jumped in Heath's cheek. "I can't say anything about the Grandins or Lattimores, however."

With his brother's ominous words ringing in his ears, Nolan got back into his vehicle and headed to the Grandin ranch. He didn't spend any energy contemplating what sort of reception awaited him there. Deep in his heart, he knew that he would do everything in his power to convince Chelsea to give their relationship a shot. She deserved nothing less that his all. He'd failed her once. Nolan was determined never to do so again.

Chelsea sat on her bed, her knees drawn up to her chest, her gaze on her laptop screen, where an image of Bora Bora glowed in all its white-sand, turquoise-blue-water glory.

Nolan had been gone for over a week, and she'd never known such misery. It made every breakup she'd ever gone through pale by comparison. In fact, this was worse than every one of them rolled into a single enormous heartache.

Worse, she couldn't even bring herself to be mad at him for ending things. Even if she'd not succumbed to her insecurities and tried to sound all tough and confident, successfully chasing him away in the process, when Nolan had invited her to come away with him, she'd been too afraid to go.

That moment had tormented her for ten days and nights. She couldn't focus on work or even summon the energy to care that in the midst of her battle for the ranch, she'd stopped fighting. The victory she'd labored long and hard to achieve no longer held any luster. What the weeks of dating Nolan had revealed was that she'd been miserable before he came along. And now that he was gone, her life was an endless, desolate landscape once again.

She'd even considered booking a ticket to Bora Bora to surprise him, but fear of his rejection kept her from acting. The whiff of distrust continued to linger. What if he'd been playing her all along? Unable to shake the anxiety that was driven by her past romantic failures, Chelsea continued to grapple with doubt. Nolan wasn't like the other men. He'd had a good reason for ghosting her at the club. Her fingers dug into the coverlet beneath her. Vic had driven him away with his sly meddling.

Still, she'd been the one who'd overreacted and failed to agree to Nolan's offer when he'd extended it to her. If she'd been brave, they could be happily ensconced in paradise together. Blissful with Nolan sounded better than heartbroken alone. Chelsea's resolve swelled. She pulled her computer onto her lap and opened a new browser window.

As she was evaluating which of the twenty-plus-hour flights would work best, she heard a soft knock on her door frame. Glancing up, she spied her dad standing in the hall and closed the laptop.

"Your mother and I are on our way to the cookout at the TCC," he said, frowning as he took in her mood. "Just checking to see if you want to ride with us."

She'd forgotten all about the party at the Texas Cattleman's Club. The all-day affair included a pool party for the kids, a barbecue and a live band. The idea of having to pretend that everything was fine made her stomach roil.

"I'm not really in the mood to be around people right now," Chelsea said.

"You okay?"

She exhaled slowly, emptying her lungs. "Fine."

Chelsea was surprised when her father didn't accept

her answer at face value and retreat. Victor Grandin was a straightforward man with old-fashioned ideas about women. The one he'd married, while not a pushover, embodied the traditional role of wife and mother. In contrast, Layla, Chelsea and Morgan had shown a strong preference for having successful careers and Chelsea was sure their father struggled to understand what drove them.

"I haven't seen you much around the ranch these last few weeks." Victor stepped inside the room and leaned against her dresser. With his arms crossed over his chest, he regarded his daughter with a solemn expression. "Some things have been slipping through the cracks."

On a normal day, this criticism would have sparked her irritation. But with Nolan gone, she couldn't summon the energy to point out just how much she did around the ranch. As long as her father was determined to give Vic control, Chelsea was more like a hired hand. Let him see what happened she stopped making decisions that benefited the ranch. Or maybe he would never appreciate how many of her changes had ended up improving things.

Chelsea shrugged, feeling no guilt for acting like a moody teenager for once in her life. "I guess I've been a bit distracted."

"That Thurston boy?"

"Among other things." Chelsea resisted the urge to throw a pillow. "Mostly I'm tired."

Tired of struggling to gain stature in her father's eyes. Tired of fighting a losing battle for a birthright that should've gone to the one who worked the hardest instead of the one who happened to be born male. Tired of telling herself that there was something wrong with the men she chose to date when she suspected that her stubbornness and ambition were the reasons they abandoned her.

"It occurred to me lately that I haven't taken any time off this year," she continued. "I thought I might go visit a friend of mine in Houston. She and her husband are having a baby, and their shower is next weekend."

"I guess you're due for some time off. You work hard around here."

Chelsea's eyebrows shot up. "I didn't realize you noticed." A month ago this admission would've been the confirmation of her worthiness that she'd craved. Today, all she felt was annoyance.

"I pay attention to everything that goes on around here."

"That's interesting," Chelsea said, in no mood to pull her punches. "Because you haven't been noticing that your son has let Layla and me handle the bulk of the problems that come up around here." Seeing her father's surprise, Chelsea warmed to her topic. "You've basically told him he will be in charge, and he thinks that gives him a free pass when it comes to doing things."

"I haven't noticed."

"You don't want to notice." The frustration she'd used to fuel her campaign suddenly had a new target. "You never want to see that your daughters are better at ranching than your son. Because we want the ranch to thrive, and we are willing to work damned hard to make sure it does."

When her father seemed at a loss for words, Chelsea kept going.

"I was willing to do whatever it took to prove to you that I deserved to be the one you should put in charge. Thinking I could save our ranch, I even went so far as to scheme to convince Nolan to talk his brother out of pursuing the oil rights claim." Chelsea's throat locked up at this reminder that her single-minded drive to win at all costs had cost her a future with the man she loved.

"I take it you couldn't."

Chelsea stared at her father in disbelief. Was that the message he'd taken away from her rant?

"More like I didn't want to in the end. Nolan and Heath don't intend to keep the money for themselves. Heath wants to use it to fund his sister's foundation. To do something wonderful in her name. We shouldn't stand in their way."

She could see her father's disapproval grow as she spoke. Chelsea wasn't surprised that he rejected her declaration of support. Her father had very strong opinions. She's been fighting against them all her life. No doubt, he viewed her as a traitor because she wasn't putting the family interest first. It was difficult to choose between two things she loved so much.

With their families on opposite sides of such a fraught issue, and neither party willing to give, they would never be able to please everyone. A relationship between her and Nolan had been doomed from the start.

His decision to leave Royal and take up his old life had probably saved both of them from even greater heartache. Which probably was a good thing, because Chelsea didn't think she could've survived a pain worse than what she was feeling at the moment.

"I'm sure you're disappointed in me," Chelsea said into the silence that had invaded her room. She struggled against the heavy emotions weighing her down. Her father's opinion had always meant so much to her, and going against his wishes added another layer of sadness to her burden of misery.

"I'm not disappointed in you," her father said, crossing to the bed and sitting beside her. He reached for her hand and clasped it in his warm palm. "Maybe I haven't appreciated your contributions the way I should. It's become pretty apparent these last few weeks just how much you do around here. A lot of things have been neglected. Your brother has had a hard time keeping up with everything on his own. Seems to me that you're an asset I've taken for granted."

Chelsea gave her father a watery smile. "I've been waiting a long time for you to recognize everything I contribute to the ranch."

"Maybe you and I should spend some more time together, and you can give me a better sense of all the things you do."

"I'd like that. Running this ranch is all I've ever wanted to do. But I've sacrificed a lot to win your approval. I think I need to find a better balance." As satisfying as it was to hear her father realize that his son wasn't the perfect choice to run the ranch, dating Nolan had awakened her to the need for fun as well as work in her life.

"Does that mean I'm gonna have to get used to seeing Nolan Thurston around here?"

"No." Chelsea dug her nails into her palms to keep from succumbing to tears. "We're over. He left Royal."

"I'm sorry." And to Chelsea's surprise, her father actually looked like he meant it. "I didn't realize what was between you was serious."

"I don't know that it was for him, but I liked him a lot." Way more than a lot. She'd fallen in love with him.

Her father seized her chin and turned her head until she met his gaze. "He's a fool if he doesn't see what a treasure you are."

"Thanks, Dad." Since Chelsea sensed that she'd made inroads where her father was concerned, she decided

she could make an effort. After all, he'd come looking
for her and had made the effort to get to the bottom of
what was bothering her. "I think I've changed my mind
about the cookout. Give me ten minutes to change and
I'll meet you outside."

After donning a white lace sundress and her favorite
boots, Chelsea tied up her hair in a messy topknot and
applied mascara, liner and lipstick. She might be miserable inside, but at least she looked good.

As she neared the living room, she heard the low rumble of conversation and paused to collect herself before
entering the room. She expected to find her parents and
maybe her brother—but stopped short at the sight of the
man who stood in the foyer.

Thirteen

Nolan hadn't known what to expect when Chelsea entered the room, but he didn't expect the flare of joy mixed with despair that erupted as their eyes locked. She looked sad and tragic, but so beautiful in a white lace dress and cowboy boots. Given that he'd thrown down an impossible ultimatum before he'd walked away, he'd half expected she would immediately show him the door. Instead, she stopped dead, as if she'd seen a ghost. Her shoulders collapsed as she reached her left hand across her body and grasped her right forearm.

"Nolan?" She said his name as if she couldn't comprehend that he was standing in the same room as her. "You're here?"

All too conscious of her parents watching the exchange, Nolan nodded. He couldn't seem to make his facial muscles work. Where he wanted to smile and welcome, all he could do was stare at her like a man possessed.

"I'm sorry I didn't call before showing up, but I was afraid you'd tell me not to come. And I needed to talk to you." Nolan shot a glance at her parents, hoping they would get the hint and make themselves scarce. When they showed no signs of moving, he ground his teeth. "Feel like taking a walk?"

"We are on our way to the TCC cookout."

"I could drive you."

Chelsea seemed to have forgotten her parents were in the room. Her gaze stabbed into him as if she could tear him open and get to the heart of why he'd returned. She looked unsure of the situation, which struck him as odd, because he'd never seen her as anything but completely confident.

"Why are you back?" Chelsea asked, showing no sign of going anywhere with him. "I thought you were supposed to be going to Bora Bora."

"I did." Nolan wanted so badly to cross the room and pull Chelsea into his arms, but he'd messed up with her. "My team is still there. I couldn't concentrate with you so far away. So I came back."

"Oh, I see." But from the subdued tone in her voice, Nolan guessed she didn't see it all. "But if there are still things to do, you must be going back."

"The scope of the project requires me to take several trips over the next few months," he said. "And I realized I couldn't stand being away from you that long."

"Away from me?" she echoed, frowning. "I don't understand. You gave me the impression we were done."

"I didn't want us to be done," he admitted, taking several slow steps in her direction.

She stared at his chest, refusing to meet his gaze, but didn't back away from his advance. He took that as a positive.

"That's not the impression you gave me. You were pretty clear that you weren't coming back. And if you did, you wouldn't be coming back for me."

"I was confused and angry. Your brother said all those things…" Nolan grimaced, all too aware of their audience. "But I should've trusted you."

He glanced toward Chelsea's parents, who were watching the exchange with avid interest, and willed them to go. He wanted this moment with Chelsea to be for just them. So much needed sorting out.

At last, Victor Grandin seemed to get the hint. He captured his wife's elbow in his hand and steered her toward the front door. "We'll wait in the car." As he passed Nolan, Victor gave the younger man a stern glare and muttered, "You be good to my daughter or I will track you down wherever you may run and make you pay."

Nolan wasn't sure if he was more shocked by the man's threat or the backhanded approval of him as his daughter's suitor. Either way, Nolan knew that regardless of the hurt feelings between them, he had to do whatever it took to win her heart.

In the seconds after he found himself alone with Chelsea, Nolan took stock of the tension in her body language. She seemed equally relieved and unhappy to see him.

"The hour I spent waiting for you in the bar was the worst. You'd never given me any doubts before that moment, and when you didn't call or respond to my texts, I didn't know what to think. I was frantic that something had happened to you. And then my insecurity kicked in, and I convinced myself that I'd pushed you into doing something you didn't want and that you'd left me like everyone else."

"I'm so sorry I did that. It was a dick move on my part.

I knew perfectly well how you've been treated in the past, and I never should've disappeared on you."

"No," she agreed, her spine stiffening. "You knew how it would devastate me."

"I'm more sorry than you'll ever know," Nolan declared, reaching for her hand. To his relief, she didn't resist as his fingers curved around hers. She seemed to be fighting herself as much as him. "Leaving you was the biggest mistake I've ever made."

"I think we've both made mistakes."

"Can you forgive me?"

"I think I would do anything to have things back the way they were," Chelsea admitted. "And that terrifies me."

"I don't want you to be afraid to be with me."

"I'm not."

"Does this have to do with the oil rights claim you and your brother are making? If it does, then you should know I've already told my dad that we shouldn't stand in your way. I just hope that we can find a way to make it so that our land isn't completely ruined."

"You did?" Nolan couldn't believe what he was hearing. "Why the change of heart?"

"I got to thinking that it wasn't fair for us to fight you when my grandfather gave your mother those rights fair and square. He must've had a reason, and knowing him the way I do, I'm sure it was a good one."

Despite what should be his success in winning her over, her explanation left him ice-cold. She obviously persisted in believing he was committed to the claim, when in truth the only thing he was committed to was making her happy.

"I really don't care about any of that." He grabbed her by the shoulders and gave her a little shake. "I came back for you. Nothing else. I don't care about the oil rights or some job waiting for me in Bora Bora. All I want is you."

"Me?"

The way she said it ripped into his heart. Here stood a woman who understood her worth, yet she questioned whether anyone else saw her value. She worked so hard to prove she was strong and competent, yet her accomplishments hadn't received anywhere near the recognition they were due.

"You." He took her hands in his and brought them to his lips. "From the minute I laid eyes on you across that Fourth of July parade, I was smitten. My feelings for you only grew stronger the more time we spent together. You are more fascinating than any exotic location could ever be."

"That's not possible. All I've done is focus on this ranch. It's my all-day, every-day fixation." She paused and bit her lip, glancing up at him from beneath her long lashes. "Or it was until you came along. Now, I realize I'd give up running the ranch to be with you. If that means spending the rest of my life on the road, as long as you were there, I could be happy."

Her willingness to sacrifice her passion made his heart clench painfully. The long flights to and from the South Pacific had given him a lot of time to think. Before leaving Royal, she'd pleaded with him to keep their relationship going, and in a moment of cowardice he'd tossed out a ruthless ultimatum, knowing she'd never agree to leave her world behind to be with him. Yet here she was, being braver than any person he'd ever known. And he adored her for it.

"You wouldn't be happy if you couldn't be here, where you belong, making Grandin Ranch the best in the county. Hell, in the whole state of Texas." Nolan put his whole heart and soul into the next two sentences. "And I'd like to be by your side, helping you with that. If you'll have me."

Her eyes went wide with shock. She dug her fingers into his. "But you left Royal because you didn't want to be stuck here ranching."

"I was eighteen when I ran off to see the world. I couldn't see a place for myself here. But now, after everywhere I've been, recognizing that there are exciting and magical destinations still to visit, I know that what's here in Royal is all I'll ever want. And that's you."

Chelsea stared at Nolan across the inches that separated them. He was telling her that not only did he intend to give up his claim on the oil rights, but he also planned to side with her and her family. Doing so would put his relationship with his brother at risk. He genuinely seemed ready to do that. For her. For them. Did she need more proof that he loved her?

"I love you," she said, willing to take a risk of her own. "It scares me how much I need you. That's why I was so stupid that day at the Texas Cattleman's Club. I fell into my old patterns of self-doubt when you didn't show up, and I went a little crazy."

"I never should have left you there alone. I knew how much it would bother you, and I was so afraid of how you made me feel that I did what I always do and ran. But it didn't take long before I realized that running didn't make me feel better. In fact, I've never been more miserable in my whole life."

"I think we might find a way to overcome our worst fears if we do it together."

Nolan nodded. "It won't be easy."

"I'm not afraid of a little work, and I don't think you

are, either." As Chelsea's resolve grew, her fear and anxiety eased. She trusted the bond between her and Nolan. That her confidence in him had developed despite the trouble between their families meant their connection was real and strong. "As long as I have you by my side, nothing else can hurt me."

"Not even if your father decides to let your brother run the ranch?"

A month earlier Nolan's question would've sparked hot emotion. Now, she saw her obsession with running the ranch as a distraction from loneliness and disappointment. She'd longed for someone to share her dreams with, not understanding that she'd lost sight of what made her happy.

"Once you and I began dating, I started to realize that I've sacrificed far too much to my ambition. I can't imagine ever not being a part of running the ranch, but I've focused too hard on changing my father's mind. It led me to think it would somehow be all right to manipulate you into turning on Heath. I'm ashamed that I went there. It's not the way I want to be."

As she bared her soul to Nolan, Chelsea felt stronger than she'd ever been in her whole life. He was a beacon of joy and delight. Together they would be a family and, hopefully one day, welcome children.

Yet, even as these thoughts popped into her mind, Chelsea wondered if she was jumping the gun.

Nolan must've seen her concern, because he cupped her cheek in one hand. "What?"

"I realized that once again I'm throwing myself into the future before I've bothered to find out what you see for us. You love to travel. I'd never ask you to give that up. I want us to explore the world, but I want to make babies with you and see them grow up here." She trailed off, unsure if he wanted to have kids. "Wow, that's a lot." She chuckled self-consciously.

"I've been running around the world for a long time, searching for a missing piece to make me feel whole and never finding it." Nolan's thumb grazed her skin, soothing her worries. "Imagine how surprised I was when I came home to the place I'd fled long ago to discover what I wanted was here all along."

When his hand dived into his pocket and produced a small black box, Chelsea's throat locked up. In that instant, she realized she no longer gave a damn about running Grandin Ranch. This man, the love glinting in his dark brown eyes, filled her with a sense of belonging she'd never known.

"I hope I'm being clear enough," Nolan said. "If not, let me state quite simply that I want you. In fact, I'm really glad that you're imagining a future with me, because otherwise this would've been really awkward." As he finished speaking, Nolan dropped to one knee and popped open the box. A sparkling ring featuring a large oval diamond sat nestled on a cushion of black velvet. "Chelsea Grandin, I love you."

Chelsea threw her hands over her mouth, reeling at his words and unable to believe what she was seeing and hearing. "I love you, too," she repeated, the fierce declaration reduced to a hoarse whisper as emotions overwhelmed her.

"I want to spend the rest of my life with you." The hand holding the ring box shook as fierce emotion burned in his gaze. "Will you marry me?"

Chelsea reached down and clasped his hand between hers, feeling her own body trembling in the acute rush of her joy. "Yes. I want us to be together forever."

Nolan plucked the ring from the box and slid it onto

her finger. Chelsea could barely see the diamond through
the tears gathering in her eyes. And then he was springing
to his feet and wrapping her in his arms. He kissed her
with blinding passion, his lips moving over hers with pos-
sessive hunger. Chelsea tunneled her fingers through his
hair and held on tight as they feasted on each other's lips.

At long last they broke apart, chests heaving as they
grinned at each other in giddy, stunned joy. They were
so lost in each other and the momentous transformation
of the relationship that they didn't realize they were no
longer alone until someone cleared their throat.

"Looks like everything's okay in here," Chelsea's father said, sounding somewhat bemused.

Chelsea turned toward her father and spied her mother
standing just behind him, looking anxious. Her expression cleared as she gazed from her daughter's face to the
man who had wrapped his arm around her and held her
possessively at his side.

"Better than okay," Chelsea said. She held out her
left hand, where the diamond winked on her ring finger, and braced herself for her parents' reaction. "We're
getting married."

"Oh, that's wonderful." Bethany Grandin rushed to
embrace her daughter, shocking Chelsea to no end. "All
I ever wanted was for you to be happy," she whispered
in her daughter's ear.

She was still absurdly perplexed by her parents' easy
acceptance of the "enemy" into their midst as her dad
hugged her tight. While Chelsea's mother gave her soon-
to-be son-in-law a warm hug, Nolan met her gaze. His
warm brown eyes and steady smile filled her with a sense
of belonging.

As her father hugged her, Nolan seemed utterly at ease
as he basked in the glow of her parents' positive reaction

to the news. Yet even as she recognized his solidarity with her family, she worried what would be the cost in his ongoing campaign to repair his relationship with his brother. The conflict drew a line in the sand. In order to be together, they would have to choose a side.

While she recognized that Nolan was willing to make that sacrifice for her without hesitation, if the tables were turned and she'd chosen to support Heath and his claim, the loss of her family would've been devastating.

She needed to make sure Nolan was completely at peace before moving forward. Twisting the ring on her finger, Chelsea prepared to take it off at the slightest indication that he would regret his decision to take her side against his brother.

"Are you sure you're okay with becoming part of my family? I know how much you wanted to repair your relationship with your brother."

"Heath is coping with his grief the best way he can, and while I appreciate that he wants to fund Ashley's foundation and create something in her memory, I can't get past the fact that our mother had the oil rights for years and never did anything about them. It seems to me that she wouldn't agree with what he is doing. If my mom wanted us to take something from you, she would've told us the oil rights existed."

While Nolan's explanation made sense, she couldn't help but argue the same thing from her family's point of view.

"Does that mean you'll talk to your brother on our behalf?" Victor asked before Chelsea could speak her mind.

"Absolutely not," Chelsea answered for him. She wrapped her arm around Nolan's waist and faced her parents. "Grandpa and Augustus granted Cynthia those oil rights. None of us understand why, but the fact is they did. The Thurstons are legally entitled to do whatever they want with them. Neither Nolan nor I will have anything more to say about the rights. You and the Lattimores can fight it, but from now on, we remain neutral."

"This is your ranch we're talking about," Nolan reminded her. "Your family's legacy."

"This is our life," she countered. They were a team now. It was no longer a situation where they sided with his family or her family. From now on, they would prioritize each other and the family they would one day make together. "As far as I'm concerned, we are what's important. Whatever it takes to keep us strong. That's what I intend to do."

Fourteen

Instead of heading to the Texas Cattleman's Club as planned, Nolan and Chelsea took a little detour to his loft. When Nolan had called from Bora Bora, the land-lord told him no one had rented it yet, so the loft was No-lan's as long as he wanted it. After a ten-day separation, they were ravenous for each other and didn't get farther than the closed front door before Nolan had Chelsea up against the wall in a hot, desperate kiss.

In minutes, Chelsea had shimmied out of her panties while Nolan freed his erection, and then he was lifting her up and spearing into her. They drove wildly toward a fast orgasm, each thrust a hungry, frantic attempt to get closer and closer still. He loved how she didn't hold back, how she told him exactly how badly she wanted him. With her hands knotted almost painfully in his hair, her breath coming in short, urgent pants against his face, she proclaimed in words and actions just how much she loved him. Nolan lost himself in her desire, and as she came apart in his arms, he was right there with her.

Afterward, they stripped bare and ran to his bed to start all over again. This time the build was slower and hotter as he relearned every inch of her body with his hands and tongue before sliding home. As she closed around him, tight and wet and warm, she gave out a giant, ragged sigh that lanced straight through his heart.

"Are you okay?" he asked, stopping all movement so he could dust kisses across her eyelids and down her nose.

"Better than okay," she murmured, cupping his face between her palms. "I'm absolutely perfect. Being with you is all I could think about these last ten days, and believing that you were gone forever was…" She shuddered. "I can never go through that again."

"Trust me when I tell you that I'm never going to leave you. You're mine and I'm yours. We belong together, and nothing will ever change that."

That seemed to be everything she needed to hear, because her arms and legs tightened around him and she began moving in a way that made every cell in his body come to life. She was perfect and glorious and Nolan knew he would never tire of making her come.

As much as he would've loved to spend the rest of the day and night in bed with her, Chelsea received several texts from her family demanding to know where she was and reminding her that she had an obligation to join them at the charity event. After grabbing a quick shower together, they managed to get themselves redressed and out the door.

Before he started his rented SUV, Nolan reached into the back seat and pulled out a long, thin jewelry box. Chelsea's eyes widened as he extended it to her.

"What's this?"

"I'm afraid this is going to be anticlimactic after this." He scooped her left hand into his and kissed the spot where her engagement ring rested. "But I thought you might enjoy wearing it to the party."

She popped open the box and gasped at the bracelet of golden Tahitian pearls that lay upon the black velvet. "This is gorgeous." She lifted the strand and placed them on her wrist. The warm gold color looked fantastic against her tan skin. "Can you help me with the clasp?"

Once the bracelet was fastened, Chelsea gave him an enthusiastic thank-you kiss that very nearly sent them scrambling back to his loft for round three. Instead, she wiped her lipstick from his lips, fixed her makeup and shot him a saucy grin.

"Shall we go face the music?"

Nolan pulled a face and started the engine. "It's not going to be that bad."

"Here's hoping you're right."

The last time he'd gone to the Texas Cattleman's Club, he'd intended to meet Chelsea and proclaim their relationship to one and all. To say things had not gone well was an understatement.

This time, as he strode hand in hand with Chelsea through the members who had gathered to eat barbecue, socialize and enjoy the music, Nolan knew a new confidence and contentment. For the first time since returning to Royal two months earlier, he felt as if he belonged in the community. If this was what the love of a wonderful woman did to a man, Nolan knew he would never mess it up.

"Mom and Dad just told me you two are engaged." Layla had appeared in their path with Joshua in tow. While the men nodded in greeting, Layla's blue eyes bounced from Chelsea to Nolan before landing on their clasped hands. Her mouth dropped open as she spotted the large oval diamond. She pointed at it. "It's true. Wow!"

"We are," Chelsea confirmed. Her broad smile was half smug pride and half amusement as her sister enveloped her in an enthusiastic hug. "Do Morgan and Vic know?"

"They do."

"How'd they take it?"

"Morgan's delighted for you, of course, but Vic…"

Layla glanced over her shoulder to where their brother stood talking with his best friend, Jayden Lattimore. The pair cast speculative glances toward the two couples. After the conversation he'd had with Chelsea's brother, Nolan wondered how Vic would react to the engagement.

"It's the whole oil rights thing," Layla continued, shooting Nolan a glance from beneath her lashes. "His family. Our family."

Chelsea stepped closer to Nolan and pressed her body against his in a show of solidarity. Her chin rose ever so slightly in defiance. "Nolan and I aren't taking sides," she said. "Eventually he's going to become part of our family. Just like I'll be part of his."

Layla looked stunned. "But the ranch—you know that if an oil company gets the right to drill on our land, it will be ruined."

"I know." Chelsea winced. "But Grandpa knew that as well, and both he and Augustus are the ones who signed over the rights to Cynthia."

Nolan squeezed her hand, offering both sympathy and support. "Heath has his reasons for what he's doing and grief is playing a big role in motivating him, but I don't want to see your family's ranch damaged."

"That's good to hear." Morgan had appeared beside

Layla. She scrutinized Nolan a long moment before adding, "Welcome to the family."

Beside him, Chelsea relaxed visibly. Despite her brave words earlier, Nolan knew it was important that her parents and sisters supported her decision to marry him. It was also occurring to him how much of a change the Grandin family would make in his life. Since leaving Royal, he'd not been a part of any family, much less one as large as this. The acceptance from Chelsea's sisters delighted him more than he'd expected.

"I love you," he murmured into her hair.

She tipped her head up, and the smile on her face made his heart soar. "I love you," she murmured back. Lifting on tiptoe to kiss his cheek, she added, "Now, let's get out of here and go do some more celebrating back at your loft."

"You do make the best suggestions," he replied with a grin.

Unfortunately, it took them nearly an hour to extricate themselves from the cookout as word of their engagement spread and more people stepped up to congratulate them.

Now, however, they were finally alone. A flush of color high on her cheekbones matched the hungry fire licking his nerve endings. Nolan kicked the front door shut behind them and took both of her hands in his, slowly backing toward his bed. Halfway there he paused, seeing she had something on her mind.

"You're thinking hard about something," he said.

She pulled his arms around her and rested her cheek on his shoulder. "Are you going to be happy here? I mean, you are used to being on the go all the time."

"Wherever you are is where I want to be. Of course, I'll have to travel for my business, but I have an excellent staff who can do most of the day-to-day operations, and LA is a plane ride away."

She leaned back and gazed up at him. "So, you're really okay with being back in Royal."

"This is your home." The ranch was important to her. Her happiness was important to him. "I want to make it mine as well."

"And I want you to know that I'm going to come with you when you travel." Her eyes glowed with fervent joy. "The ranch can survive without me better than I can survive without you."

"That's also how I feel." He framed her face with his hands and kissed her gently. "When it comes to you, I'm—always and forever—all in."

"We're going to have such an amazing life."

"I can't wait to get started."

* * * * *

ONE COLORADO NIGHT

JOANNE ROCK

To Angela Anderson,
for uplifting everyone around you.
Thank you for all you do
to support the romance community!

One

Back in Jessamyn Barclay's Manhattan home, she had never once bumped into a former lover by accident. In that most densely populated of New York's five boroughs, it was a snap for her to avoid people she preferred not to see.

Now, she'd been standing inside Yampa Valley Regional Airport—gateway to Northwest Colorado according to the welcome sign—for all of ten minutes when she spied the one man whose path she did not wish to cross. Ryder Wakefield stood at the baggage claim carousel just one over from hers. And Ryder wasn't just any old boyfriend, either. He'd been the first man to show her what passion could be like.

And the one to win the prize for most damage inflicted to her emotions. Even though he'd broken her heart as thoughtfully as possible.

Bastard. As if he'd thought she'd needed to be let down

easily like some kind of fragile creature. Something Jessamyn Barclay had *never* been.

"Damn it." She darted behind a tall kid wearing a skateboard strapped to his back like a knapsack, hoping the excess baggage would hide her from Ryder's view.

For a minute, anyway. As vice president of a multinational real estate development company, she did not "hide" from anything. And it ticked her off to think how fast a sighting of Ryder turned back the clock and made her feel like a swoony teenager instead of the badass boss she'd become since then.

Peering around the lime-green skateboard painted with skulls, Jessamyn observed the man who had been one of many reasons she'd stayed away from the tiny town of Catamount, Colorado, for the past decade. He leaned with lazy grace against a cement column, his body packed with more lean muscle than she recalled. Broad shoulders stretched the fabric of his charcoal T-shirt. Her attention shifted lower despite herself, to where faded denim hugged heavy thighs.

She dragged her attention back to his face, where his angular cheekbones and square jaw were dusted with just enough whiskers to give a woman razor burn if...

Heat rushed through her as she halted that thought in its tracks. It didn't matter that she was a powerhouse executive now, the rainmaker for her father's real estate company, onboarding more clients and business than anyone else in the firm for three years running. Clearly, she'd maintained the hormones of her eighteen-year-old self. Ryder would turn heads in any city, and no amount of time or circumstance could change the fact that he was a ridiculously attractive man.

So Jessamyn decided to act like any self-respecting corporate shark. She pretended not to see him.

Tightening her grip on her handbag, a designer leather bucket purse as thoroughly out of its element as she was, Jessamyn focused on the baggage carousel in time to spot her suitcase. Her ticket out of this place, wedged firmly between a beat-up steamer trunk and an overstuffed duffel bag, inching her way at a snail's pace.

She darted past her skateboarder shield and edged around two older women in animated conversation. With an effort, she hauled the rose-gold case off the conveyor and onto the floor. Normally, she only traveled with a carry-on, well accustomed to expedient business travel. But she hadn't booked a return flight for this trip since she had no idea how long she'd stay in Catamount to finish settling her grandmother's affairs. Packing lightly hadn't been an option.

Her sister Fleur had gotten Jessamyn's promise to spend some time in their grandmother's house this summer. Time for memories before they sold the property off. That in itself had been a tough vow to make because Jessamyn had a strained relationship with both of her sisters ever since their parents' bitter divorce drew battle lines straight through the family.

For the first few years, she and her siblings had patched together enough of a bond to limp along. But even that tenuous connection had snapped almost a decade ago. If not for their grandmother's death and their shared inheritance of her ranch, the Crooked Elm, they would have happily continued going about their separate ways. Jessamyn suspected her grandmother had skipped leaving the property to her son to ensure the sisters would have to work together.

Wheeling her bag to the rental car kiosk, Jessamyn kept her focus on her target. Obtain the SUV she'd rented and begin the hour-long drive to Catamount. She needed

to sort out her thoughts before she arrived at the ranch.
Put her game face on for a conversation with Fleur. She
couldn't afford a chink in her mental armor. Best to let
her sister think she was still well-adjusted and thriving
in their father's business even though Jessamyn was furious at Mateo Barclay for contesting their grandmother's will. Fleur hated their father, and Jessamyn refused
to give her any leverage to pry apart the bond Jess had
always had with their dad.

Somehow, she'd deal with all the other uncomfortable truths coming to the surface about their father. She
loved him, and he'd believed in her when she'd felt like
an outcast in her family—the only one who'd supported
their dad. But these past few weeks had brought some
issues to light.

"Barclay," she snapped at the young woman behind
the rental kiosk a little more sharply than she'd intended.
The stress of the past weeks had eaten away some of her
poise. And then the near miss of running into Ryder...
Amending her tone, she smiled politely. "I've got a luxury
SUV reserved for the week, but I want to leave myself
the option of extending the rental agreement."

Not that she was hiding out in Catamount, of course.
No more than she'd been hiding from Ryder behind an
unsuspecting traveler carrying a skateboard. But the
same thinking applied here. Why borrow trouble? She
didn't truly *need* to return to her office in midtown for the
next few weeks, so why step back into her father's obvious power machinations too soon? Her stomach churned
at the thought of the engagement announcement he was
dying to make for her and her potential fiancé. The man
Mateo had handpicked to be her husband and—not co-
incidentally—his successor at Barclay Property Group.

"Barclay?" The tall, reed-thin blonde in a red cardigan tapped her keys without enthusiasm. "I'll check, but we ran out of vehicles an hour ago."

"Excuse me?" Jessamyn leaned closer to the counter, all business. "I booked this a week ago. I have a reservation number." She turned the screen on her phone around so it faced the agent.

Tricia, according to the badge pinned to her lightweight sweater.

"There's a shortage," Tricia replied, her bland expression never changing as she consulted the monitor behind a clear partition. "We're out of vehicles."

In a major city, Jessamyn could have marched over to a competitor's counter. Or better yet, requested a car service that came with a driver so she could devote her full attention to shoring up her mental defenses before arriving at Crooked Elm. Here…what could she do?

While calling for an Uber would successfully deliver her home, it wouldn't solve the problem of how to get around town for the next week or two.

"What if I downgraded?" she suggested, worry pinching the spot between her eyebrows into a knot. "Took a smaller car?"

That got Tricia's attention. The agent looked up from her screen, her head tilting a fraction as she met Jessamyn's gaze. "We're out of vehicles of every size. If you'd like to leave your contact information, I can let you know when we get something in."

Anxiety stabbed her. Why hadn't she driven from Denver instead of taking that last little hop into Steamboat Springs to get closer to Catamount? Surely there were vehicles there. Should she look into flying back to the hub so she'd have a car at her disposal?

The thought of being pent up at Crooked Elm with no escape gave her that claustrophobic feeling she hadn't felt since the early days of her parents' divorce, when sharing a roof with any of the other Barclays could trigger panic episodes to the point of illness. Gulping for air, she tried to swallow the feeling as she glanced around the baggage area, buying herself some time to think.

Over at the other carousel, the crowd had diminished to just a couple of lingering passengers. Ryder was nowhere in sight, likely gone. A fact that eased her stress. A smidge.

Then again, it only put off the inevitable of seeing him again, something bound to happen in the tiny town he still called home. A fact confirmed for her on her last one-day trip when she and her father had flown in to attend Antonia Barclay's memorial service four weeks ago. Ryder had been there.

Thankfully, he'd left without seeking her out. Considering that behavior, maybe he'd also seen her today and had been content to pretend otherwise. The idea shouldn't bug her as much as it did. And damn, but she just wanted to get to Crooked Elm and sleep for the next three days. Between clearing her calendar for the next two weeks, her father's resentment that she wasn't giving in to his demands—and tossing in the thought of her potential marriage—it hadn't been an easy week. The tension between her eyes ratcheted tighter.

Turning back to the counter, she opened her lips to tell Tricia she'd find another way into Catamount when the other woman's expression brightened.

Transformed, really. The woman's pale eyes focused on a spot past Jessamyn's shoulder.

"I have your keys, Mr. Wakefield." The agent honest-to-God gave him a wink as she dug under the counter and withdrew a lumpy envelope.

Mr. Wakefield?

The hairs on the back of Jessamyn's neck rose, awareness and outrage mingling as she clocked the male presence at her back.

She didn't need to turn to know who stood behind her.

Still, her head swiveled around to glare at the man whose face had once dominated her every waking thought.

"How can *he* obtain a vehicle when I was here first?" Her eyes narrowed on Ryder's lazy smile.

His untroubled blue gaze swept over her briefly before returning to the rental car agent. "Thanks, Trish."

Before his fist could close over the packet, Jessamyn snatched it from the woman's hand.

"Excuse me?" She rounded on the agent, compressing her lips into a flat line while she attempted to rein herself in. She would not be *that* person in the airport taking out her frustrations on a customer service rep who was simply the face of their company's bottom-line-based decisions. And yet? She refused to be ignored in favor of a hot billionaire rancher. "This vehicle rightly belongs to me. I have a reservation. I am in front of this…" Searching for the right word took a moment, but she settled on something innocuous. And blatantly false. "…gentleman."

Tricia shook her head as she frowned at Jessamyn. "That's not one of our cars," she stated flatly.

Before the woman could continue, Ryder held up a hand to forestall her words. "I've got this, Trish. Miss Barclay and I are old friends."

His icy glare was none-too-friendly despite the words. But then, he knew better than to try charming her. Not after the way they'd parted.

"Hello, Jessamyn. Nice to see you again." He spoke the words like a performance art piece. All for show. No emotion.

His hard jaw flexed in a way that hollowed out his cheeks and drew her attention to his sculpted lips. It really was annoying how handsome he was. She huffed out an angry breath.

"Hardly. And before you ask, no, we can't share the ride." She shoved the heavy envelope into her bucket purse, taking full possession of the rental vehicle. Never taking her eyes off him, she addressed the agent, "Tricia, can you tell me what I'll be driving today so I can sign the paperwork and be on my way?"

Ryder's lips quirked up on one side, almost as if she amused him. Would he be amused to cool his heels in the airport for a few hours while she left him eating her dust?

"Those are the keys to Mr. Wakefield's Tesla," Tricia informed her from behind the counter. "His *personal* vehicle."

It took a moment for the words to sink in after Jessamyn had been so sure she'd bested him. Could what she was saying be true?

Ryder's mouth curved even more, threatening a full-blown grin. Jessamyn dove a hand into her bag to extract the envelope and ripped it open.

Inside, she found a shiny black fob in the shape of a vehicle with no key attached at all. Along with it, however, there was a folded note with the name Ryder scratched across the outside of the paper in a spare, masculine hand.

"My brother dropped it off for me at the airport last night," Ryder informed her, taking the fob and the note from her hands. The warmth of his touch sent a buzz through her skin in a way that proved even more humiliating than the misunderstanding over the car.

Before she could reply, he lowered his voice for her

ears alone, leaning closer to say, "And since I'm far more gracious than you, Jessie, you can share my ride anytime."

Ryder could practically hear her spitting nails as she followed him into the now-deserted airport drop-off area a few minutes later. Only about thirty flights went through the regional facility in a day, and theirs must have been the last two. Since they'd lingered in the baggage area well after everyone else had found rides home, there was no one else around to hear her tirade about men who thought the rest of the world existed to do their bidding.

"...and since when is the local car rental shop the Wakefield family valet service?" Her high heels clicked in time to her rapid-fire words as she dogged his steps away from the terminal and into the small parking lot surrounded by green fields on all sides.

He didn't need to look behind him to know she pulled her rose-gold suitcase with her. The wheels rolled over the tarmac with a constant drone. He'd offered to carry the bag for her, and she'd only yanked it closer to her side in answer.

Ten years had changed a lot about Jessamyn Barclay, but she remained as prickly and independent as ever.

She was also still smoking hot.

Now Ryder turned on his heel to answer her most recent question. "Since Tricia is my niece."

She nearly slammed into him, pulling to a halt at the last second and tilting her chin to meet his gaze.

Hazel eyes more green than brown blinked back at him, her lush dark hair beginning to pull loose from a twist she'd secured with a clip. She wore a taupe-colored suit that skimmed her curves like it never wanted to let

go, the pencil skirt stopping just above her knee while
the jacket hugged a white silk tank top that molded to
perfect-sized breasts. The outfit looked as expensive as
the rest of her. From the high heels that would serve no
purpose on her family's ranch in the western Rockies to
the even more impractical suitcase, she broadcast the cos-
mopolitan polish she'd sought when she left Catamount
ten years before.

"Your niece," she repeated, her full lips twisting to
one side as if to chew that over. "That's why she winked
when she called you Mr. Wakefield. I suppose you are
reaping the benefits of small-town life." There was a
grudging acknowledgment in her tone.

Her gaze lifted to look beyond him, roaming over
the mountain view in the distance before returning to
the cornfield nearby. Did she find any aspect of that
vista enjoyable? She'd been so hell-bent on leaving this
place once upon a time. But he knew how a town like
Catamount could suck you back in. After their parents
retired from ranching and moved to Phoenix, Ryder's
older brother had given up his share of the family ranch
to marry his college sweetheart in Idaho. Yet Trey still
visited Catamount year after year, and his college-aged
daughter picked up summer jobs in Steamboat Springs.

Ryder had taken advantage of the opportunities outside this remote corner of Northwestern Colorado, but
he always returned home.

"It's absolutely a perk. As is being able to arrive in
the airport and find someone you know to give you a
lift home," he reminded her, the doors unlocking as he
neared his vehicle.

She glanced at the car, as if surprised to see they'd
arrived at his ride.

"I really shouldn't," she began quietly, as if talking to herself.

That ticked him off. Bad enough she'd wanted to act like she hadn't even recognized him inside the airport. Yeah, he'd noticed. He'd decided to let it pass because he'd been the one to blame for their breakup. Didn't matter that it had been a decade ago, when they were both barely adults. Their connection had been real enough, and it had hurt him like hell to send her away. He'd bet anything that he'd hurt her, too. So he'd bear the weight of being the bad guy in that scenario.

But for her to play games with him about a ride home, when they were both heading to the same place? He'd be damned if he'd be her personal scapegoat for all the things that irritated Jessamyn Barclay.

"Why is that?" He edged fractionally closer. Just enough to break the barrier of her personal space. "Afraid the old chemistry is still there?"

Even as he asked, he felt the electric pulse of it leap from her flashing hazel eyes into his skin. Awareness throbbed in his veins, multiplying like a virus he couldn't shake.

Yet Jessamyn's bottom lip curled as if she found the very idea offensive. Maybe the attraction felt like a virus on her end, too.

"Definitely not." She nearly snarled the words, leaving the pointed edges on them.

"Then what's got you all worked up about riding home with me?" He raised the trunk, then lowered his bag and climbing gear into the back. He waited to see if Jessamyn would make the trip with him.

Frowning, she folded her arms and shot back, "I am hardly *worked up*, Ryder. I'm just wondering how I'll go about obtaining a rental if I leave here without one."

He could see her point. Catamount wasn't much more than a map dot.

"Fleur has a vehicle," he mused aloud, thinking through the problem. "I've seen her delivering baked goods to the Cowboy Kitchen some mornings. Aren't you staying with her?"

"I can't just borrow my sister's car. Especially when she clearly needs it." Her grip tightened on the handle of her shiny suitcase, one manicured nail tapping thoughtfully.

His attention drifted over her again, lingering on one cocked hip where the fabric of her skirt stretched to accommodate the movement. An old memory returned with sudden vividness—him pulling her closer by her hips. Her melting against him and twining her arms around his neck.

They were a long way from those days, he reminded himself, cranking his head up to meet her gaze again.

"But she could probably give you a lift back here when they have a car available." He wanted to get on the road, damn it, not argue with a woman who belonged in his past. "Do you want a ride or not? I can't hang around here shooting the breeze all day."

She only hesitated a moment before she gave a clipped nod.

"Yes, please." She smacked the retractable handle on her fancy luggage back into place, then moved to lift the bag herself.

Stifling his own tirade about hardheaded women, Ryder took the heavy bag from her and slid it into the trunk before closing the lift gate.

Jessamyn remained silent as he opened the passenger door and helped her in, then went around the vehicle to take his own seat. He'd known for weeks—ever since An-

tonia Barclay's death—that Jessamyn would most likely
show up in town again.

Until a few days ago, he'd expected they'd do their
best to avoid each other. As they had since their long-
ago summer relationship. Then Ryder heard through the
grapevine that her father was contesting Antonia's will—
a will that left the Crooked Elm Ranch to her three granddaughters, including Jessamyn. Ryder had his reasons for
not wanting to be involved with *any* of the Barclays, let
alone the woman he'd briefly hoped for a future with.
But if Mateo Barclay persisted in barring Jessamyn from
inheriting the ranch that should rightfully be hers, Ryder
knew he'd have no choice but to share information he'd
safeguarded for nine long years.

For now, however, he'd bide his time. Pulling out of
the airport parking lot and onto the main road, Ryder
reminded himself that Jess would likely iron things out
on her own. He couldn't imagine anyone shortchanging
her from what she believed should be rightfully hers. So
Ryder wouldn't have any reason to interfere in her affairs.

No reason at all to see her elegant curves and smok-
ing-hot stares again.

He'd just about firmed up that plan in his mind, when
Jessamyn's silky voice wound through the plush black
interior of his vehicle.

"Now who's worked up?" she asked mildly.

He slanted a glance her way. "Me? I haven't said a
word since we got in the car."

"That's exactly how I can tell you're annoyed." She
shifted in the seat, as if she was settling in for an inter-
rogation. "I snipe when I'm irritated. You go silent. Is it
because I said you had the world to do your bidding?" she
mused aloud as she adjusted the air-conditioning vent to
blow toward her face.

Her neck.

She plucked the silk fabric of her tank away from her skin just below her collarbone, the action dragging his attention to her breasts and the body-hugging jacket that framed them.

And shouldn't his eyes be on the road? He whipped his head around, grateful there was no traffic to speak of in this part of town. Green fields lay on either side of them as he drove west toward Catamount.

"It's been ten years since we've seen each other. You really think you know me well enough to guess what I'm thinking anymore?"

She scoffed at that, letting go of her blouse and sinking into the seat. "*You* suggested I was afraid of potential chemistry." The word dripped with disdain. "It sounds like you think we're both stuck in the past."

"Touché." He nodded, granting her the point even as he tried to recall the last time he'd had her in his passenger seat. Their history together had been brief but intense, the memories of their touches imprinted on his brain. His body. "So we've established there's no longer any attraction between us, and also that you don't know what I'm thinking." He wasn't sure about either one, but he didn't want to argue with her the whole car ride home. "Any suggestions for conversational topics to fill the void for the fifty-minute ride we're looking at? Are we relegated to commenting on the weather? Making polite inquiries about each other's jobs?"

Jessamyn picked at the button on her jacket cuff, a single gold bangle sliding down her wrist. "I'm sure you don't want to discuss my latest real estate deal any more than I care to hear about your high-tech ranch upgrades."

He raised an eyebrow at that, wondering how she knew about the changes he'd made at his ranch. Had she been keeping tabs on him? The awareness she refused to acknowledge sparked to life, warming the air between them.

How long had it been since he'd tasted her? The question made him very aware of the two years it had been since his last relationship ended. He'd been too busy with the ranch to date, a fact that hadn't bothered him much until today, when the sudden, sharp desire for the woman next to him was the last thing he needed.

"All right, then." He couldn't quite keep the gratified note out of his voice.

"I've got a conversational topic anyway," she rushed to add, sitting up straighter. Uncrossing her long legs, she put both feet on the floor mat. "In the interest of making sure you believe me that the chemistry is thoroughly dead, I can tell you about my future husband."

Two

The silence stretched.

Jessamyn watched Ryder steer the vehicle along Route 40 heading west, following the Yampa River toward Catamount. The scenery outside the car was flat and green, an empty train track snaking alongside the road. The view inside the sleek black sports coupe proved far more compelling.

Ryder's jaw ticked, a pulse throbbing there even though nothing of the rest of him moved. Even his hands were still, the highway unfurling in an easy line for miles ahead.

"Future husband? As in this guy needs to be coerced into proposing?" Cool blue eyes flicked her way before returning to the lane in front of him. "I sure as hell don't see a ring on your finger."

Glancing at her bare left hand on the armrest, she yanked it out of sight, tucking her fingers under her thigh. As soon as she'd done it, of course, she felt the flush of awkward embarrassment.

Sort of like bringing up her almost husband in the first place. How come she could play it cool with any other man in the world but this one? She'd been in his car for less than ten minutes, and she'd already reverted to the starry-eyed girl she'd once been.

"It's not official yet," she forced herself to say calmly, feigning indifference when she was actually tense as hell about the whole engagement question. She really needed to get her head on straight while she was in Catamount. "There's been no rush to announce our partnership since it will have implications at Barclay Property Group. We thought we'd save it for our next investor meeting."

She'd proposed the timeline to her father, hoping to gain some breathing room for her and Brandon to get on the same page before making an engagement official. After all these years, she'd never felt the passion she'd had with Ryder. And she'd come to believe that looking at marriage as something practical rather than romantic would be the key to success.

They'd both been too busy to date much, so taking their relationship from co–vice presidents to something romantic would require time and effort. In the meantime, her father couldn't wait to unveil Barclay's new "power couple."

"You've got to be kidding me." Ryder shook his head, sliding the fingers of one hand through his dark hair while he anchored the steering wheel with the other. "You're going to make your marriage a business decision?"

"On the contrary, I'm using my marriage announcement to further my business goals." Not that she owed him an explanation. For some reason, she resented Brandon's willingness to treat their future relationship as a business deal, even if that was her own rationalization. But the impending engagement was on her mind. And if she could use it to forestall thoughts of the man sitting beside her, all the better. "There's nothing wrong with being judicious about sharing aspects of my personal life in a way that will help my career."

"Sure there is. It's called selling out. And it's cold as hell. Too cold for a marriage." He slanted another hard look her way before his attention snagged briefly on something beyond her.

Following his gaze, she spotted a group of mule deer in the field. Two of them looked up at the car as it passed, their big ears twitching. She turned her attention back to Ryder as he passed a slow-moving hay truck towing stacked bales.

"Spoken like a man who's never had to think twice about balancing a personal and a professional life." Stabbing the button to lower the window, she inhaled the scent of green grass and trees mingled with a hint of the river. She didn't allow herself to miss Colorado very often, but the larger-than-life landscape had always pulled at her.

"Only because I don't have a personal life," he admitted. "With my parents retired and my brother off in Idaho, I don't spend much time with family. Even though I see Trish more these days, there's still a distance." Was there a hint of regret in his tone? She barely had time to weigh the words before he lowered his voice to a silky octave. "Didn't anyone ever tell you that business and pleasure don't mix?"

She'd be lying if she said the word *pleasure* tripping off his tongue in that particular tone didn't stir something deep in the pit of her belly. Good thing she had the news of her impending engagement to keep those feelings at bay.

Fighting the urge to both fan herself and check her watch to see how many more minutes they would be enclosed in this small space together, Jessamyn shifted in her seat.

"My business *is* a pleasure." She hit the button to raise her window again, then reached for the air-conditioning vent to point it at her overheated face.

She'd always loved the challenge of her job, closing real estate deals and being a part of groundbreaking new developments. But for the past eighteen months she'd been questioning her professional future. Would the same type of work make her happy forever? Maybe once she and Brandon took over the business, it would feel different. More personal.

"That's good to hear. I remember how much you dreamed of being where you are now." He eased the car around a bend in the road as they began heading south. Gentle hills hinted at the more mountainous terrain ahead, where they'd skirt the north of the Flat Tops Wilderness before reaching Catamount.

"Climbing the ranks at my father's company has been rewarding. He has encouraged my relationship with Brandon and our goals for the business," she said carefully, unwilling to think about the dreams she'd once confided to Ryder. Dreams that had her working out West in real estate instead of New York. But she would not be trekking down memory lane with him on this trip. So she reached for any other topic, seizing on the first thing that came into her brain. "What brought you to the airport today? Have you been out of town long?"

"I was in the Alaska Panhandle doing climbing of another kind for the last ten days. But I needed to come home to oversee some modifications to my house." He slowed for a group of cyclists pedaling hard as they bent over their handlebars. "I'm refitting the main home to run off solar and wind power only."

Impressive. She couldn't deny it.

"My grandmother mentioned that to me in our last

phone conversation." She swallowed past the grief that still came when she thought of how long it had been since she'd seen her grandmother in person.

"I'm sorry for your loss. I know how much you cared for her," Ryder assured her quietly. "I missed you at the memorial, but you were on my mind that day."

The sincerity behind the words reminded her of what she'd once liked most about this man. She'd thought him the kindest person she'd ever met. Until...he hadn't been. She pressed the heel of her hand to her sternum as a pain sprang up there.

She resented the physical manifestations of her emotions that made her feel out of control. Was this what her mother had felt like when she'd battled depression after her divorce? Shaking off the empathy that her mother had never wanted from her, Jessamyn stared out the window.

Ryder passed the next group of bikers, picking up speed as the sun sank lower, casting the sky in shades of pink and violet.

"I— That is, thank you." She'd only flown in for the day of the service. Knowing the sisters had lost the chance to reconcile in the presence of the grandmother who'd wanted that more than anything had lit a fire under Jessamyn. She'd vowed to get her personal life together.

With her estranged siblings, for starters. But also with her lackluster romantic life. She'd taken her father's suggestion of marrying more seriously after Antonia's death. At least Brandon understood the demands on her professional life. They could build on that. Craft a future that wasn't full of tension and combat, like her parents' marriage.

"Did your future husband make the trip with you?" Ryder asked, tone cooling.

"No. I attended with my father, which seemed fitting."

She wouldn't try explaining her relationship to Ryder since she wasn't sure he'd understand the appeal of a partner who was more a friend and teammate than a romantic attachment.

"In other words, your boyfriend sat at home in New York while you mourned one of the most significant people in your life." His grip tightened on the steering wheel as they wound through steeper hills, trees crowding closer to the car. "I don't mean to judge, Jess—"

"It sure sounds like you're judging," she shot back, crossing her legs and her arms, shifting in her seat to look out the passenger window.

Of all the people she could have possibly caught a ride with today, why did it have to be a former love? A man who could still get under her skin?

"I just hope you'll give the engagement some thought while you're in town. Marriage is a big step."

She hated that he gave her advice she'd already been planning to take. It made it tougher to argue.

"Is that why you've never taken the plunge? Not all of us can afford to wait for life to be perfect before making a commitment." As soon as the words were out there, she realized how much they smacked of sour grapes. As if she were still smarting over his dismissal of her love ten years ago. Which was laughable. So laughable, in fact, that she turned the topic to something neutral. "Tell me more about your changes. Antonia said there was a yurt?"

If Ryder noticed that she'd fallen back on the topic of conversation that she'd said earlier she wasn't interested in, he didn't comment on it. Maybe he was as eager to leave behind the more sensitive subject as she was.

With any luck, Ryder's discussion of his off-the-grid house would take them the rest of the way to Catamount. She wouldn't have to think about his objections to her

future fiancé, or the fact that she might feel the smallest
amount of chemistry around Ryder after all.

She knew, of course, what lay down that path since
she'd already foolishly followed it. Following her personal
passions hadn't paid off, so she'd find romantic happiness
another way.

This time, she'd thank Ryder for the ride home and then
there'd be no reason in the world to see him again while
she was in town.

He *had* to see her again.

Four days after dropping Jessamyn in front of the
Crooked Elm Ranch, Ryder stood in line at the Cowboy
Kitchen, the only restaurant in the small town of Catamount. At 6 a.m., the breakfast rush was on as locals vied
for the best pick of fresh baked goods handmade by Fleur
Barclay, Jess's younger sister. Fleur, a professional chef,
had turned the Cowboy Kitchen into a morning hot spot
since her arrival in Catamount last month. She'd started
out making pastries and muffins at the Crooked Elm to
sell at the eatery, but over time she'd gotten close to Drake
Alexander, a local rancher and owner of the restaurant.
Rumor had it Fleur was poised to take over the place and
expand the business.

From his spot in the queue behind a crusty old rancher
in overalls, Ryder could see copper-haired Fleur loading
more pastries into the glass bakery case perched on the
old diner counter. He'd caught glimpses of Jessamyn in
the background, carrying trays and bakery boxes to give
her sister a hand.

Just as he'd hoped. He'd mentally regrouped since their
encounter at the airport, and he recognized that he needed
to speak to her about her grandmother's will.

Sooner rather than later. The possibility that he was sitting on information that could help her in defending her grandmother's wishes was eating away at him. Hence his morning visit to the Cowboy Kitchen. His foreman was a regular here, bringing pastries back to the ranch at least twice a week, and he'd mentioned that Fleur's sister had been helping her recently.

"Next!" Marta Macon, the cheery brunette who served as both a hostess and server, called from her spot at the register, her silver name tag glinting under the counter's pendant lighting.

The line shuffled forward even as the front bell chimed behind him, signaling another customer arriving. The decor remained the same as ever—white countertops, black-and-white laminate floors, chrome barstools with turquoise seats from a bygone era. An oversize painting of a faded brown Stetson hung on the wall above the counter. Although Ryder suspected the look of the place would be changing soon with Fleur Barclay on the scene.

Except Fleur wasn't the woman who'd captured his attention this morning. Jessamyn carried out yet another tray of baked goods from a seemingly endless supply in the kitchen. She wore a white chef's apron cinched around her narrow waist, with her dark, glossy hair clipped high at the back of her head. The tennis shoes on her feet instead of high heels added to the contrast of her airport outfit. And when she turned her back to the counter, Ryder could see a pair of jean shorts and a cropped tee that had been hiding behind that industrial apron.

A hint of thigh was just visible from his vantage point on the other side of the counter before Marta shouted again, "Next!" Then, recognizing him, the woman curved her lips into a wide smile. "Hi, Ryder. Should I get your usual?"

Jessamyn whirled around at the mention of his name,

her hazel eyes homing in on him with a faintly accusing air.

Just looking at her, he found his body stirring despite everything—being in public, being on the receiving end of Jess's obvious displeasure, and needing to give his breakfast order.

"Sure thing, but can you double it today? I'm meeting a friend." He allowed his gaze to return to Jessamyn, who scowled at him briefly before pivoting away to charge into the kitchen.

He tried not to follow the twitch of her hips in those denim cutoffs, but that proved a losing battle.

"Of course," Marta answered with her usual enthusiasm, reading him his total and making change before she continued. "I'm excited about the Atlas Gala at Wakefield Ranch later this month. Congratulations on the Captain Earth Award."

He tried not to cringe at the title worthy of a comic-book hero instead of a rancher trying to do what was best for his land with sustainable development. He knew the Atlas Foundation's goal was to draw attention to their mission of protecting the planet, and if the kitschy name of an award helped them garner headlines, all the better.

"Thank you. I'm glad to hear you'll be at the gala." He slid the change into the tip jar and stepped out of the way to wait for his coffees, already wondering how he could intercept Jessamyn.

A moment later, a white paper bag and two coffees in hand, Ryder stepped outside into the parking lot in front of the Cowboy Kitchen. He'd spotted Fleur's vehicle on the way into the restaurant, so he had an advantage for knowing where Jessamyn might retreat.

Sure enough, she was already in the passenger seat of the silver rattletrap that Fleur had driven into Catamount last month. Ryder knew Drake Alexander was in the market to replace it for her, since his friend had approached him about an extra truck that Ryder kept in his equipment barn for emergencies. He would have sold it to him, too, but Fleur had wanted the satisfaction of purchasing her own vehicle.

Catching Jessamyn's eye, he held the bakery bag up in front of the windshield.

"Hungry?" he asked through the tempered glass.

Slowly, her window lowered via a hand crank.

Her hair was down now, loose around her shoulders, and she'd removed her apron so that she sat in the passenger seat in her faded red crop top and frayed jean shorts. The white edges of the denim blew along her skin as the morning breeze filtered into the car, the outfit a far cry from the sleek, expensive outfit she'd worn in the airport four days ago. Right now, she looked like the Jessamyn he remembered from a decade ago.

"I thought you were meeting someone for breakfast?" One elegant eyebrow lifted in question.

Only now, seeing her up close in the morning sunlight, did he spot the violet smudges under her eyes. Had she been losing sleep?

He passed her a coffee, hoping like hell that her grandmother's will hadn't been the source of anxiety. "That someone is you. Can you spare some time this morning?"

When she seemed to hesitate, not accepting his offering, he pressed his case.

"We need to talk. And when I left the restaurant, I noticed your sister deep in conversation with Drake Alexander. So if you're waiting for her, it could be a while before she joins you."

Jessamyn huffed out a sigh. "Once they step into each other's orbits, it's like the whole rest of the world ceases to exist." Was there a wistful note in her voice? For a moment, he wondered about that fiancé of hers if Jessamyn didn't know that same kind of gravitational pull Drake and Fleur had for each other. Before Ryder could dwell on that, she rolled up the window and pushed open the car door to step outside. "Even so, I probably wouldn't have said yes if not for the coffee."

"Cream only, no sugar," he informed her as she took the cup, her fingers brushing his briefly.

He noticed a bandage on the back of her hand as hazel eyes darted to his over the rim.

"Good memory," she murmured, sounding surprised. "Thank you."

Her praise, however small, shouldn't feel so damned good. He shook off the warmth she'd stirred inside him, reminding himself he'd sought her out for a reason, and it wasn't to indulge an old attraction, no matter how tempting that might be.

"What happened to your hand?" He pointed to the bandage, curious how she'd been spending her time for the past few days.

"Spider bite. I've been sorting through some things in Gran's attic." She took a sip of the drink, her eyes closing appreciatively.

His gaze stalled on her long lashes fanned over her cheeks, some of her tension obviously easing as she enjoyed the coffee. He decided then and there he wanted to do more things to put that expression of pleasure on her face again. Then, recalling her words, he cautioned, "I hope you had that looked at. Some spiders can be dangerous around here."

"I did a telehealth visit. It's all good." She leaned against the car's trunk, and he recalled his ulterior motive.

"Would you mind if we take the food on the road?" He

pointed toward his work truck, an old gray 4x4. "You can text Fleur that you're with me, and I'll drop you off at the ranch afterward."

For a moment, she seemed to weigh this. Was she thinking about that man in her life again? The thought ticked him off and at the same time made him all the more determined to convince her. He shouldn't care this much, yet he didn't have a chance of telling himself it didn't matter.

At her nod, relief rushed through him. He started walking toward his pickup, not giving her time to change her mind. He could hear her dictating a message into her phone as he opened the passenger door for her and assumed she was letting her sister know they were together.

A few minutes later, they were underway. Ryder headed toward a spot he frequented in the mornings when he needed time away from the ranch. Trying not to dwell on the vision Jessamyn's bare legs made where she stretched them into the footwell, he focused on his reason for seeking her out. Before he could launch into the subject that was likely to shut her down, she cleared her throat to speak.

"The suspense is killing me," she announced, planting an elbow on the truck's armrest as she tracked the rolling hills outside. "What gives with the private conversation? Especially when we had all the time in the world to talk just a few days ago?"

She'd never been one to mince words. Back when they were dating, he'd liked that about Jessamyn Barclay. He'd trusted her to be forthright. Honest. But right now, when he wrestled with his moral obligation to protect privacy as a rescue worker versus information he believed she should know, that candid quality in her made him conflicted. Uneasy.

Should he come right out and tell her he was in a dicey situation with proprietary information he wasn't at liberty to share, even though it could help her with the battle over the will? Or would that only turn up the heat on him to spill what he knew?

"I heard your father is contesting Antonia's will," he said carefully. "I always considered your grandmother a friend, and if there's any way I can help, I want you to know that you and your sisters have my support."

"That's what this is about?" She pivoted in her seat to face him, her legs shifting in a way that drew his attention despite himself. "The will?"

"Not just the will, Jess. It's about Crooked Elm and your grandmother's wishes. I know she wanted you and your sisters to have the ranch one day."

"She told you that?"

"Not in so many words, but it was obvious in the way she spoke—" He cut himself off when he realized she was shaking her head. "What is it? You don't agree?"

"Of course I agree. But a belief or hearsay isn't likely to help us in court." Abruptly, she leaned forward to point out the windshield. "Hey. Isn't this the bridge near your ranch?"

The truck trundled over the wooden structure he'd rebuilt two years ago.

"I was wondering when you'd notice where we were headed." He was glad for the reprieve in the conversation. He needed to think about what evidence he could offer first. Gather more information. "You mentioned the yurt on the ride from the airport. I figured we could have breakfast here."

He hoped she wouldn't mind that he'd brought her here. Some of their history was tied to his ranch. They'd shared a memorable first kiss on the old bridge that had spanned the waterway he'd just crossed.

Sneaking a sideways glance at her, he caught her furrowed brow as her gaze swept the horizon. Without his permission, his attention dipped briefly to her full mouth. Her tongue swept along the upper lip in a brief swipe that had his groin tightening.

Thankfully, their destination appeared around the next bend, breaking the moment.

"Oh, wow," she breathed, a note of awe in her voice as she took in the octagonal structure set in a wooded corner of his property. "It's beautiful."

Parking the truck nearby, Ryder hoped he hadn't made a mistake in bringing her here. He'd hoped he could draw her out about where things stood with her grandmother's will.

But as he shut off the ignition and gathered up the white bags with their breakfast, he was very aware of the old attraction that still simmered between them. When Jessamyn unfastened her seat belt and peered up at him from under long lashes, he could feel that she was every bit as conscious of the chemistry as he was.

Grinding his molars against the awareness jolting through him, he decided he just needed to get through this conversation and a shared meal. Then he'd have the answers he needed, and he could leave Jessamyn Barclay to her own devices until she returned to New York and her not-quite fiancé who clearly wasn't worthy of her.

Yet as he moved around to the passenger side of the truck to help her down to the ground, just one touch of her hand in his sent enough sparks through him to assure him he was lying through his teeth.

Three

How was it possible that Ryder's gaze aroused her more than any other man's touch? And more importantly, how was she going to keep her desire hidden through their breakfast? In the past week, she'd exchanged a few texts with Brandon, but they'd mostly involved work and potential public appearances. No thought of Brandon had stirred her so.

As the compelling rancher followed her to the inviting outdoor structure, Jessamyn could swear she felt his gunmetal-blue gaze on her skin as surely as a fingertip trailing up her spine. Awareness pricked along the back of her neck, raising goose bumps on her arms while she wove her way toward the glass-and-wood building reflecting the morning sunlight.

Two decks wrapped around the back, only partially visible from where she stood. One deck sprawled out at ground level, with a firepit and cushioned deck chairs.

The other had been raised as if to access an interior loft. Nearby, a brook—a feeder stream for the White River—babbled, but the soothing sound did little to settle her nerves. She'd walked beside the creek with Ryder once, and they'd paused on the arch of the wooden bridge when they'd kissed for the first time.

Was it just nostalgia and old memories making her heart pound now? Or was the attraction she felt a current, living thing? The buzz in her veins sure seemed vibrant. Fresh.

Persistent.

His voice rumbled from behind her. "Do you mind if we sit outside to eat?"

The sound of him—closer than she'd expected—sent an empty ache through her midsection.

She told herself it must be hunger for food. She just needed sustenance, right?

"That would be good," she agreed, her voice husky. Clearing her throat, she stepped onto a raised platform that wrapped around the yurt, following the planks to the back deck. "And then I want to see inside. I'm curious about why you'd build a yurt instead of—I don't know—a hunting cabin?"

He laughed, and for a moment, she let his good mood warm hers.

"For starters, City Girl, I'm too close to my own livestock for hunting." He swiped a broad palm over the cushion of one of the patio chairs, chasing away a few fallen leaves. His broad shoulders stretched the fabric of the black button-down shirt. Then he held the chair out to her. "Have a seat."

"Thank you," she murmured, lowering herself onto the plump gray cushion. A view of the mountains was framed between two tall pines some twenty yards from the deck. The effect was like looking at a three-dimensional painting. "And I do realize you wouldn't hunt this close to your grazing fields. I haven't been in New York long enough to forget my family's roots. I only meant that a yurt seemed like a surprising choice for a ranch outbuilding."

Breathing in the scent of cedar and juniper, she waited while Ryder withdrew pastries from the bags and laid them on paper napkins he arranged on the low wooden table between their chairs. Two chocolate croissants. Two *xuixos*, deep-fried and sugar-crusted confections that originated in Catalonia, Spain, the recipe arriving in Catamount via Antonia Barclay. Fleur loved baking all her grandmother's recipes, especially tapas and Spanish-inspired pastries.

"I'm hoping to rent this out for guests who enjoy ecotourism but still want a taste of ranch life." He pried the top from his coffee and took a long swallow.

Jessamyn's gaze followed the move, her eyes snagging on the hollow at the base of his throat. With an effort, she tried to conjure up an image of Brandon's face to ward off Ryder's magnetic draw.

She couldn't. Instead, she scavenged her brain to follow the conversation.

"Ecotourism? I thought that meant traveling to wilderness areas and leaving them undisturbed." Taking a big bite of the *xuixo* that she'd helped her sister bake at 3 a.m., Jessamyn hoped a sugar fix would ease the hunger for the man next to her.

"Initially, that's how the term was used. But in a broader sense today, travelers are looking for ways to see the world and use less resources while they do. I'm trying to make Wakefield Ranch a destination of interest for people who are curious about sustainable living."

She recalled the conversation she'd caught snippets of earlier at the Cowboy Kitchen and smothered a grin. "I may have overheard something about the Captain Earth Award."

Even as she teased him, she also had to admit his efforts were admirable.

A couple of friendly gray jays landed nearby and hopped closer, perhaps sensing the possibility of an easy meal.

"It's a publicity tactic for the conservation group, but I can hardly complain when they're making inroads with a younger demographic." Ryder tore off a corner of his pastry and tossed it to the pair of songbirds. "Next door to Crooked Elm, Drake is already working to restore wetlands along the river. I'm complementing the effort here to show how a ranch can work harmoniously with the environment."

"I'm impressed," she admitted honestly, watching the little jays squawk over their treat as they pecked it into bird-sized bits. "But I know that's not why you wanted to talk to me. You said you were willing to help me with my case against my father, but I'm not sure how you can."

Ryder shook his head, scowling. "I just don't understand why he would do that to you in the first place. He knew what your grandmother intended."

Tensing, she bristled at the accusation in his voice. "Wrongheaded as he may be, I'm sure he has our interests at heart." She needed to believe that. "He said he's concerned Lark and Fleur will outvote whatever I want to do with the property. He hopes to even the odds if he has a voice."

Even though she defended her dad, on the inside, she was still furious with him over it. His explanation implied that, even if he lost the case to have himself declared the primary beneficiary of the will, he would still try to obtain a portion of the estate equal to Jessamyn's and her sisters'. How could he have thought that would honor his mother's wishes?

Ryder set aside his coffee, his pastry finished. Then, he pivoted to face her full on.

"Do you believe what he said about putting your needs first?" Those cool blue eyes probed hers, seeing right through to her thoughts.

"He's given me good guidance in the past," she answered, hedging. "My career has taken off because of him."

"It's taken off because of *you*, Jess. Don't avoid the question. Do you truly believe he's looking out for you now?"

She itched to ask why it mattered to him enough to bring her here to quiz her about it. But between the concern in his eyes—for her—and the fact that she worried about this issue, too, she thought maybe she owed it to herself to answer him honestly.

"No, I don't," she confessed, agitated and feeling disloyal about having to admit her doubts. "But *he* believes it, Ryder. I'm sure of that much."

His jaw flexed, the muscle working silently as he seemed to chew that over.

"So you'll admit he doesn't know what's best for you with your grandmother's ranch," he pressed, leaning closer to lay a gentle hand on her forearm. Pushing into her personal space. "How could you believe he'd ever know what you need in a husband?"

Her mouth dried up.

At his touch. His nearness.

His unexpected counterattack on the question of her potential engagement.

A hundred responses circled through her brain. That it was none of his damned business. That Ryder didn't know what he was talking about any more than her father did with regard to her personal life. But the only reply she wanted to make was a silent press of her lips to Ryder's firm, sculpted mouth.

She wanted that so much, in fact, she shoved to her feet to escape his nearness. Escape the tangible seduction of his gaze sliding over her.

Striding to the low fence surrounding the deck, Jessamyn gripped the smooth wood handrail, her nails biting into the surface.

"I like and respect Brandon. I agreed to the match based on our common goals and interests." Even as she said it, she knew Brandon's proposal was never going to happen now.

If she couldn't even conjure up a vision of her potential life partner's face while Ryder was around, then she was doing herself—and Brandon—a huge disservice to even consider saying yes. She couldn't build a personal partnership with someone who didn't share her vision of the future, nor could she raise a family with a man who didn't share her aspirations. The loss of that dream, even if it had been a foolish one, raked out her insides, leaving her empty of everything save the heated awareness of Ryder as he left his patio chair to stand behind her.

"You can't sacrifice personal happiness for someone who checks a bunch of boxes." The warmth of his chest blocked the breeze from her back, the cedar-and-leather scent of him stealing around her as surely as a touch. "It's a bloodless way to approach a relationship."

The words rattled her even as she battled the old awareness for Ryder, a live-wire connection that had never been fully shut down.

"Bloodless?" As she spun around to face him, the word was a quiet whisper rasping up her dry throat. It held a world of ghosts in it for them, the echo of a long-ago argument returned from the dead. "You think I don't feel? That I make decisions like some kind of automaton?"

She felt the warmth of his breath on her face, the force of his frustration with her. Those gunmetal-blue eyes sparked with an internal fire, the silver streaks near his pupils turning molten.

"Don't you?"

The challenge stung like a gauntlet to her cheek.

An answering anger rushed through her, tangling up with the desire held in check for too long. Her hand fisted in the placket of his black button-down shirt before she could consider what she was doing.

"How dare you?" She vibrated with each slam of her heartbeat against her ribs, as if that vital organ wanted to get closer to Ryder, too. "I feel. I have the same hungers coursing through my veins as you."

The force of them made her feel light-headed. Dizzy with awareness of this man and all the things they'd once felt for each other.

Even so, she told herself to walk away. To relax her grip on his shirt and pull it together.

But at the same moment, Ryder's mouth descended toward hers. Gently. Slowly.

Giving her time to choose what she wanted. That searing gaze checked in with hers as he neared, seeing what she wanted. Gauging her reaction.

Something about that combination of raw attraction and his cautious approach undid her. Like he'd reached inside her and seen exactly what she needed. Craved.

When his lips finally brushed over hers, she allowed

the electric spark to open a circuit between them, the current of need fusing their months together.

Had he goaded her into the kiss?

The fear circled around Ryder's brain, warning him he needed to break the connection. He couldn't allow an impulsive moment to give Jessamyn any reason to feel regret later.

Just one more minute.

After ten years without tasting her, he couldn't let her go just yet. Not until he'd had time to catalog every delicious whimper she made in the back of her throat. Each sharp inhale that pressed her breasts to his chest. Every caress of his fingertips along her narrow waist. The flicker of her tongue along his, her hands growing bolder as she stroked up his chest and over his shoulders. Her cinnamon-sugar flavor stirred his hunger, stoking the urgency building behind his zipper.

One more minute...

A warning bell clanged in the back of his head, alerting him that his "one more minute" had already gone on too long. With superhuman effort, he forced himself to loosen his grip on her waist. He levered back to look at her, breaking the kiss.

Her hazel eyes remained heavy-lidded, her focus unclear until she pulled her attention up to meet his gaze.

"What are you doing? Why did you stop?" Her pupils dilated, her tongue darting out to moisten her lips.

His heart hammered so loudly that the nature sounds vanished. The birds, the breeze, the rustle of small animals in the underbrush off the deck. Everything seemed silent except for the roar of his blood in his ears.

"I didn't want to pressure you if you weren't ready for more." He dragged in deep breaths, willing his pulse back to normal. "About the bloodless thing…" He shook his head, disappointed with himself for needling her when she'd already been on the defensive. "You don't need to prove anything to me."

"No kidding. I'm pretty sure I have a stronger sense of self than that." Her hands began to slide away from his shoulders.

Ryder caught them, pinning them to his chest before she could take them back. "Wait a minute. If you're not proving a point, why are you kissing me?"

She stiffened. "Excuse me? *You* kissed *me*."

"I realize that. And I want to keep on kissing you. But not if you're going to fly back to the arms of some other guy tomorrow."

Her eyes narrowed a moment, scrutinizing him. He hadn't meant to reveal the dark jealousy for the man who wasn't yet her fiancé, hadn't even acknowledged that it lurked inside him until now.

Some of the tension eased from her at his admission while a breeze stirred a few dry leaves at their feet, rustling noisily. "I won't. You're right that I shouldn't accept someone as a partner just because they meet predetermined criteria. This week apart has made me reevaluate our relationship."

Relief whooshed through him at her reassurance. He hadn't realized how much he hated the idea of her marrying this guy until that moment. Since when was he so damned invested in her personal life?

She glanced at her feet, where a small whirlwind of fallen leaves danced around her white tennis shoes and his boots. When she looked up again, her eyes had a glimmer of a fire barely banked.

"Furthermore," she continued, her voice pitched low,

"I told myself if I couldn't even picture his face when you were around, I had no business getting engaged to him."

Her words were a balm to his soul one minute. And the next, they lit him on fire. He nodded his satisfaction.

"That's why you kissed me."

Her breath huffed faster as her gaze dipped to his mouth. "I didn't see the point in denying something we both wanted."

His body steeled at the implication, his grip tightening where he held her hands in his.

"Hell no, there's no point." He drew her arms up, fastening them around his neck before he skimmed his palms along her body, gliding along her curves to land on her hips.

Tug them closer.

Her breath caught. Her lips still glistening from where he'd kissed her before. Desire squeezed his middle in a tight fist.

"We never purged this from our system when we were young," Jessamyn added, her fingers tangling in the ends of his hair, her body rocking closer. "Maybe now, if we indulge the attraction just this once, we can put it behind us and move on for good."

Just once?

He didn't agree with that statement based on the hunger raging like an inferno inside him. Yet, for now, it was enough to know he could taste her again.

His body felt the pull of need radiating from her, and he was powerless to deny what she wanted. Especially when he'd dreamed about her every night this past week.

"We can indulge it all right," he muttered, lifting her higher against him so that he could kiss her without bending down. Her sweet curves dragged over him, scrambling his brain and making it imperative to have her underneath him. Or on top of him. Wrapped all around him. "I'll indulge your every last need for as long as you'll let me."

For a moment, their gazes collided. Locked.

"Yes. I want that." She cupped his jaw, her fingers stroking his cheekbone while their ragged breaths met and mingled.

He claimed her mouth the way he'd longed to in his car four days ago. The way he'd dreamed about ten years ago, before he'd let her chase her dreams.

Back then, he'd known they were both too young for anything permanent. He hadn't wanted to derail her dreams. And he knew he'd have to focus on his own goals as well. Now? She was all woman, and she knew what she wanted.

She kissed him like she'd been dreaming about this for as long as he had. Her tongue meeting and mating with his, her hips tilting toward him. The friction of her body made him forget everything but pleasing her. Providing what she needed.

Lifting her higher against him, he turned to bring her indoors. With a sexy moan, she wrapped her legs around his waist, anchoring herself to him in a way that lined up the hard bulge in his jeans with the soft warmth between her thighs.

The pressure robbed him of every thought but being inside her, a need that seized him like a biological imperative he had to fulfill *now*.

"Jess," he growled her name like a warning as he opened the French doors into the wide-open space surrounded by windows. "If you keep that up, I'll never last."

"Really?" She broke the kiss just enough to say the word against his lips. "Are you suggesting I might have some power over your legendary self-control?"

Ah, damn.

She'd once accused *him* of being the bloodless one, back when he'd told her that a relationship would never work. That he'd only get in the way of her dreams.

But they weren't delving into that ancient history now. Not when she was wriggling against him like she couldn't wait to get her clothes off. Not when they were alone with a bed just a few more yards away.

"You've always had power over me." He let his hands roam over her hips until he palmed the rounded contour of her ass. Her shorts just barely covered her, his fingers grazing the tender flesh beneath those curves. "The difference is, now I'm not fighting it."

When his shins met the barrier of the mattress on a low platform bed, Ryder dropped her onto the center of the fluffy white duvet. He backed away to work on the buttons of his shirt, his gaze never leaving her.

A sexy, speculative gleam was in her hazel eyes as she lifted her crop top tee up and over her breasts. White lace barely hid them from his view, and she wasted no time popping open the front clasp to slide off the bra, too.

His mouth dried right up at the sight of her dark pink nipples, her breasts swaying as she moved to the edge of the bed and stood up again.

He wasn't sure he remembered his own name by the time she hooked her thumbs in her jean shorts and wiggled them off her hips.

"That's a good thing," she purred as the denim slid down her thighs. "Because I'm not fighting it, either."

Four

For an instant, standing in front of Ryder in a pair of panties, Jessamyn flashed back to the last time she'd been this close to naked with him. The time she'd been ready to give him her virginity.

And he'd been too much of a gentleman to take it since he already knew they had no future together.

Ryder had shredded her heart and her pride all in one blow.

He wasn't backing out on her this time, though. She saw the fire in his eyes that told her he wanted this every bit as much as she did.

Just once, she promised herself. One time with Ryder and they would come full circle. She could move on. Excise him from her life without wondering about what they'd be like together.

Then his hands were moving, unfastening the rest of the buttons on his shirt while he toed off his boots. When he shrugged out of the shirt and moved to his jeans, Jessamyn's gaze locked on his torso, the road map of ridged muscle enticing her closer.

Closer.

As she reached to caress him, however, he imprisoned her wrist with one hand, spinning her around so that her back was pressed to him.

"Jess. Jess. I want you too much." He buried his face in her hair, his words warming her neck and her shoulder as he spoke. "Let me touch you first so I can make this last."

Releasing her wrist, his fingers drifted lower on her belly, sliding beneath her underwear.

Her head lolled back against his shoulder as pleasure and anticipation wound through her. "It doesn't matter," she protested, her breath coming in ragged puffs.

"It does to me. I need you to feel good." He scraped aside her hair with his free hand so that his lips were next to her ear. "Will you let me do that for you first?"

Her knees buckled a little as his fingers slid through her wetness, finding the pulsing center of her sex. A gasp raked up her throat at the feel of him there, circling the swollen flesh.

Over and over.

"Oh. Ryder," she managed brokenly, grateful when his other arm anchored her beneath her breasts. Securely held, she was able to remain upright while he sought out the touches that made her breath catch. "But I can't put my hands on you like this. It's not fair to you."

Her whole body spasmed as he reversed the path of his circling fingers, going backward. Fast and slow. Slow and fast. Building a fever inside her.

"You can't guess how much I want to touch you this way." His voice was pitched so low, so deep, it dragged her deeper under the seductive spell of what he was doing to her. "How much it cranks me higher seeing you like this."

She felt the pleasure tightening between her hips, knew she was close to flying apart.

"Yes. Yes, please," she murmured through the haze of desire. She couldn't stop her hips from grinding into his, taking the measure of the hard ridge pressed against her curves.

"I can't wait to watch you." The low insistence of his words made her head roll back and forth against his chest.

Then, the arm banding around her ribs shifted so that he palmed one breast. His thumb rubbed the nipple, mirroring the way he touched between her legs.

And just that quickly, she went hurtling over the edge, headlong into a fresh abyss of pleasure. Through every last convulsion, Ryder held her close, teasing more sensation from her body. She twisted against him, shamelessly seeking all that he had to give.

When she went still at last, heart slamming with the overload, she pried her eyes open and lifted her head from his shoulder, feeling unsteady on her feet.

He must have known, because no sooner had she thought it than he lifted her in both arms and carried her to the bed.

This time she lay there trying to recover enough equilibrium to pay him back for the way he'd made her feel. Dragging in deep breaths while she watched Ryder through heavy-lidded eyes.

He shoved his jeans off his hips, taking his boxers and his socks before she'd even caught her breath.

And oh. Wow.

The sight of him made her inner muscles contract again, the empty ache intensifying.

"I have condoms," she offered, remembering the strip

she'd put in her bag last winter. "I left my purse in your truck." She'd been changing them out seasonally for years even though she hadn't used one in longer than she could recall.

Was it any wonder that orgasm had felt so incredible?

And yet it hadn't been enough. She needed the deeper intimacy of him inside her. The completion of feeling him there.

"Housekeeping makes sure there are some in here," he assured her, reaching into the bedside drawer of a simple wooden nightstand. Retrieving a packet.

"Let me," she urged, taking the foil from him and ripping it open. "I want to touch you."

Kneeling up to the edge of the bed, she reached for him. She stroked her fingers along the hot length of him while his breath hissed quietly between clenched teeth. He felt so good. She hated to cover him, imagining how it might be to have him without the layer between them. But what was she thinking?

Clumsily, she positioned the protection and rolled it into place, a thrill shooting through her at the gleam in his eyes.

A shudder trembled up her spine as his arms enveloped her, his body pressed to hers.

"Do you know how many times we've done this in my head?" he asked as he guided her down to the mattress. Covering her.

Her throat dried up. His question probed at her emotional defenses, stripping away more than just her clothes.

"More times than I should admit," he continued, not requiring an answer from her. His hands guided her hips where he wanted them, his steely hardness settling against her sex in a way that made stars flash behind her eyelids.

"Ryder," she murmured softly, desperate to lose herself in the physical and ignore the warmth of feeling in her chest. "Why aren't you inside me already?"

"Look at me," he commanded, stroking her hair away from her face. "I want your eyes on me when that happens."

When she did as he asked, their gazes connected, and his hips pushed forward.

She'd never been vocal in bed before, but a shout built in her throat now, a hoarse cry of pleasure that broke free as he went deeper. Deeper.

Breathless, she gripped his shoulders tighter, her legs wrapping around his hips to accommodate more of him. All of him.

"Don't move," he rasped, his fingers sinking into her hips to keep her in place. "Need a minute. You feel too good, Jess."

Her teeth sank into her lip as she tried to hold still. In that moment, she felt his heart gallop faster while the rigid length inside her pulsed.

How could she *not* move?

"Um. Ryder?" Her breath whooshed in and out of her lungs, the vein beneath one eye ticking. She was hyperaware of every inch of her body. "The struggle is real for me, too."

He made a sound that might have been a laugh or maybe a cry of despair. Maybe a little of both. But whatever he was feeling, he seemed to give in to what they both wanted.

His hips began to move in a rhythm that made her forget everything else. Everything but this. Him.

All Jessamyn could do was hold on, letting the sensations build again, the anticipation pushing her higher. Her brain blanked of thoughts, her focus narrowing to

Ryder. To the connection that had never gone away between them.

Even now, that bond threatened to take over. To eclipse everything else until it was the only thing she could see and feel.

Overwhelmed, she had no choice but to close her eyes again, to focus on the physical part that was incredible enough without the complication of other feelings.

At the same time, Ryder slowed to reach between her thighs and massage the same spot that had given her an orgasm earlier. He grazed those places lightly at first, then picked up speed, using what he'd learned before to drive her closer to completion.

She wound her fingers in his hair, pulling too hard but unable to stop herself as he found exactly where she needed to be touched. Her feminine muscles seized, contracting over and over again in a way that must have touched off his release, because he went rigid above her a moment afterward.

His shout drowned out hers, the sound vibrating through his chest and hers, too, so that she felt it as much as she heard him. Helpless as wave after wave of release unwound, she bent her forehead to his shoulder, kissing him there. Biting gently while his body tensed and twisted through his own finish.

For long moments afterward, the only sounds were their harsh breaths and the pounding of their hearts. Hers slowed before his, but eventually, they both quieted. Ryder shifted away from her, withdrawing to dispose of the condom before falling back on the pillows next to her.

In the recesses of her brain, she knew she should probably make an excuse to leave. To resurrect the barriers that had crumbled between them this morning. But the residual effects of multiple partner-induced orgasms were too heady for her brain to pick her way through the potential land mines of that conversation.

Besides, the bed felt so comfortable, especially as Ryder flipped a quilt over her and stroked her hair from her face. She shouldn't like that so much when they couldn't be together again.

"I've been awake since three a.m. baking with Fleur," she reminded him as her eyes drifted closed. Really, she shouldn't feel this relaxed after sex with an old crush. Sex that couldn't be repeated when her stay in Catamount was very temporary, and Captain Earth would never leave his Colorado ranch. "I may close my eyes for just a second."

She would leave in a minute. Tell Ryder to take her home so she could resume her search for evidence to support her case against her father's will contest. Today was just a way to get Ryder out of her system for good. To have the closure he'd denied her ten years ago.

It would have been a hell of a lot easier to truly feel "closure" if the sex had been terrible. Especially when she feared she'd be craving a repeat of what had just happened between them and that would be unacceptable.

Luckily for her, self-discipline was Jessamyn Barclay's middle name. Because she had a mission in Catamount this summer, and it didn't have anything to do with Ryder Wakefield.

Jessamyn studied a map of Northwestern Colorado spread out on the picnic table in the backyard, two days after the toe-curling encounter with Ryder. Sun warmed her shoulders as she browsed Routt County for potential land deals—just out of curiosity, because real estate was her jam—hoping the break in her workday would take her mind off the man who loomed ever-present in her thoughts.

And it wasn't Brandon, even though her phone chimed again with a call from him. Her gaze went to her phone vibrating on the redwood table, knowing she needed to talk to him.

To tell him they couldn't go through with an engagement.

Steeling herself for the confrontation that she'd been delaying, she tipped her face up to the noonday sun and dragged in a deep breath. Then answered the call.

"Hey, B," she answered softly, the old shorthand for his name falling from her lips.

They'd met in the master's program at NYU, first as friendly rivals for top honors, later as study partners who motivated the best from one another. That dynamic had continued into their roles at Barclay Property Group, where she'd convinced her father to interview Brandon straight out of school. He was a strategist who was great with numbers. Jessamyn excelled on the client-facing side, calming high-strung investors, luring reluctant sellers into deals, and finding the elusive sweet spot that made everyone at the negotiation table happy.

She would hate to lose the synergy of their partnership. But she also couldn't afford to let him think this marriage could happen.

"Jessamyn, did you get the deal memo on the Cartwright sale?" he began without preamble, the sounds of a busy deli lunch counter echoing behind him. A bell ringing. Sandwich names shouted out over the dull rumble of a crowd. "The seller is backpedaling about every aspect she agreed to last week."

"I did. And I was just about to call her." That wasn't strictly true, but she would do that next. For now, Jessamyn folded up the map on the picnic table and pushed it aside, reminding herself that her business was still in

New York, not Catamount. "Can I talk to you about something else first? Once you have your food?"

She knew the deli close to the Barclay headquarters in Midtown Manhattan where he grabbed most of his lunches. Sometimes she joined him for a bite. In the summers, they'd walk to Bryant Park and sit outside.

"Sure thing. I'm on my way out the door now."

Her heart rate sped as she listened to the door chime as he exited. The traffic noise as he walked away from the building. This might not be the ideal time to tell him she didn't want to go through with the engagement scheme, but she'd delayed long enough.

"It's just that I've been thinking more about us as a couple long-term, and the more I consider it, the more I believe it will be a mistake." There. The truth was out.

In a nutshell, that was it.

Brandon didn't sound too pleased when he drew in a sharp breath, stifling a curse.

"Are you kidding me right now?" he asked, his voice sounding close on the phone as if he'd tucked the device under his chin. "When I've already been ring shopping and we've gone over the details twenty times, from the honeymoon in the Maldives to the home on Central Park South?"

Guilt stabbed through her.

They had talked about their plans in detail often enough. Perhaps that had been her way of putting off actually acting on them.

"I just don't think we should let my father dictate what happens with our romantic lives." Rising from the picnic table bench, she walked toward the goat pen where Gran's Nubians bleated and cavorted through the grass. "It seems sort of like…selling out. Like a cold approach to marriage."

She cringed as she heard herself use Ryder's words.

"Where is this coming from?" Brandon asked, his tone aggravated. Impatient. "Because this is straight out of left field for me, Jessamyn. We have talked this over at length."

"I realize that, and I'm sorry that I allowed my father's preferences to have such sway over me for so long." Because that's what it came down to. If not for the pressure from her dad, she would have never considered marrying Brandon in the first place. At best, they were friends with very occasional benefits. Hardly the foundation for a marriage.

Especially now that she'd known Ryder's touch and what real passion felt like.

The strangled sound Brandon made might have been another curse. Or a wry laugh.

"That's great you've figured that out. And thanks for letting me know on my lunch hour. Well done, Jessamyn. And since we're such experts in cold mergers, how about you make that phone call to the seller in the Cartwright deal now that you've given me the axe?" The fury in his voice surprised her.

She couldn't remember the last time she'd seen him truly angry. And never with her.

But she knew her timing hadn't been the best.

"You deserve better, Brandon," she said softly, reaching over the fence to pet the brown-and-white goat. "And I'll call the seller now."

She wasn't surprised when he disconnected the call without further comment.

And while one piece of her felt free from the weight of a connection that wasn't meant to be, another part of her echoed with the hollowness of a new realization.

Her father had almost talked her into an engagement

she didn't want just because it would secure the legacy of his business.

How many other times had he steered Jessamyn into something that wasn't right for her, just because it was what he'd wanted?

A week after sharing the best sex of his life with Jessamyn, Ryder recognized that she was now officially avoiding him. He didn't like being ignored, and her flagrant evasion was wrecking his morning ride with his buddy.

Reining in his sorrel stallion, Flame, alongside his best friend, Drake Alexander, Ryder could see Jessamyn's retreating figure. The Alexander Ranch butted up against the Barclay family's Crooked Elm property, and Ryder had been hoping to see Jess today since she hadn't returned his texts. Ryder had driven her home after she'd fallen asleep beside him that morning. She'd seemed okay then. A little distant, perhaps, but he'd put that down to the awkwardness of sex outside a relationship. No doubt he'd been quiet, too, since he'd been processing what their mind-blowing encounter had meant.

But he'd told her he would call her after his next round of mountain rescue training with a crew of his SAR friends in Steamboat Springs. Yet when he'd returned to Catamount two days ago, she hadn't answered his call or texts.

Drake had asked him to review his winter rangelands where he was considering installing wind turbines, and they'd been riding back to the stables when Ryder had spotted her.

Drake nudged his paint mare, Pearl, toward the four-rail fence where Ryder had slowed to a walk. "Is that Jessamyn?" he asked, following Ryder's gaze where a slender figure vanished into the tree line near the creek.

"If it had been Fleur, I'm sure she wouldn't be walking away," Ryder observed dryly, wishing he felt as composed inside about Jess's defection as he forced himself to sound.

But the truth was, she'd dominated his thoughts all week, memories of their time together so vivid he couldn't stop replaying them.

"I thought you two were ancient history?" Drake slowed to a stop, then reached forward to pat Pearl on the neck.

Until that moment, Ryder hadn't even realized he'd come to a standstill himself. But he found himself straining to see beyond the ranch grasslands in the foreground to that thicket of juniper trees. To the Crooked Elm main house.

"We are." He needed to start believing that. Hadn't she told him their time together would be just once to get the attraction out of their systems?

He should be relieved, since he wasn't ready to come forward with the story about Mateo Barclay anyhow. Keeping what he knew about her father to himself now when the guy was contesting Jessamyn's inheritance was no easy task. It would simplify things for him to keep his distance while he kept an ear to the ground about the situation. He wouldn't share what he knew about Mateo unless absolutely necessary. And even then? He struggled mightily with the ethics of sharing something learned in a triage situation.

"And yet?" Drake prodded, swatting at a deerfly. "I sense more to this story."

"There may still be some chemistry," he admitted, unwilling to deny something that would surely be obvious to anyone who observed them together. And considering Drake wanted to marry Jessamyn's sister one day, chances were good he'd see the pair in each other's company.

If Jess ever stopped avoiding him.

Drake looked meaningfully toward where the middle Barclay sister had disappeared. "Chemistry or animosity?"

Ryder gave a rueful laugh as he tipped his head to remove his Stetson and fan himself with the brim. The late-July heat had picked up since they'd started their ride shortly after noon. The sun blazed hot now.

"Chemistry doesn't change who we are or what we want out of life. Jess is hell-bent on running her father's real estate business in New York and—" He stopped himself. Shook his head. "Well, can you picture me anywhere but in a saddle or on the side of a mountain?"

Drake gave a low whistle. "Did it really come down to that? You two were that serious?"

Ryder jammed his hat back into place, uncomfortable with the sharing. Normally, he didn't feel a need to unburden himself of personal stuff. It was indicative of how much Jessamyn had gotten under his skin that he was talking about any of this now.

"Like you said, ancient history." Ten years ago, he hadn't allowed his relationship with her to progress far enough for their differences to matter, since it wouldn't work between them anyway.

And about a year later he'd discovered something about her father that could turn her life upside down. He knew he would never be able to hide something like that from a woman in his life. Even in the short time they'd been together since she'd returned for this visit, Ryder had felt the burden of it weighing him down. So why was her defection bugging him so much now?

"I'm sorry to hear it," Drake said finally, his brown

eyes assessing. "I always liked all the Barclay women. It was a damn shame Antonia's son turned out to be such a jackass. That divorce did a number on his daughters."

Ryder hadn't been as close to the family as Drake had been when they were younger. He hadn't met Jessamyn until he'd been a teen working summers at a local rodeo, but then, Jess had never been a year-round resident. She'd shown up sporadically those last summers before she relocated to New York.

He was curious about Drake's impression of Mateo. Maybe his friend would have helpful insights.

"Hey, I was—"

Before he could get the rest of his thoughts out, a woman's scream cut through the quiet afternoon.

Five

"It's okay, puppy. It's okay," Jessamyn murmured to the agitated—massive—dog whose sudden growl from the woods startled a scream out of her.

She'd been hurrying along the creek to return to the house after spying Ryder on horseback with Drake Alexander on the neighboring property. A fierce growl from a thicket had scared her, and for a panicked moment, she'd thought a wolf had been eyeing her.

But a second look at the muddied and matted beast told her it was no threatening predator, but a Great Pyrenees caught in an illegal trap. Fury seized her even as a rush of sympathy for the frightened creature forced her closer to assess the situation and see if there was any hope of freeing it without endangering herself or the animal. She already had her phone in hand to call the state wildlife department for guidance when the ground beneath her feet vibrated with the sound of approaching horses.

And even though she'd been doing her best to avoid an awkward encounter with Ryder after what had happened between them, she'd never been so relieved to see someone. Ryder and Drake Alexander approached, a matched set of sleek horses, broad shoulders and Stetsons. Yet it was Ryder who commanded her full attention. Who sent her heart tripping in spite of her fear for the scared pet nearby.

"Jess? Are you okay?" Ryder's eyes were fixed on her as he secured a sorrel stallion to a tree and then made his way down the incline toward the water where she stood.

"I'm fine, but there's a dog in a foot trap down here." Her gaze flicked to the victim, whose head swung between her and the newcomers. His earlier growl had given way to anxious yelps, his rear paws dancing back and forth while his left front paw remained caught.

"Help is here," she assured the shaggy white canine while it followed her movements with liquid brown eyes, its ears pinned back. She kept her voice low. Soothing. "They'll know just what to do, I promise."

She didn't doubt their competence for a moment. Good ranchers understood animals, and they made it their business to treat them all with care and compassion.

The Great Pyrenees answered with a frustrated whine.

"Is he hurt?" Ryder called out as he reined in a couple of yards away. He was off his horse in no time, swearing at the sight of the trap. "Those are illegal. No way anyone got the special permit required to put that on your land."

Still keeping her distance, Jessamyn focused on the spot where the trap met the paw. The fur was dirty and wet and he kept shifting around, whimpering, as if he could free himself with enough movement. A fresh wave of empathy made her wonder how long he'd been out here scared and alone.

On the hill above them, Drake dismounted a moment behind his friend. "I'll get a log or something to put the trap on. They're easier to open if you have a hard surface to slide underneath it."

In the meantime, Jessamyn returned her focus to the ensnared pet.

"He's a little muddy, so it's hard to get a good look at the paw." She'd been careful to keep enough distance so as not to get bitten if the dog felt threatened. Only now, as Ryder neared, did she glance up at him again to see the rope in his hands. "What's that for?"

"We'll need a leash after we free him. It looks like he has tags, so someone will be glad to have him back home safely." Ryder reached her side, his palm finding the middle of her back. When their eyes met, his were full of worry. Concern. "That scream of yours scared the hell out of me."

Her mouth went dry at his expression. At the answering awareness of him.

The moment lasted only a second, and then he was all business, calling up the slope to his friend. "Drake, do you have anything we could use for a muzzle while we work on the trap?"

"Sure thing," Drake answered as he strode back toward his horse, a flat gray rock in one hand.

"You'll be able to extricate him?" Jessamyn asked, needing the reassurance. "I keep wondering how long he's been out here."

"I'll bet not more than a day from the looks of him." Ryder hung the length of coiled rope on a broken pine tree branch nearby. "But I've got a half sandwich in my saddlebag if you want to grab it for him while we disengage this big guy. The container it's in would make a good water dish if you bring that, too."

"I'm on it." She hurried up the hill, glad to have a task that would help.

She passed Drake on her way up. He carried a red bandanna now in addition to the flat gray rock. Some of her worry must have shown on her face, because Fleur's rancher boyfriend gave her shoulder a pat as he walked past.

"He'll be okay," Drake promised. "And we'll find whoever laid that trap."

She'd been so concerned for the dog she hadn't thought much about the legalities of the device yet. But how had it ended up on Crooked Elm land? Fleur would never set a trap, of course, and she was the only one who had access to the property in the past month.

Besides Josiah Cranston.

She stopped for a moment, remembering the tenant for the Crooked Elm rangelands. The guy was a creep who had ignored the "vacate" order they'd given him as soon as he'd discovered that Antonia Barclay's will was being contested. He'd promptly informed them that since they weren't legally recognized as the owners of the property, they couldn't demand he leave.

Legally, he had a point. But Cranston had taken advantage of their grandmother for years, using more of the acreage for grazing than he was supposed to, and getting the land at a cheap price by promising to install an irrigation system, which had never materialized. Could he be enough of a dirtbag to set traps on the property, too? This particular acreage wasn't even the part he paid to use.

Reaching into the saddlebag on Ryder's tall sorrel quarter horse, Jessamyn found the leftover lunch and the plastic container, then hurried back down the slippery incline strewn with pine needles and dead leaves. Already, the dog had the red bandanna tied around his

snout to keep him from biting while they helped him.
Ryder stood over the furry captive, keeping the big animal still between his knees while Drake slid the rock
under the trap.

Her heart caught in her throat at the sight of them,
taking so much care with the dog. Even as she moved
down to the creek's edge to fill the plastic container with
water, she kept one eye on Ryder's hands as he steadied
the creature's shoulders and crooned words of comfort.

"…and you'll be clean and dry in no time," Ryder
told the dog while Drake pressed on the sides of the trap
with both hands. "You'll have a belly full of vittles and
a healed-up war wound that all the lady dogs are going
to swoon over."

Warmth curled through her at the gentle way he
coaxed the frightened pup. Even when the trap opened
around the injured paw, Ryder moved the limb out slowly
and carefully, keeping the rest of the big animal still.

Jessamyn hastened over with the water as Drake
tossed aside the trap. "Should I pour this on the cut to
clean him up?"

At Ryder's nod, she washed away the mud and caked
blood until they could see the wound beneath the snarled
fur.

"We could use a wrap for that raw patch," Ryder observed. "The good news is it looks like an abrasion wound
and not anything serious."

She saw a way to help. "We can use my sock to wrap
him up. I wore knee-highs today in case there were ticks.
One of these will be perfect." Her fingers moved to the
laces on her tennis shoe.

Ryder petted the dog and continued to reassure the
animal while Drake lifted the tag on his collar and ob-

served, "His name is Phantom, by the way. And there's a phone number."

"Good." Ryder stretched a hand out for the coil of rope he'd brought. "Looks like the link on his collar ought to be big enough to pass a line through."

Jessamyn noticed that the dog looked up at him, tail wagging slowly. Her heart melted a little.

Between the three of them, they got a makeshift bandage on Phantom's leg and the temporary leash secured to his collar. Carefully, they removed the muzzle once Phantom knew there was a meal in store for him in the form of the chicken sandwich. As the dog ate and drank from the refilled container, Drake contacted the owner and decided to meet at the closest nearby access road so Phantom wouldn't have far to walk. He seemed to bear weight without favoring his leg. Thank goodness he didn't need to be carried.

Jessamyn moved toward the discarded trap. Her anger returned, now that her fears for the dog had eased.

"We should bring this with us." She used a stick to lift the metal device. "No sense making it easy for an illegal trapper to reset it and use this again."

Ryder gave a grim nod as he took the contraption from her. "I'll call the wildlife department on the ride home."

Reminding her they'd be parting ways again. Soon.

She'd have to restart her mental clock on how many days she'd spent away from him. Somehow getting to seven had seemed like a feat after what they'd shared a week ago. Now she'd be back to zero and wondering how to put him out of her thoughts again.

From a few feet away, Drake moved to join them, settling his Stetson lower on his brow.

"Good news," he began, shoving his phone in his back pocket. "Phantom's owner is already on his way over here to pick him up. If I walk Phantom to the closest road, Jessamyn, would you consider riding Pearl to Crooked Elm? He'd be fine in the old pasture for a couple of hours until I meet Fleur for dinner tonight."

"Of course. I'd be happy to." She hadn't ridden since she'd returned to Catamount, but she'd been eager to be on horseback again. There'd been a time in her life when she'd ridden daily—during the school year at her family's home outside Dallas, and during the summers at Crooked Elm.

Decision made, she glanced up the hill at Drake's tall paint and prepared to take her leave of the men.

Until Ryder put a hand on the small of her back, steering her gently toward the mounts.

"I'm going with you," he announced, his tone grave. "If there's someone trapping on your land, Jess, we need to figure out who and why."

She could hardly argue with that. But for her own sanity—for the sake of getting through the next hour with Ryder at her side—she sure wished his touch didn't ignite a thrill she felt to her toes.

"You've been avoiding me."

Ryder hadn't seen a reason to mince words now that they were alone. He kept Flame to a walk as the horses picked their way along the creek toward Crooked Elm. No sense hurrying back to the Barclay place when he had a few things to settle with the woman on horseback beside him.

His gaze roved over her long legs mostly bared by trim black shorts, especially now that she'd removed both her socks—one for Phantom, and the other she must have tucked away somewhere. She wore a long-sleeved white blouse that looked like it might be sun-protective, the fabric a nouveau kind used in hiking gear. No matter that he'd teased her about being a city girl, she had maintained her outdoors smarts. And her horsemanship, for that matter. She swayed in the saddle as easily as if she'd ridden daily for years.

She returned his gaze now, her expression defiant. "I don't see the point in spending time together when we both know things between us will never be anything more than what we already shared."

Irritation flared as he ducked a low-hanging branch. "Is that because you went back to your almost fiancé?"

He'd wondered about that more than once this week. Never before had he been a jealous person, but the idea of her still seeing the Manhattan big shot ticked him off no end.

"Of course not," she retorted immediately, frowning at him. "I might have allowed myself to get caught up in the idea of marriage for a time, but once I realized he wasn't the right one, I called and told him so."

The tightness in his chest relaxed, making him too aware how much her answer had meant. "Then why do you think there will never be anything more between us?"

For a long moment, she didn't answer, the only sound the soft trudge of hooves over the pine-needle-strewn earth and the occasional twigs cracking underfoot.

"Honestly? I spent a long time being hurt by your rebuff ten years ago, Ryder." The stiffness of the admission underscored the truth of the words. "But eventually I did see your point. We want different things. Lead very different lives."

A rush of anger for his nineteen-year-old self surprised him with its force.

"Which were good reasons not to jump into a serious commitment. You were on the verge of a big future, Jess. I couldn't allow you to get sidetracked from your dreams."

"So you made the executive decision to end things with me rather than just say as much?" Her laugh was mirthless. "Not that it matters now, but I'd always prefer the truth to someone else figuring out what's best for me."

She'd meant the words to be biting. And yet Ryder knew she couldn't possibly realize how much they cut to the quick when he was keeping her father's secrets. The burden of that weighed still heavier as the main house came into view across a long, open pasture.

"All I'm saying is that we're not running the risk of falling in love anymore," he continued, readjusting the reins in his hands and steering Flame away from the creek bed to higher ground. "We're two consenting adults who happen to have a connection that nearly burned down the yurt when we were together. If you don't want any part of that—or me—again, then fine. No need to run for cover when we get within a mile of each other."

He'd never been much for casual relationships in the past, but Jessamyn Barclay wasn't just any woman. Whatever had happened between them a week ago had been special. Unique. Powerful. And he hadn't stopped thinking about her for more than ten minutes at a time this past week. He couldn't imagine not being with her again. Touching her. Tasting her.

Besides, the need to keep tabs on her father's court case hadn't gone away, and Jessamyn was his best hope of learning new developments.

"I've never run from a man in my life, Ryder Wakefield," she shot back, tossing her glossy hair behind her shoulder. "And I won't start with you. Now, don't you think we should call the wildlife department and focus on something more important, like who is setting illegal traps on my property?"

Conceding her point—even though he recognized very well that she was redirecting the topic on purpose—he withdrew his cell phone to report the incident as they neared the house. Drake had texted him a minute ago to let him know the Great Pyrenees belonged to the foreman on a neighboring ranch. The man had been overjoyed to be reunited with the dog—still technically a puppy despite his size—that had startled during a thunderstorm the day before and bolted out the front door.

Disconnecting his call as they reined in their mounts in the pasture area closest to the house, Ryder shared the response from the parks and wildlife department, which hadn't proven that encouraging. Although there were hefty fines for illegal trapping, finding the culprit often proved difficult.

"They suggested using a wireless wildlife camera." He dismounted as Jessamyn did the same. "Which is a good idea and I think I have one at the house that I can run out there later."

They ground-tied the horses while Ryder walked with her past a small shed and pen where three Nubian goats bleated noisily at them.

"Really? That would be great. If you don't mind." Something about the awkward cadence of the words, her rush to make sure it was no trouble for him, alerted him that she was still wary of getting close to him.

If he wanted to be with her again, he needed to proceed with caution.

"I want to." His own anger at the trapper added steel to his voice. "What kind of bastard traps illegally and on someone else's land to boot? You don't have any idea who would do that?"

He slowed his step as they reached the backyard, where a picnic table painted bright turquoise stood next to a birdbath surrounded by flowers in a riot of colors. Butterflies fluttered around the blooms, adding more rainbow shades to the mix.

Jessamyn lowered herself to the picnic table bench, facing away from the table to use the surface as a backrest. He took a spot by her on the bench, the old wood creaking quietly. Awareness tripped through him at her nearness, reminding him of the way they'd connected physically. Now that he had her attention again, he wasn't going to let her keep avoiding what happened between them. Sooner or later, they needed to confront it.

"I do have an idea, actually." She lifted her hair off her neck and twisted it in a complicated way that resulted in a low knot. "Or at least, I know that Josiah Cranston, my grandmother's tenant, has access to those lands. My sisters and I formally asked him to vacate when we thought we were going to clear probate and were preparing to sell the land."

He focused on what she said instead of thinking about how good her neck would taste. Or how much he ached to blow a cool stream of air to the heated place beneath her hair.

Instead, he forced his thoughts to what he knew of the disagreeable rancher—none of it good. His reputation for cheapness spilled over to his cattle, a failing that endeared him to no one. A man could cut corners with his equipment or maybe even the wages he paid his hired hands if times were really tough. But shortchanging livestock in your care?

There was no excuse for it.

"And he hasn't left?" A protective urge rose in him.

Jessamyn shook her head, crossing one leg over the

other. "No. Legally, he doesn't have to until the ownership of the land is settled."

All the more reason to make sure the will was settled sooner rather than later. The knowledge of her father's shortcomings—his unworthiness to claim any part of Crooked Elm—ate at him. Made him all the more determined to find another way to help her since he hadn't shared what he knew with her.

"I can still talk to Cranston." He relished the opportunity to confront the guy, in fact. "And if he set that trap—"

"You don't need to get involved, Ryder. I appreciate the use of a camera if you have one, but Fleur and I will manage our business." She stood abruptly, the movement jolting the knot in her hair so the dark mass came tumbling around her shoulders. "Thanks for helping Phantom today."

As social cues went, she couldn't have sent him a more obvious one that she was ready for him to leave. More avoidance, damn it.

He rose to his feet, taking small comfort at the way her breath caught when he took a step closer. Just close enough to remind her how potent that connection was between them. He wouldn't push. But he wouldn't let her forget, either.

"No need to thank me. I went into search and rescue because I enjoy helping people." A smile pulled at his lips. "Dogs, too." He remained near her, breathing in her amber-and-vanilla scent, remembering the places he'd found that fragrance when he'd had her in his bed.

Behind her ears. At her wrists.

"I don't plan on requiring any more rescues this trip." She folded her arms as she squared herself to him.

Bold as you please, the same as she'd always been.

"Then I'll give you your space," he assured her. *For now*, he added silently to himself. But, unable to resist, he dropped his head to speak near her ear. "Just keep in mind I'm available for more than rescuing. Anytime at all."

He took it as a good sign that she made no smart comeback. No sharp retort. She swallowed visibly, her hazel eyes turning a darker green as she regarded him.

At least she'd be thinking about his offer.

Still, it didn't sit well to walk away from a woman he wanted so badly he could almost taste that amber-and-vanilla perfume on his tongue again.

Six

Jessamyn couldn't recall ever feeling so thoroughly turned on from a simple conversation with a man.

She forced herself not to watch Ryder Wakefield walk away from her after he'd practically handed her an engraved invitation back to his bed. An invitation that stirred memories she didn't want to have in her head right now when she needed all her focus on gathering evidence to fight her father's contest of Gran's will.

I'm available for more than rescuing. Anytime at all.

The echoing words sent a fresh shiver down her spine as she entered the cool interior of the Crooked Elm ranch house. The scent of cinnamon and sugar lingered around the clock with Fleur's newfound baking and catering businesses, and the incredible aromas enticed Jessamyn toward the bright yellow kitchen.

She couldn't have the no-strings affair that Ryder had tempted her with, so she would fill another hunger instead. Maybe if she gorged herself on sugar in the form of Fleur's one-of-a-kind pastries, Jessamyn would quit fantasizing about taking a big bite of a sexy rancher. Reaching for a plastic storage container on the counter sure to contain something tasty, Jessamyn started back at her sister's voice.

"Sooo...you and Ryder Wakefield?" Fleur stepped suddenly from the breakfast nook, a stoneware mug of coffee in one hand. She nodded toward the bay window behind the banquette. "I might have had a view of you two from my seat."

The youngest of the three Barclay sisters, Fleur bore little resemblance to Jessamyn or their older sibling, Lark. With copper-colored hair and gray eyes, Fleur had made smart use of her natural beauty and horsemanship skills to win rodeo pageants across five states after their father had cut her off financially. Jessamyn knew it hadn't been easy on Fleur to pay her own way through culinary school, but Fleur and Lark had both refused to make amends with their wealthy father for the sake of any support from him. For her part, Jessamyn had long blamed her mother for her role in the divorce that ignited stark family divisions. These past months since her grandmother's death were giving her reasons to rethink her dad's innocence, however.

For now, she was just grateful for the chance to salvage some kind of relationship with her sisters. Even though she was unaccustomed to anyone weighing in on her relationship decisions.

"Ryder and I are not...a thing," Jessamyn objected, while her body protested the news. "We're not anything."

She couldn't help that she wanted him. That was biology. A physical craving for intimacy didn't have anything to do with what was right or what made logical sense. Ryder had never shared her dreams or her vision for the future.

Although it had certainly come as news to her today that he'd broken things off with her ten years ago precisely because he understood that fact. All this time she'd thought he hadn't wanted her the way she'd hungered for him. The revelation that he'd given her up in spite of his own desires? That put a new spin on things.

She'd need to put that in perspective at some point. Figure out what it meant for them now, if anything.

Fleur's eyebrow lifted as she took a silent sip from her mug. Still clad in pajama pants and a pink sleep tee that said Less Talk, More Coffee, she leaned a hip against an archway separating the breakfast nook from the rest of the dining area. "Well, that clears up matters nicely."

Jessamyn opened the pastry container and helped herself to a *pain au chocolat* before closing it again.

"He was just helping me free a dog—"

Fleur held up her phone. "Drake told me all about it. I'm livid about a trap on our land."

"Me, too. Ryder said he might have a wildlife camera we could use to keep tabs on the area and see who comes to check the trap." Taking a bite of the croissant-like pastry, Jessamyn caught the crumbs in her free hand.

"My money is on Josiah Cranston." Fleur set aside her coffee mug on the Mexican-tiled countertop. "He made his displeasure clear when I gave him those lease termination papers."

"For all the good it did in getting rid of him," Jessamyn muttered darkly.

All three sisters were looking forward to the income the sale of the land would bring. At first, they'd also considered selling the ranch house, but now Fleur was making a pitch to keep it in their family. Her sister's sentimentality for the place had surprised Jessamyn at first, but spending time in Catamount again, remembering the warmth of their grandmother's house that hadn't been as tainted by their parents' unhappy split, she was beginning to see the appeal.

Well, beyond Fleur's love for Drake Alexander, of course. Jessamyn could also see the draw of Catamount. There was a strength and self-sufficiency to the people who lived in the foothills of the Rocky Mountains, a sense that they could fend for themselves no matter what came their way. Ten years ago, that hadn't meant anything to her when she had her eye on the prize of succeeding in her father's world.

But sometimes she wondered if she'd been seeking success for its own sake, or for her father's approval. She was so lost in her thoughts that it surprised her when Fleur called to her from the living room.

"Jess? You should see what I've been digging out this morning. Maybe it'll help us oust Cranston sooner rather than later."

Jessamyn took another bite of the chocolate pastry before setting it on a napkin for later. She brushed her hands over the sink to remove the crumbs before following her sister's voice into the whitewashed living area. With dark wooden beams overhead and the fireplace wrapped in tile, the room had all the Spanish Colonial touches that Antonia Barclay had loved. The dark wooden floor was partially covered with a worn cream-colored carpet while oversize leather chairs alternated with white sofas around the hearth.

But today, there were also boxes everywhere. Some open, some still closed, they were stacked on the coffee table and floor. A few spilled out their contents of papers and books onto the surrounding furniture.

A low whistle escaped her as she took it in. "What's all this?"

Curious, she walked over to one of the storage bins marked "Photos, hacienda rehab" to see what was inside.

"Gran's things from in the attic," Fleur explained, dropping to sit in one of the big leather armchairs. "I started pulling down boxes so we could search for documents that might support our claim that Gran wanted the property to go to us."

"This is excellent." Surprised at her sister's initiative, she glanced from the stack of old pictures to Fleur's determined face. All week while Jessamyn worked remotely, Fleur had been busy with catering jobs and baking, giving Jessamyn the impression that she wouldn't be much help with the court case. But clearly, Fleur had made time. "I didn't know Gran kept so much."

She picked up a handful of photos of the Crooked Elm in the days before Antonia had gone to work on the interior. Her and their grandfather smiling around a tall Christmas tree. Antonia in an apron, covered in flour as she worked in the old, tiny kitchen.

"Me, either. But I went in the attic because I wondered if there was any way to convert the space into a cathedral ceiling in the great room." In her quest to keep the ranch house, Fleur had been considering ways to make space for her own restaurant on the property—either in a separate building, or in an addition to the home. "And I found all this stuff tucked under one of the eaves in a crawl space."

"All we need to do now is go through it." Jessamyn guessed it could take days. Especially if some of the documents were written in Spanish, her grandmother's native language.

Jessamyn wasn't working a full schedule for Barclay

Property Group while she was in Catamount, but she'd been juggling at least thirty hours a week since arriving. Now, she'd have to whittle that back a bit to make time for the hunt for supporting documentation of Antonia's will. Her father wouldn't be happy about that, but then, it was because of his court case that she needed to do this.

As for Brandon… He wouldn't be pleased to lose more of her time, especially on conference calls with potential new clients when she was their most efficient closer. In fact, she guessed he'd be more disappointed about a potential loss of business that her absence might mean than he'd been about losing her as a potential life partner.

"I've actually got a lot of catering commitments in the next few days, but I have some time free next week," Fleur said.

Jessamyn sank down to sit on the arm of one of the sofas as she reached into a box and pulled out a small book covered in dark leather. She swallowed a sigh, unwilling to discourage Fleur, but frustrated not to be making more headway with finding evidence. She really wanted to unearth something decisive that would show their dad he couldn't win his own way in everything.

As fun as it was to find old photos, she doubted the ones in her hand would help.

"Sounds good. I'll get a head start this week and we can finish together when you're available." An idea had been circling around her brain ever since she'd learned they'd need witnesses or written evidence to support their case. "You don't suppose Mom would have anything in her possession that would support our claim? Old letters from Dad or Gran?"

Fleur glanced up from the diary, wariness scrawled in every delicate feature. "You're not seriously suggesting I ask Mom about letters Dad sent her?"

"Right. No sense walking over a potential land mine." She set aside the old square photos she'd been holding. "It took *us* almost a decade to start speaking again. It would probably take Mom that long to think about Dad without getting angry."

She ran a finger over a cut on her hand that she must have gotten while helping free Phantom. She wished the unseen cuts her family—and Ryder—had left on her would fade as easily as this small scrape would.

"And vice versa," Fleur reminded her shortly. A little sharply. "Not only is Dad no help to us, but he's the one actively gunning for our inheritance when he knows perfectly well Gran wanted us to have Crooked Elm."

Jessamyn tensed, bristling out of old habit. But her sister had a point and it was past time to acknowledge it. "Do you know why I took Dad's side? To start with, at least?"

She hadn't planned to share this with Fleur, but then, nothing about this trip was going the way she'd anticipated—from sleeping with Ryder and ending her engagement, to finding more to love about Catamount and her family.

Her father had been pressuring her to come back to work, to give Brandon another chance, to focus on new clients. He was great at talking but not so good at listening. He needed Jessamyn at his side to persuade their clients that they understood what the clients wanted in their new property. She had the touch—personal and professional.

From the emails, texts and voice mails she was getting, Mateo was growing annoyed that she was deviating from his wishes. And Jessamyn was growing more frustrated at being on the outs with her father. Even Brandon was wondering if they should try again.

Jessamyn had to keep things under control both in New York and Colorado.

Fleur's answer came quickly as she flipped through the small volume in her hands. "Because Dad's ambitious, like you. Because you wanted to live the kind of life he was building for himself in New York instead of the slow-lane pace we lived in Texas."

"Later, maybe, those things mattered to me. But at first, during that initial awful year when Mom found out Dad cheated and she hated him so much—that didn't have anything to do with it." For a moment, the old hurt stole over her, so sharp she had to close her eyes for a moment and breathe through it.

When she opened her eyes again, Fleur stared at her curiously.

"Why, then?" Fleur ran her fingers over the cover of the leather book, then clutched it closer to her chest as she listened.

"Because she told me I was just like him." Not just once or twice. Over and over. Quickly swallowing the catch in her voice, she cleared her throat impatiently. "When I asked her to come to school for things—for myself, yes, but also in the hope of giving her something to think about besides her unhappiness with Dad—she told me I was being selfish. That I shared that in common with our father. That every time she looked at me, all she saw was him—the driven overachiever. She made me feel all the resentment she had for him. Every time I laughed or had a friend over or did well in school, she brought up how much we were alike."

And it had been no secret what Jennifer Barclay thought of her husband by then. Jessamyn had felt the pain of the words singed into her skin like a brand, along with all the ways it implied her own mother's dislike of *her*. Jessamyn had taken up her father's banner then and there, knowing she wouldn't be welcome on her mom's side.

How many life decisions had she made as a result of supporting her dad? Her career? Where she lived? She wanted to believe she'd chosen her path based on her passions and her skill set. But being back in Catamount was reminding her of other things she'd once enjoyed.

"She was battling depression, Jess," Fleur reminded her quietly.

Empathy registered along with regret for all the time she'd lost with her mother. But it hadn't been all bad. Her dad had put on a good face and shown up for her, whether it was chaperoning a Model UN field trip or driving her to dance competitions.

Although, looking back on it, had he fanned the flames of the division between mother and daughter?

"I know that *now*. But I didn't understand anything about what she was going through when I was twelve years old. Then, by the time I was old enough to realize what she'd been experiencing, we were already on opposite sides of the family battle."

The hurt and fallout of that time—learning that she'd abandoned her mom when her mother had been fighting for her health—had led Jessamyn to fall for the first man who'd treated her with kindness and understanding when she was eighteen. She'd been swept off her feet by Ryder's empathy and generous spirit, so different from the way her family members all guarded themselves. Then, when Ryder had abandoned her, too, she'd had zero emotional resources for shoring herself up afterward.

"Maybe *you* should ask Mom if she has anything to

support our claim," Fleur suggested a moment later as she
slid the leather-bound volume back into the closest box.

"Me? The Barclay daughter who has no relationship
with her?" She shook her head, not understanding.

"It could be a way to start a dialogue with her again."
Fleur held a hand up before Jessamyn could argue. "Just
think about it. I'm convinced Gran left us Crooked Elm
to help us find our way back together as sisters. Maybe
it will help us heal some of the other stuff, too."

Like her broken relationship with her mother? Jessamyn seriously doubted that. Or maybe she was simply
afraid to hope.

"First, I'm going to go through the boxes," she said
instead, unwilling to disappoint her sister when Fleur
had gone to the effort of bringing down all the papers
from the attic. "Maybe talking to Mom won't even be
necessary."

Fleur made no answer, but then, she didn't have to.
Jessamyn recognized she was hiding from confrontation
with their mother the same way she'd avoided Ryder all
week. But her coping mechanisms had gotten her this
far in life, and she was doing just fine so far, thank you
very much.

Although, as a memory of Ryder's parting words—
I'm available for more than rescuing. Anytime at all—
floated through her head again, Jessamyn wondered if
she'd be able to continue her avoidance strategy where
he was concerned. For one thing, she was curious about
his revelation today that he'd only broken things off with
her ten years ago because he'd understood she needed to
follow her dreams. She wanted to ask him more about
that, but how could she without seeming like she just
wanted another chance to tear his clothes off again?

Until she figured that out, she suspected she would

need a whole lot more *pain au chocolat* to assuage the hunger still tingling through her even now.

Have you spotted any activity on the wildlife camera yet?

Ryder read Jessamyn's text after he got out of the shower, his wet hair dripping onto the screen since he hadn't been able to wait to dry off to read it.

Respecting Jessamyn's space proved a whole lot tougher than he'd thought it would be, but then, he'd known she was a strong-willed and fiercely independent woman. She wouldn't simply fall into his bed all summer long simply because they had amazing chemistry. If anything, the strong connection had probably rattled her into keeping her distance over the two weeks since they'd rescued the dog together.

Sure, she'd helped him install the wildlife camera so they could see if anyone came to check the trap, but she hadn't indicated she wanted to see him again. And how could he press her when he'd promised to give her some breathing room? But in the ten days since they'd installed the camera, she'd gotten in the habit of texting him in the evenings to ask about the feed that was still hooked up to his personal account and easier for him to check.

Which was why he hadn't been able to wait to dry off when he'd heard the notification chime at 10 p.m. The sound had a Pavlov's-dog type of effect on him, his body going on high alert at just the thought of an interaction with her. Because sooner or later, she would want to find out if their first time together had been a fluke. He couldn't believe he was the only one reliving those hours they'd spent in his bed.

Just showered, he typed back, taking a small amount

of pleasure in putting that image into her head. Will fire up laptop in a sec and get back to you.

He could check the feed from the phone, but he was already signed in and had the page loaded on the other device.

Besides, he might have agreed to give her space, but he hadn't made any promises about the nature of their conversational topics. He didn't mind pressing a few of her buttons if it would speed her in his direction. Hell, he didn't mind pressing anything of Jessamyn Barclay's.

Maybe that was why he found himself typing again as he secured the towel around his waist and looped another around his shoulders before he walked out of the bathroom into the master suite.

I told you what I'm wearing. Or not. Care to repay me with a visual on you? He hit Send, not giving himself time to second-guess the message. If she thought for a second that he didn't think of her often, he wanted to disabuse her of the notion.

I'm covered in dust bunnies thanks to crawling in the attic. Still searching for supporting documentation of Gran's wishes.

Ouch. He felt the pang of guilt about the information he was withholding as he dropped onto the gray leather couch across from the fireplace in his suite. He used the towel around his neck to mop off his face and chest before pulling open his laptop on the coffee table.

Lucky dust bunnies. He input the words on his phone while his laptop fired to life. But sorry to hear you haven't found evidence yet.

He was certain it had to be out there. Because Antonia Barclay had definitely not wanted to give Crooked Elm to her son. Even Mateo Barclay knew that, whether or not he would admit it.

For a long moment, his phone remained silent and he wondered if Jessamyn was discouraged. He hated the thought of her wasting time looking through old papers to no avail.

I hope so, she typed finally. And something about those three lone words assured him he hadn't lost her. The connection between them was still there, and not just the on-screen kind.

Tapping the buttons on his laptop that would show him the last day's worth of camera footage in fast-forward mode, Ryder then turned his attention back to his phone. His hands might be tied as far as keeping the old confidentiality he owed her father, but Ryder could still give her a hint of where to look for answers without compromising any ethics, couldn't he?

I know you don't want to contact your mother about this, but what about one of your dad's girlfriends? he suggested, knowing which one would be ready to throw Mateo under the bus. Remember the one he was dating when you and I were together?

He told himself that wasn't pushing it. That he wasn't angling for Jessamyn to come over and see him in person for answers. With one eye on the camera footage, he was thinking about how much he wanted to see her again when his phone rang.

Caller ID showed his SAR commander.

Crap.

Stabbing the connect button, he already knew what the guy wanted. It was the only reason his SAR contact ever phoned him personally, let alone at this hour.

"Wakefield here," he answered at the same time he typed a final message of the evening to Jessamyn.

Will look at footage later, Jess. SAR duty calls.

Hitting Send, Ryder rose to dress for work. Normally, a search and rescue assignment consumed all his attention. But even after he hit the road five minutes later, his gear already in the back of his truck, Ryder couldn't shake the image of Jessamyn alone and frustrated at Crooked Elm, needing help he couldn't give her.

One way or another, when he got back he would think of a way to ensure she found the information she needed.

Seven

Blinking from the sunlight splashing over her face, Jessamyn awoke slowly from the deepest, thickest sleep of her life. Her head felt heavy. So did her limbs. What time must it be for her old bedroom at the Crooked Elm to be this bright? Birds trilled outside her window.

She never slept late.

"Jess? Can I come in?" Her sister's voice sounded outside her door.

"Of course you can," she answered, trying to sound alert since it seemed inexcusably lazy—for her, at least—to have just opened her eyes at…she lifted her cell phone to see the time…nine in the morning?

Fleur pushed the door to the small bedroom at the same time Jessamyn scrambled to a sitting position. And while Jessamyn felt sloppy in her nightclothes, Fleur wore cute denim cutoffs and a cream-colored retro blouse with crocheted squares across the bodice and gauzy sleeves.

"Sorry to bother you." Fleur stopped short at the sight of her sister still in a black tank top and pajama shorts. "I didn't mean to disturb you, but I thought you'd want to know—"

"You didn't disturb me," Jessamyn protested, still feeling "off" somehow. Not tired. Not sick. Just like she was moving through peanut butter or something. "I'm usually up for hours by now. I guess I had trouble falling asleep last night or something."

All at once, she recalled Ryder's final text to her about going out on a search and rescue assignment. She gripped her phone tighter, seized with the need to follow up on his message. Make sure he was okay.

"It's fine. I assumed the early mornings you've put in helping me bake for the Cowboy Kitchen finally caught up with you." Fleur lowered herself to sit at the foot of Jessamyn's bed, tucking her bare feet under the white dust ruffle, a decorating leftover from Jessamyn's childhood. "And I hated to disturb you now, but I thought you should know that Ryder is out on a potentially dangerous search and rescue call."

Everything inside her went still.

"What do you mean? How do you know?" Straightening her spine, Jessamyn narrowed her focus to her sister. "Who told you that?"

"Everyone in the diner was talking about it this morning. A couple of climbers got caught in a summer avalanche out in the Flat Tops Wilderness—"

"Avalanche?" Her heartbeat went into overdrive as her brain stumbled on the idea, cold fear wrapping itself around her throat. "How could that be? It's been seventy degrees out this week."

"A wet avalanche, according to everyone at the Cowboy Kitchen." Fleur scooted closer on the bed, laying a hand on Jessamyn's bare arm. "The snow on the peaks melts and makes the underlayer unstable."

"And Ryder is still out there?" Jessamyn swung her legs out of the covers, unable to sit still. "It's been almost eleven hours since he got the call. He texted me last night, and—"

Remembering their message thread, she turned on her phone's screen to see if there was anything else from him. But the last text she'd received from him had been about 10:45 p.m.

Worry sank in her gut like a stone. She opened a heavy chest of drawers near the bed and pulled out a fresh T-shirt and a pair of sweatpants.

"What are you doing?" Fleur asked, coming to her feet.

"I need to find out what's happening." The lethargy she'd felt on waking was gone, evaporating under the hot weight of regret that she hadn't followed up on Ryder's mission before going to bed. "Do you know where they are?"

"Somewhere near Pagoda Peak, I think. But you can't go out there, Jessamyn. They'll never let you near a rescue operation—"

"I know." Nodding, she pulled the sweatpants over her sleep shorts and then shimmied out of the tank top to yank the T-shirt over her head. "I was just curious. I could learn more at the diner, maybe. Or Ryder's house."

Jessamyn headed for the small Jack-and-Jill bathroom shared with the bedroom that used to belong to Lark. While Jessamyn ran her toothbrush over her teeth, Fleur smoothed the covers on the bed Jessamyn had left so hastily.

Fleur didn't ask her why she was so worried. But then, if her sister had known to wake her up with this news in the first place, obviously Fleur had a clue that Jessamyn's feelings for Ryder were more than just friendly.

So much for keeping him at a distance.

She just needed him to be okay.

"Do you want Drake to drive you anywhere?" Fleur asked, following her out of the bedroom and down the stairs. "He's worried, too."

The knowledge that Ryder's closest friend was scared as well didn't do anything to lessen her anxiety.

"There's no need." Grabbing the car keys for the rental she'd finally managed to obtain the week before, Jessamyn stuffed her phone in the pocket of her sweats and headed toward the door. "I'll be fine."

She just prayed that Ryder would be, too.

Because of their history, she told herself. Because he'd been her first love, and he was a good person. Her fears were rooted in that old bond and didn't have anything to do with what had happened between them a few weeks ago.

A sudden bout of queasiness stopped her as she put her hand on the doorknob. A wave of nausea forced her to stand still for a moment. Collect herself.

Backtracking to the fridge, Jessamyn grabbed a water bottle for the road. She'd be fine.

He'd be fine, too.

She was just being sentimental. Sensitive. The trip to Catamount was pulling all kinds of surprising emotions out of her—feeling nostalgia for a sense of family she hadn't experienced in too many years. Remembering how much she'd once loved this place. And, of course, memories of Ryder were tied up in all that.

Once she saw Ryder was okay, she would return to

working on the case she was building against her father's claim on Crooked Elm. Then her life would return to normal.

Bone-weary, Ryder breathed a sigh of relief as he steered his work truck onto the private drive for Wakefield Ranch. The search for the missing climbers had taken half the night, and the rescue operation the whole morning, both parts hampered by miserable conditions. Leaving him wet, exhausted and scraped up from scrambling around rocky terrain in the dark. He'd showered and grabbed a couple of slices of pizza at the local firehouse where his team had convened afterward, but the damp cold from the slush on the mountain hadn't left him yet.

They'd found the climbers—alive—and brought them home successfully. Any other day, that would be enough to soothe the physical toll of rescue work. But today's assignment reminded him too much of another one. That first, long-ago SAR mission where Mateo Barclay had called for help to save his girlfriend who'd fallen down a ravine in an avalanche.

A fall she'd taken because of Barclay's negligence.

Squinting gritty eyes against the bright afternoon sun, Ryder scrubbed a hand over his chest, where a thorny ache of regret had lodged a decade ago. He would have mulled it over more, except that as the main house came into view, so did an unfamiliar sedan. And a very familiar feminine silhouette.

Jess.

His exhaustion faded, replaced by a new urgency to wrap her in his arms. The adrenaline rush that came from his work on the mountain could leave him buzzing for hours afterward, and he felt that surge to life again, igniting a hunger no other woman but this one could fill.

What was she doing here? The need to find out had him slamming his vehicle into Park the second he braked to a stop. Throwing the door open, he stepped down to the stone drive that curved in front of the entryway while his gaze hungrily tracked her movement toward him.

"Is everything okay?" he asked, closing the distance between them. He couldn't ignore the instinct to touch her, not when her hazel eyes locked on his, worry etched in her features. When he opened his arms, she flew into them. "What's wrong?"

Her soft curves molded to his body, the amber-and-vanilla scent of her skin and hair filling his nostrils. She felt so good. So right. Memories of their night together stole through his brain, fanning the flame of his hunger for her.

She tucked her head into his chest, her cheek pressed to a place just above his heart, her whole body tense. "I've been worried about you. I heard about the avalanche." For two heartbeats, she took deep breaths and seemed to steady herself before peering up at him again. "The local news was giving updates about the climbers, but they didn't say anything about the rescue workers."

Touched by her concern, he wanted to believe her fears for him meant something—emotions she'd refused to show him before now. Then again, how much worse would he feel about keeping secrets from her if their physical intimacy spiraled into something deeper?

He told himself to let her go. Relinquish the hold he had on her before they wound up right back in his bed. With an effort he edged away from her a step, just enough to insert an inch of space between their bodies.

His hands remained fixed on her waist, though, his fingers not quite cooperating with the plan.

"I'm sorry you were worried. It was a long night because conditions went to crap. Too windy for the chopper to find the climbers, and too risky for the search dogs." He felt her sharp intake of breath at his words, saw the fear return to her eyes, and he quickly amended his decision to share the particulars. "But we found them. We all stayed safe, and we got them out of there without taking unnecessary chances."

By slow degrees, he felt the tension in her body relax.

"Thank God. That must have been scary." She exhaled a long breath but didn't move her hands from where they'd rested on his sides. Only now, as her anxiety seemed to lessen, did he allow himself to take in the sight of her. She'd obviously dressed hurriedly in a pair of sweats with a slightly rumpled white tee, her glossy brown hair tied in a crooked ponytail. She looked a far cry from the sleekly elegant executive he'd picked up at the airport a few weeks ago.

And damn, but he liked this side of her even more. It reminded him of the woman he'd fallen for ten years ago. The Jessamyn she'd been before she embraced a different life in New York. Dangerous thoughts when he needed to let her go.

The adrenaline still hummed inside him, needing an outlet.

"I should get in the house." He wrenched his hands away from her, a new kind of tension filling him now that hers had eased.

He took a step back, putting more space between them so her hands fell away from him. Regret for the loss of her touch crowded his insides, his body howling over the abrupt parting.

Jessamyn's forehead knitted in confusion. "I don't understand. Was it wrong of me to wait for you?"

"No," he told her vehemently in a voice too loud. Then, modulating his tone, he swallowed before he continued. "I'm flattered. I'm just—"

"Flattered?" She bristled, her shoulders straightening as she drew herself up to her full height. "Like I'm some kind of groupie?"

"That's not it," he assured her, his skin feeling too tight as he tried to recalibrate his response. But thoughts and reason failed him when all the heightened fears from the mountain—decisions he'd had to make in life-and-death situations—left him with no resources to navigate a dicey conversation.

And all the while, his brain taunted him with images of losing himself in Jessamyn's soft, giving body. Sweat popped along his shoulders as his boot heel hit a stone step. He hadn't even realized he was still backing away.

Jessamyn lifted her arms in surrender. "By all means, I'll let you get back to whatever it is you need to do. Sorry my worry delayed you—"

He stepped forward and caught whatever she'd been about to say with his mouth, sealing his lips to hers in the heated kiss he'd needed since the moment he stepped out of his truck. Knowing he didn't have the eloquence to argue right now, he just wanted this kiss to speak for him. He'd step away any second now. As soon as she got the message that he wasn't being selfish by retreating.

He was being respectful, damn it.

Except there was a chance that message was going to get lost if he continued to devour her like a starving man.

Breaking the kiss was one of the toughest things he'd ever done. But he would not take advantage of a vulnerable moment when Jessamyn had been worried about him. As he held her gaze in the aftermath of the explosive kiss, he hoped like hell his eyes did a better job of explaining that he was on edge right now.

That he needed her too much for finesse.

For a protracted moment, she stared up at him, her rapid breath huffing over his lips as she seemed to weigh what had just happened. Would she storm away, indignant that he'd kissed her into silence?

Or would some tender regard for him see beyond his knee-jerk reaction to the knot of emotions behind it? Perhaps she'd kiss him on the cheek and walk away again, return to avoiding him the way she'd done as much as possible over the past weeks. An idea that left him hollow as hell.

Ryder swallowed the lump in his throat, bracing himself for either one.

Instead, he watched as Jessamyn's hazel eyes shifted a shade greener. Brighter. The pupils dilated, the black center crowding away the mossy ring around the outside. A switch flipped inside him, his heart slugging heavy against his rib cage. His body understood that signal from her faster than his head could comprehend it. Everything inside him tightened. Tensed.

Turned hard as steel.

At the same moment, Jessamyn stepped closer to him, her gaze never breaking. With slow, deliberate movements, she laid her palms on his chest and smoothed them up and over his shoulders, leaving rippling sensations in their wake. Her hips tilted toward his, the contact eliciting a groan of pleasure from both of them.

"Take me inside with you, Ryder. Now."

Gratified by Ryder's instant response to her request, Jessamyn found herself almost running to keep up with his long strides up the covered walkway to his massive stone-and-log home. His grip on her hand was tight. Sure.

As if he had no intention of letting her go.

A shiver of anticipation tripped through her while he jabbed impatient fingers over the security keypad near the front door. The testosterone practically steamed off him in his jeans and work boots, a navy blue T-shirt bearing the logo for Routt County Search and Rescue stretched across his shoulders.

She hadn't come here for the purpose of mind-blowing sex. She'd been scared and emotional—two moods she had little experience dealing with. And maybe after the hours of fear, she was recognizing some of that adrenaline crash that seemed to take hold of Ryder now that his mission had been accomplished.

No way would she turn her back on him—on *this*— now.

"This way." He directed her through a huge foyer where glowing wood floors and high cathedral ceilings framed a small water feature in one wall, the sound of flowing water a musical greeting.

But she didn't have time to take in much beyond the split-log stairs leading up to the second-floor gallery. Ryder still gripped one of her hands tightly while she allowed the other palm to skim along the polished log handrail where elk antlers served as spindles. The scent of pine and cedar mingled in the air as she followed Ryder into the primary suite at the top of the stairs. Two patio doors opened onto a private deck from here, overlooking the green backyard, where gravel paths connected the natural stone pool area to the firepits and dining area.

Flip-flops smacked the wide plank floors as she wandered into the living area of the suite, her heart still racing. The sound of her shoes reminded her how little attention she'd paid to her appearance in the race to find out if Ryder was okay. A residual quiver of worry forced her to look at him now as he closed the door behind them, sealing them into the privacy of his bedroom.

Her throat went dry as she feasted her eyes on the ropes of muscle in his arms, the chiseled perfection of his pectorals that looked hewn from stone through his fitted cotton T-shirt. Memories of what he looked like without it put her feet in motion to meet him halfway across the room, her fingers itching to undress him.

"You're going the wrong way," he chastised her gently when she reached him.

His big palms settled on her hips as he steered her backward, deeper into the room. His thumbs strayed below the waist of her sweatpants, coming to rest in the hollow below her hip bones. Desire pooled low in her belly.

"Don't you want me walking *toward* you?" She couldn't keep her hands off him, her touch skimming up his arms to slide beneath the fabric of his sleeves.

"First and foremost, I want you in my bed." His voice was all gravel, low and rough. "Once you're there, I'll come to you."

A soft whimper escaped her, and she wondered at the plaintive sound that she'd never made before with a man. Normally, she took what she wanted in bed, comfortable with asking for what she needed. But this heady urge to give? And to feel so worked up about yielding to this man in particular?

Something about it hit hot buttons she didn't know were lurking in her sexual subconscious. She felt her defenses crumbling, but she told herself it was just physical.

They both needed this.

"I like the sound of that," she confessed as the backs of her calves hit the heavy, carved side rails of the king-size bed.

Then, pinned between Ryder and the mattress covered by white pillows, Jessamyn gave in to the urge to tunnel her fingers under his T-shirt.

She ran her fingers along the ridges of his abs, lingering briefly before she dragged the cotton up and over his shoulders. Ryder's hands followed hers, mirroring her action with her shirt until it was on the floor on top of his. He made a guttural sound of approval at her lack of bra—she'd only half paid attention to clothes this morning.

She could hardly regret the decision when the end result was his lips on her nipple all the faster, his tongue teasing circles around each taut peak, one after the other. Her breasts had never felt so exquisitely sensitive.

Winding her fingers through his thick, dark hair, she arched into his mouth, needy for more. For everything.

He seemed to understand, his hands already at work on her sweatpants, dragging them down her body along with the sleep shorts she'd been wearing underneath.

"No panties, either," he muttered darkly as he helped her out of her clothes. "Are you trying to make me lose all restraint?"

"No," she replied automatically before rethinking, her whole body tingling as he stroked a tentative touch between her thighs. Her legs went limp. She sort of collapsed into his touch. "Maybe. Yes, actually. That's my final answer."

His eyes were glowing coals when they met hers, his fingers teasing the sweetest sensations from her body.

This time, when his mouth found hers, the kiss was

a claiming. A no-holds-barred mating of tongues as they took and gave in equal measure, hungry for more.

She wrapped her arms around his neck and he lifted her onto the bed, displacing a handful of white pillows. He only paused the kiss long enough to strip off the rest of his clothes and retrieve a condom from his nightstand.

Yes, yes, yes. She thought she chanted it in her head but based on how quickly he tore off the wrapper and sheathed himself, she might have been urging him on out loud.

Either way, she knew he must get the message by the way she tilted her hips to his, seeking. She trailed kisses up his throat, reveling in the hot taste of him while she stroked her foot up his calf.

When at last he pushed his way inside her, the sensation rocked her. She hadn't realized she was already so close to orgasm from his touches. But now, feeling the warning ripples already squeezing her womb, she could only lock her ankles around his waist and hold on tight.

"Feels so good," she gasped.

"Need you," he groaned at the same moment, their words interlacing as thoroughly as their bodies.

Her fingernails dipped into the muscle along his shoulder, seeking purchase. Or maybe just hanging on to the pleasure for as long as possible.

But the tide of hunger was too strong. The next time his thumb circled the bud of her sex, she flew apart, her body gripped with delicious waves of bliss. Her head fell back, at the mercy of the sensations while Ryder found his peak a moment later.

He gripped her hips tightly, holding her where he needed her, and she melted at the sight of him lost in the same undertow as her.

For long minutes, they held each other in the aftermath. Unlike their first time together, she didn't feel
the same worry about what would happen next. Clearly,
avoiding Ryder hadn't helped her to get over the attraction to him. Once hadn't been enough to get him out
of her system.

How long would it take?

Opening eyes that had fallen shut, she slanted a
glance over at Ryder on his back now beside her. His
breathing was even, but she knew he hadn't fallen
asleep. Still, he had to be exhausted from being on the
mountain all night.

Her limbs felt heavy, too, her whole body limp and
languid. From the incredible orgasm, she guessed. Although she'd woken up feeling tired, too, which was
so unlike her.

And there'd been that weird moment of nausea this
morning. Was she coming down with something? Or
did she just need to eat?

"You must be starving," she reasoned, levering up on
an elbow. "And tired. Would it be weird of me to vol-
unteer to make us something to eat?"

His gaze flicked over her exposed breasts, and she
couldn't help the smoky wisps of pleasure that floated
through her at his attention.

"I could probably do with something more substantial
than you," he teased, his eyes darkening as he kissed
the rounded curve. "Then again, I haven't gotten my
fill of these. Or the rest of you."

Palming her breasts, he squeezed one gently, and she
relished the new, heightened sensitivity…

The thought stopped her cold.

Sensitive breasts.

Nausea.

Unusual exhaustion.

She quickly added up math that didn't compute. They'd used condoms. She was on the pill.

"Jess?" Ryder's head lifted from the sensual attention he'd been paying her body. "Something wrong?"

"I— No." She shook her head, even though a prickle of dread needled at the base of her spine. Especially when she thought about when she'd last had her period.

Back in New York. Six weeks ago?

Panic bubbled up her throat.

"Talk to me." Ryder's voice grew more urgent, his hands going to her shoulders to steady her. "What's the matter?"

Her heart raced. Her mouth felt like cotton.

"Nothing. I'm fine," she started, needing to reassure herself and failing miserably. "But I—" She swallowed hard and started again. "I should get going."

Levering herself off the bed, she bent to retrieve her T-shirt and plunged her arms into the sleeves. She needed distance from him—fast—to wrap her head around her upside-down world.

"I don't understand." He shook his head as he sat up fully, moving to the edge of the bed as he watched her with wary eyes. "Why the sudden rush?"

Pressing her hand to her head, she didn't even begin to know how to answer that.

"Just feeling a little guilty, I guess," she began again, needing to make her excuses so she could figure out a more reasonable explanation for why she was feeling off today. "I know you'd already be sleeping if not for me. You must be exhausted after the rescue."

She moved back to the bed to lay a hand on his forearm. To make him see she was okay, even though she was anything but. The warmth of his body reminded her of how recently they'd been wound around one another, finding pleasure unlike anything she'd ever known.

Hiding her thoughts from him now wasn't easy, but she needed to spare him this worry until she was certain. Until she knew what to do next.

His eyes darkened at her touch. He hooked a hand around the back of her thigh, drawing her closer so she stood between his knees.

"I was glad to see you when I got home," he admitted, his voice gravelly. "You're welcome to share my bed for as long as you like."

Her pulse skittered, her body reacting despite everything. But she bit down the response, needing to retreat before she fell any deeper under this seductive spell.

"I'll call you later." Forcing a smile, she leaned forward to brush a kiss over his lips, wishing with all of her being that she could stay, that things could be uncomplicated between them. "You should sleep now."

Blue eyes searched hers for a long moment. Then, after he kissed her a second time with thorough, knee-melting skill, his touch slid away from her slowly.

"All right. I'll let you go." A wicked twinkle lit his gaze. "If you agree to be my guest at the Atlas Gala next weekend."

Her throat went dry. She shouldn't say yes to any such thing when they could be facing a monumental problem. When she could be carrying his child even now.

But she couldn't bring herself to tell him about that before she was certain. And perhaps it was a false alarm and she could just keep things simple between them after all. So she backed up a step and forced herself to nod.

Willing her voice to be steady, she gave him the only response that wouldn't tangle them in a longer conversation. "Of course. It's a date."

Eight

Twisted in his sheets six hours later, Ryder woke from uneasy dreams.

Spearing a hand through his hair, he winced at a muscle strain in his shoulder. He must have pulled it during the rescue when he'd leaned deep into a crevice to haul one of the panicked climbers to safety. There'd been concern among the SAR team that the guy had seriously injured his legs given his lack of movement and his symptoms of shock. He'd been pale and clammy, anxious in the extreme. He was only twenty-three, and he'd fallen in an ascent with his brother. The two of them had been trying to outdo one another on the trail, racing where they should have been spotting each other. The brother's blatant disregard for his younger sibling had reminded Ryder too much of the way Jessamyn's father had behaved during a long-ago climb, bringing back too many bad memories.

Shoving out of his bed, Ryder padded barefoot toward the en suite bathroom, then flipped on the dual-head shower. While steam rose off the Calacatta marble salvaged from a home demolition, he tried to gather his bearings and shake off the nightmares. In his sleep, his brain had confused the recent rescue with his first winter mission involving Mateo Barclay on one of Colorado's most dangerous peaks. The episode where Mateo's bravado had almost cost his then-girlfriend her life.

Ryder stepped under the powerful stream of water, hoping to wash away thoughts of the incident he'd put out of his mind until Jessamyn returned to Catamount. Yet from that day forward, it had circled his head daily since Mateo's confessions on Longs Peak might be enough evidence for the Barclay sisters to win their case. With each passing hour, keeping quiet about what he knew weighed heavier on him. Especially now that they were spending time together again. He wasn't sure what the future held for them when her life was still about the real estate business based in New York. But he felt certain the connection they shared didn't come around often. He'd let her go ten years ago to pursue her dreams, only to discover he wanted her even more now than he had back then.

Still, Jessamyn deserved to know the truth about her dad, although it would hurt her deeply.

Enough to make her cut ties with Mateo and New York?

Certainly, that wasn't any part of Ryder's motive in wanting her to know about her father, but it was a real possibility. Shutting down the shower nozzles, Ryder stepped out of the tile shower surround to towel off, contemplating his options for giving her the information she needed. It wouldn't violate any standard of ethics

if she learned the truth from Mateo's ex-girlfriend. Or
better yet, straight from Mateo himself.

Tossing his towel aside, Ryder strode into the closet
where built-in mahogany shelves and racks organized
business and black-tie attire on one side, while deep
drawers on the other side contained rescue gear and
work clothes. He pulled on jeans and a long-sleeved
T-shirt before returning to the bedroom to retrieve his
phone.

He couldn't put this off any longer if he wanted any
hope of moving forward with Jessamyn. First, he typed
in the name of the woman who'd fallen during that long-
ago climb with Mateo. Finding her might have been
easier if she'd had a more unusual name than Susan
Wilson. As it stood, the number of results was stagger-
ing, even if he limited his search to Colorado, which
didn't seem realistic.

Conceding he might need to hire an investigator to
find her, Ryder closed that screen and decided to go
straight to the source first. He searched for a number
for Mateo Barclay.

After only a second's hesitation, he punched it in
and waited while it rang three times before switching
over to voice mail.

Committed to his task, Ryder delivered the message
he should have given Jessamyn's father weeks ago.

"Barclay, this is Ryder Wakefield from Catamount."
He considered that sufficient identification. There was
no way Jessamyn's father would have forgotten the man
who sat with him on a brutally cold mountainside while
Mateo confided his darkest secrets. "We need to talk
about the Crooked Elm property before this case goes
further." He halted a moment, unwilling to make ulti-

matums over the phone. Exhaling a frustrated breath, he said simply, "Call me back."

Disconnecting, Ryder wished that the effort had eased some of his unrest over how long he'd delayed taking this action to help Jessamyn. But a sense of disquiet remained.

He told himself it was only because she'd seemed unsettled when she'd left his house earlier. As if she'd been withholding something from him. But who was he to point fingers at her for that considering his own behavior?

Sinking into a leather armchair in the living area of his primary suite, he cracked open his laptop to work on finalizing plans for the Atlas Gala. The organizers had been sending him questions that he'd been too busy to field the past few days.

Now that he had lined up Jessamyn for his date, he was all the more committed to making sure the event ran flawlessly. He would romance her. Showcase Wakefield Ranch at its most impressive. Because if there was any chance the news about her father convinced her that life in New York wasn't for her, Ryder intended to make sure she saw Catamount, Colorado—and him—as too tempting to resist.

Unable to sit in the empty and echoing ranch house at Crooked Elm, Jessamyn sat outside at the picnic table in the backyard, watching her grandmother's long-eared goats play in their pen nearby. The three Nubian goats—Guinevere, Morgan Le Fay and Nimue—cavorted in the sunshine, kicking up their heels and making a happy racket as they romped around the enclosure.

Jessamyn had come home from Wakefield Ranch bursting at the seams to talk to Fleur, but her sister had been out with Drake Alexander. The only sign of Fleur had been a handwritten note on stationery dotted with daisies, saying that she was having a "sleepover" at Drake's place and was taking a day off from delivering her baked goods tomorrow. Fleur had stuck the note to the electronic tablet she used in the kitchen and had added a second sticky note underneath it suggesting Jessamyn touch base with Lark to update their sister about their progress on the case.

Jessamyn clutched the tablet now as she slid off the picnic table and walked toward the goat pen, unsure what progress she had to share about the will contest. She'd found very little evidence to discuss in a courtroom.

Besides, she'd been so full of her pregnancy worries that she hadn't been able to think about the will contest proceedings coming up. She'd briefly considered stopping at the local market on the way home for a pregnancy test, but Catamount was such a small town she feared the rumor mill would be full of the news before suppertime. And, maybe a little part of her feared making the news official. Once she did the test, there was no going back. It wasn't like her to avoid uncomfortable truths, but Jessamyn really didn't feel ready for baby news.

Was it foolish to cross her fingers that her period was just late? They had used two forms of contraception after all. Although in thinking about it, she recalled that she'd been on antibiotics for that spider bite around the time she'd first been with Ryder. So there was a possibility that had lowered the effectiveness of the pill.

Stopping near the fence enclosure, she watched the little black-and-white one trot over to greet her. She reached between the taut wires to stroke the animal's warm fur as she glanced down at Fleur's note again, still stuck on the tablet in Jessamyn's other hand. The news that Fleur was taking a day off from baking came as a surprise. Fleur had worked tirelessly to build her local following as a caterer and baker, hoping to launch her restaurant business on the reputation of her sought-after foods.

Also a surprise? How disappointed Jessamyn had felt about her sibling's absence. She couldn't deny that she was growing closer to Fleur, the way their grandmother had always wanted all three of them to heal their differences. In Antonia Barclay's absence, Crooked Elm still seemed to work its old magic, making Jessamyn feel the pull of "home."

The thought of her grandmother and the wishes she hadn't lived to see fulfilled had Jessamyn pressing the button on top of the tablet, opening the screen for a video call to Lark. Not to share her pregnancy fear, but maybe just to…check in.

"I was just thinking about you—" Lark's voice sounded while her image came into view a moment behind. When the video connected, her older sister squinted at the screen. "Oh, wait. Jessamyn?"

A moment of self-consciousness made her defensive.

"Sorry to disappoint you," she snapped, straightening from where she'd been petting Nimue. "Fleur thought I should touch base to update you on the will contest case."

"Okay, sounds good." Lark stood in her closet dressed in gym clothes and looking like she'd just returned from a workout. Behind her, Jessamyn could see a selection of somber pantsuits in grays, blues and browns.

Her sister's eyes were a deep, mossy green, her dark hair a glossy braid that snaked over one shoulder. Lark was a natural beauty without trying, but she absolutely did not ever try. Jessamyn had never understood why her older sister rejected all things traditionally feminine or delicate with both hands, embracing form and function over all else.

"Honestly, I'm discouraged as we have very little." Jessamyn came straight to the point. "I've spent every free hour going through Gran's old journals and letters, hoping for concrete evidence we can use, but she only talks about the gardens and cooking. There's not much that's personal."

Lark frowned as she looked into the camera and toed off her black tennis shoes. "Surprising given how vocal she was with us about her hopes for the ranch in the future. How she wanted it to help us realize our dreams."

The disparaging note in Lark's voice caught Jessamyn off guard.

"You sound like you're not interested in coming back here." Jessamyn knew that her older sister had rarely visited Crooked Elm. Once Lark had checked out of Catamount, she was done. "Were you just humoring Fleur when you told her you'd try to visit the ranch before the end of the summer?"

Fleur had elicited a promise from both of them at Antonia's memorial service. Their younger sister had been determined to carry on their grandmother's efforts to heal their differences.

Lark grabbed a gray blazer and pants from a hanger and laid them over her arm before moving out of her closet into an all-white bedroom. "I'll be there next week. I won't miss the court case."

Vehemence underscored the words.

"I'm glad," Jessamyn told her honestly, sensing Lark

would be formidable in court if she had any testimony to offer. "Will you be submitting a statement?"

"I'm working on it." Lark tossed the suit on the crisp white blanket that served as the bed's only ornament, corners tucked so tightly a stranger might have guessed Lark had been in the military. "Have you seen my ex-husband around town since you've been there?"

"Gibson?"

The corners of Lark's lips quirked. "Thankfully, I only have one ex-husband."

Jessamyn stifled a smile. Lark was a hard-ass by anyone's standards, but she had a quiet sense of humor that could catch a person by surprise.

Los Angeles–based Lark had been briefly wed to a hockey player who—at that time—had skated for a West Coast team. Lark had been working as a sports psychologist back then, and the two had connected immediately. But the relationship wore away under the strain of Gibson's travel, according to Lark's extremely limited commentary on the marriage. And Jessamyn had only heard that much secondhand since she'd had a strained relationship with her sisters until recently.

Interestingly, Gibson had been in the process of buying a ranch close to Crooked Elm at the time of the divorce. Jessamyn had assumed that they were going to live in Catamount, but as far as she knew, Lark had never set foot in the place. Gibson, however, had been known to pop into town in the off-season, staying for two months at a time while he fixed up the place.

"Right. A good thing." Jessamyn leaned against a wooden post for the goat enclosure, setting aside her own worries to concentrate on her sister. "I haven't heard or seen Gibson in town, and I would think if the local hockey star was in residence, there would have been talk of it at the Cowboy Kitchen."

"Excellent news." Lark nodded her satisfaction as she tugged the band off her braid and began unthreading her hair. "I'll try to get my statement submitted to the attorney by the weekend so you can preview it, and I'll see you next week."

Jessamyn recognized the phrases that signaled the end of the communication and, disheartened to have made little progress on extending an olive branch to her older sister, she signed off and shut down the tablet.

Their relationship remained functional but unfulfilling, and Jessamyn wondered if Lark kept everyone at a bit of a distance anyhow. It seemed like that would be her way. Although maybe Lark thought the same thing about her.

Considering Jessamyn hadn't shared so much as a hint about her own woes, maybe that was true. But she didn't want it to be anymore. She was tired of following their father's example of having relationships serve a purpose.

She didn't want that any more than she'd wanted to marry Brandon. Returning to Catamount had reminded her she wanted deeper connections.

Just maybe not co-parenting type deep.

Her gut cramped at the thought of a possible pregnancy, and she turned the tablet on to the calendar function to count days and recalculate when her period was due.

She'd never been very regular in the first place, so she might be worrying for nothing. In the meantime, she had a lot on her plate to finish going through Antonia's boxes. She'd wait a few more days before she went rushing off two towns over to buy a pregnancy test kit.

It was early yet.

Better to put the worry—and Ryder—out of her mind.

She closed the tablet just as her phone vibrated in her back pocket.

Ryder's name appeared on the screen, but it wasn't a call.

Your tenant Josiah Cranston just showed up on the wildlife camera to check the trap.

She'd forgotten all about the illegally set trap. Anger fired through her now at the reminder. At herself for being so caught up in Ryder that she'd allowed the trapper to slip from her mind. And at the thought that their tenant was the very same person committing criminal acts on their property.

Memories of Phantom whining and scared in that snare made her determined to prosecute the one responsible.

She typed a note back to Ryder, furious fingers stabbing the screen.

Heading over there now.

Darting inside the house to retrieve the rental car's keys, Jessamyn calculated the best route to put her closest to the site. Ryder had taken the device for evidence, of course, but they'd monitored where it had been with the cameras.

Ryder's text was almost immediate.

Do NOT confront him. I'm calling the parks and wildlife department.

And risk having Cranston gone by the time they got there? At least this way, Jessamyn could be sure to find the guy in the vicinity of his wrongdoing. Maybe he would lead her to more of his illegally set ambushes.

Besides, after a day of gut-wrenching worries, the possibility of having an outlet for some of her frustrations practically pushed her into the driver's seat of her rental.

Defensiveness for Crooked Elm and her grandmother's land fueled her anger, calling her to protect this place. Not just for her, but for Fleur and Lark, who both needed the healing this place might offer.

Crooked Elm had given Fleur the gift of a fresh career path and new love. Jessamyn knew she wouldn't find either of those in Catamount since her life and work would always be in New York. If anything, Barclay Property Group would be the legacy she had to offer a child if—and it was a big if—she really did turn out to be pregnant.

But even so, life in Catamount had given Jessamyn a smaller gift that was no less wonderful. The possibility of a family in her sisters, who still might become her friends again.

Fueled by that hope, and the need to ensure Crooked Elm was a safe place for Lark to find whatever she needed from the quirky ranch where they all had roots, Jessamyn pressed the accelerator harder. The sedan bounced over the rough road, spitting gravel out the tires as she steered along an access route toward the feeder creek that led to the White River.

For a moment, she had a passing fear that all this passionate defensiveness of her home was some kind of pregnancy hormone gone wild. A nesting instinct nine months too early. But that was absurd thinking.

She was overtired and letting her imagination run away with her when her period was just late.

End of story.

What was more important was that this little corner of the world had come to mean something to her. And she'd be damned if she let anyone steal the tenuous sense of peace, healing and—yes—*family* she'd found here.

Nine

By the time Ryder reached the spot in the woods where his battery-operated camera was located, two Colorado wildlife officers were already on the scene.

Ryder had spotted the government agency's Jeep on the trail closest to the creek, with Jessamyn's rented white sedan parked nearby, mud-spattered from the trip through the fields. Now, after leaving his truck on the trail, Ryder made his way toward the group standing beside the slow-running stream. The sun was setting on the summer day, the sky already more pink than gold.

Two agents in matching khaki uniforms—a slim, dark woman with steel-colored hair in a razor-sharp cut and a round-cheeked younger man with thumbs hooked in his belt—flanked Jessamyn. And it was a damned good thing they did. Because Ryder did not like the look of the grizzled rancher in dirty coveralls standing across from them.

Ryder had run into Antonia Barclay's tenant in town enough times to know Josiah Cranston was unfriendly to the point of rude. But right now, the man's pale blue eyes were narrowed in fury as he glared at Jessamyn in a way that made him seem more than just rude.

The man looked outright dangerous.

"It's against the law to film me without my consent," the rancher shouted, cords standing out from his neck as he leaned toward her. "I know my rights."

Protectiveness surged, quickening Ryder's step. He didn't trust Cranston. And why were the wildlife officers letting the guy yell at Jessamyn? Shouldn't they be intervening?

"This is my land—" Jess began calmly, her tone tougher to hear from a few yards away.

But the old-timer didn't let her finish.

"That I pay good money to use," Cranston argued, voice rising another octave as he pointed toward the camera mounted to the trunk of an old alder tree. "I have a right to privacy on this property when I'm paying rent, and that means you can't record me."

"Don't blame her, Cranston." Ryder joined the conversation as he arrived at the group. He made a place for himself between the young officer and Jessamyn, placing a protective hand at the small of her back. Or a soothing one, maybe. He wanted Jess to know he was there to give whatever help he could. "That's my camera, and I mounted it after finding my neighbor's dog caught in your trap. The animal was fortunate we came along when we did."

Jessamyn's spine was rigid beneath his touch, and he hated that she had to listen to Josiah Cranston at all, let alone that she had to suffer him continuing to rent grazing acreage when they knew him to be a miserable guy. He'd cheated Antonia Barclay out of an irrigation system he'd promised to build in a verbal agreement in exchange for cheaper rent. More recently, he'd been ignoring conservation warnings to change his grazing practices for the sake of the wetlands, much to the frustration of Drake Alexander, who'd devoted years of hard work to improve the ground as well as the water quality of the local creeks that fed the White River.

Ryder told himself not to let the guy's anger spur his own, however. He calmed himself by breathing in the scent of Jessamyn's hair as he stood beside her.

Cranston wasn't anywhere near calm, however.

"I don't care who mounted it," the rancher continued loudly, startling a couple of birds from a branch overhead. "The fact is, I've been illegally recorded. I've been a paying tenant on this land for five years, and I know my rights." Cranston stamped his foot for emphasis as he repeated himself. "I can trap nuisance animals on my own land."

Jessamyn's already straight spine tensed further at the words. She hauled in a breath as if to take him to task. No doubt she wanted to remind him that he was using more of the Barclay lands than what he'd paid to rent, but the female officer intervened first.

"We have no record of a relocation permit for taking nuisance animals, Mr. Cranston," the woman told him, her voice neutral and her face impassive. "Furthermore, leghold traps are outlawed in this state."

"Not when it's a matter of human health and safety," Cranston roared, spittle flying. Then, swinging back toward Jessamyn, he leveled his gnarled finger at her. "And I've got permission to trap here firsthand from your daddy."

Ryder felt the jolt of surprise ripple through Jessamyn, though she hid it well. He would have been glad to settle this with Cranston himself, but he knew better than to step on Jessamyn's toes when she'd been working hard for weeks to secure the rights to Crooked Elm for her siblings.

Instead, he turned to address the female wildlife officer, whose demeanor made him guess she was the senior of the pair.

"Would it be easier for you to speak to both parties separately?" he asked, hoping it came across as a strong suggestion. At the same time, he slid his hand around Jessamyn's hip, reminding her he was beside her.

Trying his damnedest to help without interfering.

It spoke to how rattled she must be that she allowed him to take the lead. He guessed hearing her father had involved himself in her dispute with Cranston had cracked a bit more of her faith in her old man.

"That would be best." The woman's name badge glinted in the last rays of the setting sun showing through the trees. N. Davies. "If you wait by the vehicles, we'll join you in a few minutes."

Once Jessamyn nodded, Ryder led her up the hill toward his truck, hating the way the confrontation had left her pale, her lips pursed.

"You okay?" he asked once they were out of earshot of the party near the creek.

Behind them, he could hear Cranston still ranting. But at least at a distance, the other sounds of the wooded thicket became audible. A rabbit rustling in dead leaves nearby. A dead branch creaking softly in the slight breeze.

She wrapped her arms around herself and Ryder fought the urge to wrap her in his instead.

"I'll feel better once Dad tells me that Cranston made

up the part about obtaining permission to trap from him," she admitted, stopping beside his truck bed to lean on the fender. "The guy is a piece of work."

"No doubt." Ryder agreed with the latter, though he had his doubts about the former. He found it all too easy to believe Mateo Barclay had conversed with his mother's tenant in recent weeks. "And I hope you're right about your father. But it would be foolish of Cranston to make claims that would be so easy to disprove."

He propped his elbow on the ledge of the cargo box, wishing he could take her home and help her forget the unpleasantness of the day.

"Dad wouldn't do that," she told him impatiently, straightening to reach in the back pocket of dark denim jeans to withdraw her phone. "I'm calling him so we can confirm that right now."

His gut knotted at the thought of her finding out what a creep her father was. As much as Ryder wanted her to know the truth, he hated that it would hurt her.

But before Jessamyn could dial, the younger of the two officers scrambled up the hill toward them.

"Officer Davies said you don't have to stay, ma'am." The man thumbed up the brim of his pale beige Stetson as he addressed Jessamyn. His badge read B. Jenkins. "We have a record of the complaint called in by Mr. Wakefield, and we'll write up a citation."

"You will?" Jessamyn's eyebrows lifted. "Even though my tenant says he had permission to trap?"

While she spoke, Ryder reached into his truck bed to retrieve the trap he'd confiscated the day they freed Phantom. He'd held on to it until the officers could come out to the land.

Officer Jenkins nodded, his thumbs returning to hook on his belt. "We take this sort of thing seriously.

Of course, Mr. Cranston can opt to argue it in court, so it may come down to a judge's discretion. Especially if he obtained permission from Mr. Barclay."

Ryder saw Jessamyn's fists clench. Hoping to save her the aggravation of arguing the point, he passed the device to the guy. "I'd like to turn this in to you as evidence. We took it with us to keep pets and wildlife safe from potential harm."

"Sure thing. Thank you both." With a tip of his hat, the officer ambled to the Jeep, carrying the trap.

Leaving Ryder alone with Jessamyn as she rubbed her temples between her fingers and thumb.

"I think we've done all we can for today." He glanced to where Josiah Cranston still spoke emphatically to the senior officer. "Can I make you dinner tonight? I'd like to treat you to something nice to get your mind off this."

Hazel eyes snagged on his, and for a moment, he thought he saw a hint of yearning in them. But she nibbled her lip before shaking her head. "Thank you. But I really do need to speak to my father about everything that's happened with Cranston. If my dad's working against me somehow on this, too...well, I need to know what he's about."

Guilt wrenched his insides. But damn it, he wanted her to find that out. Even though it would hurt to hear, delaying would only magnify the pain.

It didn't bode well that Barclay had never phoned him back after Ryder left a message. No doubt Mateo Barclay would be just as glad for Ryder to forget about that long-ago conversation they'd had on the mountainside.

"Fair enough. How about later this week? I know you might not stick around Catamount for long after the Atlas Gala since the probate court case is on the docket for the week after that." He'd looked it up since he wasn't about to let her go into that courtroom without more evidence. Even now, his investigator was looking for Susan Wilson, who could at least offer evidence of Mateo Barclay's darker deeds. "I thought maybe we could do some of the things that we used to do together. Go hiking or horseback riding?"

Twilight had faded into near darkness while they'd been standing there, leaving them in shadows. Jessamyn's pale face was still visible, though, her eyes searching his.

"Don't you think that will complicate things unnecessarily?" She shifted on her feet uneasily.

But she hadn't said no.

"I think we could both use some fun." He was determined to keep things light. To show her they could have a good time together outside of sex.

To romance her?

Yes, exactly that.

"I guess that would be all right. I can't spend all of my free time reading Antonia's papers," she conceded. "Maybe a hike on Wednesday?"

Ryder's chest thumped with the victory. He wanted to haul her into his arms and kiss her breathless in response, but with the voices of the officers and Cranston still nearby, he refrained.

For now, her agreeing to the date would be enough.

"Sounds good." He couldn't stop himself from rubbing his hands down her arms, though. Squeezing lightly while he breathed in her amber-and-vanilla scent. "I'll see you then."

Letting her go wasn't easy, but he told himself it was only for a couple of days. Maybe by then, he'd have found a way to relate her father's misdeeds in a manner that wouldn't compromise his ethics or—he sincerely hoped—wouldn't cause Jessamyn too much pain.

Jessamyn didn't wait long to try calling her father.

After the debacle with Josiah Cranston, she drove her rental car home with more care than she'd taken on the way over there. Arriving back at the Crooked Elm main house, she lingered outdoors in the light of a pale moon, taking a seat on an old swing in the sprawling box elder tree out front.

The house was quiet behind her. Fleur must still be with Drake.

Her father answered in two rings.

"Jessamyn. We need to talk." Her father's voice was all business, like always. For years, she'd told herself she admired that about him—his way of coming to the point quickly worked to his favor in business and saved time in meetings. But tonight, when she felt shaken for too many reasons to count, she really wished he was the sort of parent who took time to ask how she was doing.

But she knew he was the same Mateo Barclay as always. It was Jessamyn who'd changed this summer. Still, she knew how to operate in his world. She was good at it.

"Indeed we do." The clipped manner of her New York speech had everything to do with content, not accent. It felt unnatural to use that language as she sat on the swing, moonlight bathing her bare calves in white light where her cropped jeans ended on her legs. "Josiah Cranston claims you gave him permission to trap on our land. Is that so?"

The extra second of silence answered her question before her dad spoke.

"What if it is? Crooked Elm is my mother's property,

Jessamyn. And it should legally come to me upon her death now that her will has come into question."

Fury ripped through her at his cold about-face from the answers he'd given to her about his challenge before.

"So you've abandoned the tactic of inheriting a share of the property along with my sisters and me?" She rose from the swing to pace the driveway, her feet covering long strides to work off the angry energy. "Now you're going for the whole thing in spite of Gran's wishes?"

"My attorney says it's cleaner that way." In the background, Jessamyn could hear an evening news program. No doubt he sat in his study with his nightly glass of scotch and his review of the day's business deals. "When a woman without a spouse—like my mother— dies intestate, her property goes to her children. In this case, me."

She heard ice cubes clinking against a glass as he rattled his drink. He'd always found it hard to sit still, jingling his keys, his coins, his ice.

"But she *didn't* die intestate. You know as well as I do that Gran had a will." Jessamyn couldn't hold on to her clipped, all-business facade now. Not when her dad was threatening something that her sisters were counting on.

And now, she counted on it, too. Not that she needed the income from the estate. But because of what it signified. A place where they'd all been happy once. A home where good memories had been made.

Maybe even for her, because Catamount was where she'd first fallen in love. For the only time in her life. Her throat felt raw to think on that time and how easily she and Ryder had walked away from those early passions. Yet she'd been comparing men to him ever since.

"If the will was important to her, she would have made it ironclad," he reasoned, referring to the fact that Gran had changed the will several times over the years through an online program, not always taking the time to have her lawyer review the revisions. "Because she didn't, I will assume she intended for the estate to fall to me."

This time, it was her turn to allow an extra beat of silence as she absorbed that blow.

The revelation that her father was every bit as much of a selfish bastard as her mother and sisters had always believed him to be. Why had she refused to recognize it before now? He didn't even bother to couch his greed in more palatable terms. Didn't try to justify his actions as anything other than a money grab. Jessamyn felt like the foundation beneath her feet had fallen away. The one family member she'd always counted on to have her back didn't care for anyone but himself.

"Have you been this awful all these years, and I didn't see it until now?" How many times had her sisters told her that their father only looked out for himself?

Maybe she hadn't wanted to see it because it might mean—like her mom once told her—that Jessamyn was that selfish, too.

But she wasn't a kid anymore. And she knew that wasn't true.

"Do you think I've built Barclay Property Group by being the nicest guy in the room, Jessamyn? Or have I built it by being the smartest?"

Anger simmered hotter.

"Neither. You've built it by being ruthless. And it's one thing to be a shark in business. It's another to be that way with family." She quit pacing the driveway to look back at the house where her grandmother had built a life on her own for years after her husband died. She'd raised goats and made cheese. She'd nurtured granddaughters when her son left the ranch to pursue his business. And she'd wanted her granddaughters to enjoy the same peace and contentment she'd found here. Even now in the moonlight, Jessamyn could see Antonia Barclay's fanciful touches. A bright orange tile inlaid with a yellow sun set into a stucco archway near the front door. Turquoise and yellow pillows spilling off a painted green bench to welcome visitors.

Arriving here was still like walking into a hug. And if there was any chance that Jessamyn carried a child, she would want to raise a baby in that kind of environment. One that felt like a hug and not a race to the fattest bottom line. She would still be proud of her legacy in real estate development, but that didn't mean she needed to live and breathe it.

"Catamount has turned you sentimental." Her father lobbed the accusation with distaste, his words dragging her back to the conversation. "Is that why you told Brandon you won't go through with the marriage? An attack of sentiment?"

Closing her eyes, she refocused on her parent, understanding at last that he didn't have her best interests at heart now. He might have, at one time. But the will contest was all about him.

"Brandon and I work well together," she told him tiredly. "We don't need to muddy our professional relationship with matrimony."

"You may need the marriage to hold on to the company, though, since I consider Brandon my heir apparent. Since the new fiscal year started, he's bringing in more business than you." More ice rattling. His glass sounded empty.

Sort of like Jessamyn's heart right now.

At one time, she might have leaped to prove him

wrong. But she didn't want any part of those competitive games tonight.

"Whatever you do with the company, Dad, make sure your wishes are ironclad. You wouldn't want a conniving offspring to undermine you." She could almost hear his displeasure. Perhaps it was in the way he stopped shaking his tumbler. "I'll see you in court."

Disconnecting the call, she felt a tremor go through her at her own nerve.

No. At *his* nerve.

Because he was the one responsible for his behavior. For giving Josiah Cranston permission to trap on Barclay land that Gran had meant for her granddaughters. For trying to make Jessamyn marry his choice of husband. For undermining his own mother to obtain Crooked Elm for himself.

Jessamyn wouldn't do any of those things. And it was past time she straightened out her life and her priorities. Not just because she might be expecting a child.

Her hand skimmed over her flat belly at the thought that had shaken her earlier in the day. There might not be anything inside there. Perhaps the pregnancy scare was the universe's way of making her see what—and who—was really important in her life.

Her sisters.

Ryder?

His name bubbled to the surface of her thoughts before she had time to hold it back.

But she wasn't ready to think about that right now. Pocketing her phone, she marched toward the house to finish going through her grandmother's boxes. Because one way or another, she would make sure the Barclay patriarch didn't get his hands on Crooked Elm.

Even if she had to personally call everyone Antonia

mentioned in her journals. Everyone she'd ever corre-
sponded with. Someone out there must be familiar with
what her grandmother wanted to happen when she died.
  She just needed to find that person.

Ten

After days of preparing for the Atlas Gala and tracking down Mateo Barclay's ex-girlfriend, climbing Sawmill Mountain seemed like a cakewalk for Ryder.

Although it would be more enjoyable if Jessamyn would talk to him.

"We're almost there," he observed in yet another effort to draw her out.

He glanced over at Jessamyn beside him, a lightweight backpack strapped to her shoulders. The sun lit her dark hair with copper, the long strands twisted into a braid and clipped at the end with a gold clasp.

She'd seemed preoccupied ever since he'd picked her up for their hiking date, but he'd credited her distraction to thoughts of finding evidence for the case against Mateo's will contest. At least she covered the terrain with ease, keeping a brisk pace in hiking boots and khaki cargo shorts. Her legs had distracted him more than once, the sight of her bare thighs reminding him how badly he wanted them around his waist again.

Yet that wasn't all he wanted from her. Her happiness mattered to him. More than he would have expected. In fact, *she* mattered.

Was something else bugging her that she wasn't sharing with him? He tried again to nudge along conversation.

"Remember when we climbed Devil's Causeway?" he asked, drawing on an old memory.

"It was a beautiful sunrise that day," she admitted, the smallest smile curving her lips. The mint blouse she wore made her hazel eyes look greener as she met his gaze.

"I was thinking less about the sunrise and more about when I tried to impress you with how fast I could sprint up the exposed ridge." He laughed to think of how young he'd been.

How crazy about her.

"You *were* very impressive before you lost your footing near that ledge." She ducked under a low-hanging pine branch. "But who would have expected the tourist to scream at you like that for running on a trail?"

"Obviously she couldn't wait for karma to take me down and had to help it along by scaring ten years off my life with that holler." He nodded at a couple of teenage boys hiking in the other direction, their hats pulled low to ward off the sun of a bright day.

"Good thing your catlike reflexes kicked in just in time," she teased, flipping her dark braid behind her shoulder. "You escaped with just a scratch on your knee."

"Which you nursed very tenderly, now that I think about it." He recalled sitting with her at the end of the ridge overlooking the Flat Tops Wilderness. She'd poured water from her insulated bottle over the cut and then grazed her lips over his mouth until he forgot everything but her. "Definitely worth risking my neck."

She ducked her head as if to study the trail in front of her feet, but he thought he'd seen a trace of a smile before she went quiet again.

Could it really be the court case causing her so much distraction?

He wondered if he should bring up Susan Wilson over the picnic lunch he'd planned, or if he should simply wait for Mateo Barclay's ex-girlfriend to get in touch with Jessamyn as she'd promised. He was still mulling over his best course of action when they cleared the trees to step onto the summit of the mountain. Here, a rocky outcropping offered a view of the wilderness and the creek that fed a nearby reservoir, the water glittering blue under the clear sky.

Ryder breathed deep, pulling in the fresh air along with new optimism that a picnic would put Jessamyn at ease enough to confide in him whatever was bothering her. His plan to romance her necessitated another date. Another chance to remind her how good they were together. While attending the Atlas Gala with her would be an opportunity to pull out all the stops, he feared it could mark the end of their time together unless he gave her a reason to spend longer in Catamount.

"Should we lay out the blanket under that tree?" He pointed to a cluster of lodgepole pines providing a patch of shade.

The trail was quiet aside from the teens they'd passed on the way up, and for now they had the summit area to themselves. Plus, the pines were situated away from the best view the peak offered, so they wouldn't be in the way of other hikers.

At her silent nod, they worked in tandem to drape a bright blue quilt over the pine-needle-covered sand. Then she helped him unload the food he'd brought in his pack—lobster rolls he'd special-ordered, a light salad, peach handheld pies that were one of her sister's most popular bakery items.

To top it off, mint iced tea. And he'd brought real china and silverware for the occasion so he could make the settings elaborate. Memorable. He hoped.

"Ryder, this is beautiful," she acknowledged as he handed her a white linen napkin. "You've gone to so much effort."

They settled beside one another to eat, and he hoped the tense, quiet mood might lift now.

"My pleasure. I remember how much you used to love hiking."

"I forgot how much I enjoyed it," she said as she filled her plate, her attention straying to a blue butterfly moving through a patch of wildflowers. "I have a good life in New York, but it's very focused on work."

Taking a bite of his lobster roll, he tried not to think about how close she'd come to hitching herself to a colleague for the sake of business, but the thought of the other guy still darkened his mood a fraction.

"And you're still enjoying the job?"

She smoothed the napkin over her lap, finger tracing the stitching on the edge. "I thought I was. But lately I wonder if I've just been using work as an escape mechanism for other areas of my life where I'm less successful."

His fork stalled on the way to his mouth. Could this

be why she'd been withdrawn today? He forced himself to think carefully about his response before he spoke.

"Tough to picture you failing at anything you set your mind to. You're one of the most driven people I've ever met." And that was saying a lot considering the passion he'd seen people put into search and rescue.

She sipped her tea from one of the insulated tumblers he'd brought to keep the drinks cold. "Professionally speaking, maybe. Not so much personally."

Surprised to hear her speak so candidly about perceived shortcomings, he wondered what she referred to specifically. Was it insensitive to push her for answers? A meadowlark sang sweetly in the nearby tall grass while he thought over the best response.

"I hope you're not referring to your family," he replied finally. "Because your parents bear a lot of the burden for expecting you and your sisters to choose sides."

Of course, he ascribed more of that blame to Mateo Barclay, but he was still uneasy telling her that. She'd know the truth about him soon enough.

Shrugging, she chased an arugula leaf around her plate before spearing it with her fork. "I regret not making more of an effort to patch things up with them long before now. I should have prioritized that. It's occurred to me recently that family should be—"

Stopping herself, she looked up at him quickly with an unreadable expression.

"What?" he prompted, feeling like he was missing something today.

"I've just realized that I want to place more importance on family," she finished.

Her bare knee grazed his denim-covered thigh as she repositioned herself to get more comfortable. He wanted to haul her into his lap and feed her himself before he feasted on her lips. But he knew he needed to focus on learning what was troubling her.

Before he could speak, though, she returned her attention to her meal.

"Thanks again for the picnic." She spoke in a rush in a transparent effort to change the subject.

Which was fine with him since he hadn't been able to glean what was unsettling her from that line of conversation anyhow.

"Still trying to impress you," he admitted, his eyes roaming over her face, searching for clues to her peculiar mood. "Just like on that Devil's Causeway climb."

"It's working." She licked her thumb after a bite of her lobster roll. "This is delicious."

His gaze stuck on her still-glistening thumb for a moment before he dragged his attention back to her face.

"Is everything all right? I keep thinking things seem a little...off somehow today."

Hazel eyes shot to his. For a moment, she almost looked...

Panicked?

"Jessie?" The former nickname slid from his lips without a second thought. The old care for her was still there, too. And he hated to see her troubled. "What's wrong?"

She pushed her plate aside. Knotted her napkin in one fist.

"I've been trying to find the right time to tell you," she began. "But I guess there's no perfect way to do this."

Was she leaving Catamount sooner than he'd anticipated? Breaking things off with him before he'd even had the chance to woo her at the Atlas Gala? Wary of whatever announcement she needed to make, Ryder slid his plate out of the way as well, focused on her.

"No need to couch your words with me. I can handle it." He sure as hell hoped he could, anyway.

She gave a brusque nod, her braid falling forward over her shoulder again. The little meadowlark that had been in the grass near them trilled again, giving Jessamyn's words an unexpected drumroll.

Licking her lips, she met his gaze. "I took a pregnancy test last night, Ryder."

The words were so unexpected he figured he'd misheard. They made no sense for long, slow seconds.

"Excuse me?" he said finally, his heartbeat quickening.

"I missed my period and was worried that somehow—" She shook her head impatiently before blurting, "Look, there are no two ways about it. I'm pregnant."

Impossible.

Ryder thought it, but at least he had the wherewithal not to say it out loud.

Heart banging like off-tempo cymbals, he stared dumbfounded at Jessamyn. Just a couple of minutes ago he'd been worried she was distracted. Now that he'd learned *why*, he couldn't believe she'd kept silent about it all this time.

He was used to Jessamyn being relentlessly forthright. Candid. And she expected the same honesty from the people around her. A thought that caused him another, unrelated pang considering his own secret. He forced himself to refocus on her revelation.

"We were careful, though," he reminded her, his brain unable to wrap around this bombshell. "Weren't we?"

"I realize we used condoms, and I was on the pill." She nodded quickly, straightening the leftover dishes from their picnic. "That's why I wasn't worried at first when I was late. But it occurred to me later that I was on antibiotics briefly after that spider bite."

He recalled the day he'd seen her at the Cowboy Kitchen and she'd had a bandage on her hand.

The same day he'd taken her to the yurt and they'd ended up tearing each other's clothes off. Guilt at not protecting her better speared through him. He'd thought he'd taken care of her.

"Even so, we used condoms," he reminded himself more than her, recognizing he was too rattled to weigh in intelligently on this news. "So if one failed, the other works. That's the whole point."

She quit packing up the dishes to frown at him.

"I'm totally familiar with the process," she snapped, folding her arms across her midsection where—wow—she was now telling him his child could potentially reside.

He closed his eyes, warning himself to pull it together fast for her sake. Later, he could figure out how he felt about all this. Right now, he needed to be there for Jessamyn.

Of course she was every bit as stressed about this possibility as him.

"I realize that," he conceded. "I'm sorry I'm not processing this quickly enough."

He needed action. Movement. A way to show her his support.

A marriage proposal was the only answer in his mind. And he was about to ask her to cement their relationship that way when she spoke.

"I understand." Her tone gentled, her hazel eyes turning warm. Kind. "I already went through the denial stage, so I can hardly blame you for a knee-jerk reaction that is completely relatable."

Grateful for her easy forgiveness when his first reaction had been less than stellar, he shoved aside the open backpack she'd been refilling for their trip down the mountain and edged closer to her on the picnic blanket. As he took her hands in his, he wanted to get this next part right. He wasn't about to leave her with the burden of his child. He knew his obligation. If anything, he was grateful that she'd discovered she was pregnant while she was still in Catamount, where he could at least learn the news in person.

"Thank you. But it wasn't denial so much as surprise. I promise you I will be by your side every step of the way—"

He stopped himself since she was already shaking her head. Withdrawing her hand from his.

"That's not necessary, Ryder. I've had time to think about it, and I'm ready to take full responsibility for this child." She met his gaze directly. "I'd be glad to assume sole custody."

Judging by Ryder's expression, Jessamyn guessed she hadn't handled any part of relating the baby news well.

A blue vein ticked in his temple. A light throb of a fast, furious pulse. She'd meant to relieve him of responsibility, not frustrate him more, but she guessed that was all she'd managed to accomplish with her suggestion.

"No." His answer was the sharpest he'd ever spoken to me. I *will* be."

"No." His answer was the sharpest he'd ever spoken to her. "That is completely unacceptable to me. I want to be a part of our child's life, Jess. I *will* be."

Huffing out a sigh of frustration, Jessamyn rose to her feet and shouldered her small pack so they could begin the trek down Sawmill Mountain.

"Certainly you have the right if you wish—"

He was on his feet a moment after her, his expression tight as he gathered the remaining items from their abandoned picnic, rolling the blanket into a haphazard bundle and stuffing it into his pack. "I do wish. Hell, I demand it."

Nearby, voices sounded as another party of three hikers—two older women and a teenage girl—broke through the trees to the summit, delaying Jessamyn's answer.

Perhaps it was just as well that they each had a moment to regain composure. Silently Ryder zipped up his backpack for their descent.

Wishing she'd waited until they'd finished their picnic to share her news, Jessamyn headed for the trail to lead them back down to where they'd parked. She nodded at the new arrivals on her way past them. A moment later, she heard Ryder's heavier steps behind her as he caught up.

She knew perfectly well that a baby bombshell wasn't what he'd been expecting on a hiking date. So she didn't blame him for being caught off guard. She understood all too well that he must be reeling, the same way she'd been when she took that pregnancy test alone in her bathroom last night.

Then again, she'd had a few days before the test to roll the idea around in her mind. To rail against the possibility and debate what it might mean. To think about changes she'd have to make to her life to accommodate a child.

Ryder was having to condense all those reactions into seconds instead of days. Plus, he was forced to experience those responses in front of her, whereas at least she'd been able to digest it privately.

Turning on the heel of her hiking boot, she glanced

back at him striding down the trail behind her, greenery slapping his legs as he passed.

"I'm sorry—"

"I'm sorry—"

They began at the same time.

It was enough to make them both smile. A moment to ease the thick tension.

"You first," he urged, quickening his pace to match hers where the trail was wide enough to walk two astride. There were only a few places that required climbing or walking one behind the other.

"I only wanted to say that you can be a part of your child's life. I didn't mean to suggest otherwise." She swatted a deerfly from her forehead as the sun sank lower on the horizon.

"Thank you." He sounded relieved. Sincere. "Can we stop for a second?"

He took her hand, and she pivoted to face him, following him to sit on a moss-covered fallen tree beside the trail. She couldn't deny the small thrill she took from having his palm wrapped around hers, his thumb stroking the back of her hand.

"We can. But considering that you just found out about the baby, I wonder if it would be wisest of us to table any discussions until you've had more time to get used to the idea?" She hadn't really thought through how awkward it might be to share the news while hiking today. She'd only known she couldn't delay relating something that affected him deeply.

"This isn't about the baby." His blue eyes looked indigo in the sunlight, his focus all on her. "This is about us."

His words seemed to reverberate through her, the

deep tone of his voice almost a caress as she sat inches from him on the fallen oak.

"Us." The word whispered from her a little too softly and she could hear something in it that sounded almost wistful. So she blustered on, hoping to cover up the telltale note in her voice earlier. "You mean shared parenting? Because we should probably wait to think about that, too."

"Nothing like that." He reached for her free hand and took that one in his other palm so they sat with both sets of fingers laced. Nearby a stream babbled a soft tune. "I know this is unexpected, but considering the monumental life change we're facing, I'd like to ask you to marry me, Jessamyn."

Shock robbed her of speech.

It was her turn to search for words that wouldn't come. Her turn to reel with news she hadn't prepared for. He was only suggesting this because of the baby, of course. But there was a part of her—the old, sentimental part that had fallen for him ten years ago—that swooned a little at the idea.

And how dangerous was it to feel that way when she needed to keep her wits about her with a baby on the way? Frustration tensed her shoulders.

"Ryder—"

"Please. I want you to think about how much we cared about one another once." Releasing her hands, he moved to cup her shoulders so that they faced each other full on where they sat. "How close we came to committing ourselves to each other."

Her pulse stuttered at the mention of caring for her in the past tense. As if his feelings for her had faded long before now.

"That was a decade ago," she protested, her heart

speeding in response to words that sounded almost romantic when they needed to be practical. She'd learned to guard her heart against this man the first time he'd walked away from her. It was a lesson she would need more than ever now, with a child's future at stake. "And it fell apart in the most painful way imaginable for me."

She got to her feet, surprised to realize she was a little unsteady. She steadied herself on a tree trunk before charging forward.

"Jessamyn, wait."

"No." She called on all her defenses to stay strong in the face of Ryder Wakefield's appeal. "We knew all along this was temporary between us. We're not a couple because we didn't have anything in common back then, and nothing's changed."

"A baby changes everything."

"Not what we want out of life. You're still rooted deep in Catamount, and I'm still committed to making my mark on the world in my father's business." She knew now that her father wasn't as trustworthy as she'd once believed, but that didn't make Barclay Property Group any less important to her. She'd poured her heart and soul into making the company a success. "Now it's not only about what I want to achieve. It's about creating a legacy I can be proud of to pass on to my child."

Just saying the words still felt surreal. But she needed to get used to this new turn her life had taken.

"We have plenty of things in common," he fired back. "And we can find compromises where we don't."

"Not on the big issues." She shook her head sadly, her heart aching at the thought of leaving Ryder behind again when she returned home after that will contest case. "Compromise isn't going to make New York a realistic place for you to run your ranch any more than

Catamount is a potential home for a woman with an international business based in Manhattan."

A breeze stirred the leaves of the aspens overhead and one floated down to land on Ryder's broad shoulder. She smoothed it away, her fingers drawn to him even when they argued.

He tipped her chin up to his face.

"Four weeks ago you were contemplating marriage to a man for business purposes, but you won't consider marriage to me for the sake of a child?" Blue eyes bore into hers.

"You told me I'd be selling out if I wasn't marrying for love," she reminded him, even though his words stung. Her chest ached with too many emotions crowding inside. "And I decided to take your advice. Then, and now."

This time when she turned to walk the rest of the way down the mountain, Ryder didn't stop her.

She knew they still had a lot of decisions to make between them, but she was relieved to have the baby news out in the open. It was real now. Ryder knew about it.

They could decide from here what was practical.

And Ryder would quit offering up empty gestures that would only shred at her heart for all they would never have.

Eleven

"You're carrying Ryder Wakefield's baby?"

Fleur, seated on the end of Jessamyn's bed in the small bedroom at Crooked Elm, repeated the words slowly back to Jessamyn as if to ensure she had them exactly right.

The day after her hike with Ryder, Jessamyn stood in front of the room's cheval mirror, dressed in a plain black cocktail dress that seemed all wrong for the Atlas Gala. She'd been waffling over outfits for the event, torn between longing to dazzle Ryder and not wanting to look as though she'd tried too hard. Perhaps she was being a little too prideful to want her dress to slay when she walked into the event, but some part of her feminine self-confidence had taken a hit when Ryder hadn't even hinted at deeper feelings for her in his perfunctory marriage proposal.

So a black cocktail dress would not do. She reached around to her back to unzip.

"That is correct. I'm pregnant. He's the dad." While she tried on outfits, she'd decided to give her sister a bare-bones recap of the huge development in her life and how things stood with Ryder. Because soon enough, people would learn of Jessamyn's pregnancy, and she needed to get comfortable with sharing some details about that and the inevitable questions that would follow about her baby's father. "I'm only four weeks along, so maybe that's too early to broadcast the news. But it's very much on my mind, to the detriment of everything else I'm supposed to be focused on. Such as the court case."

She should have been reading more documents now, in fact, but she hadn't been able to concentrate on the cache of old letters Antonia had written. Instead, she'd been thinking about Ryder and how radically their relationship was about to change from exploring their attraction to consulting each other about nap times and nanny qualifications. Skipping right over the opportunity to develop deeper feelings for each other. The way she feared she already had for him. Was that why it had stung her so much when he hadn't seemed the least little bit optimistic about proposing to her? Because he hadn't felt the emotional tug of their relationship the way she had?

She shouldn't have been surprised, given the way he'd walked away from her a decade ago, too. Apparently she never learned.

Unwilling to spiral into anxiety and sadness over a relationship that seemed destined not to blossom into more, she'd come upstairs to try on gowns for the gala instead. Fleur had followed, quizzing her about why she'd seemed so distracted. Making Jessamyn realize just how grateful she was for her sister's presence and support.

Shimmying off one strap of the black taffeta, she would have reached for the next hanger on the heavy iron hook installed on the back of the bathroom door. But Fleur threw her arms around her before Jessamyn could grab the garment.

"Jess, that's amazing! I'm so happy for you." Fleur's copper-colored hair tickled Jessamyn's nose as her sibling squeezed her tight. "A baby." She breathed the word reverently. "Wow. Gran would have been so thrilled about this."

For a moment, Jessamyn relaxed into the unexpected jolt of love and familiarity for her sister. Nostalgia for the way they'd once been enveloped her along with Fleur's roses-and-vanilla fragrance. The slender arms and graceful figure that had won Fleur Miss Rodeo crowns all over the West when she'd had to finance her own college tuition. Fleur's beauty and grit had taken her from scrappy fighter to accomplished woman with a rapidly growing business of her own. And Jessamyn couldn't be prouder of her.

How long had it been since they'd connected—really connected—like sisters? One old ache in her heart soothed away, a new world of possibility crowding out the hurt.

"Thank you," Jessamyn told her sincerely, her voice a little wobbly as they let go of each other. "I've been so busy worrying about the logistics of the pregnancy and what it means that I haven't taken any time to celebrate."

Taking a step back, Fleur lifted one eyebrow as she studied her. "But Ryder must be excited about it?"

Was he?

Jessamyn had been too nervous about sharing the news with him to properly gauge his reaction. Then, just when she'd been relaxed enough with Ryder to turn their baby discussion toward practical elements like how to share custody, he'd stunned her with a marriage proposal that had been purely utilitarian.

How ironic for him to seek marriage with her when he had been *adamant* that she not wed someone else for business reasons. Besides, her parents' unhappy marriage had caused her and her sisters so much grief and upheaval. She wanted better for her baby, which meant she'd need to proceed carefully with Ryder.

"I think he's still adjusting to the idea, too," Jessamyn explained carefully, turning to retrieve a pale green crepe-and-sequin gown she'd special-ordered along with three other dress possibilities for the gala.

After she stepped out of the black taffeta, Fleur rehung the piece while Jessamyn slid into the new outfit.

"I saw the way Ryder looked at you that day he came into the Cowboy Kitchen. And it was just the same way he looked at you during the summer you two were dating." Fleur rezipped the taffeta dress before turning around to help Jessamyn with the hook-and-eye closure on the crepe gown.

"Yes, well, chemistry has never been an issue between us," she acknowledged as she straightened slender tulle straps embellished with lustrous faux pearls and beads. "That doesn't mean he's ready to celebrate co-parenting with me."

She didn't mention the half-hearted marriage proposal as it didn't seem relevant. Even though she'd been thinking about that today as much as the pregnancy.

Why had he suggested such a thing when he didn't love her even a little? Were his values so traditional that he thought parents should be married to raise a child? Had he assumed she *expected* him to propose? She wished she'd thought to ask him his reason, but she'd been too shocked at the turn in the conversation.

Fleur's hands moved to Jessamyn's shoulders as Fleur stood behind her, both looking into the old cheval mirror, the glass a bit cloudy from age. "Don't discount chemistry. Ever consider that it exists to help direct you toward people who might be The One? Sort of like nature's version of a flashing neon sign that says Potential Mate?"

"Seriously?" Jessamyn laughed, pivoting on her heel to face her sister. "Lust is the new love?"

"Well, maybe not exactly that." Fleur shrugged as she turned a critical eye over Jessamyn's gown, straightening the draping at the neckline. "All I know is that I had it with Drake forever, but neither of us would acknowledge it. So for years, all of the misplaced chemistry turned into arguments and sniping."

"I remember how much you two bickered." Jessamyn watched Fleur closely, curious about how her sister had navigated confusing romantic waters. "When did you realize there was more to it?"

The transformation in her sister's expression about took Jessamyn's breath away. One moment Fleur was straightening a dress. The next, she practically glowed with giddy love.

"It was a shared horseback ride." Her cheeks even turned the slightest bit pink. Another minute and Jessamyn figured her sister's eyes would go heart-shaped. "There was an almost kiss during that ride that was... well..." Fleur fanned herself. "Suffice it to say some close proximity alerted me to a wealth of feelings that were all wrong for a guy who was supposedly my enemy."

"I can't believe you're blushing like a sixteen-year-old," Jessamyn teased, although truthfully she felt a sharp pang of envy for the obvious love Fleur had for Drake. "And I'm really happy for you. But Ryder and I—we've been down this road before ten years ago and it didn't work out then, either. I think he's too practical to consider me a romantic prospect."

"*He's* the practical one?" Fleur's eyes went comically wide. "Okay, that's saying something, coming from you when your lists have lists. Last I knew, you've never veered from a goal or a task once it's on paper."

Defensiveness straightened her shoulders and she spun away from Fleur to assess the gown in the mirror again. "Professionally, that's not a bad quality to have."

"Agreed," Fleur offered more gently, taking a step forward to stand by the reflective glass so Jessamyn had no choice but to see her. "I'm just saying that maybe you're both being so careful that you're not seeing the romantic possibilities. And since you're having a baby together— honestly—why not consider them?"

The defensiveness deflated right out of her at the wise words, delivered with nothing but kindness. Jessamyn nibbled her lip, considering.

Fleur held up a hand. "No need to answer. Just think about it. This gown is the one, by the way," she added, perhaps guessing that Jessamyn needed processing time for the deeper questions on her mind. "You're a total knockout in it, and Ryder will *not* be thinking practical thoughts when he sees you in this. If that's what you're going for."

Jessamyn glanced from her reflection in the mirror to her sibling, who stood with arms crossed over her pink apron, which said Kiss the Cook.

"That is sort of what I was going for," she confessed. "I really have no idea where to go from here with Ryder or how to handle this pregnancy. But I definitely want to look good."

Fleur winked. "That's one task you can check off the list."

Grinning, she was about to ask for Fleur's opinion on shoes when her cell phone buzzed.

"Susan Wilson." Reading the name aloud, she would have let it go to voice mail, but Fleur gripped her arm.

Halting her.

"Oh my God. That's Dad's old girlfriend," Fleur reminded her, voice lowered while the phone vibrated again. "The woman who was injured hiking with him."

"The same girlfriend who broke up with him while she was still in the hospital?" Jessamyn started to ask, but her words faded as she recalled the source of her information about that breakup—her father.

Her self-serving father.

Was there a chance Mateo Barclay had told Jessamyn a skewed version of those events? She needed to get it through her head that her dad was not the man she had believed him to be.

And didn't she want to hear from people who might know more about the Barclay patriarch as the will contest case began next week?

Taking a deep breath, Jessamyn swiped to answer the call.

"Congratulations on a stellar turnout, Ryder." Drake Alexander shook his hand. The two men stood on the red carpet that led into the event tent outside Wakefield Ranch's main house on the night of the Atlas Gala. "Although I have to admit, I thought Jessamyn would be on your arm tonight after the way you two have been circling each other these last few weeks."

Ryder straightened an obsidian horseshoe-shaped cuff link as he peered through the crowd inside the specially constructed venue for the Atlas Foundation's annual black-tie evening. Everything had kicked off as planned.

The caterers had been on-site all day, including Fleur Barclay, who he'd insisted be in charge of tapas for the appetizers course of the meal. The charity's event organizer had taken on the brunt of the work throughout the day to prepare the space, but Ryder had double-checked things for himself since Wakefield Ranch would be showcased as a model of ranch-style sustainable living.

He'd long wanted to show that raising cattle could be managed with respect to the animals and the land alike, and he was proud of his efforts here. The only thing missing in an otherwise perfect evening to cap off his accomplishments?

Jessamyn. The mother of his child. The notion still leveled him.

And filled him with a protectiveness that had him awake every night thinking through how to best provide a good future for their child.

"She'll be here any minute, I expect." Ryder had faith in that, as Jessamyn Barclay was not a woman who backed out of her commitments.

He just wished he hadn't spooked her with the marriage proposal on their hike earlier in the week. Afterward, he backed off, remembering the way she'd needed space when she'd first arrived in Catamount. He'd given it to her, and she'd come around eventually, throwing over her almost fiancé to spend time with Ryder instead.

But had that approach backfired this time? It didn't bode well that he hadn't heard from her since their outing to Sawmill Mountain. Had he lost any chance he might have had of pressing the marriage question to his advantage? The thought had kept him awake every night— even more so than the fact that Jessamyn carried his baby. Because how could he even think about raising a child until he'd done everything necessary to make the mother secure?

And damn it, when was she going to show tonight? He refrained from checking his watch, aware that the cocktail hour was still in full swing and that guests were still arriving.

"Have you heard anything more about Josiah Cranston's citation from the parks and wildlife department? I don't suppose there's any chance that will set a fire under him to vacate the Crooked Elm rangelands," Drake muttered darkly, drawing Ryder's thoughts away from Jessamyn where they tended to dwell the majority of time.

On the far side of the open-air tent, chamber musicians swapped their elegant classical numbers for a spirited country tune that earned a few appreciative whistles from the cocktail hour crowd. Waitstaff were busy passing Fleur's tapas as hors d'oeuvres, trays emptying quickly. He glimpsed her across the room overseeing the presentation. And something hit him as he saw the glance—both tender and lustful—that she shot to Drake.

"I rode by his place two nights ago," Ryder admitted as he waved to one of the Atlas Foundation's founders and her husband, a couple who'd provided him with encouragement throughout his efforts to transform Wakefield Ranch. "But his truck was still there along with his equipment, so it didn't look like he'd made plans to leave anytime soon."

He didn't mention he'd only made the trip over to Crooked Elm in the hope of running into Jessamyn. His gaze flicked up to check for her arrival again.

Drake waved off a server's offer of champagne. "Maybe we won't get Cranston to budge until after the court case and ownership of the ranch is definitely awarded. I just hope the Barclay sisters win their fair due."

Surprised at the bitterness threading through his friend's voice, Ryder hauled his full attention back to Drake.

"Spoken like a man who knew Antonia was going to leave her land to her granddaughters. Are you going to be able to take the stand to that effect next week?" Ryder had been hoping he wouldn't have to test the legality of doctor-patient confidentiality. While that protection extended to EMS workers, which Ryder technically had been on Longs Peak nine years ago, there was a gray area about what kinds of information could be protected. It's not like he'd share Mateo Barclay's health history, which was strictly safeguarded by law.

But an admission made while he was in shock? An ambiguous set of circumstances as far as ethics were concerned.

So if Drake knew something that would keep Ryder from having to come forward, that would be a huge win.

"I believe so." Drake lowered his voice as a foursome of gala ticket holders arrived on the event's red carpet, shaking hands with various organizers before giving their names at the check-in table. "I submitted a statement of support. I confirmed her healthy state of mind and that her granddaughters never had undue influence over her. And I told the lawyers that when I offered to buy Crooked Elm one day, she'd laughed and said I'd need to deal with her granddaughters."

"That sounds definitive to me." Ryder's gaze shifted away from the event under the tent where the sounds of laughter, music and glasses clinking in celebration had grown in the past ten minutes. Instead, he looked down the access road leading into the ranch, hoping for a sign of Jessamyn. "I would think that weighs strongly in favor of the sisters over Mateo."

"It would carry more weight if I weren't already involved with Fleur, or if anyone else could offer similar evidence." Drake stopped one of the servers passing *croquetas de jamón* and took two along with a napkin. "But apparently I'm the only one Jessamyn has located who heard that straight from Antonia herself."

Right. And if she couldn't find anyone else, Ryder needed to step up regardless of the potential conflict of interest. He wouldn't allow her father to squeeze her out of an inheritance that rightfully belonged to her and her sisters. His obligation to speak out had doubled now that Jessamyn carried a child who would have a stake in Crooked Elm, too. He owed it to their baby to secure the rightful legacy.

"She'll find more evidence," Ryder assured him just as he spotted a familiar white rental car rolling to a stop in front of the valet stand.

Jessamyn.

Anticipation fired through him, even as he knew he'd have to come clean with her tonight. Tell her everything about that conversation with her father, offer to give evidence about his own knowledge of what Antonia Barclay intended for Crooked Elm.

Only then would he be able to turn his attention toward convincing Jessamyn to marry him. And bottom line, that was his number one objective this evening.

He couldn't imagine having his child out in the world somewhere without him. He needed to be at Jessamyn's side to raise their child together. And he knew her well enough to know that, deep down, she wanted that, too. They shared those values.

You didn't fall for someone at nineteen years old and not understand some key things about their character. Jessamyn was a family-oriented person whether she wanted to admit it or not. Now, he just needed to convince her that he was, too.

Yet, as Jessamyn stepped from her automobile, all thoughts of babies and values faded to the back of his mind.

She pivoted on her heel, sunlight catching her sequin-covered dress in a way that cast prisms everywhere. Her own personal special effects lighting that followed her wherever she went. And never had a woman been more worthy of a spotlight.

Dressed in a pale green gown that skimmed her curves like a lover's hand, darting in at her waist and hugging both her hips and her breasts, she was a vision that took his breath away. A high slit gave him glimpses of her toned thigh as she strode up the red carpet toward him. Silver, strappy heels elevated her already tall frame, giving her an elegant presence to go with her confident walk. By the time his gaze made it up to her face, framed by a dark tumble of glossy curls, he was already moving forward to meet her.

Vaguely, he heard Drake give a low whistle of appreciation. But knowing Drake, that ode to how good Jessamyn looked was most certainly just to needle Ryder. As if anything could distract him from intercepting her.

When he was a step away, he held his arms out to her, kissing her cheek.

"Wow." He breathed the word into her ear after the kiss, holding on to her a moment longer than was strictly polite. "You look good enough to eat."

He felt her cheekbone shift against the side of his face and hoped that she'd smiled. Her amber-and-vanilla fragrance called him to seek out a taste of her. To trace his tongue over the places she'd spritzed the scent that teased him.

"Thank you. But you should probably let go before you cause a scene." She didn't sound overly concerned, however.

For that, he was grateful. Tonight would be difficult enough for them both when he confided what he knew about her dad. He didn't want to go into the evening with her already keeping her guard up around him.

He longed to ask if she'd reconsidered his marriage proposal, but of course, that would have to wait. First, they needed to get through the gala.

"Didn't you hear I'm Captain Earth tonight?" he returned, squeezing her waist briefly before finally releasing her. "The title should come with a few extra privileges."

He held his arm out to her to escort her into the gala now that the event was in full swing. Jessamyn slipped her fingers around his biceps.

Only then did he truly meet her hazel eyes and see the subtle glint in them. For a moment, he glimpsed the Jessamyn Barclay who'd challenged him at the rental car kiosk weeks ago, a woman with her guard up.

"And so it does come with privileges." There was an edge to her words. "I'm still your date tonight even though our time together should be sitting down to make practical plans for our baby."

All at once, he guessed that he shouldn't have given her space. He should have shown up at her door every day to discuss the huge change in their lives that neither one of them had anticipated.

"Jessamyn." He stopped on the red carpet, his dress shoes grinding to a halt. He was unwilling to enter the event when they needed to discuss this first. "I already planned to speak to you after the gala—"

"And we will talk." She smiled with a cool politeness

that told him he'd have a long way to go to convince her to marry him. He already missed the warmth of the connection they'd shared right up until she'd told him she was pregnant and he reacted in all the wrong ways. "Just not right now. We've both earned an evening of fun after a difficult week. We may as well make the most of it."

Around them, the volume of the party spilling out into the evening was increasing. The chamber musicians had given up the platform to a country rock band who were already launching into their first tune and attracting couples to a dance floor lit by twinkling blue and yellow lights hung in the rafters to look like fireflies.

Tours of his house were being given to select parties throughout the evening. But he couldn't enjoy a moment if she was unhappy.

"Let's discuss this now." He laced his fingers through hers and pulled the back of her hand to his lips so he could place a kiss there. "Nothing is more important to me than ensuring we're on the same page for our child's future."

Some of the steel left her spine at his words.

"Thank you." She gave a nod of acknowledgment. An acceptance, perhaps. "But after the gala is soon enough. For what it's worth, I am proud of you and what you've accomplished here, Ryder. Let's celebrate that first, and then we'll work through the rest."

The kindness in her eyes—the willingness to compromise—touched him deeply. And in that moment, he recalled all the reasons he'd fallen hard for her ten years ago.

Jessamyn Barclay was a woman of substance. A fiercely independent, loyal, strong person, and any man who could attract her would be beyond fortunate to keep her.

Yet as he walked through the Atlas Gala with the most

beautiful woman in the room on his arm, he feared he didn't stand a chance with her. Not when he'd withheld what he knew about her father for this long. Maybe if he'd been up-front earlier, things could have been different. But he'd screwed up. Royally. How would he ever persuade her to trust him now?

What a time to realize that he loved her. Right when he was poised to lose her forever.

Twelve

"Champagne?" A bright-eyed server with a curly ponytail presented a tray of crystal flutes to Jessamyn.

Nearly two hours into the Atlas Gala, Jessamyn had her first moment alone after spending most of the time at the side of her highly sought-after date. As a host of the event, Ryder had been in demand all evening by guests interested in both his sustainable home and ranching practices. Her appreciation for his work at Wakefield Ranch had only grown as she'd listened to him explain the systems for reducing water use, recovering rainwater and sourcing gray water for irrigation. And that was just the beginning. He'd harnessed sun and wind energy in ways that made the ranch far less reliant on fossil fuel, and his efforts were attracting nationwide attention.

What woman wouldn't have been proud to be at Ryder's side this evening? Then, there'd been the way his hand had frequently sought the base of her spine as he'd guided her from one group of guests to the next, the warmth of his touch an ever-present reminder of the connection they'd shared. Throughout the night, he'd included her in conversations, given weight to her thoughts, highlighted her experience. It was obvious he respected her as well as liked her.

And she watched carefully as he interacted with his brother and sister-in-law. He cared about his family and enjoyed celebrating with them. He'd be a good father, caring and concerned. Much more than her own had ever been.

Could this connection grow into something more for the sake of their child, the way Fleur had suggested? Jessamyn found herself considering it more and more as the evening wore on, especially now as she stood alone near the chocolate fountain, breathing in the decadent scents of ripe berries and dark cocoa. Or at least, she had been until the waitress appeared with her champagne offering while the country band rocked on.

"No, thank you." Jessamyn held up a hand to refuse the alcohol, knowing she should start considering more facets of her diet than just avoiding champagne now that she was expecting a child. Her to-do list seemed to expand by the minute ever since she'd learned about the pregnancy.

It still felt surreal—and exciting—to think she carried a new life inside her. Ryder's baby.

As she plucked a raspberry from the dessert buffet, Jessamyn's gaze sought her date again. He stood near the now-vacant podium where the Atlas Foundation's president had made a short speech about Ryder's contributions to environmental awareness. Ryder was in conversation with a younger couple dressed in matching tuxedos who, she'd learned earlier in the evening, were significant donors to the charity.

She popped the berry in her mouth just as Ryder's blue eyes met hers across the photo booth area set up in front of a digital backdrop of Wakefield Ranch.

How was it that even so far from him, she experienced the tug of heated male interest? Rolling the berry on her tongue, she felt the answering awareness for Ryder, her skin flushing as he broke away from the pair he'd been speaking with to head her way.

She bit into the fruit as he stalked closer, never taking his gaze from her.

How could she be so breathless at the thought of touching him when he'd made it clear that his proposal was for a marriage of convenience because of their baby? Shouldn't that have dulled this fiery response to him? All at once she recalled Fleur's idea that sexual chemistry was nature's flashing neon sign to point her toward someone who could be The One.

Sage advice or silly?

As Ryder reached her, his palm slid around her waist to the small of her back. He leaned down to whisper, "I'll admit I'm curious about what thoughts put that particular expression on your face as I walked over here."

Her heart thumped harder. "Just wondering when we'll have time to talk." She tried to swallow down the breathlessness to focus on what was important tonight. "I received a phone call from Susan Wilson. Apparently you encouraged her to phone me?"

Ryder tensed beside her, guiding her a few steps away from the music and chatter growing louder as the dancing wore on. "She told you about the rescue on Longs Peak?"

She leaned back to gauge his expression as he continued to lead her out of the tent and onto the expanse of lawn that led to his house. If she didn't know better, she would think he sounded wary. Guarded. But her father's ex-girlfriend had spoken warmly about the search and rescue team she credited for saving her life.

"She did." Jessamyn had listened in growing anger to the woman's story as Susan explained how Mateo Barclay had led her up a path he was unfamiliar with, expecting her to make a climb well above her skill level. "I knew you were a part of the rescue team that day, but until I spoke with her, I had no idea how difficult it must have been for the first responders."

As Ryder moved them farther away from the party tent strung with white lights, it became more difficult to see his face under the quarter moon. He gestured toward a wrought iron bench near a windmill built to look antique, but Jessamyn had learned this evening that it provided considerable power for the house's electrical systems.

"I can't take any credit for the rescue," he clarified, shaking his head as he claimed a seat beside her, his knee brushing hers where the long slit of her dress bared one leg. "I was still learning and didn't play a prominent role."

She studied him in the moonlight as he tucked a finger into his bow tie, loosening it a fraction. The action prompted her to put a restraining hand on his.

"I didn't mean to steal you away before the party ended. Should we wait to speak further until we say goodnight to your guests?"

She breathed in the pine scent of his aftershave while the minty aroma of bee balm drifted up from the flower beds nearby. She knew that it was more than just heightened senses from pregnancy that made her crave more of him.

His gaze swung to hers, his jaw flexing. "No. I've had

this on my mind for a long time, Jessamyn. We need to talk now."

Wariness curled through her as she let go of him. Did he mean he wished to discuss the pregnancy instead? The idea didn't quite connect since he couldn't have had the baby on his mind for a long time. He'd only just found out she was expecting his child days ago.

Plus, his tone didn't bode well for the romantic possibilities of a future with Ryder that Fleur's encouraging words had led Jessamyn to start thinking about. Had she been foolish to begin hoping that he could have deeper feelings for her one day?

"All right, then, we can talk." She crossed her legs to make herself more comfortable on the cool metal seat. Fearing any real comfort wasn't in the cards for her this evening. "You know about Susan Wilson's call since you urged her to contact me. And while her take on my father affirms he's not the person I believed him to be, his behavior on the mountain that day won't help me win the court case."

In the brief silence after she spoke, the country band switched to something more down tempo, quieting the distant crowd underneath the glowing white pavilion. Jessamyn could see couples pairing off on the dance floor, heads inclining toward one another. She wished she was there with Ryder, still enjoying the feel of his hands on her instead of wading through whatever he had to say to her. Everything about his stiff shoulders and serious tone told her she wasn't going to like it.

"But I know something that will help you win the case, Jess." His voice was pitched low. He shifted on the bench to look her squarely in the eye, and she could see him better now that her vision had adjusted to the grayed-out shades of moonlight. "I learned something from your father while we waited for the rest of the search and rescue team to pull Susan up from the ledge where she'd fallen."

"*You* know something," Jessamyn repeated, regrouping mentally. "So you didn't bring me out here to talk about the baby?"

"I need to tell you this first." He swiped a hand through his dark hair, a horseshoe cuff link catching the party lights as he mussed sleek strands. "I hoped Susan might have been privy to the same information I learned that day, since she wouldn't have been under the confidentiality restrictions that have held me back."

Frowning, she tried to follow what he was saying. "I don't understand. What restrictions?"

He looped one arm over the back of the bench. "As a first responder, I operate under doctor-patient confidentiality expectations. It's more of a gray area for EMS workers, but courts have ruled that patients have a right to privacy during emergency care."

Her mind jumped ahead now, making new connections. "You learned something on the mountain that day? While treating my father? And her?"

As she swiveled in her seat toward him, her sequins caught awkwardly in the wrought iron, but that was the least of her concerns. What did Ryder know that could help her case?

"I had the least experience of the search and rescue crew, so I was tasked with keeping your father stable while we waited for the others to bring up Susan." He hadn't answered the questions, clearly having his own plan for sharing what he knew with her. Ryder's gaze slid from hers to look off into the distance, as if seeing other mountains in his mind. "Your dad was exhibiting symptoms of shock and distress."

"According to Susan, he hadn't checked her equipment before they started rappelling. And he had taken them on the wrong trail, so they were coming down a much tougher route than they'd climbed up." Jessamyn had learned this from the phone call. Also, that her father had been the one to end the relationship in the hospital, not the other way around. Susan had sustained multiple breaks in her legs and back and hadn't been able to return home for weeks. "I know that much."

Jessamyn owed her sisters and her mother an apology for ever taking their dad's side in the split. He'd kept a very dark side hidden from her. The call from Mateo's ex-girlfriend had underscored that, strengthening Jessamyn's resolve to distance herself from him.

Professionally, that might take time. But she refused to associate with someone who continually put selfish interests above hers.

Ryder shook his head slowly. "That's not the half of it."

"Tell me." Tension drew her whole body tight. Her relationship with her father had taken one hit after another ever since he'd filed the paperwork to contest the will.

Now it felt like she'd never known him at all.

"Mateo was wound up. Talking fast." Ryder's tone softened as his attention returned to her. He laid a hand on her arm, the warmth of his skin failing to ward off the chill of premonition that she wouldn't like what was coming. "He was expressing frustration with Susan, saying he preferred—his words—'strong women who could keep up.'"

Her throat hurt, sensing that this was going to get worse before it got better. "That doesn't surprise me, ugly though it may be. Go on."

How many times had her father expressed approval for her when she came into work sick or stayed in the office for long hours on the weekend to force through a deal? His brand of "win at all costs" wasn't healthy, but for years it had forced her to achieve more. She'd bought into the whole "live to work" idea hook, line and sinker, never making herself a priority.

Ryder scrubbed a hand over his face before continuing quietly. "Mateo confessed that's why he left your mom once she began to struggle with depression. He didn't have the time or patience for her illness."

A small sound escaped her throat. An echo of the despair her mother must have felt at being abandoned by the man who was supposed to care for her most in the world. God, Jessamyn had been so wrong to listen to his glib bs. And she'd been even more wrong to follow in his footsteps, putting work and a bottom line before family.

That hurt. But there was also another hurt underneath that. Another layer of raw ache as she met Ryder's eyes.

"All this time you knew how awful he was," she mused aloud, pulling away from his touch. How many bad decisions could she have avoided if she'd had this knowledge nine years ago. "And you allowed me to go on believing—"

"Wait." He cut her off, his voice sounding— impossibly—more tortured than her own. "Please. There's more."

She couldn't catch her breath, her whole world effectively rearranged by this conversation already. And there was more? She wrapped her arms around her midsection, as if she could protect the life inside her from this night of awful revelations.

The band in the pavilion was saying their goodnights to the remaining guests before recorded music switched on over the outdoor speaker system, an old-time country-western ballad. Guests were leaving the party, laughter and talk spilling out onto the pavement near the valet stand.

Beside her in the shadows, Ryder continued.

"Finally, Mateo told me that he knew his own mother disinherited him for being a jackass to his wife."

Everything inside her went still.

"He said those words?" She rounded on him, relief and anger knotting her insides. Ryder had just offered her the key to winning the will contest case. Too bad he'd withheld it from her for weeks while she turned Crooked Elm upside down for evidence he'd had all along. "Dad knew even then that Gran wasn't going to leave Crooked Elm to him?"

"That was my understanding. Yes."

"And you didn't tell me because of my father's right to confidentiality?" Her voice went higher, disbelief creeping in.

She wasn't well versed in the law. But Ryder understood how much she'd followed in her father's footsteps. Knew how much doing so had cost her relationships with the rest of her family. And he'd chosen not to tell her a word of this when any one piece of it would have changed so many decisions she'd made since then. There had to be dozens of ways he could have steered her to the information about her father without outright telling her.

"Yes. A court could still refuse to admit a confession made during a time of duress—"

"Screw the court, Ryder." The angry words shot out before she could temper them. "What about *me*? Did I mean nothing to you once I left Catamount? Were you so hell-bent on breaking my heart ten years ago that you decided I didn't deserve to know this? That my father admitted all those awful things to you firsthand?"

Her sisters had always believed as much of their father, of course. But that was different than hearing her dad admit it all in his own words.

Thinking back to the timeline of when Ryder would have been on that mountain with her dad, Jessamyn realized they would have been broken up for a year at the time. Probably less. She'd gone to college in New York City specifically to live closer to her dad and to start interning at Barclay Property Group.

"I didn't even know if *now* was the right time, Jess." Ryder spread his arms wide, a gesture of surrender. As if he was throwing himself at her mercy now that she couldn't feel any. "Even if the letter of the law is gray, the spirit of the law says I shouldn't be telling you."

Cold hurt split her in half. How could she have thought that he might grow to care for her just because they shared a physical connection? How many times did Ryder have to prove that he would never put her first before she got it through her head?

"Yet you decided to break nine years of silence *now*, just when you find out I'm carrying your child?"

He started to speak, but she held up a hand, not finished. Anger building.

"Could your sudden attack of scruples have anything to do with the fact that our child will be a future beneficiary of Crooked Elm if I win my case against Dad?" Unable to sit beside him another moment, she stood quickly.

Started walking.

She needed to go home. Now.

"Jessamyn. Wait." Ryder's steps vibrated the ground behind her. "It's you that I'm thinking of, you, first and foremost. You that I want to protect—"

"By making me spin in circles for weeks trying to find evidence that you've had all along?" She kept coming back to that. "My father was not a patient. He was the man responsible for injuring his girlfriend. And it's not like he confessed to something that could come up in court. So I fail to see the big ethical dilemma here. You didn't owe him anything, as far as I'm concerned. But me?"

She felt the burning behind her eyes. Knew she needed to get away from him before he saw how much he'd hurt her.

Deeply. Irreparably.

Gathering the last of her strength, she continued, "You did owe me something, Ryder. And you simply didn't care enough to make me a priority. Then. Now. Or ever."

What had he done?

Ryder banged his fist on the steering wheel of his truck half an hour later, pushing the accelerator too fast as he drove away from the party.

Thick darkness enfolded him as he rounded a bend above Wakefield Ranch, the truck whipping past trees as he wound toward the mountains. Climbing higher above Catamount.

He wanted to go to Jessamyn. Needed to talk to her. Explain himself in a way that would somehow make her understand—

But he couldn't go to Crooked Elm like this. Half out of his mind with fear that she would push him from her life for good. What about the child she carried?

He'd figured a drive would clear his head first, so he'd walked away from his duties as one of the Atlas Gala hosts and left his departing guests to the care of the foundation organizers. Jessamyn needed to be his priority, damn it. But he couldn't go to her until he sorted out his thoughts. Until he found the right words that would make her see that he'd done his best—

Another bend in the road came up too quickly. His

headlights flashed onto tree trunks instead of twin yellow lines.

Braking too late, Ryder yanked the steering wheel hard to the left. Tires squealed. The truck cab tilted.

The whole vehicle lurched toward the trees and the mountain precipice beyond—

Before the truck stopped. Inches from the trunk of a gnarled old pine tree.

Ryder clutched the steering wheel in both hands, engine running but his anger gone. What the hell was he doing? He could have gone over that cliffside in a moment of anger and stupidity. He'd been moments away from needing a search and rescue team himself.

Like so many people he'd saved on the mountain over the last nine years, he'd taken his focus away from what was important.

Banging his fist on the steering wheel again—more gently this time—he knew he couldn't go to Jessamyn's tonight. He had no idea how to rescue this relationship, but he wouldn't find the answers in the dark tonight.

He would never forgive himself if he lost her. So he'd simply do whatever it took to win her back.

Thirteen

Eyes still burning from bitter tears even two days later, Jessamyn ignored the knocking on her bedroom door. Sliding a pillow over her head, she burrowed deeper in her covers, oblivious to the time of day.

She'd hardly left her bed at Crooked Elm since she'd returned home after the gala, barely speaking to Fleur since she couldn't talk without crying. Instead, she'd sent her sister texts from the privacy of her own room relating the gist of what had happened with Ryder. After half a lifetime of being one of those "strong women" her stupid father admired, she'd caved in on herself and could hardly draw a breath without falling apart. For herself. For the relationships she'd torched with her mom and sisters because of a man who hadn't deserved her faith. For the loss of what might have been with Ryder if he hadn't kept secrets from her. And, contrarily, she cried for the loss of Ryder's arms around her, too.

Ryder.

Just thinking about him made the tears threaten again. Wasn't there a limit to how much water could express through those tiny ducts in her eyes?

The circle of her futile thoughts was broken by more knocking at her door. Louder this time. *Rat. Tat. Tat.*

"Jess? It's Lark." Her sister's voice drifted through more softly. "Can I come in?"

Lark was here?

Jessamyn slid the pillow from over her head, sitting up in bed. A faded T-shirt from a long-ago summer camp fell in wrinkles. Her head pounded. Even her body ached from the monsoon of emotions brought on by Ryder's revelation.

"Lark?" Her voice scratched as she spoke for the first time in two days.

"I'm coming in," her older sister announced as she turned the handle, her voice as no-nonsense and authoritative as Jessamyn remembered from childhood. Lark had long taken her role as oldest Barclay sister seriously. "We need to talk."

Yes, they did. Jessamyn owed both of her sisters—and her mother—long and thorough apologies for not listening all the times they'd tried to tell her their father wasn't a good person.

And for so much more. She'd abandoned them on Christmases and birthdays. She hadn't attended Lark's wedding or been there two years afterward when her older sister had gone through a divorce. Jessamyn *had* tried to send Fleur financial help for college over the years, but that was as much effort as she'd made, and Fleur had always sent back those checks.

Money was a poor excuse for connection. Real connection.

Now, as the bedroom door opened, Lark stepped onto the old blue-and-yellow braid rug, with Fleur on her heels. Lark wore a black knit sleeveless dress and matching sandals, her straight dark hair in a braid that lay on one shoulder. No jewelry. No makeup. Her bright green eyes were all the more noticeable for the lack of decoration, and a hundred old memories swept over Jessamyn. Lark bandaging skinned knees and kissing them better. Lark at the stove, just two years older than Jessamyn but light-years wiser, stirring the butter into their macaroni and cheese lunches. Lark dressed as a wicked witch for Halloween while Fleur and Jessamyn flitted around as good fairies.

She owed her big sister so much better than she'd given back. A wave of love flooded through her as Lark sank onto the foot of the bed without fanfare.

"How are you feeling?" Lark asked, green eyes running over her but taking in what must be an extraordinarily disheveled appearance without comment.

"Hungry, actually." Her hand went to her belly as she recalled her biggest responsibility. "I should probably get something—"

"I'm on it," Fleur volunteered, still on her feet near the door. "You may recall I've tried to tempt you to eat about five different times, so I've got some really good things ready."

Their younger sister darted out through the open door, her copper-colored ponytail swishing as her bare feet moved soundlessly into the corridor.

Lark cleared her throat quietly. "Congratulations on the pregnancy." At Jessamyn's questioning look, Lark hastened to add, "Fleur filled me in on everything. And although you're obviously distressed today, I'm hoping you're feeling okay about the baby?"

More love bubbled up inside her. Not just for Lark being here with her, but for the child she carried.

"The pregnancy is definitely a good thing." Grabbing a downy pillow, she dragged it over her belly and hugged it to her, a small comfort for both her baby and her, too.

Lark's steady gaze was as calming as her voice when she pressed, "But Fleur said you haven't come out of your room for two days."

It was easy to envision her sister in her role as a therapist, helping people to navigate problems and relationships.

"I've been reeling since Ryder's disclosure at the Atlas Gala," she confessed, swiping a hank of unwashed hair from her face. "While I wish I could say it's been pregnancy hormones that have turned my emotions into a waterfall for days, it has more to do with learning the truth about Dad. And learning it from the father of my child, who's known what a sorry excuse for a human being our father has been this whole time."

Nodding slowly, Lark seemed to take this in. She didn't comment at first. Getting to her feet, she walked to an open window and rolled up the shade where sheer curtains filtered the pinks and yellows of a setting sun.

"Why do you think you found it tougher to hear the truth about Dad from Ryder?" Lark asked as she adjusted the curtains, carefully spacing them on the rods, so they billowed evenly in an evening breeze.

Jessamyn blinked at the unexpected question. She was grateful that Fleur reentered the room with a tray, buying Jessamyn time to think about her answer while the scents of yeasty bread and warm ginger swirled under her nose.

Fleur settled the red metal tray on the nightstand. "I have more nutritious things downstairs, but I wasn't sure if you were having morning sickness so I didn't want to overwhelm you with anything that might trigger your stomach."

"Thank you so much." Jessamyn reached for the warm French bread and took a bite.

"That's ginger tea, by the way. It's supposed to be good in early pregnancy." Fleur folded her legs beneath her as she settled on the bed in the spot Lark had vacated.

Fleur's turquoise bead bracelets and white eyelet top reminded Jessamyn of the way their grandmother had always dressed, although Fleur paired hers with denim cutoffs instead of the long jean skirts Antonia had favored. Or maybe it was the freshly baked foods and perpetually warm kitchen that had Jessamyn thinking about Gran.

"So?" Lark's voice interrupted the run of nostalgia. "Is there a reason it bothered you so much more to hear about Dad from Ryder than it did from us? Or Mom? Or his ex-girlfriend?"

Jessamyn set aside the bread she'd been eating, recognizing that this wasn't Lark's counselor voice. This was her annoyed-sister voice. And with good reason.

"I am deeply, genuinely sorry I didn't listen all the times you tried to tell me about him. I think I saw what I needed him to be, and maybe it will take time for me to understand why." Perhaps she really had seen herself in him, and considering what she knew about him now, that was a gut punch.

Still, she thought—she hoped—she was a good person. Her father had broken up with his injured girlfriend in the hospital when he'd been to blame for the woman's fall. Jessamyn would never end a relationship when someone needed her—

A flicker of memory from the night of the gala returned. Ryder's voice sounded in her mind.

Nothing is more important to me than ensuring we're

on the same page for our child's future. They never had gotten around to discussing the baby after the gala. Regret for her emotional departure niggled. As a mother, she needed to start putting her child first.

And about how she'd treated Ryder...?

"Mom and Dad's personal war did a number on us all, Jess," Lark assured her as she moved to the next window and repeated the procedure—shade up, curtains precisely adjusted. "Since moving to specialize in child therapy, I have all the more appreciation for the emotional hellfire we waded through as kids, so this isn't about blame. I'm genuinely wondering why you were able to finally recognize the truth when Ryder said it?"

Because she trusted him deeply. She'd recognized his innate goodness and caring at eighteen years old and she'd loved him even then. But she'd loved her sisters, too. Even when she didn't trust their view of their father.

"Maybe because he was outside the family." Tentatively, she picked up the mug of steaming tea and took a sip, hoping to warm the chill from her heart. "He didn't tell me to try to make me abandon Dad. Ryder shared it because the court case is coming up, and he knew that Antonia wanted the land to go to us."

The tea was delicious, and she drank a little more.

"Ryder has no horse in the race. He's just a good person trying to do the right thing." Lark repeated it simply. As if it were a statement of fact. "If anything, his keeping the secret that long speaks to his character...the kind of character anyone would want in a man."

Jessamyn bristled. She jostled the mug a little and had to set down the tea.

"Keeping me in the dark while I made bad decision after bad decision was the right thing to do?" The frustration stirred again. "He could have told me—hinted to me—nine years ago, but—"

"But he tried to keep an oath he swears in his profession. The confidentiality clause isn't there as a suggestion or a guideline. It's a law." Lark's green, older-sister eyes bored into hers with the same wisdom she'd always possessed. "And knowing the kind of man Mateo Barclay is, Ryder could face a lawsuit from Dad if he makes those words public for our sake."

The idea made her ill.

"God." She retrieved the mug again, craving the tea to soothe the sudden nausea that was more about Ryder's predicament than any morning sickness. "Dad is lawsuit-happy."

"So maybe you shouldn't be too hard on Ryder," Fleur suggested, laying a hand on Jessamyn's ankle through the blankets. "If he comes forward, we definitely have a stronger shot of defending Gran's will. But it could come at a cost to Ryder."

Fleur's eyes were as kind as her gentle words.

"Maybe I lashed out where I shouldn't have." More qualities she shared with her dad? Steeling herself to do better, Jessamyn forced herself to dig deeper. To share the feelings under the anger. "I was just so hurt that he kept it from me when I wanted—for once—to feel important to him."

Ryder was a good man. She'd known it a decade ago, and he'd apparently been wrestling with ethical issues she hadn't fully appreciated. Perhaps instead of seeking a declaration from him—hoping he'd declare feelings for her that he just didn't have for her yet—maybe she should be more focused on being worthy of him.

She'd been toying with the idea of staying in Catamount. Living closer to Ryder so he could be a part of their child's life. Besides, she'd dreamed of coming back here one day, before her life became one endless list of achievements to accomplish.

There were opportunities for creative real estate development here. Ways Jessamyn could make her mark on this part of Colorado.

"You are important to him," Fleur promised. "He called the house phone earlier when you didn't reply to his messages. He sounded worried about you."

Or worried about the baby.

Which was his right, as the child's father, even if it hurt that his concern was more for the pregnancy.

Whatever happened between them, Jessamyn couldn't simply ignore him because she was hurt that he didn't love her back. She owed him more than that.

"I'll call him." Setting aside the tea, she slid out from the covers, knowing she needed to make things right with a lot of people. "But first, I want you both to know that I'm going to put in hard work to fix my relationships with you and with Mom. And if there's one thing I'm good at, it's hard work."

Lark folded her arms, assessing her. "In that case, I'll look forward to being impressed."

Fleur made a dismissive sound as she rose to hug Jessamyn. "I'm already on board, Jess. I wanted us all at Crooked Elm this summer so we could patch up our differences and be a family again."

Jessamyn's throat closed up at her sister's easy forgiveness. A few more tears came, but this time, she didn't mind. If only one person was ready to forgive her, that was progress.

She squeezed her sibling tightly. "I never stopped loving you, even when I wasn't in your life. I hope you know that." Cracking open one eye, she glanced at Lark over Fleur's shoulder. "That goes for you, too."

"Excellent." Lark gave a satisfied nod but didn't move closer. "I'm facing the worst summer of my life now that Gibson is returning to Catamount while I'm here. So you can start showing the love by lying to him every single day he asks about me and telling him I'm *not* here."

Jessamyn let go of Fleur, her mind filling up with questions. Star hockey player Gibson Vaughn was in Catamount? She knew that was big news. There'd been rumors he would take a contract as a free agent, but maybe he was retiring at last. But even as she wanted to quiz her, their truce was so new—fragile—she accepted this wasn't the time to push Lark.

Before she even finished the thought, Fleur caught her eye and gave a discreet shake of her head as if to keep her quiet. A moot point since Lark walked out of the bedroom, back straight and chin high.

Jessamyn didn't envy her sister having to face her famous ex-husband. The sports media hadn't been kind to her during her brief marriage to Gibson.

"I'll fill you in another time," Fleur whispered as she picked up the abandoned food tray. "You should go see a man about a baby."

The reality of what Jessamyn needed to do returned, weighing down her feet.

She knew she needed to see Ryder. To smooth things over for her outsize reaction to an admission that hadn't been easy for him. No matter how much it hurt to face a man who didn't love her—who'd only proposed because he was the most kind and honorable of men—she still had to own up to make things right between them.

She would preserve a friendship between them. Open communication and goodwill for the sake of their child.

Not for anything would she repeat her parents' mistakes. Somehow, she would pull herself together to visit Ryder.

They had their baby's future to plan.

Standing inside a quiet paddock as night fell, Ryder waited impatiently for a veterinarian to arrive to help him with a mare ready to foal. He stroked the nose of the agitated dun while a warm night breeze blew through her dark mane.

At least Coco's foaling would give him something to occupy his thoughts tonight. Maybe the birthing would buy him a few hours that weren't filled with regrets about how he'd handled things with Jessamyn. Had there been a minute so far that he hadn't thought about her walking away from him after the Atlas Gala? The ache in his chest hadn't eased for even a second since he'd watched her fight back tears because of him. He'd gone to sleep both nights since the evening of the gala knowing he'd put that hurt in her eyes and hating himself for it.

Coco snorted and pawed at the grass, reminding him to keep his focus. Where was the vet? He'd thought the doctor had arrived a few minutes ago when he spotted headlights by the main house, but there was no sign of the woman yet.

In the meantime, Ryder had turned the animal out into the clean grass for foaling since the mustang had a history of difficult births and she liked her space to roll around at the end. He hoped the paddock would be the right choice for her.

At least he knew something about mares and he could offer some help. Unlike with Jessamyn, who didn't want to see him or talk to him after he'd withheld what he knew about her father.

The horse paced away from him to kick at her belly, her unrest driving his own.

Checking his phone, he tracked the vet on the app for the animal practice and saw the woman was still half an hour away. So who had been pulling up to the main house a little while ago?

"Ryder?" A familiar woman's voice called from the far side of the barn.

Jessamyn.

Was he dreaming that he heard her voice now? Or was it possible she was really here?

"Back here," he called through the dark, wishing he'd switched on the outdoor lights over the paddock. He'd flipped them off earlier in Coco's labor, hoping it might relax her.

"It's hard to see," Jessamyn remarked, her voice registering surprise but no anger. No coolness.

"Sorry about that. I switched the lights off in the hope of settling an anxious mare ready to foal tonight." He knew better than to hope she'd forgiven him for staying silent about her dad. But if there was any chance she would hear him out again about a future together, he intended to remind her why they should be in each other's lives.

And he'd do a better job of it than he had on Sawmill Mountain when he'd first learned about the baby. He'd processed the news. Understood there was nothing more important to him in the world than being there for his child.

Except being there for Jessamyn. Whatever it took.

"It's fine. I've got my phone's flashlight."

Ryder turned on his phone again and raised it over his head to help her see. "I'm by the paddock."

He spotted her shadow moving closer and the blue

light of her cell phone as well. She shone the flashlight feature at the ground, illuminating her legs in dark jeans and boots. A far cry from the way she'd been dressed the last time he'd seen her. Yet, as she came fully into focus by the light of his phone, every bit as beautiful and more.

His heart gave a rough thump at her nearness. But these days, it beat for her.

"Is this a bad time?" she asked, her voice betraying trepidation.

Nerves?

He didn't think that could be the case. Still, he reached a hand automatically to steady her step. Or maybe just because he was dying to touch her, however briefly.

She wore a pale-colored T-shirt, so her arm was bare where he touched her. The skin so smooth and soft it took all his restraint not to pull her closer.

"Not at all," he reassured her, ignoring his impulses to guide her toward the paddock rail so she could orient herself. "Just watching over Coco until the vet gets here. The mare has had trouble foaling in the past, so I don't want to leave her."

"Do you think she'll mind that I'm here?" she asked, turning off her phone and slipping the device into the back pocket of her jeans. "I don't want to upset her."

"Maybe she'll appreciate a woman's presence," he mused, settling against the paddock rail beside her. It felt right to stand next to her, to share his daily concerns with her.

"I only know a little more about horses than I do about giving birth, so I'm not sure how helpful I'll be." Jessamyn folded her arms over the top rail, leaning into the fence. "I didn't pay much attention to farm life back then."

He could see her clearly now in the moonlight, her

delicate features calling to his fingers to trace them. Part of him was dying to know why she was here and if she felt even a fraction of the regret he did about their parting the other night.

But the other part of him feared she was coming to tell him goodbye.

"You know plenty about horses." He wished he'd taken more time to reminisce with her while he'd had the chance. To bring to mind the fun things they'd done together that summer when they'd fallen for each other, back when Jessamyn had still worn her heart on her sleeve. "I used to love watching you barrel race in the junior competitions."

Coco still paced the paddock, but she seemed less agitated now. Was she comforted by their low voices?

Jessamyn turned to him, her brows raised. A half smile kicked up the corner of her lips. "You never told me that."

"You were just a kid then," he reminded her. "So it was hardly the kind of thing I'd say to woo you when you were eighteen and I was an oh-so-smooth nineteen. But yeah, I remember you barrel racing. You did it like you tackle everything—focused, determined. Hell-bent."

He was enjoying the memory so much he didn't realize she'd turned away from him again until her voice sounded sadly. "Ha. Sounds like me. All about the accomplishment. Never about the people."

Surprised, he laid a hand on her arm again, hungry to correct the impression.

"Are you kidding me? That couldn't be further from the truth." Another old memory stirred. "Do you remember the year you won the juniors?"

He could feel her pulse thrum at her wrist and couldn't resist the urge to stroke his thumb lightly over the spot.

"The day my parents got into a screaming match in the stands, and Fleur launched into a rendition of 'America the Beautiful' to try to take the arena's focus away from the brawl breaking out?" Jessamyn shook her head, her loose hair glinting in the moonlight. "Unfortunately, yes."

Squeezing her arm gently, he leaned closer to make his point.

"When the whole arena was gossiping about Fleur's performance, whispering about the precocious nine-year-old in spangles for somehow hogging the spotlight, I saw you give her the trophy you won to cheer her up." It had been a sweet moment. A brief glimpse he'd caught of a dejected nine-year-old being comforted by her big sister.

He'd been fourteen at the time, sitting in the mostly empty arena eating as much fried dough as his bottomless stomach could hold. And he'd never forgotten that small moment of kindness.

"I'd forgotten that," she admitted, straightening as Coco paced toward them, head down. "I can't believe you noticed us that day."

Jessamyn held her free hand out to the mare, letting Coco's restless nose move over her palm. Jess hadn't moved her other arm away from him where his fingers still circled her wrist. Thumb still hovering over the pulse point.

"I've always noticed you. And you're good with people." He needed her to know that. No matter if she was here to tell him goodbye, he had to make sure she understood what he saw in her. "I don't need to live in New York to know that's why you excel at your job there. People put their trust in you because you earn it, and that's a very attractive quality."

Her eyes remained on Coco as the mare whinnied softly. Jessamyn comforted her with a stroke down her neck.

The moment was broken by the momentary splash of white headlights across their faces. The sound of crunching gravel on the far side of the barn.

"That must be the vet." Letting go of Jess's arm, he moved toward the barn. "I'd better turn on the lights so she can see her way back here."

Ten minutes later, he had the lights on and the doctor set up in the paddock to check Coco. The vet had brought a student intern with her to help with the birth, so Ryder hadn't bothered calling in anyone else to sit with them.

Giving him the time he craved with Jessamyn.

"Would you like to sit on the porch swing?" he suggested, gesturing toward the back of the main house where a wide veranda wrapped the whole length. "I can get us drinks, or—"

He trailed off since she was shaking her head.

"I'm fine. But if you think it's okay to leave Coco, the porch swing sounds good."

Ryder glanced back toward the paddock, now well lit by the exterior barn lights. "Coco is in good hands. She looks more comfortable this time. I think she'll like being outdoors instead of the birthing stall."

They walked side by side in silence for a few moments, stars winking overhead, night bugs humming. Tension ratcheted higher inside him as he braced himself for whatever she'd come here to say.

He glanced over at her to see her frowning. Biting her lip.

Was she wondering how to say she was leaving?

By the time they reached the porch swing, he couldn't hold back his own words any longer.

Steadying the chain swings so she could make herself comfortable, he blurted, "Jess, I'm so sorry I didn't tell you about your father sooner. You were right—"

"No." She ignored the swing seat to clutch his shoulder where he stood. "No, I *wasn't* right. You were, Ryder. I came here to apologize to *you* for making it all about me when you were torn between ethical responsibility and wanting to help me."

His grip on the chain tightened. He couldn't quite believe what she'd just said, which seemed like a total about-face from the other night.

"But what you said about your father not being the patient, that was true. I don't think he was ever technically admitted to the hospital." Ryder had revisited the encounter so many times in his mind, trying to untwine what he owed to Mateo Barclay versus what he owed to Jessamyn.

Every time, he wished he'd spoken to Jessamyn sooner. Because right or wrong, he was glad she knew now.

"He was in shock." Jessamyn's fingers dug lightly into his shoulder as if she could press the idea into him. "Lark thought Dad could even sue you if you made a statement about—"

"Let him." He waved it off, unconcerned with whatever civil nonsense Mateo cooked up with an expensive attorney. The only thing he cared about right now was having Jessamyn here, her hands on him. Her hazel eyes full of concern for him. "I will go on record in court about what I heard that day, and I hope like hell it helps you and your sisters win your case because I know what Antonia wanted for Crooked Elm. I've done my best to uphold the oath of providing emergency care, but if I lose my certification over this, it's still a choice I will stand by because you're my priority, Jessamyn. You and our baby."

Crickets chirped and branches rustled overhead to fill the silence as the words seemed to settle around her.

Was it his imagination, or did her expression soften

somehow? Her hold on him eased, her hand sliding down his arm with slow care.

"Ryder." A wealth of emotion hid behind the single word.

He was certain of it.

Because she was leaving Catamount and him for good?

Or because she might give him another chance?

Before he could find out, she continued, "One way or another, my sisters and I will defend Gran's will. Call it pregnancy intuition, but I feel it in my bones that we're going to prevail." A small smile lifted one side of her mouth. "My sisters and I are coming together in a way I would have never predicted. And it just feels—right. Like together, we're going to win this thing and prove to Dad that he can't call the shots forever."

She sounded certain. Confident.

And he was glad for her. But she hadn't said anything about staying in Catamount. With him.

"Jessamyn. I'll do everything I can to help. I promise you." His hands went to her waist in his need for her to listen. To make her see they weren't finished here yet. "But it's also important to me that you know we belong together. We always have. Please don't leave Catamount without giving this—giving us—one more chance to be a family."

"I want that, too, Ryder. So much." Her eyes turned brighter, the tears pooling without falling.

"So what's holding you back?" He stroked her dark hair, hating that he'd brought her a moment's unhappiness. Not knowing what he was missing. "I'd give you my name. My whole world. I'd give up the ranch for part of the year to be in New York with you if that's what it takes—"

"I'd never ask that of you." A tear spilled down her cheek, and he captured it with his thumb, wishing he could stop the flow forever. "You belong here."

You do, too. But he wouldn't be the one to tell her that if she didn't see it yet.

"Then let's get married and make this work," he urged, his hand cupping her face. "And know that I'm willing to do whatever it takes."

He could swear they were on the verge of understanding one another. Of being the family that he knew they were meant to be.

Her fingers fisted in the front of his T-shirt.

"I love you, Ryder," she admitted with a fierceness he'd never heard in her voice before. "And as much as I want that future with you, I won't marry you until you return some of the love I have for you. That I've had for you since I was eighteen years old."

Her fingers twisted the fabric tighter and he wondered how she could not know that she had his whole heart right in her hand? How could he have missed saying those words, especially since he knew the scars left by her parents' loveless marriage?

She needed—deserved—the reassurance.

"Oh, Jess." His forehead fell to hers, the relief of her words damn near taking his knees out from under him even as he grieved his blindness in missing what she needed from him. "How can you not know how much I love you, too?"

She edged back to study him, hazel eyes wide. Confused. Wary.

He cursed himself to hell and back.

Then, cradling her beautiful face in his hands, he looked into the eyes that held his world and repeated the words that gave shape to everything he'd ever felt for this woman.

"I love you, Jessamyn Barclay. Forever and for always." His thumb stroked her cheek. He kissed one eyelid and then the other. "And that love is going to burn bright for you until I have you in my arms every day and in my bed every night."

He felt her shiver against him and pulled her tighter.

"You won't have long to wait," she promised, tilting her head to slant her lips over his. She kissed him with slow deliberation, tongue twining around his and turning him inside out before she edged back again. "Because I want that as soon as possible, do you hear me?"

He wasn't losing her. She was here to move into his life and she was never leaving it again.

Joy speared his insides.

"I hear you." He tugged her lower lip into his mouth, needing to taste more of her. "And I want to work out all the logistics of this new life of ours with you in the morning over breakfast, because we have a lot of figuring out to do for us and for our baby, too."

"Good. I've already figured out that I want to start my own development group out here so I can make Catamount my home. I'll still maintain a share of Barclay Property Group since I won't allow my father to shut me out of a company I helped him build. But there's nothing stopping me from starting another business of my own here." She wound slender arms around his neck, her breasts pressing against his chest. "But together, you and I can fine-tune all the necessary plans to be together."

They would face the future—whatever it held— side by side.

He shook his head, mesmerized by this fearless, ambitious woman. "I'd love that. But first, I'm taking you upstairs—"

"Less talking, cowboy," she purred against his lips as she tilted her hips into him. "More taking."

Counting his blessings, he swept Jessamyn Barclay right off her feet and did exactly as the lady asked.

* * * * *

COMING SOON!

We really hope you enjoyed reading this book.
If you're looking for more romance, be sure to
head to the shops when new books are
available on

Thursday 7th July

To see which titles are coming soon, please visit
millsandboon.co.uk/nextmonth

£2·95

The author lives in East Anglia with her husband and two dogs. Her favourite hobby is visiting churches.

A Drink of
Deadly Wine

Kate Charles

HEADLINE

First published in 1991
by HEADLINE BOOK PUBLISHING

First published in paperback in 1992
by HEADLINE BOOK PUBLISHING

10 9 8 7 6 5 4

ISBN 0 7472 3767 0

Printed and bound in Great Britain by
Mackays of Chatham PLC, Chatham, Kent

HEADLINE BOOK PUBLISHING
A division of Hodder Headline PLC
338 Euston Road
London NW1 3BH

For Simon

Author's note: I have taken a few ecclesiastical liberties for which I hope I will be forgiven. St Anne's Church, Kensington Gardens, does not exist, nor does St Dunstan's Church, Brighton. I have also elevated two towns to cathedral cities for reasons of plot: Selby Abbey of course exists, but is not a cathedral, and likewise Plymouth has been elevated.

Thou hast shewed thy people heavy things:
thou hast given us a drink of deadly wine
Psalm 60.3

Prologue

*Keep me from the snare that they have laid for me:
and from the traps of the wicked doers.*

Psalm 141.10

Emily put her head around the study door. 'The children are ready, darling. Shall we go?'

With an effort, Father Gabriel Neville smiled at his wife. 'You and the children go on ahead. I want to have a last look at my sermon – people will be expecting something special today!'

'And I'm sure you won't disappoint them. See you in a bit, then.'

As the door closed behind her, the smile faded from Gabriel's face, and he stared unseeing at the piece of paper in his hands. An ordinary piece of paper, with no distinguishing marks. He could throw it on the fire and get on with his life, with his career. But the words that were written on that paper were already incised on his heart, and the threat behind them would not go away.

Ugly words, words full of hate, and malice, and hurt. His carefully ordered world . . .

A shaft of morning sunlight broke through the study window, and his desk was momentarily dappled with pools

1

of colour from the inset pane of stained glass. Cool blue lapped his sermon notes, while a finger of red touched the smooth rock paperweight. The past . . . he would not allow himself to think of the past. Gabriel shuddered and reached convulsively for the silver-framed photo of Emily and the children. A beautiful family – any man would be proud. Lovely Emily, with her glossy dark hair and her glowing brown eyes. Viola and Sebastian, the twins. People often stopped Emily on the street, astonished by their beauty. Beauty in duplicate it was, with their perfect heart-shaped faces, Emily's shining dark hair and his sapphire-blue eyes. He gazed gratefully at them. The past, threatening to crowd in on him, was held at bay by their smiling faces. The present, yes, the present was all that mattered – that, and the future.

He looked around the study as he contemplated his future. When the time came, he would be sorry to leave this place; of all the rooms in the vicarage, this was his favourite, his sanctuary. All was in order: his books, lined up alphabetically on the oak shelves; the mantelpiece with its carefully arranged treasures; the beautiful Queen Anne desk, polished to a mellow sheen and clear of all save the sermon notes and the photo; the Persian carpet, its colours still rich and vibrant despite its great age. It was all of a wholeness, just like his life.

And now this. Gabriel opened the top drawer of his desk and thrust the folded paper in, then hesitated. No one else should be opening his desk drawer – the children knew they were not to enter his study, and the daily would never look inside his desk when she polished it, but it didn't do to take chances. He fiddled with a bit of wood, and a secret drawer slid silently out. The paper thus safely dealt with, Father Gabriel Neville prepared himself to go to church.

PART I

Chapter 1

*Take the psalm, bring hither the tabret: the merry
harp with the lute.
Blow upon the trumpet in the new-moon: even in
the time appointed, and upon our solemn feast-
day.*

Psalm 81.2-3

In the moment of expectant pause before the entry of the
procession, Emily looked up from her prayers. The church
had never looked better – Gabriel would be so pleased.
The six silver candlesticks gleamed on the high altar and
the figures on the newly cleaned rood screen virtually
shone. Even the stained-glass windows, begrimed by London
traffic, had been cleaned for the occasion, and were jewel-
like in their brilliance. The sun streamed through; it seemed
a good omen after several weeks of almost unrelieved
rain.

The Feast of St Anne, the church's annual Patronal Festival. It had always been the highlight of Emily's year, as
long as she could remember. As a small girl growing up in
this church she'd loved the sights, the sounds, the smells
of this day – the cloth-of-gold, the choir, the incense. She
loved the banner carried in procession, the one with St

7

Anne, mother of Our Lady, teaching the young Mary to read. That banner, weakened by age, was now only brought out once a year, on this feast day.

She drew in her breath in anticipation as the doors at the north-east of the nave opened and the procession entered. Sebastian, making his first appearance as boat boy, walked solemnly beside the thurifer. He'd been looking forward to this day for a long time. Emily felt Viola tense beside her, and gave her shoulder a little squeeze of sympathy.

The thurifer swung the heavy silver thurible straight in front of him, releasing an aromatic cloud of smoke. By the time the choir entered, behind the crucifer and acolytes, it was becoming difficult to see. But there it was – the banner. And there, just ahead of the Bishop, resplendent in cloth-of-gold, was Gabriel.

Beautiful Gabriel. That first time, ten years ago it was, she hadn't even seen him at first, so entranced she'd been with the banner. But once she'd seen him she hadn't taken her eyes off him for the rest of the service. Gabriel had been thirty then, but looked younger. His was the heart-breaking androgynous beauty of a Burne-Jones angel: tall and slender, luminous pale skin, high cheekbones, long straight nose, deep-set eyes, startling in their blueness and fringed with dark thick lashes, lips that were soft and rounded without being full. His hair was auburn, wavy and worn a fraction longer than the current fashion, but it suited him so completely that it never occurred to anyone to criticise it. And now, after ten years, he was little changed, his hair perhaps shorter but without a touch of grey, his face smooth and unlined, his figure slim as ever. As he passed by, Emily smiled at him with love.

Involved in his own observations, Gabriel missed her smile. The church looked splendid, he thought – full marks to Daphne, who was chiefly responsible, and to all the ladies who'd worked so hard cleaning and polishing. He'd have to remember to thank them. The procession passed under the rood screen; each person moved smoothly to his appointed place. The servers were doing uncommonly well – he'd have a word with Tony later to compliment him. Now he smiled at Tony as he brought the book forward for the collect; the young man returned his smile discreetly. Sebastian, clutching the silver incense boat, was behaving beautifully, conscientiously following the thurifer's every move. It was a shame that Viola had taken it so hard, but she had to understand that there were still certain things that girls couldn't do.

As the choir began the Gloria and he settled into his seat, Gabriel's eyes moved over the congregation. His thoughts, so carefully under control until now, moved back inexorably to that piece of paper. He finally articulated to himself the terrifying question: who had sent it? Who had crept up to his door early this morning and slipped the envelope through the letter-box? Who could hate him that much? And most frightening of all, who could possibly know about that terrible time in Brighton, so long ago?

He collected himself during the readings, concentrating very hard on the words, and prepared himself for the sermon. The choir chanted the psalm set for the day; its words reinforced his calm.

Blessed are all they that fear the Lord: and walk in
his ways.
For thou shalt eat the labours of thine hands:

O well is thee, and happy shalt thou be.
Thy wife shall be the fruitful vine: upon the walls
of thine house.
Thy children like the olive-branches: round about
thy table.
Lo, thus shall the man be blessed: that feareth the
Lord.
The Lord from out of Sion shall so bless thee: that
thou shalt see Jerusalem in prosperity all thy life
long.
Yea, that thou shalt see thy children's children:
and peace upon Israel.

As he stepped into the pulpit, Gabriel was well in control.
The congregation settled back with a collective sigh for
one of his famous sermons. He was justly famed, for he was
a spellbinding speaker. Although he was a scholar of some
note, with an impressive intellect, his sermons were never
dry exercises in scholarship. He had a gift for making the
most abstract and esoteric concept understandable, and in
a way that made his listeners feel that they not only
understood it, but had known it all along. With his compelling
beauty and his eloquent and charismatic delivery, it was
said that no one had ever slept through one of Father
Gabriel Neville's sermons. Today he spoke movingly on
the subject of Grace, the literal translation of the Hebrew
name Anne.

As he preached, he made eye contact with the congregation, one after another, though their presence barely registered with him. Emily, near the front, gazing at him with
rapt love, with Viola beside her. The churchwardens, flank-
ing the aisles. Lady Constance, in her customary pew on

the left. Daphne at the back. The Dawsons, their usual dis-approving looks softened by his rhetoric.

One of his gifts as a preacher was knowing when to stop, and he sat down leaving his listeners wanting more. The choir sang the Credo, the Intercessions were made, the Prayers of Penitence said, and the Bishop stepped forward for the Absolution.

Forgive us all that is past . . .

The Mass. The Bishop was celebrating, so Gabriel could stand to the side and let the familiar words of the Prayer of Consecration slip through his mind like rosary beads through his fingers. With angels and archangels . . .

The Agnus Dei soared high into the polychromed roof as Gabriel took the silver chalice and moved to the rail. His mind was numb, the twin questions beating a painful tattoo in his head: Who hates me? Who knows?

They came forward and knelt one by one, and he looked searchingly at each one as he proffered the chalice. The servers knelt first. Ahead of Gabriel, Sebastian gazed up suitably awe-struck as the Bishop's hand rested momen-tarily in blessing on his dark head. Old Percy 'Venerable' Bead. 'The blood of Christ.' Who knows? The two young-sters, Johnnie and Chris. 'The blood of Christ.' Who hates me? Tony Kent. 'The blood of Christ.' Who knows? Lady Constance the next to receive communion from the Bishop, as was her due. 'The blood of Christ.' Who hates me? Miles Taylor, down from his perch in the organ loft. 'The blood of Christ.' Emily. The Dawsons, two little grey people, together as always. 'The blood of Christ.' Who knows? Daphne Elford, solid and comfortable. 'The blood of Christ.' Who hates me? The churchwardens at the end, Wing Com-mander Cyril Fitzjames and Mavis Conwell. 'The blood of

Christ.' Who knows? Who hates me? Who knows? Who knows?

Chapter 2

Thou shalt hide them privily by thine own presence
from the provoking of all men: thou shalt keep
them secretly in thy tabernacle from the strife of
tongues.

Psalm 31.22

The Bishop had managed to arrive and robe with a minimum
of fuss, but after the service he found himself the object of
Percy Bead's hovering ministrations. 'Right Reverend Father,
let me take your mitre. If I may say so, it's a lovely one.'
Percy's short fingers lingered over the rich gold embroidery.
'May I help you with your cope? We have to take particular
care with this gold set.'

'It's a beautiful Mass set – one of the finest I've seen in
a long while. You're very lucky to have it.'

Percy, characteristically, took that as a personal compliment and beamed. 'Yes. It was a gift from Lady Constance Oliver, just after her husband died, so that goes
back a long way. We'd never be able to replace it today.
You just can't get materials like that any more.' He grew
confidential. 'There aren't many left in the church who remember back that far. I'm one of the old ones, you see.
Me, Lady Constance, Cyril Fitzjames.'

13

Percy Bead, known to all as 'Venerable', was possessed of strongly held opinions about everything, and he never hesitated to share them. The Bishop, who had only recently become Area Bishop, realised that this could be a valuable asset on his periodic visits to St Anne's, Kensington Gardens. He measured up the old man, squat in his black cassock. 'I suppose you've seen quite a few Vicars come and go.'

'Oh, yes, I've seen them all. We had a grand tradition here in the old days. Mind you, we manage to keep things up a lot better than they do most places nowadays.' His disapproving sniff conveyed a great deal. 'You've got to hand it to Father Gabriel – he does insist on maintaining standards.' A crafty look crossed his face. 'Of course, he might not be here that much longer. With the Archdeacon retiring . . . some people think he's about due for a promotion.'

The Bishop smiled non-committally. He'd been right – there was speculation in the church. They'd be looking for an announcement soon. How would the news be received? Ten years was long enough for a priest to stay in a parish. Would Gabriel Neville's departure be mourned?

The other servers, awed by the Bishop's presence, stayed out of the sacristy, so their conversation had been conducted in some privacy. But at that moment Mavis Conwell, one of the churchwardens, bustled in and hurried up to the Bishop. 'Your Worship, it's so wonderful to have you here today!' She grabbed his arm. 'Come along and have some sherry – I'm sure there are people you'd like to meet.'

She walked with him to the church hall. 'Actually,' she said confidingly, 'I'm glad to have a chance to have a word with you. Did you see the *News of the World* last week?'

The Bishop permitted himself an ironic smile. 'No, I'm not a regular reader of that publication. But I've heard about the fuss.' Indeed, it would have been difficult for anyone to have been unaware of the 'Pervie Precentor of Plymouth' scandal, rocking the Church of England for the past week.

Mavis, impervious to the irony, went on, 'Well, of course I don't read the *News of the World*, either, but I know people who do. And I think it's just disgusting.'

'What's disgusting, Mrs . . . er, Conwell?'

'That people like that are allowed to remain in the Church. Honestly! That's what's wrong with the Church today – there's not enough plain talk about what's right and what's wrong. And for a man of the cloth – a man of God – to tell a journalist that he has fantasies about choirboys – well! I know what I'd do with people like that!'

The Bishop replied mildly, 'And what would you do, Mrs Conwell?'

'Why, kick them out of the Church, of course! Just think about our young people, and the example that's being set for them. They're being corrupted and led astray by all these . . . people, and the Church is making it easy.'

Attempting to change the subject, the Bishop asked, 'Do you have children?'

A look of pride transfigured her plain face. 'I have a son, a good boy.' She frowned. 'But if I ever thought that anyone . . . well, their life wouldn't be worth living.' She was not easily diverted. 'What I really wanted to say was that we're very lucky here at St Anne's. Father Gabriel

may not always speak out as frankly as I'd like about
these things, but he's a good family man himself – not like
so many of these priests you hear about.' Here she stopped
in her tracks, faced him, and lowered her voice confidingly, fixing him with her gimlet eyes. 'There are rumours
. . . well, everyone says that he may be made Archdeacon
soon. And I just want you to know that I for one think it's
very important that our new priest, when we get one, should
be a family man.'

Taken aback, the Bishop replied, 'You know, don't
you, Mrs Conwell, that I don't have the patronage for this
appointment?' His natural discretion asserted itself. 'Even
if there were going to be a vacancy, and certainly no announcement has been made about that, the gift of the
living belongs to Lady Constance Oliver.'

Mavis Conwell was undeterred. 'Yes, but surely you
have some influence. I'm sure that Lady Constance would
listen to you. She knows how I feel, but if she were to hear
it from someone like the Bishop . . .'

'I'll keep it in mind,' he replied non-committally, resuming his progress towards the church hall.

Most of the congregation had already gathered there,
and were standing about in small groups, sipping sherry
and dissecting the service according to their own particular interests.

In one corner, Miles Taylor, the organist, was holding
forth to Wing Commander Cyril Fitzjames. 'You just have
no idea what I have to put up with,' he asserted earnestly.
'You churchwardens just have to parade around with your
staffs – or is it staves? – and look dignified. I have to hold
the entire service together. *And* cope with priests who
can't sing. We don't realise how lucky we are with Gab-

riel – he has a beautiful voice. But did you hear the Bishop? Sheer agony!'

Cyril Fitzjames made the appropriate noises of sympathy, though his attention was elsewhere. No one actually listened to Miles Taylor any longer. He'd been organist at St Anne's for several years now, but had run out of original conversational topics within the first few days. It must be said that he was a man of considerable musical talent, and had raised the standards at St Anne's noticeably. And he was not without charm, after an eccentric fashion. Many of the elderly ladies at St Anne's had been captivated by this young man's manner – they of course thought of him as a young man, though he must be over thirty. Tall, lanky and sandy-haired, he seemed to be all arms as he gesticulated wildly through every conversation.

'Of course the choir sounded all right – they know the Byrd four-part Mass backwards – though I can never understand why Gabriel insists on all that ancient stuff! It's just not moving with the times! There's so much good music being written these days that's never performed, because of old-fashioned priests who won't let a chap get on with his job! Now, at Selby . . .' He lifted his arms dramatically, exuding a faint whiff of cigarette smoke. 'If I've told the Vicar once—' He broke off and looked around suddenly. 'Where is the Vicar?'

Sensing his opportunity for escape, Cyril said quickly, 'I'll go and look for him,' and shambled off. Miles, temporarily thwarted, shrugged and went outside for a cigarette.

Emily chatted with the Sacristan, Daphne Elford, her mind only half on the conversation. Just after the service, Gabriel had slipped up to her and whispered that he had a

17

terrific headache and was going home. Poor Gabriel, the stress of the service had obviously been too much for him, though he had always enjoyed it in past years. Maybe this year was different, knowing that it was probably his last.

'Aren't you required in the sacristy? Putting away the vestments and the silver, and all that?' Emily asked.

Daphne snorted. 'You'd never know I was Sacristan, the way Venerable Bead takes over after Mass. He makes me feel like a trespasser in the sacristy, so I just stay away until after he's gone. Especially with the Bishop – he's acting like he's his personal property.'

Just then Emily noted the Bishop, pinned in the corner by the earnest Mavis Conwell. 'Oh, the poor Bishop. He'd be better off with Venerable Bead – look who's bending his ear.'

'No doubt telling him that the Church of England is going to the dogs. Perhaps I'd better rescue him and see that he meets a few people,' Daphne suggested.

The Bishop was drowning in a barrage of words, now centred chiefly on the weather. 'It's been a dreadful summer. When Craig was younger and my husband was alive we used to have some lovely holidays at the sea, but this year – why, I was hardly out of the hotel for the whole fortnight, it rained so much. It's got something to do with the ozone layer, I think, don't you?'

He was saved the necessity of a reply by the welcome intervention of Daphne, bringing him a glass of sherry. Mavis hung on doggedly for several minutes, then admitted defeat and marched over to where her friend Cecily Framlingham stood with the Dawsons. Cecily, a tall, hatchet-faced woman in her early fifties, was describing the difficulties she'd encountered in finding the flowers she'd wanted for today's service. 'You'd think, wouldn't you, that in the middle of summer you'd be able to get white roses? But there just aren't any to be had this year. And I did so want some for in front of the statue of Our Lady of Walsingham. White roses are just the thing for Our Lady. Chrysanths just aren't the same. I told my Arthur . . .'

'It's the ozone layer,' Mavis interjected. 'I was just telling the Bishop . . .'

Roger Dawson wrung his hands. He had a perpetually disgruntled look on his face. 'It doesn't really matter what flowers you use, as long as Our Lady of Walsingham is stuck in that corner where no one can see her. It's a disgrace. I shall tell the Bishop—'

'I really think that red roses are better for Our Lady,' interrupted Julia Dawson earnestly, her receding double chin quivering with emotion. 'They represent her suffering – the Sacred Heart, you know.'

'But white roses represent her purity,' explained Cecily. 'It's most important. Remember that sermon that the Vicar preached last year about Our Lady? How her purity was . . .'

'Where *is* the Vicar?' queried Roger Dawson. 'I haven't seen him since Mass.'

'Purity!' announced Mavis triumphantly. 'Now *that's* a quality that's lacking in the Church of England today! If only the Vicar would have the courage to preach about that! He should have been up there today denouncing that disgusting "Pervie Precentor" instead of talking about . . . whatever he was talking about. How can we expect proper standards to be upheld when clergy – even respectable married clergy – close ranks around their own? It's cowardice, I say.'

Meanwhile, in their favourite corner near the drinks table, the servers were also finding the 'Pervie Precentor' a fascinating topic of conversation.

In keeping with his position as head server, Tony Kent was as usual the spokesman for the group, and the leader of opinion. In his late twenties, Tony was also the oldest of the servers, with the notable exception of Venerable Bead: most of the servers were in their late teens or early twenties. Tony was a handsome young man with grey-blue eyes and straight, fine fair hair worn in a floppy fringe; well educated and articulate, he was a teacher of history and geography.

'Poor Old Norman Newsome – you've got to feel sorry for him,' he stated. 'Though talking to that journalist wasn't the smartest thing he's ever done.'

Venerable Bead, who had just joined the group after his self-imposed toils in the sacristy, nodded vigorously. 'I've met Norman Newsome, you know – last year, or was it the year before, when the Society of the Most Holy Blood had its annual do at Plymouth. He celebrated at the service, and he was brilliant. Biretta, lace down to his knees, and the liturgy . . . well, the man really knows what he's doing. It would be a crime for the Church to lose a man like that.'

'What will happen to him? Will he resign?' These questions were from the young ginger-haired server named Johnnie – or was it Chris? No one but Tony ever seemed to remember which was which. Close friends and always together, they were referred to indissolubly as 'Johnnie 'n' Chris' by those who knew them, and 'the dark one and the ginger one' by those who did not.

'Hard to say,' ventured Tony. 'The Dean says he won't

20

force his resignation, but the pressure is pretty strong. I don't know if he can hold out against it.'

'If he does resign, he'll never get another job in the Church of England,' Venerable stated.

The dark one – Chris – added, 'But it's not as if he's actually *done* anything! How can they hound him out of the Church just because he's had fantasies? I mean, who's perfect? The first stone, and all that?'

Tony shook his head. 'It's not what you think – or even what you do – that matters. Most people' – he shot a look at Mavis Conwell, still holding forth to her friends – 'most people don't really care, as long as they don't have to know about it. Some, of course, make an occupation out of knowing other people's business.'

Emily caught the end of this as she approached the cluster of servers, and exchanged smiles with Tony. 'Morning, Mrs Vicar,' he said, tugging on his floppy forelock. 'To what do we owe this favour?'

Emily played along, greeting him with a royal flourish. 'I don't want to interrupt anything, but I wanted to tell you all how excellent the serving was this morning. I didn't see a single mistake, and I know Gabriel really appreciated the care you've taken.'

'Where *is* Gabriel?' asked Venerable, looking around. 'I haven't seen him since he left the sacristy.'

'Oh, he's gone home with a headache.' Emily tried to look unconcerned. 'I suppose the pressures of the service – with the new Bishop and everything – must have caught up with him. And of course things are very difficult for him now, between curates. All the workload is falling on him.'

'Well,' said Venerable, with a cagy expression, 'I suppose the pressure really is on, with the Archdeacon retiring. The Bishop must be taking a very close look at Gabriel right now.'

Discreet as always, Emily changed the subject quickly. 'Thank you especially for looking after Sebastian. He's been looking forward to this day for a long time. I hope he didn't give you too much trouble.'

'Oh, no, he was as good as gold. He knew he wouldn't dare misbehave, and I don't think he would have wanted to,' replied the thurifer.

'Well, he's certainly pleased with himself now,' Emily said. 'Next week he's going to want to be crucifer!'

'I think he might find the cross just a bit heavy for him,' laughed Tony. 'But I'm sure he won't be boat boy for ever. Was Viola upset to be left out?'

'Dreadfully. I've always told her she can be anything she wants to be. So now she wants to know why she can't be the first female server at St Anne's.'

Venerable bristled angrily. Before he could speak, Tony interposed, 'Can you imagine what the Dawsons would say?'

Emily laughed. 'They don't even approve of *me*, you know. Married clergy are definitely not the thing, in their book.'

The Bishop was at that moment enduring a session of hearing the Dawsons' views on the sad state of the Church of England, and most particularly Anglo-Catholic worship at St Anne's. Their main grievance, as far as he could tell, was that Father Neville failed to treat the Walsingham Cell, of which Roger was clearly the leader, with the due respect and deference it deserved, or indeed to accord it any pre-eminence among Church organisations.

Mary Hughes, a gentle spinster of the parish, joined them and tried to turn the conversation in a more positive direction. 'Don't you think we're fortunate to have such a good choir – and such a gifted organist?' she asked. The Bishop nodded and she went on, 'And of course there's that clever little machine on the organ.' Before the Bishop could respond, an extraordinary-looking old woman hobbled up and confronted them. 'It's Beryl Ball,' Mary Hughes whispered warningly. 'Don't pay any attention to what she says.'

Beryl Ball was, as always, very smartly dressed in the cast-off clothes which she purchased at the jumble sales of the fashionable London churches. But the overall effect was just slightly bizarre, set off with the bright green moonboots which she always wore. She fixed the gathering for a moment with a stare, her eyes magnified alarmingly behind thick spectacles. Then she startled the Bishop by thrusting out her false teeth with her tongue, and settling them back into place, before she spoke. 'It won't do you any good, you know,' she announced. 'I can tell that you want me, but I'm telling you right now that I'm pure. No man has ever touched me, and no man ever will.' She looked at the Bishop challengingly, defying him to deny it. 'I've been in this church for a long time, and every Vicar who's been here has wanted me, but I've kept myself pure.' She lowered her voice, shooting a look at Emily. 'Not that I wasn't tempted by this last one. Oh, he was a beautiful young man, and he didn't half want me. I very nearly gave in to him. But then *she* came along and stole him away from me. No better than a prostitute, is that one. She came between me and the Vicar, and that's no mistake.' Her expression was pure venom. The Bishop gazed

23

with repelled fascination at the magnified eyes with their dilated pupils.

Mary Hughes tried to intervene. 'Beryl, now you know that's not true . . .'

Beryl Ball turned on her fiercely. 'Shut up, Mary Hughes! Everyone knows that you wanted him for yourself! All the women wanted him, but he wanted me, until that whore made him marry her!'

The Bishop opened his mouth, then shut it again. He knew it wasn't true, but what sort of man was this who inspired such passionate feelings? What sort of man was he about to recommend to be Archdeacon?

Chapter 3

*O go not from me, for trouble is hard at hand: and
there is none to help me.*

Psalm 22.11

After the splendours of the morning service, and later Solemn
Evensong and Benediction, the seven forty-five Low Mass
was a welcome relief. Gabriel conducted the service quietly,
his head still throbbing with a dull pain behind his eyes.
This wasn't like him, to feel unwell. Not like him, either,
to dwell on negative feelings. What shall I do? he thought.
There's no one I can talk to, no one who can help me. No
one who would understand. If only I could confide in
Emily, and she could tell me what to do . . . And then a
name came into his mind unbidden, and resounded there.
David. I must talk to David.

The congregation was small, but Lady Constance was
there as she usually was. After the service, Gabriel waited
for her to finish saying her rosary in the Lady Chapel, and
approached her as she rose to her feet. She was an impos-
ing woman, rather tall and with a stately carriage. Her
silver hair was immaculately waved above her fine-fea-
tured face, delicate fair skin webbed with the tiny lines of
old age. 'I want to apologise to you for this morning,' he

began. 'I'd intended to have a glass of sherry with you and the Bishop, but I got a terrific headache during the service, and had to go straight home.'

She looked closely at him, noting the faint purple marks of pain under his eyes. 'I do hope you're feeling better now,' she said with concern.

He smiled with an effort. 'I tried to get some rest during the afternoon, and of course Emily did her best to wave her magic wand and make it go away. She fixed me some foul-tasting herbal brew, and kept the children quiet – and that was quite an accomplishment, believe me.'

'Your wife is a treasure. I hope you realise that,' said Lady Constance with a smile.

'My greatest asset,' Gabriel agreed. 'I don't know where I – or the parish – would be without her.'

A good choice . . .

It was probably because he was so unaccustomedly thinking about the past that when Emily's face appeared in his mind's eye, it was not the self-assured Emily of today that he saw, but the Emily of ten years ago, at their first meeting.

Cyril Fitzjames, churchwarden even then, brought her over to him with a faintly proprietary flourish. 'Father Gabriel, I think you should meet Miss Emily Bates. Her father is an old friend of mine.' Shy, quiet Emily, just down from Cambridge with a First in English. She looked up at him, her small heart-shaped face framed by sleek wings of dark hair, her dark eyes glowing with a quick intelligence, and with something more . . .

Was it from that moment that he had determined the shape of his future?

The future, the past . . .

David.

Gabriel hesitated for a moment before the Sacristan's flat. He occasionally turned up for a quiet drink after the evening services, so Daphne wasn't likely to be suspicious of ulterior motives. But how exactly was he going to bring up the subject of David, without making it seem forced? He'd have to play it very carefully, make it look like her idea somehow. He rang the bell deliberately.

Daphne's round face creased with pleasure as she opened the door. 'Why, Gabriel! Do come in.'

Daphne's flat was as homely and welcoming as she was; Gabriel felt instantly at ease in its comfortable shabbiness. He sank gratefully into an armchair and accepted a drink with thanks. Having women fussing around him was a constant feature of his job, and one Gabriel could very well have lived without, so Daphne's matter-of-fact treatment of him was always a welcome relief.

She wouldn't be described as feminine in any conventional sense: short and plump without any of the curves that might once have softened 'plump' into 'voluptuous', Daphne had a blunt, open face and roughly cut grey hair with no pretence of style. Her manner, too, said, 'Here I am – take me for what I am, or leave me.' And yet there was an essential vulnerability about her that tempered the honesty into something even more appealing. She could be counted on never to be small-minded, petty or judgemental. Gabriel, in common with most people, liked her very much.

He sipped his whisky for a few moments before speaking. 'I didn't have a chance to tell you this morning how much I appreciated all your hard work in getting the church ready for today. Everything looked absolutely splendid.'

'I can't take all the credit. You know I had a lot of help.'

'Yes, but I also know that you won't let anyone else touch the silver. You must have worn your fingers to the bone polishing it all.'

'Not exactly,' she replied, holding up stubby hands for inspection. 'But it does seem to multiply on these occasions.' She looked at him thoughtfully. 'That reminds me – I thought that Mavis Conwell was going to give us a new silver alms dish in memory of the late, lamented Richard. It must be nearly a year since he died – has she said anything about it lately?'

'No. Strange, isn't it? After he died, that was all she could talk about, but I haven't heard a word about it for several months now.'

'Well, the old one will do for the moment. I don't suppose we can press her on it.'

They sat in companionable silence for several minutes. Thank God Daphne's not one of those women who feels she has to fill every second with conversation, Gabriel reflected.

Daphne spoke at last. 'Have you heard anything from David lately?'

Gabriel smiled to himself. This was going to be easier than he'd thought.

'David Middleton-Brown? Not really. Of course I had an acknowledgement of the flowers for his mother's funeral, but nothing else. How is he doing? I'd meant to write him a proper letter of sympathy, but I had the Area Synod meeting that week, and the PCC . . .'

'I don't think he's handling it very well. You know

David.' She smiled fondly. 'She was a terrible old harridan, his mother, but she was all he had. It must have been hell for him, living with her, but he needs to be needed. Now he's got nothing, no one.'

'Have you spoken to him?'

'You know that David hates the telephone; never uses it unless he absolutely has to. No, I had a letter from him just yesterday. It was typical David: polished prose, all terribly light-hearted, but between the lines a real cry for help. I wondered if we might be able to help him – you and I.'

Gabriel was cautious. 'How? I realise you've known him much longer than I have, but I wouldn't have thought that he'd welcome help from either one of us.'

'Oh, I don't mean . . . Wait, I'll explain my idea,' Daphne replied. 'He seems to be at a real loose end at the moment. Apparently he'd booked a long summer holiday so he could take his mother to the seaside for a month. And now . . . well, he certainly doesn't want to go to the sea by himself, and his firm says he must go ahead and take the holiday, since they've planned the workload around him already – you know how inflexible solicitors can be.' She paused consideringly, then rushed ahead. 'I was wondering if we might invite him to come here for a while. I know he's refused our invitations before, but maybe under the circumstances . . .'

Behind the carefully maintained non-committal expression, Gabriel was jubilant. This was going far better than he could have hoped. 'You think he'd come?'

'Well, he might. If I were to write to him and invite him, and you were to write at the same time . . . We couldn't make it seem like we were trying to do him a

29

favour, or he wouldn't come. Maybe if we could let him think we needed him to do us a favour . . .' She considered, then went on. 'We could say we needed his help in sorting out something in the sacristy. Something to do with the silver, that required his expertise . . .'

'No good. You taught him practically everything he knows about church silver. Why would you need his help?'

'These old eyes aren't as good as they used to be on the hallmarks,' she chuckled. 'And you do him an injustice – he knows much more about silver than I do. But no. I've got it. The Comper crypt chapel. You know how long that project has been hanging fire! Lady Constance has offered to fund the repairs to the polychrome walls and roof, in her brother's memory. We've even been granted the faculty for the work. You know the only reason it hasn't been done yet – we need to be sure we're doing it exactly right.'

'And who better than David to advise on that?' Gabriel finished. 'I must admit, that will be pretty irresistible bait for him. He'll protest, say he isn't qualified, that he doesn't know any more about Comper or polychrome or gilding than the average man in the street – but he'll come.' He paused and took a sip of his drink before considering the next difficulty. 'Where will he stay?'

'Of course he can stay here. I have an extra room.'

'Will he think that's proper?'

Daphne smiled wryly. 'I'm an old woman. He's an old friend. Why shouldn't it be proper?'

'That's settled, then.' Gabriel was silent for another minute, thinking. This might be the most difficult part. He continued, slowly, 'One more thing. I'd appreciate it if . . . well, that is, I'd rather it looked like he was visiting *you*, not me.' She looked at him, inquiring. 'I can't really explain, but I just think it would be better if the parish didn't know generally that we knew each other. In fact, it might be better if the letter inviting him came just from you, and I kept out of it entirely. Would you mind?'

She was puzzled but compliant; Daphne had long ago learned not to ask Gabriel – or David, either – too many questions, especially when she wasn't sure she wanted to know the answers. 'I won't say a word. Would you like another drink?'

Gabriel rose with a satisfied smile. 'I'd love one, but I'd better not. I'd better be on my way – you have a letter to write, and the sooner the better.'

Chapter 4

*These wait all upon thee: that thou givest them
meat in due season.*

Psalm 104.27

The lounge bar of the country pub was almost empty, but
Emily chose a table in the back corner and sank into the
chair with a sigh, exhausted after the morning's task of
delivering the twins to her parents for a short visit. 'Sit
down, Lucy. I don't know about you, but I'm absolutely
starving.'

'Don't you want to order a drink?'

'I'd love to, but I'm driving, so I'd better not. Just an
orange juice and lemonade, I think.'

She watched her friend order the drinks, then thread her
way back to the table, balancing one in each hand. Lucy
managed to perform even such a mundane task with unnatural grace. She sat down and pushed her hair back from
her face with a characteristic gesture.

Lucy Kingsley's hair had, in childhood, been bright
red; now, in her thirties, it had faded to an attractive
strawberry blonde. But it retained all of its natural curl,
and it fell to her shoulders in a cascade of waves and
ringlets. She had a long white neck, and her colouring was

33

of the peaches-and-cream sort that so often accompanies that particular shade of hair; she accentuated her very English type of beauty by dressing in pastel-coloured floral Laura Ashley prints.

She faced Emily across the table and raised her wine glass. 'Cheers, Em. Now, what's up? Why the sudden invitation to accompany you on this mission? Did one of your men-friends stand you up?'

'Don't be daft. Let's order first – I'm really famished.' Emily applied herself to the menu. 'I'm going to be really wicked and order the kind of thing I'd never let the children have. A huge plate of fried scampi and chips, I think,' she said to the waitress who had materialised beside their table.

'And I'll have the avocado and smoked chicken salad.'

'That doesn't sound like much, Luce. Aren't you hungry?'

Lucy shook her head, then smiled mischievously at Emily. 'We could have eaten at your parents', you know. Your mother positively begged us to stay for lunch.'

Emily grimaced. 'Very funny. You don't know what it's like to have a mother who can't cook. I love my mother very much, but I have no illusions about her culinary abilities. She's the only person I know who can ruin a cheese sandwich.'

'Then how can you bear to leave your children there?'

'I'll admit it's difficult. But they're only six – too young to suffer any permanent damage from bad cooking.' She laughed. 'Of course when I was their age, I had no basis of comparison – I thought everyone cooked like that. School dinners were an absolute treat for me!'

'But Viola and Sebastian know better. You're a good

cook, Em. They're used to a pretty high standard of food.'

'Thanks to you.' She smiled reminiscently. 'It seems like such a long time ago now – those days when I was first married, and didn't have the first idea what to do in the kitchen. And you offered to teach me. I don't know how I would have managed without you, Luce.'

'You could have kept the housekeeper. After all, Gabriel got by somehow before he married you.' Lucy added, 'Anyway, I seem to recall you telling me that *his* mother was not exactly brilliant in the kitchen.'

Emily laughed. 'I never knew her, of course, but I have it on good authority that she never even knew where the kitchen was!'

'Not impossible in that sort of grand house, I suppose. Poor little Gabriel, only the cook to blame for a deprived childhood.' Lucy rolled her eyes. 'How is the Angel Gabriel, by the way?' she added ironically.

'All right.' Emily was silent for a moment, moving her glass around and leaving damp circles on the polished wood table-top. 'Men . . . you know what they're like.'

Lucy studied her bent head, certain that she was getting close to the reason for today's invitation. 'All too well. What's he up to now?'

Emily's laugh was affectionate but bemused. 'He's been in a real strop the last day or two. There's just no pleasing him.'

'What's brought it on? A week of the children's summer hols?'

'I don't think so.' She reflected. 'There was only one day last week when it didn't rain, and he went with us to Kensington Gardens. Viola insisted on looking at Peter Pan, as usual, and Sebastian wanted to sail his boat on the

Round Pond. Gabriel was fine that day – he really seemed to enjoy it.'

'And since then?'

'Well, I've managed pretty well to keep the children out of his hair when he's had work to do. He worked ever so hard on his sermon for the Patronal Festival yesterday.' She shook her head. 'He's overworked since the last curate left, of course, and the new one won't come till the end of the summer. But I'm sure it's all this pressure over the Archdeaconry. I think he felt that yesterday was the big test.'

'And was it?'

'Probably. The Area Bishop was there, of course. You know how these things work. The position won't be vacant for some months – the end of the year, I think – but I'm sure they're already close to taking a decision, and the Bishop of London will want the Area Bishop's recommendation. It's really no wonder Gabriel felt pressurised. He wants that job very badly.'

'How soon will he know?'

'Probably not for a month or so. The sooner the better, as far as I'm concerned,' Emily declared. 'Gabriel can be obsessive, but he usually handles it better. That's why I think this promotion must be very important to him.'

'What exactly has he done?' Lucy touched her friend's arm, and added facetiously, 'He hasn't been beating you, has he? I didn't really think the Angel Gabriel would resort to physical violence!'

'Hardly,' Emily laughed. 'Oh, look, here's the food.' For a few minutes she concentrated on the scampi in silence, then continued, 'You know that Gabriel is never ill. He prides himself on that – always says it's all in the mind. Well, yesterday, after the service, he went home with a headache! I've never known him to have a headache. He even missed having a sherry with the Bishop, so he must really have felt rotten.'

'That does sound like stress. Then what?'

'I brewed him up some of my herbal headache remedy – it's an infusion of lavender flowers, lemon balm and a few other bits – and the way he complained you would have thought I was trying to poison him! Honestly!'

'Was he any better today?'

'No, that's the point. I don't think he slept very well, and this morning he was singularly uncommunicative.'

'He was meant to go with you to your parents', I take it.'

'Yes, he was having a day off to take the twins to Mum and Dad's. I was really looking forward to having a quiet day with him after the big weekend. I thought that after a decent interval with my parents, we could escape and maybe go somewhere on the way home – somewhere in the country where we could have a nice long walk, if the weather was decent. But this morning he shut himself in his study, and only put his head out long enough to say that he had some very important work to do, and would I mind if he didn't go along?'

'So that's where I came in,' Lucy mused, twisting a corkscrew of hair around her finger.

'Yes. I just couldn't face the prospect of an hour in the car, with the children scrapping in the back seat, and I didn't think you'd mind keeping me company, Luce. Gabriel suggested it, in fact.'

Emily missed the quick flash of antagonism in her friend's eyes, as Lucy carefully controlled herself and said neutrally, 'I suppose he thinks I haven't got a proper job, so it doesn't make any difference.' She added more warmly, 'I'm glad. We don't very often have a day out together, Em, and I think we should make the most of it. He won't be expecting you back for a while yet, will he? Where shall we go after lunch?'

Chapter 5

*He chose David also his servant: and took him away
from the sheep-folds.*

Psalm 78.71

As usual it had been a long night, and there was nothing to
get up for. David Middleton-Brown looked up at the ceiling,
his mind blank. Gradually the noises of the postman – the
advancing steps, the clink of the gate, the clatter of the
letter-box, the retreating steps – seeped through to his
consciousness, and gave him an excuse to get out of bed.

I hate holidays, he thought grimly, slipping into his
dressing-gown. And the only thing worse than staying at
home for a holiday is going away. He padded quietly
down the hall, pausing without thinking to look into his
mother's room. The curtains were wide open and the white
counterpane stretched smoothly across the bed. The room
was empty, empty even of the force of her strong personality. David would have sworn that that, at least, would
have survived her death, would have left an imprint on
this room.

'I don't know why I bother,' he muttered to himself as
he descended the stairs. 'It's probably just bills. And ad-
vertisements for double glazing.'

Indeed, as he stooped to retrieve the pile of envelopes, he recognised an electricity bill on the top. He shuffled through quickly: another bill, a newsletter from the Kempe Society, a brochure for the Wymondham Choral Society's next season, a catalogue from an antiquarian bookseller, some communication from the Law Society. He paused as an envelope with Daphne Elford's distinctive, nearly illegible handwriting emerged from the pile. You'd never know from her writing that she'd been a school teacher, he reflected idly. The next envelope . . . his heart lurched involuntarily as he recognised the elegant pen strokes. Gabe, he thought. My God, Gabe.

With characteristic self-control, David carefully laid the letters, unopened, on the hall table and went into the kitchen to make himself a pot of tea. He concentrated almost obsessively on the ritual, willing himself not to think. He filled the kettle and switched it on, retrieved the teapot from its shelf, took a mug from a hook – Mother wouldn't approve; she insisted on a cup and saucer – and got out the little silver milk-jug, bought for next to nothing years ago at a junk shop on one of his jaunts with Daphne. But he found no milk in the fridge and had to avert his eyes from the pile of post as he made his way to the front door. The milk bottle stood in a puddle of water on the porch. Damn, he thought. Another wet day.

By the time he'd returned to the kitchen and filled the milk-jug, the kettle had nearly boiled. He poured a bit of the water into the pot and swirled it around, then reached for the tea-canisters. Two spoons of English Breakfast and one spoon of Darjeeling, a legacy from Mother. She liked her tea made properly, and wouldn't have a tea-bag in the house. As he poured the boiling water over the fragrant leaves, her words came back to him. 'Nasty things, tea-bags, and not good for you, either. Mark my words, David. Someday they'll find out that the paper in tea-bags gives you cancer.'

David put the things on a tray and carried it through to what his mother had called the sitting room. This room strongly reflected her taste, and he'd always hated it. The crocheted white doilies that to her had indicated refinement were everywhere, on the chair-arms and under the lamps. The lampshades were of a nasty pretentious sort, scalloped rose-coloured satin with little silky pink tassels. A monstrous television set had pride of place, a bland cyclops straddling the corner. Much as David had complained about having a television in the room, she had insisted. 'If you can afford to have a nice big television, what's the point of hiding it away somewhere where no one can see it?' That's what I'll do this holiday, he decided suddenly – change this ghastly room. And that television will be the first thing to go. As a first step he unplugged it, and immediately felt better.

It was time. He went into the hall for the post; while the tea steeped he looked at the Choral Society brochure – a nice programme, he thought. He laid it aside and poured the tea, then fetched the letter-knife from the ornate bureau in the alcove beside the fireplace. The fireplace – that was another of his mother's great prides. At terrific expense she'd had the efficient and homely coal fire bricked up ('So dirty, don't you think?') and a gas fire with a marble hearth and 'real flame-effect' logs installed. David despised its synthetic perfection.

He resumed his seat and opened Daphne's letter with mild curiosity. His correspondence with her was intermit-

41

tent, but had continued over nearly twenty years, and he'd heard from her several times since his mother's death.

Dear David,

You may be surprised to hear from me again so soon, but I have a problem and I hope you may be able to help me with it. I've told you about St Anne's Comper crypt chapel – I've probably mentioned that in recent years it's suffered rather badly from damp, and the paintwork is peeling from the walls and the roof. Lady Constance Oliver – I'm sure you've heard me speak of her – has offered to pay for the repairs and restoration, but no one here has the expertise to advise on what needs doing. We want it done properly, and I don't know where to begin to find the craftsmen, materials, etc. Even if you could only stay for a few days, I'd really appreciate it if you could come and have a look, and let me know what you think. Any time would be fine – my spare room is always free, and you can stay as long as you like. A few days in London might do you good! Let me know . . .

It tailed off, and was signed, Affectionately yours, Daphne.

He re-read it thoughtfully. She'd almost had him taken in, until she gave herself away with that last bit about a few days in London doing him good. A put-up job, that's what it was. Good try, Daphne old girl, he said to himself. I've got to hand it to you – the Comper chapel is a masterstroke! He'd write tomorrow and decline. Still, a Comper chapel . . . it would almost be worth going. Almost.

He took a sip of tea, then gulped down half the mug.

Out of the corner of his eye he could see it – Gabe's letter. It hadn't gone away, wouldn't go away. He couldn't put it off for ever. David picked up the stiff envelope and forced himself to study it for a moment. If Gabe's fluid script weren't so distinctive, he might not even have recognised it, so infrequently had he seen it. Letter-writing had never been Gabe's style, and the annual Christmas cards were always addressed and signed by Emily. Ten years, he thought. Ten bloody years. With a swift slash he opened the envelope, and extracted the letter. It was written on heavy notepaper with the letterhead of St Anne's Vicarage. There were only a few lines. He willed his eyes to focus on them, his brain to absorb them.

Dear David,
    You should be receiving a letter from Daphne, asking you to come and advise us on the restoration of the Comper chapel. She doesn't know that I'm writing this, asking you to please consider coming. We really could use and would appreciate your help with this. But there's another reason that Daphne knows nothing about. Something's come up and I don't know where else to turn. Please come, David – come soon. I need you. Don't let me down.

It was signed simply, G.
    David sat still for a long time, the blood pounding in his head. Through all the pent-up emotions of ten years which now raged in him – the pain, the hurt, the love, and, yes, the anger – shone that brief sentence, like a shaft of sunlight through a storm cloud, piercing in its sweetness. I need you.

43

Gabe needed him. Years ago he'd needed Gabe, but Gabe had never needed *him*. Gabe had loved him – of that he was sure. It was that certainty alone that had kept him going through much of the last ten years. But needed him? Never. No more than the planet Jupiter, cloaked in beauty and mystery, needed the tiny moons that spun around it.

Gabe needed him. If he left now, he could be in London by lunch-time. He felt in his dressing-gown pocket for his car keys; the utter ridiculousness of this action returned him to reality.

And with reality came the realisation that things had changed in ten years. Emily. No matter how or why Gabe needed him, Emily would be there.

David rose and started upstairs, unaware of what he was doing, his thoughts now centred on Emily. How could he go; how could he bear to meet her? Through ten years of imaginings she had grown in his mind into a selfish, grasping monster. How else to explain the inexplicable? She had cold-bloodedly trapped Gabe into marriage, that was clear. It was against his nature. Therefore he was an innocent victim, a lamb to the slaughter, and she was a scheming bitch. It was the money, he supposed, and the position; maybe she even fancied him – he couldn't blame her for that. But why, Gabe? Why?

As he'd done so many times before, he tried to imagine her, this woman who had captured Gabe. She must be attractive, at least in a superficial way. A Sloane Ranger type, he supposed. Blonde. Probably a lot of hair. Long red-lacquered fingernails. Hard, calculating eyes set in a pretty, vacuous face. She was supposed to be bright, something of an intellectual even, he'd heard, but he didn't believe it. Street-smart, more likely, with an eye to a good thing.

So great was his loathing of this unknown woman that he'd gone to every length to avoid meeting her. He'd declined the invitation to the wedding – of course! that was pain beyond enduring – and all subsequent half-hearted invitations from Gabe to come for a visit. He'd even refused to visit Daphne in the two years since she'd been at St Anne's, insisting instead that she come to him for their periodic reunions; he'd had his mother's bad health as an excuse, and Daphne had never questioned that. And of course he was too proud to ask Daphne about Emily, to try to find out what she was really like. How could he face Emily now?

He was facing himself now, staring at his own image in the dusty mirror. Dusty? He looked around with surprise to find that he had gone past his own room and climbed the narrow stairs into the attic room.

This room, shabby as it was, had been his only real refuge from his mother; she had been unable for years to negotiate the steep steps, little more than a ladder really. David hadn't been up there since she died – there was no more need to escape.

It was also the room which evoked the strongest memories of Gabe, and he knew, looking down at the letter still clutched in his hand, that those associations had drawn him here now. Gabe had visited this house just once, for a week's holiday, against David's better judgement. But his misgivings had been unfounded, and the week had been magic. Mother had adored Gabe. Gabe was always charming even without trying, and he'd made a special effort to be captivating that week. Even Dad, who had rarely said anything, had been drawn out by his easy manner into actual conversation, day after day.

And night after night . . . they'd been together in this room. Mother had never been one for having people to stay, and there was no spare room for that purpose. So David had given up his room to Gabe, and had moved into the attic. There, night after night, Gabe, loving him, wanting him, had crept silently up the stairs, in spite of David's initial frantic protests. There under his parents' roof, in the house of his childhood, though he was approaching thirty he felt like a naughty schoolboy, terrified of being caught.

But they hadn't been caught, and the joy was all the sweeter for the fear. It was in the early days of their love, when everything was new and each discovery brought a fresh sense of wonder.

Candlelight. Gabe, boyish, sprawling on the bed. Laughing up at him, his eyes in shadow, his soft lips curved, his hair glinting on the pillow. The arms, outstretched, inviting . . .

Their behaviour, during those enchanted candlelit nights, had been reckless, certainly; possibly even irresponsible and unwise. But an older and wiser David could not regret the most complete happiness he'd ever known. He could only regret that it had ended.

David gazed again at the mirror. He no longer felt like a schoolboy, and he recognised, with the shock of one who usually looks into a mirror without seeing, that it had been a long time since he'd looked like one. His face, never particularly handsome (why had Gabe loved him?) was at least beginning to look what people kindly called distinguished, with that hint of grey at the temples, while the fleshy pouches under his eyes spoke of long tiring days and sleepless nights. And his body, though still reasonably trim, had lost the suppleness of youth.

Gabe will be ten years older, too, he realised suddenly. Funny. He'd always pictured him looking jüst as he had then, perpetually beautiful, untouched by time. He found himself wondering exactly what he would find when he arrived in London, as he knew he must. Gabe needed him.

Chapter 6

Thy tongue imagineth wickedness: and with lies thou
cuttest like a sharp razor.
Thou hast loved unrighteousness more than goodness:
and to talk of lies more than righteousness.

Psalm 52.3–4

'So, what did you do today, all on your own?' Gabriel
asked his wife over their evening meal on the following
day, Wednesday.

Emily considered. 'Well, this morning I made a couple
of batches of jam for the fête. If I make some every day
for the next week, and maybe bake a cake or two for the
freezer, it won't be so awful at the last minute.'

'How about this afternoon? You were out, weren't you?'

She made a slightly guilty face. 'Yes, I went down to
Kensington High Street for the summer sales. It's so difficult to do the sales properly with the children along, so it
seemed a good opportunity. Lucy met me along the way,
and we had a nice tea at the Muffin Man afterwards.'

'Did you buy anything?'

'Mostly things for the twins. I got them some lovely
cotton jumpers at Marks and Spencer's – they've quite
grown out of the ones they had last year.'

49

'You miss the children, don't you?' Gabriel smiled sympathetically.

She looked at the empty chairs. 'I really do. It's so quiet in the house without them, especially when you're away in the evening. But I mustn't be selfish – my parents do so enjoy having them to stay, and spoiling them with little treats.'

Gabriel consulted his watch. 'Well, I won't be out long this evening. I need to pay a call on that new family in the parish, but the churchwardens are coming by at eight for a meeting about the Quinquennial Inspection, so I should be back by then.'

Emily grimaced. 'You'd better be. For heaven's sake, don't leave me alone with that appalling Mavis Conwell. I can't be held responsible for what I might say to one of her frightful remarks.'

'I'm sure that Cyril will be on hand, more than happy to come to your rescue as your knight in shining armour.' Gabriel's smile was tinged with malice.

Emily stuck her tongue out at him affectionately. 'Poor old Cyril – he can't help it. Anyway,' she added, 'I don't make fun of all the women who are in love with *you*.'

'Except Beryl Ball.'

'Except Beryl Ball,' she conceded readily. Glancing at the clock, she asked, 'Have you got time for a coffee?'

'Just about. I'll probably get offered one later, but it's always best not to count on it.'

Emily rose and went into the kitchen. Gabriel sat quietly, abstractedly drawing designs on the tablecloth with the tip of his knife, a small frown between his brows. The phone bleated in the hall and he jumped, startled.

'Stay there – I'll get it,' Emily called, then put her head

round the door a moment later. 'It's Daphne, she says she wants a quick word.'

'Ah.' In a few strides he was in the hall, picking up the receiver. He tried to keep the eagerness out of his voice. 'Yes, Daphne?'

'Oh, hello, Gabriel. I've been out all afternoon and just got home to find a reply from David in the second post.'

'And?'

'He's coming. On Friday, he says. I just thought you'd like to know.'

He closed his eyes and sighed, then said, 'Thanks. That's good. Will he come straight to you?'

'Yes, I expect it will be sometime in the afternoon. I'll probably take him over to the church and show him the crypt chapel.'

'Why don't you give me a ring when he's arrived, and I'll meet you there?'

'Fine. I'll talk with you then.'

'Thanks, Daphne. I'm sure it will do him good to have a change of scenery.'

'Right. Ta.'

Gabriel replaced the receiver and felt his shoulders relax. David's coming, he told himself. He'll get to the bottom of this somehow: everything will be all right.

He returned to the dining room and accepted the steaming cup of coffee with the first real smile he'd given his wife in days. 'Thanks, my love.'

Gabriel hadn't yet returned when the doorbell sounded, a few minutes before eight. Emily went to answer it with a sinking heart. If I'm lucky it will be Cyril, she thought – I can cope with him, anyway. But on the doorstep, under a

51

dripping umbrella, stood Mavis Conwell. As Emily beckoned her indoors, Mavis's small eyes, fractionally too close together, swivelled round to see if she were indeed the first to arrive. 'Am I early? Father Gabriel said eight.'

'I'm very sorry, Mavis. He's not back yet. He went out on a pastoral call about an hour ago. Can I offer you a coffee?' Emily took the proffered umbrella and the wet raincoat with a cordial smile.

'Thank you, Emily, that would be very nice.'

'Why don't you make yourself comfortable in the drawing room?' she suggested. But Mavis followed her into the kitchen and watched her fill the kettle.

'Actually,' Mavis confided, 'it's nice to have a chance to chat with you. It seems like I hardly ever see you to talk to.'

'I'm usually around,' Emily replied, with a vague wave of her hand. 'But I suppose there are always people who want to have a word with the Vicar's wife.'

'Exactly,' Mavis rejoined. 'And it's just lovely the way you try to make time for all of them.'

Emily opened a cupboard and took out the sugar basin. 'That's all I can do.'

'No, you go far beyond that. For example, I think it's just wonderful the way you've been counselling that head server, Tony Kent. Not everyone would have the courage.'

Frankly puzzled, Emily frowned. 'What do you mean?'

'Well, everyone knows he's a' – Mavis lowered her voice conspiratorially and glanced around – 'you know, a homosexual.' She almost hissed the word. 'And for a woman like you, with a small son, to counsel him – well, that's what I call an act of real Christian charity.'

'Counsel him?'

'I've seen you talking to him after church on Sundays, and I do think it's very brave. Someone must have the courage to tell these people that what they're doing is an abomination before God. I'd do it myself, but I'm sure he'd listen more to you, being the Vicar's wife and all. And a bit nearer his age,' she added.

'But Tony's a friend,' Emily protested, baffled.

'Of course he is, dear,' Mavis agreed smugly. 'They say that we have to befriend these people before we can really help them. He *does* want to be helped, doesn't he?'

'I think he's perfectly happy the way he is.'

Mavis was horrified. 'It will probably take you an awful lot of counselling then. But do be careful. I mean, you never know what you might pick up from these people. Not to mention the danger to Sebastian.'

Emily didn't know whether she wanted to laugh or to scream at her, but she controlled her expression and said mildly, 'I don't think Sebastian's in any danger. And I don't know what you think I could catch from Tony.'

'Oh, I didn't mean AIDS, though on that score I don't think you can be too careful, do you? But, well, I don't know . . . Those people go to such horrible places . . .'

Emily took a deep breath and deliberately changed the subject. 'How is Craig? I haven't seen him for quite a while.'

Mavis beamed. 'He's just fine. I know he doesn't come to church very often – it's not "his scene", as he says, but he's a *good* boy. No harm in him.' Unwilling to let the subject drop, she went on, 'Quite a one for the girls, is my Craig. I'm just so glad that I have no worries on that score.'

'But what about the girls? Don't you worry about them?'

'Girls these days can take care of themselves. They're all on the Pill, aren't they? Anyway, I'd rather have him get a girl pregnant than to be . . . the other way. I just thank God that I have a manly son!'

Emily was saved the necessity of replying by the pealing of the doorbell. 'Excuse me a moment, Mavis. That must be Cyril.'

Wing Commander Cyril Fitzjames stood on the doorstep, smiling fondly at Emily as she opened the door. 'Good evening, my dear,' he boomed, smoothing his hair carefully across his head. Although he was quite bald on top, he had cultivated a very long piece of hair on the side of his head with which he endeavoured to disguise the fact; the parting started just above his right ear. The effect was never very convincing, and at times was frankly bizarre, but it satisfied his vanity.

He stepped inside, shaking the rain from his mac like a big wet dog. Emily had often thought there was much that was dog-like about him, from his appearance to his devotion to her. He was a large man, and in his prime had been impressive, with his broad shoulders and erect carriage. But the muscle had gone to fat and the military bearing had become a stooped shamble. He had a jowly, heavy face with drooping eyelids and liver-spots, and his hands, large and mottled with age, had a slight tremble. Emily took his mac and offered her cheek for the inevitable kiss.

'So what's this meeting tonight all about, my dear?' he bellowed. 'Gabriel didn't say. You'd think a chap had nothing better to do than come out in this rain for a blasted meeting.'

'Oh, something about the Quinquennial Inspection, I think he said.'

Mavis appeared at the kitchen door, clutching her coffee cup. 'What's the Quinquennial Inspection?'

Cyril smiled condescendingly. 'Ah, Mrs Conwell! When you've been churchwarden as long as I have, you'll know what the Quinquennial Inspection is, all right!'

'Well, what is it?'

'Quin – that's five, if you remember your Latin. Every five years the diocese comes in to make sure that everything is shipshape. Looks over the building, goes over the books.' He gave a short, barking laugh and wagged his finger at her roguishly. 'So if you've been pinching money, you're sure to get caught, my girl!' He broke off as the door opened and the Vicar blew in on a gust of rain. 'Ah, Gabriel, my dear boy! Let the meeting commence!'

It wasn't until much later that Emily discovered the coffee stain on the hall carpet, but she managed to get most of it up so that it hardly showed.

Chapter 7

*I have considered the days of old: and the years that
are past.*
*I call to remembrance my song: and in the night I
commune with mine own heart, and search out
my spirits.*

Psalm 77.5–6

Driving across the Fens alone was depressing even at the
best of times, David reflected, and this wet summer day
was anything but the best of times. The low clouds were
unbroken, the rain unremitting, and there was no
compensating warmth in the air. In spite of his resolution
not to dwell on the past, David found himself remembering
a happier time, driving back to Brighton with Gabe beside
him at the end of that lovely week. The drive from Brighton
to Norfolk at the beginning of the week had been tense,
fraught with his anxieties about the wisdom of the enterprise,
and the leaden sky had threatened snow. But at the end of
the holiday they'd both been basking in the warm glow of
their love. It was an afternoon in mid-winter and the Fens
had never been more beautiful. In a cloudless sky, dusk
was closing in early; the horizon glowed like a creamy
iridescent pink pearl. Each twig on every tree – thousands,

57

millions of twigs – stood out in stark relief, like intricate black lace, against the nacreous sky, and the black birds perched in the trees were silent. David and Gabe had been silent, too.

David groaned now with frustration as a lumbering farm vehicle pulled out in front of him from a side crossing. He'd never get to London at this rate. He was unused to London traffic: it had been years since he'd lived there, as a student and as a trainee solicitor, and in the intervening years the evening rush-hour seemed to have begun earlier and earlier. By the time he'd negotiated the M25, then Finchley, St John's Wood and Paddington, it was nearly tea-time and he was in a black mood when he pulled up in front of Daphne's flat.

Daphne had been watching for several hours from her vantage-point at the window, the latest P. D. James novel unopened on her lap. In the morning she'd cleaned her flat, bathed, and taken special care with her appearance. Silly old woman, she'd grumbled wryly to herself, but she'd still put on a new coral-coloured jumper with her best summer skirt. She realised, as she sat looking out the window, that her motives in asking David here had not been entirely unselfish, but that uncomfortable knowledge did not prevent her from taking pleasure in anticipating his arrival. Self-knowledge did not always come easily to Daphne, but once it was achieved, she didn't shrink from its implications.

As the ancient brown Morris ground to a halt outside, she resisted the impulse to go outside and meet him; she remained in her chair and counted to ten after the bell went. But any potential awkwardness in their meeting was dispelled as she spontaneously burst out laughing at the sight of his grim face.

'I don't know what's so damned funny,' he said peevishly.

'You,' she chuckled. 'You look like you've lost your last friend. Oh, David, it is good to see you.'

He glowered, but unbent sufficiently to kiss her cheek with affection as he came through the door. 'Any chance of a cup of tea? It's been a hellish trip.'

'I'll put the kettle on.' She retreated to the kitchen and he followed automatically.

'Nice place you've got here,' he remarked, looking around with interest. 'This comes with the Sacristan's job?'

'Yes. I'm very fortunate. Rents are sky-high in this part of London, that is if you can even find rental property. I don't know where I would have gone when I retired and left the school if this hadn't come up.' She looked at him, hesitating. He usually accepted gratitude with bad grace. 'Have I ever properly thanked you for finding me this job? I wouldn't have ever known about it if you hadn't been such a thorough reader of the classified adverts in the *Church Times*, and I probably wouldn't have had a chance of getting it if you hadn't written such a nice letter of recommendation to Gabriel.'

He was embarrassed. 'I'm glad it's worked out for you. I didn't say anything that wasn't true.' He paused. 'How is . . . Gabriel?' he finally asked, the unfamiliar name enunciated with an effort.

'Overworked and a bit distracted these days, to tell the truth. I don't know if I mentioned that he's likely to be appointed Archdeacon in the near future. That probably accounts for it.'

'I haven't seen him in over ten years, you know.'

Daphne looked at him speculatively; she'd often wondered about that, but knew better than to ask. Finally, as if
reading his mind, she said, 'I wonder if you'll find him
much changed. I've only known him a couple of years, but
he is very well preserved for his age!' She added sincerely, 'Of course, you're not so bad yourself.'

David shrugged philosophically. 'I'm not the boy you
used to know, am I? But at least I've still got all my hair,
even if it is a bit grey around the edges.'

Daphne warmed the teapot and tore the cellophane off
two new packets of Twining's tea. 'I remembered,' she
said somewhat self-consciously. 'Two spoons of Earl Grey
and one of Assam. No tea-bags. Milk, no sugar.'

He laughed, delighted. 'I hope you haven't forgotten
the English Breakfast and Darjeeling for tomorrow
morning!'

'No, and I haven't forgotten the Scotch for tonight,
either.'

He smiled, but his thoughts were suddenly sober: I shall
probably need it by then.

Gabriel paced impatiently at the west end of the church,
glancing at his watch. Daphne had phoned a quarter of an
hour ago to say they were on their way. They were certainly
taking their time about it.

As they walked along to St Anne's, David had the curious sensation of moving in slow motion, like a fish swim-
ming upstream. Daphne's flat was not far from the church,
but their route led them from her quiet street on to a very
busy main road, the pavements clogged with people in a
hurry, the thoroughfare bumper-to-bumper with rush-hour
traffic. Then suddenly they turned off the main road, and

St Anne's Church was a short distance before them. The rain had stopped, at least for a time, and David's first glimpse of St Anne's was in a watery sunlight. Daphne chatted about the building's architectural merits, pointing out a buttress here and some tracery there with the specialised knowledge of a passionate amateur, knowledge that he shared and surpassed. He half listened and responded in kind.

Nearing the door, some instinct informed her that this meeting should not be witnessed. 'You go on in and say hello to Gabriel. I'll . . . uh, check the noticeboard in the north porch to see if there's anything I need to know about, and I'll be in directly.'

He stepped into the Pre-Raphaelite gloom of the church's interior, blinking for a moment as his eyes adjusted to the dim light, and came face to face with Gabriel. For a very long moment the two men regarded each other, the silence suspended like a crystal between them.

He hasn't changed, was David's first coherent thought, after the flood of inchoate emotion. Damn it, it's not fair. He looks exactly the same. How can I stop loving him when he's just the same?

Gabriel observed him with mixed feelings, this relict of a long-ago past. After the anticipation of the last few days, he now felt an odd detachment. This man had once meant something to him – for a time had meant everything to him – but now he seemed a stranger. Older, greyer; lines around his hazel eyes. But then at last David spoke, and the illusion of strangeness dissolved; the dry voice, the ironic self-deprecating smile instantly recalled the David of old. 'So where's this famous Comper chapel I've come all this way to see, Gabe?'

Gabriel flinched almost imperceptibly at the name. 'No one . . . calls me that,' he said in a soft, controlled voice. 'No one else ever has. Perhaps it would be better . . .'

'I'm sorry . . . Gabriel. It just came out.' David looked away, the pain almost too great to bear; he'd foolishly thought that Gabe no longer had the power to hurt him.

Daphne joined them at that moment. 'You're looking uncommonly smart today, Daphne,' Gabriel greeted her in quite a different voice. He was surprised to see her blush – something he would not have thought possible.

'You've never seen our church, David?' He assumed the comfortable official role of Vicar and tour-guide as they strolled about; he pointed out the Morris & Co. windows and the Burne-Jones reredos in the Lady Chapel, the Bodley rood screen, the Bainbridge Reynolds metal-work, before leading the way down the spiral staircase which led from the Lady Chapel into the crypt.

David caught his breath, his attention truly captured at last. 'Why, it's stunning! Absolutely stunning!' The three of them stood silently for a moment, drinking in the blue and gold richness of the chapel. After a while, David went on, 'This is even better than the one at St Mary Magdalene, Paddington. I can't imagine why it's not better known.'

'But as you can see, the damp has really got in. Here,' Gabriel pointed, 'and over here. And here on the roof, the gilding is flaking off. Something really needs to be done.'

'Yes, well. I suppose that's what I'm here for. Not that I know any more about it than either of you. I learned everything I know from Daphne.'

'Don't be daft,' she interposed. 'I may have got you started, but you passed far beyond my knowledge a long time ago.'

'And I learned everything I know from you,' Gabriel finished. 'So no false modesty will be tolerated.'

'Everything you know?' David dared, shooting him a significant look. 'I thought it was the other way around.'

Gabriel ignored the implication. 'Everything about church furnishings, certainly,' he replied neutrally. But while Daphne was inspecting a bit of peeling paintwork, he said rapidly, in a low voice, 'I must talk to you. Tomorrow. Come to early Mass. Half-past seven.'

After a simple supper, David and Daphne sat companionably in the overstuffed chairs of her sitting room, drinking and reminiscing. The rain was again beating a steady tattoo on the window, and in spite of the season she'd lit a small fire against the chill of the night air.

David sipped his whisky appreciatively. 'I've always blamed you for my taste for whisky. I don't think I'd ever tasted good whisky before I met you.'

Daphne smiled, and he regarded her fondly. To him she seemed little altered in twenty years. She had appeared old to him then, or perhaps timeless, with her cropped grey hair and her comfortably shapeless figure. Strange to think that he was now as old as she'd been then; the intervening years had somehow narrowed the gap between them.

A bright summer morning, full of promise. His cases packed, the guidebooks endlessly perused and marked. A fortnight in the churches of the West Country ahead. Then Daphne's arrival, the confused explanations and excuses. A holiday in shambles, a friendship mortally wounded. Rejection . . .

David looked at her again, wondering. They'd never spoken of it since. But why the hell not, he decided. 'Why did you cancel that holiday? Why wouldn't you ever tell me what happened?'

Daphne regarded him over the rim of her glass. 'You really don't know?'

'No. Why should I?'

She lowered her glass and looked at him gravely. Seeing him sitting there, so much the same David and yet so different, was more painful than she would have thought possible; she'd convinced herself that she'd got over these feelings years ago. But now she felt as though her heart would break all over again, as the light from the fire caught the burnished glints in his hair. 'It was all a long time ago.'

A late summer afternoon, sunlight slanting through the clerestory windows of the church, motes of dust dancing. The smell of the flowers she was arranging. The muted murmur of voices in the chapel. 'I hear they're going away together again. Doesn't she realise how ridiculous it looks?' 'Obviously not, the silly old cow.' 'Why, he's only half her age – if that!' 'She's obviously besotted with him. Well, you can't blame her for that, but honestly!' Shock, automatic denial, then . . . Sleepless night, agonised realisation . . .

She took a quick gulp of whisky to fortify herself, then said rapidly, 'People were talking. I decided it wasn't a good idea to leave you open to that.'

David stared, incredulous. 'But there was nothing to talk *about*! It's ludicrous even to suggest it! You were – well, you weren't young, and I was scarcely more than a boy, and . . .'

The hand that smoothed back her hair hid the pain in her eyes as she repeated softly, 'It was all a long time ago.' When it came to revealing the secrets of her own heart, her characteristic honesty would take her this far and no farther.

Chapter 8

Although the bed in Daphne's spare room was more
comfortable than his narrow bed at home, David had not
slept well. At six o'clock he lay awake, listening to the
rain on the window and replaying in his mind everything
Gabe had said to him yesterday, everything he'd said to
Gabe. He'd had rather too much whisky last night, and felt
that he needed some fresh air; he got up, opened the sash,
and leaned out, drawing in deep breaths of damp, smoggy
London air. Was Daphne an early riser? He thought she
was, and couldn't face the prospect of cordial chit-chat
and English Breakfast tea (with one spoon of Darjeeling),
so he shaved and dressed quietly, found his umbrella, wrote
her a quick note, and slipped out of the flat. It would be an
hour before he could decently turn up at St Anne's, but
Kensington Gardens were just around the corner, and he
spent an hour walking in the rain, thinking about yesterday,
about Gabe, about today, about . . . Emily. Today would
probably be the day he'd have to confront her, or tomorrow
at the latest.

When he arrived at St Anne's, still half an hour before early Mass, the door was unlocked, though no one else seemed to be about. Yesterday, in the emotion of meeting Gabe again, David had absorbed only a general impression of the church, even during their tour. Now he decided to explore it himself, and to concentrate on its features.

David's extensive knowledge about churches, their architecture and furnishings, was something that he had acquired on his own, through reading and through many years of visiting churches, as well as from Daphne, whose shared interest in churches had been the basis of their friendship. He was passionately interested in the subject, and he often wished that he could have made some sort of career for himself in that field. But his mother would never have approved, and somehow at the time it had been easier to take the path of least resistance and to read law.

His family had never been a church-going one, and David's first exposure to any church had been as a young boy on a school visit to Wymondham Abbey, the ancient monastic church in the town where he'd grown up. It had been a case of love at first sight; he'd wandered away from the other, bored children, entranced by the beauty of the church, hungry to explore it on his own and to learn more about it. The massive Comper screen, with its nearly life-sized figures of saints and its impressive canopy, had stunned him with its splendour, and had inspired his special interest in the work of Sir John Ninian Comper.

David had returned to that church again and again as a boy, first just to soak up the sense of beauty that was so lacking elsewhere in his young life. But eventually he'd begun to attend services; there a beauty of a different kind gripped him, and faith was born. Thus David's faith, born in beauty, was inextricably bound up with his interest in the church buildings themselves and his response to them. His God was a God of beauty; it was inconceivable to him that God could be worshipped in an ugly building.

He had found Gabriel a kindred spirit in this respect. Although Gabriel's knowledge was not so extensive as David's, he, too, was moved by the beauty of the Anglo-Catholic approach to worship, and the awe and reverence which it inspired. His sense of his vocation for the Church was strong; David had always envied him that, and envied him as well the strength of character which had driven him to follow that sense of vocation in spite of a fair amount of opposition from his wealthy, aristocratic family.

David wondered now, as he explored St Anne's, how it was that he had never been there before, especially as its Comper chapel was so splendid. He and Daphne had spent a lot of time visiting the churches of London, all those years ago, when he'd been a student. It was a lovely church – Gabe must be very happy here, he thought.

Eventually he became aware that people were arriving; it must be nearly time for Mass. Early Mass was held in the Lady Chapel, and was attended by only a handful of the faithful, David noted as he slipped into a pew near the back. There was an imposing-looking elderly woman towards the front, and a man and a woman, both in grey and looking very alike – both had the corners of their mouths turned down, permanently it appeared – in the middle. Wandering around the edges, trying first one seat and then another, was a rather odd old woman, dressed very smartly but wearing enormous padded moon-boots. An elderly man in a black cassock, small and squat with a beaky nose, small bright eyes and bushy white hair and eyebrows, bustled up to the altar and lit the candles. David knelt and tried to pray, but was distracted by the wonderful Burne-Jones reredos, the huge central panel depicting the Annunciation. Mary's face was averted, perhaps from the temptation of the terrible beauty of the angel. The Angel Gabriel . . .

When the Vicar entered, and the odd woman moved yet again, David realised that she was positioning herself to get the best possible view of him. Maybe she's not so crazy after all, he observed wryly. She's got good taste in men, anyway. Gabriel looked splendid in a silvery-green chasuble, and David had forgotten how movingly and how reverently he had always celebrated the Mass.

After the Mass, Gabriel waited at the door to greet his small congregation. The little grey couple rushed away, presumably home to their breakfast, and the odd woman was not far behind, with a last, fond leer at Gabriel. David lingered on his knees while the elegant old woman spoke with the Vicar, but as their conversation became prolonged he decided that his devotion was too conspicuous, and joined them at the door.

Gabriel welcomed him with a smile. 'Lady Constance, you must meet David – he's a friend of Daphne's. David Middleton-Brown, this is Lady Constance Oliver.'

Lady Constance extended her hand and gave him a searching look. 'You must be the clever one that Miss Elford was telling me about: the one who's going to see to our chapel for us. We're so grateful.'

'I don't know what she's been telling you about me, but I'm not a bit clever,' he protested with his self-deprecating smile.

70

'I shall judge that for myself, thank you, young man. You must come to supper some evening. You and Miss Elford. Monday?'

David glanced at Gabriel, who gave an imperceptible nod. 'Thank you, Lady Constance, I shall look forward to it very much.' He bowed slightly as she turned away.

Gabriel watched until her straight back was out of sight, then turned to David. 'Come home with me for breakfast. Then we'll talk.' David waited at the north door while Gabriel went to the sacristy, returning a moment later in a black cassock and carrying an umbrella.

'Does your . . . does Emily know that you're bringing a guest to breakfast?' David asked as they walked the short distance to the vicarage.

'No, but she won't mind.'

I'll bet she'll be just thrilled to meet her husband's old lover. Or maybe it's something she's used to, he thought bitterly.

He knew he hadn't been the first for Gabriel, as Gabriel had been the first – and only – for him. Not that Gabriel had ever been promiscuous; one relationship at a time was more his style. Gabriel had never actually told David the details of the experiences he'd had before they met, but he knew that there had been a few. Gabriel's sexual education had probably started very young, at the exclusive, expensive boarding school where he'd been sent as a boy.

The vicarage was a large brick Victorian house, just across from the church and built at the same time. David looked approvingly at its spacious aspect as they approached; in a moment they were inside. 'Come on through to the kitchen.' Taking a deep breath, David followed Gabriel through the door as he announced, 'Darling, I've brought someone home for breakfast.'

The woman who turned, smiling, from the cooker to face them was so opposite to David's expectation that he almost cried out in protest, 'But where's Emily?' He tried to assimilate her appearance, to make it fit somehow with the calculating character he was sure she must have, but his mind just wouldn't take it in. Small-boned and delicate in her dressing-gown, she wore no make-up; her dark brown hair, cut close at the nape, curved forward at chin-length to frame her face, with its small pointed chin and softly rounded cheeks, a face dominated by large, warm brown eyes and transformed by the look of love she turned on her husband. An enchanting face, without artifice and without guile. There must be some mistake.

'Darling, this is David Middleton-Brown, an old friend of mine, and a friend of Daphne's. He's come to stay with her for a visit.'

The smile of welcome that lit her face was entirely sincere; she was glad to see her husband, and she was glad to see his friend. 'David! How lovely to meet you at last! I've heard Daphne speak of you so often.'

'Oh?' was all he could say.

'In fact, don't we have you to thank for having Daphne here at all? Didn't you recommend her to Gabriel for the Sacristan's job?'

'Well, yes. I knew she was looking for something to do when she retired from teaching, and when I saw Gabe . . . Gabriel's advert in the *Church Times*, I thought . . . well, why not?'

'How thoughtful of you. We're entirely in your debt, then – Daphne is absolutely wonderful.'

'Well, she does know her stuff.'

'So do you, from what she tells me. Anyway,' she added impulsively, 'it's lovely to meet an old friend of Gabriel's. Maybe you can fill me in on what he got up to before I met him!'

David stared at her aghast, at a loss for words. She doesn't know, he thought. She probably thinks we went out looking for girls together.

She noticed his stricken expression. 'Is something the matter?' she asked with concern.

'No. That is, well . . . I mean, you're not what I expected,' he blurted.

She laughed delightedly and put her arm through Gabriel's, looking up at him; the unselfconscious intimacy of the gesture hurt David more than he would have imagined possible. 'Darling, what have you been telling this man about me? You didn't tell him about the second head, did you? I forgot to put it on this morning.'

Gabriel's answering laugh was strained, as he looked from one to the other of them, from Emily's animated face to David's curiously blank one. 'I told him . . . that you'd give us some breakfast.'

'And so I shall, in just a minute. Why don't you go into the breakfast room and sit down, you two. Have some tea while you're waiting – the kettle's just boiled.'

David sat down across the table from Gabriel and made an effort at conversation. 'The children. Aren't they up yet?'

'They're not here. Didn't I say? They've gone to Emily's parents in St Albans for a week or so. They'll probably come back spoiled rotten. You know how grandparents are.'

'I thought . . . well, I suppose I had the impression that

Emily's parents lived around here. I don't know why.'

'Oh, they used to. Emily grew up in this parish. But when her father retired a few years ago, they wanted to move out of London. They like it in St Albans, but they quite miss the grandchildren.' Gabriel poured the tea. 'Do you take sugar, David? I don't remember.'

'No, thanks.'

It wasn't English Breakfast, but it was hot and strong, and as he sipped it David felt himself reviving a bit, regaining his equilibrium. In a few moments his breakfast was before him: eggs, bacon, sausages, tomato, sautéed mushrooms, fried bread. And then there was toast and home-made marmalade. Just the sort of breakfast he loved and so seldom got – his usual fare was cornflakes – but he found he wasn't very hungry.

Emily sat down beside him. 'When did you come down from . . . Norwich, isn't it?'

'Just outside. Wymondham. Yesterday.'

'Oh, Wymondham, that's right. How long have you lived in Wymondham? You were in Brighton at the same time as Gabriel, weren't you?'

'Yes, I . . . knew . . . Gabriel in Brighton. But I grew up in Wymondham, and went back to look after my mother, when my father died. That was nearly ten years ago.'

'Wymondham is somewhere I've always wanted to see. The abbey is supposed to be splendid.'

'It is splendid. You must come up to stay some weekend,' he found himself saying, totally against his will.

'We'd like that very much, wouldn't we, Gabriel?'

'Of course.'

'Perhaps in the autumn, if you really mean it,' she went on. 'We could leave the children with my parents for the weekend. I don't imagine you're up to entertaining six-year-old twins, are you?'

The thought filled him with utter horror, but he replied politely, 'I'm sure I could manage, if you wanted to bring them.' He couldn't resist adding, 'This time I'd have a proper guest room to offer you, Gabriel.'

'Oh, have you been before, darling? I hadn't realised.'

Gabriel shot him a warning look. 'Yes, once,' he said lightly. 'Twelve or thirteen years ago – I'm surprised I've never mentioned it to you.'

David addressed himself to Emily, enjoying Gabriel's discomfiture in spite of himself. 'He was a great hit with my parents. My mother thought he was quite the nicest young man she'd ever met. She always hoped he'd come back one day; in fact, after my father died, she had his room converted into a guest room, just in case "that lovely young clergyman" came again.'

'And you never went. Gabriel, that was very naughty of you. And now your poor mother's dead,' she went on with feeling. 'David, I *am* sorry. How long has it been?'

'Almost two months.' David hated facile sympathy, but Emily's warmth nearly brought tears to his eyes. He changed the subject abruptly. 'Do you usually have a bigger congregation than that for your weekday Masses? Or is that the norm?'

'Generally a few more than that, but the weather does discourage some people. We've got quite an elderly congregation, by and large, and a lot of them don't like to come out when it's wet.'

'Who was there?' Emily asked with interest.

'A most peculiar old woman,' David stated. 'She kept swapping seats.'

'Beryl Ball,' Emily laughed. 'She has to make sure she has the best view of Gabriel.'

Gabriel nodded. 'Lady Constance, of course. She's invited David and Daphne to supper on Monday.'

'My, but you're the honoured one! I shall want to hear all about it. You must remember everything she serves so you can tell me.'

'I'll try.'

Gabriel continued, 'Aside from that, it was only the Dawsons. And Venerable serving, of course.'

They chatted back and forth, amiably, about church affairs; David stopped listening and became involved in his own thoughts. Seeing Gabe in this cosy domestic situation was infinitely more painful than the scenario he had imagined, the 'marriage of convenience' he had so desperately wanted to believe in. But confused as his emotions were, and unsure as he was about Gabe's true feelings, two things were clear to him: she doesn't know – not about Gabe and me, not about any of it; and, she really loves him. Crazy as it seemed, and with no real basis – he still had no idea why Gabe had sent for him – he suddenly found himself terrified for Emily.

He looked down and discovered that although he'd had no appetite, he had, in his abstraction, eaten every bite of his breakfast. 'Would you like some more?' Emily was asking. 'No?' She jumped up. 'Then I'll leave you two old mates to talk about past times. I've got cakes to bake – the fête is a week today, you know!'

Chapter 9

*I will acknowledge my sin unto thee: and mine un-
righteousness have I not hid.
I said, I will confess my sins unto the Lord: and so
thou forgavest the wickedness of my sin.*

Psalm 32.5–6

Gabriel ushered David into his study and into the most
comfortable chair; he himself sat in the swivel chair at his
desk. There followed a few seconds of uncomfortable silence
as Gabriel, face averted, fingered first the paperweight and
then the silver-framed photograph. 'Here are the twins,' he
said abruptly, handing the photo to David.

'You have a lovely family, Gabriel,' David stated gravely
and without a hint of irony. He was wary, expecting anything and prepared for nothing.

Gabriel hesitated. 'What . . . do you think of Emily?'

'I think she's lovely,' was the sincere reply.

Gabriel's relief was visible. 'I'd always hoped that you
and Emily could be friends,' he said awkwardly, looking
out of the window. 'Perhaps it's not too late.'

Yes, David reflected, why not? He and Emily had a lot
in common. They both loved the same man. The only
difference between them was that Emily had Gabe, and he

77

had . . . his memories. His mouth twisted bitterly at the cliché, so true and so uncomforting.

Gabriel turned back toward him. 'I was very sorry to hear about your mother, David. Please accept my sincere sympathy on your loss.'

The formal words, so devoid of real feeling, ignited a small spark of anger on his mother's behalf. It wasn't just him that Gabriel had deserted. This man had deliberately charmed his mother, won her over completely, and then abandoned her for the rest of her life. For the last thirteen years she'd been comparing him, David, unfavourably with the absent Gabriel, and blaming him somehow for Gabriel's failure to return. 'She asked for you on her deathbed,' he said softly. 'She could never understand why you didn't come back as you'd promised.'

Gabriel looked away again. 'Then she never knew . . . about us?'

'No, of course not.' He gave a short, dry laugh. 'Not that she wouldn't have believed me capable of any depravity under the sun. But not the blameless Gabriel. Funny, isn't it? When I didn't even know . . . what I was . . . until I met you?'

Gabriel made no reply; he clenched his fist around the paperweight and gazed out of the window. David looked at his exquisite profile and the words were wrenched out of him without his volition, words so heavy with pain that Gabriel flinched visibly. 'There's never been anyone but you, Gabe. Never.'

'I don't want to talk about it.'

'What *do* you want to talk about, then? What am I doing here? Why did you send for me?'

Faced with the uncomfortable reality of David, Gabriel

wondered about that himself. Was there any chance that David could actually do anything to help? Sending for him had been little more than grasping at straws: he realised that now. But it was too late to turn back.

Gabriel took a deep breath and turned to face him. 'It was an impulse, really. I just didn't know where else to turn.'

'But what's the problem? And how can *I* help?'

'I've had a letter – a threatening letter. I suppose you'd even call it a blackmail letter, though it doesn't ask for money. And I thought . . . well, I suppose I thought perhaps you could help me find out who wrote it,' he finished lamely.

'How? I'm not a detective or a policeman. I'm only a humble country solicitor.'

'But people talk to you, don't they? It's one of your great gifts – the ability to get along with so many different sorts of people, and to make them say things they wouldn't ordinarily say. That was my idea, I suppose: that you could go around and talk to people in the church, and see if you could work out who sent it. Anyway,' he added, 'when you've seen the letter, you'll understand why I couldn't possibly show it to anyone else.'

'How do you know that it was written by someone in the church?'

'It must have been. I don't see how it could be anyone else.'

'Can I see the letter? I'm not promising anything, but if it will make you feel better to let me have a look at it . . .'

Gabriel released the catch of the secret drawer, as he'd done so many times in solitude during the past few days, drew out the folded paper and handed it to David, then sat impassively as he read the typed lines in silence. Gabriel knew the ugly words off by heart.

> I know about Peter Maitland, and what you did to him. You are responsible for his death, as surely as if you had killed him yourself. You are a disgrace to your sacred calling, and have brought dishonour on yourself, the Church of England, and St Anne's. If you do not resign your living and leave the priesthood by the Feast of Assumption, I will see that your wife, the Bishop, and the national newspapers know about Peter Maitland and how he died.

David read it through several times and still the words made no sense to him. Peter Maitland. The name meant nothing at all. Peter Maitland. Dead? What did it all mean? He raised puzzled eyes to Gabriel's still face. 'Peter Maitland? Who is . . . was . . . he?'

Gabriel hardly knew how to explain. Things had always been so simple for David, he thought. His approach to life and love had always been very uncomplicated: he had loved Gabriel, and that was all there was to it. He had never been able to – would never be able to – understand Gabriel's more complex needs, never be able to understand that his love for David had represented only a part of his nature, and that there was another side of him that had needed something else. David wouldn't understand about Peter, any more than he understood about Emily. He would have to be as factual as possible, remove the emotional content from the story he was about to tell.

And so Gabriel's voice was entirely matter-of-fact as he related the story; he might have been reading Emily's grocery list for all the emotion he displayed. 'He was a boy I knew in Brighton. You never knew him. I met him . . . well, it doesn't really matter how I met him. He was young, inexperienced – but he pursued me – he thought he was in love with me. Maybe he was. I thought it was a lark. Things were . . . well, things had got a little stale, a little predictable . . . between you and me, and I was ready for a bit of excitement. It was fine at first. I was intrigued by him – he was very beautiful, very eager. But he didn't know how to handle it. He wanted more and more. He didn't understand that making love to him was . . . fun, but it just wasn't that important to me. I was afraid that he might become indiscreet. I told him I wouldn't see him again. He wrote to me, asked me to meet him on the beach one night. He said if I didn't come he'd kill himself. I didn't go. I thought he was just being dramatic to get my attention. Two days later his body washed up. I read about it in the newspaper. There were no signs of foul play, as they say, and the inquest recorded a verdict of accidental death. My name was never mentioned. I knew it wasn't my responsibility – it was his own choice. I was guilty of bad judgement and foolish behaviour, nothing more. But it hit me pretty hard, I don't mind telling you, and I wanted to get away, to have a fresh start. I pulled every string I could to get out of Brighton. My spiritual director . . . well, I was lucky enough to get the living of St Anne's very quickly. So I came here, I met Emily. I started again. There's no point in living in the past, David.'

David remembered reading somewhere that men who have limbs blown off in battle don't feel a thing at the time; the only way for the body to cope with such intense, immediate pain is to postpone it. With great detachment, he thought that the mind must be the same. He heard Gabriel's terse words, he understood their meaning perfectly well, and yet . . . Later on this is going to hurt, he realised. Later on, when I've absorbed it, I will wish I were dead.

He had no consciousness of speaking; he heard his own voice from far off as though it were coming from another room. 'Emily. What does she say about this?'

Gabriel's face and voice finally registered emotion. 'Good Lord, David! How could you even imagine that she could know about it? She just couldn't cope with it!'

What about me? 'Then how do you propose to explain to her what I'm doing? My going about asking questions won't work if people know that I know you. Emily knows that we're friends – what's to stop her telling the whole parish?'

'I'll have a word with her – that won't be a problem. Emily can be very discreet.'

'I can see you've made a good choice for your wife.' David closed his eyes briefly, then continued, 'There's not much time. The Feast of the Assumption is only two and a half weeks away. Do you have any idea who might have written the letter?'

Frowning, Gabriel replied slowly, 'I haven't thought about much else all week. And I'm at a total loss. First of all, there's the question of motive. Who could hate me that much, and why?'

'And?'

'I just can't think. That's where you come in, really. Maybe you can catch someone in an unguarded moment.'

'But that's not the only question, is it?'

'No, and this is the real problem.' Gabriel spread his hands, palms up. 'You see, until a few minutes ago, I have never told a living soul about Peter Maitland. Who could possibly know?'

After David had gone, Gabriel sat for a very long time, looking out of the window. Eventually there was a tap on the door.

'Oh, David's gone, has he? I was going to offer you some coffee.' Emily entered the study, encircled her husband with her arms, and laid her cheek on the top of his head. He pulled her on to his lap and kissed her, lightly at first but with increasing urgency; presently he murmured, 'Forget the coffee, my love. Let's go upstairs.'

Chapter 10

For it was not an open enemy, that hath done me
this dishonour: for then I could have borne it.
Neither was it mine adversary, that did magnify himself
against me: for then peradventure I would have
hid myself from him.
But it was even thou, my companion: my guide, and
mine own familiar friend.
We took sweet counsel together: and walked in the
house of God as friends.

Psalm 55.12–15

David had left his umbrella at the vicarage, but he was
oblivious to the soft rain which fell as he walked blindly
through Kensington Gardens. There were many more people
about than there had been earlier that morning, in spite of
the weather; however, no one gave a second look at the
solitary man, hands jammed in his pockets, who walked
back and forth, up and down. At one point the thought
crossed his mind that Daphne might be wondering where
he was, might have breakfast – or lunch – waiting for him.
But he knew also that Daphne would never ask questions,
and so he walked on.

After a while, he left the park and wandered instead

through the streets of Bayswater, up the main roads through bustling crowds of people, past greengrocers and gourmet delicatessens, antique shops and wine merchants, fast-food take-aways and pizzerias, and then around the back streets, past row upon row of terraced houses, bleak in the rain. Ordinarily he would have taken a great interest in the multi-faceted personality of London, but today he was completely unaware of his surroundings.

Without conscious thought, he found himself eventually back in front of St Anne's for the second time that morning. After a moment's hesitation he went in, realising suddenly that he was quite wet. The church seemed empty, though someone was playing the organ softly; David thought the piece sounded like Messiaen. A lingering scent of incense mingled with the smell of fresh flowers and the lemony tang of furniture polish. With no sunlight to illuminate them, the stained-glass windows looked muddy, the faces lifeless. But a spotlight on the rood screen emphasised its rich colours while casting distorted shadows high up on the chancel wall of the crucifix, with its limp tortured figure, and the mutely agonised postures of Our Lady and St John. David genuflected to the altar and the flickering Sacrament lamp, then crossed into the Lady Chapel. He automatically went to the votive rack, felt in his pocket for a coin, and lit a candle for his mother. She wouldn't have approved of such popish nonsense, he knew, but it made him feel better to have done it.

When he turned around at last, he discovered with a start that he wasn't alone in the chapel. A sharp-featured woman with drab grey hair was looking critically at a half-finished flower arrangement on a large pedestal. She added another spray of greenery with a stabbing motion of ill-concealed hostility. David would have fled, but she caught his retreat out of the corner of her eye and turned to speak to him. 'It's no good, is it?' she demanded.

'It looks just fine to me. Of course, I'm not much of a judge,' he replied diplomatically. 'What seems to be the matter with it?'

'I just don't have enough flowers. The Vicar's wife was supposed to bring in some from the vicarage garden, and help with the arranging, I might add, but she hasn't shown up!'

David felt absurdly defensive on Emily's behalf. 'I'm sure there must be a good reason,' he offered. 'Perhaps some emergency . . .'

The woman snorted dismissively. 'This younger generation just has no sense of responsibility. As my Arthur says, a man's word should be his bond. If you say you're going to do something, you must do it.'

David, seeing that this conversation was leading nowhere, said, 'Well, I think the flowers look fine,' and made his escape towards the stairs down to the crypt chapel. But before he'd reached his goal, an absurdly tall, thin man with enormous round gold-rimmed spectacles came hurtling towards him from across the chancel. 'I say, you don't have a fag on you, do you?' the man accosted him fiercely.

'I beg your pardon?' David replied, startled.

'A fag!' the man repeated, a little more loudly, as though David were deaf.

'No, I'm sorry. I don't smoke.'

'Damn. My wife must have pinched mine from my jacket pocket, and I'm absolutely gasping for a smoke!' The man, towering above him, flung out his arms in a massive gesture of despair. 'Wives!' he groaned dramatically. 'Are you married?'

'No, I'm afraid not.'

'Well, if you're smart you'll keep it that way. They're more trouble than they're worth!' And with that the man turned and sprinted back across the chancel; shortly the tones of the organ were once again heard.

David stared after him a moment, bemused, then went down the steps to the crypt. The sound of the organ faded gradually as he descended, and when he reached the chapel he felt a welcome solitude surrounding him in the blue and gold silence. The gilded angels on the riddel posts of the altar, and the serene saints in their niches, were his only companions. He knelt.

For a long time his mind remained mercifully blank, empty of thought and empty of emotion. But suddenly, blindingly, it was all there. All the knowledge, all the pain that his mind had been suppressing in the hours – how many? – since this morning. As he replayed in his head all that Gabriel had said, the terse sentences exploded one by one like fireworks in his mind, illuminating corners that had been dark for over ten years. It explained everything. Why had he been so blind at the time? Why had he not sensed Gabe's boredom with their relationship, understood his need for excitement? How had he failed to read all the signs? It must have been his inexperience, his natural inclination to take people at face value, his belief in the uniqueness and completeness of their love – for both of them. All the pieces fell into place; the inexplicable was explained. Gabe's absences, his excuses, his gradual withdrawal. Those few terrifying weeks of alienation and silence, and then . . . Gabe was gone. Practically overnight, gone from his life with scarcely a word; the first communication he'd had from him had been the wedding invitation, a few months later. All these years he'd lived with the fear that it was his fault somehow, that he'd failed Gabe, hadn't loved him enough, and now . . . was he free of blame? If he'd understood Gabe half as well as he'd loved him, would all this have been prevented? 'There's no point in living in the past, David.'

That was easy enough for Gabe to say. Gabe, who had an enviable present and a bright future. But David's past was Gabe, and his present was . . . emptiness. His future? He didn't even want to contemplate that. His impulse was to flee right now, back to Wymondham, back home. But was there any escape from the pain? Or, for that matter, from the love? Could he stop loving Gabe now, even if he wanted to?

He lost track of time as he stayed on his knees, trying to work out what to do. Did he owe it to Gabe to stay and help him, to make up for the way he'd failed him? Or did Gabe deserve to be abandoned to his fate? And what about Emily? She was truly the innocent party in all this – she must be protected. But Gabe had married her – let him deal with it. She was Gabe's responsibility, not his.

A soft step on the stairs tore his eyes from the crucifix on the altar and he half rose, looking at the door, as Emily tentatively entered. 'Oh, it is you, David,' she greeted him. 'Cecily said that a man had come down here, and I thought it might be you. I didn't mean to disturb your prayers.'

'Oh, that's all right, Emily. I had finished.' He smiled at her. 'So you finally made it with your flowers? That woman wasn't very happy with you.'

Emily looked embarrassed. 'I was . . . delayed.'

'I told her that probably something had come up at home.'

She bit her lip to suppress a smile. 'Yes, you could say that. But I've made my apologies, and I think I've been forgiven. Cecily's a bit intimidating, but I'm used to her. I hope she wasn't too hard on you.'

'Not at all. But that chap – I think he was the organist –'

She laughed. 'Oh, no, Miles hasn't been having a go at you, has he?'

'He was trying to scrounge a cigarette. I thought he was a bit peculiar.'

Emily shook her head. 'Don't worry about Miles – he's perfectly harmless. Just a bit obsessive, that's all. And he smokes like a fiend.'

'He's a good organist.'

'Yes, very good. He was the organist at Selby Cathedral, before he came to us.' She made a comical face. 'According to Miles, everything at Selby was absolute perfection. He almost expects you to genuflect when he mentions the sacred name of Selby.'

'If it was so wonderful, why did he leave?'

Emily laughed again. 'Oh, here he has so much more scope for complaint! And complaint is what he lives for.'

David marvelled at the sympathy that there was between them, as she sat down next to him. 'Gabriel's very lucky to have a wife who can share his work,' he said impulsively.

She smiled and looked thoughtful. 'But he doesn't really have what I'd call friends. That's why I'm so glad you've come. I think it will do him a world of good to have you to talk to.'

'He talks to you.'

'Yes, but that's not quite the same. There are some things that I can only tell my friend Lucy, and I'm sure there are some things that he'd only tell another man. You're good for him, David.' She regarded him earnestly. 'I can tell a difference in his mood already, since you've been here. He's explained to me that you're on a little private mission, and you don't want people in the church to know that you're friends. But I must tell you how grateful I am for your friendship, and how glad I am that you're here.'

Although his better judgement told him to get in his car and drive away while there was still time, as he met her brown eyes, David knew that he had no choice but to stay.

Chapter 11

O remember not the sins and offences of my youth:
but according to thy mercy think thou upon me, O
Lord, for thy goodness.

Psalm 25.6

The remains of a veritable orgy of Sunday paper reading
were strewn about the sitting room. Daphne, sated, looked
over the tops of her half-moon reading glasses at David,
nearly asleep in his chair. 'Are you ready for some tea?'

'Mm.' He roused himself a bit when a fragrant mug of
Earl Grey appeared in front of him several minutes later.
'Sorry, Daphne. All of a sudden I just couldn't keep my
eyes open.' He yawned. 'It was that excellent lunch, I'm
sure – I suppose I ate too much. And you shouldn't be
waiting on me like this, cooking for me, and bringing me
tea. I'm perfectly capable of helping, you know.'

Daphne looked horrified. 'But you're my guest! I wouldn't
dream of allowing you to help! Anyway, it's a pleasure to
have someone to fuss over, for a change. I must admit, I
don't usually bother with a proper Sunday lunch, just for
myself.'

'But how can you manage for the rest of the week,
without left-over joint? Not that you've got much left over

this week! It's a good thing we're going to Lady Constance's tomorrow.'

'I wouldn't be surprised if you're asked out every night,' Daphne teased him. 'There seems to be a great deal of interest in the parish in that handsome young man who's come to take a look at the crypt chapel.'

David grimaced. 'Not very handsome, and not very young, but thanks anyway, Daphne.'

'Miles Taylor seems to look on you as almost a personal protégé. He was going around telling everyone this morning that *he* discovered you.'

David shook his head. 'You certainly have a few odd characters at St Anne's. The churchwardens, for instance – they're a strange pair, aren't they?'

'Cyril is an old dear, but I'm afraid he's a bit past it. He's got more and more vague over the last few years, but he won't even consider giving up the wardenship.'

'Was it my imagination, or was he following Emily around the church hall after the service this morning?'

Daphne laughed indulgently. 'That's not exactly a well-kept secret. He's adored her for years, or so I've heard. She's very patient with him.'

'Well, he seems a harmless sort, anyway. There's something a bit terrifying about the woman.'

'Mavis Conwell? Well, I'll admit, she's not exactly tact personified.'

'I get the feeling that people don't like her much.'

'That's probably a fair statement. She puts a lot of people's backs up with her comments sometimes. She's fairly renowned for her insensitivity.'

'How on earth did she ever get elected churchwarden, then?'

'It was a sympathy vote, I suppose. Her husband died about a year ago, and she was at a loose end and really wanted the job – something to keep her busy, or maybe it was the prestige, or the power, that she wanted. There's certainly still a bit of both connected with being church-warden, isn't there? Anyway, when the Annual Parochial Meeting came round, I don't think anybody else was that keen to do it, except perhaps Roger Dawson, and his wife is Mavis Conwell's friend, so he stepped aside. But a few people have lived to regret it, I dare say. Anyway, I try my best to keep out of parish politics. I'm only the Sacristan.'

'You don't usually go to the eleven o'clock Mass, do you?'

'Not generally.' She grimaced guiltily. 'I must admit, I usually stay home and listen to the *Archers Omnibus* on a Sunday morning! The Sacristan's job is really a doddle, with Venerable Bead always around wanting to take over. I polish the silver and look after the other bits during the week, though he takes care of early Mass every day, so I don't even have to deal with that. I usually go in on Saturday night and get things laid up for the eleven o'clock, and let Venerable have his fun clearing up afterwards. It all keeps him happy!' She shook her head. 'I prefer the seven forty-five low Mass in the evening, anyway. But I must admit I'm glad that I've got it over with this morning and don't have to go out tonight.'

'Then you're not going to Solemn Evensong and Bene-diction?' David asked.

Daphne raised her eyebrows. 'You should know that SE and B has never been my style. I didn't think it was yours, particularly.'

'Oh, well,' he said, slightly shamefaced, 'it isn't really,

not in my own church anyway. But I think I'll go along, just the same, to see what it's all about.'

She laughed. 'David, I do believe that you're a spiritual thrill-seeker. Pass me your cup – it looks like you need more tea.'

Solemn Evensong and Benediction might not be his favourite, but David had to admit that it was done very well at St Anne's. The music was superb, the serving was flawless, and of course Gabriel handled the whole thing beautifully.

After the service, as he rose from his knees, David was approached by a young fair man dressed in a cassock. 'Hello, we haven't yet been introduced. I'm Tony Kent.'

'David Middleton-Brown. You're the head server, aren't you? I must congratulate you on your team of servers – I think they're the best I've ever seen.'

Tony beamed; he took great pride in his servers, and spent much time training and rehearsing them in the complex choreography of the Mass. 'It's very kind of you to say that. A lot of credit has to go to the Vicar – he sets very high standards. Fortunately, we're not short of volunteers, so we can pick the best.' He paused, then went on impulsively, 'Listen David, why don't you join us at the pub? We usually have a pint down at the Rose and Crown after SE and B. How about it? I'll buy you a drink.'

'The magic words. Yes, why not?'

'Terrific. I'll be with you just as soon as I can get out of this gear.'

David wondered briefly about the wisdom of falling in with this high-spirited young crowd, as they chattered their way down the road to the Rose and Crown. But it was all in the interest of information-gathering, after all, and he felt that he could use a drink.

They quickly settled in the corner of the pub with their drinks. Most of the young men were drinking pints; his double whisky made David feel far removed from their generation. But they welcomed him readily.

'Where are you from, David?' the young ginger-haired chap asked.

'Wymondham, near Norwich.'

'The abbey?' inquired Tony with interest. 'I'll bet the serving there is of a pretty high standard.'

'Yes, it's not bad.'

'Were you ever a server there?'

David twisted his glass around on the table. 'A long time ago,' he admitted. 'When I was in my teens – a little younger than most of you. And I served for a while at . . . a church in Brighton.'

'Oh, our Vicar did a curacy in Brighton,' interposed the dark-haired one called Chris (or was it Johnnie?). 'At St Dunstan's, I think.'

'There are a lot of churches in Brighton,' David said quickly – almost too quickly. 'And I was there a very long time ago.'

'You're not *that* old! You talk like you're about as old as Venerable Bead!' said the ginger-haired one.

David welcomed the opportunity to change the subject. 'Is he the old chap? Where is he now? Or does he stay away from these gatherings?'

'He insists on doing the seven forty-five low Mass,' Tony explained. 'He'll be along as soon as it's finished. Gabriel never lingers long over the seven forty-five.'

'Before he gets here, tell David the story of Venerable

and the Bishop,' urged one of the young servers who hadn't spoken before.

Johnnie and Chris both leaned forward eagerly. 'Yes, you must hear this one,' the dark-haired one began.

The ginger-haired one continued, 'It was a visit by the Area Bishop a few years ago.'

'Not the one we've got now – he's new.'

They tossed the narrative back and forth between them. 'This one was a veritable prot – a real evangelical.'

'He didn't even like to wear a mitre . . .'

'He wore a little, apologetic one – it looked more like a tea-cosy!'

'Anyway, the Bishop pulls up in front of St Anne's in his car.'

'It was a really ordinary car, too – a Sierra or something.'

'He gets out of his car. You can only just about tell that he's the Bishop and not the chauffeur . . .'

'Because he's wearing a purple shirt with a dog-collar.'

'Not even a cassock!'

'Well, Venerable's been hanging around the west door, waiting for the Bishop.'

'He's all dressed up in a cassock and cotta . . .'

'With a couple of feet of lace on it at least!'

'Old Venerable goes dashing out . . .'

'Just as the Bishop's getting his case out of the boot.'

'And right there in the middle of the road . . .'

'He goes down on one knee!' they both roared together.

'And grabs the Bishop's hand . . .'

'And kisses his ring!'

'You've never seen anything like the look on the Bishop's face!'

'Pure horror!'

'Then Venerable says, "My Lord, let me take that," and grabs for the Bishop's case.'

'But the Bishop won't let go . . .'

'And the case goes flying into the road!'

David joined in the contagious laughter. Tony shook his head at the two ebullient story-tellers. 'Poor old Venerable, he'll never live that one down.'

Presently, David looked around and said, 'It looks like it's time for another round. I'll buy.' His head full of drink orders, he made his way towards the bar.

Before he reached his goal, he encountered a most unlikely patron of the Rose and Crown – it was unmistakably Mavis Conwell, with her close-set sharp eyes, her inexpertly dyed rusty-black hair, and her rat-trap mouth. She was looking around with a furrowed brow, and didn't see him at first. But just as he thought he might slip by unnoticed, she grabbed his arm. 'Mr Middleton-Brown!'

'Good evening, Mrs Conwell.' He thought with a sinking heart that she was going to expect him to buy her a drink.

But his fears were unfounded. 'I'm looking for my son – my boy Craig. He hasn't been home this afternoon, and I thought maybe he'd come down to the local. But you don't know my Craig, do you? So that's no help. And I'm certainly not going to ask *them* if they've seen him,' she added, with a malevolent look at the servers in their corner. She lowered her voice and looked earnestly at David. 'Would you like a word of advice? Stay away from *them*. Everyone knows what they are, and if you're seen with them, people might think you're . . . well, like that.'

99

She bared her teeth in a smile. 'And I know you're not.'

David regarded her with bafflement; he didn't have any idea what she was hinting at. 'It's very kind of you to take such an interest in my reputation, but . . .'

'Even the Vicar knows better than to be seen with *them*, and no one would ever think of saying that the Vicar was . . . like that. He leaves it to his wife to counsel them. A very wise man, our Vicar.'

'Well, it was nice seeing you, Mrs Conwell. I'm sorry I can't help with your son. I hope you find him,' he said, disengaging himself and continuing towards the bar, desperate by now for another drink. He found her attitude toward the servers inexplicable: they exhibited youthful high spirits, certainly, but nothing more sinister than that. What was the woman going on about?

The servers greeted his return with increased hilarity. 'Trying to pick up women, are you, David?' laughed the ginger-haired one.

'Couldn't you do any better than Mavis Conwell?' the dark-haired one added.

'She was looking for her son, she said.'

'Oooh, the manly Craig,' said the ginger-haired one.

'What is this Craig like?' David asked curiously.

'He's a very nasty piece of work,' Tony replied. 'She thinks that the sun rises and sets in him, as you might have guessed, but he's a right little bastard.'

'Who do you suppose I've just seen on my way in?' interrupted Venerable Bead as he plodded up to the table, drink in hand. 'Mavis Conwell! She was going on again about Norman Newsome. She thinks he ought to be kicked out of the Church. Imagine – a man with such a gift for liturgy!'

'And such an eye for choirboys,' added Johnnie wickedly.

Tony looked stern. 'Boys, this is all very funny, I'm sure, but we have a guest tonight. What will he think of us?'

'Not at all,' said David. 'It's all been most . . . illuminating.'

Chapter 12

*Yea, because of the house of the Lord our God: I
will seek to do thee good.*

Psalm 122.9

Having resolved to spend the day on Monday on his
ostensible mission of the crypt chapel, David found himself
in an absurdly good mood. The servers' high spirits of the
previous evening had been contagious, and after all he was
engaged in work in which he had a passionate interest. So
he pottered about the chapel contentedly all morning, making
notes on a pad of paper and whistling something that sounded
curiously like Byrd's 'Ave Verum' under his breath. Of
Gabriel and his problem he thought not at all.

The only interruption to his concentration came when
Percy Bead, hearing suspicious noises coming from the
chapel, made his way down the stairs to investigate.

'Oh, David, it's you.'

'Good morning, Mr Bead,' David greeted him cheerily.
'Lovely day, isn't it? It actually looks as though we might
get some sun.'

'Call me Venerable, please. Everybody does.'

'Do you mind that?'

'It's an honourable title,' the old man chuckled. 'There

103

are some, our Vicar for one, who would give a great deal to be called Venerable,' he added slyly.

Recalled unwillingly to thoughts of Gabriel and his responsibility to him, David decided to make the most of the voluble old man's presence.

'And do you think that's likely to happen? That he'll be named Archdeacon?'

'I don't know why not. He's served ten years at St Anne's – that's a long time in this diocese. He's well regarded by the powers-that-be, I think.'

'What sort of reputation does he have?' David asked curiously. 'In the diocese, I mean.'

'I know a lot of the bigwigs – I get around, you know,' explained Venerable with a falsely modest smile. 'Father Gabriel is considered to be a hard-working priest – a good parish priest – and something of a scholar. He's written a couple of obscure theological books, you know.'

'No, I didn't realise that,' David replied, surprised. He knew, of course, that Gabriel would excel at anything to which he applied himself, but somehow he'd never imagined him getting involved in the finer points of theology. 'And what about the congregation? What do they think of him?'

Venerable was not the least suspicious of this line of questioning; to him this type of clerical gossip was the most natural thing in the world. 'His sermons are famous – he's the best preacher I've ever heard, and I've heard a few! Personally, he's very well liked. Loved, I'd say. Especially by the ladies, who can't resist those blue eyes!' he added with a chuckle. 'My wife – God rest her soul – used to say that no man ought to have eyes like that! And more charm than a man ought to have! It's a lucky thing for him he's got a wife – and I have to say, he didn't waste any time finding one after he got here – or he'd have ladies on his doorstep day and night.'

'Then he didn't have a wife when he got here?' David asked ingenuously.

'No indeed. One or two people even thought he might be . . . not the marrying sort, if you know what I mean. But he soon proved them wrong. Almost indecent haste, it was. But they make a lovely couple, don't you think? Or haven't you met the Vicar's wife?'

'Yes, I have. I've found her very . . . pleasant.'

'Emily's a good sport. She's always been nice to the servers – and she and Tony are good friends.'

'Tony seems a very nice chap,' David remarked.

'Oh, Tony's the best. He really knows about serving. Of course, I've taught him a lot, but he's got a real gift for it. He keeps the other chaps in line.'

'He's not married?' David asked.

'He may as well be: he's got a boyfriend, if that's the correct term, that he lives with. Ian – that's the chap's name – often joins us down at the pub on a Sunday night, but he didn't come last night. He's not a church-goer, so you won't see him around here.'

'I quite enjoyed myself last night,' David admitted. 'I haven't laughed so much in years.'

Venerable smiled in a paternal way. 'Yes, the boys are a lovely bunch. We do have some good times.' He didn't seem to find it at all unusual to include himself in their ranks.

'Mavis Conwell warned me about being seen with the servers. I didn't understand what she meant – they seemed fairly harmless to me.'

The old man's eyes snapped. 'Oh, she thinks just because Tony . . . that we're all that way! But she's wrong! Poisonous old . . .' He pursed his lips virtuously. 'But I'm a Christian man, and I won't say what I think of her. Well, I'd better get back upstairs. The church wants tidying up after the weekend. People *will* come in and disturb things.'

In the early afternoon, David decided to clear up a few obscure points by paying a visit to the reference collection of the Conservation Department at the Victoria & Albert Museum. He would cut through Kensington Gardens, he decided, skirting the Round Pond and emerging near the Albert Memorial, where he could cross Kensington Road and head down Exhibition Road to the V & A. It was a rather pleasant day, and he found himself walking slowly through the park, reflecting on the state of his inquiries to date.

On the whole, he decided, while he'd met some interesting people and learned some fascinating things, he had made no progress at all in finding the blackmailer. No one seemed to have any negative feelings about Gabe . . . rather the opposite, in fact, he reflected somewhat sourly. The man was apparently universally loved by his parishioners; no one would say a word against him. Perhaps his best bet would be in following the other line of inquiry: trying to discover who, by some means, had found out about Peter Maitland. It was all very well for Gabe to say that no one could have done; someone clearly had. Probably the boy had talked to somebody, had mentioned Gabe's name, and somehow it had got to the ears of . . . whom? David wished that he could talk it over with someone; Daphne's common sense would be a great help in sorting out the options, but of course that would be impossible. Gabe would never agree, and he couldn't really blame him.

He dashed across Kensington Road, barely escaping death under the wheels of a red double-decker bus coming from the right, and a taxi coming from the left. After catching his breath, he noted a small florist's shop in a side street. He'd have to remember that on his way back – he must pick up some flowers for Lady Constance. Freesias, it would have to be – carnations just wouldn't do for someone like Lady Constance. He'd better get some for Daphne, too, while he was at it.

'Tell me a little bit about Lady Constance,' David requested as they walked the short distance from Daphne's flat to the exclusive square, surrounded by tall white houses. 'She's a widow, I assume?'

'Yes, for many years, apparently. Her husband was a wealthy industrialist – his family made their money from Victorian sweatshops, I would have thought. It was their conscience-money that built St Anne's.'

'Oh, really?'

'Yes, it was her husband's grandfather or great-grandfather who founded and built the church, and obviously he was willing to pay for the very best. Lady Constance has continued to take a close personal interest in St Anne's – we've been very lucky. Whenever we've needed money for anything, from new vestments to cleaning the rood screen, she's been more than generous. And of course most of the silver has been given by the Olivers, through the years.'

'Does she have any money in her own right?'

Daphne considered. 'No, I don't think so. I believe that her father was some impoverished baronet, with hundreds of years of history but no money. But I'm not really sure about that.'

A maid opened the door as soon as he'd rung the bell, at eight o'clock sharp; they were ushered into the entrance hall of the Georgian house, as gracious on the inside as it was impressive on the outside.

Lady Constance met them at the door of the drawing room. 'So nice to see you, Miss Elford, Mr Middleton-Brown. Oh, freesias, how very lovely. My favourite. Thank you so much.' An old gentleman rose as they entered the room. 'Mr Middleton-Brown, have you met Wing Commander Fitzjames?'

'Yes, we met briefly on Sunday. How nice to see you, Wing Commander.'

'My pleasure, my boy. Do call me Cyril. Good evening, Daphne. You're looking charming tonight, if I may say so.'

Invitations to sup with Lady Constance were not commonplace, and Daphne had made a real effort. Although she'd entertained fleetingly – then rejected – the radical notion of visiting the hairdresser, she had actually set her hair on rollers, and the result was not unbecoming. She had applied a bit of make-up, and was wearing her best dress; the dress had been bought several years ago for a nephew's wedding, and although its cost had seemed at the time, on her teacher's salary, somewhat excessive, it had seldom seen the light of day since. She'd felt slightly foolish taking the extra trouble with her appearance, but now was relieved that she'd done so – at least David wouldn't be too ashamed of her.

Lady Constance, of course, was her usual picture of un-selfconscious elegance, in a well-cut dark dress and pearls. Sherry was offered and accepted, and there was the inevitable slight hesitation before polite conversation was initiated.

'Have you always lived in London, Lady Constance?' David inquired.

'My girlhood was spent in the country,' she replied. 'But I've lived in this house since my marriage, and I'm afraid I've become a real Londoner. One does become spoiled by all the amenities – the galleries, the concerts, the ballet, and of course the shops. One misses it all dreadfully, I fear. I've only been away from London once for more than a short holiday, when I looked after my brother in his final illness. I tried to get him to come here, where he could be properly seen to, but he just wouldn't leave his parish, even at the end. Lewes is not a bad place, but it was such a relief to get back.'

'Oh, I remember!' Daphne exclaimed. 'That must have been my first summer here, two years ago. There was all that problem with the fête because you weren't here to open it!'

Cyril gave a loud, throaty chuckle. 'That fête! What a disaster! At the PCC meeting, when we realised that we had no one to open the fête, everyone had their little idea about who should be asked. The argument went on for hours, as I remember it, and afterwards everyone thought that someone else was taking care of it, but in the end no one did, so no one showed up on the day to do the honours!'

'And it rained,' Daphne added.

'Didn't it just!' Cyril chortled. 'Absolutely teemed, all

day. Had to have it in the church hall, and of course no one came that didn't have to.'

'The "fête worse than death", Father Neville still calls it,' Lady Constance said with a wry smile. 'I'm sure he still holds me personally responsible.'

'You *will* be doing the honours this Saturday, I assume?' Cyril laughed.

'Oh, certainly. I wouldn't miss it. I do hope we have good weather this year. It's so much nicer when the teas can be held in the vicarage garden.'

In due time they moved into the dining room. 'Just a simple cold supper,' Lady Constance apologised. 'I do hope you don't mind.' The 'simple cold supper' included asparagus vinaigrette and smoked salmon, as well as a bottle of a fine vintage wine, and finished with an exquisite home-made sorbet, so David minded not at all.

'I'm curious,' Cyril said, as they neared the end of the meal. 'How did you and Daphne get to know each other?'

'Oh, we go back a long way, don't we, Daphne?'

'Over twenty years,' she confirmed.

Lady Constance looked interested, though her good breeding prevented her from asking any probing questions. Cyril, though, had no such inhibitions. 'Where did you meet?'

They looked at each other and laughed. 'In a church, of course!' Daphne replied. 'Here in London.'

'I was at university, and Daphne was teaching. We found that we had a mutual interest in churches – architecture, furnishings, the lot – and we became great chums. I was a young ignoramus – I loved it all, but I didn't know much about it – and Daphne knew so much. She took me under her wing. We did quite a bit of travelling, exploring . . .'

'And before I knew it, he had passed me by!' Daphne added ruefully.

'Which brings us to the crypt chapel,' Lady Constance interposed. 'What do you have to tell me about that, young man?'

David pulled some papers out of his breast pocket. 'I must warn you that I'm not a professional,' he said with a self-deprecating smile. 'I've never done anything like this before. But I'm tremendously excited by it.' He indicated the papers. 'I've brought a few notes to show you. I must tell you I'm very impressed by the chapel. It was done fairly early in Comper's career, before he reached his mature genius, but it shows all the marks of his style, in the very best sense of that term. His characteristic use of blue and gold, the lavish, not to say reckless, application of gold leaf, the wonderful angels . . .' Soon he was involved in technical detail about paint and gilding, fabrics and embroidery.

Lady Constance asked intelligent questions but mostly listened, impressed by his expertise. At last she said, 'You clearly know what you're about. Go ahead and engage whatever craftsmen you need to do the work, and I will happily pay the bills. All I ask is that you supervise the work to make sure it's done properly.'

David nodded, satisfied.

'And now, Miss Elford, don't you think we ought to leave the gentlemen to their port for a while?'

After the ladies had gone, David said conversationally, 'I understand that you've been churchwarden at St Anne's for a long time.'

'Donkey's years, my boy. I've seen Vicars come, and Vicars go.'

'I've heard rumours that Father Neville might not be around much longer.'

Cyril sighed lugubriously, and shook his head. 'I dread the thought. Don't get me wrong, my boy. He's a jolly good priest, and I like him very much. But I just can't imagine life around here without . . . Mrs Neville. Emily.'

'You've known her a long time?'

'Practically all her life, I suppose. I remember her as a girl – a tiny little thing she was. Her father and I were great friends. He lives in St Albans now – I don't see him very often. But in those days . . . well. As I say, she was a lovely little thing. Enchanting girl, Emily Bates. And then, after my wife died it was, she came back from university, and I was just bowled over! She was still tiny and delicate, but she'd grown into the most exquisite young woman.' He looked at David over his wine glass; his rheumy old eyes were filled with misty tears. 'I had a bit more to offer in those days. And I thought . . . well, I don't mind telling you, my boy. I had my hopes.'

'What happened?'

He shook his head again, more slowly. 'He came. Gabriel Neville came. No other man stood a chance against him. I don't blame her, mind. But . . . well, I had my hopes,' he repeated forlornly.

David topped up the port glasses and made meaningless comforting noises. He realised with a start that this old man was the first person he'd found who actually had a reason to hate Gabriel. The oldest motive in the book . . . But what could he possibly hope to gain by driving Gabriel (and Emily) away from St Anne's? And how could he know about Peter Maitland?

Chapter 13

Let his children be vagabonds, and beg their bread:
*   let them seek it also out of desolate places.*
Let the extortioner consume all that he hath: and let
*   the stranger spoil his labour.*

Psalm 109.9–20

'Isn't it dreadful,' David commented, buttering a morsel of toast and heaping it with marmalade. 'I haven't been able to get myself up for early Mass yet this week.'

'I shouldn't feel too guilty about it,' Daphne replied as she poured him another cup of tea. 'After all, it is your holiday.'

'You should know by now that "guilt" is my middle name,' he said lightly. 'I can feel guilty about anything. Sins of omission, sins of commission – they're all grist for my mill.'

'So what are you going to do today?'

'Get to work making arrangements about the chapel, I should think. I say, Daphne, I couldn't talk you into making some phone-calls for me, could I?' He looked slightly sheepish; she couldn't help laughing.

'I'll be glad to do what I can, but don't you think it would save a lot of time and effort for you to talk to these

113

people yourself?' she said sensibly.

'I suppose you're right,' he agreed reluctantly. 'Maybe I could nip around and see some of them in person.'

She shook her head in affectionate amusement. 'Suit yourself. But don't forget that Tuesday is the day that they serve lunches in the church hall. You might enjoy coming – if you think you can stand another session with the inmates of St Anne's.'

'Perhaps I will put in an appearance,' he said. 'Though I don't suppose I can expect gourmet fare.'

'Quiche and salad, most likely. But it's usually very good. It's all home-made, and the sweets are generally excellent.'

'You've convinced me. I'll catch up with you at lunch-time, then.'

David entered the church hall, balancing a plate of quiche in one hand and an incredibly rich and delicious-looking sweet in the other. He was relieved to see a number of familiar faces in the crowded room, though, naturally enough on a weekday, there was a dearth of men. They mainly seemed to be concentrated at one table, and he started towards them. Venerable Bead was conversing earnestly with Tony Kent – David remembered that Tony was a teacher, and would be on his summer holidays – and Cyril Fitzjames sat with them, not joining in and evidently not even listening. David instinctively followed Cyril's gaze to another table. Yes, there was Emily, and with her Gabriel, and Daphne, trying to catch his eye and gesturing towards an empty seat. He sighed and made his way over to join them.

'David, sit down quickly!' Daphne greeted him. 'I've

had to fend off all sorts of people from your seat. I've just been telling Emily about our evening with Lady Constance.'

'Hello, David,' Emily put in. 'She's got me drooling over the smoked salmon.'

Gabriel acknowledged him with a nod. 'Daphne tells me you've been hard at work over the chapel.'

'Yes. It's a slow time of year for the workmen, and I think they'll actually be able to begin work by next week sometime.'

'That's splendid news,' Gabriel said heartily. 'And now, if you'll all excuse me, I want to get home and start on my sermon for Sunday. I can't afford to leave it to much later in the week, with the fête coming up. See you later, darling,' he added to his wife; they all watched his tall cassocked figure leave the room before resuming their conversation.

'Oh, the fête,' Emily grimaced.

'Well, it can't be as bad as the "fête worse than death",' Daphne observed comfortingly.

Emily came back quickly, 'No, but I'll still be glad this time next week when it's a "fête accompli".'

David laughed in appreciation. 'What are your responsibilities?'

'Well, in the afternoon I have to oversee the teas in the vicarage garden, though I should have quite a few helpers. And in the morning I'm lumbered with the jam stall as usual. Lucy's offered to help me with that, fortunately. That way I can start getting organised for the teas in plenty of time.'

'Is this one of Lucy's quiches?' Daphne asked, as she took a bite.

'No, it's one of mine, which means it's still Lucy's recipe,' Emily replied. She explained to David. 'My friend Lucy's a superb cook. She taught me how to cook when I got married. That sweet you've got is one of her specialities.'

He eyed it with anticipation. 'It looks wonderful. Just the sort of thing I shouldn't eat. Can't I meet this great gourmet chef?'

'Oh, she's not here today. If you want to meet Lucy, you must come to the organ recital tomorrow. That's something she never misses – Lucy's a real music-lover.'

'Then I shall definitely come. Is this something that happens every week?'

'Yes, every Wednesday at lunch-time.'

A woman approached their table, looking anxious. Initially David didn't recognise her, then realised that he'd never seen Julia Dawson without her husband before; she looked incomplete somehow. Her face reminded him of some nocturnal woodland animal, with its wide, startled-looking eyes, its long, pointed nose, and its receding chin. She didn't really look exactly like her husband, he decided: Roger Dawson had more resemblance to a predatory creature, a wolf perhaps, with his sharp, prominent teeth. It was their identical curdled-milk expressions and the overall greyness of them that gave that impression of likeness; both had straight, iron-grey hair, an unhealthy greyish tinge to their skin, and a way of moving that was both self-effacing and obtrusive. Julia Dawson was dressed in an unseasonal murky-coloured jumper, as she sidled up to Emily purposefully.

'Have you been baking cakes?' she asked, with an intense quiver in her voice, completely out of proportion to the question.

'Oh, yes,' Emily affirmed. 'But my freezer's getting full, I'm afraid. I don't know if I'll have room for the ones I did this morning.'

Julia stood stock-still, her face registering horror. 'But that's terrible! What are you going to do?'

'Put them in someone else's freezer, I imagine.'

'I can put them in mine. I can get them right now, if you're finished here.' She looked at Emily's empty plate. 'Running the cake stall is such a *responsibility*. You just can't imagine.'

Emily rose, with a regretful smile for David and Daphne. 'I'll see you tomorrow at the organ recital, then.'

'She won't see me,' Daphne stated as Emily departed.

'Why not? Don't you like Miles Taylor?'

Daphne looked at him shrewdly. 'I'm not one of the old ladies in his fan club, if that's what you mean. He knows I haven't got any money, so he never bothers being nice to me.'

'Are you saying . . .'

'I'm saying that he makes a great fuss over some of the old ladies, and they all adore him.' She smiled blandly, inviting him to draw his own conclusions.

The two empty chairs at their table were now being claimed by Cecily Framlingham and Mavis Conwell. Mavis barely acknowledged their greeting; Cecily, too, virtually ignored their presence, but chatted volubly to Mavis. 'It's too crowded today. I just don't know where all these people come from. I suppose it's this nasty weather that brings people indoors. It's just ruined the flowers, the frightful weather we've had this summer. I simply don't know what we'll have to sell on the flower stall at the fête.' She turned to Mavis. 'What have you got in your garden that might do?'

'Oh, I don't know,' she replied offhandedly. 'Not much, I suppose.'

'How about the lobelia? Or the dianthus? I wish your antirrhinum were better this year. Maybe some of that artemisia – people like that for drying, don't they?'

'You can have whatever you like.'

'We can always try to sell some of Arthur's marrows, if the worst comes to the worst. The rain doesn't seem to be doing *them* any harm.'

Mavis made no reply. Frustrated by her friend's lack of response, Cecily tried a topic calculated to engage Mavis's interest. 'Did you see that Norman Newsome has resigned? Arthur read it in this morning's newspaper.'

Mavis's reaction to this bombshell was less than gratifying. 'Oh, really?'

'Yes. Apparently the Dean decided there was no smoke without fire, if you know what I mean. That's what you've said all along, Mavis. No smoke without fire.'

David, intrigued by her uncharacteristic silence, observed Mavis out of the corner of his eye as he ate – with great appreciation – his sweet. She seemed to be watching the entrance; she gave a little start and David raised his head in time to see a young man hesitate for a moment at the door, then slouch towards her. He was a well-built and good-looking young man, with coal-black hair worn very short, but there was an indefinable weakness around his mouth, and his posture was appalling. The manly Craig, David concluded, as he reached the table.

'Craig,' his mother said flatly.

'Mum, where's the ten quid I asked you for? I need it now.' He spoke in a low, urgent voice.

'I haven't got it, Craig. I told you I didn't have it.' She looked frightened.

'But I need it! Well, give me a fiver then.'

She scrabbled in her brown vinyl handbag, looking for loose change. A couple of pound coins appeared, and a few odd coppers. 'This is all I've got. You can have it.'

He looked at the proffered coins with scorn. 'Is that the best you can do? That's not much bloody good, is it?' His voice was low, but it carried.

'Craig, please! Not in church!' she hissed in an agonised whisper.

'Maybe I can help,' Cecily interposed, pulling a five-pound note out of her handbag. 'Consider it a loan, Mavis.'

Craig took it from her, inspecting it with care. 'I'll expect the other fiver tonight, Mum. Don't forget,' he muttered ungraciously, and, glowering sullenly, turned and made his way out.

Most people who were close enough to hear anything of this exchange were looking down at their plates in embarrassment, but Beryl Ball, who had just come into the room, observed his departure with frank enjoyment.

She shuffled up to their table. 'That's a fine boy you've got, Mavis. Quite a high-spirited lad.' She nodded, smiled, and thrust her teeth out with her tongue.

David couldn't help raising his head and looking at her. She was dressed all in yellow, with a large-brimmed yellow hat. He stared involuntarily at the glassy-eyed canaries perched on its brim, as if ready to burst into song, or into flight.

'What are you looking at?' she challenged him loudly. 'I know that look – you want me, don't you? Well, you can't have me! If I don't give in to the Vicar, I certainly won't give in to you! I've kept myself pure for over fifty years, young man! I have never been touched by a man!' With a majestic toss of her head, which sent the canaries bobbing, she turned and hobbled out of the room. Mavis took advantage of the distraction to escape, with Cecily close behind her.

David looked at Daphne with a bemused smile. 'Well, I must say. You certainly put on a good show for visitors at this place. And I thought I was going to have a quiet lunch!'

Daphne shook her head. 'Anything to keep you amused. It looks as though you're ready for a cup of tea. Shall I get it? Or would you rather have a coffee?'

'Tea would be lovely, thanks.' He watched her make her way to the table with the urn. She stopped to speak to a woman who had just come in, and David observed the newcomer with quiet amusement. Barbara Pym, he thought. She looks exactly like someone out of Barbara Pym.

She was a large woman, tall and well upholstered though not fat. All of her clothes were just a bit too small for her; her dress encased her body tightly, and stopped just short of the knee, where a lace petticoat peeped out coyly, and she wore a white vinyl raincoat, also very tight and a bit shorter than the dress. Her face, topped by tightly permed white hair, was large and round, like an undercooked dumpling, with small features and pale gooseberry eyes. Her shoes were an old-fashioned brown, and as she approached with Daphne he noted that she walked slightly pigeon-toed, with small mincing steps that seemed quite out of keeping with her substantial frame.

Daphne introduced them. 'Mary, this is my friend David Middleton-Brown. David, Miss Mary Hughes.'

'Hello, David, it is so nice to meet you.' Her voice was also unexpected: it was precious and slightly breathless.

'My pleasure, Miss Hughes. Are you joining us?' David rose gallantly and pulled out a chair for her.

He was rewarded with a look of extreme gratitude. 'Oh, thank you. You're most kind.' She sat down and leaned toward him confidingly; he got a not-unexpected whiff of Pears' Soap. 'I do hope that Beryl hasn't upset you. Daphne tells me that you've had a little encounter.'

'I've been assured that she's harmless,' he replied.

'Oh, she is. I've known Beryl since we were girls together, if you can believe it!' She giggled in a coy way. 'We were confirmed together in this church. That's been a few years ago, of course.'

'Has she always been . . . like this?'

'Oh, Beryl has always been a bit peculiar, if you know what I mean. I suppose you've heard about all the men who have been in love with her. I wish I could tell you it was true!'

'You mean it's not?' Daphne was disillusioned, if not surprised.

'No, indeed. But she's always had a fixation about clergymen. All men, really – it's quite dreadful. *Sex*,' she whispered furtively. 'It's unhinged her mind. Not having any, I mean.' She blushed at her own candour.

'A whisky before bedtime is something Mother would never have approved of,' David said, stretched out on Daphne's sofa.

Daphne refrained from saying that Mother was no longer around to approve or disapprove of anything that her son did. From her own observations, Daphne had concluded that Mother had done much more of the latter than the former, and not to her son's benefit. 'Well, I approve heartily,' was all she said.

'Tell me about Mary Hughes. She's so Barbara Pym.'

'Yes, isn't she? One of her "excellent women" types, but we have a lot of those at St Anne's.'

'What's her story?'

'I don't think there's that much to tell. Spinster, obviously. She looked after her aged parents until they died a few years ago. They left her well cared-for financially, so she can now devote herself to the church and other "good works". She still lives in the house where she was born. She's a very well-meaning person, and usually gets lumbered with all the jobs that nobody else wants.'

David pondered the events of the day. 'I know I've promised Emily to go to that organ recital tomorrow, but in the morning I fancy getting away from it all. Do you realise that we haven't looked at a single London church since I've been here? How about it, Daphne? It's been years since we've done a London church crawl. You can show me all your favourites. Let's get an early start. Well, a civilised start,' he amended.

Chapter 14

*Therefore will I praise thee and thy faithfulness, O
God, playing upon an instrument of musick: unto
thee will I sing upon the harp, O thou Holy One
of Israel.*

Psalm 71.20

Wednesday morning had passed too quickly; David and
Daphne agreed to continue their leisurely progress through
the London churches on the following day, and David
arrived at St Anne's in good time for the organ recital.

Mary Hughes handed him a programme at the door.
'This is your first time, isn't it, Mr Middleton-Brown?
You're in for quite a treat, I can tell you.'

He glanced down the list of pieces. 'Mm. Sounds very
nice. A most ambitious programme. Mr Taylor is a very
accomplished organist, I believe.'

'Oh, yes, he's wonderful!'

He was surprised to see a sizeable audience gathering
in the nave. There were many people he didn't recognise,
and he assumed that the weekly event must draw in many
regulars from outside the congregation.

Emily was waiting for him inside the door. 'Here you
are, David. The best seats are going fast!' She led him up

the aisle and selected three seats. 'We'll save one for Lucy.'

'Is it always this well attended? I'm amazed to see so many people here on a weekday!'

'Oh, definitely. See that group over there?' She indicated a section of the prime seats, distinguished chiefly by the uniformly white heads of the inhabitants. 'Lucy and I call that the Fan Club. They're all here every week.'

David looked around curiously. 'Is Miles's wife here?'

Emily laughed. 'The mysterious Mrs Taylor? Not a chance!'

'What do you mean?'

'Would you believe that no one at St Anne's has ever seen his wife? Lucy and I think that he keeps her hidden away, so as not to damage his mystique with the Fan Club. The old ladies love him, you know.'

David nodded. 'So it would seem.' He went on, 'This really is an impressive crowd. Do you get many people from outside the church?'

'Well, there are quite a few people who work around here who come regularly, and then there's always the odd tourist who wanders in.'

'You ought to charge admission.'

'That's what Miles says. We do take a retiring collection, but he thinks that's not good enough.'

An expectant hush had fallen; a few of the more eager members of the Fan Club were craning their necks towards the chancel. Mary Hughes abandoned her post at the door and hurried up the aisle to her seat amongst the Fan Club.

'Looks like Lucy's going to be late,' Emily whispered.

Lucy slipped into the church halfway through the Bach

Prelude and Fugue and decided to stand at the back until the end of the piece. She spotted Emily, with the empty seat beside her; on her other side there was a man she'd never seen before. She observed him with interest and wondered who he was.

During the applause at the end of the fugue, she moved to claim her seat beside Emily, and whispered introductions were made. There was just time enough for Lucy to get a quick impression of the man Emily said was called David Middleton-Brown. He was quite ordinary-looking, distinguished by no particular beauty of form or feature. He appeared to be of an average height, and had brown hair, dusted with grey at the temples, and pleasant hazel eyes. But it was a nice face, Lucy decided – above all a kind face.

The recital continued. The final piece was a very dissonant and somewhat formless work that David found much more difficult to appreciate than the Bach. After he'd finished, the lanky organist descended into an eager crowd of admirers; Mary Hughes was in the forefront. 'I didn't realise that Miss Hughes was such a great fan,' David remarked, as they stood up.

'Definitely,' Emily replied. 'She thinks that our Miles is the "bees' knees".'

He turned to Lucy for the first time. 'Emily tells me that you come every week. Don't you count as one of the Fan Club?'

She laughed. 'No, not I. The man's organ playing is superb, but . . . well, he's just not my type. For that matter, I don't think I'm his type, either.'

'Then that is his loss,' David said gallantly, feeling a bit foolish as he said it. She smiled at him almost conspiratorially as Emily asked her a question about jams, and for a moment the two women were involved in a technical discussion of boiling points and pectins. Though he hadn't given her a great deal of thought prior to this meeting, Lucy wasn't really what he'd expected, David decided, watching them with their heads together, one dark and one rosy. He'd thought she'd be much like Emily, he supposed, but the two were very different, and not just in colouring. Emily was wearing what David had come to recognise as her preferred everyday garb – jeans and a loose cotton jumper – whereas Lucy was elegant in an ivory lawn blouse with a delicate antique lace collar and a calf-length flowered skirt in shades of willow green and apricot. There was something so graceful in the way she pushed her hair back from her face with her long tapering fingers. That incredible aureole of hair! She wasn't a girl, David realised. The network of tiny lines around her greeny-blue eyes told him that she would never see thirty again. But the quality of her beauty was not dependent on youth.

'Do forgive us, David,' she said, turning to him with a charming smile. 'We've been very rude, talking about jams like that! But this fête seems to be overshadowing everything that happens around here at the moment.'

'Why don't you both come back to the vicarage and have some tea?' Emily suggested. 'Gabriel's out this afternoon, and with the children away it would be nice to have some company.'

'That would be very nice,' David accepted. 'I don't think Daphne's expecting me back just yet.'

Lucy looked regretful. 'I'm sorry, Em, but I really can't. I started a painting this morning, and I must get back to it. I'll tell you what, though – could you both come to me for tea tomorrow afternoon? It might be finished by then, and you can tell me what you think.'

'Super, Luce. David, how about you?'

'I'd love to come, thank you.'

'Lovely. I'll see you both tomorrow, then. It was very nice to meet you, David.' She smiled as they parted at the church door.

'And you.' His eyes followed her involuntarily as she walked down the street and around the corner.

Emily tugged at his arm. 'Come on, David. You can't get out of having tea with me so easily.'

He smiled down at her. 'That's the farthest thing from my mind.'

In a few minutes they were settled in the drawing room at the vicarage, sipping tea. 'Have some of this cake, David.' She pulled a slightly guilty face. 'If Julia Dawson finds out I've been raiding the fête cakes . . .'

'She won't hear it from me,' he assured her. 'You can consider it advance advertising. It's absolutely delicious, and when the great day comes I intend to buy one exactly like it.'

'You'd better get there early, then. The cakes sell out quite quickly.'

'I'm sure I'll be there early. Seriously, is there any way I can help on Saturday? I suppose all the stall assignments have been fixed for months, but if there's anything I can do . . .'

'Thanks, David. I'm certain that no volunteers will be turned away! If you'd be willing to go where you were needed . . .'

'Yes, of course. I'll leave myself entirely in your hands.' He looked around the drawing room with interest; it was the first time he'd been there. 'This is a lovely room,' he said. 'Have you decorated it? Or was it like this when you moved in?'

'No, it was awful when I came – very dark and gloomy. It had been that way for years, I think, and Gabriel hadn't really been here long enough to do anything about it. But I couldn't bear it. It was my first try at decorating, with lots of help from Lucy.'

'I suppose she's good at that sort of thing?'

'Very. Wait till you see her place – it's stunning.'

'Did I understand correctly that she's some kind of artist?'

'Oh, yes. She does water-colours. Didn't I tell you? But they're not the sort of thing you'd expect. She'll show you some of her work tomorrow, if you're interested. Lucy's extremely talented. Her things are very much in demand, in certain circles – she makes quite a nice living from it, too.'

He absorbed all this information in silence. 'Does she live alone?'

'She's not married, if that's what you mean,' Emily replied with a knowing smile. 'She was married once, when she was quite young, but I don't think it lasted very long, and she never talks about it.'

'Not even to you?'

'Not even to me. Lucy is a wonderful listener – people are always telling her their problems – but she very rarely talks about herself.'

'Then she must be in much demand at St Anne's. There seem to be a great many talkers there, and very few listeners.'

'She doesn't spend a great deal of time at St Anne's, to

be honest. She's very much on the fringe.'

'Why is that?'

Emily shrugged. 'I'm not really sure. Her work, I suppose – it keeps her quite busy. And her father was – still is – a Vicar, so maybe she's all churched out.'

'Do you think she feels . . . well, would being divorced make any difference, as far as St Anne's is concerned?'

Emily considered. 'No, I don't think the divorce thing really bothers her much. A few of the congregation would mind about it: the Dawsons, for example, wouldn't approve at all. But Lucy wouldn't care if they approved or not – she'd think that was their problem, not hers.'

'It's easy to cast the first stone, isn't it?' David mused. Emily looked at him questioningly, and, afraid he'd betrayed something, he quickly changed the subject. 'Well, I'm looking forward to our tea tomorrow. I'm going out with Daphne in the morning, and don't know when I'll be back. Shall I stop by for you, or just meet you there?'

'It will be easier for you if you don't have to worry about me. I'll tell you how to get to Lucy's – it's not far.'

Chapter 15

Thou hast loved to speak all words that may do hurt: O thou false tongue.

Psalm 52.5

That evening, David felt a bit unsettled and restless, for no reason he could put his finger on. He tried to read the newspaper, and found it boring; he even attempted to watch television, something he rarely did. Finally he suggested to Daphne that they go out for a meal. 'Forget about cooking tonight, why don't you. Let me take you out, Daphne. Do you have a favourite place?'

'We could get a Chinese take-away, and eat it here,' she suggested.

He grimaced. 'No, I'd like to go out. What's the matter – are you ashamed to be seen with me in public?'

'Oh, all right. I just thought . . .'

'Come on, then, Daphne. Where shall we go?'

'There are several pizza places down along Kensington High Street, if you like. Cheap and cheerful.'

'It doesn't have to be cheap and cheerful. I'm quite happy to take you somewhere nice, if you like. You've been spoiling me – let me spoil you for a change!'

Daphne pulled a face. 'Pizza is also quick, and I've just

remembered that I promised to call and see Mavis Conwell this evening. We could stop there on the way back, if we don't take too long over our meal.'

'Mavis Conwell? Whatever for?'

'I'm not sure,' she replied. 'She rang this afternoon, and was quite insistent that I come to see her. Or at least she wanted to see me, and I suggested that I go along there, rather than have her come here. I thought I might never get rid of her if she came here.'

'Yes, at least we can make a speedy exit. She didn't give you any idea what it was about?'

'No. Just said she wanted to see me, and it had to be tonight. Well, we'll soon find out.'

'Right, then. Let's go have a pizza, and maybe a bottle of wine, to fortify us for the loathsome Mrs Conwell. Perhaps if we're lucky we'll have another glimpse of the manly Craig . . .'

The Conwells' house was a small terrace, in a street surprisingly close to St Anne's and the splendid homes that surrounded the church. Property values in this part of London were so high that it was still worth a considerable amount of money, David surmised; he wondered what the late Mr Conwell had done for a living.

Mavis opened the door to them quickly, almost as if she'd been waiting. Perhaps she'd seen them coming from a window.

'Oh, Daphne. Thank you for coming. And you've brought Mr Middleton-Brown with you.' She smiled her fierce, false smile at them. 'You'd better be careful, Daphne. People will start talking about you. You wouldn't want that, would you? I mean, having a man to stay with you in your flat! Some people might think there was something in it! Of course, if anyone said anything like that to me, I'd set them straight for you.' She looked back and forth between them speculatively, showing her teeth.

David could feel Daphne tense beside him; she was so furious that she was unable to speak. He had never known her to be at a loss for words, and marvelled at Mavis's ability to get at her.

'Good evening, Mrs Conwell,' he said smoothly. 'I'm so sorry to come along without being invited, but we've just been out for a meal.'

'Come in,' she beckoned. 'Have you been to someone's house, then? I know you were invited to Lady Constance's on Monday. Cyril told me. I'm sure that lots of people are jealous of Daphne, having you all to herself.' She smiled at him again, coyly this time. 'Especially when there are other eligible women around who are closer to your own age!'

He was repelled by her implication, as she stood there grinning at him, and he felt incensed on Daphne's behalf. When neither of them spoke, Mavis ushered them into the room on the right of the entrance hall. It was a small sitting room, neat as a pin.

'Would either of you like a coffee?' Mavis offered.

David nodded, out of a desire to get rid of her for a few minutes rather than from a need for coffee.

Daphne nearly exploded when she'd left the room. 'Of all the damn cheek!' she whispered fiercely.

David put his hands on her shoulders to calm her, and pushed her down into a chair. 'Down, girl. Consider the source.'

He moved around the room, pretending to examine things,

and tactfully allowing Daphne a moment to collect herself.

It was obvious from the condition of the room that Mavis was a house-proud woman. Everything was in its place, and dusted meticulously. He picked up a 'Souvenir of Brighton' ash-tray, with a picture of the Royal Pavilion stamped in the centre. 'How tasteful,' he murmured. More promising was a photo on the mantelpiece. He strolled over and examined it: in a plastic frame, the manly Craig sulked petulantly on a beach somewhere. Mavis also had a large television set, similar to the one at home in Wymondham. In many ways, David reflected, looking around the tastelessly tidy room, Mavis was like his mother. That didn't bear thinking about.

Craig in the flesh was nowhere in evidence, David noted with regret. He might have provided a diversion from Mavis's relentless awfulness. And from what David had seen on the previous day, the boy seemed to have a dampening effect on her that couldn't help but be an improvement.

By the time Mavis returned with the coffee, Daphne had regained a semblance of her usual manner. She still looked a little white around the mouth, but at least she was able to speak. 'What was it you wanted to see me about, Mavis?' she asked in her blunt way, unwilling to spend any more time than was necessary with this odious woman.

Mavis tried to look offhand. 'Oh, it was nothing, really. Nothing important.'

'What, then?' Daphne demanded.

'Well, I just wondered about something. The church books – they're usually kept in that drawer in the sacristy. But . . . well, they aren't there now.'

'No, they're not,' agreed Daphne, perversely forcing Mavis to be more direct.

'Well, where are they then?' Mavis finally asked. Her attempt at appearing disinterested was not very successful.

'You know the Quinquennial Inspection is coming up. Gabriel's asked me to lock them in the safe until then. To make sure they don't fall into the wrong hands,' she added with a look at Mavis's anxious face.

'But I'm a churchwarden. I have a right to see them,' Mavis insisted.

'Of course you do. No one said you didn't. You know where the safe key is kept, don't you?'

'I'm not sure. You showed me once, but . . .'

'It's in the vestment cupboard, the one nearest to the safe. On a hook. Would you like me to get the books out for you tomorrow?'

'Oh, no, thanks. I just wondered. Just in case . . .' Mavis bit her lip and was silent for a moment, then changed the subject quickly. 'Did you hear that Norman Newsome has resigned? That's one way to get that kind of filth out of the Church of England. The *News of the World* has done us a great service, don't you agree?'

Chapter 16

*O sing unto the Lord a new song: for he hath done
marvellous things.*

Psalm 98.1

Thursday was a day in which bursts of heavy rain had
alternated with brief and glorious sunny spells. For once,
none of the churches that he and Daphne had visited had
been locked, so David was in a rather cheerful mood as he
walked in the sunshine to Lucy's house. She lived in a
small mews, just south of Kensington Gardens, and with
Emily's directions he had no difficulty finding it. The
narrow house had a minute garden in front, imaginatively
laid out and immaculately tended.

'Hello, David,' she greeted him, opening the door with
a welcoming smile. She was dressed in primrose yellow
today, and the effect was an entirely different one than
Beryl Ball's yellow ensemble, he noted with approval. She
led him into a small sitting room, flooded with the afternoon sun; it seemed to be full of fresh flowers.

'What a very lovely room,' he said impulsively. It had
none of the grandeur of Lady Constance's drawing room,
or the one in the vicarage, but it was totally in harmony
with itself and with its owner, reflecting her sense of gra-

cious serenity in every detail, and he appreciated its warmth and its integrity.

'I'm glad you like it.' She smiled. She had a deliciously enigmatic closed-lipped smile which David found enchanting. 'Please sit wherever you like.' He chose a small but comfortable armchair covered in flowered chintz. She left him looking around the room and returned a few minutes later with a tea-tray, which she perched on an overstuffed footstool.

'I hope you don't mind too much,' she said, curling into a chair. 'It seems that it will just be the two of us this afternoon. I suppose I should give you the opportunity to escape, if you want to.'

'Not at all. But what's happened to Emily?'

'She rang me this morning – apparently she'd forgotten she'd promised Julia Dawson that she'd join her in a cake-baking session all afternoon. She was sure we'd understand. It doesn't do to upset Julia Dawson, after all.' She rolled her eyes.

'And I think that Julia Dawson is rather easily upset,' he observed. 'Well, it's Emily's loss, but I think we can manage without her.'

She poured the tea into antique china cups. 'It's Earl Grey. Would you fancy a slice of lemon instead of milk?'

'That sounds lovely for a change.'

She passed him his tea, then produced a plate of delicious-looking finger sandwiches. 'These are prawn and avocado, and the others are smoked salmon and cucumber. Rather monotonously fishy, I'm afraid.'

'They look marvellous. Emily told me that you were a gourmet cook.'

'Emily flatters me. I just enjoy pottering about in the

kitchen, that's all. And I love good food,' she added.

He savoured the sandwiches, noting that there were more delicious-looking things on the tea-tray – several sorts of cakes and pastries. 'I could easily get spoilt by this kind of treatment. I'm usually lucky to get a biscuit out of a tin with my cup of tea.' He felt vaguely disloyal to Daphne as he spoke, but the feeling was dispelled by Lucy's warm smile.

'Maybe it's about time you were a bit spoilt. I don't think it will do you any harm at this stage.'

A small marmalade-coloured cat crept from under the sofa and looked hopefully at the sandwiches. 'Sophie, I don't think so,' her mistress said mildly.

He extended his hand tentatively towards the cat, who sniffed it, then, satisfied, jumped on his lap and immediately began purring loudly.

'Sophie is quite fussy about laps. You should feel very honoured.'

He stroked the cat's warm fur, eliciting even louder purrs. Her contentment communicated itself to him, and together with the tasty food, the afternoon sun, the cosy room, the smell of fresh flowers, and the congenial company, produced in him a feeling of great well-being. The empty house in Wymondham, the clamour of egos at St Anne's – they all seemed very far removed.

'You seem used to cats, David. Have you got one?'

'No. I always thought I'd like to have one, but Mother would never allow animals in the house. She's dead now, so I suppose I could get a cat if I wanted to.'

'Has it been very long since she died?'

'No, only about two months. I still haven't got used to living without her.'

139

'I don't know anything at all about you, David. Where do you live?'

'Wymondham, in Norfolk. It's a market town, quite near Norwich. A lovely town, really, with a beautiful abbey church.'

'And what do you do in Wymondham?'

'Well, I work in Norwich, actually. I'm a solicitor. Nothing special. It's just a job, and a pretty tedious one at that.' He sighed.

'And have you always lived at home . . . with your parents, your mother?'

'Not always. I read law at the University of London, and my first job was in London. But my father died about ten years ago. I was living and working in Brighton at the time. My mother . . . well, her health wasn't good. It seemed like the only thing to do at the time, to move back home. It's a very boring story.'

'I'm interested,' she said firmly. 'You're an only child?'

'Yes. My parents married quite late in life. There was only me.'

He found himself talking at length about his childhood, telling her stories only dimly remembered and never before shared. She listened intently, twisting a lock of hair around her finger and asking questions to draw him out. When the mantel clock gently chimed six, he looked at it in surprise.

The cat was still on his lap, but the sandwiches and the cakes had all been consumed. He smiled a little self-consciously at Lucy. 'I seem to have done a lot of talking, and a lot of eating. Look at the time! I really should be leaving you in peace. But you promised to show me your paintings. Will you?'

'Of course, if you'd like.' She rose, and he regretfully deposed Sophie and followed her out of the room and up the stairs. 'I've made the second bedroom into a studio,' she explained. 'It's in the back, so it gets the northern sun – when there is any, that is – and I've had a skylight put in. This time of year I can work well into the late afternoon in natural light.'

There were several paintings in various stages of completion about the room. The medium was watercolour, but her works were far from the bland impressionistic flower paintings he'd halfway expected. The paintings were stylised and highly individualistic, featuring abstract motifs repeated in clear colours. It was obvious that she had a great deal of talent and skill, and David could see why her work was in demand. 'Why, they're brilliant!'

'Surprised?' she asked wryly.

'Not at all. But . . . well, they're just so unusual. Wherever do you get your ideas?'

'That's a well-kept secret, but I think I can trust you!' She smiled. 'Most of my inspiration comes from the good old Victoria & Albert. I'll never run out of ideas as long as the V & A is right around the corner! All those patterns, all those incredible designs.' She pulled out a sketch-book filled with pencil drawings of Egyptian antiquities, Indian textiles, Chinese porcelain.

'Well, for whatever it's worth, I'm impressed.'

She led him back downstairs.

'How long have you lived in this house?' he asked. 'You've done it up so beautifully.'

'Oh, about twelve years now. It's taken most of that time to get it fixed up to suit me.'

'How do you . . . well, don't you hate living alone?' David blurted.

'Well, I'm used to it,' she replied candidly, pausing at the foot of the stairs and looking up at him. 'And, after all, what choice do I have? It's just one of those things.' She laughed and added without a trace of self-pity, 'You know what they say, and I'm afraid it's true: by the time you get to my age, all the good blokes are either married or gay.' Pushing back her hair, she went on, 'But I'll tell you what I *do* hate, and that's eating alone. If you don't have any plans for this evening, David, how about doing a lonely spinster a favour and staying for a meal?'

'I'd love to,' he replied instantly.

'It won't be anything special,' she warned. 'Just whatever I've got on hand.'

'You can't talk me out of it that easily.'

'Good.' She led him into the kitchen at the back of the house. It had been extended and fitted to her specifications. He looked around, impressed once again.

'It will be a privilege to watch you at work in this place. You will let me watch, won't you?'

'You do talk rubbish sometimes, David.' She laughed affectionately. 'You won't be watching, you'll be helping.'

Chapter 17

*The ungodly borroweth, and payeth not again: but
the righteous is merciful, and liberal.*

Psalm 37.21

Mavis Conwell fitted the large key into the sacristy door
and turned it with great care. No one was in the church at
that time on a Thursday evening, she knew, but you couldn't
be too careful. There was enough illumination coming in
the window so that she could avoid turning on a light. She
shut the door behind her and locked it with the key, then
located the key to the safe on its concealed hook in the
vestment cupboard. From the safe she drew out the large,
heavy ledger book, bound in blue cloth, and carried it over
to the desk in the corner.

She turned rapidly through its pages until she reached
the entries she was looking for. Very deliberately, she
took a small penknife from her pocket and neatly slid it
down the full length of the page. There! You could scarcely
tell that a page was missing. She folded the page up and
put it in her pocket along with the knife, before repeating
her steps in reverse. The whole operation had taken less
than five minutes.

*   *   *

The wine was unashamed plonk, but it tasted good, and the food was delicious. Lucy, with a little help from David, had concocted a pasta dish with browned butter and feta cheese, and a big leafy salad. Served with fresh French bread and plenty of sweet butter, and followed by fruit and cheese, it was a filling and satisfying meal. They talked and laughed without a pause through the preparation and consumption of it, then returned to the sitting room with their coffee.

David was amazed to realise that the subject of St Anne's had scarcely come up. 'Emily tells me that you manage to keep your distance from St Anne's,' he began.

'Yes, well, the Angel Gabriel manages to run it pretty well without my help,' she replied.

There was something in her tone of voice that piqued his interest. He looked at her guarded expression with curiosity. 'You don't like him much, do you?'

She shrugged, not bothering to deny it. 'No, not especially.'

'Why not?'

'Emily is my best friend. She worships the ground he walks on. I think he's a . . . well, I won't say it.'

David was intrigued. Was it possible that Lucy was one of those women who cherished an unrequited passion for the Vicar? Somehow he couldn't imagine it. 'But why?'

She shrugged again. 'For one thing, there's something . . . unsettling . . . about a man of forty who only looks half his age, don't you think?'

'That's hardly a reason to dislike him, Lucy. I wish I looked half as good as he does.'

She looked at him in the darkening room. 'I don't know why you always put yourself down,' she said shortly. She liked his air of maturity, the nice lines at the sides of his eyes when he smiled, the hint of grey in his hair. 'I like the way you look.'

He leaned over and switched on a light to cover his embarrassment. 'Father Gabriel,' he pursued. 'He . . . treats Emily well, doesn't he?'

'As well as a clergyman ever treats his wife, I suppose. I know that I'd never want to be married to one. I saw what it did to my mother, and I know how hard it is on Emily to share her husband with every lunatic in the parish.'

'But she doesn't seem to mind.'

'She minds, all right. Do you have any idea what she gave up to become Mrs Gabriel Neville?'

He was puzzled. 'No. She was quite young when they married, wasn't she?'

'She was twenty-one, and had just taken a first-class degree at Cambridge. She'd been offered a research fellowship to go on and take her doctorate. But the Angel Gabriel put an end to that.'

'Surely it was her decision?'

'But she was madly in love with him, and he didn't want to wait. They were married within six months.'

He was silent, remembering.

'And then, after she lost the first baby . . .' An involuntary noise from David stopped her and she looked sharply at him. 'Oh, you didn't know about that? I shouldn't talk about it, then.'

'Please,' he urged. 'I want to know.'

'The year after they were married. She carried it nearly to full term, then something happened. Well, she's so small, you see. Narrow-hipped – she's built almost like a boy.'

He wished that she hadn't put it quite like that.

Lucy's voice was full of pain for her friend. 'The doctors said that she'd never be able to carry a baby to term. They said it could kill her to try. But she was determined to give Gabriel a child. We talked about it often. She wanted children too, of course. But I think that she felt she had failed him, and that somehow she owed it to him.'

'And?' He was almost afraid to speak.

'A couple of years later she became pregnant again. They found out very early that it was twins. The doctors wanted to terminate the pregnancy. They said her chances of surviving and giving birth to two healthy children were . . . well. She was determined, as I said. She spent almost the entire nine months flat on her back. She was absolutely huge – you can just imagine. I'll give Gabriel credit – he brought in the best specialists that money could buy, and she came through it all right in the end. She nearly died, but she gave Gabriel his children, his precious Neville heirs.' The bitterness in her voice was unmistakable.

'I see.' He paused. 'I had no idea.'

'No, most people don't. She doesn't talk about it.' She refilled his coffee cup from the cafetière and forced a smile. 'Anyway, let's talk about something more cheerful. Any suggestions?'

'Well, I'm curious to know what you do with yourself on a Sunday, if you don't go to church? It's very difficult for me to imagine Sunday without it.'

She laughed more naturally. 'That's what I used to think, till I discovered a big wide world out there, outside the four walls of a church.' She looked at him as an idea occurred to her. 'I'll tell you what. If you want to know what I do on Sunday, why don't you join me this week?'

'Give me a hint what it is before I commit myself,' he said with a smile.

'Well, first of all, I go out for breakfast.' At his shocked look she went on, 'Yes, I know that's terribly decadent, but there's nothing quite like eating eggs that you haven't cooked yourself! Later, I go and spend most of the afternoon at the V & A, mainly sketching. I usually take along a sandwich or something, and when I get hungry I take a break. If the weather's nice I eat it in Kensington Gardens or Hyde Park and have a little walkabout, then go back to the V & A. When it closes I come home, and fix myself a nice supper.'

'You've talked me into it,' he affirmed. 'It never hurts to see how the other half lives . . .'

Walking back to Daphne's late that evening, David's route took him past the vicarage. He saw a light on in Gabriel's study, and on impulse he went up and looked in; Gabriel was writing at his desk. David tapped on the window. Gabriel looked up in surprise, then gestured towards the front door.

He opened the door quickly and quietly. 'Emily's gone to bed early – a bit of a headache, I think. Come in, if you like.'

David was suddenly awkward. 'No, that's all right. I didn't mean to bother you. I was just passing by, and thought . . .'

'No other at all. Come in and have a drink. We haven't really talked all week. I'm afraid I've been very busy this week . . .'

David followed him into the drawing room, bemused. Gabriel was behaving more naturally towards him than he had since his arrival; he didn't quite know how to react.

'Have a seat, David. Whisky? Or something else?'

'Whisky is fine.'

Gabriel took two glasses and a decanter out of a cupboard and poured generous measures of drink. 'Here, David. Well, here's to . . . whatever.'

He almost said 'old times', David thought. Not a good idea. He acknowledged the toast with a nod.

'Well, what have you been up to this week? Meeting lots of people?'

'Yes, I've met quite a few.' In a half-conscious gesture of something, he wasn't sure what, he added, 'I've spent this afternoon and evening with Lucy Kingsley.'

Gabriel nodded approvingly. 'How nice. She's a very charming woman.'

'Yes, I like her very much. She's very fond of Emily,' he added.

'I believe so.'

There was a short silence. 'Do you know anything about . . . well, have there been a lot of men in her life?' David asked, hesitating, not sure himself why he was asking.

Gabriel considered the question. 'I'm not really sure. You'd have to ask Emily. Wait, I remember there was one, quite a few years ago. I think he was actually living with her. And then, a couple of years ago, there was another one. That one was serious too, I think. She brought him round to dinner here one evening. Nice chap, I thought.'

'But what happened to him?'

Gabriel looked at him blankly. 'I have no idea. I don't think I ever saw him again after that. Emily would know.'

A fine pastor to his flock he is, was David's quickly stifled disloyal thought.

'Why do you want to know?' Gabriel asked.

'Oh, I just . . . wondered. She seems . . . oh, I don't know. Vulnerable, but wary.'

'Well, Lucy Kingsley surely wouldn't be any help when it comes to finding out about . . . the blackmail letter,' Gabriel stated.

Of course. The letter. Peter Maitland. No wonder Gabriel wanted to talk – no wonder he was interested in what he'd been doing.

'Have you found out anything at all?' Gabriel pursued.

'Very little that sheds any light, I'm afraid. I've talked to a lot of people. And the only person I've found who has any reason to dislike you at all seems to be Cyril Fitzjames, for pinching the woman he wanted.' And Lucy Kingsley, for the way you've treated that woman, he refrained from adding.

'Cyril,' Gabriel sneered dismissively. 'He hardly seems a likely blackmailer, does he?'

'Not at all. But . . . well, I've been thinking. So far I've got nowhere in trying to find a motive. So I need to concentrate on the other angle. Who could have found out about Peter Maitland?' He deliberately kept his voice neutral, treating it as an abstract problem.

'No one. I told you—'

'Don't be silly, Gabriel,' he cut him short. 'It's obvious that someone has. If you didn't tell anyone, then Peter must have.'

'Yes, I suppose so. But who . . .'

David came to an instant decision. 'I don't know. But I intend to find out, one way or another. There's less than a fortnight left. Tomorrow I shall go to Brighton.'

Chapter 18

*Yet do I remember the time past; I muse upon all thy
works: yea, I exercise myself in the works of thy
hands.*

Psalm 143.5

Friday morning dawned clear and bright, with the promise
of very warm temperatures. Forgoing early Mass yet again,
David climbed in the brown Morris and set off for Brighton.
Very soon he began to regret his lack of planning; the first
truly summer-like day of the school holidays had brought
sun-seeking families out in their thousands, and the roads
were jammed with cars. Even before he cleared the London
traffic, he realised that he should have taken the train.
From Victoria he could have been in Brighton in under an
hour and a half. At this rate he would be lucky to be there
in three hours.

Telling himself that it did him no good to fret and raise
his blood pressure, David tried to remain calm in the crawling queue of cars that stretched the entire length of the
A23.

For the first hour or so out of London, he thought about
the previous day's visit with Lucy Kingsley, replaying in
his mind the conversations they'd had and trying to recap-

ture the sense of peace he'd felt in her presence. But the nearer he got to Brighton, the more inevitably his thoughts turned to Gabe; unwillingly, he found himself remembering their time there together. This was getting him nowhere, he decided. He forced himself to consider the problem which was the reason for his journey. He must think about it objectively, as having nothing to do with himself, nothing to do with Gabe. It was about a boy who'd died, that was all. An unfortunate incident. A tragic accident. A mystery to be solved.

If he were a young boy in that situation . . . whom would he tell? In whom would he confide about the man he'd fallen in love with? He'd never found out how old the boy was. Still in school, perhaps. Would he possibly tell a trusted teacher? That wouldn't be impossible, especially if he were a bit disturbed. What teachers did David know at St Anne's? Daphne. Well, that was pretty ridiculous. Tony Kent. He wasn't old enough – he was probably, in fact, about the same age as Peter Maitland would have been. He wasn't sure about anyone else.

Friends? He wouldn't know where to begin to look. Gabriel had been very vague about the circumstances of meeting Peter. He claimed that he couldn't really remember where they'd met or how they'd become acquainted. David didn't deceive himself that Gabriel was trying to spare his feelings – he was probably just blocking a memory that had painful associations.

This trip to Brighton had been an impulse, and not a very well-thought-out one. What could he possibly hope to discover, with only a few hours, and nothing to go on? His mood was approaching despair by the time he arrived, faced with the prospect of searching for a place to park.

But luck was finally with him: as he drove along the sea-front, a family with several children, sticky with Brighton rock and candyfloss, piled into their car and pulled out of their parking space.

He hadn't been back to Brighton since . . . then. Not since his father died. There had been no reason to come back. There was his friend Graham, a colleague from work, who still lived in a Brighton suburb with his wife and family. But he and Graham had never been that close. They'd often had lunch together, and had shared an occasional drink after work; he'd enjoyed Graham's company, but they didn't have that much in common. Now they kept in touch only with annual Christmas cards. On an impulse, he thought that he might look Graham up later on, when he'd got something to go on. If he needed any sleuthing done on a local level, Graham would be very keen to help. And Graham had never met Gabe, so no awkward explanations would be necessary.

He got out of the car and walked aimlessly for a while along the beach. He scarcely noticed the thousands of people who jealously guarded their small rocky patches of ground, their pale white flesh exposed to the relentless sun. He wished it were raining. In his memories of Brighton, his memories of Gabe, it was always a day like this, a day bright with sunshine, and alive with joy. The summertime scent of Brighton – the tang of the salt air, the sickly sweet smell of candyfloss, all the mingled odours of hot bodies and sun-tan lotion – evoked such powerful memories. And the smell of fish and chips, redolent with vinegar. He realised that it was past lunch-time and he was hungry, and he turned his steps automatically towards his favourite fish and chip shop. Yes, it was still there, still serving steaming paper cones of succulent freshly caught fish with thick greasy chips. He ordered a large portion and ate it greedily, sitting on the beach.

The library, he decided. When in doubt, go to the library. It was a good place to start.

It took him a moment to orient himself. The library had entered the modern age, with computer terminals where ranks of card files had once stood. But eventually he located the periodicals department, still where it used to be, and found the newspaper archives, where back issues of the *Brighton Beacon* were stored on microfilm; Gabe had said that he'd read about the death in the newspaper. David thought for a moment. He didn't actually know the date when Peter Maitland had died, but he would be able to get pretty close by reconstructing his own painful memories of that time. Damn Gabe, he thought. He could have at least told me the date. And of course he hadn't thought to ask.

Spring, ten years ago. He'd start with April and see what he could find. He located the spool and wound it on to the cumbersome machine. It was like entering a time-warp. The events recorded on these newspaper pages were things that he remembered, practically his last memories of Brighton. He was fascinated, and, absorbed in the past, nearly forgot what he was looking for. He found it almost by accident – a small paragraph, tucked on a back page. 'Body Found on Beach.' His heart jumped; he read and re-read the brief account.

A body, identified as Peter Maitland, aged eighteen, was discovered early Monday morning on the beach to the east of the town. Maitland had been reported

missing on Saturday. The body had been in the water
for some time, and drowning appears the probable
cause of death. There were no signs of foul play. An
inquest will be held after a post-mortem examination
has been completed.

Until he saw the words, even on this distorted screen,
David had believed somehow that it was all a terrible
mistake, a bad joke. There was not, had never been, a
Peter Maitland, and those unthinkable things that Gabe
had said were not true. Now his mind had to accept it.
Peter Maitland had lived, had died. Gabe had been involved.
No matter how strongly he tried to deny responsibility, he
had been involved. And someone had found out.

He continued to scan the newspaper pages, one after
another. A fortnight after the initial account, the results of
the inquest rated a brief mention.

An inquest has been held into the death of Peter
Maitland, aged eighteen. Maitland's drowned body
was found washed up on Brighton beach in the early
hours of the morning on 7 April. The post-mortem
examination revealed no evidence of foul play, and
Maitland's room-mate testified that no suicide note
was found. Verdict: accidental death.

Accidental death. David rewound the microfilm, replaced
it carefully in its drawer, and went out for a cup of tea.
The afternoon was getting on; his labours over the microfilm
machine had taken longer than he'd realised.

Death notice, he thought suddenly. He hadn't even looked
on the obit pages. If Peter Maitland was anybody at all,

there should be a death notice. He quickly paid for his tea and returned to the library. It was nearly closing time, but he might just about manage. He relocated the reel of microfilm and turned the handle rapidly. April. Nothing on the 7th, of course, and nothing on the 8th. The 10th – there it was.

> Maitland, Peter. Suddenly on 5 April, in his nineteenth year. Beloved son of Susan and George Maitland of Croydon. Funeral will be held at 10 a.m. on Monday, 14 April, at St Mary's Church, Croydon. No flowers please. Memorial gifts to the Selby Cathedral School's chorister fund. 'His voice will be heard in heaven.'

For a long moment, David stared at the words. Selby Cathedral. Chorister. My God.

The librarian came by with a pleasant smile. 'We'll be closing in five minutes, sir. If you don't mind finishing up . . .'

He shook himself out of his trance. 'Is it possible to get copies from the microfilms?'

'Certainly, sir. I'll just pop it on this machine for you. If you'll show me what you want copied . . .'

Ten minutes later he returned to the car, photocopies of the three pieces in his pocket. As he went by a phone box he fleetingly considered ringing Gabriel, but his aversion to the telephone overcame his desire to share his incredible find. If all went well, he could be back in London in a couple of hours, with plenty of time to see Gabriel tonight.

All did not go well. The thousands of cars which had rushed, lemming-like, to the seaside that morning were wending their way back to London that night. Near Crawley, there were major road-works in progress, bringing the north-bound traffic nearly to a complete halt. David drummed his fingers on the steering-wheel in frustration, but to no avail. It was well past midnight before he pulled up at Daphne's; good thing she'd given him a key, he thought. Tomorrow morning would have to do. He'd set his alarm and get up for early Mass. Then he could tell Gabriel that there was a light at the end of the tunnel.

Chapter 19

*It is but lost labour that ye haste to rise up early,
and so late take rest, and eat the bread of care-
fulness: for so he giveth his beloved sleep.*
                                                    Psalm 127.3

The alarm went off at half past six. Its harsh buzz came as
a shock to David, who hadn't needed to set it since he'd
been in London. Friday's good weather was forecast to
continue through the weekend, he heard as he switched on
the radio.

He lay in bed for a few minutes, savouring the thought
of telling Gabriel of his discovery. He'd be relieved, grateful . . . Of course there were a few loose ends to be tied
up. They'd have to contact Selby Cathedral School, confirm that Peter Maitland had been a pupil there, and a
chorister, find out if he'd been there when Miles Taylor
was organist and choirmaster. And after that – he didn't
know how Gabriel would want to handle it. It was still a
very delicate matter. But he'd done his part, and he was
pleased.

Early Mass was once again quite poorly attended. The
regulars were all there – Lady Constance, the Dawsons,
Beryl Ball. Mary Hughes was there, too, and Cecily Fram-

lingham, with a man he assumed must be Arthur. David barely noticed them. After the service, he hung back until they'd all filed past Gabriel at the door, with a handshake and a murmured word.

He approached, and Gabriel grasped his hand automatically. It was like an electric shock; Gabriel's hand was cool and smooth, and David realised that it was the first time they'd touched since he'd been there. Those hands – those well-known, well-loved hands . . .

He took a deep breath to collect himself and looked Gabriel in the eye. 'I have something very important to tell you,' he said. 'Can we go somewhere and talk?'

Gabriel looked at him as if he'd taken leave of his senses. 'Talk? Now? David, don't you realise that the fête will be starting in under an hour?'

The fête! How could he have forgotten so completely that today was the day? 'It's important,' he repeated lamely.

'Tonight, then. After the fête. Come round to the vicarage tonight.'

'I suppose it can wait till tonight . . .'

'Right, then. If you'll excuse me, David . . .' and Gabriel was gone.

The church courtyard was transformed. Colourful stalls had appeared, and people dashed about with armloads of assorted goods in a flurry of last-minute preparation. David stood dumbly watching, trying to get his mind in tune with what was happening. 'There you are,' Daphne greeted him. 'It seems like I haven't seen you for about two days. You crept out this morning before I was up, but I guessed I'd find you here.'

'The fête,' he said stupidly.

'Yes, once a year, whether we like it or not,' she chuck-led. 'You've been to Mass? Have you had breakfast?'

'No. It doesn't matter.'

'I suppose you can fill up on cakes, in due course.'

He looked at the large table which the Dawsons, as-sisted by a very plain teenaged girl, were rapidly covering with vast numbers of cakes. 'Yes. Everyone's been busy, haven't they?'

'Frantically.'

'What stall are you doing, Daphne?'

She grimaced. 'The jumble stall. Bric-à-brac, they call it. Everyone's cast-off rubbish, in other words. I've been through everything – you can be sure there's nothing you'd want.'

'No unrecognised treasures? Bits of tarnished silver that someone thought were plate?'

'I'm afraid not. But perhaps you'd be interested in a "Souvenir of Scunthorpe" egg cup, only slightly chipped? Or maybe a complete set – near enough anyway, give or take the odd piece – of genuine plastic picnic cutlery?'

'How tempting. I'll have a look later. But now I'd better report for duty to Emily and see if she has anything for me to do.'

He moved towards the stall where the two women were lining up jars of jewel-toned jams in neat rows. They were both looking extremely attractive today, he observed. Emily had given up her jeans for the day and was wearing a very flattering simple white cotton summer frock, while Lucy's dress was covered in tendrils of deli-cate pink and blue sweet peas. David felt a bit self-conscious, in a pleasant way, at the warmth of both their greetings. He realised, with an odd shock, that it was just a week since his first anxious meeting with Emily. Now, astonishingly, she seemed an old friend. And Lucy . . .

'Well, the weather is certainly cooperating,' he said.

'I can't believe how lucky we are,' Emily replied. 'It's not supposed to rain all weekend.'

'Do you have anything for me to do? I'm at your service.'

'You can help us get the jams set out.' There were boxes of them: orange marmalade, lemon marmalade, apple jelly, strawberry, raspberry, greengage and ginger, gooseberry, damson, apricot. Then there were jars of lemon curd and chutney to fit on the stall. David wondered if the lemon curd was as good as his mother's.

'I'll have to buy a good selection to take back home with me,' he said, when they had finished.

'Why don't you pick out what you want now, and we'll put it away for you?' Lucy urged, handing him an empty box. 'You'd be surprised how fast they sell out.'

He filled his box and secreted it under the stall. 'Now what?'

'Why don't you go over and give Tony a hand with that sign? It keeps falling down,' Emily suggested.

Tony was struggling with the large square of cardboard which announced: 'Tombola – 25p a ticket or 5 for £1'. David held it for him while he secured it with strips of sellotape.

'Thanks. I needed three hands for that job,' Tony said.

'How are you, Tony? I haven't really seen you this week.'

'Very well, thanks. Enjoying my summer hols. And are you having a pleasant stay? How much longer will you be with us?'

'Yes, I'm enjoying it very much. I should be here another week, at least – until I'm satisfied that the crypt chapel restoration is well under way and in good hands.'

'That's good. Maybe we could get together sometime next week for a drink or something,' Tony suggested.

'I'd like that,' David responded, looking around at the increasing levels of activity. 'Who is the girl with the Dawsons?' he asked idly.

'That's Teresa, their youngest daughter.'

David looked surprised. 'I didn't realise that the Dawsons had any children.'

'Heaps, actually. Nick, the oldest, is around my age. Then there's Benedict, and a few more, and finally Teresa. She's the only one still at home.'

David laughed, delighted. Nicholas, Benedict, Teresa. 'Are all of them named after saints?'

'Of course. What else would you expect from the Devout Dawsons?'

'I would think the Dawson boys would have been servers. Have you had to deal with them?'

Tony rolled his eyes. 'That's a story in itself. The two oldest boys, Nick and Ben, were apparently pretty good servers. But the youngest, Francis – well, it's quite a tale. I must tell you about it sometime.'

'I can't wait.'

Tony paused. 'I'll tell you what – why don't you come to me for lunch next week? Then we can have a good gossip. Could you bear to pass up lunch here on Tuesday, and come to me instead?'

'I'd love to.' He looked over at the Dawsons. 'Teresa's no great beauty, is she?'

'The Dawson offspring are a singularly unprepossessing lot,' Tony replied. 'Not really surprising, considering their genetic make-up.'

Emily was gesturing to him. 'I suppose that's my cue,' David apologised. 'I'll see you later.'

'Thanks for your help with the sign.'

'Don't mention it.'

Before he could reach the jam stall, David was waylaid by Mavis Conwell. 'Mr Middleton-Brown! We missed you yesterday!'

'Yesterday?' He was baffled.

'The final preparations for the fête – all day yesterday. Everyone was here. Everyone but you, that is.' She looked accusingly at him. 'No one seemed to know where you were. Have you got a girlfriend somewhere in London that nobody knows about?' she added, with a ghastly attempt at a coy smile.

He didn't bother to answer. 'Emily needs me. Goodbye, Mrs Conwell.' Mavis is certainly back on form today, he reflected as he strode away.

Emily was looking at her watch. 'It's just about time to begin. Lady Constance should be here any minute.' As she spoke, Gabriel and Lady Constance came out of the church together and walked formally to where the ribbon stretched across the courtyard gate. An expectant hush had descended; in clear tones she made a little speech, welcoming everyone and thanking them in advance for their generous purchases in aid of St Anne's Church. Gabriel handed her a pair of scissors and she cut the ribbon smartly, to polite general applause. Then, as the general rush to the cake stall began, she and Gabriel strolled over to the jam stall where David stood with the two women.

'Young man, I require your assistance,' Lady Constance addressed David.

'How can I be of help, Lady Constance?'

'I need to visit each of the stalls and make my purchases. Will you please accompany me, and carry the things for me?'

He looked to Emily for confirmation; she nodded encouragingly. 'Yes, Lady Constance, I'd be delighted to walk with you,' he replied. Gabriel produced a large wicker basket and handed it to him.

'Excellent. We can begin here.' She considered the array of jams while David attempted to compose himself into a suitable posture. But Lucy caught his eye, and he could have sworn that she winked at him. 'Now, what do you recommend, Mrs Neville?' Lady Constance inquired gravely.

'The apricot looks quite good,' Emily replied seriously. 'And Lucy's greengage and ginger is always delicious.'

Lady Constance looked dubiously at Lucy, but nodded, and David put the two proffered jams in the basket. 'And how about some marmalade?' Lady Constance added.

'Do you prefer thick-cut or thin-cut?' Emily asked. 'The thick-cut is Mary Hughes's speciality, and I've made the thin-cut myself. Or there's some very chunky marmalade made by Mr Bead.'

'The thin-cut would be very nice, thank you, Mrs Neville,' she concluded, handing her a five-pound note. 'Do keep the change.'

'Thank you very much, Lady Constance, and I hope you enjoy them.'

'Oh, I'm certain I will.'

As they approached the cake stall, the crowds fell back like the parting of the Red Sea. Lady Constance carefully considered the large array of cakes. 'I shall have one of these fruit cakes, and a lemon sponge. Perhaps a dozen rock cakes, a plate of shortbread, and . . . yes, I'll take this chocolate gâteau.'

'Yes, of course, Lady Constance. Is that all? Let me just show you this . . .' Julia Dawson was volubly obsequious, while her husband wrung his hands in an agitated manner.

While these transactions were taking place, David smiled encouragingly at Teresa Dawson. She hung back and looked at him with bulbous eyes, made even less attractive by her almost invisible eyelashes. She looked like nothing so much as a frightened rabbit, David decided, with those eyes, her mother's receding chin, and her father's sharp, protruding teeth; her stringy hair was even a rabbity-brown colour. Decidedly unprepossessing.

Lady Constance paid Roger Dawson, and Julia turned to David, anxious to be seen to be on good terms with one who was so obviously in favour with Lady Constance. 'Mr Middleton-Brown, how very nice to see you today. We did all wonder where you were yesterday!'

He smiled non-committally, unwilling to enter into any explanations. 'Good morning, Mrs Dawson.'

'Roger and I . . . that is, we were wondering . . . we'd very much like to invite you to join us for a meal next week. When are you free?'

There's no escaping from this one, he told himself with resignation. 'Most evenings, I should think.'

'Oh, good! Would Wednesday be possible? Our son Francis will be home that night, and it would be so nice for you to meet him.' This was delivered with great emotion.

'Yes. I'll look forward to it very much,' he fibbed.

Lady Constance had turned to him. 'Mind you put the cakes in here very carefully, young man. I don't want anything crushed.'

'Yes, of course.' He put the shortbread on the bottom and the chocolate gâteau on the top.

The servers were manning the side-shows, and Johnnie and Chris greeted David with cheerful waves as he and Lady Constance passed by. The side-shows were beneath her dignity, but she stopped at Tony's tombola stall. The most coveted prize was a bottle of very good whisky, David noted approvingly.

'I shall have ten tickets, please, Mr Kent,' she announced, handing him two pounds. He offered her the bowl of tickets, and she pulled them out one by one. Two of the numbers were winners, and she collected her prizes – a pair of bright orange tights and a packet of custard powder – with gracious thanks. David and Tony exchanged smiles as the prizes went into the basket.

The next stop on their progress was Cecily's flower and produce stall. 'Those are uncommonly fine marrows, Mrs Framlingham,' Lady Constance pronounced.

'Arthur grew them himself,' Cecily volunteered eagerly.

'What a pity I don't care for marrow. Perhaps a bunch of those sweet peas, and a pound of tomatoes. Did Arthur grow the tomatoes?'

'No,' replied Cecily, crestfallen. 'They're from Mavis's greenhouse.'

'Oh, Mrs Conwell. I see.'

Mary Hughes was at the next stall, selling handicrafts.

'Good morning, Lady Constance,' she said, a bit over-enthusiastically. 'I have some lovely things this year.' Lady Constance inspected the array of hand-knitted baby sweaters, embroidered needle-cases, and multicoloured knitted tea-cosies; they all looked indistinguishable from last year's and the year before's. She tried to remember what she'd bought the previous year. A tea-cosy, probably. Or perhaps that had been the year before.

'Bedsocks,' she intoned judiciously. 'Have you any bedsocks?'

'Oh, yes, Lady Constance. What colour do you fancy? These blue ones are nice. Or these pretty lilac ones – they match your dress!' Mary Hughes stammered, blushing at her boldness.

Lady Constance turned to David. 'What do you think, Mr Middleton-Brown? Blue or lilac?'

'I'd choose the blue, I think.'

'Yes, I believe you're right. Thank you, Miss Hughes, for your help. They're two pounds fifty, I believe? Keep the three pounds.'

'Oh, thank you, Lady Constance. I do hope you'll be happy with the bedsocks.'

The Mothers' Union were traditionally in charge of the 'nearly new' clothing stall, which was their next stop. Mavis Conwell, who, in her role as churchwarden, would shortly retire to the sacristy to begin counting the takings, was doing an early stint at the stall. She'd done some very good business already, selling a number of items to Beryl Ball. Beryl had bought several hats, an evening gown, a Harris tweed coat, and a silk dressing-gown. Now Mavis greeted Lady Constance. 'You'll have a hard time making your mind up, Lady Constance.

Wait till you see what we've got!'

Lady Constance tended to agree that she'd have a difficult time, but perhaps not for the same reason that Mavis
intended.

'Thermal underwear!' Mavis announced. 'Just look at
the quality of this thermal underwear. It will keep you
nice and toasty warm next winter – and it's hardly been
worn! I'll bet that big house of yours is cold in the winter.
I'd hate to pay the heating bills, anyway.'

Lady Constance looked at all the garments strewn about
by Beryl Ball in her enthusiasm. Beryl Ball's rejects of
someone else's cast-offs – it didn't bear thinking about.
'Yes, I'm sure that will be most . . . suitable,' she agreed
repressively. 'Could you please wrap them up?'

'Of course, Lady Constance. Thank you very much.
And may I say . . .'

Lady Constance turned away without hearing what Mavis
wished to impart. 'Dreadful woman,' she murmured under
her breath so that only David could hear.

The book stall was nearly all that remained. Lady Constance passed quickly, with a delicate shudder, over a pile
of detective novels with lurid covers. She inspected a complete set of the *Waverley* novels. 'A bit too heavy to carry,'
she concluded, looking farther. She looked at a 1967 Al-
manac and leafed through an old medical text-book.

'Poetry?' David suggested. 'How about Keats?'

'I'm too old for Keats, I'm afraid. Is there any
Tennyson?'

'One is never too old for Keats!' Cyril Fitzjames protested from behind the stall. 'Especially not you, Lady
Constance,' he added gallantly.

David unearthed an old leather-bound volume of George

Herbert and showed it to her. 'That's just the thing,' she agreed.

'Let me buy it for you,' he said impulsively.

'You're very kind, young man,' she said, bestowing a rare smile.

Daphne stood behind the final stall. Business had not been good, and David could see why. The egg cup was still there, and the plastic cutlery. They were indeed among the more choice items available. There was a box of jumbled-together rhinestone jewellery, all with stones missing, and a stack of stained beer-mats. Lady Constance was looking bemusedly at a framed picture of the Sacred Heart of Jesus, throbbing with three-dimensional blood, while David inspected a lamp made out of a wine bottle. 'Not even a very good wine,' he muttered; Daphne stifled a chuckle. Then Lady Constance pounced thankfully on a box of dusting powder, unopened – someone's unwanted Christmas gift. 'This will do nicely, Miss Elford,' she proclaimed. David added it to the collection in the basket.'

'Well, that's over for another year,' Lady Constance said to him in a low voice as they walked away from the stalls. 'Would you be so kind as to help me to my car?'

He took her arm and walked with her to the elegant old Bentley, parked just around the corner. 'I usually walk,' she said apologetically. 'But I was a bit tired this morning, and then there are these things to be got home . . .' She paused as her chauffeur climbed out of the car and efficiently dealt with the basket of purchases. 'You really have been most kind,' she continued. 'I like you, young man. Will you have tea with me next week?'

'Yes, of course. It would give me great pleasure, Lady Constance.'

'Shall we say Thursday, then? Perhaps you'll have something to report about the work on the chapel by then.'

'I will look forward to it.' He handed her into the car, and saluted respectfully as she was driven away.

Chapter 20

They talk of vanity every one with his neighbour:
they do but flatter with their lips, and dissemble
in their double heart.
The Lord shall root out all deceitful lips: and the
tongue that speaketh proud things . . .

Psalm 12.2–3

The jams were looking decidedly depleted by the time
David returned; he was glad he'd selected his in advance.
Emily was relieved to see him. 'Oh, you're back – good.
Would you mind giving a hand on the book stall for a
while?' She lowered her voice. 'Miles was supposed to
help Cyril, but he hasn't shown up yet, and dear old Cyril
– bless him – keeps wandering off to buy another jar of
my jams.'

'Or a cake that she's baked with her own fair hands,'
Lucy added, smiling.

'So poor Daphne's had to cover the book stall, as well
as her own, half of the time.'

'Where is Venerable Bead?' David asked curiously, looking about. 'I would have thought he would be here in the
thick of things.'

'Oh, he's giving conducted tours of the church. Much

more his line,' explained Emily.

'Of course. I should have guessed. Well, I'm off to Daphne's rescue.'

Daphne gave him a look of gratitude as he stepped behind the book stall. Cyril was just returning from the cake stall. 'You're here to help, are you, my boy?' he boomed. 'Just look at this marvellous cake I've bought. Almond and cherry. Emily baked it herself.'

'It looks delicious.'

The morning went by quickly; David was kept busy making change, wrapping up parcels of books, and listening to Cyril's chatter. Periodically, Gabriel's black-cassocked figure appeared as he relieved them of their accumulated cash and took it to the sacristy, where Mavis remained to count it. 'We're doing very well,' he said on one visit. 'Well ahead of last year, Mavis says.'

'I used to count the money,' Cyril told David when Gabriel had passed on to Daphne's stall. 'That was always my job, year after year. But now they think I'm past it, so they've given it to that woman to do. Maybe I am past it, my boy. Maybe I am.'

David was on the point of reassuring him when Miles Taylor rushed up to them, completely out of breath.

'Wouldn't you know!' he expostulated. 'Wouldn't you just know! My alarm didn't go off this morning! Well, all I can say is, thank God it didn't happen on Sunday morning!'

'No problem, my boy,' Cyril responded. 'This fine young man and I have managed splendidly, haven't we?'

'Oh!' Miles drew back and looked at him, gravely offended not to have been missed. 'Well, if you knew how late I'd been up last night – I was out very late indeed.' He paused to allow them the opportunity to ask where he'd been, but again he was disappointed.

Cyril chuckled condescendingly. 'Ah, out sowing your wild oats, were you, young man? Well, I suppose at your age that's to be expected.'

Miles drew himself up to his full height and looked at him stonily, the light glinting on his round lenses. 'I was not sowing wild oats! I am a married man! I was . . .'

Mary Hughes touched his arm diffidently and he spun around. 'Oh, Mr Taylor, I'm so sorry to interrupt you! But I just wanted to ask – you are doing a recital in church this afternoon, aren't you? I've been so looking forward to it. When you weren't here earlier I thought perhaps . . .'

He gave Cyril a triumphant look. 'Yes, my dear Miss Hughes,' he replied expansively. 'I will be giving a recital at half past four. And I shall play some of your favourite pieces, just for you.'

'Oh, *thank* you!' She turned quite pink with pleasure, and hurried back to her stall.

Miles turned back to David. 'You can go now,' he said with a dismissive wave of his hand, then drew a cigarette out of his breast pocket and lit it nonchalantly, taking a deep drag and blowing the smoke in David's face.

David shrugged, and took his leave. 'Thank you for your help, my boy!' Cyril called after him.

He stopped by the tombola stall to see how Tony was faring. Incredibly, the bottle of whisky was unclaimed. 'Do you feel lucky?' Tony greeted him, holding out the bowl of tickets.

'Well, you never know. Today may be my lucky day.' David fished in his pocket and found fifty pence. The first ticket got him nothing, but the second one he drew bore the number on the whisky bottle.

'Well, I never!' exclaimed Tony. 'I've been waiting for that to happen all morning!'

'I suppose I owe you a drink for this,' David said, tucking the bottle under his arm. 'Daphne will be pleased!'

He turned around to see that Lucy had come up behind him. 'Emily's sent me to find you. The jams have sold out, so we've packed up, and now she wondered if we could give her a hand setting up the vicarage garden for the teas.' She didn't touch him, but there was something about the way David looked at her, about the familiar, almost intimate, way that she spoke to him, that piqued Tony's interest and caused him to watch them as they walked together to the vicarage. Maybe I was wrong about him, he speculated.

Emily was waiting for them with a plate of sandwiches. 'I suddenly realised that I was starving!' she said. 'And I wondered if you two would join me for a sandwich before we get down to work.' So they sat in the vicarage kitchen for a few moments, eating ham sandwiches and drinking lemon squash.

'When are the children coming back, Em?' Lucy asked.

'We're going to fetch them on Monday,' Emily replied, her eyes alight with pleasure. 'I have missed them. They will have been gone a whole fortnight!'

'It's a shame for them to have missed the fête,' David remarked.

'A shame for them, but actually much easier for me. I have so much to think about today, and they would have been bored after the first hour or so. Once they've done all the side-shows, there's nothing much for them till tea. And my parents promised to take them to the Woburn

Safari Park today, so missing the fête was the last thing they were worried about!'

'Have you talked to them, then?' David asked.

'Oh, yes, every day. I'm sure that I miss them more than they miss me, but they are only six!'

'I'm sure their father misses them too,' said Lucy, her face turned away from David.

'Yes, of course he does. It will be lovely when we're all together again.' Emily smiled, a far-away look in her eyes.

'And I look forward to meeting these wonderful children,' David said, much too heartily.

'Of course, you haven't met them! How very odd that seems!' Emily looked at him with wonder.

Gabriel came through the door. 'I wondered where you were.'

'Just having a bite to eat with Lucy and David, darling. Have you got time for a sandwich?'

'Yes, I suppose so. I've just taken Mavis the latest batch of money.' He sat down at the table and helped himself to a sandwich. 'It's really going very well. The cakes have sold out, and the jams, of course. Even Daphne's managed to shift a lot of her rubbish.'

'I suppose there's no accounting for taste,' David remarked. Gabriel looked at him sharply but David only smiled.

The vicarage garden looked lovely. David had set up all the tables, and the women had covered them with snowy white cloths and decorated them with nosegays of flowers. Stacks of crockery were at the ready, all the cakes had been sliced and the sandwiches cut, the urns were on the

177

boil, and all that remained was to make the tea when the moment arrived. The helpers began trickling in – Julia and Teresa Dawson, assorted members of the Mothers' Union. Roger Dawson came too, announcing that he would be happy to take the money.

'I think I can manage now,' Emily said to Lucy and David. 'You've both been a great help, but now you're entitled to a break. Relax and have some tea, won't you?'

They escaped gratefully, and joined the crowd that was gathering outside the vicarage garden, waiting for the gate to open. Restive murmurs of 'I could murder a cup of tea right now', 'Isn't it about time?' and 'I'm perishing for a cup of tea', were heard on all sides. In a few minutes Emily opened the gate and the rush began.

Lucy hung back, laughing. 'Let them have their tea first, if they want it so badly. I'm sure there will be some left for us in a few minutes.'

'Why don't we go to Kensington Gardens for a while?' David suggested.

'Oh, yes. Why not?'

They'd gone farther than they'd intended, all the way down the Flower Walk, so they were ready for their tea by the time they returned. They found a small table at the edge of the garden and settled down with their tea and cakes, oblivious to the speculative stares they were beginning to draw from various members of the parish.

'Were you planning to go to the organ recital?' David asked, looking at his watch. 'It's nearly half past four.'

'Oh, I suppose so. Though it seems such a shame to go indoors when it's so glorious outside.' Lucy stretched luxuriously in the sunshine and pushed her hair back with both hands. 'Well, never mind.'

'We can wait a few minutes more. It won't hurt to miss the beginning, will it?'

'Not at all. It's the kind of thing where people come and go, anyway.'

'Then let's have another cup of tea.'

'Oh, yes.'

Gabriel had quite a heavy-looking bag of money when he stopped by their table a few minutes later.

'Enjoying yourselves?' he asked in his most cordial Vicar-voice.

'Yes, thank you,' Lucy replied coolly. 'Your wife has worked very hard to make this a success.'

'I know she has. And of course the wonderful weather hasn't hurt.'

Emily appeared beside him quite suddenly, looking very worried. 'Oh, Gabriel, could you come? Teresa Dawson has just fainted!'

'Yes, of course. I was just taking this money to the sacristy . . .'

'I'll take it for you,' David offered quickly.

'Thanks, David.' Gabriel handed him the bag and disappeared with his wife.

'Finish your tea, why don't you?' David suggested to Lucy. 'And when you've done, I'll see you at the organ recital.'

He could hear the sound of a Franck chorale as he approached the church. Reluctant to go through the church while the recital was in progress, he walked around the north side of the building and found that the small side door was unlocked. It led directly into the corridor where the sacristy was located, he discovered to his satisfaction.

179

He tapped lightly on the sacristy door.

'Come in, it's not locked.'

Mavis looked up as he entered. On the table in front of her were piles of notes, stacks of coins, and a ledger sheet where she was entering hourly totals. 'Oh. Where's Father Gabriel?'

'He had an emergency. I offered to help.'

'Put the money right here,' she directed. 'Mind you don't knock anything over.'

It was the first time David had been inside the sacristy, Daphne's domain, and he looked around with mild interest. It was a fairly large room; in the centre was the heavy oak table where Mavis sat with the money. Set into one wall was a large old-fashioned safe, and the other walls were lined with tall, upright oak cupboards for hanging copes and albs, and stacks of big, shallow drawers for storing chasubles, stoles, and linen. In the corner opposite the door there was a small desk, on which were an ancient manual typewriter, Mavis's brown handbag, and a collection of assorted prayer books and hymn books. It was a tidy, well-kept room, which David attributed more to Gabriel's influence than to Daphne's inclinations. He could imagine what Gabriel would say – it was a room for holy things, therefore it was proper that it should be kept neat.

'Father Gabriel says we're doing quite well,' he said, glancing at the ledger sheet.

'Oh, yes. I've been comparing the hourly figures to last year's, and we've been well ahead all along. It's the good weather that's made all the difference. We've gone over two thousand pounds already!'

'That's very good. Well, I won't keep you from your counting any longer, Mrs Conwell.' He retreated, shutting the door behind him. Instead of leaving by the side door, he went down the short corridor which led to the church. Beryl Ball, dressed in blue, passed him with a nod and a friendly waggle of her false teeth as he went through the door.

He looked around for Lucy. She certainly wasn't with Mary Hughes and the Fan Club. Tony Kent caught his eye and gestured tentatively, but he shook his head as he saw Lucy slip in from the north porch. For an instant the sun coming in the west window behind her turned her hair into a halo of rose gold, and he drew in his breath sharply.

They met at the back, smiling silently at each other, and found two seats. Half an hour later, after a slightly flawed performance of Bach's Great G Minor Fantasia and Fugue, they agreed to call it quits and see if they could get another cup of tea before Evensong.

'Miles isn't at his best today,' Lucy remarked. 'He must have something on his mind.' David had to agree.

Venerable Bead was weary after a day on his feet, taking group after group of people around the church. He wasn't as young as he used to be, he reflected, and he hadn't even had his tea. There just hadn't been time for such self-indulgence. He wished he didn't have to serve at Evensong, but if Father Gabriel couldn't count on him, who could he count on? He looked at his watch. Half past five. There was certainly no time for a cup of tea before Evensong. He'd have to start laying out the things for Father Gabriel any minute now – his cotta would probably need a quick press. And the candles on the altar were getting low – he'd better replace them before the service. He hoped that fool organist knew that he'd have to stop playing – showing off, more like it – quite soon to allow for the preparations for the service. He sighed, and got to his feet; with a heavy tread he made his way through the door at the north-east end of the church and down the corridor to the sacristy. He tried the door tentatively; it was locked. With another heavy sigh he retrieved his ring of keys from his pocket and fitted the large key into the lock.

The teas were winding to a close. David and Lucy had begged a final cup from Emily, and were enjoying it in the late afternoon sunshine. Julia Dawson had taken the ailing Teresa home, so Gabriel had been pressed into service clearing tables. Lucy pointed out to David how ridiculous he looked, carrying around trays of dirty crockery in his black cassock. But he bore the ignominy with the good grace of a parish priest who often has to do many tasks that he considers beneath him.

No one really saw him coming. Certainly David and Lucy did not. But suddenly Venerable Bead was there, in the vicarage garden, clutching his chest and breathing raggedly. His face was white, and large beads of sweat stood out on his clammy forehead. He staggered to Gabriel, nearly collapsing.

'He's having a heart attack,' Lucy said quickly. 'Someone get a doctor.' David rose, then paused as the old man spoke with a great effort.

'Come!' he said. 'The sacristy. You must come, Father. She's in the sacristy. Mavis Conwell. She's hanging. She's dead!'

PART II

Chapter 21

*They smite down thy people, O Lord: and trouble
thine heritage.
They murder the widow, and the stranger: and put
the fatherless to death.*

Psalm 94.5–6

David didn't understand why the police wanted to talk to
him – he had scarcely known Mavis Conwell – until it was
explained to him that he was the last person to admit to
having seen her alive.

To admit it. That meant that they thought someone else
had seen her later, David reasoned. Someone who wouldn't
admit it. Someone who had . . . killed her. So they think
it's murder, he told himself as they escorted him into the
sacristy.

Several hours had passed, during which the efficient
police teams had done their work: fingerprints, photographs,
and finally the removal of the body. A small crowd had
gathered in the street outside St Anne's, as inevitably happens when the police barriers go up, but they'd dispersed
by now, with the departure of the ambulance. David had
remained at the vicarage, drinking black coffee supplied
by Emily, while Gabriel had joined the police in the church.

And now they'd sent for him.

The sacristy looked different in artificial light than it had in the afternoon. Two policemen sat at the table where so recently Mavis had counted her money, and their notebooks and bits of paper replaced the piles of notes and coins. Both of the policemen had anonymous, kindly faces. They rose as he entered.

'Mr Middleton-Brown? Thank you for coming. I'm Detective Inspector Pierce, and this is Sergeant Gordon. We'd just like to ask you a few questions about this afternoon.'

'Of course. I understand.'

A chair had been placed in front of the table. Detective Inspector Pierce motioned for him to sit and he complied.

'Now, Mr Middleton-Brown. You came into this room this afternoon. At what time was that?'

'It was just after half past four. Probably twenty-five to five.'

'How can you be sure about the time?'

'The organ recital began at half past. He was playing the first piece, the Franck Chorale, when I arrived. I'd checked my watch at about twenty past, and it couldn't have been much later than that.'

'And how long did you stay?'

'Just a few minutes. Three or four at the most.'

'And what route did you take to get to this room?'

'I didn't want to walk through the church during the recital, so I came around the side and in the little door.'

'You found that door unlocked?'

'Yes.'

'And the sacristy door as well?'

'Yes. I knocked, and Mrs Conwell asked me to come in.'

'Now, I understand that Father Neville had been bringing the money in to be counted all day. Why, on this particular occasion, were you bringing it?'

'There was an emergency at the vicarage – a girl had fainted. I offered to bring it over, to help him out.'

The Detective Inspector jotted down a few notes, then looked up again. 'What did Mrs Conwell say to you?'

'She asked me why I'd come instead of Gabriel – Father Neville. I told her the same thing. That there'd been an emergency and I was helping out. We chatted for a minute or two about how much money we'd taken in – that sort of thing. Just chit-chat.'

'And how did she seem? How would you describe her?'

David thought for a moment. 'Very ordinary. She didn't appear to be upset or agitated. If anything, she was just a bit more subdued than usual, but she was involved in counting the money, and not really interested in conversation.'

'How well did you know Mrs Conwell?'

'Not very well at all. I first met her . . . last Sunday, it must have been. I've seen her briefly once or twice since then.'

'And what seemed to be the general opinion, among people you know, of Mrs Conwell? Was she well liked?'

'No, I wouldn't say so. She had her friends – Mrs Framlingham and Mrs Dawson – but most people . . . well, they tended to steer clear of her.'

'And why was that?'

'Well, I think she was regarded as a gossip, and she was very judgemental about . . . people's lifestyles, if they didn't agree with her . . . moral standards.'

'Very good, Mr Middleton-Brown. Now, I'd like you to take a look around this room. Look very carefully. Does it look the same as it did this afternoon?'

David stood up and studied the room. Desk, typewriter, prayer books, safe, cupboards, table. 'The money, of course. The money was on the table.'

'Yes. We've recovered the money. You needn't worry about that.'

'Aside from that, it looks the same to me. But I've only been in here the once.'

'Well, thank you, Mr Middleton-Brown. I don't think we have any further questions for you at this time. Father Neville would be able to tell us where you could be reached, if it were necessary?'

'Yes, he would.'

'Thank you for your help.'

David left the church through the north porch and walked the short distance to Daphne's.

It had been a very long day. He wasn't thinking clearly, he knew. He hadn't really absorbed the fact that Mavis Conwell was dead, murdered, and that he'd seen her less than an hour before she died.

Why? And who? He had a feeling that it was all tied up with the blackmail somehow. In a day or two he'd be able to think about it, maybe sort it out. And he had faith in the police; in his professional dealings with them he knew them to be competent, thorough, and honest. So why hadn't he mentioned the blackmail to them? They hadn't asked – but that was a ludicrous excuse. Why on earth would they ask? He hadn't been thinking clearly. He'd answered the questions they'd asked, straightforwardly, and for tonight that was enough. Tomorrow he'd talk to Gabriel. Tomorrow he'd know more, understand more. But tonight all he wanted was a drink, and his bed.

Chapter 22

In the multitude of the sorrows that I had in my heart: thy comforts have refreshed my soul.

Psalm 94.19

David's sleep had been laced with nightmares of Mavis Conwell, grinning at him with a rictus-like smile, but in the morning he was no closer than he'd been the night before to understanding or even apprehending her death.

Daphne was up before him, and had brewed a pot of black coffee. He accepted a mug gratefully, but neither one was particularly inclined to talk about the events of Saturday. They sat silently for a few minutes, drinking their coffee.

'Let's go to eight o'clock Mass,' he suggested. 'And then . . . well, I'm not sure. I was going to spend the day with Lucy, you know, but . . . under the circumstances, maybe . . .'

'I think you should go ahead,' Daphne said sensibly. 'Why should you change your plans? You've said your piece to the police, and if they need you again, they'll find you soon enough. Anyway, it will take your mind off things.'

'Yes, I suppose you're right. But it just doesn't seem . . .'

'Respectful to the dead? I wouldn't worry about that.'

'Hm. Well, I'll try not to be back too late. Will you wait up for me?'

'If you like.'

Eight o'clock Mass was a hurried affair. Gabriel's heart just wasn't in it; he looked harassed and preoccupied, and rushed through the service with a totally uncharacteristic lack of feeling. But everyone made allowances – it wasn't every day that a priest had a member of his congregation, and a churchwarden at that, murdered in his sacristy. And the silent, but visible, presence of the police during Mass was a constant reminder to everyone that this was not a normal Sunday.

Gabriel didn't even remain to shake hands with his departing congregation. 'I don't suppose he can face all the questions,' Daphne whispered as they left the church.

'I'm sure he doesn't have any more answers than anyone else at this stage,' David defended him half-heartedly.

They parted, and David tried to shake himself out of his mood of foreboding as he walked to Lucy's house. It shouldn't have been difficult: the weather was even more glorious than the day before, a perfect summer's day. But in the back of his mind was the uneasy feeling that this death was just the beginning of even more terrible things to come. Tomorrow. Tomorrow he must talk to Gabriel. But today . . .

Realising that it was still quite early, David took the long way through Kensington Gardens, stopping for a few moments to sit on a bench and watch the antics of the birds. The swallows were chasing each other across the wide expanse of grass, skimming over the ground, swooping and diving in perfect unison, their wings scissoring the azure sky. Kensington Gardens represented an anomaly, a bit of the country in the heart of London, a bit of peace in the midst of chaos. He looked at his watch. Nearly time. He thought suddenly how glad he would be to see Lucy. She would banish his morbid thoughts if anyone could.

Her front door was ajar, and he tapped tentatively. 'Come on in, David,' she called from within.

He stood in the entrance hall for a moment, looking about for any clues to her whereabouts. 'I'm just about ready,' she said as she came from the kitchen, pushing back her hair. 'David, just look at my nose!' She stood before him, lifting her face.

'What's wrong with it?'

'What's wrong with it?' she echoed disbelievingly, moving to the mirror and peering at herself with horror. 'Why, it's all red! It was that walk in Kensington Gardens before tea that did it, I think. I look just like a clown.'

'Not to me you don't. I think you look beautiful,' he said with sincerity. She did look beautiful, in a creamy cotton dress strewn with roses just the colour of her hair.

She turned from the mirror and smiled at him. 'Well, I don't know about that. But maybe if I wear a hat, you won't be ashamed to be seen with me.' She rummaged in the cupboard under the stairs and emerged a moment later with a broad-brimmed straw hat, which she clapped on her head. 'There! If I keep it on when we're outdoors, at least it won't get any worse. What do you think?' she demanded, facing him.

'You look beautiful,' he repeated. 'But I wish you didn't have to cover your hair.'

'It can't be helped. Not unless you're particularly anx-

ious to see me looking like a beetroot by the end of the
day,' Lucy said, going into the kitchen. She returned shortly
with a large wicker hamper. 'Do you mind carrying this?'
He took it from her as she collected her sketch pad and a
clutch of pencils from the hall table. 'There now – off we
go. I hope you're ready for breakfast.'

'Where do you go for breakfast around here?' he asked
as they walked along.

'The Muffin Man. It's not far. They do a lovely breakfast.' She turned off Kensington High Street – congested
with sightseeing buses even on a Sunday morning – and
led him down a side street. 'You wouldn't find this if you
didn't know it was here,' she commented as they went
into the small restaurant. They found a table in the corner.
It was covered with a flowered tablecloth and located under a hanging basket trailing with ivy. Lucy wasted no
time. 'We'll have two breakfasts – the works,' she in-
structed a passing waitress, dressed in a pinafore to match
the tablecloths.

'I've been to eight o'clock Mass,' he confessed. 'And
I'm starving. I've been up since – well, early.'

She looked concerned. 'Mavis Conwell. Of course you
must be upset about that. The police only had a few questions for me – I wasn't really involved. But you . . . Did
you have to talk to the police last night?'

'Yes,' he replied shortly, unwilling to go into details.
'But it wasn't too bad. It's just . . . well, there's something
about the whole thing that bothers me. But I don't want to
talk about it today. I want to forget that St Anne's exists,
for the rest of the day. Will you help me to do that?'

She smiled into his eyes. 'You've come to the right
person.' She reached across the table and gave his hand a

gentle squeeze. 'Oh, look. Here's the orange juice.' Raising her glass, she toasted him. 'Here's to today, David Middleton-Brown.'

After the creamed eggs, and the toast with marmalade, and the pots of tea, they were finally ready to move on. 'When does the V & A open?' David asked.

'Oh, not for hours yet. Shall we go to the park?'

'How about Hyde Park? I'll tell you what – I've always wanted to go in a boat on the Serpentine.'

'A rowing boat? Oh, what fun! Can you row?'

'I suppose I can learn,' he said doubtfully. 'At least it will help to work off breakfast.'

There were quite a few other people with the same idea, but they managed to hire one of the turquoise boats for an hour, and David somehow successfully piloted them around the Serpentine without mishap. Rowing was hard work, but he alternated with periods of lazy drifting. Lucy trailed her hand in the water and laughed tolerantly at his efforts from under the brim of her hat.

When their hour was over, they walked about for a while in the brilliant sunshine, until David declared himself unable to continue. 'You won't believe it, but I'm hungry again!'

They found a secluded, shady spot of grass under a silver birch tree and Lucy discarded her hat. 'You've worked hard,' she said. 'You're entitled to be hungry.' She spread out a cloth, and began to unpack the hamper.

'I thought you said a sandwich,' David remarked, eyeing all the lovely things that were beginning to appear.

'That's when it's just me. I love having someone to cook for, and a picnic is one of my favourite things.' Lucy pulled out a bottle of champagne and David popped the cork as she produced two carefully wrapped long-stemmed glasses.

They had chilled watercress soup from a thermos, then little savoury parcels of filo pastry filled with cream cheese, a roulade of chicken and crab meat, and other various delicacies, finishing with a mango soufflé.

'That was the nicest picnic I've ever had,' David declared, when the last bite had been consumed. He lay back in the grass and closed his eyes. The grass was warm, even in the shade, the quiet murmur of the insects was soporific, and the half-bottle of champagne he'd drunk was making him drowsy.

'You just rest a while,' Lucy said soothingly. She got out her sketch pad and spent some time on a drawing of David in repose. The tense expression was completely gone from his face as he rested peacefully, in that half-aware state between sleep and wakefulness. He knew that he was well fed, and that Lucy was there. He knew that he was ... happy. He knew ...

He opened his eyes with a start, not at all sure how much time had passed. Lucy was working on a close-up sketch of him, and was sitting very near. She smiled at him as he opened his eyes; he reached out a disembodied hand and gently pulled on a ringlet of her hair. It straightened out, but snapped back as soon as he released it. 'What wonderful hair,' he murmured.

'You should have seen it when it was really red,' she laughed. 'When I was ... young.'

Eventually they made their way to the Victoria & Albert Museum. 'My turn to do some real work,' said Lucy with regret. She settled down with her sketch-book in the Islamic gallery. David made himself comfortable against a nearby pillar and watched her with fascination. He was now wide awake, but kept very still to avoid breaking her concentration. She drew rapidly, skilfully, and very quickly filled several pages. After a while they broke for a quick cup of tea in the museum café, then Lucy returned to work until closing time at six.

The sun still shone brightly as they walked slowly back to her house, David carrying the empty hamper. 'It's really hot,' he said. 'I could use a cool drink about now.'

She took off her hat and fanned herself with it. 'Coming right up,' she promised. 'We're almost there.'

'How fortunate you are to live practically around the corner from the V & A.'

'Oh, I know. I love living in London. And this is such a wonderful area. There are all the museums, the shops are good, and then there's the Royal Albert Hall nearly on my doorstep.'

'Yes, the Proms. Do you ever go?'

'Of course,' she replied. 'Several nights a week, usually. I always buy a season ticket, then if it's anything good I go and queue up. You have to get there early to get a decent spot, but if I don't have anything better to do . . .'

'Could I come with you some evening?' he asked impulsively.

'Certainly, if you like. You can take a look at the book when we get home, and see if there's anything you fancy.'

Sophie was waiting for them when they came in, mewing querulously. 'Oh, poor Sophie, she wants her dinner,' Lucy murmured. 'David, you can go in the sitting room and make yourself comfortable, if you like. I'll get you a drink, and feed Sophie. How about a Pimms?'

'That sounds lovely.' He sat down in his favourite chair and put his feet up on the footstool. A moment later she'd brought him an icy drink and the Proms book; he turned to the programmes for the coming week.

'Have you found anything tempting?' she asked when she returned with her own drink.

'Yes, definitely. Tuesday sounds very good, and so does Thursday. Were you going to go on Tuesday?'

'That's the all-Mozart programme, isn't it? Yes, I thought I'd go to that one. A little Mozart goes down well on a nice summer evening.'

'Do you mind if I tag along?'

She smiled. 'I think I could put up with you.'

In another minute Sophie had finished her dinner, and was curled up on his lap.

Chapter 23

*The sorrows of death compassed me: and the over-
flowings of ungodliness made me afraid.*

Psalm 18.3

There were two glasses and a bottle of whisky on the
table, awaiting his return; Daphne looked up from her
book as David came in just after eleven. 'Have you had a
good day?'

'Lovely, thanks.'

'Do you want anything to eat?'

David groaned. 'I don't think I shall want to eat for a
week. I've been eating practically non-stop all day.'

'Anything good?'

'Oh, yes. All of it. And I've just had a marvellous
supper.'

'Well, have a drink, then. Or would you rather have tea
or coffee?'

'This looks good to me.' He poured himself a generous
whisky. 'What have you done today?'

'Not much. I read the papers, had a sandwich, started
reading this Ruth Rendell novel.'

He imagined Daphne eating her solitary sandwich while
he was indulging in culinary delights, and had a brief pang

197

of guilt. 'Anything exciting in the papers?'

'There was just a paragraph in the *Independent* about . . . Mavis.'

Mavis. It was time to start thinking about Mavis. He sighed as the foreboding, the feeling of vague fear descended on him again.

'What did it say?'

She leafed through the paper and found it for him. 'The body of Mrs Mavis Conwell, aged forty-eight, was discovered in St Anne's Church, Kensington Gardens, London, late Saturday afternoon. The police are making inquiries,' she read.

'That's the *Independent* for you,' he said dryly. 'To the point.'

'Yes, I can imagine what the *News of the World* had to say about it. "Lonely Widow Slain in Church Bloodbath" or something like that.'

'You know,' he said suddenly, 'it just occurred to me. If she died in the sacristy – wouldn't it have to be reconsecrated before Mass could be celebrated?'

Daphne laughed. 'Full marks to you on that one. I found out this afternoon what happened: Gabriel had to bring the Bishop in last night to do it, after the police had finished in the sacristy. The Bishop was at a dinner party, and was none too happy about being called away, or so Emily says! I must admit, I had never even thought about reconsecration.'

'So,' David said, taking a fortifying gulp of his drink, 'what do you make of this business?'

'Mavis, you mean?'

'Yes. You must have your ideas about it. After all, you read all those crime novels.'

'So you're assuming it's murder.'

'Yes, of course,' David asserted with a nod. 'It certainly wasn't an accident, and Mavis didn't seem the type to kill herself. Too self-satisfied by half. She wouldn't hesitate to suggest that entire . . . groups of people . . . should go out and kill themselves en masse, but not her.'

'I think you're right,' Daphne admitted.

'Then who killed her?' he posed bluntly.

'Ah, that's the real question, isn't it?'

'Well, what do you think?' he demanded.

'Of course you have to think about the two big questions: motive and opportunity. Opportunity is easier to deal with,' Daphne said in a detached, mystery-fan way, making herself more comfortable on the sofa.

'I should think that's a pretty wide-open field,' David commented.

'Yes, in this particular case, anyway. All sorts of people were around, and any of them could have nipped in and done it.'

'The sacristy door wasn't locked when I left.'

'And neither was the side door, was it?'

'No, it wasn't.'

'And anyway, even if the sacristy door were locked,' Daphne added, 'half the people in the church have a key, and the other half know where to find one. So that wouldn't eliminate anyone.'

'Are you assuming it was someone from the church?' As he said it, he realised that it echoed his question to Gabriel about the blackmailer. He wished he could tell Daphne about the blackmail letter.

'Most likely. A stranger probably would have been noticed by someone, and a stranger wouldn't have known that they'd find her in the sacristy.'

'Unless it was a simple robbery?' he suggested. 'And she just happened to be the one there when someone went in to steal the takings from the fête?'

Daphne considered the possibility. 'Now we're on to motive, aren't we? That's not impossible, in theory. There was a lot of money there, and that wouldn't be too difficult for a lot of people to have figured out. But in that case, the *modus operandi* – she laughed self-deprecatingly at the phrase – 'just doesn't fit. A casual thief might shoot someone who stood in his way, or even stab them, but hanging – no. Hanging implies that it was someone who knew her well enough that she wouldn't be suspicious. Someone who could get behind her with a noose . . .'

David shuddered at her detached tone. She'd read too many mystery novels.

'Anyway,' she added, 'the money wasn't taken, was it? Didn't the police tell you that it was all accounted for?'

'Well, what about other motives then?'

Daphne laughed dryly. 'You know yourself in your short acquaintance with her that Mavis wasn't the best loved person at St Anne's. There were plenty of people with reason to dislike her.' David looked at her pointedly; she merely raised her eyebrows and went on. 'But murder? That requires more than just dislike.'

'Such as?'

'Well, if you remove money from the list . . . you're left with things like jealousy, revenge, thwarted love, blackmail, the thirst for power. Power – now there's an idea. Who do we know who desperately wants to be churchwarden?' she asked humorously. 'Roger Dawson, maybe?'

He smiled, but another word in her list had inevitably

caught his attention. 'Blackmail,' he said slowly. 'What do you mean? How could that be a motive?'

'Oh, blackmailers very often get themselves murdered – in books that I've read, anyway. Blackmail is a very dangerous business. If the victim finds out who his blackmailer is, he can kill the blackmailer to protect himself. Self-preservation is a powerful motive for murder.' Daphne talked on at great lengths about the other possible motives, but David was no longer listening. As soon as he could, he made his excuses and went to bed.

But not to sleep. He lay awake for hours as the enormity of the situation dawned on him. Mavis Conwell had been murdered. She'd been murdered by someone she knew, someone at St Anne's. Someone she'd blackmailed. Gabriel. After his first visceral acknowledgement and simultaneous denial of the possibility, David thought about it logically. Gabriel could not have killed Mavis. He'd been at the vicarage when she was killed. He, David, had taken Mavis the last bag of money that had been delivered. Thank God for that, he thought. Thank God Gabe was out of it. Emily would be able to give him an alibi for the whole period. He'd been helping with the teas, with the clearing up. Any number of people would have seen him.

He had no difficulty in accepting instantly his instinctive feeling that Mavis had been Gabriel's blackmailer. She had the essential self-righteous mind-set, he knew. That was all the motive necessary for the letter she'd sent – ridding St Anne's of an impure, unworthy priest. She wouldn't care that it was ancient history, that Gabriel was now a respectable and respected married man. If she'd found out . . . But how had she found out? Something nagged at his brain. It would come to him. She must have found out.

If she were blackmailing Gabriel, would she stop there? Or would she be blackmailing other people too? That must be the answer. She'd blackmailed someone else, and they'd killed her. He could imagine Mavis Conwell sitting over her typewriter, pouring out poisonous suggestions and self-righteous demands to those who had somehow offended her moral code. Someone else with a secret . . .

He'd almost made a fool of himself, he'd been so ready to accuse Miles Taylor of being the blackmailer, just because Peter Maitland had been a chorister at Selby. Clearly he had been wrong – it was a coincidence, nothing more than that. Mavis Conwell had been the blackmailer, and now she was dead.

Tomorrow. He must talk to Gabriel tomorrow. In the dark, he peered at the clock. Today.

Chapter 24

He shall deliver me from my strongest enemy, and
from them which hate me: for they are too mighty
for me.

Psalm 18.17

David looked out of his window at an overcast sky and
decided not to go to early Mass. Instead he walked to the
vicarage, arriving just after eight. Emily, dressed already
in jeans and a striped shirt, answered the door. 'Good
morning, David. Is Mass over? Have you come for
breakfast?'

'I haven't been to Mass,' he confessed. 'I've come to
have a word with Gabriel. But I wouldn't say no to breakfast.'

'Come on in, then. Gabriel's not back yet.' She looked
at her watch. 'He might be delayed by the police. But I
hope he won't be too long – we're going to St Albans
later.'

'Yes, of course. The children.'

'I can't wait to see them,' she confided. 'Come into the
breakfast room, David. Would you like some cereal?'

'Yes, thanks.' He discovered, improbably, that he was
very hungry.

'And how about a boiled egg?'

'That sounds delicious.'

'We won't wait for Gabriel. He can have his when he comes,' Emily said, joining him.

When Gabriel arrived, nearly half an hour later, he was looking relaxed and happy; all the tension of the past day, of the past weeks, was dissipated. He greeted Emily with a kiss, and David with an open, friendly smile, then ate his breakfast heartily.

'Are you coming with us to St Albans, David? We could take you to the Cathedral, if you've never been,' he offered.

'Oh, do come, David!' Emily urged. 'That would be great fun.'

'I couldn't possibly intrude on your family reunion,' he protested, embarrassed.

'Don't be silly!' Emily said fondly. 'You're practically one of the family.'

'No, really. I couldn't.'

'Well, what can I do for you, then?' Gabriel asked with good humour. 'We want to leave by mid-morning, don't we, darling?'

Emily nodded.

'I'd like to speak to you,' David replied awkwardly. 'It's . . . well, could we talk in your study?'

Gabriel looked puzzled, but not annoyed. 'Of course. If you don't mind, darling?'

'Go right ahead, you two. Have your secret chat. But just don't be too long about it!' she said with a smile.

They went into the study and sat down. 'Now, David, what's this all about?' Gabriel inquired genially.

David felt acutely uncomfortable. A woman was dead –

why was Gabriel so cheerful? 'About Mavis's . . . death,' he began.

Gabriel frowned. 'What about it?'

'I've been thinking about it. Has anything . . . struck you, Gabriel?'

Folding his hands on his desk, Gabriel looked at him and said formally, 'I have just finished speaking to the police about Mrs Conwell's death. It is their conclusion, based on the post-mortem examination and other evidence, that her death was . . . self-inflicted. That is to say, she hanged herself.'

David stared at him. 'Hanged herself? But you don't believe that, do you?'

'What reason would I have to disbelieve the police?'

'But surely . . . she was murdered? I mean, why on earth would Mavis kill herself?'

Gabriel spoke slowly and deliberately. 'The police spent the day in the church yesterday. A great deal of evidence has come to light. There's no reason why I shouldn't tell you. It would appear that Mrs Conwell had been . . . appropriating church funds for her own use . . . for some months. There have been some discrepancies that various people have noted, and a page has been removed from the current ledger book. Mrs Conwell's fingerprints were found on the book.'

'Mavis stealing money! But if it's been going on all this time, why should she kill herself now?'

'The Quinquennial Inspection is due to begin within the next few days. The police believe that she panicked and tried to cover her tracks, and when she realised that it wouldn't work, and she was bound to be discovered, she couldn't face the shame.'

'Is that all the evidence they've got?'

'Not at all. The sacristy door was locked, and the key was in Mrs Conwell's pocket.'

'But you know very well that doesn't mean anything! The door can be locked from the outside as well as the inside, and according to Daphne, half the people at St Anne's have got a key.'

Gabriel looked pained. 'David, I do think you should let the police do their job. They have found no evidence at all to point to . . . murder. The position of the body, the lack of signs of a struggle – all perfectly consistent with suicide.'

David took a deep breath. 'But you know better, don't you?' he said softly. 'You know that she was . . . the blackmailer.'

Gabriel recoiled. 'Are you suggesting that I killed her?'

'No, of course not. I know that you were at the vicarage when she was . . . killed.'

'Then what do you mean?'

'That you weren't the only one she was blackmailing. That she was playing a dangerous game, and it backfired on her. It all fits, Gabriel. And you believe it too.' As he said it, David realised that there was no other explanation for Gabriel's ebullient mood and behaviour: he believed that he was no longer in any danger.

Gabriel struggled for control. 'The police are satisfied. They are not pursuing the case any further.'

'Did you tell them about the blackmail letter?' David demanded.

'There was no need. It has nothing to do with . . .'

'Bloody hell, Gabriel! It has everything to do with it! Mavis Conwell attempted to blackmail you!'

206

'How can you be sure of that?' Gabriel challenged him. 'What proof do you have?'

'No proof,' admitted David, more quietly. 'But it all fits. She had the motive – she hated . . . queers, and especially queer priests.'

Gabriel winced at the description. 'Perhaps. But how would she have known about . . . Peter?'

'I'm not sure,' David began, then the thing he'd been trying to remember during the night came to him in a flash of memory. 'Wait. She's been to Brighton – I saw a souvenir ash-tray in her house. Obviously she met someone in Brighton, somebody who knew Peter. That's got to be it.'

'Even if that were true,' Gabriel said, 'and I'm not saying it is, why does that mean she was murdered? She could have been the blackmailer, and committed suicide.'

So that was what he wanted to believe, David reflected. Gabriel, too, had come to the conclusion that she had been his blackmailer, but had convinced himself that that fact was irrelevant to her death. He thought about it for a long moment. 'But Gabriel, if she killed herself over money, why couldn't she have just taken some of the proceeds from the fête, before the money was counted? No one but Mavis knew how much was coming in. It was all there, I assume? All the fête money? It tallied with the ledger sheet?'

Gabriel looked at him. 'There was no ledger sheet,' he said guardedly. 'There was just over eighteen hundred pounds on the table.'

'No ledger sheet?' David tried to assimilate the implications of that statement. 'But that means . . . that means that someone was in the sacristy after I left! The person who murdered Mavis Conwell!'

207

'The police are satisfied,' Gabriel repeated stubbornly. 'Leave it, David. You can only cause problems by stirring up all these questions.'

David's legal training, his strong sense of justice, asserted itself. 'How can you ask me to leave it?' His voice neared hysteria. 'A member of your congregation is dead. Another member of your congregation murdered her. Someone else she was blackmailing. Someone else with a secret to hide. I intend to find out who it was! With or without your cooperation! With or without your permission!'

Gabriel raised his voice for the first time. 'The police are satisfied! The investigation is closed!'

'I don't give a damn about the police!'

'Why don't you go home now, David? Forget about it all!'

'All you care about is your bloody reputation! You don't care about justice, about the truth!'

Gabriel had regained his self-control. 'The police are satisfied,' he repeated in a soft, steely voice. 'And would you please lower your voice? My wife might hear you.'

'The police can go to hell. And you can go to hell, *Father* Neville!'

Emily paused outside the study door, about to offer the men coffee. Though she couldn't hear their words, something in the quality of their voices made her hesitate. This was no friendly discussion, she realised. In spite of herself, she remained for a moment. Their voices were now raised in real anger, and several words resonated through the door: murder, police, secret, blackmail. Troubled, she retreated to the kitchen to puzzle about what she'd heard. Gabriel and David rowing. What did it all mean? Gabriel had been so ... cheerful this morning. What could David have said to make him so angry?

After a few minutes she heard the front door slam. When there was no other sound, she went to investigate. The door to the study was open, and Gabriel was sitting, rigid, at his desk. His face was white and set, and his hand was clenched around the paperweight as though he were ready to hurl it through the window.

'Gabriel, what's wrong? What's happened?' she asked with concern, entering the study hesitantly.

'Nothing,' he replied evenly, relaxing his body with a great effort and replacing the paperweight on the desk. 'Nothing at all.'

'But David – he was shouting at you.'

He laughed tightly. 'David tends to – overreact sometimes, that's all. He thinks that Mavis Conwell was murdered.'

'And was she?'

'No, of course not. The police have closed the investigation. They're quite satisfied that it was suicide.'

'But why should he care? He scarcely knew her. Why is he so upset?'

'God knows. David's a funny chap. I stopped trying to understand what makes him tick a long time ago.' He said the words lightly, but there was something in his voice that set off an alarm in her brain.

'He was shouting something about ... blackmail,' she said slowly. 'Won't you tell me what it's all about, Gabriel? I'm your wife. If you're in any sort of trouble ...'

'Don't be ridiculous,' he snapped. 'You're overwrought. He didn't say anything of the kind. Why should I be blackmailed?'

Emily turned and left the room in a kind of daze. Why, indeed? She went back into the kitchen and gripped the counter edge, taking a deep breath. She knew her husband well enough to know quite clearly that he was not telling the truth. What was Gabriel hiding? Why was he lying to her? What was the terrible secret he felt he had to protect her from?

It was something that had started a long time before today, she was sure. David. How was he involved?

If Gabriel wouldn't tell her, maybe David would. She had to know.

Chapter 25

Then thought I to understand this: but it was too hard
*   for me,*
Until I went into the sanctuary of God: then understood
*   I the end of these men . . .*

Psalm 73.15–16

The way Gabriel had said David's name, just now; the
look on his face . . . Emily thought of it again, as she
walked across the road from the vicarage to the church.
Suddenly her conscious mind apprehended, with an icy
shock, something that her unconscious must surely have
known or suspected for a very long time. Gabriel . . . and
David.

She knew, somehow, that she would find David in the
crypt chapel. He turned to her light step as she came down
the stairs. Still trembling with anger, he tried to calm
himself as he saw the haunted, strained look on Emily's
face.

'David, can we take a walk in the park? I need to talk
to you.'

'Of course,' was all he said.

They walked in silence for a long time as Emily tried to
summon the courage to frame the question that must be

asked. Her need to know was now greater than her over-whelming desire not to know. When they'd passed Peter Pan, Emily abruptly pulled him down on to a bench and looked searchingly into his face.

'David, we're friends, aren't we?'

'You know that we are.'

'If I ask you a question – a difficult question – will you promise to answer it?'

A trickle of fear reached his heart. 'If I possibly can.'

'David . . . were you and Gabriel . . . lovers?'

He caught his breath sharply, but managed to maintain eye contact with her. 'Don't you think you ought to ask Gabriel that?'

She looked away suddenly, biting her lip. 'You've just answered my question.'

He looked at her mute misery for a long moment. 'Emily, I . . . that is, what do you want to know?'

Her voice was almost inaudible. 'When? Where? For how long? Please, David. I have to know.'

'Let's walk,' he suggested. She walked deliberately, head down and hands in her pockets. At her side, David matched his pace to hers and kept his eyes straight ahead.

After a moment he began. 'It was in Brighton. He was the curate at St Dunstan's, and I was a server. We got to know each other. We . . . fell in love.' He sensed rather than saw her flinch. 'I didn't know what was happening at first. I was very innocent.' He rushed on, thinking of Gab-riel's lack of innocence. 'I was twenty-eight years old. Gabriel was a little younger. It lasted . . . for about three years. We were very discreet. No one else ever knew. It ended . . . when he came to London, to St Anne's. I never saw him again.'

She touched his arm gently; he stopped and faced her. 'I'm glad, if it had to be somebody . . . that it was you, David,' she said awkwardly. He waited, hoping and praying that she wouldn't ask him if he'd been the only one; he didn't know how he would answer. Above all, he didn't want to tell her about Peter Maitland. Misunderstanding his silence, a look of painful comprehension crossed her face. 'You still love him, don't you?' she whispered.

'I've never loved anyone else.' It was said simply, without self-pity.

Her quick mind, stunned as it was, reached the next inevitable conclusion with a surge of sympathy for him, sympathy that showed on her face as she said softly, 'How you must have hated me.'

He managed a smile. 'For ten years. Silly, wasn't it?'

'Oh, David.' They resumed walking, in silence.

Eventually they arrived back at the church, and went down to the chapel together. 'What are you going to do now?' David asked. 'You really should talk to Gabriel.'

Emily couldn't bear the thought of facing Gabriel now, while this knowledge was so new to her. 'Not now,' she said swiftly. 'I need time . . . to think. To try to understand, to make sense of it all. I thought I knew him . . .' Her voice broke. She hadn't cried till now, but the realisation of her short-term dilemma was too much for her. She wept, and David, who was unused to women's tears, held her gently, stroking her hair, reflecting bitterly on the irony of the situation.

When her tears were spent, she raised her eyes to him. 'Will you help me?' she appealed.

'Anything that's in my power,' he promised.

'I need to get away for a few days. I just can't face him now.' Her voice trembled again.

He understood her need to escape. 'Where will you go? To your parents'?'

'No, not there. I need to be alone, where I can think.'

'What about the children?'

She bit her lip. 'They'll be fine with my parents for a few more days. I just can't . . .'

'No, of course not,' he said, thinking quickly. 'I could take you to a place I know – a community of Anglican sisters, just outside London. They'd look after you, and you wouldn't have to talk to anyone.'

'Oh, David, would you?' She looked at him with gratitude.

'Of course. I think that would be best. You can stay as long as you like, and when you're ready . . . well, when you want to come back, I'll come and get you.'

'And you won't tell Gabriel . . .'

'Not if you don't want me to.' I don't think I'll have the chance, he added to himself. Not after the way we parted.

'I must write him a note – so he won't worry,' she said. David found her a piece of paper, and she wrote, 'Dear Gabriel, I have a lot of thinking to do, and am going away for a few days. Please ring my mother and ask her if she will keep the children for several days longer.' She hesitated, then added, 'Don't worry about me, and don't try to find me.'

Emily sat quietly beside him in the car. After a while David spoke. 'How did you . . . I mean, what made you . . . why now?'

She smiled ironically. 'After all these years, you mean? Yes, I must seem pretty stupid to you.'

'I didn't mean that.'

She thought for a moment, then explained, 'I heard you shouting. I was concerned to hear the two of you rowing. So I asked Gabriel what it was all about. He wouldn't tell me anything. It was nothing, really. Just something in the way he talked about you. Suddenly everything . . . well, it all made sense.'

'And you never suspected anything before?'

'Never. I was so naïve when I met him. And from the very beginning, our relationship was so . . . so physical. I just never dreamed.' It was David's turn to flinch. 'I suppose I didn't want to know, really,' she went on, clinically. 'He was the first man I ever loved, and he told me I was the first *woman* he'd ever loved.' She laughed bitterly. 'I just didn't ask the right questions. I wanted to believe it. It's silly now, when I think about it. To imagine a man as . . . beautiful, as . . . passionate as Gabriel, could reach the age of thirty . . . That he was waiting around for me, all that time . . .' She sighed. 'I wanted to believe it. That was my only excuse.'

'Don't blame yourself.'

She closed her eyes. 'How very foolish you must think me.'

It seemed like something from another world, the rambling house set on the edge of rolling green hills. Emily felt enveloped by its tranquillity even before they were in the door. Perhaps it was just that shock was setting in, she realised; she was drained of emotion now, and just wanted to rest.

David was so kind. He took care of the technicalities: he spoke to the head of the community, who was apparently a long-time acquaintance, and arranged for an open-ended stay for her in one of the rooms set aside for retreatants. Emily sat by numbly while he did all the talking. Finally it was time for him to take his leave of her.

'You'll be all right here, Emily,' he said awkwardly. 'They'll take care of you. And you can stay as long as you need to.' She nodded. 'When you're ready to . . . come back, just ring me at Daphne's and I'll come for you.'

'You won't tell him?'

'No, of course not.' He took her hand; it was like ice. He squeezed it. 'Listen, Emily. If there's ever anything you need, anything I can do for you . . . you know where to find me. I'll come in a minute if you need me.'

She looked up at him with gratitude. 'I'll be all right, David. Don't worry about me. And – thank you. For everything.'

A sweet-faced nun came forward. 'I'll take you to your room now, Mrs Neville.' Emily was silent as they passed down the corridor. 'I'm Sister Mary Grace.' She opened the door to a small, plainly furnished room. 'If you ever need to talk to someone, just ask anyone to find me for you. Any time.' With a sympathetic smile, she left Emily alone in the room.

Emily sat on the bed. That was all she wanted right now – to be alone.

Chapter 26

*Who will rise up with me against the wicked: or who
will take my part against the evil-doers?*

Psalm 94.16

Having left Emily in the capable hands of the good sisters,
David set off on the return journey into London. He very
quickly became entangled in traffic, but his thoughts were
in such turmoil that he scarcely noticed his lack of progress
on the road.

He was more than ever determined to follow through
on his threat to Gabriel to investigate Mavis's murder. He
hadn't much liked the woman, but it went against his
lawyer's instincts to let a murderer go scot-free, just because the police were too incompetent to recognise a murder when they saw one. To be fair, he reasoned, it wasn't
entirely the police's fault – they didn't know about the
blackmail. Damn Gabriel.

He felt an enormous need to talk to someone about it. It
was clear that he could no longer talk to Gabriel, and even
if Emily were available it would hardly be fair to burden
her with it. Lucy? He considered the possibility carefully.
He'd like to tell Lucy. She would be a good listener, and
would probably be able to offer some helpful insights. But

she was entirely too close to the situation. Her protective feelings for Emily would get in the way, and her dislike for Gabriel would predispose her to think the worst of him. And how could David explain to her his own place in the scheme of things? No, it would never do.

Daphne. That was the only possible answer. Daphne would listen, and not pass judgement. With her incisive understanding of people and her vast experience of crime novels, she could be of real help in puzzling things out. She knew all the people involved, and could probably shed some light on them in a concrete way. And he could trust Daphne. Of that he was sure. He could trust her completely with his innermost secrets. And he'd have to begin with his innermost secrets, or she'd never understand what was at stake.

Once that decision was made, he became impatient with the traffic. He wanted to talk to her now. He hoped she'd be home when he arrived.

He was in luck. She was in the kitchen, boiling the kettle for tea. 'Just in time,' she greeted him with a smile. 'I wasn't expecting you for tea.'

'I suppose you'd think it was too early for something . . . stronger?'

'Whatever you like,' she agreed, switching off the kettle and reaching for the whisky. 'Has it been that sort of day?'

'Absolutely.'

'Do you want to tell me about it?'

'I'd like nothing better,' he confessed, leading the way to the sitting room.

Daphne made herself comfortable and looked at him over the tops of her glasses. 'Fire away,' she urged.

David sat awkwardly on the edge of his chair, twisting

the glass in his hands. 'I don't know where to begin.'

'The beginning is generally as good a place as any,' Daphne suggested with an encouraging smile.

'The beginning. Well.' He took a gulp of whisky and tried to relax in the chair. 'We've known each other a long time,' he started, self-consciously. 'Oh, hell, Daphne! I just don't know how to tell you this. I've never told anyone before in my life.'

'Told anyone what?'

'Well, it's just that . . . that is to say, there's something about me that you don't know. I don't . . .'

'Do you want me to make it easier for you?' she drawled. 'Are you trying to tell me that you're gay?'

His body sagged in relief and amazement. 'Daphne! How long have you known?' he gasped.

'Probably a lot longer than you have, if you must know. I always had a feeling you were . . . that way inclined.'

'My God. And you never said a word.'

'It was none of my business, was it?' she said imperturbably. 'The question is, why are you telling me this now?'

'That's another difficult thing to explain. It has to do with Gabriel.'

'I thought it might.'

'You know about . . . me and Gabriel?' He stared at her.

She smiled calmly. 'I guessed. As soon as I met Gabriel. There was something about the way he talked about you, and about the way you talked about him. It was obvious there'd been something between you. Obvious to me, anyway,' she added quickly, to forestall alarm. 'I don't think anyone else has guessed. No one else around here knows you as well as I do. Anyway, I didn't see you very often during those years you were in Brighton. I had a feeling you might have . . . met someone special.'

David felt limp. 'I'm speechless. Daphne . . .'

'Well, go on. What's the problem?'

'When you wrote and asked me to come, to see about the chapel . . .'

'Yes.'

'Gabriel wrote at the same time. He said he needed my help.'

'I rather thought it might be something like that,' she mused. 'He came round here to see me one night, the night we decided to invite you to come and help with the chapel. I wondered what was up. He jumped at my suggestion so eagerly, and he was most anxious to conceal from the parish that you knew each other. So what was it all about? And does he know that you're telling me now?'

'No, he doesn't. I'll get to that. The day after I'd arrived, after early Mass, he showed me a letter he'd received. I suppose you'd call it a blackmail letter.'

Daphne raised her eyebrows. 'Blackmail?'

'Yes. It didn't ask for money, but there were . . . certain demands. I can't really tell you what it was about, but suffice to say that it was written by someone who'd found out . . . something . . . about Gabriel's past. Nothing to do with me,' he added quickly. 'But he thought I might be able to help him find out who'd written the letter.'

'And did you?'

'I thought I had, a few days ago. But since then . . . well, I think it's quite clear that it was Mavis Conwell.'

She nodded thoughtfully. 'Certainly that would be right

up her street, if the subject matter was what I think it was.'

'Yes. When you said, last night, that blackmail was a motive for murder – well, everything fell into place. I realised that she'd probably been killed by someone she had blackmailed.'

'Surely you're not suggesting that Gabriel . . .'

'Good Lord, no!' he denied too quickly. 'That's unthinkable, as well as being impossible – he was at the vicarage helping with teas when she was murdered.'

'Then who . . .'

'I believe that she was blackmailing someone else, as well as Gabriel.'

'What do the police say?'

He sighed. 'That's the problem. The police believe she committed suicide! They've closed the case.'

'But they don't know about the blackmail, presumably?'

'No. Gabriel didn't tell them, naturally enough.' David poured himself another drink. 'This morning he and I . . . we had a terrific row.' He closed his eyes for a moment at the memory. 'I'm sure he believes that she was the blackmailer – he was so relieved, so cheerful. But he's convinced himself that she wasn't murdered.'

'How does he reckon that?'

'Well, apparently she's been pinching money from the church.'

Daphne gave a low whistle. 'Is that so?'

'Yes. That's mainly why the police think it was suicide. Remorse, fear of exposure, all that. And Gabriel's buying it. At least he says so.'

'And you think . . .'

'That she was murdered. By another blackmail victim.

221

After all, if she was blackmailing one person, why not more than one?'

'Why don't you go to the police?'

He shook his head. 'I've thought about it. But it really would be damned awkward, without any evidence, now that they've closed the case.'

'So what are you going to do?'

'I want to make a few discreet inquiries, like I was doing before, about the blackmail.'

'To what end?'

'I'd like to find out, if I can, who murdered Mavis Conwell. What I'm looking for is someone with a secret – a secret worth killing to protect. I'm not pretending it will be easy . . .'

'It could be dangerous, David,' she warned. 'If this person has killed once . . .'

'I know. I'm not going to ask you to help me, Daphne. I wouldn't put you in that position. But I need someone I can talk to about it. Two heads, and all that. You know the people, you know the set-up. What do you think? Will you be my sounding-board?'

'You're not going to relegate me to that role, now that you've brought me this far! We're in this together now, David.'

'So you think I'm right?'

'I think that between us we can come up with an answer that makes more sense than the police's solution. And then . . . well, we'll see, won't we?' Daphne topped up her glass, then settled back. 'This *is* decadent, drinking whisky at four o'clock in the afternoon. Cheers, partner,' she saluted him.

'Where do we start?'

She thought for a moment. 'I don't suppose we can do much today besides explore some of the possibilities. Let's try to think who might have something to hide. Something that Mavis might find . . . of interest.'

'Do you think it has to be a man?'

'I think it probably is,' Daphne replied. 'From a purely practical standpoint, it would take a fair amount of physical strength to . . . well, to hang someone. Lifting the weight, and all that. Mavis wasn't a particularly big woman, but just the same . . . I don't think I could have done it, and I don't know many women who could.'

'Well, that makes it easier, if we can eliminate all the women.'

'Mavis would have been much more likely to be interested in the . . . secrets . . . of the men, anyway, I should have thought. Think about her obsession with "manliness", and lack of it, in the Church.'

'The servers,' David said, thinking out loud. 'She despised them. She seemed to think they were all suspect, because of Tony Kent. Tony. Everyone seems to know he's gay.'

'Yes, but that's the point. Everyone does know it. He's never made any secret of the fact.'

'Unlike others we know,' David said with a wry smile. 'Maybe it's the difference between his generation and mine, or perhaps just his upbringing and mine.'

'Well, it might be worth while talking to Tony, anyway. He may well know something that could help us.'

'I'm having lunch with him tomorrow,' David remembered suddenly.

'That could be useful.'

'Roger Dawson. I can't imagine him having any guilty

secrets. He seems as dull as ditch-water to me.'

'But you know about still waters running deep,' Daphne cautioned. 'Don't dismiss him on that account.'

'What does Roger Dawson do?'

'He's some sort of a minor civil servant. Works in the local DSS office, I believe.'

'Hm. Well, I'll find out probably more than I want to know about Roger Dawson soon, too. I'm going there for dinner on Wednesday,' he said with a grimace.

'Now *that's* suspicious in itself! I wonder why they've asked you? The Dawsons have never been well known for their hospitality!'

'I'm sure I'll find out in due time. But I don't think we have to worry about the Dawsons.' David held his glass up to the light and squinted through the amber liquid as he worked through the possibilities in his mind. 'How about Cyril?' he asked.

'I shouldn't think so. I don't think he'd be physically strong enough, in the first place. I'd say the same about Venerable Bead. And Cyril's too . . . candid for me to believe that he has any terrible secrets. I mean, everyone knows how he feels about Emily! And he doesn't seem at all embarrassed that it should be that way.'

'Do you know who I'd like it to be?' David confessed. 'Miles Taylor. I just don't care for the bloke. What secrets is he hiding?'

'Funny you should ask that,' said Daphne, with a speculative look. 'As a matter of fact, there is something distinctly suspicious about Miles Taylor.'

'Tell me.'

'Well, you know that he used to be organist at Selby Cathedral.'

'I had heard,' he said, rolling his eyes.

'Yes, I suppose it would be difficult to be around Miles for five minutes without learning that fact,' she acknowledged humorously. 'Anyway, Miles left Selby very suddenly about five years ago, and came here. Now, St Anne's is a lovely church, and has a lot to offer a musician, but it's not a cathedral.'

'No . . .'

'And there have been a few people who have wondered why a man with Miles's talent would have left a cathedral to come here. It's rather a step down in the world for a cathedral organist.'

'Does anyone know why he left Selby?'

'He never talks about it. But I think there's something in it, something he's hiding.'

'I wonder.' David looked very thoughtful.

'Secrets,' Daphne mused. 'Everyone has them, I suppose.'

'Even you, Daphne?'

She smiled enigmatically. 'Even me. The things we think other people wouldn't understand . . . It's all perception, you know. The faces we show to the world . . .' Suddenly practical, she sat up. 'We must make a plan. You will have lunch with Tony tomorrow, and talk with him. See what you can find out.'

'I'd like to talk to the manly Craig, if I could. I'm not suggesting that he had anything to do with the murder – Mavis would hardly have blackmailed her own son, after all! But I might learn something about Mavis and her preoccupations from him. I don't know how I'd manage it, though. He's not exactly the sort one would pay a sympathy call on!'

225

'As a matter of fact, I'll be seeing Craig Conwell to-morrow,' Daphne revealed with satisfaction. 'He's coming in to discuss the arrangements for the funeral with me and with Gabriel.'

'Excellent. Then I'll leave him to you – he's your assignment for the day.'

'Then what?'

'I would dearly love to have a word with Miles Taylor. At the moment, my money's on him.'

'I doubt that he'd be very forthcoming. You know how he is. Well, you can see him on Wednesday at the recital, anyway.' Daphne suddenly looked very sheepish, then burst out laughing.

'What's so funny?'

'Oh, David. I've just realised something. Miles Taylor is the one person who couldn't possibly have killed Mavis!'

'Why not? If this motive turns out to be anything . . .'

'No, David, you don't understand! Miles was playing the organ, wasn't he?'

'Yes,' David said slowly. 'The recital had started when I left Mavis alive in the sacristy . . .'

'And he was still playing when Venerable opened the sacristy door an hour later! Whether you like it or not, David, Miles is in the clear!'

'Damn,' said David, crestfallen.

Chapter 27

Who imagine mischief in their hearts: and stir up
strife all day long.
They have sharpened their tongues like a serpent:
*   adder's poison is under their lips.*

Psalm 140.2–3

The workmen were due to begin their repairs in the crypt chapel on Tuesday morning, David remembered. He'd promised Lady Constance that he would oversee their labours. So the morning before his lunch with Tony went by quickly, with scarcely time for thoughts of murder and blackmail. But inevitably before the morning was over, Venerable Bead puffed his way down the stairs to find out what was happening, his little eyes bright with curiosity. 'Oh, I wondered if the workmen had started,' he addressed David.

'Yes, just this morning. It's going to take some time, I think. The work is very delicate.'

'Well, when you have to leave London, you can leave it in my hands,' Venerable said with eagerness. 'When are you going back home?'

'I've got a month off from work,' David replied vaguely. 'So I can stay a bit longer if necessary.'

Venerable stood for a moment observing the workmen.

'Mind you watch what you're doing!' he said sharply to one of them at some imagined infraction. The man glared.

David stepped in quickly to distract the old man's critical eye. 'That must have been quite a shock for you on Saturday, finding the body.'

'Oh, it gave me quite a turn, I can tell you! Not what I was expecting to see, when I went to get ready for Evensong!' He was enjoying himself immensely, David could see, and he wordlessly encouraged him to go on. 'Terrible, the sight was! I've never seen anything like it! She was hanging from that long bracket, the one for the statue of Our Lady, and the chair was knocked over on the floor. Her eyes were staring right at me! And she was all limp, and her tongue . . .' He shuddered deliciously, and demonstrated the expression on the dead woman's face. Venerable Bead's fund of stories had been enriched immeasurably – he'd be dining out on this one for the rest of his life, David thought.

When the time came, David was glad of the chance to escape from the church, and from the daunting prospect of the weekly lunches in the church hall.

Tony lived in a flat outside St Anne's parish in Notting Hill Gate, not far from the Portobello Road. David had known the Portobello Road fairly well in his early days in London with Daphne, but hadn't been there for years, so he self-consciously consulted his *A to Z* before setting off. He was glad he'd done so, as Monday's overcast skies had turned at last to steady rain, and the pavements seethed with umbrellas. A taxi passing too close to the kerb soaked his trouser-legs, and he cursed silently.

Tony seemed glad to see him. 'Hope you didn't have

too much trouble finding it, David. You look like you
could use a drink. Sherry? Or would you prefer whisky?'

David looked at him gratefully. 'You read my mind.
Whisky, please.' While Tony fixed the drinks, he observed
the flat with interest. It was really only one room, cleverly
divided into areas for sitting, cooking and eating, and sleeping. The sleeping part consisted of a loft, reached by a
ladder and containing an oversized bed. The walls of the
sitting area were lined with bookcases, and the whole of
the flat was dominated by a sophisticated stereo system
with multiple speakers. It was decorated with innovative
but simple good taste. 'I like your flat,' he said sincerely,
crossing to the purpose-built record shelves for a browse.
A little Vivaldi might be just the thing, he thought, but he
was disappointed: the record collection seemed to be dominated by rock music by people he'd never heard of.

'Sorry about that,' Tony apologised, turning and seeing
his furrowed brow. 'My . . . flatmate . . . has rather esoteric tastes in music, I'm afraid. The sound system is his. I
like a bit of jazz, myself – my records are there at the
end.'

David thought he might just about be able to endure
jazz, if he had to. Tony put on some Dave Brubeck, turned
the volume down low, and they sat on the low-slung chairs
with their drinks.

'Your . . . flatmate's not here?' David asked conversationally. 'Ian, I think his name is?'

'Ah, so someone's been talking, have they?' said Tony
tensely.

'Only Venerable Bead,' David reassured him.

'That's all right, then.' Tony relaxed. 'No, Ian's at work.'

'Oh, isn't he a teacher, too? I just assumed he was.'

'No. Ian . . . well, he drives a taxi.'

'Ah! Maybe he's the one I have to thank for this, then!' David surveyed his damp ankles ruefully.

They both laughed, and the potential awkwardness was dispelled.

'The flat really is lovely,' David reiterated. 'Have you lived here long?'

'About six or seven years, I suppose. I've gradually fixed it up the way I like it.'

'You're not actually in St Anne's parish here, are you? Did you used to live in the parish?'

'No, I'm not a native Londoner. I grew up in Croydon – there's a good High Church tradition there, as you may know, so when I moved to London to teach, I looked around for a church nearby with the proper churchmanship. St Anne's was just what I was looking for, and they happened to need servers very badly at that time. So I've been there ever since. It's suited me very well, and it's quite close by.'

'I would have thought St Anne's would never suffer from a shortage of servers.'

'Well, not too long before I came, they'd lost the two oldest Dawson boys, Nick and Ben. They'd gone off to university. Venerable says they were both pretty good servers – very conscientious, anyway.'

'But Francis?' David prompted. 'You said you had a tale to tell about him.'

'Oh, Francis. You haven't met him, have you? He's absolutely gormless. And as a server . . . Well, let's just say his career was short-lived but memorable.'

'What on earth did he do?'

'He very badly wanted to serve. I wasn't keen on having him – I knew how clumsy he was, but Gabriel insisted that I at least give him a chance.'

'Fair enough, I suppose.'

'I gave him plenty of training, and thought he might be able to start as an acolyte. But the very first Sunday, he bent too close to the candle, and set his hair on fire!'

'That must have been quite a sight!'

'It was at the high altar, so I don't think too many people saw it. I'll never forget it, though! Next I tried him as crucifer – I thought that would be safer. But he led the procession off in the wrong direction. There wasn't anything that anyone could do but follow him. So much for being crucifer.'

'You didn't let him be MC, did you?'

'Just once. He opened the book at the wrong page, and Gabriel read out the wrong collect. He wasn't very amused – I think he was beginning to realise he'd been too charitable in his assessment of Francis's abilities.'

'So that was the end of his career?'

'Oh, no. He went out with a mighty bang. Literally. His ultimate ambition was to be thurifer, so I thought I'd give him a go at it on a weekday, at a Saint's Day service. I figured he couldn't do much harm there, but I was wrong. He was swinging the thurible, and got up such a good head of steam that he let it go. It went flying, with incense and charcoal landing all over the sanctuary carpet in flames. Gabriel didn't miss a beat. He stomped it all out while he intoned the Gospel. But that was well and truly the end of Francis's serving career. Gabriel put his foot down, so to speak.' Tony shook his head. 'You've got to laugh.'

'Are those the only boys in the family?'

'Yes. Then there are the three girls. Bridget, Clare, and

Teresa. Thank God no one has ever seriously suggested allowing girls to serve at St Anne's, or Teresa would be the first to sign up! That girl is completely clueless.'

'Well, I shall certainly look forward to my dinner with the Dawsons – it should be worth a great deal in entertainment value. I'm even promised a chance to meet the famous Francis!'

'You're going to dinner at the Dawsons'?'

'Yes, tomorrow. Didn't I tell you?'

Tony looked amazed. 'Well, I never. I can't imagine what that will be like. The Dawsons never have people over for a meal.'

'Really?'

'No. Their meanness is legendary when it come to hospitality, or lack thereof. You know, whenever I've been at their house for a meeting – servers, or whatever, the big event is the unveiling of the sacred Postman Pat biscuit tin. I think it must be a family heirloom. It's brought out with all due ceremony, and everyone present is invited to help themself to one biscuit, and one biscuit only.'

'Maybe I'd better eat before I go.'

'That wouldn't be a bad idea, probably! Speaking of food, though, are you ready for some lunch?'

'Any time.'

'It isn't anything fancy,' Tony warned. 'Just plain food – not the airy-fairy sort of thing you'd get from Lucy Kingsley,' he added, tongue-in-cheek, and watching surreptitiously to see his reaction.

David refused to be drawn. 'I imagine you're a very good cook,' he said blandly.

That proved to be true, and the tales of the Dawsons resumed over an excellent steak and kidney pie.

'Have you noticed Roger Dawson's liturgical ties?' Tony asked. 'Probably not. It's a lot more noticeable when you get the whole family there, wearing their ties in seasonal colours.'

'Do you mean to tell me the Dawsons wear neckties in liturgical colours? Every day?' David inquired, bemused.

Tony laughed. 'Not every day, no. Just on Sundays and Feast Days. We've had a pretty long spell of green ties now, except for gold on the Patronal Festival. But if you're still here next week for the Feast of the Assumption, you'll get to see the rare blue tie, in honour of Our Lady.'

'I don't believe it.'

'Oh, it's true all right.'

'But what about the women?'

'The girls generally wear hair-bows, and Julia wears a silk scarf. There's no one more properly Catholic than the Devout Dawsons.'

After lunch they relaxed over coffee. David had tried very hard to think of a way to introduce the subject of the blackmail letters in a natural way, but finally he gave up and plunged in. 'Tony, you may think this is a strange question. It *is* a strange question, but I have reasons for asking it.'

'Go ahead,' Tony said, somewhat apprehensively.

'It's just . . . well, I wondered if you had any knowledge about . . . that is, do you know anyone who has received any . . . threatening letters? Letters that might have been written by Mavis Conwell?'

Tony stared at him in amazement. 'How did you know?'

'Know what?'

'About the letter?'

'You've had a letter?'

'Yes, of course. How did you find out?'

David took a deep breath, stunned. 'Tell me about it, please.'

'It came – oh, a fortnight or so ago. Maybe longer.'

'Have you kept it?'

'No. It was – horrible. I tore it up and threw it on the fire.'

'Did you know it was from Mavis?'

'I assumed it was. I threw it away, and tried to forget about it.'

'But what . . . can you tell me what it said?' Tony looked stricken. 'I wouldn't ask if it wasn't important,' David added gently.

'It said . . . that I was a disgrace to the Church.'

'But there was a threat?'

'Yes.' Tony hesitated fractionally, looking down at his clasped hands. 'About Ian.'

'I don't understand.'

Tony turned and met his eyes. 'Ian is only nineteen,' he said in a low voice. 'I could go to prison.'

Walking back to Daphne's in the rain, David went through the Portobello Road market to look for a florist. The flower-sellers on the market, discouraged by the weather, had long since packed up and gone home, but he found a florist shop around the corner. Roses for Lucy, he thought. Long-stemmed roses, the colour of her hair. He chose them with a feeling of anticipation. Tonight he'd give her the roses, and they'd listen to Mozart, and he'd forget about murder for a few hours.

In the meantime, though . . . He picked out a sturdy

bunch of mixed summer flowers for Daphne, and went back for tea.

'So how is the manly Craig taking his mother's death?' David asked while the tea steeped. 'Prostrate with grief, is he?'

'He doesn't seem to be particularly bothered,' Daphne said in her detached way. 'He didn't have much to say for himself, but he's not especially verbose at the best of times.'

'When will the funeral be?'

'Next week – probably Tuesday. I think the inquest will be Monday, and they'll release the body for the funeral then.'

'Are there any other relatives?'

'I believe that Mavis had brothers and sisters, but there's no one close enough to be involved in the planning. Craig wants it as simple as possible, he says. Actually, he wants it as cheap as possible,' she added cynically. 'It will be a plain Prayer Book funeral, no frills at all.'

'No servers?'

'No.' Daphne laughed. 'This is the other interesting bit. He says he doesn't want any servers – not even a crucifer. He said that his mother hated "those poofs" and wouldn't have wanted them "prancing around" at her funeral!'

'And what did Gabriel say about that?' David smiled in spite of himself.

'He didn't say a word, but he looked extremely pained.'

'I should think he did.'

Chapter 28

*Upon an instrument of ten strings, and upon the
lute: upon a loud instrument, and upon the harp.*
                                                    Psalm 92.3

Daphne had already finished her breakfast and was nearly
done with the newspaper by the time David emerged,
yawning and rubbing his eyes. 'Would you like a cooked
breakfast?' she offered.

'No thanks, Daphne. I really can't have you waiting on
me all the time. Just toast and tea will be fine.'

'You must have been out quite late last night. How was
the Mozart?'

'Oh, splendid,' he replied with a reminiscent smile.
'The worst part was queuing in the rain. I swore it was the
last time I'd ever do that – and I'm too old to stand
through a concert, anyway.'

'I thought you said you were going to go again tomorrow night.'

'Yes, but I've splurged, and bought seats in the stalls. It
will be worth it.'

'Are you going to the organ recital today?' she asked.

'Yes. Do you want to come?'

'No, thank you. I heard a bit of the one on Saturday,

237

and a little of Miles goes a long way with me.'

He frowned pensively. 'I really wish I could pin the murder on him.'

'Well, you can't. We've established that. Have you had any further thoughts on what Tony told you?'

'I've been thinking about it. I think that the fact that he was so open about the letter he received puts him in the clear. If he'd murdered her, he wouldn't have told me about the letter.'

'Not necessarily. He might have been trying to throw you off the scent. After all, you didn't actually see the letter. You don't know what it really said.'

'Oh, Daphne, your mind is too devious for me. Is there anybody I can cross off the list of possible suspects?'

'Yes, Miles Taylor,' she chuckled.

The sun had returned, at least intermittently; Lucy was waiting for him outside the church, shading her eyes against the bright light. 'You're early,' he greeted her.

'Yes, it was such a pleasant day that I couldn't really get started working, so I came out and walked over through the park. Anyway,' she confessed, 'I didn't get up very early this morning, so there wasn't time to do much painting, even if I'd been inclined.'

'I didn't either,' David admitted. 'Poor Daphne, I don't know how late she waited up last night.'

'You couldn't talk her into coming with you today?'

'No, she wasn't all that keen.'

Lucy hesitated. 'Emily won't be coming today, either.'

'Oh?' David said, as non-committally as possible.

'No. I had a letter from her in this morning's post. You know I said last night that I hadn't talked with her since

Saturday? Well, apparently she's gone away for a few days.'

'By herself?' he asked, hating himself for his dishonesty.

'Yes.' Lucy didn't say any more, and he could only guess at how much Emily had revealed to her. Not very much, he surmised. Lucy would be loyal and discreet, but surely Emily wouldn't have . . .

People had been steadily streaming past them into the north porch of the church. Now Beryl Ball approached, shuffling up in her moon-boots. But instead of going past, she stopped and looked at David, then at Lucy, with her magnified eyes. 'You just can't stay away from the women, can you?' she asked maliciously. 'When I wouldn't have you, you went after that whore the Vicar's wife. She's not particular – she'll take any man! But she's gone now, isn't she?' she announced with triumph.

'Is she?' David said faintly.

'You know she is – that's why you've got this one now! You're a sex maniac, that's what you are!'

'How do you know she's gone?' Lucy asked.

'The Vicar told me himself! Yesterday, at lunch. I asked him where she was, and he said she'd gone off to take care of a sick relative. But I knew he was lying. She's gone for good, is that one. Run off with another man. No better than she should be, I always said.' She nodded her head vigorously. 'Sick with worry, the Vicar looked. Not that I didn't warn him, before he married the slut. I told him it would end in tears.' Beryl looked back and forth between them, daring them to challenge her, then grinned suddenly as a new thought occurred to her. 'To tell the truth, I wouldn't be a bit surprised if it was Mavis's boy that she's run off with! He wasn't half upset when I turned him down on Saturday! It was my new hat, you see – he just couldn't resist me in it. But I told him no, and he must have run off with her instead!'

'Miss Ball,' said David finally, 'I don't really think—'

'You can count on it. That's just what happened,' she interrupted, with a self-righteous thrust of her dentures, and shuffled off into the church.

David had a guilty pang at the thought of Gabriel, sick with worry. Should he say something to him, just to ease his mind? No, he decided. Emily's needs were more important at the moment. She'd never forgive him if he betrayed her trust.

To David's disappointment, the penultimate piece on the programme was the same piece – the Great G Minor Fantasia and Fugue – that Miles had performed on Saturday. Apparently he had not practised it in the meantime, David noted; he was making exactly the same mistakes. The mistakes were not glaring ones, but they were evident to anyone who knew the piece well, and they grated. After several minutes, he whispered to Lucy, 'Why don't we make our escape now? I've heard enough of this.' She nodded agreement, and they slipped out of the north porch.

'Why don't you come to my place for some tea,' Lucy suggested. But David made no reply; stopped in his tracks, he was staring with disbelief at Miles Taylor, who leaned nonchalantly against the church, smoking a cigarette.

'Come on,' she urged. 'Miles is just cheating again,' she added in a whisper. 'He must have the Great G Minor on the computer. You know, the machine that plays the organ for him.'

David turned to stare at her. He deliberately marched her around the corner of the building, out of Miles's hearing, and said slowly, 'Would you please repeat what you just said?'

'I said he must have the Great G Minor on the computer. Surely you know about his fancy machine – he brags about it enough. He loves all that high-tech gadgetry, you know. And this is the latest thing.'

'And what exactly does this machine do?'

'It plays the organ for him. I'm not sure about the technical details. But apparently it remembers all the registrations, and the key-strokes, and plays it back exactly – actually plays the pipes, just as if he were sitting at the console. Miles is a chain-smoker, surely you've noticed that. He can't get through an hour without a cigarette, so he's got some of his favourite pieces stored on the machine, and he usually puts at least one of them on every recital programme, so he can sneak out and have a fag. When he's having a real nicotine fit, he doesn't have to play a note himself. Most people never know the difference.'

David closed his eyes and leaned against the warm stone. 'Lucy, you're wonderful.'

'Why, thank you. I think you're rather nice yourself. But to what do I owe that compliment?'

'I can't really explain now. But I need to have a word with Miles. Would you mind going on ahead and putting the kettle on? I'll be along in just a few minutes.'

'Whatever you say. See you shortly, then.' With a quizzical look over her shoulder, she departed, and he watched her graceful walk as he had watched her the week before, the day they'd met. Only a week? he thought. Impossible.

* * *

The rest of the recital seemed to take hours, though in reality it was less than ten minutes. David waited at the back of the church in a fever of impatience while the applause went on, the organist took repeated bows, and finally descended to feed his ego on the adoration of the Fan Club.

But David reached him first, with a smooth smile. Flattery would get him everywhere with this man, he had decided; the direct approach would never work.

'Mr Taylor – may I call you Miles? – that was a splendid programme!' he enthused.

Miles turned to him, beaming. 'I'm glad you liked it. It was rather good, wasn't it?'

'Splendid! Splendid!' he repeated, steering Miles past the waiting women and leading him outside. 'It's a very fine instrument, isn't it?'

'Well, it has its strengths. Of course there are little problems that only an organist would understand. You're not an organist, are you?'

'No, just an appreciative listener,' David gushed.

Condescendingly, Miles explained, 'It's a fine organ. But some of the registrations just don't – well, I mustn't get too technical.'

'I suppose no organ is perfect, but it's the mark of a professional to be able to work with the imperfections to achieve such a magnificent sound!'

Miles's thin chest swelled. 'You're right, of course. Though I must say that the organ at Selby Cathedral is as close to perfect as I've ever found. Sheer heaven, that organ. Mechanical action, beautiful voicing, incredible stops. Absolutely perfect for contemporary music.'

'Of course, you were at Selby. That must have been a wonderful experience for you.'

Miles flung out his arms in an expansive gesture. 'Yes, those were the best years of my life! That magnificent organ! The wonderful music! And the choir – brilliant!' He beamed seraphically in nostalgic remembrance.

Having led him so satisfactorily up the garden path, David was ready for the kill. 'St Anne's is so lucky to have a man of your . . . experience,' he said ingenuously. 'Tell me, how did you come to leave Selby for St Anne's?'

The smile froze on Miles's face, his eyes glittered behind his spectacles, and his arms dropped to his sides. 'I'm afraid that as a non-musician, you couldn't possibly understand. Now I really must be going. The ladies will be so disappointed if they don't have a chance to see me. Do come again next week, won't you?'

David watched his retreating back with satisfaction. Daphne had been right: he was definitely hiding something. But Daphne had been wrong about the other thing. Miles Taylor was not off the list of suspects, not by a long shot. At the moment, he was well ahead of the pack. With a thoughtful shake of his head, David resumed his journey towards Lucy and tea.

Chapter 29

Lo, children and the fruit of the womb: are an heri-
tage and gift that cometh of the Lord.
Like as the arrows in the hand of the giant: even so
are the young children.
Happy is the man that hath his quiver full of them:
they shall not be ashamed when they speak with
their enemies in the gate.

Psalm 127.4–6

Tea had stretched out over the afternoon, and the Dawsons
had invited him for the unbelievably early hour of six, so
David barely had time to stop at a wine merchant's to pick
up a bottle and to call in on Daphne before hurrying to his
dinner date. She told him how to find the Dawsons' house
– a semi-detached, a few streets away from Mavis Conwell's
terrace – and promised to wait up for his return, intrigued
by his hints of revelations to come. 'I can't imagine that
you'll be very late,' she called after him.

He was not really looking forward to this evening, David
reflected, wondering again why he'd been invited. The
Devout Dawsons were not his cup of tea. According to
Tony Kent, the Dawsons were totally without any sense of
humour, and paradoxically it was that quality alone that

made them amusing, in an entirely unintentional way. But with people who took themselves so seriously, any temptation to share the joke, as it were, would have to be firmly suppressed. He practised looking solemn, and pious. He hoped it would be a short evening. Five minutes late already – damn. With the Dawsons, he didn't imagine that six meant anything but six sharp.

Julia Dawson opened the door to him with her customary anxious expression.

'I'm so sorry I'm late,' he began as he handed her the bottle of wine.

'We were beginning to worry,' she said, ushering him in. 'I was afraid you'd got lost, and Roger thought perhaps you'd had an accident.' She announced his arrival in the lounge. 'It's all right, he's here.'

A small dog of indeterminate breed appeared as if from nowhere and hurled itself at David's legs, yapping frantically. David liked dogs, but he didn't much like the look of this one. Shaggy and unkempt, it resembled the business end of a well-used mop. 'Ignatius!' Julia shrieked. 'Leave the man alone! I thought I'd shut you outside!' She grabbed the dog by its collar and dragged it away. 'I'm so sorry, David. Ignatius doesn't like strangers,' she apologised over her shoulder. He stood a moment, bemused, then entered the lounge.

Roger Dawson rose, and extended his hand. Teresa, sitting in the corner, turned her head away in embarrassment at David's acknowledgement. And then there were the introductions to Francis, the man enshrined in serving lore for ever.

Francis Dawson was pretty much exactly what David would have expected. Unprepossessing, in the honoured family tradition. He wasn't tall, but neither was he short. His hair was the colour and texture of wet straw – David had to bite his lip to suppress a chuckle at the thought of that hair blazing away, ignited by a candle; he could just imagine the look on Gabriel's face. Francis had mild blue eyes, not as protuberant as Teresa's, and his mother's thin, pointed nose. A tuft of scraggly beard gave him the illusion of having the vestige of a chin. His voice, when he spoke, was soft and diffident.

Julia returned, breathing heavily. 'Do sit down, David,' she urged, then struck by her own presumption, added anxiously, 'May I call you David?'

'Yes, of course . . . Julia.'

'Now, what would you like for your tea?' she addressed her children. 'Remember that we have a guest. Would you like fish fingers and chips? Or beans on toast?'

'Spaghetti on toast?' suggested Teresa hopefully.

Julia shook her head. 'I'm afraid we're out of tinned spaghetti.'

'Fish fingers, then,' Francis said, and Teresa agreed. 'After all, we have a guest.'

Julia looked to David for his approval; he could only nod mutely. Tea, he thought. Not dinner – tea. No wonder they'd said six o'clock. With all those children stretched over so many years, they'd apparently never got into the habit of eating dinner like civilised adults. And they clearly didn't realise that the children had grown up. He shuddered inwardly at the thought of frozen fish fingers, but had to admit that they were preferable to the alternative of beans on toast. At least he wasn't too hungry – he mentally blessed Lucy, and the lovely sandwiches and cakes she'd fed him that afternoon. He gave up any hopes he'd cherished of being offered a sherry, and sat back to await his fate.

Filling the time until the food was produced proved to be a little difficult. Roger Dawson had the disconcerting habit of refusing to make eye contact: all his remarks were addressed to David's left shoulder. Teresa huddled in her chair, trying to make herself disappear. That left Francis as the most likely source of conversation.

'So, Francis,' David began heartily. 'What do you do?'

'I'm at university,' he replied. 'I've just finished my first year.'

'He's followed his big brother Nick to the University of Sussex,' Roger added in his dry, slightly raspy voice, overlaid with a faint sibilance. 'We're proud of our boys.'

'And what are you reading?'

'Philosophy and Artificial Intelligence.'

David hardly knew what to say to that. 'That sounds an interesting combination,' he managed.

'Yes.'

There was an awkward silence, then Roger asked his son a question about his course-work, and they carried on a two-sided conversation for several minutes. That gave David the opportunity to observe the room surreptitiously. He concluded that it resembled nothing so much as a corner of the Shrine of Our Lady of Walsingham, a place he loathed, finding it tacky and tasteless. There was actually a statue of Our Lady of Walsingham, smirking child on her lap, surrounded by red and blue votive candles, on the mantelpiece; the walls were covered with cheap reproductions of bad religious paintings, adorned with old palm crosses. And the furniture was covered with dog hair – long, dingy-grey hairs. David inconspicuously, he hoped, picked a few off his trouser-legs.

Mercifully soon, Julia reappeared to announce the meal. They trooped into a dining room dominated by a huge family-sized table; places were set around it at widely spaced intervals. Passing the salt could be interesting, David envisioned.

The fish fingers were fully as appalling as he had imagined, but surprisingly the addition of Julia to the gathering improved the conversation considerably.

'I'm so sorry about Ignatius,' she began. 'He really is a very naughty little doggie.' She put her head to one side, listening to the persistent and hysterical barking from somewhere outside. 'Do you like dogs, David?'

'Yes, very much,' he replied without thinking, then, afraid she would interpret his reply as an invitation to bring Ignatius back, quickly changed the subject. 'How did your cake stall do at the fête?'

'Oh, very well indeed. We sold out before the afternoon, and took in nearly five hundred pounds. It's the best we've ever done.'

Unthinkingly, he responded, 'Mrs Conwell said that the fête had raised more money than ever before. When I saw her in the sacristy,' he added lamely, when he saw their horrified faces staring at him. Julia's mouth hung open like a fish, and her chin trembled. Roger licked his lips nervously. Francis looked blank, but Teresa had at last, bizarrely, come alive. Her eyes glittered avidly.

'I heard that when Mr Bead found her, her lips were blue, and her eyes were popping out,' she whispered intensely, in the first complete sentence David had heard her utter.

Startled, he said, 'Yes, I believe that's true.'

'Teresa! That's quite enough!' her mother quavered. 'Poor Mavis! How could you be so callous!'

Teresa looked down at her plate, but not before David caught the look of satisfaction in her eyes.

'David,' Julia appealed to him. 'Has Daphne said anything to you about the funeral arrangements?'

'She mentioned that there were some preliminary plans. I think it's to be next Tuesday.'

'At St Anne's?' Julia asked, her eyes wide.

'That was certainly the impression I got.'

'Shocking!' was Roger Dawson's reaction, addressed to the potted lily on the sideboard.

'Why . . .'

'A suicide! A woman who killed herself – to be given a Christian funeral, and her ashes buried in consecrated ground! I just don't believe it!'

'Whatever can Father Gabriel be thinking of?' Julia added with a shaking voice.

Teresa raised her eyes again. 'Maybe it wasn't suicide,' she announced with relish. 'Maybe it was . . . murder!'

After a sweet of tinned fruit with ice-cream, they returned to the lounge. David wondered how soon he could decently escape, but Julia had other ideas. 'We thought you might enjoy looking at some family pictures,' she suggested, hauling out a mammoth album.

'Oh, yes, that would be lovely,' David lied. He settled the album on his lap. Julia and Roger flanked him on either side of the sofa, and Teresa returned to her chair in the corner. Francis disappeared, and shortly David could hear the faint sound of a television from somewhere else in the house. Outside, Ignatius's frantic barking had transmuted into a steady howl.

He opened the album to be confronted by a mind-numbing array of Dawsons, at all stages of life and in every possible combination. There were baby Dawsons – unmistakably Dawsons, all of them – in prams, in cots, in pushchairs. Toddler Dawsons in the park, on the beach. Dawsons in school uniforms. Dawsons in cassocks and albs. Dawson dogs, of course, each one more unappealing than the last. And innumerable Dawson relations. 'That's Uncle Edmund,' Julia pointed out.

'He's dead,' Teresa said in sepulchral tones. 'He got run over by a train.'

Dawson cousins, Dawson grandparents. 'Grandmother Dawson,' indicated Roger.

'She died last year,' added Teresa. 'Blood poisoning.'

Dawsons on holiday, Dawsons standing in front of churches. David occasionally stopped to ask a question, to identify a person or place.

He looked at a photo of two young Dawson girls, dressed in virginal white with wreaths of flowers in their hair, posed in front of St Anne's with another little girl, similarly attired. 'Bridgie and Clare,' Julia explained, 'after they were in the Procession of Our Lady one year. The girl with them is Cecily Framlingham's daughter.'

'But she died,' Teresa announced. 'She drowned, on holiday at Bournemouth.'

'How terrible,' said David. He turned the page and looked at a picture of the Dawson he had come to recognise as Nick, sitting with a good-looking young man who was clearly not a Dawson, not even a Dawson cousin.

'That's Nick and his room-mate, his first year at university,' Roger explained.

Teresa opened her mouth, and David anticipated her words. 'He's dead, too. He . . .'

'Teresa, that's quite enough of your morbid stories,' her mother said shrilly. With a sulky yet venomous look, Teresa got up and left the room. Julia turned to David apologetically. 'I'm sorry about Teresa. You know how teenagers are.'

'Yes, of course.' And David settled back for yet more of the pictorial Dawson chronicles.

'Poor David. The didn't even offer you a drink?' Daphne sympathised later.

'Not a drop. Not a sherry before . . . the meal – I won't call it dinner – and the bottle of wine I took disappeared without a trace. Nothing after, either. Just a cup of insipid instant coffee.'

'Well, no one said it would be a fun evening,' she said, pouring him a generous whisky. 'But did you actually find out *why* they'd invited you?'

He laughed. 'Eventually. After an agonising evening of looking at family pictures, they finally got around to the reason for the invitation.'

'Which was . . .?'

'They were after some free legal advice, of course. I should have suspected it! It was something to do with Grandmother Dawson's will – they were just too mean to pay a solicitor, and thought I could help them.'

'Of course,' Daphne chuckled. 'That makes perfect sense.'

'They're the strangest family I've ever met.' He shook his head, remembering. 'Roger gives me the creeps, the way he never looks straight at you. Julia seems like she's

always about to burst into tears. Francis — well, gormless
is the right word for him. And that girl . . .'

'Teresa?'

'She's the most peculiar of all — she's a right little
ghoul. What a household.'

'Does that mean you're not going to invite them to stop
for a visit on their next trip to Walsingham?' Daphne
asked with a straight face. 'They go on the National Pil-
grimage every year.'

'Yes, I'm sure they do,' he groaned. 'Promise you won't
tell them where I live.'

'I'll draw them a map to your front door, unless you
stop all this Dawson talk and tell me right now what all
this is about Miles! I've been sitting here all evening trying
to decipher your hints!'

'Ah.' He smiled, immensely pleased with himself, and
leaned back in his chair.

'What on earth have you found out, David?'

'Only that Miles is no longer off the list of suspects.
He's back at the top of the list!' She looked dubious but
fascinated, as he went on to explain his discovery about
the organ-playing computer, and his subsequent conversation with Miles.

'Oh, David. This changes everything.'

'Absolutely.'

'He could so easily have gone down the stairs from the
console — they're right there in that corridor — and nipped
into the sacristy without anyone seeing him. All the while
the organ was playing. How long is that piece, by the
way? The one he had on the computer today?'

'Twelve or thirteen minutes, I suppose. That would give
him plenty of time. Or he could even have taken longer if

necessary. Lucy says he can programme in a whole se-
quence of pieces for the machine to play. I should have
known,' he added. 'When he "played" the Great G Minor
today, all the mistakes were exactly the same, just like a
recording. I just thought he hadn't practised.'

'But how could you have known about the machine? I
certainly didn't, though I suppose I should have. I just
never pay that much attention to Miles and his antics.'

'Lucy says it's the latest thing. Emily told her that he
went to the PCC and said he had to have it, and threatened
to quit if he didn't get it.'

She snorted. 'Thank God I'm not on the PCC. I'm
afraid I wouldn't have been keen to spend that kind of
money, just so Miles could have a smoke! He probably
spun them some plausible tale about being in the forefront
of technological progress . . .'

'But the question is, Daphne, what do I do now? He's
hiding something, but there's no way I'm going to find out
what it is. Not here in London, anyway.'

'I think you'll have to go to Selby,' Daphne said practically. 'That's where the answer is.'

David nodded. 'Yes, you're right. The sooner the better, I suppose. Will you come with me?'

She thought for a moment. 'I don't think I should; you
don't know how long it will take, and I need to be here on
Sunday. Anyway, it's better for me to stay and keep an
eye on things here.'

'I can't go tomorrow,' he remembered. 'I'm having tea
with Lady Constance, and I wouldn't want to stand her
up.'

'And don't forget stall seats at the Proms tomorrow
night.'

'Of course. But Friday – I can go on Friday. You'll have to help me think of a strategy. Miles Taylor may think he's clever, but between us, Daphne, we'll outsmart him.'

Chapter 30

Forsake me not, O God, in mine old age, when I am grey-headed: until I have shewed thy strength unto this generation, and thy power to all them that are yet for to come.

Psalm 71.16

The contrast could not have been more marked, David reflected, between yesterday and today: between the tasteless clutter of the Dawsons' lounge and the understated elegance of Lady Constance's drawing room, between the nasty frozen fish fingers and the tasty finger sandwiches, between, indeed, the twitchy peculiarity of the Dawsons and the calm patrician aura of Lady Constance herself.

He had found Lady Constance looking rather tired, the lines on her face more pronounced than on previous meetings, and he inquired with concern. 'It's nothing, young man,' she reassured him. 'Old age, that's all. I find I tire so quickly these days. It's a terrible thing to get old.'

'But it's better than the alternative,' he replied lightly.

'Sometimes I wonder,' she said softly, but the smile belied her words.

'Perhaps Saturday was too much for you,' he suggested. 'Walking around in the hot sun.'

257

'Perhaps,' she agreed. A shadow fell over her face. 'A terrible business, that on Saturday. It has quite upset me.'

'Oh, Mrs Conwell's . . . death. Yes, it was. But you said she was a dreadful woman.'

'And indeed she was. But . . . I certainly never wished her dead. For the woman to take her own life like that – how desperate she must have been. That must surely be the worst thing in the world, to feel so . . . trapped, that to make such a choice seems the only way out.' Lady Constance's voice was soft and troubled, and David was touched by her deep empathy with a woman she hadn't even liked.

'But are you sure she took her own life?'

She looked at him with surprise. 'Father Neville came to see me on Monday. He explained what the police had found – that Mrs Conwell had been taking money from the church, and when faced with . . . exposure . . . she had . . . hanged herself. Is there any reason to believe . . .'

Impulsively, he leaned forward. 'Would you feel any better about it if she hadn't killed herself? If . . . there was another explanation?'

Lady Constance was alert, intent. 'Young man, what do you know about this? Please tell me.'

He was already beginning to regret his impulse, but decided that there was no reason not to tell her, if it would somehow lessen her distress. 'I can't tell you the details,' he explained, 'but I have very good reason to believe that Mrs Conwell was murdered.'

'Murdered!'

'Yes. I believe she was.'

'But have you told this to the police?'

'No, I haven't. I didn't think they'd listen to me, without any hard evidence. But I've been making . . . certain inquiries myself, and I think I'm getting close to an answer. When I have something concrete, then I'll go to the police. The inquest isn't until next week, so the case is still technically open, even though they're not pursuing it.'

'But what have you found out?'

David hesitated. 'I can't say, until I'm sure myself, or at least until I have some proof. I'm going to leave London for a few days, to do some . . . research elsewhere, but I hope to be back by the beginning of next week.'

She smiled with an effort. 'I hope this doesn't mean that the chapel is being neglected,' she said lightly.

He answered her smile, and matched her tone. 'Not at all, Lady Constance. I have it well in hand.'

'Very good. What can you tell me about it?'

'The workmen began on Tuesday,' David explained. 'I was there all morning to get them started, and showed them exactly what to do. They're very good, though, and seem to know what they're about. This morning I checked on their progress. They've done the damp-proofing where necessary, and are working on the replastering.'

'How long will it take?'

'I'm afraid that once they've done the plaster, which they ought to finish within a day or so, they'll have to leave it for six weeks before they can apply any paint to that bit. But there's still a few days' work for them now with the other painting, and the gilding. Some of it needs retouching. That's a very tricky business.'

'You will be able to supervise that?' she asked with concern.

'Yes, next week. I'll be back by then. I'll make sure they do it properly,' he reassured her.

Her face relaxed into a smile. 'It's very good of you,

Mr Middleton-Brown, to humour an old woman like this.
You must think me very silly to worry about it so.'

'Not at all.'

She looked out the window, in the vague direction of St
Anne's. 'That church means very much to me,' she explained softly. 'My husband and I – we never had children. St Anne's has been almost like my child. I care very
much about what happens to it.'

'I understand.'

'Yes, I believe you do.' She looked at him shrewdly.
'You're a very sensitive young man. You love beautiful
things. I trust you . . .'

After the sandwiches, after the scones, when the maid had
brought in the cakes and a fresh pot of tea, David led the
conversation around to the subject of Miles. 'I went to the
organ recital yesterday,' he remarked casually.

'Oh, you did? Did you find it enjoyable?'

'Yes, indeed. The quality of the music at St Anne's is
most impressive.'

'In spite of the Director of Music sometimes,' she replied somewhat tartly. 'Though that's not really fair of
me. My taste in music and his are very different, I'm
afraid.'

'Why, what does he like?'

Lady Constance sniffed disparagingly. 'Modern music.
Dissonant noise, I call it. He's forever pestering the Vicar
to let the choir sing things that were written five minutes
ago. I'm afraid I don't approve of things that haven't stood
the test of time. As long as I have anything to say about
what happens at St Anne's, you won't be hearing the music that Mr Taylor prefers.'

'And he complains about that?'

'He complains about it all the time. Not to me, you understand,' she added with a wry smile. 'He's not that reckless.'

'What do you mean?'

'Mr Taylor may be a somewhat outspoken young man, but he's not stupid. He's never less than completely courteous to me. I think he would dearly like to number me among what Mrs Neville quaintly calls his "Fan Club".'

'And are you among them?' he asked boldly.

'No. I'm not as easy to get around as someone like Mary Hughes. I can see quite clearly what he's up to.'

'And what is he up to?' David queried with an innocent air.

'Come now, young man. You're not that naïve. Mr Taylor is what one might call an opportunist. His primary concern is always what's best for Miles Taylor, and nothing else. He has all the time in the world for the elderly ladies at St Anne's, especially if they have a bit of money and no one in particular to leave it to when they're gone.'

David admired her candour, and her shrewdness. 'Has he been successful with many of them?'

'Oh, yes. He's had several rather nice little legacies over the past few years, both for the music fund and for himself personally. And I wouldn't be a bit surprised if Mary Hughes were to make him her primary heir. She thinks he's marvellous.'

'Is Miss Hughes well off?'

'Well enough. She has a private income, and a house in

Kensington. That would suit Mr Taylor very well, I'm sure.'

David spoke even more frankly. 'Has he tried . . . to make up to you?'

'He's tried, all right. He's revoltingly ingratiating to me, and that I can't abide. He hasn't quite had the cheek to invite himself to tea, but he's dropped enough hints.' She smiled suddenly. 'No, you're much more my style, young man. And I do hope you'll come again.'

'Of course, whenever you like,' he replied.

She closed her eyes briefly. 'Let me see. Today is Thursday. Could you come next Wednesday? That's the Feast of the Assumption, so we'll have to make it lunch – if we're going to Mass in the evening, there will be no tea for us that day.'

'I'll look forward to it,' he said, taking the hint and rising. 'And now I think I had better leave you, Lady Constance. You're looking a bit tired.'

'Please forgive me, Mr Middleton-Brown, but I am suddenly quite weary.' She put her hand to her head. 'And a bit dizzy.' She rang for the maid as he bent over her with concern. 'No, young man, it's nothing for you to worry about. Molly, would you please see Mr Middleton-Brown out, and then help me upstairs?'

As she opened the door for him, Molly hesitated for a moment; David sensed that she had something to say. 'What is it, Molly?'

'I wouldn't normally say anything, sir, but . . .' The girl spoke in a troubled whisper.

'Yes?'

'Lady Constance, sir. She's not been herself lately. She's really not well.'

'She *is* an old lady, Molly.'

'But she accused me of pinching her cameo brooch, sir. And I never.'

'You're sure, Molly?'

The girl was indignant. ''Course I'm sure. She'd just put it in the wrong drawer, was all. She found it the next day.'

David smiled and patted her arm. 'Don't worry about it, Molly. Old people often forget things. My mother was the same way. Lady Constance knows you wouldn't take her brooch . . .'

'Thank you, sir. But . . . I just thought as you ought to know, that's all. Her ladyship sets a lot of store in you. If you could kind of keep an eye on her, like . . .'

'Yes, I'll do that. I'm very fond of Lady Constance, Molly. Thank you for telling me.' He didn't mean it as empty reassurance; he was genuinely concerned about Lady Constance's health.

But as David reached the end of the street, he was already thinking ahead to the evening, and Lucy.

Chapter 31

For he maketh the storm to cease: so that the waves thereof are still.
Then are they glad, because they are at rest: and so he bringeth them unto the haven where they would be.

Psalm 107.29–30

In his favourite armchair in Lucy's sitting room, David was relaxed but by no means sleepy. The concert had been excellent, and the late supper at a cosy French restaurant, accompanied by a couple of bottles of champagne, had been delicious. Now he swirled the brandy around in his glass, and inhaled its aroma with sensuous pleasure. He glanced idly around the now-familiar room, realising in a strange detached way that it was only a week since he'd first sat there, stroking Sophie.

Lucy was smiling at him from her chair. She was looking especially beautiful tonight, he thought. She was wearing black; it was the first time he'd seen her in a dark colour, and he found that the contrast with her fair colouring only emphasised her loveliness. Tonight had been the first time, too, that he'd been conscious of being seen with her. Though they hadn't seen anyone that they knew, he had been aware that other people were looking at her, admiring her, and he'd been proud to be with her.

Sophie, who had been sleeping elsewhere in the house, materialised silently and jumped on his lap. She arched her back luxuriously, kneaded his trouser-leg with her paws, and curled up in a small orange ball, purring loudly. He automatically put a hand on her silky fur.

Lucy, too, was relaxed, after the music and after the champagne. He has nice hands, she thought, watching him stroke Sophie. Not for the first time, she noticed that his fingernails were chewed down to the quick. 'You ought not to bite your nails,' she said without thinking.

He was not offended. 'You sound like my mother,' he replied good-humouredly.

She stretched and pushed back her hair. 'You never talk very much about your mother,' she said. 'Tell me about her. What was she like?'

He thought for a long time before answering. 'It's difficult to say. A very strong personality. Domineering, I suppose you'd say. She always ran my father's life, poor man.'

'And your life? Did she run it, too?'

'Well, she tried. I was a great disappointment to her. I was never as rich or successful as she wanted me to be.' He paused for a moment, looking into space and reflecting. 'It's funny, isn't it? She always said that she wanted me to have a backbone, to be independent, but of course all she really wanted to do was control me, mould me in her image. She said that she wanted grandchildren, but she wouldn't have known what to do if I'd married and moved away from her. And she always said that I was a failure, and should be making more money, but whenever I talked about selling the house and moving . . .'

Lucy said gently, 'It sounds like you have a lot of unresolved feelings. Your life with her must have been very difficult.'

He'd never talked about these things with anyone before. Suddenly he was telling her everything: about the constant belittlement, the sense of failing to live up to expectations, about the petty-minded morality and ugly middle-class values and all the resultant guilt, about the anti-intellectual snobbery that he'd battled against to go to university and educate himself. His mother had been extremely pretentious in her own way, but had always dismissed his more cultured tastes as 'just showing off'. And his church-going she had found effeminate and unnecessary. 'You can be just as good a Christian in your own home as you can in a church full of hypocrites,' she'd often said.

'I loved my mother, but I never liked her,' he blurted out at the end, and as he said it he knew it was true. He felt cleansed, freed by the admission and the realisation.

Lucy had said very little, but somehow she'd been with him through every step of his confession. Suddenly, fancifully, he imagined that Lucy was like a deep pool of tranquil water, hidden in some leafy glade. He could cast his problems, like stones, into her calm depths, leaving not even a ripple on the serene surface.

'But you never talk about yourself,' he said. 'I want to know everything about you.'

'What do you want to know?' she asked calmly.

He was emboldened by the rapport that had grown so naturally and so warmly between them. 'Emily said that

267

you'd been married. Tell me about that. Who was he? What happened?'

Perhaps it was the champagne that made her unusually candid, or perhaps it was the incredible feeling of affinity between them. She looked into space thoughtfully, winding a strand of hair around her finger. 'His name was Geoffrey. It seems like such a long time ago. I was very young – only eighteen.' Lucy tossed her hair back. 'As you know, my father is a Vicar in a rural parish, in Shropshire. I was the only girl in the family, with three brothers, and I was very protected. You can imagine.' She smiled. 'All those wholesome country values. My experience of life was quite limited. But I always wanted to be an artist. When I was eighteen, I left home and went to art college. I met Geoffrey there. He wasn't like anyone I'd ever known – certainly nothing like my family. We had nothing in common except art, but that didn't matter to me. He was brilliant, and I was dazzled by him. We married very quickly, and of course it was a disaster. It only lasted a few months. I haven't heard from him in years.' She added frankly, 'It almost seems like something that happened to someone else, maybe in a book that I read a long time ago.'

It was David's turn for silence. After a few minutes he said, 'And after that? A beautiful woman like you, surely . . . Have there been other men?' He marvelled at his own daring, and thought perhaps he'd gone too far. He wasn't even sure why he was asking: was it only simple curiosity?

But she, too, was finding release in honesty. 'A few,' she said. 'There was one, quite a while ago now. He ran an art gallery, and I met him when he had an exhibition of my works. We lived together for over a year.'

'What happened?' he asked when she paused for a sip of brandy.

'He left me for another artist. A man,' she finished candidly. 'I was pretty devastated. It was worse than the divorce. We'd been together a lot longer than I'd been married to Geoffrey, and – well, I don't know. It didn't do much for my self-esteem.'

He stared at her, stricken, but she just shrugged. 'It was a long time ago. But it put me off men for quite a while – it was years before I got involved with anyone after that. Then a couple of years ago I met this chap.' She laughed ruefully. 'Believe it or not, I met him queuing for the Proms. I used to see him most nights in the queue, and we'd often have a chat, or sometimes a drink in the interval. One night I invited him back to the house for a drink after the concert. They'd played the Dvořák Cello Concerto,' she explained, as if excusing herself. 'We were both pretty emotional after that. He . . . well, I let him stay the night.' She stopped, then went on matter-of-factly, 'I was lonely. It had been a long time. It just happened.' Her face was in shadow as she paused again. 'Anyway, after that, we saw a lot of each other. We both enjoyed music, and we got on very well. It looked as though there might be a future in it. I even took him round to the vicarage for dinner once. After the Last Night of the Proms, he told me that he had a wife in Manchester. I never saw him again.' Lucy smiled, without self-pity or bitterness. 'And there you have it. The story of my love life. Oh, I've been out with other men, of course,' she added. 'But those were the ones that mattered – the ones I cared about.'

David gripped Sophie so hard with his fingers that she gave an angry yelp, jumped up, and with an annoyed lash of her tail, disappeared. He was overwhelmed by a jumble of emotions. First of all, he was incensed on her behalf at the treatment she'd received from these men – it just wasn't acceptable to use people like that, and especially someone as vulnerable as Lucy. And he felt her pain keenly, empathetically. Though it was all in the past, there were clearly lasting scars: how she must have suffered. Finally, he realised with surprise, there was a large element of jealousy in his reaction. He was improbably jealous of those men she'd spent time with, had cared about, had . . . slept with. He didn't want to think about it.

After what must have seemed like a very long silence, he simply said, 'Thank you for telling me. Can I have another drink?'

The atmosphere eased. They had more brandy, and talked about inconsequential matters, and later she put on some music and they simply sat and listened.

Sophie had forgiven him and returned to his lap, and David was completely at peace. His body melted into the chair; he felt that he never wanted to leave that chair again. It was at that moment that the idea entered his mind for the first time: why should he leave? Why couldn't this go on for ever? Why shouldn't he . . . marry Lucy?

Marry Lucy. It pounded in his brain, in time with the music. He couldn't think properly – not now. Not with the music, and the brandy, and this room, and Lucy so near. Marry Lucy. He'd think about it tomorrow. And now . . . if he didn't leave now, he never would. He put Sophie off his lap and stood up. 'It's very late. I must go.'

He lingered by the door, not really wanting to leave, knowing he must. 'In the morning I'm going away for a few days,' he told her. 'Business. But I'll be back as soon as I can. And then. . . well, I think there are some things we need to talk about.'

She stood close to him, not touching him but smiling into his eyes and willing him to make love to her. Almost without volition, he entwined his fingers in her hair, and brushed her soft, fragrant cheek with his lips. 'Good night, my lovely Lucy,' he murmured. And then he was gone.

Chapter 32

I am weary of crying; my throat is dry: my sight faileth me for waiting so long upon my God.

Psalm 69.3

In the middle of a lovely dream, Emily turned over and reached for Gabriel. He wasn't there; she awoke with a start and all the pain flooded back. The vividness of her dream made the reality even harder to bear. She was not in her own comfortable bed, with her husband curled up warm beside her; she was alone in a hard, narrow bed. And this was not their spacious room, with the wallpaper they'd chosen together, and their lovely antique furniture: this was a small cell, whitewashed and sparsely furnished. Her eyes focused on the plain wooden crucifix on the opposite wall. It was her fourth morning waking in this bed.

She'd spent much of the last three days here in this room, on her knees in front of the crucifix, lying on the bed thinking, or sitting in the hard chair writing: writing to Lucy, writing to the children, writing endless letters to Gabriel and tearing them up. But now she felt that she needed to escape from the confines of this room, the room that had seemed such a welcome refuge a few days ago. She pulled on her jeans and shirt and slipped down the hall quietly to the chapel.

The chapel was as unadorned as her little room, with its white walls and its large, stark crucifix. But somehow its simple piety, so different from the gilded gothic splendour of St Anne's, was just what she needed at this moment. It was empty when she entered; she knelt near the back and poured out her heart in prayer. After a while the tears started to flow, and though she tried to choke them back at first, she was soon overwhelmed with misery. I should go back to my room, she thought, and rose to go. Her eyes blinded, she almost ran into a nun who was just coming in.

'My dear,' said the nun with concern. 'Are you all right?'

Emily blinked, and recognised the sweet-faced sister who had been so kind to her on her arrival. 'If you ever need to talk . . .' the nun had said that day. Suddenly it seemed the only thing to do. 'Oh, Sister.' She took a deep breath. 'Sister Mary Grace, isn't it? I'd really like to talk to you. But if you're busy . . . maybe later . . .'

'There's nothing more important right now,' the sister said firmly, putting her arm around Emily and leading her to a small private room, furnished with only two chairs. 'Now, my dear. What is it that makes you so sad?' she began, proffering a clean white handkerchief.

With an effort, Emily controlled her tears. She wiped her eyes and blew her nose, and looked gratefully at the nun. Sister Mary Grace was of an indeterminate age – she could have been anything from thirty to sixty – with smooth, unlined olive-toned skin, compassionate eyes, and a kind smiling mouth. Emily felt that nothing she could say would shock or upset this calm, gentle woman. 'Sister, I've made such a mess of my life, and I don't know what to do.'

'Why don't you tell me. Start at the beginning, if you like.'

The beginning. When was that? Ten years ago? Or longer?

'My husband is . . . well . . . I don't know if I should . . .' She hesitated.

'Nothing you say to me will go any farther than this room, my dear. You don't have to be afraid to tell me anything.'

'My husband is a priest.' The nun nodded encouragingly. 'We've been married for nearly ten years. I love him very much. I've always thought he was everything a priest should be, and everything a husband should be.'

'Then you've been very fortunate.'

'Yes, but now I've found out that I didn't know him as well as I thought I did. From the very beginning. He lied . . . no, he didn't lie to me. He just didn't tell me the truth.' Her mouth twisted at the fine distinction. 'I was very foolish. I took him at face value, because I loved him and because I wanted him to be the man I thought he was.'

'That's only natural.'

'But he never was what I thought he was. That's what hurts me so much – realising that for ten years, I never really knew him.' She sat silently for a moment, searching for the courage to tell the story. 'My husband was thirty when I met him. A bachelor. I did think it a little unusual that a man of that age . . . well, I asked him if he'd ever thought of marrying before. He said that he hadn't – that there had never been another woman in his life before he met me. I believed him. I wanted to believe him. I wanted to think that I was as unique and special for him as he was for me.'

'And it wasn't true?'

'Oh, that part of it was true, I think. As far as it went. But I didn't ask the other question, because it never occurred to me, and he didn't tell me.' The sister waited; finally Emily went on. 'He didn't tell me that he had been in love before – with a man.' There, it was out. Still the sister said nothing. 'I know a lot of gay people; some of them are good friends of mine. I don't have a problem with it at all, in theory. But . . . he didn't tell me. And I don't really know how I would have handled it if he had. He never gave me a chance to try to understand, to come to terms with it. I loved him very much – I don't think it would have made a difference. But I don't know. My marriage: it's been very happy. But has it been based on a lie? Has he really ever loved me at all?' The last terrible question came out on a sob.

'Have you asked your husband that question?'

Emily looked at her, horrified. 'Oh, I couldn't! Not yet, anyway. I don't know if I could bear it . . .' She wept.

The sister squeezed Emily's hand until she regained control and was able to go on.

'My dear, have you been wrestling with this by yourself all this week? Why didn't you come to me sooner?'

'I just couldn't. I was in shock. I had to try to sort it out, to make sense of what's happened and my feelings about it.'

'What you haven't told me is how you found out about this. Did your husband tell you?'

'No, that's what makes it worse. He's in some kind of trouble – I know it. But he wouldn't tell me, so it must have something to do with all this. He's been distracted and upset for weeks, and still I haven't understood. I've been so stupid, so insensitive to him.'

'How did you find out?' Sister Mary Grace repeated patiently.

'Finally, I just . . . guessed, I suppose. The other man. The one my husband . . . loved. I think my husband is being blackmailed about their affair. I'm not explaining this very well,' she apologised. 'The other man came for a visit about a fortnight ago. I'd never met him. I'd heard his name, as an old friend of my husband, that was all. I didn't suspect – why would I? He's a nice man, David. I like him very much. But then he and my husband – they had a row about something. I overheard a bit, just enough to make me think about it. I asked my husband. He wouldn't tell me anything. I think that's when I knew, suddenly. It was just an intuition. I had to be sure. So I asked David. He was honest with me, admitted they'd been . . . lovers. I don't blame David,' she burst out. 'I don't blame him for loving Gabriel. Why shouldn't he love him? And he's been hurt too, poor David. I don't blame Gabriel for loving him. But why didn't he tell me? Why didn't he tell me?'

'Only he can answer that question, my dear. You must ask him. You must go to him and ask him.'

'I just can't. Not yet. Please let me stay here a little longer.'

'You can stay here as long as you like. But it mustn't be for much longer, my dear. Have you given any thought at all to how your husband must be suffering without you, not knowing where you are? I'm sure he loves you very much.'

'Oh, poor Gabriel!' Emily wailed. 'I've been so selfish! Thinking only about myself!'

The sister took both Emily's hands in hers, and gazed at her with compassion. 'Perhaps not yet,' she agreed. 'Before you're ready to hear the answer from him, there's something you must ask yourself.'

'I don't understand what you mean.'

'You must ask yourself who you really are angry with. The things you've told me – you're in a lot of pain right now, but there's also a lot of anger there. And what I'm hearing is that you're angry with your husband, for not being honest with you. But mostly you're angry with yourself, for not understanding him better, for having unrealistic expectations of your relationship, for not asking the right questions, for failing him somehow, for being hurt even. And the anger brings guilt. My dear, you are full of guilt.'

'Yes,' Emily admitted.

'You must come to terms with that. Before you talk to your husband, you must come to terms with yourself. You must forgive yourself before you can forgive him.'

Emily covered her face with her hands.

Chapter 33

Thou art fairer than the children of men: full of
grace are thy lips, because God hath blessed thee
for ever.

Psalm 45.3

'I think that the Three Swans looks your best bet,' Daphne
concluded, poring over her AA hotel guide. 'It's right in
the market-place, very near the cathedral. And they've got
a car park.'

'That sounds fine,' agreed David.

'Would you like me to ring and book a room for you?'
she offered.

'Don't bother, I can take my chances.' He reconsidered. 'Well, actually it might be a good idea. That way
you'd know for sure where you could reach me, in case
there are any developments here.'

'You never know. Miles might make a dramatic confession, and jump from the church tower.'

'Ha. Well, anyway, I *will* answer the phone if you ring.
But don't expect me to ring you, no matter what happens,'
he warned.

'I know better than that. Using the telephone is against
your religion. But I've never known why.'

'I'm not even sure of that myself,' admitted David. 'I must have been bitten by one when I was a child.'

'How long do you think you might be away?'

'Probably not more than over the weekend. I'll be back when I'm back, is all I can say. Don't rent out my room while I'm gone!'

Daphne shook her head. 'Never think it! All shall be kept in readiness for your return.'

'Will you light a little candle in the window each night?'

'Get out of here.'

'I'll see you in a few days, then, Daphne.' She lifted her cheek for his affectionate kiss, and watched him from the window until the brown Morris was out of sight.

Negotiating Friday morning London traffic, and then finding his way to the A1, required all David's concentration; once he was in Hertfordshire he began to think about where he might eat lunch. He couldn't abide the multitudinous roadside restaurants that proliferated along the A1, with their identical synthetic food. Stamford would be nice, he thought – the George ought to serve a decent lunch. That was nearly halfway, and would be a good break. It was a pretty town, too, with its church spires, its twisting streets and its warm beige stone buildings. If he wasn't in a hurry to get to Selby, he might easily spend some time there exploring the churches.

Lunch plans thus disposed of, his mind turned to the subject he'd been avoiding since last night's brainstorm. It was time to think about it. He asked himself, finally, the big question: should he marry Lucy Kingsley?

She was a beautiful woman. It would not be true to say that her beauty, which was so much more than skin-deep, left him unmoved. On the contrary, his response to it was deeply emotional, as it would have been to a stirring performance of Bach's B Minor Mass, the Sistine Chapel ceiling, or an exquisitely fashioned piece of silver.

He wished that he wanted to make love to her. But physical lovemaking had never been that important to him. Even with Gabe – especially with Gabe – the emotional closeness, the tenderness, were more important than their physical expression. No, sex wasn't all that central to his life. If it had been, he realised, he would never have lived for twenty-eight years before discovering his orientation, would never have been able to live the last ten years celibate as a monk, would not now be able to contemplate the step he was so seriously considering. And he was considering it very seriously indeed.

He thought about the implications for his lifestyle, the changes that would take place in his life on a practical level. The house – it certainly wouldn't suit Lucy as it was now. But she could redecorate it. It wasn't a bad house – it had potential, anyway. Once they'd eradicated all traces of Mother, Lucy could make it a showplace, with her exquisite taste. The money was available, and she could do whatever she liked. He'd be quite happy to leave it to her, or they could work on it together. Make it reflect both of them. That might be nice. She'd need somewhere to work. The attic room could easily be converted into a studio for her, with a skylight added. Or if she didn't like the house, he could sell it and they'd find something else, get a fresh start. Maybe something in Norwich, with its easy access by train to London. They'd keep Lucy's house in Kensington, he imagined. She'd probably want to keep it. They could go to London for the weekends, so she could keep up her weekly visits to the V & A. It would be nice to spend weekends in London: they could go to concerts, art galleries and the theatre, eat at good restaurants.

Maybe Lucy wouldn't want to live in Norfolk at all – perhaps she wouldn't want to leave London. Well, he could always find a job in London. That wouldn't be difficult. And to be quite honest, having a beautiful, accomplished wife wouldn't do him any harm in furthering his career. He'd loved living in London when he was younger. Moving to London would be fine. He'd see more of Daphne, of Emily.

And they could travel. He'd seen a fair bit of England, especially during his years of travelling with Daphne, but his dislike of travelling alone had kept him from spending time abroad. With Lucy he could go to Italy, as he'd always wanted to do. Perhaps she'd been there before and could show him all the art treasures. They could go to France, to Switzerland, even to Greece or Egypt.

But whether they lived in Wymondham, in Norwich, or in London, he would no longer have to be alone – that was the main thing. He hated living alone. He loathed preparing meals just for himself and eating by himself, almost as much as he hated dining in restaurants alone. If he married Lucy, he would never have to be alone again.

He tried, then, to imagine what life would be like with Lucy as his wife. It was one thing spending time with someone when you were on holiday, as he was now. But to live with them, every day . . .

He wasn't at his best in the mornings, David realised that. He hoped that Lucy would be able to make allowances for that. He'd be more than willing to make an effort: he'd get up and make the tea, and bring her a cup in bed, as he had for years with Mother. He didn't require much breakfast, or much in the way of conversation in the morning, so she could lie in as long as she liked.

The evenings would be lovely. When he came home, they'd have a glass of sherry together and a chat. She'd talk about her day, and show him the painting she'd done. He could tell her about all the annoying people he'd had to deal with, and she'd soothe him with sweet reasonable words. Now there was no one to calm him down – he could only brood, and feel even worse. Then when they'd relaxed, they'd have a delicious dinner, and a good bottle of wine. They'd prepare the meal together: he enjoyed cooking when he didn't have to do it by himself and for himself only, and it would be great fun working with someone as accomplished in the kitchen as Lucy was. After dinner they'd retire to the sitting room, where they'd spend a companionable evening talking or listening to music. Perhaps they might read to each other – Jane Austen, or Barbara Pym, something deliciously entertaining and not too demanding. They might have a drink, a brandy or a whisky.

And later, after the long companionable evening, when he went to bed with . . . his wife: he supposed it wouldn't be so bad, though he couldn't really imagine the act. At least he didn't find the idea repugnant, only uninteresting. So that would be all right. If he were lucky, he might even get to like it. Gabe apparently had, at least enough to convince and to satisfy Emily.

It all sounded wonderful, too good to be true. What could he be leaving out of his calculations? It suddenly occurred to him that he had never asked himself what his feelings for Lucy really were. Did he . . . love her?

Lucy made him happy. It wasn't the wild, blood-pounding joy he'd found with Gabe, but that kind of happiness belonged to youth, and could never be recaptured. It was a quiet, contented sort of happiness. Her serenity, her tranquillity enveloped him with a feeling of well-being. He felt that he could be with her for ever, and never tire of looking at her, listening to her, laughing with her. Wasn't this love, or at least a kind of love? He was so used to defining love in terms of his feelings for Gabe that he wasn't sure.

But did it really matter, after all? They could be happy together, he was sure of that. Lucy had a salutary effect on him; he thought that he was a nicer person when he was with her. As far as he could tell, there was every indication that she was fond of him, she even seemed to find him attractive, for some unknown reason. And he knew that whatever name you attached to it, he was very fond of her. Wasn't that enough? He and Lucy weren't a couple of kids. They were both too mature to be hung up on romantic terminology. He had been offered a chance of happiness that was as unexpected as it was enticing. Wouldn't he be very foolish indeed to turn his back on it?

Chapter 34

*One deep calleth another, because of the noise of
the water-pipes: all thy waves and storms are
gone over me.*

Psalm 42.9

David counted the cathedral bells as they tolled; one, two,
three, four. In a few more hours he could get up. He had
not stopped to consider the consequences of the guidebook
term 'very near the cathedral' in choosing his hotel. The
cathedral bells were very pleasant to hear in the evening,
sitting in one's room, but in the wee hours of the night
they were less than welcome.

Not that it really mattered, he reflected. He'd complained about the room he'd been given – he would have
preferred a view of the cathedral to a view of the car park
– but had been told it was the only single room available
at such short notice. And now the lack of a view had paled
into insignificance beside the room's more noticeable draw-
back. It was located adjacent to the boiler room, and the
clanging of the water-pipes had provided an unmusical
counterpoint to the striking of the bells throughout the
night. To top it off, the rumble of thunder had recently
been added to the cacophony, and a few moments ago a

terrific storm had let loose its fury on the cathedral city of Selby, in West Yorkshire.

Why couldn't Miles Taylor have been organist in a more civilised place? David asked himself savagely. He hadn't been to Selby for years, and belatedly he remembered why. It was really nothing more than a small Yorkshire market town, elevated to city status by virtue of its magnificent abbey cathedral. There were no decent restaurants – it didn't even rate a mention in the *Good Food Guide* – and David had been reduced to dining on fish and chips. Tomorrow night – tonight, he amended, remembering the four bells – he didn't know what he'd do. Drive into York, maybe. He certainly wasn't going to be staying in Selby any longer than absolutely necessary. If he couldn't find out something tomorrow – today – he'd be inclined to give it up as a bad job.

He'd only had one tenuous lead in his search for Miles Taylor's hidden past. After Evensong, he'd lingered near the organ during the final voluntary. Close to the entrance to the console was a board with a list of the cathedral's past organists, their names painted in red, and he'd studied it with ostensible interest as a fresh-faced young man emerged from the console.

'The voluntary was excellent,' he remarked as the young man passed him.

The young man stopped. 'Oh, did you really think so?' His round face went pink with pleasure.

'I've rarely heard it performed so well,' David replied gravely.

'Oh, well. I wasn't sure about the registration in the final bit. But if you say it was good . . .'

'It was superb. Are you the organist here? Mr . . .

Moffat?' he added, looking at the board.

The young man smiled in a flustered fashion. 'Oh, good heavens, no. Just the assistant.'

'You're certainly very accomplished for an assistant. How long have you been at Selby, Mr . . .?'

'Thompson. William Thompson. I've been here for nearly three years now.'

Damn, thought David. 'Well, I'm sure you'll be going on to bigger and better things very soon, Mr Thompson.' He looked again at the board, and said casually, 'I see that Miles Taylor was organist here before Mr Moffat. But that was before your time.'

'Yes. Though of course I've heard plenty of stories about Miles Taylor. He was a real legend around here.'

'Then I suppose there are still people in the choir who remember him?'

'Oh, yes. Why? Do you know him?'

'I've heard of him,' David hedged. 'His name . . . in musical circles, you know . . . the friend of a friend . . . that sort of thing.'

'I see. Well, you won't find anyone here at the moment who knew him – the choir is on holiday. That was a visiting choir at Evensong, you realise.'

'Yes, of course.' David hadn't really thought about it.

'Of course, the person to talk to about Miles Taylor is Miss Somers. I don't believe she was here at Evensong to-night – she's getting on in years now, and doesn't always make it.' The young man turned his head guiltily as a man in a cassock beckoned frantically from the transept. 'Oh, excuse me, Mr . . . um. I really must go. Frightfully nice to meet you.'

And the young man had scurried off, leaving David

little more enlightened than he'd been previously.

Now, as the wind-driven rain lashed the window, its wooden frame rattling in the onslaught, David recalled again the young man's words. Miss Somers. He'd had enough hints from Daphne, and from Lady Constance, about Miles's predilection for wealthy old ladies. Was Miss Somers one of his conquests? Or one with whom he'd failed? Someone like Lady Constance, who saw through his manoeuvres and his facile charm? If he could, he would like to meet this Miss Somers.

To David's dismay, his alarm clock had been left on the bedside table of Daphne's spare room, so he marked time by the striking of the bells until they tolled seven; having nothing particular to get up for, but no compelling reason to remain in bed any longer, he rose, showered, shaved, and dressed. The room's shower, as he would have expected, was less than efficient, and he endured alternating trickles of hot water and jets of icy spray. But the kettle provided in the room seemed functional, and he decided to fix himself a cup of tea. Too late he realised that it would have to be made in the cup, with a tea-bag, and that the only milk available was of the powdered variety. Giving up in disgust, he went down to a breakfast of runny scrambled eggs on soggy toast.

The day could only improve, he decided, leaving the hotel immediately after breakfast. The night's storm had been short-lived in its intensity, leaving the sky a bright, cloudless blue. David walked along by the river for a long while before heading back to the cathedral.

Selby Abbey was a splendid building, he reflected as he approached. Unfortunately, its monastic past meant that it was stranded in the middle of the town with no cathedral close to insulate it from traffic. The monastic buildings had all been knocked down, leaving only the church, which had survived as a parish church for several centuries before its elevation to cathedral status in the late nineteenth century. In the meanwhile, building had gone on all around it.

But inside the cathedral, one of the best-preserved monastic churches in the country, it was easy to forget its surroundings. There were several small clusters of tourists looking about, and near the south transept entrance a party was forming up around a guide. David decided to join them.

The guide was a small, elderly woman with untidy hair, bright eyes, and a strong Yorkshire accent. She was giving an account of the founder of the abbey.

'I suppose you can say that this is an institution founded on a theft,' she said. 'When Benedict fled from his abbey in France, he pinched the finger of St Germanus, and that became the chief relic of the new abbey he founded here, in 1069. But Benedict didn't take kindly to others following his example – at least not that example. When two monks were caught stealing some silver, he had them castrated! He was so unpopular that he was finally forced to resign.'

Sounds like a jolly chap, David reflected. He probably would have approved of his church employing a bloke like Miles Taylor.

When the tour was over, David stayed behind and spoke to the guide. 'Thank you for a most interesting tour. What a fascinating history this place has!'

'Is this your first visit?'

'No, but I haven't been here in nearly twenty years. It's a splendid building.' The woman smiled and nodded in agreement. On an impulse, David asked her, 'Do you know a Miss Somers?'

'Yes, of course. Everyone at Selby knows Miss Somers. Why, is she a friend of yours?'

He thought quickly. 'No, but someone from my local church knows her – a distant relative by marriage, I believe. They asked me to look her up.' He smiled ingratiatingly, and, he hoped, convincingly.

'Well, if you want to see Mildred Somers, just come to Evensong this afternoon. She never misses it on a Saturday. If you'll come up to the chancel with me now, I'll show you where she always sits.'

David looked at his watch. Only a few more hours to kill in Selby before Evensong.

There wasn't even a market in Selby on a Saturday. Walking aimlessly through the streets of the town, David resorted to people-watching. Everyone he saw seemed to be in pairs: teenaged couples, spotty and unattractive to anyone but each other, smooching unashamedly on the street corners; young married couples, their arms entwined; middle-aged and older husbands and wives, less affectionate but comfortable together as they accomplished their weekend shopping in tandem. Even the swans on the river were in pairs, he noted glumly: swans, he knew, mate for life. For the first time since his mother died, David realised, on an emotional level, how very alone he was.

He spotted a Teleflora sign in a florist's window. Without stopping to think about what he was doing, he opened the door of the shop and went in; the bell on the door roused the clerk from dreamy contemplation of a potted fern. 'May I help you, sir?'

'If I were to place an order now, could something be delivered to London this afternoon?'

'I don't see why not. What would you like?'

'Roses. Long-stemmed roses – a dozen. No, make it two dozen.'

'Red roses, sir?'

'No, not red. Not pink. That sort of peachy-gold colour. You know the colour I mean.' He wrote Lucy's name and address on the form the clerk handed him.

'And the message on the card, sir?'

David smiled a bit self-consciously; he was new at this sort of thing, after all. 'Lucy, will you marry me?' He added, 'No signature. I think she'll know who it's from.'

Chapter 35

*Whoso hath also a proud look and high stomach: I
will not suffer him.*

Psalm 101.7

David was back with plenty of time to spare before Evensong.
He went into the cathedral gift shop and bought a souvenir
book with coloured pictures of the cathedral to take back
to Daphne. As an afterthought, he selected a couple of
picture postcards, one of the west front of the cathedral
and one of the high altar, to send to Daphne and Lucy. I'll
be back before they get them, he thought, but at least it's a
gesture. I should have done it yesterday.

'Did you need stamps for those, sir?' inquired the helpful young woman who took his money.

'Yes, that would be most useful.' She smiled at him in
a very friendly way and he was emboldened to ask her a
question. 'Do you know . . . a Miss Somers?'

'Yes, of course. Everyone does.'

He hesitated. 'You must think me frightfully ignorant,
then, but who *is* she? Why does everyone know her?'

The woman laughed easily. She was younger than
Lucy, but there was something about her laugh that
made David think of Lucy, and miss her. 'She was an

293

institution around here for years, that's all. Miss Somers was the secretary to the Provost for as long as anyone can remember. Everyone knew that she really ran the cathedral – Provosts came and went, but Miss Somers remained.'

'And now?'

'She finally retired, a year or so ago. She didn't want to, I can tell you. But they gave her no choice.'

A customer behind David made an impatient noise, and he looked around guiltily. The woman laughed again. 'Here I am, standing here gossiping when there are people to be served. I'll probably get the sack.' She didn't look too bothered at the prospect, so with a quick nod of thanks, David moved away from the till.

He took a seat in the choir stalls, strategically chosen so that he could observe Miss Somers when she had arrived. He knelt to pray, and when he looked up again, she was there.

Formidable was the word. The only thing really reminiscent of Lady Constance about her was her erect carriage. She sat ram-rod straight, her eyes closed. Her hair, which remained quite dark with just a few streaks of grey, was parted in the centre with military precision, and scraped back into a tight bun at the nape of her neck. Her eyebrows were pencilled on in thin lines above steel-rimmed spectacles, and her mouth had a no-nonsense set to it, even in repose. She had large ears, made even more prominent by her severe hairstyle, and in their fleshy lobes she wore, incongruously, oversized gypsy-like gold hoops.

Today's visiting choir, from a parish in the diocese, had more enthusiasm than skill, and David found himself unable to concentrate on the service. He watched Mildred

Somers discreetly, from under half-closed lids, and wondered what she could tell him about Miles Taylor. She didn't look at all the sort of person to be taken in by Miles, and that would affect the manner in which David approached her.

In the end he decided on the direct approach. After the service, as she got to her feet with the aid of a stick, David waited to catch her eye. 'Miss Somers?' he began tentatively.

'Yes?'

'So sorry to disturb you. I was told that you were the person to speak to about a former organist here, Miles Taylor.'

She looked wary. 'Why? Are you a friend of his?'

He thought quickly. 'No, not at all. It's just that . . . well, a friend of mine is a churchwarden in a parish that's thinking of employing Mr Taylor, and he asked me if I might make a few discreet inquiries. Nothing official, you understand. I thought you might be the best person to ask, on that sort of basis.'

She nodded, her earrings bobbing, and sat down again, gesturing for him to sit beside her. 'Yes, of course, Mr . . .'

'Middleton-Brown.'

'Mr Middleton-Brown. I'll be happy to help in any way I can, of course. What did you wish to know about Mr Taylor?' Her voice, when she spoke the name, was decidedly frosty.

'Forgive me, Miss Somers, but you don't sound very enthusiastic about him.'

She flashed him an acerbic glance. 'Clever boy. No, I have to tell you that I never got on with Miles Taylor.'

'Could I ask why?'

'Well you might ask. For one thing, the man was far too fond of himself for my taste. If you didn't know how wonderful he was, he would be happy to tell you, at great length. And I couldn't abide his arrogance.'

'Did he know his job?'

'His, and everyone else's too, if he was to be believed. He thought he knew better than anyone how the cathedral ought to be run. As far as the music was concerned, he was in charge, and there was no arguing with that. But worship, and administration – those things were none of his affair, but he couldn't help interfering, putting his oar in. No, I didn't get on with Miles Taylor.'

David could well understand that, if the man had been foolish enough to try to meddle in this woman's sphere of influence. 'He was organist here for . . . several years, I believe?'

'Yes, four years.'

'And he left about five years ago?'

'That is correct.'

'Might I ask . . .' he hesitated delicately, 'about the circumstances of his leaving? Were there any . . . causes?'

Miss Somers fixed her gaze on the organ console just above them. 'There were . . . disagreements about the music. He was very keen on experimenting with new things, and the Chapter felt . . .'

'But that's not the real reason, is it?' David asked gently but firmly. 'You just said that he had final authority as far as music was concerned.'

She compressed her lips, and regarded him keenly, shrewdly for just a moment. Making up her mind, she nodded again suddenly. 'Yes, I think you . . . your friend . . . have a right to know. I don't know what Mr Taylor has told anyone about why he left here, but it could have a direct bearing on someone's decision to offer him a post.' David held his breath and waited, not daring to speak. 'The truth is that Mr Taylor falsified his credentials when he came here.' David let his breath out in a long hiss, almost a whistle. Miss Somers raised her eyebrows significantly and went on. 'We never questioned it initially, of course. You do take a lot on faith in this business, if you'll forgive the pun. In this particular case, that was a mistake. Miles Taylor lied to the Cathedral Chapter, to the Provost, to me. When it all came out, he tried to deny it – he was very brazen about it. We finally had no choice but to dismiss him, and to warn him that if he tried for another cathedral post, we would have to apprise them of the situation.'

'I see.'

'In the end he went to a parish church in London. They never asked for a reference – I suppose they thought they were lucky to be getting someone of his calibre. I don't know what we would have told them if they had asked. Is he still there, do you know? Somewhere in Kensington, I believe?'

'Yes, I think so.'

'And this church that's considering him . . .?'

'I doubt very much if they'll be interested, when they've heard this,' he said hastily.

Miss Somers nodded again, satisfied.

So old Miles had lied about his credentials. Gabriel might be very interested to hear that, and so might the police.

He sat in a little café drinking a cup of tea. It was quite stewed, and obviously made with cheap tea-bags, but at least they'd used fresh milk, and it had to be an improvement over what he could have made himself in his hotel room. He'd return to London first thing in the morning. He was half tempted to go back tonight, but he'd already had the young man at the hotel reception book him a table for dinner at a restaurant in York, a restaurant that had been quite favourably reviewed in the *Good Food Guide*. He'd have a good meal tonight, and first thing tomorrow he'd go back.

Gabriel tossed sleeplessly in the comfortable bed. Never in his life had he had problems sleeping, until this week. His head hurt. He got up and took some paracetamol tablets; if he'd had sleeping pills, he would have taken them. At the first morning light, he rose and went downstairs to make himself a cup of tea.

There was a white envelope on the carpet, just inside the door. As he picked it up, his heart lurched apprehensively. The envelope had a familiar look. He went into his study for his letter-knife and slit it open with mounting dread.

The letter was on the same paper as before, neatly typed.

This is to remind you. You have until the end of the day on Wednesday, 15 August, the Feast of the Assumption, to resign. It would be very foolish of you to ignore this warning.

PART III

Chapter 36

*When thou with rebukes dost chasten man for sin,
thou makest his beauty to consume away, like as
it were a moth fretting a garment: every man
therefore is but vanity.*
*Hear my prayer, O Lord, and with thine ears con-
sider my calling: hold not thy peace at my tears.*
Psalm 39.12–13

David probably would have sworn that he hadn't slept a
wink all night, between the water-pipes and the cathedral
bells, but the jangle of the telephone jolted him awake.
Damn, he thought. Time to get up already. Without his
alarm clock, he'd asked the hotel reception desk for a
wake-up call, so that he would be sure of making early
Mass at the cathedral and thus could get an early start
back to London. He hadn't actually believed that they'd
carry out his request, so his second thought was mild surprise
at their efficiency. He reached for the receiver. 'Yes?' he
growled.

The voice on the other end was tentative. 'David?' He
didn't recognise it, but it clearly was not his wake-up call.

'Speaking.'

'David, this is Gabriel.'

Suddenly he was wide awake. Gabriel's voice sounded strained – not like him at all. David replied cautiously; the last words they'd exchanged had hardly been cordial. 'Yes, Gabriel?'

'I'm so sorry to disturb you. I rang Daphne, and she gave me this number where you could be reached. I wouldn't bother you like this, but . . . it's rather important.'

It must be, for Gabriel to be ringing him in Selby at seven o'clock on a Sunday morning. 'What is it?'

'David . . . there's been another letter. This morning.'

'What on earth do you mean?'

'Another blackmail letter. Like the first one.'

David struggled to comprehend Gabriel's words. 'But that's impossible. Mavis is dead.'

'You were wrong. Mavis couldn't have written the letters. I tell you, I've had another one.'

'But that's impossible,' David repeated stupidly.

'David, please come back.' Gabriel paused awkwardly. 'I'm sorry about . . . the way we parted last week. About the things we said in anger. I need your help now, more than ever. Please come back.'

'I'll be there in a few hours.' David hung up, then stared at the telephone for a moment. Gabe needed him. Again.

Gabriel must have been watching for him from the study; he opened the door before David could ring the bell. 'Come in, David. Let's go into the study.'

Once they were out of the dim light of the entrance hall, Gabriel turned to face him. 'I'm glad you've come,' he said simply. David caught his breath at the change in Gabriel's appearance. It had been less than a week since he'd seen him, in this room, but Gabriel had altered subtly yet noticeably in that week. He was immaculately groomed and attired as always, but he looked tired and – yes, older. There were tiny lines around his eyes where none had been before, and a pinched look around his mouth. This business has really hit him hard, David concluded, with a stirring of compassion.

Gabriel gestured him to a chair, and sat himself as usual at his desk. He seemed at a loss for words.

'Show me the letter,' David said, without preliminaries. This time there was no need for concealment; there was no one else in the house. The letter lay folded on the desk, and Gabriel handed it to him silently.

David studied it for a moment. 'It does seem to be from the same person,' he admitted at last. That destroyed his pet theory, formulated on the drive from Selby, that there were two blackmailers. 'So it wasn't Mavis. I was wrong. I'm not much of a detective, am I?'

'We were both wrong,' Gabriel said with a bitter smile.

'Then who?'

Gabriel shook his head hopelessly. 'I wish I knew. I've been over and over it in my mind, and I just don't know. And time is running out.'

'Three days, give or take. What are you going to do?'

Gabriel looked at him pleadingly. 'Won't you help?'

'All right, what are *we* going to do?'

'Thank you, David.' His smile, though strained, was genuinely grateful. 'Isn't there any way you can find out? You've been to Brighton – was there anything . . .?'

David covered his face with his hands and thought hard. It was difficult changing gears like this, back to Peter Maitland and Brighton. 'You'll have to help me, Gabriel.

You'll have to think about this. Before, you didn't tell me anything about his background, his friends. I know nothing about him that would lead me to someone who knew him, someone to whom he might have mentioned your name. Did you ever meet any of his friends?'

'No, that wouldn't have been a good idea.' Gabriel looked away. 'And it wasn't that kind of relationship.'

David suppressed a pang. 'Try to think. Did he ever mention any friends – *anyone* he knew – by name?'

Gabriel furrowed his brow in concentration. 'It's been so long ago. I can't remember. He had a sister somewhere, but I don't know her name. Maybe it was Kathy, Karen, something like that. His room-mate's name was Dominic, I think. And I think he talked about someone named Anthony. Is it really that important?'

'I have nothing else to go on. And time, as you said, is running out.'

They talked around in circles for a long while. Gabriel was too upset and bewildered to be of any real use; finally David said, 'I will do my very best. But it's so difficult on my own – I really haven't been a very clever detective so far. May I ask for Daphne's help?'

Gabriel was horrified. 'Tell Daphne? What would she say? What would she think of me?'

David hesitated. 'She already knows about . . . us. I didn't tell her – she guessed. And I don't believe she thinks the worse of either of us because of it. Daphne is discreet, you know that. And she never judges. It would be a great help to me to be able to talk it over with her: Daphne's very shrewd about people. I won't tell her all the details, just the bare facts.'

'If you think it's best, then,' Gabriel nodded listlessly,

playing with the paperweight. 'I don't care how you do it, but just find out by Wednesday.'

'I'll do my best,' David repeated gravely and, he hoped, reassuringly.

Gabriel roused himself. 'Would you like a sherry? Or maybe a cup of tea?'

'I'd love a sherry. I didn't stop to eat.'

'Then you must be hungry. I haven't eaten, either. Maybe I can find us some food – you stay here.'

David was happy to remain, and occupied himself looking around the study. It was a lovely room, with the Queen Anne desk and the Persian carpet. He glanced at the photo of Emily and the children. Dear Emily – he wondered how she was. He must go to see her and find out. He browsed for a few minutes among Gabriel's books. Some of them he remembered, but many he did not. Gabriel's reading habits had always been catholic, with a small 'c', so amongst the books on theology and exegesis were a sprinkling of the classics, and a few modern novels. And there, under 'N', were Gabriel's own books; David took them down and looked at them with interest. *Transubstantiation: An Anglican Perspective*, followed by *Sacramental Confession: A Spiritual Imperative*, by Fr Gabriel Neville, MA Oxon. He was surprised that he hadn't seen them reviewed in the *Church Times*. They looked suitably learned, but written with a certain popular appeal for a particular brand of churchmanship. He returned them to the shelf almost guiltily as Gabriel, bearing a tray, pushed the door open.

'I found a tin of tuna,' he announced, indicating a plate of inexpertly-made sandwiches. 'Would you like a sherry first?'

'Yes, please.'

'Amontillado?'

'Lovely.'

They sipped sherry and munched sandwiches almost companionably for several minutes. They were both so hungry that the sandwiches tasted rather good. Gabe had never been much use in the kitchen, David recalled. But then, he'd never needed to be. There'd always been someone else to keep him fed: the succession of cooks at home, at boarding school, at university, at the clergy house in Brighton, then the housekeeper at St Anne's vicarage, and finally . . . Emily. He wondered how Gabriel was faring without her on a purely practical level. Probably not too badly, if the story he'd concocted about Emily nursing an ailing relation had gained very wide circulation amongst the ladies of the parish.

'Would you like a piece of cake?' Gabriel asked, confirming his suspicion. 'I think I've got a bit left from the one Mrs Framlingham brought me the other day.'

'No, thanks. I'm fine.'

'She – Mrs Framlingham, that is – said that she'd seen you at the Royal Albert Hall with Lucy Kingsley,' Gabriel remarked casually.

'Oh, did she?' was David's calm reply. Interfering old cow, he added to himself furiously. None of her bloody business.

'You've been seeing rather a lot of Lucy Kingsley, from what I hear.'

'And who are all these sources of information, who are taking such an interest in my life?' Although he struggled to keep his tone light, his voice was beginning to take on a hard edge.

'Various people. In a parish like this, it's bound to

306

happen. Let's just say that people have noticed. Don't get me wrong, David – I think it's great,' Gabriel remarked heartily. 'It's about time you found yourself a nice wife and settled down.'

'A wife?' His expression was dangerously calm; Gabriel should have been warned.

'Yes. I can't recommend marriage too highly, David. Have you thought about it at all? Lucy would make you a good wife. She's an excellent cook, and good company, and quite pleasant to look at. You could do much worse.'

David struggled with himself for a moment before replying. 'How dare you,' he said, very quietly. 'How dare you presume to tell me what I should do with my life?'

'I only meant . . .' Gabriel stammered, startled. 'I just want you to be happy, David. I just thought . . .'

'Anyway, I don't see that you're exactly a walking advertisement for the joys of wedlock. You seem to have cocked up your marriage pretty badly,' David said brutally.

The face that Gabriel turned on him was white, as he struggled with a dawning realisation. 'You know where Emily is, don't you?'

'What if I did?'

'If you know, David, for God's sake tell me! Don't you know that I can't live without her?' There were tears in his eyes.

David looked at him for a long moment. He knew then that Gabriel's haunted look, the changes he'd noted in him, were caused by Emily's absence, and not by the second blackmail letter. Gabriel had suffered, was still suffering, and he hadn't been able to share his agony with anyone. He must love her very much. David knew then what he had to do. Emily might never forgive him, might not understand why he'd done it. But Gabriel deserved a chance.

'Yes, I know where she is,' he said. 'And I will tell you.'

Chapter 37

*But lo, thou requirest truth in the inward parts: and
shalt make me to understand wisdom secretly.*

Psalm 51.6

David had been walking aimlessly in the park for a long
time – he had no idea how long. So many things crowded
his mind, demanding attention: the blackmailer, Gabriel,
Gabriel and Emily. Lucy. He had to talk to Lucy.

It was Sunday afternoon. He would find Lucy at the
V & A.

He went to the gallery where she'd been working at
closing time the week before. She was there, alone in the
gallery, intent on her sketch pad. David stood immobile
for a long time watching her. There was such grace in her
every movement, her every gesture, and as she paused
momentarily, unconsciously to push her hair back from
her face, he felt his chest constrict painfully. She was so
very beautiful, sitting there on a bench at the V & A, with
her red-gold curls shimmering in the late afternoon sunlight. He felt that he could not bear what he now had to
do. His nerve failed him, and he half turned to go.

The movement caught her eye; she looked up and saw
him, and her face illuminated with pleasure. David thought

that as long as he lived he would remember that look, as if a light had been switched on inside her. In a continuous fluid motion she rose and came to him, checking herself at the last moment as she saw the expression on his face. 'Hello, David.'

'Lucy.' He smiled, painfully, and took her hands in his. 'How have you been?'

'All right. I missed you. How was your trip?'

'Fine. The weather was miserable, the food was awful, and the bloody pipes banged all night and kept me awake, but aside from that . . .'

She laughed. His heart constricted again, and he dropped her hands. 'Listen, Lucy, we have to talk,' he plunged in. It was now or never. 'The roses I sent you . . . I thought I meant it, but . . . I just can't do it. I feel terrible about this . . .'

She interrupted him softly, 'You don't have to say anything, David. Let's just leave it. We've had some lovely times together, so let's not spoil it now by saying anything we'll be sorry for.'

'But I want to make you understand why . . . it has to be this way. It's not you, Lucy, it's me that's the problem.'

'I do understand,' she affirmed, raising her eyes squarely to meet his. 'You're a lovely man – you deserve the best that life has to offer. I know it sounds terribly trite, but I hope that someday you'll meet somebody special and he'll make you very happy.'

'How . . . how did you know?'

She laughed quietly, wryly. 'I've known a lot of men, remember? I told you once that all the good blokes around my age were either married or gay. You're a damn good bloke, and you're definitely not married.'

'You knew all along.'

'I suspected. And the other night I knew for sure, when I wanted you to stay, and you wouldn't . . . couldn't.'

'I didn't know that you wanted me to stay,' he breathed with wonder.

'That's just it, isn't it? You didn't know.'

'Then why . . . I was going to . . . I asked you to marry me!'

'Ah, David.' She touched his cheek with great tenderness. 'I was going to say no. I was very tempted, but I would have said no.'

'But why?'

'Don't you see, David? Marriage with you . . . well, it would have been very nice. Comfortable. An end to being alone. But that's not enough. There always would have been . . . something missing. It would have been a mistake for you, and it would have been a mistake for me.'

'But, Lucy, I do love you.' As he said it, he knew it was true.

She smiled into his eyes. 'Yes, I believe you do. But maybe not in the right way, or maybe not enough. Marriage isn't a game, David. It's not an escape from anything – not even from loneliness. Some of the loneliest people in the world are married. Your loneliness is inside you, David, in a place I could never reach.'

His eyes filled with tears; he found he couldn't speak.

'I've been there before,' she went on. 'Years ago I married for all the wrong reasons, trying to escape from my past, from . . . myself. It didn't work. But at least I've learned from my mistake. I won't do it again. And I care about you too much to let you . . .' She smiled through her own tears. 'But let's not close all the doors yet, David. Please?'

His voice, when he finally spoke, was choked. 'Lucy Kingsley, did anyone ever tell you that you were a wise woman?' He took her gently in his arms and, for the first and possibly the last time, kissed her on the lips, with a kind of love and with infinite regret.

Chapter 38

They that sow in tears: shall reap in joy.
He that now goeth on his way weeping, and beareth
forth good seed: shall doubtless come again with
joy, and bring his sheaves with him.

Psalm 126.6–7

Emily was drowsing in bed. She'd spent much of the past two days sleeping, a healing sleep, and when she woke she thought about her past, and her future. Soon she would have to make some decisions and face the future, whatever it held. But first, in this limbo-like present, she must try to come to terms with the past, her past and Gabriel's.

In thought she'd gradually worked her way back through the years, the years of happy memories. The last few years, when the children were small, and needed so much attention and love. Before that, the incredible joy of their birth, after they'd both wanted them for so long. And the not-so-happy memories of the time before that, when she'd lost the baby, and disappointed Gabriel so terribly. But always, through it all, the love they'd shared . . .

Outside her window it was a golden August afternoon. It was on just such an afternoon that he'd first asked her to marry him. Emily closed her eyes.

It was his afternoon off, and they'd driven out into the country for a walk. They'd known each other only a few weeks. At the top of a hill, he suddenly stopped and said, 'Emily, I want to marry you.'

Breathless after the climb, and with surprise, she replied, 'I just don't know, Gabriel. I have other plans for my life. I never counted on meeting you – I need some time to think about how you fit in. There's Cambridge, and the fellowship . . . I'm just not sure yet.'

But later, back at the vicarage, the housekeeper away, he took her in his arms and kissed her, and from that moment on nothing else mattered. He'd kissed her before, but this time he meant business. His lips, his arms around her – she didn't want him to stop. He didn't stop. Afterwards, in bed, he smiled down at her, tenderly brushing a strand of dark hair from her cheek. 'Now you'll have to marry me, my darling Emily.' And, looking into his eyes, loving him, of course she said yes.

It was just after that, she recalled now, that she'd asked him the question: why hadn't he married earlier? 'Because I've never met a woman like you before. You must believe me, my love – you're the first woman I've ever loved.' Had there been even a shadow of concealment on his face when he'd made his reply? She couldn't remember. She got up and splashed some cold water on her face at the basin, trying to stop the racing of her pulses at the vivid memory of his lovemaking. She scrubbed at her face with the rough towel, squinted at herself in the small mirror, and ran a comb through her tousled hair. Perhaps she'd go out in the garden and get some air.

There was a quiet tap on the door. 'Mrs Neville, there's a man here to see you,' said a soft voice. David, Emily thought with a smile. It would be nice to see David. She turned as the door opened.

Gabriel! Her heart lurched with a wild joy and she instinctively moved towards his open arms, but she checked herself in time and retreated. 'No, Gabriel. That would be too easy.' She faced him across the narrow bed. 'What do you have to say to me?'

He looked at her, stunned. 'Say to you? Don't you understand, Emily? I've come to take you home.'

'I'm not sure I'm ready to go home, Gabriel. There are a lot of things we have to talk about first.'

His hands dropped to his sides. 'All right, then. Let's talk.'

'How did you find me?'

'David told me . . .'

She laughed harshly. 'I should have known that you men would stick together.'

'It wasn't like that. He didn't want to tell me – I begged him. He finally realised how important it was – that I should at least have a chance to see you.'

'Did he also tell you why I left?'

Gabriel looked away. 'Yes. But you must believe me . . .'

'How can I know what to believe, when our marriage was based on a lie?' she asked with heart-rending honesty.

'I never lied to you, Emily.'

'No, you didn't, did you? "Economical with the truth" is the phrase they use these days, I think. "The first woman you ever loved", you said. I suppose I was naïve not to ask about the other half of the human race.' The bitterness in her voice touched him on a raw nerve.

'Don't you understand? I couldn't tell you – I was terrified of losing you. I didn't think you'd be able to accept it, to accept *me*, believe that I'd changed and that all I wanted was you.'

'Did you have so little faith in me, then?'

'You were so young, so innocent. I couldn't take the risk that you . . . would be disgusted by my past.'

She was silent for a moment. She'd asked herself so many times over the last few days how she *would* have reacted. 'And since then?' she asked finally. 'Surely you could have found a moment, over the last ten years, when you might have told me. It wasn't fair of you to deny me that knowledge, not all this time. I just can't help feeling that our marriage has been a dishonest sham.'

He recoiled. 'Never that, Emily. Don't the last ten years mean anything? I've loved you, I've been faithful to you for ten years. David and the others – it was all a very long time ago.'

She looked as if she'd been struck, but her voice was deadly quiet. 'Others? There were others? How many?'

Oh, wonderful, he thought. 'Didn't David tell you? I assumed . . .'

'No.'

'Not many. Before David. Three, four . . . several. David was the only one who really mattered.'

'Oh, Gabriel, it's all too much. How can you expect me to believe anything you say any more?'

He sat down heavily on the bed, burying his head in his hands. At last he raised his face, wet with tears, and said in an anguished whisper, 'How can I make you understand? I'm so sorry that I've hurt you. I was foolish, and selfish. But I didn't want to lose you then, and I couldn't bear to lose you now. I love you, Emily. Please come home with me.' She'd never seen him cry before, not even when she'd lost the baby. His tears reached her as his words could not, and in the end she was comforting him, stroking his head and murmuring her love.

In the car, on the way home, he told her everything: about David, and how he'd loved him, about the others, and finally about Peter Maitland, his death, and the blackmail letters.

She cried a little, but her love for him was very strong, and his honesty meant everything to her; by the time they reached the vicarage he had gained the most stalwart ally he could have. 'If only you'd trusted me sooner,' she said. 'So much pain could have been avoided.'

He took her hand, lacing his fingers with hers. 'I think I can face whatever happens, now that I've got you back. Don't ever leave me again, my love.'

Chapter 39

My lovers and friends hast thou put away from me:
and hid mine acquaintance out of my sight.

Psalm 88.18

Daphne probably wouldn't know he was back in London,
David thought: he'd left his car in front of the vicarage,
and unless she'd been down to St Anne's for some reason
that afternoon she wouldn't have seen it. In any case, he
didn't think he could face her – or anyone he knew – just
yet. He took the Tube to a far-flung corner of London and
found a quiet pub where he could sit in a dark corner and
drink anonymously.

Daphne wasn't expecting him. She looked over the tops
of her spectacles in surprise when he let himself into the
flat.

'All right, what is going on?' she demanded immediately. 'Why was Gabriel trying to reach you? What's so
urgent that he'd ring here at seven o'clock on a Sunday
morning, looking for you?'

David sat down and put his feet up. 'It's a long story.'

'We've got all night. Do you want a drink?'

'Actually, I'd like something to eat, if it's not too much
trouble. I haven't had anything but a tuna sandwich all

day. And a few glasses of whisky,' he added candidly.

'I could grill you a chop, if you like.'

'Thanks. That would be lovely.'

'Come through to the kitchen, then. You can talk to me there.'

He followed her to the kitchen. It was a fairly small room, so to stay out of her way he leaned against the door jamb and watched her as she quickly and efficiently put together a meal for him. Dear old no-nonsense Daphne, he thought. What a treasure. Maybe I should marry *her*. But then there's no reason why she would have me, either, he reflected in a half humorous, half self-pitying way. By now he'd almost forgotten that he'd done the rejecting – that he'd decided he couldn't possibly marry Lucy. He remembered only that she'd said she wouldn't marry him. And he remembered that he'd said he loved her. It all seemed quite extraordinary, and a very long time ago.

'If you aren't going to tell me about Gabriel, maybe you'll tell me about your trip,' Daphne prompted him. 'Did you find out anything about Miles?'

'Yes, I certainly did.' He told her with great relish about Miss Somers, and the circumstances of Miles's departure from Selby Cathedral.

'But that's incredible! It really does give him a motive for murdering Mavis, if she'd found out about it, and was blackmailing him about it.'

David shook his head sadly. 'That's what I thought, but unfortunately it didn't happen that way. It would seem that we've – I've – been barking up the wrong tree all along, so to speak: Mavis wasn't the blackmailer.'

Daphne, on the way to the table with the plate of food,

stopped in her tracks and stared at him. 'Not the black-mailer? How on earth do you know?'

He sighed and took the plate from her. 'That's what Gabriel was in a flap about this morning. He's had another blackmail letter, and it obviously didn't come from Mavis.'

Daphne sat down at the table. 'I think you'd better start again. Gabriel's had another blackmail letter?'

'Yes, today. And it was very clearly from the same person who'd written the first one. So that means Mavis couldn't have written either one.' He looked a bit sheep-ish. 'It's my fault – I was the one who assumed she was the blackmailer. I just jumped to the wrong conclusion, that's all. So all this business about Miles has been in the nature of a wild-goose chase.'

'In other words, the blackmailer is still alive.'

'And has nothing to do with Mavis's death.'

Daphne chewed on her lip for a moment, thinking. 'So where do you stand now? What does Gabriel want you to do?'

'He wants me to find the blackmailer. And there isn't much time – the deadline he's been given is Wednesday.'

'This Wednesday?'

'I'm afraid so. The Feast of the Assumption.'

'Can you tell me what it's all about, or would Gabriel rather you didn't?'

David smiled. 'I told him that you and I work as a team, and if he wanted my help, he got yours as well.'

She returned his smile, gratified. 'Thanks, partner. So what is it about?'

He thought about how to begin. 'As I told you last week, the letter was about something that happened before Gabriel came here. Just before, in fact. There was a boy in

321

Brighton – his name was Peter Maitland – who drowned. Gabriel had . . . known him. Gabriel has reason to believe that the boy committed suicide, though the verdict of the inquest was accidental death. I think he felt in a way responsible – he might have been able to prevent the boy's death, but didn't. I think it upset him more than he's willing to admit.'

Daphne nodded gravely.

'After that, he was anxious to leave Brighton, and got the living here through some connections he had, quite quickly. But apparently someone has found out about what happened – someone at St Anne's.'

'What is the threat?'

'That unless he resigns from St Anne's and from the priesthood, he'll be exposed. The letter said that they would inform the Bishop, the national press, and . . . Emily.'

She raised her eyebrows and whistled soundlessly. 'The national press. After the smear job they did on Norman Newsome, Gabriel wouldn't have a chance. Just a hint of a juicy scandal like this, even it it's ten years old, and they'd be howling for his blood.'

'Poor old Norman Newsome only had a few fantasies about choirboys, and look what they did to him,' David mused. 'I can just imagine the meal they'd make of Gabriel.'

'Right,' said Daphne, businesslike. 'What have we got to go on? Who could have known about this boy?'

'That's the difficult bit. Gabriel says he never told anyone, and I have no reason to disbelieve that. I don't know who he would have told, anyway.' He added, so quietly that she almost didn't hear, 'He didn't tell me, and

I knew him better than anyone. At least I thought I did.'

With a quick look of sympathy, she went on. 'Then the boy must have told someone. He must have mentioned Gabriel's name to a friend, a relative, a teacher . . .'

'Yes, that's what I thought. Before, that is. Before Mavis died, and I got side-tracked down that blind alley.'

'And did you find anything? You went to Brighton, didn't you?'

He frowned, trying to remember. 'I thought it was Miles,' he said. 'Funny, isn't it? Poor old Miles! I keep trying to pin everything on him!'

'Why did you think it was Miles?'

'I found a death notice in the local paper. It implied that Peter Maitland had been a student at Selby Cathedral School, even that he'd been a chorister there. Naturally I thought of Miles – I thought that Peter must have confided in him. I was all ready to tell Gabriel that I'd found his blackmailer, then the next day Mavis was killed, and Miles didn't seem relevant any longer.'

'Did you get a copy of the death notice?'

'Yes, if I can remember what I did with it . . . I don't suppose I threw it away.'

'Well, finish your meal, and then you can look for it. Anything else?'

'There was a newspaper report of the drowning, and an item about the inquest. Not a great deal to go on.'

'So what we're looking for is a connection between this boy Peter Maitland and someone at St Anne's,' Daphne summarised.

'Exactly. And we have three days to find it.'

'Tomorrow morning is Mavis's inquest, so we can't do much till after that.'

'Mavis. I'd forgotten about that. Well, that has nothing to do with us now.'

'You'll have to go, you know. They'll want you to give evidence, pinpointing the time when you saw her alive.'

'Bloody hell. Well, I suppose it can't be helped.'

'Anyway,' said Daphne, 'you're forgetting something else. You know that Mavis was murdered, because of the missing ledger sheet. You weren't the last person in that sacristy. So even if Mavis's murder had nothing to do with this blackmail . . .'

'She *was* murdered! Well, I'll just testify about the ledger sheet being missing, and then it will be the police's business to find who killed her.'

Daphne leaned back in her chair. 'So we'll forget about Mavis, and concentrate on the blackmailer.'

A few minutes later, David had located the photocopies of the newspaper articles, slipped into the pocket of his suitcase for safe-keeping over a week ago.

Daphne read them in silence, concentrating on every detail that might be of importance. 'Are you quite sure that Miles isn't involved? It does say Selby,' she pointed out.

'I'm not sure about the timing, but it doesn't look promising. I'm sure Miss Somers said that Miles had been at Selby for four years, and she would be very precise about things like that. If he's been here at St Anne's for five years, that would mean that Peter left Selby before Miles arrived.' He frowned, remembering. 'In fact, I spent a great deal of time studying the board with the list of past organists at the cathedral, and I'm positive that Miles didn't start there till the year after Peter died. Unfortunately.'

'Then Miles is out. Again.'

'It looks that way.'

Daphne scowled. 'Croydon,' she said. 'Do you know anyone in Croydon?'

Something teased at David's mind. 'I can't think. There's someone who's recently mentioned Croydon to me.'

'Maybe it will come to you, if you don't try too hard.'

'I'm just not thinking very clearly tonight. I'm sorry. Do you think I could have that drink now?'

'Of course. Help yourself.' She looked at him intently. 'Are you all right, David? You really do look unwell.'

He poured himself a drink and sat down. 'It's been a long day. I've driven two hundred miles, and have had rather too much to drink. I've had a row with Gabriel, and . . . oh, hell. You don't want to hear my problems.'

'Of course I do.' She dropped the clippings and came over to him, bending over him clumsily. 'Tell Auntie Daphne all about it,' she urged with a self-deprecating smile. 'My shoulders are very broad – along with the rest of me.'

Oh, why not, he thought. It would be good to tell someone about it. And Daphne had always been a good listener.

'It's about Lucy,' he began. 'Lucy Kingsley.'

Daphne sat down across from him and leaned forward. 'Yes?'

'I . . . well, as you know, I've spent rather a lot of time with her since I've been here.' Daphne nodded. 'She's a beautiful woman, we have a lot of interests in common, and I've enjoyed her company. Last week, before I went to Selby, I thought . . . well, I thought that maybe it would be an idea for me to marry her.'

Daphne's face remained impassive, and David, looking into his glass, didn't see that she gripped the arm of her chair. 'Yes?'

'I thought about it a lot while I was gone. It seemed like a very good thing to do. I hate living on my own, you know. And even though I . . . well, I thought the other things wouldn't matter so much.'

'Did you ask her?'

'Yes, I sent her some roses, and on the card I . . . But today . . . well, when I was talking to Gabriel, he said that he'd heard rumours about us – about me and Lucy.' Daphne nodded; she too had heard talk. 'He tried to talk me into marrying her, said it would be a good idea, that I needed a wife. That's when I knew I couldn't do it.'

'I see.'

'Do you see?' he demanded passionately. 'Do you really? Gabriel – that was the one thing I couldn't cope with. Gabriel. After everything we'd . . . been to each other. I know it was a long time ago. I know he's got Emily now. But damn it, how could he tell me I should find myself a wife?'

Daphne bit her lip and resisted the impulse to reach out and touch him. 'So what did you do?'

'I went to see Lucy. To tell her.' He sighed deeply. 'It was all for nothing in the end. She said that she wouldn't have married me anyway. I don't suppose I ever had any reason to think she would. After all, what on earth would I have to offer to a woman like that?' Laughing bitterly, he added, 'I'm pretty hopeless, aren't I? I'm a failure as a detective – haring all over the country on a false trail. And I'm a failure as a . . . lover – I couldn't even manage a proper renunciation scene.'

Daphne swallowed, cleared her throat, and asked quietly, 'Do you love her?'

'That's the damndest part of it. I think I do.'

'And have you told her so?'

'Yes.'

'Then why wouldn't she marry you? Doesn't she love you?'

He closed his eyes, remembering. 'She made a long speech about marriage not being an escape from anything, not even from loneliness. About not wanting to make the same mistake twice. It all made sense, but it hurt like hell.'

'It sounds to me like she's a very perceptive and sensible woman,' said Daphne. 'You weren't going to marry her, anyway,' she added reasonably.

'No, but . . . oh, I don't know, Daphne. None of it makes any sense at the moment. Give me some good advice. You can tell me now to forget about her, and get on with my life.'

The expression in her eyes was unreadable. 'No, I won't tell you that. I don't think you should burn your bridges, not just yet.'

'That's funny. That's almost exactly what Lucy said. I'm not sure what it means.' He took a gulp of his drink. 'Thanks for listening, Daphne. You're a real friend.'

Unable to meet his eyes, she leaned over and patted his hand awkwardly.

Chapter 40

The ungodly are froward, even from their mother's
womb: as soon as they are born, they go astray,
and speak lies.

Psalm 58.3

The room where the inquest was being held was not large,
and it was nearly full when David and Daphne arrived, a
few minutes before ten. Although the case was not a
sensational one, it was sufficiently bizarre to have attracted
a fair crowd of thrill-seekers, in addition to the interested
parties.

When they'd found seats, David spent the remaining
minutes before the opening of the inquest studying the
crowd. Venerable Bead was there, of course, in the front
row: fairly bursting with self-importance, he continually
turned around to see who else was there. Cecily Framlingham, dressed in black and looking fairly subdued, sat with
Mary Hughes near the back. And David was not surprised
to see Teresa Dawson there with her mother. Teresa had
also dressed in black for the solemn occasion, but she
looked anything but subdued: she was virtually licking her
lips in anticipation. David didn't see Craig Conwell, but
assumed he'd be there.

'Did you see Teresa?' Daphne whispered.

David nodded. 'She's enjoying herself already.'

'So is Venerable Bead.'

'But where is Beryl Ball?'

'Oh, she'll be here. She wouldn't miss a show like this.'

But she hadn't arrived when the inquest opened. Craig Conwell was the first witness to be called. He came from the back of the room, hands in his pockets and shoulders hunched, and when he was seated he seemed ill at ease. The questions he was asked were of a perfunctory nature, attempting mainly to establish his mother's frame of mind before her death.

'She seemed OK to me.' He shrugged. 'Just like usual. Of course she was always getting worked up over something, but that was the way she was.'

'And was she "worked up over something", as you put it, that morning?' asked the coroner.

Craig shrugged again. 'Oh, just some bill in the post. I think it was the phone bill. She said she couldn't afford to pay it.'

'And when exactly was this?'

'Saturday morning, early. About eight o'clock.'

'She left the house shortly after that?'

'About half past. To go to that church fête. She was a big shot at the church.'

'That was the last time you saw your mother, when she left the house at half past eight on Saturday morning?'

His eyes darted around the room at the watching faces. 'Yeah, that's right.' David wondered if he had cultivated the Americanised drawl, or if it was just a reflection of a television-influenced youth.

'Thank you very much, Mr Conwell.' Craig returned to his seat at the back.

Next the coroner called David to give evidence. This, too, was fairly routine. He was asked to verify his statement to the police, particularly regarding the time that he'd left Mavis. This line of questioning had just begun when the door opened and Beryl Ball walked into the room. David saw that she was dressed entirely in pillar-box red, except for the green moon-boots. He stopped in mid-sentence; people became gradually aware of her as she made a stately but purposeful progress up the centre aisle. She nodded and waggled her teeth knowingly at Craig Conwell as she passed him, then headed straight for the coroner's chair. She thrust her hand and her teeth out simultaneously; taken totally aback, he took her hand and shook it cordially. She turned to David with an exaggerated wink, then hobbled to an empty chair in the front row and sat down with a flourish.

The coroner regained his composure, and the attention of his audience, after a brief struggle. 'So, Mr Middleton-Brown, you left Mrs Conwell in the sacristy at approximately four forty-five.'

'No later than that, certainly. Possibly a few minutes earlier.'

'And you are satisfied with your statement as it now stands?'

David hesitated. 'With the statement, yes. But there's something I'd like to add – something that I think is rather important.'

'Yes, Mr Middleton-Brown?'

'I was asked by the police to look around and confirm that the sacristy was as it was when I left it. In fact, something was missing from the room, but I only realised that later.'

'And what was that?'

'The ledger sheet on which Mrs Conweil had recorded the hourly totals for the money she was counting. It was on the table when I was there, and I assumed that the police had it, along with the money. But I . . . was told later that no ledger sheet was found.'

'Is that all?'

'Yes, but—'

'Thank you, Mr Middleton-Brown. You've been most helpful.'

People were becoming anxious for what was undoubtedly the centrepiece of the day's proceedings – Venerable Bead's testimony. There was a noticeable stir of interest as Percy Bead's name was called. Teresa Dawson was leaning forward so far in her seat that she was in danger of falling off.

'Mr Percy Bead?'

'That's right.'

'I'd like to ask you a few questions about that Saturday afternoon, the fourth of August. What was your business in the sacristy?'

'I was getting ready for Evensong.'

'Doing precisely what?'

'Well, I was going to put out some fresh candles. I'm not the Sacristan, you understand, but . . . well, I like to help out when I can. And I saw that the candles were getting rather low.'

'Interfering old busybody,' Daphne muttered.

'And Father Gabriel likes me to lay his cotta out for him – sometimes I give it a quick press before he comes in.'

'So what time was it precisely when you went to the sacristy?'

'Just after half past five. I looked at my watch, and wondered when the organ recital would finish. Evensong starts at six, and I like to be ready in plenty of time.'

'You found the door locked, I understand. Were you expecting it to be locked?'

'No. It usually is, of course, but I assumed that with Mrs Conwell in there . . .'

'And you have a key.'

'Yes, of course.' He looked affronted at the question. 'I have a position of great responsibility at St Anne's.'

'Could you describe what you saw when you entered the sacristy?'

Teresa Dawson's eyes glowed as Venerable Bead launched with great relish into his description of the lolling head, the blue lips, the staring eyes, the limp body.

'And you knew that she was dead?'

'Yes, of course I did.'

'You didn't touch or move the body?'

'No.'

'What did you do?'

'I went immediately to the vicarage to fetch the Vicar. I thought he'd know what to do.'

'Going back a bit, Mr Bead. The . . . object around Mrs Conwell's neck. How would you describe it?'

'She was hanging on a black girdle.' Some of the older and more secular members of the audience chuckled with discreet amusement; Venerable Bead glared. 'A girdle,' he amplified with dignity, 'is a sort of rope belt, worn with an alb.'

'And this . . . girdle. It was kept in the sacristy?'

'Yes, in a drawer.'

'Mrs Conwell would have known this?'

'I should have thought so.'

'Thank you very much, Mr Bead.'

The rest of the inquest was an anticlimax. Cyril Fitzjames was called to answer a few questions about the church finances. He launched into a complicated explanation of the book-keeping system; he became hopelessly entangled in his own verbiage and had to begin again. David's attention wandered and he idly watched the woman who was making the transcript of the proceedings. What a waste, he thought. All those words. Next week they'll be forgotten, and the transcript will be filed away somewhere with thousands more just like it, and no one will ever look at it again. Unless . . . He sat up straight as an idea came to him, and he was in a fever of impatience as the inquest wound down with expert testimony from police, doctors and pathologists, all concluding that the state of the body was perfectly in keeping with suicide. He hadn't heard a word since Cyril Fitzjames was speaking, and so he was possibly the only person in the room who was surprised when the coroner announced a verdict of self-inflicted death.

'Suicide?' he exclaimed to Daphne as soon as they were outside. 'Is he mad? Didn't he listen to what I said about the ledger sheet?'

'He must not have thought it was important. All the expert witnesses agreed.'

'Fine experts they are! Honestly, Daphne!'

'Well, I suppose the funeral goes ahead tomorrow.'

David looked at his watch. 'I don't have time to worry about this now, Daphne, there's something I need to do. I may be back quite late tonight. But promise you'll wait up for me. I shall need your clear brain by then, I think.'

Chapter 41

When thy word goeth forth: it giveth light and understanding unto the simple.

Psalm 119.130

David's last trip to Brighton had taught him a lesson; this time he took the train from Victoria, and arrived by mid-afternoon.

It was with a degree of reluctance that he approached his old offices. He hadn't been back since he left Brighton nearly ten years ago. Things were bound to have changed.

The first change was evident on the outside: Graham's name, on a brass plate, was now among those of the partners. He and Graham had started with the firm at just about the same time, nearly fifteen years ago, and now Graham had received his reward for faithful service.

David paused for a moment outside, contemplating Graham's name, and summoning the courage to enter those doors again.

The interior looked much the same as he remembered, though the girl answering the phone at the desk was not familiar. She looked about eighteen. She would have barely been out of nappies when he was here, he realised with a faint shock. When she'd finished dealing with the phone, she turned to him with an inquiring, professional smile. 'Yes, sir?'

'I wonder if Mr Crawford is free?'

'Do you have an appointment?'

'No, I'm afraid not. I'm an old friend. I was hoping he might have a minute to see me.'

'You might have rung,' she reproved. 'Mr Crawford is a very busy man.'

Suitably chastened, he persevered. 'I am sorry. But would you ask Mr Crawford if he could see Mr Middleton-Brown, just briefly?'

With a disapproving look, she rang Graham's office. 'Mr Crawford will see you,' she told him a moment later. 'He'll be down in a moment.'

'Thank you very much.' He smiled at her in a conciliatory way, but she turned away and applied herself to some papers while he waited.

He didn't have long to wait. Graham burst into the reception area, a delighted smile on his face. 'David, my dear chap! What a lovely surprise! What brings you here?' He clasped David's hand warmly.

'I came to see you. Have you got a moment?'

'For you, old chum, any time! Is this official, or shall we pop out for a drink?'

'Oh, please.'

'The pub round the corner is open all afternoon now. I love these new licensing hours! Miss Morris, please take any messages that come in for me. I'm not sure how long I'll be.'

David couldn't resist a slightly triumphant look at the disgruntled receptionist.

'Where did you get her?' David asked as they went

around the corner. 'What happened to old Miss Bradgate?'

'Miss Bradgate, bless her, retired a few years ago. Michelle's not so bad when you get to know her – she just takes her responsibilities very seriously.'

'I suppose that's no bad thing. But for a young girl she's damned intimidating.'

'You've always been easily intimidated, David.' They reached the pub and went up to the bar. 'What are you drinking, my good man?'

'Whisky, please. I'm not driving today.'

Graham ordered the drinks, then turned to him. 'How did you get here?'

'I came down by train from London.'

'Damn, it's good to see you, David. It's been a long time.'

They appraised each other for a moment while they waited for their drinks. Graham looked decidedly middle-aged, David thought. He'd always been boyishly handsome; now his fair hair had thinned noticeably and his hairline had receded well back from his forehead. The moustache also made him look older. David assumed that Graham was drawing similar conclusions about him.

'So, how are things?' David asked. 'How are Fiona and the children?'

Graham grimaced. 'To tell you the truth, David, Fiona and I have split up.'

David could have kicked himself. 'I'm so sorry. I didn't know.'

'No, of course you didn't.' Graham paid for the drinks and led the way to a table. There was an awkward silence as David tried to think of something to say; Graham finally answered the unasked questions. 'Things hadn't

339

really been right between us for quite a while. I moved out this spring, and a divorce is in the works.'

'I'm really sorry. I always liked Fiona.' David remembered all the occasions when Graham's wife, feeling sorry for a lonely bachelor, had included him in family get-togethers.

'Yes, so did I,' Graham said with a wry shrug. 'Don't ask me what went wrong. But there you are.'

'Where are you living? It's a good thing I didn't go to the house to find you.'

'I've taken rented accommodation here in town for the time being, until I get myself sorted out.'

There was another pause. 'And the children?' David asked.

'James is at university now, and Sarah is still at home with Fiona. She's entering her last year at school this autumn, doing her A Levels.'

'Good Lord. I still think of them as being about this high.' David indicated the height of a small child.

'They probably were, the last time you saw them. God, it has been a long time! How has life been treating you? You're still in Wymondham?'

'Yes.' He paused. 'Mother died about two months ago.'

'Now it's my turn to say I'm sorry. I didn't know.'

'No.'

'Are you keeping the house?'

'For the moment. Like you, it's a bit soon to decide where I go from here.'

'Well, if you ever want to come back to Brighton, there's a job for you at the old firm. I can guarantee that.'

'Thanks, but I doubt it somehow.' David smiled.

'Is there . . . anyone special in your life right now?'

Graham asked discreetly. Graham, bless him, had never pried into his private life, for which David had always been grateful. Fiona had occasionally tried to fix him up with one of her single friends, but Graham had shielded him. David wondered whether Graham suspected the truth – he'd have to be pretty naïve not to – but Graham had never said a word to indicate any possible suspicions.

'No, not really.' On impulse he added, 'I met a lovely woman recently. I thought . . . anyway, nothing has come of it. Nothing will,' he finished, embarrassed.

'Oh, you never know, old chap.' Graham looked interested and, yes, possibly a bit surprised. 'I must say, I'm rather enjoying the single life myself. There are a lot of women out there – God, I had no idea! All those years of marriage, and now . . . well, it's a whole different world! Women these days aren't ashamed to take the lead, to let you know what they want!' He smiled a self-satisfied smile.

'Another drink?' David suggested. 'Or do you have to get back to work?'

'Bugger work. It's not every day I have a chance to see an old friend.'

'I won't tell Miss Morris you said that,' David said over his shoulder as he went to the bar.

Graham lifted his glass when David returned. 'Cheers. So, David, what brings you to Brighton? It's a damned odd time for a social call, if I may say so.'

David took his measure carefully before replying. Except for the inevitable physical alterations, Graham hadn't changed since he'd last seen him. He thought he knew the best way to approach his problem. 'I want to ask you a favour,' he began. 'I need you to do a bit of spying for me.'

Graham immediately looked interested. He'd always been fascinated by espionage, devouring spy novels in his spare time. He'd sometimes lamented the fact that he'd missed out on a career in MI5. 'Yes? What sort of spying?'

'It's a delicate matter,' said David temptingly. Graham leaned forward. 'I need some information from the transcript of an inquest.'

'But they're not available for public inspection. You know that.'

'That's where the spying comes in. I need you to infiltrate the coroner's office and take a look at this transcript for me.'

Words like 'infiltrate' were calculated to pique Graham's curiosity.

'Is this top-secret stuff?' he asked eagerly.

'Top secret. Very important, too.'

Graham leaned back. 'The coroner's office. I just might be able to manage that. There's a sweet girl who works there – Denise. I have reason to believe that she might be willing to bend the rules a bit to do me a favour.' He nodded in satisfaction.

David smiled. 'I knew that your charms would come in handy some day.'

'When do you need it?'

'Uh . . . tomorrow,' David replied. 'If that's not asking too much.'

'That should be no problem,' said Graham expansively. 'Tell me what you need to know.'

David had declined an invitation from Graham to stay and join him for a meal, promising to return at an early date.

The train was not an express, so he had time for a quick meal from the buffet car. 'East Croydon,' came the near-unintelligible announcement over the loudspeaker, and David stopped in mid-bite. Croydon. Of course.

He was back in London much earlier than he'd antici-pated, and walked the short distance from the Tube station to the flat quickly, full of his new revelation. Daphne was not at the flat when he arrived; he got himself a drink and settled down impatiently to wait for her.

She was surprised to see him back already when she returned. 'I've been down at the church getting things ready for the funeral,' she explained. 'I didn't think you'd be back yet.'

'No, neither did I. I hope you don't mind.'

'Of course not. Have you eaten?'

'More or less.' He grimaced. 'I had a bite on the train. Delicious British Rail cuisine.'

'Train? Where have you been, then?'

'Brighton.'

Daphne looked interested. 'Have you got a lead?'

'That remains to be seen. Just a little idea I had – I'll tell you when and if it pans out.'

'Be that way.'

'Oh, it will probably come to nothing. But I'll tell you what I *have* remembered: I remembered who was talking about Croydon. Just as you said, it came to me when I wasn't thinking about it, tonight when the train went through East Croydon.'

'Tell me! Who was it?'

'It was Tony Kent, last week when I had lunch with him. He mentioned that he'd come from there – talked about the High Church tradition he'd grown up with.'

'Well, well.' Daphne sat down. 'So Tony comes from Croydon.'

'I've been thinking about this all the way back. Tony is about the same age that Peter would have been . . . if he'd lived. They might have known each other.'

'Tony Kent.' Daphne considered the possibilities.

'Wait a minute,' David said slowly. 'Tony. What is his proper name, do you know? Is it Anthony?'

'It could be, I suppose. You just never know with nicknames. I've never heard him called anything but Tony, but it probably is Anthony. Why?'

He rubbed his forehead. 'Did I tell you? I asked Gabriel if he knew the names of any of Peter's friends. He couldn't remember much, but he did mention that Peter had a friend called Anthony.'

Daphne looked at him for a long moment. 'You might be on to something, my boy. You just might be on to something.'

Later, they discussed the morning's inquest. 'I just can't believe they still think it's suicide,' David groaned, shaking his head. 'After what I told them about the ledger sheet.'

'The ledger sheet,' said Daphne. 'Let's think about the ledger sheet. Why would anyone take it?'

'To hide something?'

'To hide what? Something about the figures on the sheet.'

'Like . . . that they didn't tally with the money on the table!' David exclaimed, with dawning comprehension.

'Exactly!' Daphne agreed.

'And they wouldn't have!' he added, his excitement increasing. 'I just remembered – Mavis told me when I saw her that they'd already raised over two thousand pounds! I'd forgotten completely that she'd said that!'

'And how much was there when the body was found?'

'I think Gabriel said it was around eighteen hundred pounds.'

'So someone took some of the money – not enough that it would be obvious as robbery, and took the sheet so that no one would know any money was missing.'

'And they wouldn't have known that she'd told me about the two thousand pounds . . .'

Daphne nodded. 'It fits perfectly. The murderer goes in the sacristy, kills Mavis, takes some of the money and the ledger sheet, and makes it all look like suicide. If they'd taken all the money, it would have been obvious that it was murder.'

'Then who?' asked David.

'Who, indeed? That's the question.'

'Someone she would have let in the sacristy, someone who could have got behind her unawares . . .'

'Someone who needed money. Maybe not a lot of money, but . . .'

'Craig,' stated David. 'We ruled him out as a possible murderer before, but that's when we thought the motive was blackmail. But if the motive was money, theft . . .'

'But would he kill his own mother for a couple of hundred quid?' Daphne asked.

'From what I've seen of that young man, I wouldn't find it a bit hard to believe. He probably would have killed her for tuppence. She had to have been a frightful parent – there must have been a lot of bottled-up hostility on his part.'

'We're forgetting something,' Daphne put in reluctantly.

'Craig wasn't at St Anne's on Saturday. He said he wasn't, and no one saw him there.'

David sat very still for a moment, searching for an elusive memory. 'Oh, yes they did,' he said slowly. 'Beryl Ball saw him.'

'How do you know?'

'She said so, a few days later. Before the organ recital. It was one of her usual stories – I wasn't paying much attention. You know, about every man in London being after her body. She said that Craig had wanted her. *On Saturday*, she said. 'On Saturday.'

'Maybe it was earlier in the day. Or later.'

He thought a bit longer. 'No. It was then, all right. When I left the sacristy and went through to the organ recital, I met Beryl Ball in the corridor.'

'And the little outside door was unlocked.'

'Yes. Craig could have – must have – come in right after I left.'

They stared at each other. 'Good Lord,' said David at last. '*Good Lord.*'

Chapter 42

Daphne had gone to the church early, to make sure that all was in order for the funeral, so David walked to St Anne's alone. He looked automatically at the vicarage as he passed; Emily was just coming out of the front door, so he stopped and waited for her self-consciously. He'd heard from Daphne that she was back, but had not yet plucked up the courage to seek her out; he told himself he'd been too busy.

She smiled at him without reservation. 'Good morning, David.'

'I'm glad you're still speaking to me.'

'Of course I am.'

He plunged in immediately. 'Emily, I want to apologise for betraying your confidence and telling Gabriel where to find you. It was very wrong of me, but my only excuse is that I thought I was doing the right thing. I should have contacted you first, and asked your permission to tell him.'

She put her hand on his arm. 'It's all right, David. I was a little upset at first, but it all turned out for the best.'

347

'He was so devastated. I thought – well, I felt that if you saw him like that, you'd know how much he cared.'

Emily turned grateful eyes on him. 'That was very . . . unselfish of you, considering how you feel.'

'He does love you very much, you know,' said David impulsively. 'I knew it that day.'

She smiled. 'Yes. We're not out of the woods yet, Gabriel and I, but things are better between us now than they've ever been. For the first time in our relationship, he's been totally honest with me.'

'I'm glad, Emily. I mean that. You deserve all the happiness . . .'

'Thank you, David. I know what it must cost you to say that.'

They walked towards the church together. 'You're going to the funeral?' he asked after a moment.

'Yes. I thought I really should go.'

'The children?' he inquired.

'We fetched them yesterday morning, first thing. Oh, it was good to see them again! For us all to be together again, as a family!'

'Where are they now?'

'They're too young for an ordeal like this. I've taken them to Lucy's for an hour or so.' She looked at his profile closely as she said the name. He kept his face impassive. How much had Lucy told her of what had passed between them? Very little, if he knew Lucy – she was always disinclined to talk about herself. He didn't want to think about Lucy now.

Venerable Bead was at the back of the church, solemnly passing out hymn books and prayer books. He regarded this particular funeral as his personal property, by virtue of his role in finding the body; ordinarily, he would have been among the first to condemn Gabriel's decision to allow a church funeral for an apparent suicide, but he wouldn't have missed this for the world. Cyril Fitzjames, as the surviving churchwarden, assisted him; he would have contrived to give a set of books to Emily, and possibly have a word with her, but Venerable Bead was too quick for him.

Emily and David sat together near the back; it was early yet and the church was just beginning to fill up. At the front of the nave, in front of the rood screen, was a bier, ready to receive the coffin. 'So they didn't bring her in last night?' David whispered.

'No. Craig didn't want it, and Gabriel wasn't very keen either, under the circumstances.'

They watched the other mourners arrive. Teresa Dawson led her parents as far towards the front as she dared. Cecily Framlingham, in a black pill-box hat, seemed genuinely grieved, leaning on Arthur's arm. Miles Taylor began playing soothing chords on the organ and Mary Hughes nodded approvingly as she entered and found a seat. Not surprisingly, Tony Kent was nowhere to be seen. Just before the appointed hour, Lady Constance, holding herself very erect and looking straight ahead, walked slowly down the centre aisle and sat near the front; David thought that she appeared very frail indeed. Then Craig slouched in, looking thoroughly bored. The people with him, leading him to the front row, were apparently aunts and uncles, siblings of Mavis. And at the very last minute, Beryl Ball hobbled down the aisle, sheathed in rusty black from head to toe. She smiled and nodded to the assembled congregation, and took a seat in the front row, on the opposite side from the family.

There was a hush, then Gabriel's resonant voice sounded from the back of the church. 'I am the resurrection and the life, saith the Lord: he that believeth in me, though he were dead, yet shall he live: and whosoever liveth and believeth in me shall never die.' He swept solemnly up the aisle, majestic in a cope of rich black brocade, followed by the sombre men with the coffin on their shoulders. 'I know that my Redeemer liveth, and that he shall stand at the latter day upon the earth . . .' They rested the coffin on the bier and Gabriel turned to face the congregation. 'We brought nothing into this world, and it is certain we can carry nothing out . . .'

He read the psalm.

> 'I said, I will take heed to my ways: that I offend not in my tongue.
> I will keep my mouth as it were with a bridle: while the ungodly is in my sight.
> I held my tongue, and spake nothing: I kept silence, yea, even from good words; but it was pain and grief to me.'

David and Emily exchanged a look; nothing could have been less applicable to the dead woman.

'For man walketh in a vain shadow . . .'

After the service, Craig was nowhere to be seen among the family, gathered in the north porch to greet the mourners. David caught a glimpse of him lurking around the corner outside the church, smoking a furtive cigarette; on impulse he made a hurried excuse to Emily and strolled up to him.

'Hello, Craig,' he greeted him. 'May I offer my condolences on this very sad occasion?' The words were perfectly straightforward, but his voice held a hint of irony as he observed the sullen young man.

Craig eyed him suspiciously. 'Who are you? I've seen you before, haven't I?'

'I was at the inquest yesterday. I saw your mother a few minutes before her . . . death. My name is Middleton-Brown.'

'Oh, yeah.' Craig took a drag of his cigarette and observed David through the smoke as he exhaled.

David's expression never altered. 'Why didn't you tell the coroner that you were in the church that afternoon? In the sacristy, in fact?'

Craig went white, and choked on the cigarette smoke; David waited patiently while he prolonged his coughing to cover his agitation. 'I wasn't,' he said finally, belligerently.

David decided to bluff a little. 'I saw you,' he said calmly. 'You came in that side door, and you went into the sacristy. The door wasn't locked – I'd just left there myself. I saw you. So did Beryl Ball. You know she did – you saw her, too.'

'You mean that crazy old bag in the funny hat?' Craig said without thinking.

David smiled and Craig blanched. 'That's right, Craig. You saw her, all right. Why did you kill your mother? Was it just for the money? I know that you took the money. And you took the ledger sheet, because you thought that without it no one would know that any money was missing.'

Craig no longer looked defiant. His hand, as he raised

the cigarette to his lips, was trembling. 'I didn't kill her,' he said at last. 'Yes, I was there.' He hesitated. 'I don't know how you know so much, man, but I was there. And I – I took the money. And the piece of paper. But I didn't kill her – you have to believe me!' His voice had become a high-pitched whine. 'She was a miserable old cow, but I didn't kill her! She was still alive when I left that room! She locked the door behind me, and then she . . . she hung herself. I know she did! I didn't kill my mother! Please don't go to the cops, man! They'll think I did it! That's why I couldn't tell them I'd been there. Please, man! I'll give the money back, if that's what you're after, only please don't tell the cops!'

David went to the sacristy then, and found Daphne putting away the funeral cope. 'How did you manage to keep Venerable Bead from doing it for you?' he asked.

'With great difficulty,' she chuckled. 'But I think he's followed them to the crematorium.'

David told her, as succinctly as possible, about his confrontation with Craig.

'What are you going to do?' she asked.

'I really don't know. The police will have to be told eventually, of course, whether he gives the money back or not. But I'm not sure I believe him – I still think there's a good chance that the little sneak killed her.'

'Then why would he admit he'd been here?'

'He had to. He thinks I saw him, and he knows that Beryl Ball did. But of course he wouldn't admit killing her, even if he'd done it.'

'You'll have to go to the police.'

'Yes, but not today. We've only got another day to get

this blackmail problem solved. Then it will be time enough to deal with Craig Conwell.'

It was late that evening when the phone rang. Daphne answered it. 'David, for you. Graham Crawford.'

He took the receiver. 'Hello, Graham.'

'Hello, David old chap. Sorry to be so late ringing – I had to take Denise out to dinner. Quid pro quo, you know. You owe me.'

'I'm sure you'll get your own reward, if you haven't had it already.'

Graham laughed. 'Fair enough. But she came through with the inquest transcript that you wanted. Even made me a photocopy, the angel. I've put it in the post to you already. First class. No expense spared for you, old boy.'

'You're wonderful, Graham. I knew you could do it.'

'Can you at least tell me what it's all about?' he asked plaintively.

'Sorry, Graham. Too secret.'

'Oh, well.' Graham was philosophical. 'I'm sure it's all in a good cause.'

'Can you tell me the answer to the specific question? Maitland's room-mate testified that there was no suicide note?'

'Yes, that's right.'

'And the room-mate was named in the transcript.'

'Yes, of course. The room-mate's name was . . . just a second, I've got it written down here somewhere. The room-mate's name was Dominic Dawson.'

'I got the idea yesterday that the transcript of the Maitland inquest would tell us his room-mate's name. I thought that might shed some light, give us a lead. But I don't understand. Dominic Dawson,' said David slowly, trying to make sense of it. 'Peter Maitland's room-mate was Dominic . . . Dawson.'

'Do you mean Julia and Roger's son Dominic?' Daphne asked, puzzled.

'They have a son Dominic? I know Francis, of course, but I thought the others were Nicholas and Benedict. Nick . . .'

'Oh, Nick's not Nicholas, he's Dominic.'

David stared at her. 'Dominic. I just assumed that Nick was short for Nicholas.'

'As I said last night, you never know about nicknames, do you?'

'But . . . Nick! Daphne, I've been so stupid! Of course it had to be Dominic!'

'You should have known,' she agreed bluntly. 'Dominic, Benedict, Bridget, Clare, Francis, Teresa.'

'They're not just saints' names, are they?' He shook his head at his own failure. 'They're all founders of religious orders. Only the Dawsons could name their children like that . . . Even the bloody dog, Daphne! Ignatius! But I should have known! Nicholas just doesn't fit with the rest.'

'But how did you know the Dominic part of his room-mate's name?'

'Gabriel told me. He said that Peter's room-mate was named Dominic.' He rubbed his forehead. 'Nick Dawson went to university in Brighton, to the University of Sussex, like Francis. I knew that – Roger told me.'

'Nick's about the right age, isn't he?'

'Tony Kent said that Nick was around his age. We've already decided that Tony was about the same age as Peter.'

David went for the whisky bottle. 'This really does explain everything, Daphne.' Suddenly a picture flashed across his brain, a clear image of a good-looking young man with dark eyes, and he stopped in his tracks. 'My God, Daphne, I've seen his photo!'

'What?'

'Peter Maitland's photo! That interminable evening at the Dawsons! I saw his photo. It was one among hundreds – it seemed more like thousands. Nick and his room-mate, they said. And Teresa said . . . he's dead. They were all dead, Daphne. How was I to know?'

She shook her head. 'The question is, now that you know, what are you going to do about it?'

'Tell Gabriel, of course. First thing in the morning. Then he can deal with it. I don't know what he ever intended to do, if and when I found the blackmailer – go and talk to them, I suppose. Try to convince them not to go ahead with their threats. Well, it will be up to him now.'

'Which Dawson do you suppose it is?' Daphne asked. 'Roger?'

'Probably. I don't think Julia would have the nerve. And I doubt that Francis would have the brains.'

'Why now, do you suppose? After all these years?'

He shook his head. 'Maybe the Norman Newsome affair triggered it off. Or maybe the possibility of his promotion to Archdeacon. Or maybe they hadn't put everything together before now, and Francis found something out in Brighton . . .'

'Well, congratulations, David. You may have waited until the eleventh hour, but Gabriel's confidence in your abilities was well placed.'

'With a lot of help from you,' he added with satisfaction. 'But I must admit, I am pleased. I've been down a few blind alleys, but this is finally one that takes us somewhere.'

Chapter 43

*For thou, O God, hast proved us: thou also hast
tried us, like as silver is tried.*

Psalm 66.9

'I should have cleaned the silver yesterday,' Daphne admitted
over toast and tea on Wednesday morning. 'But with the
funeral, and all the excitement – I'm afraid I just didn't
get round to it. I'd better get an early start on it this
morning.'

'Would you like a hand?' David offered. 'I have a few
hours free before my lunch with Lady Constance.'

She smiled her gratitude. 'I usually don't let anyone
else touch the silver . . . but in your case, I'm prepared to
make an exception.'

'I'm honoured.' He raised his eyebrows ironically.

'You haven't really seen the silver, have you? We have
some rather nice pieces.'

'I'll look forward to seeing it. With everything else
going on, it hasn't exactly been on the top of my list, but
now that things are falling into place . . . well, I shall
enjoy looking at some silver,' he said with real
anticipation.

'And cleaning it, don't forget.'

'And cleaning it,' David grimaced. 'But on the way, I'd better stop at the vicarage and have a word with Gabriel.'

'Oh, David, I'm sorry, but you've missed him,' Emily said with a frown. 'He's gone to Brighton, of all places.'

'Brighton? Whatever for?'

'To preach at the noon Assumption Day Mass at St Dunstan's.'

'St Dunstan's?' David repeated stupidly. 'He never told me he was going to St Dunstan's.'

'No, he didn't know it himself until yesterday,' Emily explained. 'They had a last-minute problem, and thought of their old curate as a final resort. The churchwarden rang yesterday afternoon.'

'But what happened?'

She laughed. 'Apparently a certain Area Bishop of the London diocese – I need mention no names – was scheduled to do it, but he discovered at the last minute that he was double-booked. He couldn't be at Walsingham and in Brighton at the same time, so poor old St Dunstan's drew the short straw, and got Gabriel instead.'

'I dare say they've got the best of it,' David responded. 'Gabriel's a much better preacher than the Bishop of . . .'

'But Gabriel doesn't have a mitre, and that's what they all come to see. Or am I being cynical?'

'Give him time,' smiled David. 'Your husband will wear a mitre one day. But when is he coming back? I need to see him.'

Emily looked at him searchingly. 'You have good news for him, don't you? Oh, David! I knew you could do it! He'll be so relieved! He was in such a state this morning –

it was all I could do to get him to go, in the end, with this thing hanging over his head.'

'When will he be back?' he repeated.

'Probably not much before the Mass here – it's at half past six. He's gone in the car, and you never know what the traffic will be like. But as soon as he comes in, I'll tell him to ring you.'

'If he doesn't catch me, tell him I'll see him before the service. Or after.'

'You can't tell me who it is, can you?' she asked curiously. 'No . . . I don't really want to know. Not yet.'

At that moment they were interrupted by a small body hurling itself at Emily's legs. 'Mummy! Viola's taken my teddy – again! Can't you make her stop?'

'Sebastian, darling. We'll deal with that in a moment. But now, won't you say hello to your Uncle David?'

The boy looked up at him with frank curiosity. Looked at him with Gabriel's dark-lashed blue eyes: it was a most extraordinary sensation for David, who had not really been prepared for it. 'How do you do, Uncle David,' said the little boy solemnly, extending his hand. Sebastian clearly had also inherited his father's self-assurance.

David took his hand, recovering himself quickly. 'It's very nice to meet you at last, Sebastian.' Instinctively he bent down on a level with the boy. 'May I meet your sister, too?'

Sebastian looked scornful. 'Oh, you wouldn't want to meet her. She's just a *girl*.'

'Girls do have their uses, Sebastian,' Emily said fondly, her hand on his tousled dark head.

Daphne opened the safe with her own key; David waited

in anticipation as the items of silver came out on to the table, one by one. 'It's a shame we can't leave the candlesticks on the altar all the time,' Daphne commented. 'But that would be asking for trouble. So many London churches have lost their best pieces that way.'

'How sad. Country churches, too, from what I hear. They have to be so careful these days. So many churches are locked all the time now.' He leaned back in the chair. 'Remember the good old days, Daphne? When we used to travel the countryside, and never find a locked church in a whole week?'

She nodded briskly, not looking at him. 'We saw some lovely churches.'

He caught her hand impulsively. 'Daphne, what do you say? Let's do it again! That trip to the West Country that we never took – do you fancy giving it another go?'

She stopped. 'Well, I don't know. At my age . . .'

'Your age! You're only twenty years older than I am – you're in the prime of your life!'

Only twenty years, she thought. 'I suppose I could get away from this place for a few days.'

'Of course you could. Venerable Bead would be more than happy to fill in for you, I'm sure. Oh, let's, Daphne.'

'I never could say no to you, David. Almost never, anyway.' At last she smiled at him. 'Yes, I'd like that.'

'Great. We'll set a date before I leave.'

She put her head in the safe before she asked, 'And when are you leaving?'

'Maybe tomorrow. I'll have a word with the police about Craig, then . . . well, there's nothing to keep me here after that. I've taken advantage of your hospitality long enough.'

'You know I've enjoyed having you,' she said, her head still hidden in the safe.

Most of the silver had been inspected, appreciated, and cleaned. 'I've saved the best for last,' Daphne confessed. 'The festival thurible, only used for high days and holy days. The other one we use every Sunday, but this one is special.' She brought it out with pride. It was an extremely handsome piece, hand-fashioned of solid silver and very heavy.

David's eyes lit up. 'I say. That is splendid. Where did it come from?'

'Lady Constance, of course. She gave it a couple of years ago, in her brother's memory. I think it might have been his: he was a priest, you know, and undoubtedly a man of taste.'

'Of course.' He screwed one eye up and examined the hallmark with the other. 'Definitely a man of taste. Just like his sister.' He started. 'What time is it, anyway? I don't want to be late for lunch with Lady Constance.'

Daphne consulted her watch. 'You've got plenty of time. But go ahead if you want to – this is the last thing I've got to do.'

'Wait a minute.' He lifted the pierced lid of the thurible. 'When's the last time this was used? There seems to be something inside.'

'It shouldn't be incense, or charcoal. I certainly cleaned it out after the Patronal Festival, and it hasn't been used since. What is it?' Daphne's bent head joined his over the thurible.

With two fingers he extracted a charred piece of folded

paper. 'It looks like someone was trying to burn something in it.'

Daphne was indignant. 'Well, it certainly wasn't me! Of all things!'

He looked at the paper with a furrowed brow. 'What . . .' It was charred around the edges, but relatively undamaged; he unfolded it carefully.

It was a letter, typed on ordinary paper. David looked at it with a sinking feeling of recognition.

> I have good reason to believe that you have been taking money from St Anne's. You have abused your office of churchwarden in a most shameful manner, and I will not stand by and allow that to happen. You must resign your office, and repay the money you have taken, before the Feast of the Assumption, or I will inform the Bishop.

Daphne took it from him. 'David! I don't believe it!'

'It's true, all right,' he said softly, shaking his head. 'I was right that her death had something to do with the blackmail. But Mavis wasn't the blackmailer – she was one of his victims! She must have tried to destroy the letter that day, the day she . . . died.'

'She must have put it in the thurible and lit it, then shut it in the safe, not realising that it would soon go out without oxygen. And then . . .'

'And then, Daphne . . . she killed herself.' He sat immobile for a very long moment, staring at the paper; when he spoke again, his voice was very quiet, very measured. 'Oh, Daphne, I've been so frightfully stupid about this whole business. I've been wrong about everything, all along

the way. I've looked at it all the wrong way up. But now
. . . now I understand everything. Or nearly everything . . .'

Chapter 44

There be some that put their trust in their goods:
and boast themselves in the multitude of their
riches.
But no man may deliver his brother: nor make
agreement unto God for him;
For it cost more to redeem their souls: so that he
must let that alone for ever;
Yea, though he live long: and see not the grave.
                                        Psalm 49.6–9

He had stopped along the way and bought several bunches of freesias. Lady Constance opened the door herself, looking a bit stronger than she had on Tuesday. 'You remembered that I liked freesias. How very kind of you, Mr Middleton-Brown.'

'How are you feeling today, Lady Constance? Better than last week, I hope?'

'Yes, thank you. The lovely weather . . . well, it does make one feel better. And I do find your visits a tonic, young man. I hope you'll be staying in London for a long time.'

'I'm afraid not, Lady Constance,' he said regretfully. 'I'll be returning home to Wymondham tomorrow. I've

been here nearly three weeks already – that's a long time
to impose on Daphne's hospitality, and I've accomplished
what I came to do . . . with the chapel.'

She looked genuinely distressed. 'You must come for
regular visits, then,' she said. 'You will always be welcome to stay in this house. I'm sure you would be more
comfortable here than at Miss Elford's.'

'Thank you, that's most kind.'

They had lunch in the garden. Lady Constance's garden
was surprisingly large, and received the afternoon sun.
They sat in the shade of a tree, as it was a very warm
afternoon. Lunch was a smoked chicken salad, with a chilled
bottle of white wine – a very good wine. 'In your honour,
young man,' she pointed out. 'On the very sad occasion of
your last day in London.'

If I didn't know better, I'd almost think she was flirting
with me, David thought as she raised her glass to him. He
looked at her, almost as if for the first time. She must have
been quite a stunner when she was young, he reflected; he
tried to imagine her, with the silver hair dark, and the
beautifully modelled features unlined. The beringed hand
in which she held the glass was purple-veined now; once it
must have been smooth and white. Like Lucy's, he thought
with a quickly suppressed twinge.

'How is the work progressing on the chapel?' she asked
him. 'You're satisfied enough to leave it?'

'Oh, yes. The workmen are excellent, they don't need
any help from me. I watched them start the gilding yesterday. They're doing a superb job.'

'I can't thank you enough for your part in it,' she said
warmly. 'I've wanted to have it done for several years

now, but no one had the expertise to supervise it. It's a memorial gift for my brother,' she added. 'I shall want to have a plaque put up to say that the restoration was done in his memory. I would have liked to have had it finished by now – he died two years ago today.'

'I saw the silver thurible you gave in his memory. It's an exquisite piece of work.'

She smiled. 'Lovely, isn't it? I'm glad you've seen it. Edward bought that himself, quite a few years ago. I thought it right that St Anne's should have it, and use it.'

Apparently Lady Constance did not find it too painful to talk about her dead brother, so David encouraged her. 'He was a priest, I understand?'

'Yes, he was – an excellent priest. One of the old school, brought up when things were done properly, and nothing less was tolerated.'

'I'm surprised that he didn't have the living at St Anne's; I would have thought that you would have wanted him here,' David probed.

'Nothing would have pleased me more,' she admitted. 'I tried so many times to persuade him to take the living here. How I wish he had . . . Over the years, he sent us a few of his protégés' – she gave the word its proper French pronunciation – 'but of course that wasn't the same as having dear Edward here.'

'Why didn't he want to come?'

She smiled in fond remembrance. 'He was a keen boats-man, and didn't want to leave the sea. I don't think he ever lived more than five miles away from the sea in his life.' Her eyes followed the progress of a bird from tree to tree at the end of the garden, but her mind seemed else-where for a time, until she began speaking again. 'Edward was everything a priest should be: loving, compassionate . . . and holy. My brother was a very holy man. If he had any fault, it was that he was rather too inclined to think the best of people, even in the face of evidence to the contrary.'

'Surely that's what priests are supposed to do?'

She sighed and shook her head. 'This is the real world, young man. People aren't always what you would wish them to be. A priest, of all people, ought to understand that fact.'

It was a perfect afternoon in high summer. They sat for a long time over their lunch, enjoying the warmth of the sun. A few butterflies fluttered desultorily over the multicoloured flowers of the garden, but otherwise it was very still, with barely a breeze to stir the leaves of the trees. The heavy scent of the roses blended with the smell of freshly cut grass to make a powerful perfume. The maid brought them raspberry mousse in stemmed crystal dishes, but afterwards Lady Constance waved away the coffee. 'Too hot for coffee today, Molly. Bring us some mineral water instead. With lemon, please. Unless you'd like more wine?' she addressed David. 'But I think we've had rather too much wine already.' The sunlight through the tree dappled her pale mauve dress with gently moving shapes, and gave her skin an even whiter cast than usual. She stretched out a hand toward David. 'I do hope you don't feel that you have to run off immediately, young man. I'd like you to stay for a while.'

'Of course I'll stay,' he reassured her. 'I just don't want to tire you. Perhaps you ought to have a rest before the service this evening.'

'Ah, yes. The Feast of the Assumption of Our Lady.'

'I'm looking forward to it,' he said. 'I haven't seen a proper festival service in St Anne's. I'm sure they do it very well.'

'Yes, Father Neville makes sure of that.' A small smile curved her lips as she looked beyond David at the garden. 'Proper appearances mean a lot to our Father Neville.'

'He certainly did the funeral beautifully yesterday,' David said deliberately.

Lady Constance sat up even straighter, and turned her gaze from the butterflies. She looked penetratingly at David. 'Last week when you were here, you told me that you thought Mrs Conwell had been murdered. You said that you were doing some investigations on your own. Can you tell me what you've found?'

He held her gaze steadily. 'I was wrong,' he said, firmly but gently. 'I realise now that she killed herself. In many ways it was more . . . comfortable to believe that someone else had done it. Suicide is such a terrible act – it's difficult to think of someone being that desperate. And sometimes it's even more difficult to comprehend the . . . forces that would lead someone to make that choice. But I've come to understand that Mrs Conwell was under more pressure than anyone knew.'

She looked away, finally. 'I see,' she said softly. Somewhere a bird burst into full-throated song. Neither one moved for a very long time; at last Lady Constance stirred. 'Perhaps it would be best for you to go now, young man. I am rather tired, and I have a letter that I must write this afternoon.'

David stood. He bent over her, taking her hand in both of his. 'I'll see you at Mass this evening, Lady Constance, but I'll take my proper leave of you now. Thank you so much for this lovely afternoon, and for the many kindnesses of the last few weeks. It has been a real privilege to know you, and I shall always remember with pleasure the time we've spent together.' His words were formal, but there was real warmth behind them.

She looked up at him; her eyes met his in a searching look. 'It is I who must thank you, Mr Middleton-Brown. Your kindness to an old woman has been . . . more than I deserve. I'm very grateful for that.'

He raised her hand to his lips in silent tribute, then turned away. She watched his back until she could see him no longer.

Chapter 45

As soon as they hear of me, they shall obey me: but
the strange children shall dissemble with me.
The strange children shall fail: and be afraid out of
their prisons.

Psalm 18.45–46

Craig Conwell didn't have a job, as far as David knew, so
there was a chance of finding him at home in the afternoon.
With a little thought, he was able to remember how to find
the Conwell house.

He rang the bell. After a rather long delay, just as
David was about to give up, Craig opened the door to him.
The young man was looking rather unwell; his skin had an
unhealthy pallor, and this intensified when he saw David.
The hand clutching a can of lager trembled. 'Go away and
leave me alone,' he muttered, swinging the door shut.

David put a foot in the door. 'Good afternoon, Craig,'
he said smoothly as he forced the door back open. 'Mind
if I come in? I won't take up much of your valuable time,
but I have something important to say to you. I think it's
something you'll want to hear.'

'Suit yourself.' Craig shrugged, giving up. He turned
and slouched into the room on the right of the entrance

hall, without looking to see whether David was following. When David entered the room behind him, he was already slumped in a chair, swigging lager from the can.

David looked at the room in amazement. Mavis had been a house-proud woman, just like his own mother. But ten days after her death, she probably wouldn't have recognised her own sitting room: it bore no resemblance at all to that tidy room he had seen on his visit with Daphne. There was an indefinably musty feeling about the room, as though it hadn't received any fresh air in ten days. In spite of the warmth of the day, the windows were shut and the curtains were drawn; it felt oppressively hot. And strewn about the room were bits of dirty crockery, some containing half-eaten food; David looked with disgust at the dried, curling remnant of a cheese sandwich and the attendant flies. Everywhere there were empty beer cans, and ashtrays overflowing with cigarette butts. The television was on; already Craig's eyes were fixed on the antics of cartoon animals.

David crossed the room and switched off the television. Craig scowled, but couldn't be bothered to argue. Removing what looked like a collection of dirty clothing from one of the chairs, David sat down opposite Craig and leaned forward. 'Craig, I want you to listen to me. I know now that your mother wasn't murdered.'

Craig shot him a triumphantly venomous look. 'I told you so.'

'Yes, and you were right. She killed herself.'

Craig lit a cigarette and took a long draw. 'So, tell me something I don't know.'

'What I want to know, Craig, is *why* she killed herself.'

'How the hell do I know? She was taking money from

the church, wasn't she? I guess she had a guilty conscience.' He spoke the last two words with a sneer of distaste, as if it were a particularly nasty social disease.

David drew back and looked at him. 'She took that money for you, didn't she?'

'So what? A guy needs money to live. Since Dad died, there just hasn't been that much dough around. And she was too busy being Mrs Bloody Churchwarden and poking her nose into other people's business to go out and get herself a job.'

'And you couldn't get a job? You're an able-bodied young man,' David said with ill-concealed contempt.

Craig shrugged nonchalantly. 'I tried it for a while, but I just couldn't stick it. They wanted me there every day at nine o'clock, for God's sake. I couldn't be bothered. Anyway, it was up to the old bag to support me – I didn't ask to be born, did I?' He puffed on his cigarette and blew a cloud of smoke at David.

David shook his head in despair at the young man's callous selfishness. 'What are you going to do now? Now that she's dead, and can't support you any longer?'

'Maybe there's some insurance, I don't know.' He lifted his shoulders. 'If not, I'll just sell the house. I can live for a long time on the price it'll fetch. Get myself a bed-sit somewhere. I'll manage.'

'No one's going to buy the house looking like this,' David couldn't help remarking, as he glanced around at the filthy squalor. Craig merely shrugged. 'Maybe one of your girlfriends would like to come in and clean it up,' David added maliciously.

'Yeah, maybe,' Craig nodded thoughtfully, flicking some ash on to the carpet.

Leaning forward again, David said abruptly, 'But what I want to know, Craig, is why your mother *really* killed herself.'

'I told you. It was because of the money.'

'It couldn't have been just the money. Not even the money you took that day. I'm surprised that she let you have it, by the way. How did you talk her into it?'

Craig smirked. 'I didn't talk her into it, I just took it. When she wasn't looking. I figured a rich church like that would never miss a couple of hundred quid.'

'Why *did* you go there that day?'

'To get some money. I knew she was counting the dough and figured I could talk her out of a fiver. I never figured there'd be so much cash! She got all self-righteous with me, and said I couldn't have any of it. So as soon as her back was turned, I just helped myself to a bit of it. She never knew.'

'Until you were gone, and she missed the ledger sheet.'

'No, I didn't take it then.'

David stared at him. 'When did you take it?'

'Later. A few minutes later. I got to thinking about it, and figured I'd better take that piece of paper, or somebody would twig. So I went back.' He paused. 'I went in. She was . . . dead. Hanging there. So I took the paper and got the hell out of there. I took her handbag, too, just in case there was any money in it.'

'But you said she'd locked the door behind you when you left!'

Craig looked defiant. 'She did. I . . . had a key cut. I took all her church keys out of her handbag once, and had copies cut; you never know when something like that might come in useful. And it did. I locked the door behind me when I left.'

'What have you done with the keys?'

'I threw them in someone's rubbish bin, along with the handbag – there was no money in it, anyway,' he added in disgust.

David suddenly remembered the brown vinyl handbag, sitting on the desk in the sacristy during his visit there. And that evening it had been gone. He berated himself for being so unobservant.

He turned his attention back to Craig, who was lighting another cigarette. 'Craig,' he said firmly. 'There's something you're not telling me. What in God's name did you say to your mother when you were there? What did you say that would make her kill herself, in those few minutes before you came back? If she didn't even know you'd taken that money . . .'

Craig didn't respond right away, and when he did speak he didn't answer the question directly, but said in a self-pitying whine, 'You just don't know, man. You don't know what it was like, living with her.' He tilted the beer can back and poured the last few drops down his throat, then tossed the empty can on the table with its fellows. 'You don't know what it's like having a self-righteous old bitch like that trying to run your life.'

David looked at him with loathing, but there was a kind of pity there too. 'That's where you're wrong, mate,' he said in a soft, steely voice. 'I know exactly what it's like. I've been there, too. Now tell me the truth, or I'll have the cops here so fast . . .'

Craig jerked into an upright position. 'Not the cops!'

'Then tell me.'

Slumping back down, Craig turned his head away under David's relentless stare. Unwillingly, he began. 'It was the bloody phone bill. She was at me in the morning about it. Then that afternoon she started in on me all over again.' He picked up a beer can and absently crushed it in his fist.

'What about the phone bill?'

'It was too high, she said. She couldn't afford to pay it. She wanted to know who I'd been phoning. Girlfriends, she said.' He laughed mirthlessly. 'She thought she knew everything, the old cow. She said I'd been ringing girlfriends. That's what she wanted to believe.'

David held his breath; he had a premonition what was coming.

'I was really pissed off with her then. I thought, what the hell. She thought she knew everything!' His voice shook; he pulled the tab on another can of beer and took a deep swallow. 'I told her it wasn't a girlfriend I'd been calling – it was a boyfriend. I told her all the details. I enjoyed that, enjoyed seeing her cover her ears with her hands, say that it wasn't true, that I was just making it up to get at her. She cried a lot. In the end she believed it.' He paused and smirked, the smoke wreathing his head. 'I knew that she was upset, but I didn't think the stupid cow would go and kill herself! I was surprised when I went back in and saw her hanging there. But I guess that was the one thing my mother couldn't live with – the idea that her son was a bloody queer.'

David stared at him; suddenly, improbably, he was filled with empathy for this troubled young man. What would his own mother have done? 'Craig . . .' he began, not sure what to say.

Sneering, Craig laughed at him. 'You believed me! So

did she, the gullible old cow! And killed herself over a lie!' There was no mirth in his laughter. 'Me, a queer? Give me a break, man! Not in a million years!'

Chapter 46

*Thou hast turned my heaviness into joy: thou hast
    put off my sackcloth, and girded me with glad-
    ness.
Therefore shall every good man sing of thy praise
    without ceasing: O my God, I will give thanks
    unto thee for ever.*

Psalm 30.12–13

Kissing the cross on his stole, and putting it around his
neck, Gabriel automatically said the set prayer to himself.
But the prayer in his heart was wordless: a prayer of
thanksgiving for his deliverance. His vesting for the Mass
was nearly done; he turned with a radiant smile to take the
cloth-of-gold chasuble from the hovering Venerable Bead.

He'd only had time, after his hurried return from Brighton,
for a brief word with David, but that had been enough. He
was free. David had done it somehow. Gabriel knew none
of the details, not even the name of his blackmailer. But
he had David's assurance that the threats would not be
carried out. He wasn't even going to need to confront
anyone. It was all over. David would come and see him
tomorrow, and tell him the whole story. But for now, that
was enough – it was all over.

* * *

The sun was still high in the sky; its light streamed through the west window as the sounds of the Palestrina introit soared to the roof: '*Assumpta est Maria in caelum*'.

In his stall, Gabriel closed his eyes and absorbed the beauty of the music. It would be a long service: the Palestrina 'Missa Assumpta est Maria' was nearly thirty minutes long, apart from anything else. They were very fortunate to have a choir capable of performing a Mass like that, Gabriel reflected. He opened his eyes and observed Miles Taylor, conducting the choir with characteristic enthusiasm, his long arms flailing away. What a very peculiar man, always moaning about something and wittering on about contemporary music. But one could put up with a great deal of personal eccentricity for the sake of music like this.

After the Kyrie, during the Gloria, Gabriel took the thurible from Johnnie – or was it Chris? – and censed the altar reverently. The puffs of fragrant smoke rose to join the music, high above their heads. Then came the first lesson – read by the curate he'd borrowed for the occasion from a neighbouring parish – followed by the psalm.

> Thou hast loved righteousness, and hated iniquity:
> wherefore God, even thy God, hath anointed thee
> with the oil of gladness above thy fellows.
> All thy garments smell of myrrh, aloes, and cassia:
> out of the ivory palaces, whereby they have made
> thee glad.

The servers moved out of the chancel: Johnnie, swinging the thurible, with Sebastian once again beside him with the incense boat, Chris with the processional cross, flanked by two acolytes, and Tony, bearing the large book. Gabriel came forward to intone the Gospel, and for the first time he was able to see the congregation. It was a respectable crowd. Most of the regulars were there, he ascertained with a quick glance. And, inevitably on these festal occasions, the numbers were swelled by a few out-of-town punters, drawn to St Anne's by the music, or the ceremonial, or something else indefinable.

Gabriel was not aware, even as he was delivering it, that tonight's sermon was anything out of the ordinary. He'd given it once already that day – how fortunate for St Dunstan's that he'd had one prepared – so the delivery was practised and the words flowed smoothly. But it was his overwhelming sensation of joy and relief that infused it with special power, and made it a sermon that the parishioners of St Anne's would later talk about as one of the finest they'd ever heard. Even the Dawsons admitted as much. Roger Dawson flaunted his Mary-blue tie that night, disgruntled that Gabriel had once again not allowed them to take the statue of Our Lady of Walsingham around the church in solemn procession. And cloth-of-gold vestments were all very well and good, but by all rights Our Lady should have blue and silver.

After the Credo, and the Prayers of Intercession, the congregation made their corporate Confession. 'Forgive us all that is past; and grant that we may serve thee in newness of life . . .' As Gabriel made the sign of the cross and spoke the words of Absolution, he felt personally cleansed, and ready for a fresh start.

The offertory party came forward then. Usually, for a festival service such as this, it was the privilege of the two churchwardens to bring the elements to the altar. But there was now only one churchwarden. Cyril Fitzjames's jowly countenance was transformed by a rare smile; he had asked Emily to assist him. Viola went in front of them, proudly and carefully bearing the silver ciborium with the wafers. As they entered the chancel, she couldn't resist a sideways look of pure triumph at her brother.

The sun dipped lower; the light coming through the west window had a dreamy golden quality, trapped in the clouds of incense that now filled the church.

'Though we are many, we are one body . . .' All those unique individuals, somehow united in this place, and at this moment. And then, once again, they were all coming up to the altar to receive communion. Gabriel experienced a sense of *déjà vu* as he waited for them to kneel: it was so like the Patronal Festival, such a short time ago, yet so unlike. So much had happened in the intervening weeks, and so many things had permanently changed. For one thing, there was no Mavis. Someone else was missing, too – he couldn't quite think who. Gabriel noted each person as he administered to them. The servers received first: Tony Kent, Johnnie and Chris, Venerable Bead, the acolytes, and little Sebastian, bowing his head for his father's blessing. Miles Taylor, still for just a moment. Hobbling up ahead of everyone else, Beryl Ball, grinning at him and wiggling her dentures. The Dawsons, Roger, Julia, Teresa and Francis, defiant in their blue ties and bows. A horde of white-haired old ladies, led by Mary Hughes. Cecily Framlingham, staring with pointed satisfaction at the flowers as she came up. Reliable, unflappable Daphne. 'The body of Christ,' he said to each one. Cyril Fitzjames came near the end, with Emily behind him. His own beloved Emily, and their daughter. And David. Dear David. He hadn't been here that other time.

When he'd reached the end, Gabriel realised who was missing. He hadn't given communion to Lady Constance.

Chapter 47

For he seeth that wise men also die, and perish to-
*   gether: as well as the ignorant and foolish, and*
*   leave their riches for other.*
And yet they think that their houses shall continue
*   for ever: and that their dwelling-places shall*
*   endure from one generation to another; and call*
*   the lands after their own names.*

Psalm 49.10–11

David was up very early the next morning. He hadn't slept
particularly well, and he was anxious to get to the post
before Daphne arose.

The letter was there on the mat, as he had expected. He
picked it up and made sure that it had his name on it, then
took it to his room to read in privacy. Opening his curtains, and seeing that it was a beautiful clear morning, he
decided to postpone the moment for a bit longer. He shaved,
dressed, and packed his case, to save time later, and went
out into Kensington Gardens, as he had on his first morning in London, nearly three weeks ago.

Although there were few people about, he avoided the
publicly visible benches, found a spot in the grass, and
leaned against a tree. It was going to be another hot day;

already the sun had evaporated the dew and the grass was quite dry. Sitting on the grass in a park was not something he'd been particularly fond of before he met Lucy, he thought, then put the thought away from him quickly. He still wasn't ready to think about Lucy.

He examined the envelope carefully before opening it. It was square, and made of a heavy bond paper; the writing was much as he would have expected, spidery and fine yet definite, the letters well formed and not in the least wavery, reflecting the writer's personality.

David slit the top with his pocket-knife and extracted a rather thick sheaf of papers. The writing paper itself was not perfumed, but it exuded a faint scent of lavender. David sighed and unfolded the letter. It was dated the previous day, 15 August.

My dear Mr Middleton-Brown,

I am sure you know why I am writing this letter – perhaps you are even expecting it. At any rate, much of what I have to tell you will come as no surprise to you. But after your kindness to me, I owe it to you to tell you the whole story, so there will be nothing left unexplained.

You are aware, I am sure, that I have been unwell lately. I have suffered from spells of dizziness, and feelings of depression. These leave me quite exhausted and frightened. But more frightening still have been periodic episodes of dementia and paranoia, during which I have, apparently, done things about which I later have no recollection. My servants assure me that this is so, and there is other evidence. It would seem that recently I have written several letters during these spells. I do not remember writing these letters, but, with my customary thoroughness, I have kept carbon copies which I have later discovered. All of the letters seem to have been prompted, in my subconscious, by my concern for the future of St Anne's Church, but that does not excuse the abominable things that I said in them.

One of them, of course, was to Mrs Conwell. I don't know how you discovered the truth about her death, but you are a very clever young man to have done so.

Not so long ago I began to suspect, from various discrepancies, that someone was taking money from St Anne's. There were few people in a position to do this, and from conversations with Mrs Conwell and others I concluded that she was in fact the person. It was a simple matter for me to do a check of the books, and to confirm my suspicions: I of course have a key to the sacristy, where the ledger books are kept. The discrepancies were fairly minor, but her attempts to cover her tracks were crude. I meant to confront her with the evidence, and to ask her in a reasonable fashion to restore the money. But events took a different course.

As you are aware, I profoundly regret Mrs Conwell's death. I never meant for her to take her own life, but I accept full responsibility for it. Mrs Conwell died because of the letter I wrote – that fact seems inescapable, and nothing will explain it away. The guilt is mine.

The second person to whom I wrote a letter was young Tony Kent. I had been worried, in the light of the Norman Newsome affair, that his living arrangements might lead him into trouble, and thus cast discredit upon St Anne's, where he holds a position of great responsibility. I find Tony Kent a very pleasant young man, and profoundly regret any embarrassment or pain that I might have caused him.

Then there is the matter of Father Neville. I am not sure whether you know about this or not, though I suspect that you may – as I said, you are a very clever young man. But I shall tell you about it in any case, and perhaps you will tell him as much as you think is right. I rather think that your acquaintance with him is of longer standing than I have been led to believe.

In this instance, my concern for St Anne's was only part of the underlying cause. Just as important was my love for my brother Edward.

Just over ten years ago, the living at St Anne's was vacant. Edward was nearing retirement age, and was happily settled in his last parish in Lewes, so I'd given up hope of his accepting the living himself. But he rang me one day and said that he had a candidate for me – a very bright, very promising young priest in the diocese, one of his protégés. The man had been serving a curacy in Brighton, but was ready, even anxious, to move on. I don't need to tell you that priest's name – Father Gabriel Neville. Father Neville came to see me, and I was very impressed, but my brother's recommendation was all I needed. I trusted his judgement. As there was a vacancy, the appointment went through very quickly and Father Neville was installed here inside of two months. Up until about two years ago, I was very happy with him as a parish priest, and felt that he served St Anne's ably. I also very much like and approve of his wife, whom I have known all her life, and feel that she has been a great asset to him, and to St Anne's.

Over two years ago, my brother fell gravely ill. Edward and I had always been very close, and I felt that I wanted to care for him myself. I tried very hard to persuade him to come to London, where he could be close to Harley Street and receive the best private treatment available. But he didn't wish to leave his parish, and I respected that wish. So for several months I nursed him through his final illness.

He had a terrible disease, and he died a very protracted and painful death. Even now I can scarcely bear to dwell on it, but it is important for you to understand. He was in much pain, yes. But the worst part of it was that he was not himself by the time the disease had truly taken hold. After he lost the use of his limbs, he was still aware of what was happening. It was about that time that I contacted an organisation that makes it possible for people to die peacefully – and when they are ready – rather than waiting for disease to do its worst. They provided him with the means to accomplish that. But Edward wasn't ready to make that choice then, and after that – after that he lost his mind. It was a terrible thing, and as I said, he was not himself. He said things that Edward would never had said. It was appalling to hear him, day after day. At first I thought he was just hallucinating, and that the things he was saying were coming out of some dark corner of his imagination. But as he repeated himself, I realised the truth behind what he was saying.

He talked about a boy named Peter Maitland, who had drowned. And about a young priest who had come to him, his spiritual director, for Confession, with that death on his conscience. He had tried to help that priest, first by hearing his Confession, then by counselling him, and finally by helping him to find a new position and to start a new life. Of course that priest was Gabriel Neville. My brother believed in him. He believed that he was a good priest, and deserved his help. But at the end of his life, the tragic things he'd heard in that Confessional came back to haunt him and torture him.

In his right mind, my brother would never have broken the seal of the Confessional, I can assure you of that. But his disease robbed him of his reason, and so I learned things I never wanted to know about my own parish priest.

I've lived with this knowledge for two years, and have done nothing. Consciously, I knew that Gabriel Neville was not to blame for my brother's distress, but subconsciously I suppose I held him responsible. I knew it was the disease, but if Edward hadn't had that burden to bear . . .

And now I can see my brother's dementia, in the form of paranoia, exhibiting itself in me. I can assure you, though, that at the moment my mind is very clear, and I know exactly what I am doing.

I nursed my brother, and know very well the symptoms of his disease. Although I have not been to a doctor, I recognise these symptoms in myself, and know that I have contracted the disease that killed my brother.

You will surely realise that when you receive this I will be dead. I am assured that it will be a peaceful and painless death, unlike my brother's. Edward lost his mind before he could make the choice to end his life, and that was not a decision I could take for him. But I have kept the drugs that the society sent him. I make my choice in full possession of my mind, and knowing that it is proper for me to do so. Mavis Conwell died because of an action I took, and that is not something with which I can live. The remainder of my life would have been short and painful, and I might have done more regrettable things, caused pain to others. It is best that I go so.

There is one other matter I need to mention, though I am almost embarrassed to do so. It is the matter of my will. I have no family left, and have always intended to leave the bulk of my estate to St Anne's. This is still my intention. But since I realised that I was terminally ill, I have been most grieved by the thought of my beloved home being sold, and probably converted into flats. This is surely what would happen if I were to leave it to St Anne's. This house has been in the Oliver family for generations, and deserves a better fate than that. Therefore, I am going to ask you to look after my house for me. As I've come to know you over the past few weeks, I've realised that you have a rare appreciation for beauty, and the taste to match. And so I will trust you with my house. I have just written a codicil to my will, which has been signed and witnessed by my servants. It gives you my house, along with a capital sum in trust, the income from which should be more than sufficient for its upkeep and maintenance, on the condition that the house is not sold in your lifetime. You need not live in it, if that is not convenient for you, but only look after it. I hope this is not too great a burden for you, and that you will care for it and love it as I have.

I ought to tell you not to grieve for me. But I am a selfish old woman, and I would like to think that you might grieve, just a little. Goodbye, my dear young man, and thank you again for your kindness and your sensitivity.

It was signed with a flourish: Constance Oliver.

David sat under the tree as the sun climbed higher in the sky, the tears wet on his cheeks.

Chapter 48

*My covenant will I not break, nor alter the thing
that is gone out of my lips: I have sworn once by
my holiness, that I will not fail David.*

Psalm 89.34

David parked his car in front of the vicarage. He'd said his
farewells to Daphne; his case was in the car and all that
remained was the final interview with Gabriel. Although
he hadn't allowed her to read the letter, he'd told Daphne
everything – about Craig, and about Lady Constance; he
felt that he owed her that, after all her help and support.
But he was as yet undecided about how much he needed
to tell Gabriel; perhaps he'd just see how their conversation
went. He didn't know whether Gabriel would even have
heard yet of Lady Constance's death: if not, he didn't
want to be the one to tell him, especially if there was a
chance that the death could be construed as accidental, or
occurring from natural causes. Lady Constance deserved
his discretion, and his silence.

Emily and the children were on their way out as he
arrived, bound for Kensington Gardens and the Round Pond,
if Sebastian's sailboat were any clue. The children waited
impatiently while David took his leave of their mother.

'I'm so glad you caught us before we left!' she said. 'I couldn't bear the thought of your leaving town without saying goodbye.'

He smiled. 'I would have waited, Emily.'

'David.' She took his hand. 'I can't thank you enough for what you've done for him – for us. You've been a real friend to both of us.'

Embarrassed, he looked away.

'Mummy, can't we go now?' Sebastian demanded.

'Just a moment, darling. I'm saying goodbye to your Uncle David.'

'Is he going away?' Viola asked, staring at him with frank curiosity. 'Where's he going?'

'Uncle David lives a long way from here. He's going home. It might be a long time before we see him again.'

'I wouldn't be too sure of that,' he said with a smile. 'Remember that first morning I was here? You said you'd come to Wymondham to see me.'

'And so we shall, if you still want us.'

'Please do, soon. And I'm sure I'll be back in London,' he added. 'I have a lot of friends here now.' He frowned, thinking of Lady Constance, then of Lucy.

She looked at him inquiringly, not sure how much she could say. Finally she ventured, 'Lucy?'

Again he looked away, then forced his eyes back to hers. 'Lucy,' he said. 'Tell Lucy . . . Tell her I'll be in touch,' he finished awkwardly.

Emily nodded. 'I'll tell her.'

As Sebastian and Viola looked on balefully, they regarded each other for a moment, neither one quite knowing how to say goodbye. Suddenly Emily threw her arms around his neck. 'Dear David,' she said softly. 'I'm so glad we've become friends.'

'It took ten years, but . . .'

'It was worth waiting for.' She kissed him on the cheek, then disengaged herself. 'Take care of yourself, David.'

'You take care of yourself. And . . . take care of Gabriel.'

'I will.'

'Mummy, let's go now,' Viola insisted. 'Or I'll tell Daddy that you were hugging Uncle David,' she added slyly.

Emily laughed. 'I don't think your father would mind. Goodbye, David. Gabriel's waiting for you in the study.'

'Goodbye, Emily.'

Gabriel paced up and down the study restlessly. 'There are so many things I don't understand. I think you'd better start at the beginning.'

'Which beginning? Your story, or Mavis Conwell's?'

'Start with Mavis. Was she murdered, or not? I still don't know.'

'No, she wasn't murdered. She killed herself, just as the coroner said, just as the police said.'

'Then why . . .'

David gave a self-mocking laugh. 'It was my blind stubbornness. I got it into my head that she was murdered, and nothing would convince me otherwise. Not even the evidence.'

'The medical evidence at the inquest was quite clear. There was no indication that it was, or could have possibly been, anything but suicide.'

David looked sheepish. 'I'm afraid I wasn't listening during that part. My mind was made up.'

'So what made you change your mind?' Gabriel asked.

David answered indirectly. 'Did you ever have one of those kaleidoscopes when you were a child?'

'Yes. Sebastian and Viola have one now. You turn it around, and the shapes change.' He looked puzzled.

'My problem was that I was looking through the wrong end of the kaleidoscope,' David explained. 'I was looking in the back end, and all I could see were bits of coloured glass falling about. No pattern, no sense to it. Just bits of coloured glass. But when I turned the kaleidoscope around, and looked through it the proper way, all the bits of coloured glass formed a pattern, and the pattern made sense.'

Gabriel nodded. 'I see. So Mavis's death had nothing to do with the blackmail.'

'No, that's not true at all. It had a great deal to do with it. But I was looking at it backwards, assuming that Mavis must be the blackmailer. It was only later that I realised the truth – Mavis was also being blackmailed.'

'Good Lord.' He stopped in his tracks, then sat down at his desk. He considered this knowledge a moment. 'What about?'

'About her taking the money. She was threatened with exposure to the Bishop.'

'Of course. So that's why she killed herself. She couldn't face the humiliation of public exposure. Poor woman.'

David hesitated. 'It wasn't quite as simple as that. There was also . . . Craig.'

'Craig?'

'Yes. She was taking the money for him, of course. She was terrified of him, for some reason – I saw her absolutely cowering one day, when he came looking for her at

St Anne's, demanding money. I think he's a pathetic snivelling little creep, but he frightened her.' He made his mind up, and continued, 'He went to the sacristy that afternoon.'

'The afternoon of the fête?' Gabriel frowned. 'No one's ever said they saw him that day.'

'Beryl Ball saw him. She told me so, and he's admitted it. He took some money – about two hundred pounds – and the ledger sheet, so no one would realise that anything was missing.'

Gabriel rubbed his chin thoughtfully. 'I see. So that's why she killed herself.'

David didn't meet his eyes; he didn't want to say any more, but he was uncomfortable telling less than the whole truth. 'Yes. He's admitted it all to me, and promises to give the money back, if only we won't turn him over to the police.'

'You agreed to that?'

'I told him it would be up to you.'

Nodding, Gabriel assented. 'That seems reasonable to me. As long as we get the money back, it need not be a police matter. I'll deal with Craig myself.' He paused. 'But how did you find out that she was being blackmailed? That was jolly good detective work!'

'Not at all,' David disagreed with a self-deprecating smile. 'That was the easiest part of all – I had it handed to me on a silver plate. Or in a silver thurible, to be more precise.'

'What?'

'Just before she . . . hanged herself, Mavis tried to destroy the blackmail letter. But she bungled it, otherwise we would never have known. She tried to burn it, in the festival thurible. But she shut it in the safe before it had properly started burning.'

'And didn't realise that the fire would go out quite quickly,' Gabriel reasoned. 'Good Lord.'

While he sat in stunned silence, David thought carefully how to go on, anticipating the next question. It wasn't long in coming. 'So can you tell me now? Who was the blackmailer?' Gabriel turned puzzled blue eyes on him.

After a moment's hesitation, David said simply, 'Lady Constance.'

There was a sharp intake of breath, and a look of incomprehension. 'Lady Constance?' he said, after a long pause. 'But how . . .? Why . . .?' Gabriel massaged his forehead with the palms of his hands. 'I really don't understand. I don't understand how she could have found out about . . . Peter Maitland. He wouldn't have told anyone who knew Lady Constance . . .'

'No, but *you* did.'

Gabriel stared. 'I never told a soul. I swear to you, David . . .'

David smiled a bittersweet smile. 'And that's what had me looking in the wrong end of the kaleidoscope all this time. There was one person you told – your spiritual director.'

'But I didn't *tell* him! I made my Confession, of course, but that . . .' He stopped. 'Lady Constance's brother,' he said slowly. 'I made my Confession to Lady Constance's brother. But the Confessional is sacred – he would never have told anyone something that was revealed to him under the seal of the Confessional.'

'I should have realised,' David mused, glancing up at the bookshelves, and Gabriel's book, *Sacramental Confes-*

sion: A Spiritual Imperative. 'Of course you would have made your Confession. And I should have figured out that you had a connection with Lady Constance to get the living at St Anne's so quickly. I knew about her brother. But I just never put it all together. I was so busy looking for someone Peter Maitland might have told . . .'

Gabriel, stunned, listened to his musings without saying a word.

David explained it to him then, about the illness and its effects, and Lady Constance's reaction on receiving the knowledge, and the circumstances under which she'd written the letters. Gabriel sat in silence, shaking his head, and turning the paperweight around and around on his desk. He asked no questions after that, so it was not necessary to evade; Gabriel would find out about Lady Constance's death in due time, when he was safely gone.

Finally, Gabriel asked one last question. 'Is it really over? I mean, you're sure she'll take no further action?'

'I can say with certainty that you have nothing more to fear from Lady Constance,' David replied. 'She would never have followed through with the threats she made in the letters.'

Gabriel sighed. 'That's that, then.'

'Yes, that's that.'

He turned to David. 'How can I thank you? Without your help, I don't know where I'd be right now. David . . .'

Embarrassed, David looked down at Gabriel's hands. 'You don't have to say anything, Gabriel. I'm glad I was able—' He stopped suddenly, staring at the paperweight, his throat constricting. It was a smooth rock, about the size of a fist, but curiously shaped like a heart. He'd seen it on Gabriel's desk on all his previous visits, but this was the first time he'd actually looked at it. In an instant he was transported thirteen years back in time.

They looked into each other's eyes.

'I don't understand what's going on, Gabriel,' David said softly. 'I'm afraid.'

'You should never be afraid of love, my darling David.' When David said nothing, he went on gently, 'I do love you, you know. But I won't rush you — you must choose the time.' Still David was silent. 'We don't have to talk about it now if you don't want to. Let's take a walk.'

It was an unseasonably warm afternoon in late autumn. The season for holiday-makers and day-trippers had long since ended, and Brighton beach was virtually empty except for the two young men. Not daring to touch, scarcely daring to look at each other, they walked along the rocky beach for what seemed like miles, speaking hardly at all. David was intensely, acutely aware of Gabriel's nearness. He felt more alive than he ever had before, as half-realised, long-denied feelings came to the surface at last.

Finally, in the early dusk, David stopped suddenly, bending down. He plucked the heart-shaped stone from the beach and held it in the palm of his hand, feeling the weight of its smooth coolness.

'I love you, Gabriel . . . Gabe,' he said, shyly, extending his hand.

Gabe touched the rock with a finger, then took it from his palm. 'I'll treat it with care,' he promised, putting it in his pocket.

There was no one else in sight. Gabe kissed him then, and for a long moment they clung together on the deserted beach.

Gabriel followed his gaze; he held the stone up with a

bemused smile. 'No, David, I haven't forgotten,' he said softly. 'No matter what you may think, I've never forgotten.'

It was David's turn to be speechless. Finally he said, 'All these years. You've kept it all these years?'

'Yes. You can't just forget the kind of love we had, David. Things change, and life goes on, but there are some things . . .'

David found it hard to speak. 'But . . . Emily.'

'Yes, Emily.' Gabriel's voice was gentle. 'I told you once that you can't live in the past. And we live in a world that forces us to make choices. I regret that fact, but I don't regret the choice I made. My life is with Emily now. She's my present, and my future. I love her very much. I can't really explain it to you – my love for Emily is . . . different. It's very real, but it's different. And it in no way replaces what we had, or invalidates it. You were very special to me, David. You still are, in a certain way. Nothing will change that. I think Emily understands that, and accepts it, and I hope that in time you'll be able to understand it too. Our love was real, David. And I'll never forget it.'

David stood, swallowing hard. 'I think I'd better go now, Gabriel.'

Gabriel rose too, and offered his hand, his lips curving in a painful smile. 'You can call me Gabe.'

David sat in his car for a long time – he had no idea how long. For ten years he'd clung to the knowledge – the certainty – that Gabe had loved him. Over the last few weeks the question he hadn't dared to ask himself was whether it were true, or just a figment of his imagination that he'd needed to believe in. Now he had his answer: his affirmation, and something more. In a funny sort of way, he'd got Gabe back. He'd lost him completely, bafflingly, for ten long years, but now he'd got him back, and nothing could take him away again.

Suddenly, unbidden, a picture of Lucy came into his mind, painfully vivid – lovely Lucy, with her serene secret smile and her rosy corona of hair. He found that he couldn't bear the thought of never seeing her again. Without a conscious decision, he started the car and turned south towards Kensington instead of north towards Wymond-ham. It was Thursday – Lucy would be at home, painting. As he approached the entrance to her mews, he slowed the car, then went on to the next roundabout, and made his way north. Not yet, thought David Middleton-Brown. Soon, I'll get in touch with her. But not yet.

Epilogue

*Hope thou in the Lord, and keep his way, and he
shall promote thee, that thou shalt possess the
land: when the ungodly shall perish, thou shalt
see it.*

Psalm 37.35

It was a Sunday late in September, with the first crisp hint
of autumn in the air; St Anne's Church was celebrating the
feast of St Michael and All Angels. Before Mass, Gabriel
Neville, in a snow-white chasuble, stood at the front of the
nave. Beside him was St Anne's newly elected churchwarden,
Roger Dawson, who paused momentously, inflated with
self-importance and the gravity of his task. Unconsciously
he wrung his hands. 'I have an announcement to make,' he
intoned in his dry, raspy voice. 'The Bishop of London
would like me to announce that as of first January next,
Father Gabriel Neville will be the Area Archdeacon.' He
waited for a moment for the message to sink in, then continued. 'I'm sure you will all wish to join me in congratulating
Father Gabriel, and wishing him all the best for the future.
He will be very much missed here at St Anne's.'

From the front row, Emily smiled at Gabriel with love,
and with pride.

403

In the shadow of honey-coloured Medewich Cathedral, amidst the perfect lawns of the Cathedral Close, the diocesan office of St Manicus should have been a peaceful if not an especially exciting place for nineteen-year-old Julia Smith to start her first job. Yet she has been in its precincts for less than an hour when she stumbles on a horror of Biblical proportions - a severed head in the Cathedral font.

And she has worked for the suave Canon Wheeler for less than a day when she realises that the Dean and Chapter is as riven by rivalry, ambition and petty jealousy as the court of any Renaissance prelate. In this jungle of intrigue a young deaconess, Theodora Braithwaite, stands out as a lone pillar of common sense. Taciturn but kindly, she takes Julia under her wing, and with the assistance of Ian Caretaker - a young man who hates Canon Wheeler as much as he loves the Church - they attempt to unravel the truth behind the death of a well-meaning man, the Reverend Paul Gray, late incumbent of Markham cum Cumbermound.

FICTION/CRIME   0 7472 3582 1

More Crime Fiction from Headline

KATE CHARLES

Appointed to Die

A clerical mystery

Death at the Deanery – sudden and unnatural death.
Someone should have seen it coming.

Even before Stuart Latimer arrives as the new Dean
of Malbury Cathedral shock waves reverberate
around the tightly knit Cathedral Close, heralding
sweeping changes in a community that is not open to
change. And the reality is worse than the
expectation. The Dean's naked ambition and ruthless
behaviour alienate everyone in the Chapter: the
Canons, gentle John Kingsley, vague Rupert
Greenwood, pompous Philip Thetford, and Subdean
Arthur Bridges-ffrench, a traditionalist who resists
change most strongly of all.

Financial jiggery-pokery, clandestine meetings,
malicious gossip, and several people who see more
than they ought to: a potent mix. But who could
foresee that the mistrust and even hatred within the
Cathedral Close would spill over into violence and
death? Canon Kingsley's daughter Lucy draws in her
lover David Middleton-Brown, against his better
judgement, and together they probe the surprising
secrets of a self-contained world where nothing is
what it seems.

FICTION / CRIME 0 7472 4199 6

A selection of bestsellers from Headline

ASKING FOR TROUBLE	Ann Granger	£5.99	☐
FAITHFUL UNTO DEATH	Caroline Graham	£5.99	☐
THE WICKED WINTER	Kate Sedley	£5.99	☐
HOTEL PARADISE	Martha Grimes	£5.99	☐
MURDER IN THE MOTORSTABLE	Amy Myers	£5.99	☐
WEIGHED IN THE BALANCE	Anne Perry	£5.99	☐
THE DEVIL'S HUNT	P C Doherty	£5.99	☐
EVERY DEADLY SIN	D M Greenwood	£4.99	☐
SKINNER'S ORDEAL	Quintin Jardine	£5.99	☐
HONKY TONK KAT	Karen Kijewski	£5.99	☐
THE QUICK AND THE DEAD	Alison Joseph	£5.99	☐
THE RELIC MURDERS	Michael Clynes	£5.99	☐

All Headline books are available at your local bookshop or newsagent, or can be ordered direct from the publisher. Just tick the titles you want and fill in the form below. Prices and availability subject to change without notice.

Headline Book Publishing, Cash Sales Department, Bookpoint, 39 Milton Park, Abingdon, OXON, OX14 4TD, UK. If you have a credit card you may order by telephone – 01235 400400.

Please enclose a cheque or postal order made payable to Bookpoint Ltd to the value of the cover price and allow the following for postage and packing:

UK & BFPO: £1.00 for the first book, 50p for the second book and 30p for each additional book ordered up to a maximum charge of £3.00.

OVERSEAS & EIRE: £2.00 for the first book, £1.00 for the second book and 50p for each additional book.

Name ....

Address ....

....

....

If you would prefer to pay by credit card, please complete:
Please debit my Visa/Access/Diner's Card/American Express (delete as applicable) card no:

Signature .... Expiry Date...............